THE
Prairie
DREAMS
Trilogy

A Cross-Continent Search Spans
Three Historical Romances

THE
Prairie
DREAMS
Trilogy

SUSAN PAGE
DAVIS

BARBOUR
PUBLISHING

Print ISBN 978-1-63058-169-5

eBook Editions:
Adobe Digital Edition (.epub) 978-1-63058-538-9
Kindle and MobiPocket Edition (.prc) 978-1-63058-539-6

All scripture quotations are taken from the King James Version of the Bible.

This book is a work of fiction. Names, characters, places, and incidents are either products of the author's imagination or used fictitiously. Any similarity to actual people, organizations, and/or events is purely coincidental.

Published by Barbour Books, an imprint of Barbour Publishing, Inc., P.O. Box 719, Uhrichsville, Ohio 44683, www.barbourbooks.com

Our mission is to publish and distribute inspirational products offering exceptional value and biblical encouragement to the masses.

 Member of the
Evangelical Christian
Publishers Association

Printed in the United States of America.

THE LADY'S MAID

CHAPTER 1

Come with me, Elise. I can't face him alone."

Lady Anne gripped her hand so hard that Elise Finster winced. She would do anything to make this day easier for her young mistress.

"Of course, my lady, if they'll let me."

They walked down the sweeping staircase together, their silk skirts swishing and the hems of their crinolines nudging each other. Lady Anne kept her hold on Elise's hand until they reached the high-ceilinged hall below.

At the doorway to the morning room, Lady Anne straightened her shoulders. A pang of sympathy lanced Elise's heart, but she couldn't bear this burden in the young woman's place. Anne Stone had to face the future herself.

"Good day, ladies." Andrew Conrad, the Stone family's aging solicitor, rose from the velvet-upholstered sofa and bowed. "Lady Anne, you look charming. Miss Finster."

Elise murmured, "Hello, sir," while Lady Anne allowed Conrad to take her hand and bow over it.

From near the window, a tall, angular man walked forward—Anne's second cousin, Randolph Stone. Ten years older than Anne, the studious man lived in a modest country home with his wife and two young children and eked out a living on the interest of his father's meager fortune. Elise gritted her teeth, a reaction he always induced in her. With great effort, she had managed to keep Lady Anne from guessing how much she loathed Randolph.

"Anne." Stone took his cousin's hand and kissed it perfunctorily. He nodded in Elise's direction but didn't greet her.

"Randolph. I didn't expect to see you here." Lady Anne arched her delicate eyebrows at the solicitor.

"Mr. Stone had some questions, and I invited him to come with me today so I could explain the situation to both of you."

Lady Anne said nothing for a long moment then nodded.

"Er, if it pleases you, my lady, this is confidential business." Conrad shot a meaningful glance Elise's way.

Elise felt her face flush but held her ground. She wouldn't leave until Lady Anne told her plainly to do so. Besides, he'd brought along an extra person. Why shouldn't Lady Anne have that right as well?

"I would like Elise to stay." The lady smiled but with a firmness to her jaw befitting the daughter of an earl.

Conrad nodded. "As you wish. Shall we begin, then?"

Lady Anne sat on the upholstered Hepplewhite settee and signaled for Elise to sit beside her. Elise arranged her voluminous skirt and lowered herself, avoiding the direct gaze of Randolph Stone. He didn't care for her either, and Elise knew exactly why, but she didn't believe in letting past discord interfere with the future.

"You must have news," Lady Anne said. "Otherwise, you wouldn't have come."

"That is astute of you, my lady." Conrad reached inside his coat and brought out an envelope. "I've had news that is not really news at all from America."

"America?" Lady Anne's tone changed, and she tensed. "Is it my uncle David?"

Conrad sighed and extracted a sheet of coarse rag paper from the envelope. "You are aware, dear lady, that I sent letters the week after your father died, hoping to locate your uncle—that is, David Stone."

"Earl of Stoneford," Lady Anne said gently.

"Yes, well, that's the point, isn't it?" Conrad sounded tired and the tiniest bit cross, as though he hated being beaten by the Atlantic

Ocean and the American postal system. "If your uncle were alive, and if he were here, he would inherit your father's estate and be acknowledged as earl of Stoneford, it's true. But after three months of dillydallying, all we have is a letter from the postmaster in St. Louis, Missouri, declaring that while a Mr. David Stone did reside in the city some ten to fifteen years ago and apparently ran a business at that time, no one by that name lives there now."

Anne's shoulders sagged. "Surely they're mistaken. The last word we had from him came from there."

Conrad shook his head. "I'm afraid we've reached the end of our resources, my lady. I had that letter a couple of weeks ago stating that the city had no death record for your uncle."

"That was a relief," Lady Anne said.

"Yes, but all it tells us is that he did not die in St. Louis. Now, the courts agree on the procedure. The trustees will continue managing your father's estate, but the peerage will remain dormant until your uncle is either found or proven to be deceased."

Lady Anne stirred. "And why is Randolph here?"

"Your cousin is next in the line of succession, provided David Stone is proven dead and does not have a male heir. However, it is my duty to tell you both that those things may be impossible to prove."

"And the title will stay dormant and the estate unclaimed for how long?"

"As long as it takes." Conrad brought out a handkerchief and patted his dewy brow. "There are titles that have been dormant for decades—one for more than a hundred years. It will probably never be claimed."

"But the estate, the property—"

"The Crown may decide to dispose of it in time."

"Surely not, if Uncle David is still out there."

"The trustees will not spend your father's fortune in an attempt to find his heir. If you or Mr. Randolph Stone wants to spend your own money trying, that is your affair."

Lady Anne and her cousin glanced at each other. Randolph looked away first.

"And my situation is as you indicated previously," Lady Anne said.

"Yes. You will have the modest fortune your father left to you. The bulk of the estate will remain in trust for the proven heir."

"Then I cannot stay here any longer."

Conrad lifted a hand. "The trustees might allow it, but you would have to pay all household expenses and the wages of any staff you wished to keep, other than the minimum they would retain to maintain the property."

Elise schooled her features to remain impassive, as she'd been taught since she entered domestic service more than two decades ago, but her heart was in turmoil. Her own fate was closely entwined with Lady Anne's. Her mistress's inheritance would hardly enable her to keep living in this huge manor house or to pay the staff that would require. She and Lady Anne had discussed it several times in the past three months, since the earl's death. The young mistress would probably lease a cottage somewhere or go to stay for a while with friends.

"I cannot do that," Lady Anne said. "I shall have to make other arrangements."

Randolph leaned forward. "Surely you've been expecting this outcome, Anne."

Lady Anne's chin shot up. "No. I did not expect it at all. What I expected was that my uncle would be found and that he would come home and take his rightful place as head of the family."

"That isn't going to happen," Randolph said.

"It seems most unlikely." Conrad's voice held a tinge of regret.

Elise felt great sadness for her young mistress, but she could do nothing but sit beside her now and be available later when she cried.

Randolph shook his head. "So there's no hope of my ever inheriting."

"None, unless you can prove that David Stone is dead and has no male children."

They sat in silence for half a minute.

"Your uncle David was much loved," Conrad said at last. "Let me

add my condolences, my lady. This must seem a fresh bereavement to you, on the heels of your father's death. I had hoped for a better outcome."

"As did we all," Randolph said hastily.

Lady Anne looked impassively at Conrad. "I shall let you know what I decide to do."

"Thank you. Then I shall be going." Conrad rose.

Elise stood, along with Lady Anne and her cousin.

"Thank you for your work on this," her mistress told Conrad.

Again he bowed over Lady Anne's hand. "I hope I can continue to be of service, my lady."

Elise stood slightly behind Lady Anne and did not offer her hand. It wasn't her place.

Randolph said, "I wish it were otherwise, Anne."

"Of course you do."

Randolph's mouth twitched, but he didn't respond other than to clasp her hand and take his leave with Conrad. How was his wife taking the news, Elise wondered. In the past year, since Anne's other uncle, John, had died in battle, Randolph and Merrileigh must have speculated much on their chances of becoming Earl and Lady Stone. Now it seemed that would not come about. Merrileigh, who loved to entertain beyond the means her husband's current income afforded, must be distraught.

Elise walked into the great hall with the visitors and opened the front door, rather than summoning the one remaining housemaid to show them out. The butler and three quarters of the staff had already left to seek other positions before the money ran out, and Lady Anne had bid them sincere good-byes and Godspeeds. Some had served the family all their lives—and many since before Anne's birth.

Elise herself had started as a parlor maid at sixteen, hired by Anne's mother. What days those were! Elegant house parties at Stoneford and social seasons at the town house in London. When the mistress died three years ago, the family had lost much of its sparkle, but Elise had stayed on with Anne out of love as much as convenience. The seventeen-year-old girl had blossomed into a lovely, refined woman of twenty, and Elise felt that Anne relied on her almost as much as she once had her mother.

When she got back to the morning room, Anne sat once more on the settee. She looked up at Elise with a thoughtful gaze. "I shall have to make plans, Elise. I should have before now, but I couldn't believe Uncle David wouldn't turn up."

"He'd have let you stay here," Elise said.

"Perhaps. Who knows? And I admit I've never given much thought to his hypothetical offspring."

"No need to."

"Isn't there?" Lady's Anne's brown eyes widened. "Uncle David might be dead, though I don't want to think that. Still, he could have children. Father didn't hear from him once in the last ten years. He might have married and settled down to raise a passel of little Yankee Stones. There could be half a dozen of them out there, standing between Cousin Randolph and the peerage, though they have no inkling."

Elise cringed at the mention of Randolph's name. She'd done rather well in concealing her dislike of him while he was in the room, but she couldn't hold it in forever. Best to change the subject.

"Would you like your tea now, my lady?"

"I can't stay here, Elise."

For a long moment neither of them spoke. At last, Elise said, "I understand."

This was Lady Anne's way of saying she could no longer afford to keep her on. Elise's wages were near the top of the scale for lady's maids. The Stones had always prided themselves on paying their staff well and treating them humanely. Should she offer to work for less? If she took another position—and Elise had no doubt she could find one, with Lady Anne's recommendation—Anne could hire both a general maid and perhaps a cook-housekeeper, though not a very good one, for the price. If she wanted to keep a frugal household in the country, Anne could live in comparative comfort. Nothing like what she was used to of course, but she could be independent.

Lady Anne rose. "I believe I shall lie down. If I don't ring for you, please wake me in an hour. I shall take my tea then and—and lay plans."

"Yes, my lady."

Anne walked slowly into the hall and up the stairs. Her steps dragged, and her chin nearly touched her chest. Her heart aching, Elise descended to the servants' hall, where the last kitchen maid jumped up from a chair in the corner. Her eyelids were puffy from weeping.

"The mistress will take tea in an hour," Elise said.

"Yes, mum." Patsy sniffed and wrung her hands in her apron. Her hair looked disheveled, and several strands hung down from her cap. "What's to do, Miss Finster? Should I give my notice?"

"If you hear of another opening, it might be wise."

"Would you tell me if you learn something, mum?"

"Yes."

Patsy nodded. "Thank you."

Elise suggested Patsy serve a simple meal of fruit, cheese, and scones. "If there's any butter or honey in the pantry, so much the better. If not, perhaps Hannah could run to the grocer's."

"Hannah's left, mum, and Lucy is packing."

"Indeed?" That was bad news. They would be left in the huge house without servants—only Patsy. "Is Michael still out at the stable?"

"He came in for breakfast this morning, but he said if the mistress hasn't any horses to keep, he might as well go with the rest. He went out to look for a new position."

Elise went up to her room, her heart heavy, opened the doors of the large cedar wardrobe, and took out her best silk and wool gown. If Lady Anne was going to move to different quarters, Elise would have to pack all of her mistress's clothing, which comprised much more than her own. She might as well pack her personal things now and have it out of the way, so that she could give her full attention to Lady Anne's wardrobe when the time came.

How would she bring up the subject of a letter of

recommendation? She hated to ask, but certainly Lady Anne would give her one. And she probably knew of several highborn ladies who would love to have a maid of Elise's experience—although lady's maids usually retired by the time they reached Elise's age. Ladies going out in society liked to have a pretty young woman accompany them.

Elise tried to put that depressing though out of her mind. Lady Anne had once told her she wouldn't part with her no matter what the fashions were. But now, Elise was nearing forty. Her savings wouldn't be enough to retire on, and she had no prospects of marriage. Necessity would force her to remain in service, but in what capacity? She didn't know if she had the energy to work as a housemaid. Perhaps one of Lady Anne's acquaintances was in need of a companion or a governess. Neither would pay much, but she'd be comfortable and have lighter duties than most house servants.

Elise shook off the thoughts and went to the large room down the hall designated as Lady Anne's wardrobe. The room was filled with racks of gowns and petticoats. Cupboards along one wall held shoes, lingerie, and tools of the lady's maid's trade. Elise fetched a bundle of tissue paper and carried it to her room. She had a valise in her armoire, but she'd have to get a trunk down from the attic. Too bad she hadn't thought of getting out the trunks before all the menservants left. Perhaps she and Patsy could manage.

She put the clothing from her dresser into the valise and nestled the gown on top. The rest of her dresses and other clothing would go into her trunk.

Of course Lady Anne hadn't instructed her to pack, but what else could she expect? The earl was dead, and Anne would inherit nothing but the meager fund her father had set up for her. He'd expected his only daughter to marry a rich man before he died, and failing that, to have her two uncles to depend on.

Tears spilled over. *David, David, why did you leave us?* And now John was gone, too. And the earl—Anne's father and the eldest of the three brothers—had succumbed to pneumonia three months past, and Anne was alone. But Elise was alone as well—and perhaps

in a worse predicament. She snatched a handkerchief from her dressing table and blotted her cheeks carefully before reaching for her rouge pot. She would *not* feel sorry for herself.

A quick tap on her door stayed her hand, and she turned toward it, recognizing Lady Anne's method of announcing herself when she was in a hurry, rather than using the bell pull in her chamber. So close they'd become that this seemed normal. Elise would have to get used to new ways and a new mistress, one who would probably not be so lenient and informal as Lady Anne.

She opened the door. "What is it, my lady?"

Anne stood in the doorway, her chin high. Her eyes gleamed, though the whites were reddened from her recent weeping and her eyelids puffier than usual.

"Elise, I need your help."

"Anything, my lady."

Lady Anne's gaze lit on the piles of garments scattered over the bed and Elise's open valise. "What are you doing?"

"Packing. I assumed. . . ." Elise faltered to a stop.

"But. . . You can't leave me now!"

"Of course not, my lady. I'll stay with you for as long as you wish."

Lady Anne sobbed and lurched forward into Elise's arms.

"There, there, my dear." Elise patted her heaving shoulders. "I shan't leave you unless I have to. Nothing would please me more than to stay with you. I only assumed. . . ."

Lady Anne sniffed and pulled away, wiping her face with the back of her hand. "You assumed I'd toss you out? I should hope not."

Elise grabbed one of her daintiest lawn handkerchiefs from the stack on the dressing table and held it out to her. "I'm sorry. I know things will be difficult for you, and I didn't want you to feel guilty if you couldn't keep me on."

"Not keep you on? Elise, I should die without you. How would I live?"

It was true, Lady Anne depended on her lady's maid a great deal—perhaps overmuch. The thought of the twenty-year-old, pampered girl facing the harsh world alone made Elise shudder. Yet she hadn't dared hope Lady Anne would find a way to support them both, let alone maintain the lifestyle she'd lived since birth.

"I'm sure I don't know," Elise murmured. "Should I unpack, then?"

Lady Anne sighed and wiped the tear streaks from her cheeks. "I wish I could say yes, but you heard what Mr. Conrad said. Though we throw in our fates together, we cannot stay here. I'm afraid my income won't stretch to cover the coal and servants' wages."

"Yes, I suspected that." Elise frowned. "What do you suggest, then?"

"Let's go down to the little drawing room, shall we? I think a cup of tea would do us both good, and I shall tell you what is on my mind."

"That sounds most practical, my lady. I've told Patsy to have tea ready about now."

"Ah, so Patsy hasn't left us yet?"

"No, she's out in the kitchen, alone and frightened about to death. She asked me if she ought to give her notice, too. I counseled her not to ignore any opportunities that came her way. Perhaps I spoke amiss."

Lady Anne sighed. "I wish I could keep her, though she's clumsy. She has a good heart. But I fear she'd be better off if I give her a referral. And Michael is going to the Blithes."

"He's spoken to you?" Elise asked.

"Yes, he came in a few minutes ago and asked to see me. Hemmed and hawed, and I told him to speak up. I gave him his wages and a sovereign extra. I'm glad he's found a place."

Elise nodded. Michael would be happy with the Blithes. The viscount was fond of racing and owned several blood horses. It seemed all the Stones' domestics were landing on their feet, and she was glad.

A few minutes later, Elise and her mistress sat opposite each other on rosewood chairs before a very small coal fire, each sipping tea from a delicate china cup. Elise was thankful for both the tea and the coal, and for the fact that she hadn't been forced to make the tea herself.

Lady Anne set her cup and saucer on the side table with a gentle sigh. "Elise, the thought that you might leave me terrified me."

"I shall stay at your side as long as you want me, my dear."

"Thank you. I believe you and I may continue to dwell together—quite frugally of course." She waved a hand, encompassing the elegant room. "We'd have none of this, but we could take a small house together, and I believe we'd have enough to get by, just the two of us."

Relief washed through Elise. Security was high on her list of life goals. "But would you have to give up your place in society, my lady?"

Lady Anne shrugged. "We shall see. I suppose some of my friends will invite me to house parties and such, but maybe not, now that Father is gone. I may have to wear this year's gowns for several seasons." She gave Elise a rueful smile. "Perhaps I shall learn now who are my true friends."

"To be sure." The idea of setting out as two independent, if impoverished, women, had a certain appeal that bolstered Elise's stifled longing for adventure. That side of her nature seldom stood up and spoke to her, but she felt almost as excited as she had twenty-four years ago when she'd boarded the ship that brought her here from Germany to enter domestic service at Stoneford. And Elise had often been certain that Anne longed to defy convention and try an adventure of her own. Life with Lady Anne, outside the strict confines of high society, might be rather fun.

"There's another, more pressing matter," Lady Anne said.

"Oh?" Elise watched her over the rim of her cup as she sipped her tea.

"Yes. You know the situation Mr. Conrad detailed to me today, and you are aware that my father had two brothers."

"Yes." Elise hoped she wouldn't flush at the mention of Lady Anne's uncles. So unseemly.

"Since my uncle John died last summer—"

"That awful battle in the Crimea. So tragic."

Lady Anne nodded. "So that leaves David."

Now the telltale blush crept into Elise's cheeks. She could feel it spread upward and quickly raised her cup again.

"David is now the earl of Stoneford," Anne said. "At least he is if he can be found."

"Ah. But David Stone hasn't set foot in England, so far as we know, for twenty years." Elise set the cup back on the pink-and-white saucer with a slight clatter. "It was my impression that Mr. Conrad intended not to expend further energy looking for your uncle."

"That is true." Anne looked down at her cup, as though studying the bits of tea leaves as they settled in the bottom, to seek her future there. "And yet, so many lives are affected by his existence—or lack of it."

Elise swallowed with difficulty. Throughout these twenty years, she'd pined for David. For Anne it was perhaps a more academic matter, since she was an infant when David sailed for America. Of course she'd heard stories of her dashing young uncle, then third in line for the earldom. But Elise had known him personally, had thrilled to the timbre of his voice, had delighted in every glimpse of him when he came to his brother's house. Her lip quivered, and she thought it best to remain silent.

"Perhaps I'm not thinking clearly," Lady Anne said, "but I see only one course of action."

That caught Elise's attention. The young mistress had considered her options and had already made a decision. A cottage in some small village, no doubt. They could be quite cozy together, as Lady Anne had said.

"What course is that, my lady?" she dared to ask.

Lady Anne raised her chin and looked Elise in the eye. "We must find him, of course. Elise, you and I are bound for America."

CHAPTER 2

March 1855
St. Louis, Missouri

Elise held to the railing as she moved down the gangplank from the crowded riverboat. After the jolting, plunging river crossing, her gratitude on landing dwarfed all else.

"Elise?"

Lady Anne's wail brought her up short before her feet touched dry land. She turned and peered up the gangplank. Her mistress stood at the top, clutching the railing. The cold wind tossed the young woman's light veil and fluttered the decorative capes on her overcoat.

"Come along, my—my dear. It's perfectly safe."

Lady Anne's face held remnants of the terror she'd expressed on the ocean voyage. Elise shifted her valise to her other hand and hurried back up the ramp. With her large skirt, distended by six stiff petticoats and whalebone hoops, Lady Anne had effectively blocked all the other passengers' exit from the river steamer.

"Take my hand, dear." After a week's practice, Elise could still barely restrain her tongue from uttering "my lady" each time she addressed Anne. But the behavior they'd experienced in New York had made it clear that they'd be wise to travel as friends, not titled lady and servant. People who perceived that Anne was wealthy—something Elise would debate, depending on the definition of wealth—did their utmost to extract her fortune from her. As just plain Miss Anne Stone, she was less likely to be extorted.

Elise reached out and pried Anne's gloved fingers from the rail. "It's all right," she said softly. "Just a few steps and we'll be on good, solid earth again. Don't look over the side." She tugged gently on Anne's hand.

Anne took one mechanical step.

"That's good. Let's go." Elise tucked her hand firmly under Anne's elbow and threw an apologetic glance at the couple standing behind them. She couldn't help but notice the man behind them in line. He was staring at her, and Elise shivered. She'd seen him on the train yesterday, and again on the steamboat that brought them across the Mississippi. He seemed to lurk wherever she and Anne went on the steamer—in the cabin or up on deck, it didn't matter. He was always there: a thin man with an equally thin mustache. He hadn't approached them, but his presence made her uneasy. The best thing she could do was get Anne off the gangplank and into a hackney.

"Come along now, dear." Each step took an effort on Anne's part and constant praise from Elise, but at last their shoes—sturdy walking shoes Elise had insisted upon, but fine quality—touched the ground.

"Good day, ladies." One of the ship's stewards stood at the foot of the ramp, for all the good he'd done.

Elise nodded to him and pulled her mistress hastily to one side so that the other passengers could disembark. The couple bustled on toward a liveried coachman waiting with an open carriage. The thin man who'd watched them strode on and disappeared in the crowd. Elise hoped she'd never see him again.

"We're finally here." Anne looked about the busy wharf.

"Indeed, we are. St. Louis, Missouri." Elise noted that most of the passengers climbed into carriages, some of which appeared to be hackneys. "Come. I think we can find transportation."

A disembarking gentleman spoke to the steward, and the steward hurried out among the conveyances and returned a moment later.

"Right over there, sir. The team of black horses."

The gentleman passed him a coin.

"Thank you, sir. Have a good journey." The steward smiled as he tucked away the coin.

Elise opened her reticule. "Pardon me, but my companion and I shall need a hack that can take us and our luggage to a suitable hostelry."

"Yes, ma'am. Wait right here, and I'll fetch someone for you."

While he was gone, Elise fingered her available coins. She was still getting used to the American currency. The train trip from New York to the Mississippi had given her a quick if spotty education, and she selected a quarter dollar. She would have to give the fellow who loaded the luggage even more. When they reached their hotel, she must ask Lady Anne for more pocket money so that she could continue dealing with the laborers they found necessary to their journey.

"Here you go, ma'am. This fellow will take you in his cab to any hotel you please."

"Thank you." Elise slipped the quarter into the steward's hand, and he promptly pocketed it and abandoned her.

The newcomer, a short, lithe man of indeterminate age dressed in a rough jacket and trousers, whipped off his shapeless cloth cap, exposing a head of thick, dark hair.

"Afternoon, ma'am. At your service."

"Thank you." Elise pulled Anne forward. "This lady and I want you to collect our baggage and drive us to a decent hotel. Not the most expensive in the city, you understand, but a *nice* one."

"Yes, ma'am. I understand perfectly. You got trunks?"

"Er—yes." Elise peered down the wharf to where the stevedores were unloading luggage from the hold of the steamer. "Perhaps we could put the lady into your cab first? Then I could go with you to claim our things."

He nodded. "That's it right there, with the horses tied to the lamppost."

Elise lowered her voice. "Would the lady be safe if we left her there?"

"I think so."

"I'm feeling much better now," Anne said. Her face still looked pale, but she managed a smile. She'd always been a sturdy, healthy girl. Who would have thought she'd have gone all green about the gills as soon as they left the dock in England?

Elise had waited on her constantly for a week before Anne had gotten her sea legs, and they'd thought all was well. The voyage could have been worse, though they were always cold, and the ship's plunging still sent Anne to her berth on occasion. After landing in New York, they'd endured a jolting, smoke-filled journey on the train to the bank of the Mississippi and spent a night in a marginally clean hotel in the riverside town. But when they'd embarked on the river steamer that morning, Anne's queasiness had returned in full force.

Elise took her elbow. "Let's get you into the hackney."

She and the cabby put Anne in his coach and ventured onto the pier. The wind seemed to grow stronger as they got farther from shore, pulling at Elise's full skirts. She was grateful for the hatpins that securely anchored her chapeau.

The cab driver set a brisk pace to where the travelers' chests were piled. Elise pointed out her own steamer trunk and Anne's three. From another pile, she collected four smaller bags. The driver eyed the heap askance.

"I'll have to get a handcart. Are you sure this is everything?"

Elise almost thought he was joking. "Quite."

He nodded. "You go get in my cab. I'll be there shortly."

Elise didn't wait to see what heroics he'd have to perform to get a cart and load their trunks. She thrust a dollar into his hand and hurried back down the wharf.

Reaching the cab, she opened the door and gathered her skirts as best she could. She placed her foot on the step. The hoops in the hems of her petticoats eased through the doorway. She thought she was safe when she stumbled and catapulted into the coach, landing unceremoniously across Anne's lap.

Anne gasped. "Are you all right?"

"I believe so. Let's close the door so that I can bear my humiliation in relative privacy."

Anne giggled. "I'm sorry, but you did look funny." She managed to grab the door handle and swing it closed. The absence of wind immediately brought a comforting sense of warmth.

"Elise." Anne frowned and stared out the window.

"What is it, my lady?"

"Aside from the fact that you're not supposed to call me that, did you notice that man?"

"What man?"

"I thought I saw that annoying gentleman from the train—the one who ogled us so rudely."

Elise hesitated. She'd hoped Anne hadn't noticed him on the steamer. "What about him?"

"I thought I saw him just now—across the way. He was talking to another man—a tall, gangly fellow."

Elise leaned forward and peered from the side of the window opening.

"He's gone," Anne said.

Leaning back against the seat, Elise tried to breathe calmly. She'd told herself not to be suspicious when she saw the man on the steamer. Many people probably took the same train they had and then crossed the river to St. Louis. But this man had lingered about the docks while their luggage was being fetched.

"I expect it's nothing," she murmured, but her chest felt tight.

Wheels rattled nearby over the cobbles. The carriage swayed, and she grabbed the edge of the seat.

"Up, up," said a man's voice outside. "Heavy, ain't it?"

Elise caught her breath. Anne's eyes were wide with alarm.

"That's our cabby," Elise said. "He's loading our trunks, I'm sure."

"Of course." Anne took off her hat and smoothed her hair. "I admit I'm tired of traveling."

"We should be able to stay in St. Louis a few days," Elise said. "We'll rest this evening and put out inquiries for your uncle tomorrow."

All indicators pointed to David having left St. Louis several years ago, but it was their only clue. Had he gone back to the Atlantic coast, where business might be brisker? Or had he pushed on, into the western frontier?

"There should be some people in St. Louis who remember him," she said. "People the postmaster didn't talk to. Perhaps we can stop here a few days just to get our feet back under us."

"That sounds attractive. I wouldn't have thought it, but I'm quite exhausted."

The coach dipped on its springs and swayed again. A few moments later, the cabby appeared outside their door, smiling.

"All loaded, ladies. And where did you say I will be taking you?"

Elise smiled at his cheerful voice and Irish cant. "Well, sir, we hoped you could suggest a place." She looked around. "Suggest it quietly though, if you please. We do not wish to broadcast our lodging place."

Anne leaned forward. "Surely you know of a nice, clean place where ladies can stay without worrying every minute."

"To be sure," the cabby said. "I'll have you there in twenty minutes."

He disappeared, and the springs gave as he climbed to his perch on the driver's box. The horses set out at a good clip, and the cab rolled along with a minimum of jostling. Elise sank back with a sigh. Weariness seeped through every muscle. She closed her eyes and opened them, startled, when Anne spoke.

"Do you think we'll find him?"

Elise fought back her sleepiness and sat straighter. "Yes, I do."

"We've both prayed so hard," Anne said.

"The Lord will honor that."

"I wish I fully believed that. But if not, perhaps we can at least get the documentation needed for the peerage to remain active. It would be a pity for the house to sit there empty until the Crown takes it over and for Randolph to miss out on the title if it truly should be his." Anne reached out a hand as though to stop Elise's thoughts from running astray. "I haven't always been courteous to Randolph. For some reason I always found it difficult to like him."

Not "for some reason," Elise thought. *There are plenty of reasons, and I could personally name half a dozen.* But she wouldn't. Anne's vague dislike of her cousin was far better than certain knowledge that the man was a scoundrel.

The cab slowed, made a turn, and at last rolled to a stop.

24

"There we go, ladies. If this place is not to your liking, there's another not far from here that we can try. But this one is very genteel, they say."

Elise took the hand the cabby offered and climbed down, wishing she weren't so stiff. These long days of travel made her feel like an old woman. She surveyed the hotel as he helped Anne down. The broad, three-story clapboard building had a wide covered porch. Two elderly women sat there in rocking chairs, bundled up against the cool late March air, and a man in a beige suit lounged against the pillar near them. Shrubs lined the walk to the steps, and baskets of budding plants sat on the window ledges. A sign at the edge of the lawn read CINDERS HOTEL.

"It looks well kept," Elise ventured. "Shall we go in and see what it's like inside?"

"Would you like me to accompany you?" the cabby asked. "If you take a room, I'll come back out and unload your trunks."

"Splendid." Elise was thankful they'd found a reliable man. So far the Americans she'd dealt with ranged from blatant rapscallions to suave gentlemen. The cabby, to all appearances, was an honest and hardworking fellow.

Twenty minutes later, she and Anne had been shown to rooms on the second floor, and the hotel owner's son, with the cabby's help, had delivered their ample baggage. Elise tipped them generously and looked about Anne's room as the lady removed her hat and gloves.

"Perhaps we should have taken but one room," Elise said. "We need to conserve your funds."

"We may come to that," Anne said, gazing at the stack of trunks. "But for now, at least, we'll maintain our privacy."

"As you wish. But do tell me when we need to make a change." Elise walked over to her. "Here, my lady. Let me help you undress and get to bed. I'll have some supper brought up for you."

"I'm so tired," Anne admitted. She held up her arms and allowed Elise to pull her gown over her head. "Thank you. I know I shall feel better once I'm out of these crinolines and my corset."

As quickly as she could, Elise helped her change into a nightdress and wrapper then sat her mistress down so she could brush her hair.

"I could have a bath drawn for you."

"No, I'll wait until tomorrow. I want only to sink into that bed."

The single beds in both rooms had iron head- and footboards. Elise wasn't sure how comfortable they would be, but they did seem to have plump mattresses, and the bedding looked clean.

She helped her mistress into bed and turned the lamp low then walked down to the dining room where only a few customers lingered.

"Am I too late to dine?" she asked the waitress.

"No, ma'am. We've got roast beef and potatoes, or chicken stew. Take a seat anywhere you like."

"Thank you. And could I get a tray afterward for Miss Stone?"

"You sure can."

Elise hid her smile at the woman's broad accent. She supposed that she and Lady Anne sounded odd to these Yankees.

As she waited for her meal, she observed the other diners. None of them, to her relief, resembled the man she and Anne had seen earlier—*Mustache*, as she'd begun to think of him.

She supposed her suspicions were brought on by fatigue. He was only a traveler, like her, headed in the same direction. She unfolded her napkin and laid it across her lap, determined to think of more pleasant things.

David Stone, for instance. "Tell me about Uncle David," Lady Anne had said on the train. Elise had gathered her rioting thoughts and complied. David Stone was a handsome young man when last she'd seen him. Anne, of course, was too young to remember him, but she'd seen his portraits countless times. One of the three brothers hung in the hall at Stoneford—Richard, the eldest, at twenty-one, John at nineteen in his uniform, and David a lad of fourteen. He was the fairest, the most likable, and the most charming.

A second portrait of David hung in the small drawing room. He had sat for it the winter before he left England. He had grown only more handsome in the intervening eight years.

"Everyone liked him," Elise had told Anne. It was true. David had myriad friends and no enemies. Every woman who laid eyes on David Stone adored him. Elise was no exception.

But she was only the maid. At that time, she'd served Anne's mother, Lady Elizabeth Stone. She'd loved her mistress. And her mistress's brother-in-law.

David hadn't really noticed Elise—not in that way. He'd always been nice to her and even joked with her occasionally, but he'd never approached her romantically. The one man in the world she wished would do so treated her like a sister. On the other hand, Elise had needed to fight his cousin off whenever Randolph visited Stoneford.

Life wasn't fair.

Her meal came, and she savored it. The long, arduous day had taken its toll. She almost doubted she'd be able to waken Lady Anne long enough for the young woman to eat her dinner, but the plain, tasty food would be worth it and would give her strength for tomorrow—no doubt another long day.

Would they find David tomorrow?

Elise's pulse raced, though she calmly cut her roast beef and chewed one small bite at a time. It was unlikely that they'd catch up to him so soon. David had lived in this city for several years, but then he'd written to his brother Richard that he was moving on. The earl hadn't heard from him again, or if he had, the rest of the household wasn't told. If David had moved back to St. Louis, the postmaster would have informed Mr. Conrad. He must have gone somewhere else. But still. . .they might find some hint of his whereabouts among people in the city who knew him. Someday, and soon, God willing, they would find him.

Would she shortly stand face-to-face with the man she'd held in her heart all this time? David would have changed—Elise understood that. And if he'd changed for the worse, perhaps seeing him again would cleanse her mind of him. Maybe she'd be able to think about someone else now, after all these years.

She wanted a love. She wanted a home of her own. Perhaps it was too late to hope for children. But with Lady Anne's change in circumstances, Elise felt free to decide her own future. Would she remain with Anne for the rest of her life and serve her quietly? Or did something bigger await her? David? Or someone else?

CHAPTER 3

W e'll start with the last known address," Lady Anne said the next morning.

They'd both slept late and had breakfast sent to their rooms. Then they'd bathed and taken great care with their morning toilette. It was nearly noon before both felt ready to venture out and begin their search.

The hotel's owner came from behind his desk, smiling as they descended the stairs.

"Good day, ladies. How lovely you both look."

"Thank you," Elise said. Lady Anne merely nodded with a faint smile.

"How may I help you?" Mr. Williams asked.

Elise drew a slip of paper from her pocket, though she knew the address by heart. "Perhaps you could tell us where Union Street is. If it's not far, we might walk there."

"To be sure, ma'am. If you go down to the corner and turn left, then go two blocks—you might want to cross the street though, because it's muddy, and there's no cobbles here and no sidewalk on the near side—and get down to Walnut and turn again. Then it's not far. You'll see a laundry on the corner. That's the street you want."

Elise nodded slowly.

"And the livery?" Anne asked. "How far is that?"

"Perhaps half a mile."

After more discussion and repetition of the directions, the two ladies opted to walk rather than hire a hackney or a buggy. They set out on foot for the address where David had lived ten years ago, with Elise carrying a furled umbrella. The early morning fog had lifted some, but gray clouds hung low overhead. The streets were already muddy from the last shower, and the ladies were grateful for

the board sidewalks that led from the hotel to the corner. As Mr. Williams had foretold, however, on the next street they were forced to pick their way across the muddy thoroughfare, and the hems of their skirts grew filthy.

At last they arrived at the address, only to find that it was occupied by a tobacco shop. Lady Anne looked at Elise in dismay.

"Have we got it wrong?"

"I don't think so. The city is growing quickly. It's more likely that sometime in the last ten years your uncle's old house was torn down and this shop put here in its place."

Rain pattered down on them, and Elise raised the umbrella. "I suppose we can ask the shopkeeper if he knows anything about the building's history." The rain increased as she spoke, and that sealed their choice for taking shelter inside the shop.

No one stood behind the counter in the small store, but two men sat in chairs near an upright heating stove, and a third stood nearby, in conversation with them. All three had their pipes lit, and the air was hazy with aromatic smoke.

"Well, ladies!" One of the men, with luxuriant gray hair and a short-cropped beard, stood and gave a slight bow. "How may I assist you, or are you merely seeking a roof until the rain stops?"

Elise handed the collapsed umbrella to Lady Anne and stepped toward him. "We're looking for a gentleman who used to live at this address."

"Ah, an English lady seeking a gentleman." He smiled and ran a hand over his beard. "How long ago did your friend reside here?"

"At least ten years. This was the address he gave."

"Probably dead," the man still seated said dolefully. "Them was rough times."

The man who had first addressed Elise scowled at him and cleared his throat. "Pay no mind to him. This did used to be a private residence. I bought it about four years back. Before my shop, it was a bakery, or so I'm told. But it was a house once." He nodded, looking around him as though expecting to see the old furniture and residents emerge through the smoke.

"How would I find out more about the man who used to live here?" Elise could scarcely credit David, the son of an earl, living in such a small, rough building, but what did she know of life on the edge of civilization? David might have lived in poverty and not hinted of it to his family.

"What's his name?" the man asked.

"David Stone."

"Don't know him." The bearded man took a puff on his pipe and looked at his two companions, but they shook their heads.

"Might ask at the post office," said the younger man, who still stood by the stove.

Elise nodded and did not volunteer that the Stones' solicitor had done that already.

"You could ask around," said the third man. "Old Henry Cobb across the street has been here as long as anyone."

"Thank you."

Lady Anne began to cough. Rain or no rain, Elise decided it was time to get out of the tainted air.

"Good day, gentlemen." She took the umbrella and opened the door. Anne dived through it as though desperate to escape.

As she closed the door behind them, Elise heard the seated man say, "Dutch, you're lettin''em get away."

The wind blew a torrent of raindrops over them, and Elise angled the umbrella against it.

"What do you think, my lady? Should we seek out this man named Henry Cobb?"

"I'd feel we were remiss if we didn't." Anne had to raise her voice against the wind.

"I don't want you to catch a chill," Elise said.

The wind whipped Lady Anne's short veil and a few tendrils of hair escaping from beneath her hat. The fetching bonnet would be ruined if they stayed out long in this weather.

"Perhaps we should go back to the hotel until this blows over."

"No," Anne said. "I want to find Uncle David as quickly as possible."

"All right, then we'll make inquiries across the street."

Smoke rose from the chimney of the house directly across. The two women picked their way between ruts and puddles. They were nearly across when a laden wagon slogged down the way, throwing muddy water across the lower half of Elise's skirt. The driver shrugged and lifted his hat, grinning.

Elise held in the response she wanted to make and took Lady's Anne's elbow, guiding her up onto the stoop of an unpainted house that looked as though the wind might blow it down.

Anne rapped timidly with her gloved hand.

After a few seconds, Elise said, "We shall have to knock louder, I'm afraid." She used the umbrella handle to rap smartly on the weathered planks of the door.

She saw movement through a window to one side and waited, with the rain sheeting off the umbrella. The door swung open.

"Ladies! How may I help you?" An elderly man with several teeth missing and thinning white hair appraised them with an eager smile.

"Mr. Cobb?" Elise asked.

"Yes. Come in. Don't get company often, and the day's not fit for a three-legged dog. Come in and dry off, ladies."

Grateful for the prospect of a few minutes' warmth, Elise stepped in cautiously. She saw nothing to alarm her and beckoned to Anne to follow. With the door closed, the heat of the small room enveloped them. A fire blazed in a brick hearth, and a lamp burned on a small, bare table.

"Will you take a seat?" Cobb gestured toward a rocker positioned near the fireplace and a ladder-back chair near the table.

"Oh, no, thank you," Elise said. "We only wanted to inquire for my friend's uncle." She turned and nodded toward Anne. Despite her normal reserve, the lady had drifted toward the hearth and stood shivering before the fire.

"The young lady's uncle?" Cobb asked. "Do I know him?"

"Well, we hope so," Elise replied. "He used to live across the way, where the tobacconist's shop is now."

"Ah, that would be in the old days. And his name?"

"David Stone."

Cobb's brow furrowed. "Did he speak cockney like you?"

Elise flushed. The man obviously had no idea of the differences between a cockney accent and that of a cultured English gentleman, let alone a woman whose German tongue had taken on the British slant. "He was English, yes."

"Ah. Seems like I recall a gent living yonder."

"His family had a letter from him about ten years ago. Do you know when he left, or where he went?"

Cobb shook his head. "He's been gone a good many years. Ten sounds about right. Talked about going farther west, I think."

"Farther west?" Elise swallowed hard. Their journey had already taken them into conditions more primitive than she had ever imagined. St. Louis was reportedly one of the jumping-off points for even wilder country. "Do you have any idea how we can find out where he went? Were there other people he was friendly with?"

"I'm sorry, ma'am. I can't help you there." A gleam came into Cobb's eyes. "But I can offer you a glass of ale and a biscuit."

Lady Anne actually raised her chin at his words, and Elise realized she was exhausted and famished. "Uh, no, but thank you kindly, sir."

He winked at her. "If you're in town long, come back and visit with Henry Cobb. I always have a jug of ale put by."

The ladies ventured out again. The rain had slackened, but the drizzle and the deep mud made their trip back to the hotel miserable.

"I'm going to put you right to bed for a nap, and we'll continue our inquiries tomorrow," Elise said as they climbed the stairs. "In a few hours, we'll go down to dinner, or I can bring up a tray."

"I'm sure I'll be fine by then," Lady Anne said, but as Elise unlocked their door, she let out a delicate sneeze.

Elise spent an hour removing the mud from their skirts and petticoats. The hotel owner allowed her into the kitchen to use a flatiron, after which she returned to her room to clean and oil their shoes.

She ended up dining alone that evening and carrying up a bowl of soup, a coarse bread roll the Americans called a biscuit, and a cup of strong tea. After half the soup was gone, Lady Anne insisted she couldn't eat another bite. She rolled over and went back to sleep.

Elise turned down the lamp and went to her own room, where she undressed wearily in semidarkness. She prayed silently that her mistress would not be very ill. She'd been foolish to take Lady Anne out in such foul weather.

Dear Lord, she pleaded as she climbed into the narrow bed and drew up the piecework comforter, *please, please, let us find David soon.*

Thomas G. Costigan leaned on the bar in the Horsehead Saloon, sipping a beer. He couldn't afford whiskey anymore, so he bought beer one glass at a time and drank it slowly. He wished he'd never come east of Fort Laramie.

"You Costigan?"

He turned at the voice and faced a stranger. This fellow looked like a dandy—not unusual for St. Louis—but generally his kind patronized a higher class of watering hole. The slender man wore a suit and necktie and a bowler hat. On his feet were low-cut shoes, not boots. His mustache was more of a dark ink line across his top lip. A sissy mustache. Still, could be trouble.

"Who wants to know?" Thomas asked.

"My name is Peterson."

Thomas thought he caught a hint of New York in his accent, but he wasn't sure. Folks came to Saint Louie from all over.

"What do you want from me?"

Peterson gestured to a table at the side of the room. "Care to sit and discuss it? I'll stand you another one of those." He nodded toward Thomas's glass.

"Make it whiskey."

"Certainly."

Thomas stood and shuffled toward the empty table, taking his beer with him. A moment later, Peterson joined him and set down two glasses. Abandoning his beer, Thomas took a small sip. Now that was the real thing.

He set the glass down and looked at Peterson. "So what do you want?"

"I need a man to do a job, and I was told you might be the one."

Thomas wasn't against working, though he'd rather it didn't get too strenuous. But who would recommend him for a job? And what sort? He'd been in the brig for two days once at Fort Benton—up in Montana. Didn't like it and had determined never to be confined again. That experience had grown a little caution inside him.

"Depends. What do you need done?"

"It's what you might call a surveillance job."

Thomas squinted at him. "What's that?"

"Where you watch someone and report on their activities."

"Is that against the law?"

"No, absolutely not." Peterson seemed almost happy about it. "You simply follow the person about—without them realizing it of course—and make note of where they go, to whom they speak, and so on. Then you tell your employer what you've learned, and you get paid. Simple."

Thomas hesitated. It sounded like a job that would require staying sober, but he never got thoroughly drunk, anyway. That would likely end him up in some jail.

"How much?"

"Oh, I'll make it worth your while. Two dollars a day, plus any legitimate expenses you incur. And it won't be an unpleasant job. The people I need you to observe are quite pleasant to look at."

"That so?" The man wasn't making a lot of sense, to Thomas's way of thinking. Seemed like good wages for easy work. He took another sip of the whiskey.

"Are you interested?"

"I might be."

"Absolute confidentiality is required. You must tell no one either whom you are following or to whom you are reporting. Understood?"

"And how long does this go on?"

"I don't know yet. Perhaps a week or more."

Thomas nodded. "Sounds all right. But I can quit any time I choose."

"So long as you inform me. Don't just stop shadowing them without letting me know."

Thomas nodded.

Peterson slid a dollar across the table. "That's in advance. I'll pay you again at the end of a week or when the job ends, whichever comes sooner."

"All right—so who's the gent I'm following?"

Peterson smiled.

CHAPTER 4

Elise opened the door between her hotel room and Lady Anne's carefully, but it creaked on its hinges anyway.

"Welcome. Did you learn anything?" Lady Anne smiled at her from the chair by the window, where she sat fully clothed. Her prayer book lay open on the small table before her.

Elise closed the door and stripped off her gloves. "I'm afraid not. The postmaster was no help, as we feared. He only repeated what he'd said in his letter to Mr. Conrad. There's no record of David inquiring for general delivery mail since he left the city ten years ago. The postmaster did send me to the police station, however."

"The police?" Anne's rich brown eyes darkened in dismay.

"Only because he thought they would have a record if anything untoward had happened to your uncle. I spoke to one of the constables there, but they knew even less than the postmaster. The consensus is that your uncle David left St. Louis of his own free will and either returned to England or went farther west."

Lady Anne sighed. "Well, we know he didn't go back to England."

"Do we?"

Her young mistress considered that while Elise opened her reticule and took out the folded sheet of paper on which she'd written the names of the people she'd questioned.

"We know he never contacted the family again," Lady Anne said at last. "I can't imagine Uncle David setting foot in England again without letting Father know."

"I agree. So, barring a shipwreck, he's still in America someplace, and that place is most likely westward." *Whether dead or alive,* Elise added to herself, but she wouldn't speak the thought to poor Anne, who had already lost so many loved ones.

"Why west? Isn't it possible he went back to New York or one of the other cities on the East Coast?"

"Yes," Elise said, "but everyone seems to think his more probable course was westward. I found out where his store was located. It was a sort of general store, selling a variety of goods—groceries, tools, yard goods."

Lady Anne inhaled deeply and leaned her head back, closing her eyes for a moment. "So what do we do now?"

Elise took the Windsor chair opposite her and spread her skirts around her. "I have a few suggestions. Some may be practical, some not."

Anne studied her face. "Proceed."

"We can inquire of the people who now run the store. It's given over to furniture and cabinetry now, but it's possible they might know something. And the constable suggested we send letters to officials in several western cities—San Francisco, Oregon City, and so on—making inquiries about David Stone. That would take time—we'd have to wait here for replies—and is a very uncertain method of locating a person of whose whereabouts we have no clue."

"True. Unless we find evidence that he went to a particular location—"

"Precisely." Elise smiled at her. "Which is why I recommend a different course. If we stay in St. Louis a couple of weeks, we can make a more thorough inquiry. We know David left here ten years ago, but we still might turn up someone who knew him better than Mr. Cobb or the postmaster. Someone to whom he mentioned his plans."

"How likely is that after all this time?"

"I don't know. However. . ." Elise leaned toward her, holding Anne's gaze. "The constable told me that wagon trains will be forming as soon as the ground is dried up enough for travel westward. Most of them leave from Independence or St. Joseph, which are two other towns on the western edge of Missouri. But many people will pass through here on their way to the encampments. Hundreds of families will be crossing the Great Plains, going to Oregon or

California, and we might make inquiries among them."

Anne cocked her head to one side, causing her fetching curls to sway. "Why would people going west know about someone who went ten years ago?"

"Not them. The ones organizing the wagon trains. The outfitters."

"I see. Uncle David may have gone west on a wagon train."

"Yes, and one of the outfitters may have met him or perhaps even guided him. Or they might have met him in their travels, since some of these men go back and forth across the plains almost yearly."

"I like it," Anne said.

"Good. Then we need to bide our time, decide whether to keep these lodgings or look for something more economical, and inquire at places like stables and wainwrights' shops about how to contact the outfitters. As a start, I saw a broadside hanging outside the emporium today, announcing a gathering of emigrants in Independence the first week in April. Those interested in joining the expedition were urged to contact a Mr. Robert Whistler, who will be at the Riverside Hotel afternoons this week. He will take a small caravan of people to Independence soon, where they'll join a larger group."

Lady Anne clapped her hands together. "Elise, you are so clever. Whatever should I have done without you? Surely if we seek out these wagon guides, we'll learn something."

"I hope so. And in the meantime, we pray."

"Of course. And eat. Are you hungry, my dear?"

"Yes. Are you?" Elise asked.

"Starved."

"You look much better than you did yesterday."

"I feel better, too. I would like to go down to the dining room with you and partake of luncheon there."

"All right. Just let me freshen up." Elise stood and went to the door.

"Elise," Lady Anne said.

"Yes?"

"Did you have a third plan?"

Elise chuckled self-consciously. "I did have a rather nebulous

thought—but it's so farfetched that I wasn't going to suggest it unless this other plan fails."

"Oh?" Lady Anne nodded slowly. "Perhaps that is best. We have our course laid out for us."

Thomas G. Costigan sat on a keg of nails in Wyatt's General Merchandise, laconically watching the checker game in progress a few feet away and absorbing heat radiated by the tall stove in the center of the store. As long as the clutch of loiterers didn't get too big, the owner of the store encouraged them to stop by and socialize. That suited Thomas's plans perfectly.

His seat on a keg at the fringe of the hardware area allowed him a clear view of the counter to his right and several aisles of merchandise that ran the length of the store. James Wyatt, the store owner, had deliberately placed the most frequently purchased items at the far end of the room so that people in need of flour, cornmeal, or rolled oats had to walk through the store and pass displays of his most alluring merchandise—colorful woolen fabrics from New England; bulk tea and spices from the Far East; new books; medicines for man and beast; ready-made shoes; and the latest gadgets, tools, and notions.

Thomas could hear not only the talk around the stove, but also much of what was said at the counter without appearing to eavesdrop. And he could keep an eye on the tall woman with the brown hat as she moved about the store.

On this chilly morning in late March, the stunning woman had entered the store alone. He'd never seen her before. He would have remembered. But from the description Peterson had given him, he was sure. The cut of her clothes and her accent gave her away. She was the older of the two. The younger woman might have come out of the hotel and gone somewhere on her own—he had no idea. But he could only follow one at a time.

She browsed the textile display while Wyatt helped another customer, but she kept looking toward the counter. Thomas had no doubt she'd step up to have a word with the storekeeper as soon as he was free.

She stood halfway down the store and one aisle over from where Thomas sat. Even when she walked behind a tall rack of ready-made garments, he could see the top of her distinctive hat. She rounded the display and headed across the row, past the bolts of cloth, high-topped shoes, and bins of ginger roots and walnuts. When she glanced his way, Thomas averted his gaze to the checker game. The checker players and the hangers-on were watching her, too. A faint scent wafted toward him, overcoming the cinnamon, coffee, and pickle brine just for a moment. Lilacs?

Thomas sneaked another glance. In the dim recesses of the emporium, her hair looked to be a light, golden brown, but he'd be willing to bet that on a sunny day outside, it was more blond. The woman carried herself well. Thomas was thirty-nine. She looked to be a little younger, but she also seemed to be one who took care of herself.

The checker players resumed their game. One of them made a move, and the spectators crowed. The other customer went out the door, and the woman strode toward the counter. Thomas strained to hear what the lovely lady said to James Wyatt.

"Oh, he's been gone a long time, ma'am," Wyatt said. "I do remember him. He was my competition for a while. He must have been in business about five years. He seemed to be doing all right. They say he imported some fancy goods from England, and some of the ladies liked his shop because of that. But one day, he decided to close up and leave."

"Did he sell the store?"

"I don't think he owned the building. It's a furniture store now." She nodded.

"Seems to me he held a sale when he went out of business, to sell off his inventory. That was a slow week for me, but I knew that once he was gone, I'd pick up some of his regular customers, so I rode it out."

"You've no idea where he went, or if he opened another store

somewhere else?" the woman said.

The lady had a pronounced English accent—though a cultured one—and it was difficult to catch some of her words. To make matters worse, the chatter around the stove grew loud again.

Thomas stood and eased into the tool aisle and sauntered casually toward the entrance, keeping the row of display shelves between him and the counter. He paused before a rack of harness fittings, about four yards from where the lady stood. Her pinkish-tan skirt stood out around her. It looked to be velvet, or maybe a soft woolen material. Only the well-to-do women of St. Louis would wear something as fashionable. The poorer housewives wore plain wool or cotton dresses without those puffy petticoats underneath.

Over her dress, she wore a dark-brown, caped overcoat, and the matching brown hat sat atop her golden hair. She looked better than the sugar buns in Lars Neilsen's bakery window.

"I wish I could help you," Wyatt said, "but when Mr. Stone left, I didn't hear where he was going. Did you say you're a relation of his?"

"No," the lady said. "I'm a friend of his family. They've been trying to locate him for some time."

Wyatt nodded sympathetically. "I suppose you asked the postmaster if he left a forwarding address."

"Yes, that was one of the first things we did." The lady bowed her head for a moment. "Thank you for your time. Would you have any advice for someone in my situation?"

Wyatt shook his head. "Sorry, ma'am. If I was to guess, I'd have thought he went back to England. But from what you say, I'll have to change my theory. He might have gone west. Could have gone to California during the gold rush a few years back—lots of men did. And there's a lot of things that can keep a man from coming back."

A middle-aged woman with her arms full of sewing notions swooped down the center aisle toward the counter. Miss Finster, the Englishwoman, paid for a small purchase she'd apparently picked up during her wait. Thomas slipped out the door and across the street.

He leaned against the wall of a dentist's office and waited. A minute later, he was rewarded.

The Englishwoman came out of the emporium, carrying a small parcel wrapped in brown paper. She headed up the boardwalk. Thomas followed on his side of the street. When she turned a corner, he dashed across the cobbled thoroughfare and up onto the sidewalk where she'd been. Around the corner, he quickened his steps. For a moment, he'd lost her in a rash of pedestrians. Then he saw her again, near the end of the block. She walked quickly. No nonsense, that gal.

He hurried along, careful not to break into a run and attract attention. Three blocks later, he slowed. She'd turned in at a doorway. He sauntered along until he could read the sign clearly: MISSOURI DEMOCRAT. She'd gone into a newspaper office. Across the street was a bakery. The scents of yeast and chocolate hung in the air. Just the place he needed to keep watch in comfort.

Ten minutes later, Miss Finster came out of the *Democrat* office and retraced her steps a few blocks. Thomas had finished his sweet rolls and kept her in sight without difficulty. When she'd made two turns, he slowed down with a satisfied smile. She was headed for the Cinders, as he'd expected. Not the most plush hostelry, but a cut above what he'd be willing to pay for, and two above what most of the poor emigrants heading west could afford. He wondered if the younger woman, Miss Stone, was still inside. He looked around for a spot out of the wind where he could wait.

Eb Bentley sauntered across the paved street to the Riverside Hotel. He hated cobblestones. Hated cities. Hated big buildings. Give him the open West. Big sky, a good horse, distant mountains, and home waiting at the end of the day. Why had he let Rob Whistler talk him into doing this again, anyway?

As he dodged wagons and horsemen, he knew the answer. He needed the money. Enough to buy cattle to stock his ranch. The land was his, and his little house was built, but he needed cattle

and fencing and a bigger barn and a thousand other things. Seemed the surest way to accomplish that was to do one more run across the plains with a wagon train—or perhaps a crawl across the plains was more accurate. Nothing moved slower than an emigrant wagon pulled by oxen.

He strode up the steps and into the hotel's lobby, taking his hat off as he ducked instinctively beneath the lintel. He rarely bumped his head on doorways here, but it had become a habit from entering small cabins and low-ceilinged ranch houses.

"Eb. Over here."

He swung toward the familiar voice. Rob was sitting on a horsehair sofa in an alcove across from the front desk, talking to two men in rough clothes. They all stood as Eb approached them.

"This is our scout, Eb Bentley," Rob told the others. "He'll be with us from Independence all the way to Oregon City."

The two nodded at him, and Eb sized them up. Farmers, both with brown hair and eyes, both solidly built. Brothers, maybe.

"These gentlemen are outfitting their wagons here. They want to bring their families with me to Independence," Rob said.

Eb nodded, keeping his own counsel. Most folks took the riverboat to Independence, up the Missouri. But some—usually those trying to save money—drove their wagons the two hundred miles across the state. The river journey on a steamer was certainly easier, and faster, too. But it did cost money, and some people didn't want to be confined so closely with others that long. He recalled a few years back when cholera ran through the ranks of emigrants and decimated the passenger population on the riverboats. Personally, he'd rather take his horse and make his own peaceful way to the rendezvous. Never liked boats much.

"Well, sir, I guess we'll see you tonight," one of the men said.

"Sure enough. Be at the field where I told you by sunset. Eb and I will come around and make sure everyone's ready. We head out at dawn." Rob shook hands with the two men and waved them off as they left the hotel.

"How many wagons?" Eb asked, plopping down in the chair one

of the men had vacated.

"Eight so far, and I've sent several families on ahead by boat."

"There'll be three or four times that waiting when we get to Independence."

"I expect so." Rob put two fingers in his vest pocket and extracted a folded paper. He opened it and squinted down at the writing. "I've had thirty-three families speak for a place on the train so far. There'll be more, and some of them will have more than one wagon."

"Don't let it get too big," Eb said.

"I plan to cut it off at fifty."

"Lot of wagons, even so. It'll be hard to find grazing."

"We'll be one of the first trains out."

Eb shook his head. "I dunno, Rob. You go too early, and there's no grass yet."

"Go too late, and it's all eaten up," his friend retorted. "It's all in the timing, and I think we've planned it just right this time. Not like last year. Waited too long last year, that's for sure. Now, I'll head out with these eight wagons tomorrow morning, and you make sure you're here every afternoon for three more days, in case anyone else comes to see about joining the train."

Eb nodded. They'd been over the plan a dozen times. Any latecomers would have to take the riverboat to Independence or catch a later wagon train.

Rob's forehead wrinkled as he gazed toward the entrance.

Eb swung around and looked over the back of his armchair. Rob was watching two women who had come into the lobby and now approached the desk.

They looked like quality—Eb wasn't an expert, but the fabric of their skirts looked rich and ample. They wore the spreading crinoline skirts that at first had seemed to him such an outlandish fashion. Every time he came to a city, he had to get used to the style again. The ladies seemed to puff their skirts out wider every year. They must have to work hard, carrying all those starched petticoats around with them. It made him wonder if the ladies wore those huge skirts to keep fellows a good distance away. They both wore bonnets,

too. Not cotton poke bonnets, like the women on the wagon trains would wear, but fancy things with short netting veils and furbelows that probably served no practical function. Those hats wouldn't keep either sun or rain off the women's faces, so what good were they?

"That's a sight to behold," Rob said softly.

"You got no call to stare."

"No, you don't." Rob chuckled. "Did you get our supplies all laid by?"

"Sure did. I got a little extra horse feed."

"Good. We'd pay more in Independence. I've arranged with one of the wagon owners—a Mr. Leonard—to stow our grub in his wagon. It's just him traveling alone. He was glad to get a bit of cash for the space."

Rob raised his chin and stopped talking. Eb turned to see what he was staring at now.

The two women had walked over and now stood close behind Eb's chair. One hung back, a young woman of twenty or so, and pretty as a spring morning in the mountains, with dark hair, huge brown eyes, and a flawless complexion, so far as he could tell through the little veil. The older woman was past the flower of youth, but she'd held on to her beauty, with golden hair and rosy cheeks. Handsome woman, some would say.

"Mr. Whistler?"

Rob jumped up. "Yes, ma'am, I'm Robert Whistler."

Eb unfolded his long frame and stood, too.

"I am Elise Finster." The older woman sounded just a mite stuck-up, but in a flash Eb realized it was her accent. She sounded like a Britisher. She held out her gloved hand, and Rob took it—just the fingertips—and nodded.

"Ma'am."

"My friend and I"—she glanced fleetingly at the young woman—"have come to inquire about the wagon trains."

Eb almost choked. These two? On a wagon train?

Rob kept his composure. "Won't you sit down, ma'am? I'd be happy to answer any questions you may have."

Before Eb could have tightened a saddle cinch, the two ladies were seated on the chairs the farmers had sat in earlier. Rob resumed his seat, but Eb moved over near the wall and leaned against it, studying the two women. True quality, unless he was missing something, and definitely English. What on earth were they doing here?

"Allow me to introduce our scout, Mr. Edwin Bentley, usually known by his initials as 'Eb.'"

Both women looked at him. Eb nodded but said nothing. When he caught the older woman's frank gaze, he wished he'd put on his other shirt and washed off a layer of trail dust. Blue eyes with mysterious shadows in them—like the Blue Mountains in eastern Oregon, when you saw them from a distance.

"We understand you've led many wagon trains over the plains, Mr. Whistler," Miss Finster said.

"That's right." Rob leaned back a little and smiled. "This summer's trip will be my ninth across the plains." He craned his neck around. "What is it for you, Eb?"

"Seven."

Rob nodded. "Between us, we've got more experience than most anyone else you'll find, ma'am."

"That is just what we hoped for. You see, we're seeking a gentleman—my companion's uncle, actually—who we believe may have immigrated to Oregon. Or California. Or. . .well, you see our dilemma. We don't know exactly where he's gone. But we hoped you might, in all of your travels, have come across him."

Eb let out a deep sigh. So they weren't planning on going west themselves. That was a huge relief. All he and Rob needed was a couple of tender-skinned ladies to look after on the trail. But Rob wouldn't accept women unless they had men to drive and do for them. They'd talked about that after their first trip together and decided it was imperative that every wagon have at least one man attached to it.

"Ah, so you don't wish to make the journey yourselves," Rob said.

"Oh no, sir."

Rob nodded. "What is the name of the man you're looking for?"

"David Stone."

Rob's brow furrowed, and he shook his head slowly. "I don't recall anyone by that name." He looked over at Eb again. "Eb? Have you—"

"Don't think so. What'd he look like?"

Miss Finster smiled. "Miss Stone has a small portrait. Of course, the picture was made twenty years ago."

The younger woman opened a fancy mesh handbag and extracted a framed miniature portrait. Her friend took it and handed it to Rob.

"He's tall," Miss Finster said. "Your height or taller, and a very handsome young man. Well proportioned."

Was she blushing? What stake did she have in this quest other than acting as spokesman for the man's niece, who seemed quite timid?

"Did he have an English accent?" Eb asked.

Both women stared at him.

"Well, yes," Miss Finster said. "I suppose he did, though by then he'd been in America ten years or more. He owned a store here in St. Louis for a few years." She glanced at the younger woman and went on. "You see, he left England shortly after his niece was born. The family had several letters from him over a period of ten years. Half a dozen in all, perhaps. And then they stopped. The last one came from St. Louis, in early 1845."

Miss Stone nodded. "That's correct. We haven't heard a word from Uncle David since then."

Rob leaned back in his chair. "Ladies, I wish I could give you some definite news. I don't recall having this man along on any of my emigrant trains, and I think I'd remember an Englishman like that. But I have met a few English fellows in my travels." He turned to Eb. "Do you recall those two fellows who tagged along with us in 1850 until we came to the cutoff? They were headed for California, hoping to find gold."

"Irish," Eb said.

Rob frowned. "Are you sure? I thought they were from England."

Eb shook his head.

Rob shrugged. "Oh well. There are a lot of British people out in Oregon. England used to lay claim to the territory, you know."

Something stirred in Eb's memory. "I remember one fellow who had a general store in Oregon City for a while. You said this Mr. Stone ran a store here in Saint Louie?"

Both women turned eager faces toward him, and Eb's heart twanged. *Lord, don't let these ladies land on a wagon train. None of the men would want to do a lick of work between here and the Columbia. They'd all stand around gawking at the pretty faces.*

"The last time I was in that store must have been two or three years ago." Eb rubbed his chin and frowned, trying to think what the man had looked like.

"Do you recall his name?" Miss Finster asked.

"No, ma'am."

Rob said, "You must mean the man at Valley Mercantile."

"Right." There was no use getting the ladies' hopes up, but still . . .it could be the man they were looking for. Miss Stone's poignant expression heightened Eb's anxiety.

Nope, can't let our herdsmen get a look at these two.

Rob's face wrinkled. "I only saw that fellow once or twice."

"Same here," Eb said. "But he was tall, ma'am. Had light hair."

"That sounds like Uncle David," Miss Stone said.

Eb shrugged. "I don't know if he looked like that picture you have. Of course, I didn't know him well. I went in his store a couple of times. But it almost seems as though the last time I went in, somebody new was running the place."

Rob said, "You ladies are welcome to talk to the folks preparing to go with us on the wagon train. They're forming up at a field west of town."

"When will you leave?" Miss Finster asked.

"Early in the morning. It's not likely any of them knows Mr. Stone, but you never can tell who has connections out West these days."

Eb pushed away from the wall. "One other thing you could do."

THE LADY'S MAID

"Yes?" Miss Finster and Miss Stone swiveled toward him.

"Seems to me that one Englishman would gravitate toward another. You could ask around for other English folks in the city. They might know your gentleman."

"Yes," said Miss Finster. "We could ask the hotel keeper and the postmaster and the police department for names of other British people. That makes sense, Mr. Bentley." She gathered her skirts and stood. "Thank you so much, gentlemen."

Miss Stone rose as well, holding her ridiculously tiny handbag before her.

"You're very welcome, ladies," Rob said heartily as he rose. "If you want to go out to the rendezvous field this afternoon, you'll find several emigrant families there you can talk to, but you might have better luck following Eb's suggestion. We pull out for Independence at dawn. That is, I do. Eb will be here a few more days, and then he'll catch up to us at Independence. If he can be of further assistance to you, just come here between one and four in the afternoon."

Miss Finster shook his hand as Rob rambled. Then she turned toward Eb and held out her dainty hand. He looked down at her spotless white glove and slowly reached out to grasp her fingers.

"Thank you, too, Mr. Bentley. You've been most helpful."

"It's nothing."

"Oh, it's something indeed. It's sound advice and courage you've given us. Isn't that right, Anne?"

The girl nodded—she wasn't much more than a girl. Though she was pretty, Eb felt she hadn't the substance her companion had. Miss Finster might be a highfalutin' lady, but there was something real about her. She probably couldn't make pie worth eating, but she wasn't going to quit looking for this David Stone until she'd exhausted all avenues. Whether her resolve was for the young lady's sake or her own, he couldn't tell.

"Good day, gentlemen, and thank you," Miss Stone said.

Neither Rob nor Eb pretended not to watch them as they glided smoothly toward the hotel entrance.

Rob let out a deep breath. "Now, those were ladies, Eb."

49

CHAPTER 5

W e have to go to Oregon."

Lady Anne nodded slowly, surveying Elise with troubled eyes.

"That was my third plan all along," Elise said. "I know it's crazy, but we've tried everything else." She sat on the patchwork counterpane in her hotel room and spoke earnestly. If she couldn't persuade Anne now, the adventure was over, and David's fate would remain unknown. "We can't learn any more here, and we can't go home empty handed."

Lady Anne swallowed hard. "It's such a foreboding thought. I don't know if. . ."

"If what, dear?" Elise rose and went to stand beside her. They'd drawn so close over the last few weeks, sharing close quarters and their hopes and dreams. She laid a hand gently on Anne's shoulder. "What is it?"

Lady Anne's eyes glistened. "I'm not sure I'm strong enough."

Elise pressed her lips together for a moment, considering what she was asking of the young woman. "Before we left England, I might have agreed, but you're stronger than you were. I have confidence that you'll be able to find David. You were magnificent when we questioned all those people yesterday. I could see how the gentlemen at the newspaper office admired your pluck."

"I did feel as though they truly wanted to help us. It's a shame no one answered your advertisement."

"Yes. I had such hopes for that possibility." It seemed David Stone was forgotten in St. Louis. Elise tried to summon her own courage so she could keep buttressing Anne. "My dear, I don't think you could be content to go back across the ocean without knowing you'd tried everything."

Lady Anne drew in a shaky breath. "Perhaps you're right. But

I was so seasick. . . ."

"You're over that now."

"I know, but to catch Mr. Whistler and his caravan, we'd have to go to Independence. The only way to get there quickly and have time to buy a wagon and outfit it would be to go by riverboat, and I'm afraid I'd be ill again."

"The trip to Independence is only a few days. You can survive that. And you've done so much better since we arrived in St. Louis. Well, except for that one rainy day."

"Yes. Since the sun came out, I've felt quite well." Lady Anne stood and walked to the window. "Do you really think we could survive the rigors of the trail, Elise? The men we've spoken to have talked about huge mountains, and wolves, and—and Indians." She swung around and faced Elise. "What about the savages? Do you believe the stories?"

"I'm not sure."

Anne's eyes brightened. "Maybe we could go see Mr. Bentley again. We could ask him how difficult the trip really is."

"I fear we're too late. They said he'd be at the hotel three more afternoons. Wasn't today his last day?"

"Too bad."

"Yes. But Mr. Whistler's made the journey nine times." Elise smiled. "Either those men are superhuman, or the trip is doable for mortals like you and me."

Lady Anne squared her shoulders. "Well, we can't give up now. If we sail to Independence and can't find Uncle David, we have no other choice. We haven't any other promising leads. Only the man who rented the store to him."

"Yes." The man running the furniture store had directed them to his landlord, and that man had remembered one vital bit of information. "He sent David some money in Independence."

"But that doesn't mean he stayed there." Anne eyed her bleakly.

"No, and the store owner thought he recalled David saying he wanted to see Oregon. He sold the last of David's inventory for him and posted David's share to him in Independence. It's the first clue we'd found that named a destination."

Anne grimaced. "I had hoped that couple from Dorset could be of more help to us. And the newspaper ad didn't help. I'm sure if Uncle David was still in the vicinity, we'd have caught wind of him by now."

"I think so, too. So then. . .we're agreed?" Elise watched Lady Anne's face carefully.

Her young mistress nodded. "I only hope I shall not fail you, Elise. You've done so much for me."

"But this is for you. For the Stone family."

Lady Anne's smooth brow furrowed. "It's for both of us. I dare you to say otherwise."

Thomas G. Costigan looked over his shoulder before entering the Horsehead. No one was following him—but then, why would they? He smiled grimly and ducked inside. The low-ceilinged room was dim and smoky. He saw Peterson at a small table in the back corner. Thomas stopped at the bar for a glass of whiskey and carried it to the table and sat down.

"Well?" Peterson asked.

"They've made inquiries all over town, but they haven't turned up anything solid."

Peterson swore. "My own efforts have been no more successful. Where did they go today?"

"They hired a buggy and driver and went to several private residences and a few shops. And they went back to the newspaper office. I was able to hear a snatch of their conversation when they left there. Seems that ad they took out a few days ago hasn't gained them anything."

"I was hoping."

Thomas fished a folded piece of paper from his pocket and passed it to Peterson. "Here's where they went today." He smiled at the memory of the afternoon he'd spent trailing them about the city. "The older one—Miss Finster?"

Peterson nodded.

"She had the driver give her a lesson on the way back to the livery."

"Really? A lesson in driving?"

"Yup. Independent, that one. She's a fine-looking woman though. They both are." Thomas had to wonder why the handsome Miss Finster was still unmarried. Those fellows in England must be blind.

Peterson lifted his glass and took a swallow. "All right, stay on the job."

Thomas nodded. "They seem to make an early night of it."

"As proper ladies should."

Peterson didn't suggest that he should keep watch once the ladies retired to the hotel in the evening, and Thomas was glad of that.

"What if they give up and go back to England?"

"Then your job ends." Peterson scowled. "And mine will have only begun."

Thomas inhaled slowly as he watched the thin man. Peterson definitely hoped these two women would lead him to David Stone. But why? What was so important that this man would continue the search even if Stone's loved ones gave it up?

Independence was a rough and rowdy town with growing pains. No cobblestones here. No horse cars or fancy shops.

Eb's boot heels thudded on the bare boards as he mounted the steps to the Kenton House. Rob Whistler was still on the road with the emigrant train they'd formed in St. Louis. He didn't need Eb to scout for them on this leg, so he'd ridden past the caravan and on ahead to check on the rendezvous field and secure permission to use the hotel lobby as an office for a few days.

"Mr. Bentley!" The desk clerk's call drew Eb's attention, and he strode over to see what the fellow wanted.

The short man behind the desk smiled at him. "You have some callers."

"Already?" Eb wished they'd wait for Rob to arrive. He didn't have the easy manner with farmers and haberdashers that Rob had.

The clerk nodded toward the sitting area behind him. "Yonder. I must say they're classy ladies."

Ladies? Eb turned slowly. A woman in a gray-and-cream-striped silk dress with an emerald-green cape and a green hat rose from one of the chairs and smiled at him. Her full skirt swayed gently, and her blue eyes sparkled.

"Hello, Mr. Bentley."

"Miss Finster?"

She nodded. Beyond her, Miss Stone sat demurely on another chair.

A week had passed since he'd seen the two women in St. Louis, but here they were in Independence, looking as lovely and well groomed as ever. He'd been sure they'd give up the search for Miss Stone's uncle.

"We decided to continue our journey," Miss Finster said.

Eb did some quick calculations. He'd have seen them on the road if they'd driven. "You must have taken the steamer."

"That's correct." Miss Finster's face skewed for a moment, and he gathered that the voyage had been cramped and unpleasant, but she said no more about it. "The best information we could gather was from you, sir, with your description of the Englishman in Oregon City. That and a possible clue from the gentleman who owns the building David Stone leased for his store in St. Louis. We've pinned our hopes on those bits of news."

Eb's heart sank. He didn't want to be responsible for their disillusionment. "Now, ma'am, you've got to understand, I'm not at all sure that was him. I don't know his name or where he went to or anything."

"We realize that. But La—that is, my companion, Miss Stone, feels very strongly that she must do everything within her power to locate David. It's a family matter, you see."

Eb didn't see at all. He had a raft of cousins back in New Hampshire himself, but he didn't feel compelled to go see them.

He'd had no news of his family in years.

Miss Stone came over to stand beside her friend. "We did seek out other British citizens as you suggested. We found several during our time in St. Louis. One woman who married an American attorney remembered David Stone."

"Well now. I expect that was an encouragement."

"Yes."

Miss Finster smiled, and the transformation of her face almost made Eb glad she'd found him again. Her features formed such a pleasant view that he could stand and watch her face for a long time, the way he did sometimes in the Cascades, watching the sun dip behind the high peaks, leaving purple and orange streaks on the snowcaps.

"Indeed it was, sir. Mrs. Stanley told us that she and her husband invited Mr. Stone to dinner once so that they could talk about England, and a pleasant evening they had."

"But she didn't know what became of him?" Eb asked.

"We feel that what she told us confirms—or at least adds to—what you said. David Stone decided about ten years ago to sell his business and go farther west." Miss Finster shrugged. "The Stanleys couldn't tell us any more. They'd never heard from David after he left, but they were sure he would head for the Pacific and probably open a store there, as he'd done fairly well here in that line."

"I guess that makes sense, but I still—"

"Which is why we want to join the wagon train for Oregon." Miss Stone's eyes widened as though she was shocked at her outburst. Her gloved hand flew to her lips.

Miss Finster smiled. "Yes. That's exactly what we want to do. It's why we came here to see you, Mr. Bentley. What do we need to do to join your wagon company?"

Eb stared at her. "You...uh...you want to—" A vision of the two refined ladies gathering buffalo chips for their campfire flickered across his mind. "Oh no, ma'am. That's not possible."

"The nerve of that man." Elise could barely contain her ire as she and Lady Anne marched down the boardwalk in search of a livery stable. "He has no right to tell us we can't go."

Lady Anne scurried to catch up.

"I'm sorry." Elise slowed her pace. "I'm so incensed with that—that—scout."

Lady Anne chuckled. "Dear Elise. I felt certain you'd come out with some vulgar name, but it isn't in you, is it?"

"I guess not, but if we start hobnobbing with teamsters, I may learn a few earthy expressions to use on Mr. Bentley."

"I know it's upsetting," Anne said, "but if it's Mr. Whistler's policy, we'll have to abide by it."

"I think Eb Bentley's making it up." Elise paused at the end of the boardwalk and peered at the rutted dirt street below them. At least the roadway they had to cross wasn't a river of mud like the one they'd encountered in St. Louis two weeks ago.

"He said Mr. Whistler has made it his policy since his first trip across the plains, when he had so much trouble with a widow woman who couldn't control her own livestock." Lady Anne's reminder came out gently, in a ladylike tone.

Elise frowned. "I know, but I intend to go ahead with our plans. If we need a man to drive our wagon, we'll hire one." She threw Anne an apologetic glance. "That is, if you wish to and you think we can afford it."

"I believe we can. Once we know how much a wagon and team will cost, we'll have a better idea."

Elise nodded. Lady Anne would not be able to collect more money from her trust until the first of the year—a long nine months from now. She'd taken all she could from the bank before they left England. They had to plan carefully, or they might run out of funds in the middle of the wilderness. If only they didn't need to hire a man. She'd learned the rudiments of driving a horse. Surely it

couldn't be that difficult—after all, the wagons would move slowly.

"Well, Mr. Whistler should be in Independence the day after tomorrow. We'll get the full story from him on what's required."

"Yes. I'm sure he'll let us go if we just adhere to his rules." Lady Anne patted her arm.

"There's a bakery shop," Elise said. "Let's stop there and ask directions to the nearest stable. That Eb Bentley was rather vague about where we could buy our equipment. I'll tell you right now, I don't trust him."

CHAPTER 6

Eb was surprised at the relief he felt when the wagon train came in sight. He'd ridden out two miles from town to meet Rob and the emigrants. The white dots crawling down a hill in the distance were covered wagons approaching from the east. He trotted his spotted gelding, Speck, toward them and soon distinguished Rob's form at the head of the convoy. The man on the tall chestnut horse wore his usual wide-brimmed black hat and a red neckerchief that stood out from the dullness of the scene.

Speck cantered willingly toward the train. Eb pulled him up and swung around to ride side by side with Rob.

"Howdy," Rob said.

"You made it."

"Sure did."

Eb looked over his shoulder at the wagons that were strung out single file behind them. "Looks like more than eight wagons."

Rob grinned. "Twelve. The Harkness family added one, so they've got three in all, and the Adams brothers each have their own wagon. We added two more families between St. Louis and here."

Eb nodded. It happened a lot. Families who'd been waiting for the season to start joined up with the first train that came through.

"There's already twenty-eight at the field. More coming in every day."

"Good," Rob said. "Can we pull out Monday?"

Eb grimaced. "Not sure. Several people have come to ask me about going. Some of them aren't ready."

"Did you give them the list of supplies and equipment?"

"Yup."

Rob nodded. "If they're ready by next Monday, we'll take 'em. But I won't let anyone start off half-cocked. Not on my train."

"Well. . ."

Rob's eyes narrowed as he studied Eb. "What?"

"Those ladies."

"What ladies?" Rob scowled at him fiercely—a sure indicator his patience was wearing thin—probably as thin as the seat of the twill pants Rob favored when he rode horseback all day. Not a good sign when they hadn't even reached Independence.

"The English ones."

"English?" Rob pulled his head back, and his eyebrows nearly collided. "You mean those two gals in St. Louis? Miss Stone and Miss. . .Miss Finster, wasn't it?"

"They're the ones. Only they're not in St. Louis anymore. They're here."

Rob jerked back on his reins, and his chestnut stopped abruptly. "How can they be here? I left them healthy and beautiful in Saint Louie last week."

"Took the steamer." Eb let Speck keep walking, and Rob had to trot Bailey to catch up with him.

"All right, so they're here. What's going on? Are they still looking for Miss Stone's uncle?"

"Yup."

They went on in silence for a few steps.

"Well?" Rob's voice rose.

"Well, what?"

"Edwin Bentley, you are the most irritating man I know. If you weren't such a good scout, I'd trade you in for someone else. Someone who'd speak up and say what he meant instead of dropping little nuggets on the trail."

Eb had to chuckle at that. "You know me, Rob. I ain't no prospector, and I ain't a big talker."

"You're also not usually a man who butchers the English language. What's up with those English ladies? There's got to be some reason you brought up the subject, or were you just awestruck by their pulchritude and had to share your devotion with me?"

"Haw. They want to get a wagon and go west."

Rob's jaw dropped.

Eb said quickly, "I told them you'd say no, on account of they've got no man to drive them."

"Whoa, whoa, whoa." Rob's gelding stopped dead. "Not you, you lunkheaded nag!" He kicked Bailey, and the chestnut began walking again.

Eb shoved his hat back. "They're single ladies. I told them it's your longstanding policy not to let women attempt the crossing without a man to handle their livestock."

"Well, yes, but—"

"What do you mean, 'but'?" Eb glared at him. He'd had a bad feeling about this. Ever since they'd met the ladies, Rob had kept bringing up how dainty and courteous they were, almost like he wished he'd see more of them, which didn't make sense, because Rob had a perfectly good wife waiting for him at home in Oregon. Maybe Miss Stone's story had stirred his heart and he was feeling magnanimous. Eb hoped it wasn't something more than that.

Ever since he'd gotten his wife, Dulcie, safely to Oregon a couple of years ago, Rob had hinted that Eb should find married bliss as well. He wouldn't be thinking along those lines now, would he? Miss Stone was too young for men their age—Eb was pushing forty pretty hard, and Rob was a couple of years older. But Miss Finster—well, if the herd was culled according to age, he suspected she'd be in the holding pen with him and Rob. And if Rob was getting notions about having an eligible woman in Eb's age range along on the trek to Oregon, he would have to put a stop to that right now.

"You can't think of letting them set out alone. Why, those women have never done a lick of work in their lives. They're ladies."

Rob smiled. "Oh, I suspect they can ply a needle and maybe even bake a cake."

"Ha! Not likely."

Rob was unsuspecting; that was it. When it came to dealing with men, he knew a pickpocket or a professional gambler when he saw one, and he could weed out the greenhorns on the wagon

train quicker than you could wolf down a flapjack. But women? His friend had a soft spot. He always voted in favor of helping widows and ladies in distress. And when a woman started crying, watch out! That's why Rob had made the policy in the first place—so he could invoke it when his emotions threatened to beat the stuffing out of his logic.

"So you discouraged them?" Rob asked.

Eb thought about that. The ladies hadn't looked too glum when they'd left him. In fact, Miss Finster had an irate spark in her eye that made her look, if anything, more handsome.

"It wouldn't surprise me if they came 'round to question you about your rules. They're set on going out to look for Mr. Stone."

"They should go by ship," Rob said.

"Around the horn?" Eb couldn't imagine the proper ladies undergoing that ordeal.

Rob shrugged. "They sailed across the Atlantic, and you said they took the steamer here. Sounds like they're right at home on boats."

"Why don't you suggest that to them?"

"Maybe I will."

"Good."

The buildings on the outskirts of Independence came into view, and Eb shot Rob another glance. Better be on hand when the ladies confronted him, or that old soft spot might come to the fore. And Eb was determined not to guide a gaggle of helpless females through Indian Territory.

Try as she might, Elise hadn't been able to discover where the wagon master and his scout were lodging. She'd thought they must be at the Kenton House, since that was where she and Anne had found Mr. Bentley a couple of days ago. But this morning the clerk told her the gentlemen weren't actually staying at the hotel, and he didn't think they'd be in today.

The town was half-grown and a bit on the wild side. The ladies had traipsed about to several hotels and boardinghouses and found no trace of Whistler and Bentley.

"You might try out at the rendezvous field," the owner at the last place had suggested. "If they've got a wagon train that's leaving soon, they're probably sleeping right there on the ground."

And so they went to the livery stable and inquired about renting a horse and buggy with a driver.

"Got no driver available," the liveryman said.

Elise swallowed hard. "Well, then I suppose I shall have to drive myself."

Anne's eyes grew round, but she kept her peace, for which Elise was thankful.

The liveryman looked her over doubtfully. "Are you sure, ma'am?"

"Yes, sir, I am. I should like a well-behaved horse though."

"Yes, ma'am." He named a price which seemed to Elise exorbitant.

"That's more than we paid in St. Louis, with a driver included."

The man spat on the ground. "This ain't Saint Louie, ma'am. Do you want the rig or not?"

"Yes."

Elise and Anne waited while the man harnessed the horse to a small single-seat buggy with a black cloth top. At least they would have some protection from the fickle sun.

"Are you certain it's safe to go alone?" Anne whispered.

"I learned the rudiments of driving," Elise said. "We need to consult Mr. Whistler today. I don't feel we have another choice. And with a calm horse, what can go wrong?"

The owner led out the sorriest-looking animal Elise had ever seen. Its back curved lower than normal, and she could easily count its ribs behind the leather tugs.

Anne, who had regularly ridden her father's hunters to hounds, also eyed the horse askance. "That animal doesn't look healthy," she ventured.

"Take it or leave it."

Anne looked to Elise with questioning eyes.

"We'll take it." Elise was surprised by her own grim determination. She went to the buggy, held up her skirt, and climbed in. The liveryman had the grace to give Anne a hand up on the other side.

"Good day, ladies. I'll expect you and Prince back before sunset."

Elise decided it would do no good to comment on the pitiful horse's regal name. "Shouldn't I have a whip or something?"

The man frowned at her. "Naw, you'll be all right. Just snap the reins on his flanks and he'll go."

"All right," she said dubiously. "And if you'd be so kind, sir, would you repeat the directions to the wagon train's field for me one more time?" He did, and Elise tried to memorize the roads and landmarks he named.

"You can't miss it," he concluded.

Elise gathered the reins. With her mouth, she made the clicking sound she'd heard coachmen make many times. When Prince didn't move, she jiggled the reins and then flicked them so that they slapped against the horse's thin rump. Prince walked toward the street.

"There." Elise smiled over at Anne. "We should be there in no time."

She soon discovered that Prince had a mind of his own. Whenever Elise pulled on one rein, indicating he should turn, he obstinately tried to continue in a straight path. If they came to a broad, open place, he curved around, trying to head back toward the livery stable.

As they reached the outskirts of town, the horse veered to the edge of the road to avoid an oncoming wagon and sent one wheel off the edge and into a shallow ditch. Elise gasped and snapped the reins.

"Get up, you!"

Startled, Prince leaped forward and hauled the buggy back onto the roadway. Elise let him continue at a trot and concentrated on keeping him moving straight. After a few yards, however, he dropped back into his sluggish walk.

She looked over at Anne, who still clutched her hat to her head. "All right?"

Anne nodded and straightened on the seat. Her countenance smoothed out. "I'm sure we're fine."

They continued on sedately, but the moment's terror was not easily forgotten. Elise's confidence flagged. Her arms ached from tugging on the lines and flicking them often in her futile efforts to convince the horse to trot again.

They'd been out an hour when Anne looked uneasily toward the small copse of trees they were passing. "Perhaps we missed it after all. They can't be this far out of town, can they?"

"As soon as I find a place wide enough, I shall turn this animal around." Elise gritted her teeth. There might be highwaymen lurking about, or even savages. She'd been foolish not to insist on a driver, even if that meant finding a different livery stable. The open country seemed limitless, and she shivered.

She found a place where she could turn safely off the road and guide the horse around in a wide circle. When they had lurched back onto the road, she flicked the reins. Pointed toward home once more, Prince stepped out in a smarter walk.

Eb was checking over a New York family's oxen when the buggy rolled into the field. He nodded to Mr. Woolman and wandered over to where Rob was talking to the Adams brothers. Eb began whistling "London Bridge Is Falling Down."

"Hmm?" Rob arched his eyebrows at Eb then looked beyond him. "Aha." He strolled toward the buggy, driven by a windblown and very attractive Miss Finster.

Eb tore his gaze away and nodded to the Adamses. "So, you got your supplies all laid in?"

"Mostly," said Hector, the elder brother. "We need to pick up a few more foodstuffs between now and Monday." The "boys" were in their thirties, and Daniel usually let his brother do the talking while he stood by and nodded.

"Good work." Eb ambled on to the next wagon, a little closer to where Rob was engrossed in conversation with Miss Finster and Miss Stone. He stooped and pretended to examine the axle nut on the wagon's front wheel.

"Well, now, Eb tells me he informed you about my rule," Rob said. "Ladies who haven't got a man along to drive and do the heavy work for them aren't allowed."

"He did mention it," Miss Finster replied, "but you must have a way for women to circumvent that. There must be women who need to go out and join their husbands, or widows who want to take their families out and begin farming."

"Not so many as you'd think," Rob said. "They know how hard it is without a man along. I've had a few instances where a man died along the trail and his womenfolk had to continue on without him. That's a little different. But it's always hard, and it puts hardship on the others in the train to look out for them."

"We're self-sufficient, I assure you, sir."

Rob shook his head. "I'm sorry, ladies, but it would be asking for trouble. Neither of you has much experience in overland travel, and it would slow us down. Maybe you should think about going downriver to New Orleans and taking a ship."

"What if we could hire a man to go along and work for us?" Miss Finster asked. "Is that ever done? Get someone who can tend to the animals and do some of the driving?"

Rob pushed his hat back on his head. "Well, yes, it's possible. You might find a man who wants to go west but hasn't the money to outfit a wagon for himself. But you need to make sure you get someone you can trust and who'll work hard."

Miss Finster glanced toward her companion and cleared her throat. "That's what we'll do. Can you recommend someone?"

"Why, ma'am, I don't live here. I don't know too many people in town. But you could ask at the livery or put up a broadside at the post office. But you'll have to get right on it. We pull out Monday morning, no matter what."

"Oh dear," said Miss Stone.

"That is soon," Miss Finster agreed. "What exactly would we need, assuming we found a driver?"

"Well, ma'am, I can give you a list of supplies. You'd have to figure foodstuffs for yourselves and your hired hand. Of course, the first thing you'd need would be a wagon and a team of oxen or mules."

Eb straightened and stared at Rob's back. He couldn't be doing this—but he was. Probably they'd wind up with a couple of old mules with heaves. Someone wanting to unload some bad stock would see them as an easy mark. The swaybacked horse they drove today was proof of that.

Rob left them and strode to where he'd tied his saddled horse. Eb intercepted him while he fished in his saddlebag.

"What on earth are you doing, Rob?"

"I'm getting a copy of the supply list for the ladies."

"You can't let them go with us."

"They said they'd hire a driver."

"Oh, I suppose they'll find a man of sterling character on three days' notice."

Rob shrugged. "I can't refuse them if they meet the requirements."

"Of course you can."

"I won't."

Eb nodded in silence. Rob had tossed his good judgment aside because of a couple of pretty faces with a tragic story. Poor Miss Stone had her heart set on finding her long lost uncle, and they'd convinced Rob that, with his help, they could find him.

"Excuse me," Rob said with exaggerated politeness. "I need to explain to these ladies what they need to do in order to join this wagon train."

Eb watched him go. The ladies bowed and simpered when he gave them the paper—or so it seemed to Eb.

Miss Finster's smile faded as she perused the list. "Oxen? Oh dear. Must we?"

"Or mules," Rob said affably. "Oxen cost less and hold up better on grass. Mules generally need some grain, so you'd have to buy that

and carry it along."

"Neither of us has much experience with cattle," Miss Finster said.

Her young companion asked, "Couldn't we use horses, Mr. Whistler? I've been around horses since I was a child."

Rob shook his head. "Horses don't generally last well on the trail. It's a very rough trip, pulling a heavy wagon. They need too much feed and too much rest. Sounds like you'd do best with mules though, if you've never been around cattle."

"Mules would do the job, would they?" Miss Finster asked. "Aren't they balky?"

"They can be, but generally they'll follow along if the other animals are moving."

"Where would we buy a mule team?" Miss Stone asked.

"There's a couple of livery stables in Independence, and you'll find other traders about if you look. But be careful they don't try and fleece you."

The two women looked at each other doubtfully.

"How would we know?" Miss Finster asked.

"Well, right now a good mule oughtn't to cost you more than seventy-five or eighty dollars. Oh, they up the prices out here. You might have done better in Saint Louie."

"Yes, but we didn't know for certain then that we wanted to make the trip." Miss Finster looked so sad that Eb almost wished he could cheer her up. But he didn't really want to mix with them any more than he had to. He still hoped they would see the folly of attempting this adventure and back down.

"Of course, if you use mules, you'll need harness, too," Rob said. "All of that costs money."

"Oh well, that…" Miss Finster threw Miss Stone a quick glance. "I believe we're all right in that department, sir."

Rob looked over his shoulder and called, "Say, Eb."

Eb kicked himself for not making himself scarce. He walked over and touched the brim of his hat.

"Good day, Mr. Bentley." Miss Finster almost smiled but then seemed to think better of it. No doubt she remembered his words of discouragement.

"Eb, you told me which stores have the packages of supplies all made up for the emigrants," Rob said. "Whyn't you tell these ladies so they can save some time over shopping for all the individual items?"

"Well now, that'd be Ingram's or Blevin's. Of course, they don't sell wagons or livestock."

"No, but once they have their wagon, they'll need to fill it quickly, so they'll be ready to pull out with us."

Eb nodded, still unconvinced. "You ladies sure you're up to this? It's an arduous undertaking."

"Why yes, Mr. Bentley, I believe we are. I guess our ability to find and outfit a wagon in the next few days will be a test of sorts." Miss Finster's blue eyes held a spark, or maybe they just caught the glint of the sun.

"I guess it will." Eb held her determined gaze.

Miss Stone leaned toward her friend and peered at the list. "Bacon. Do we really need that much?"

"Well, bacon will keep a long time if you pack it right," Rob said. "The men on the train will hunt some fresh meat, but it's good to have enough staples along in case we don't get any game for a while."

"What about chicken?" Miss Finster looked at the younger woman with a worried frown—almost like a mother worrying over her child.

"Some folks take chickens in a coop tied to the side of their wagons," Eb said. "But are you ladies up to butchering your own fowl?"

Miss Finster glared at him. "We dainty things are up to whatever is necessary, Mr. Bentley."

"I see." Eb glared back, until Rob jabbed him in the ribs with his bony elbow.

"One hundred fifty pounds of flour. . .each?" Miss Stone turned her questioning gaze from the list to the wagon master.

"That's right." Rob shrugged. "Of course, that's an average. You ladies might need a bit less, but to be on the safe side. . . And that way, if you have a little extra, you can share with those who meet with misfortune."

"Corn *and* cornmeal," Miss Stone muttered. "Saleratus?" She looked up at Rob with a look of confusion.

"For cooking, miss. Baking soda."

"Oh."

"And we need all these tools?" Miss Finster asked.

"Every wagon needs to carry spare parts and tools to fix their gear with," Rob said. "But since you ladies don't plan to settle in Oregon, you won't be hauling furniture or farming equipment like some do. You might be able to sleep in your wagon all the way, but I'd bring a tent. An extra wagon cover, too."

"Such a lot of stuff," Miss Finster said as she looked down at the paper.

Miss Stone caught her breath.

"What is it?" Miss Finster asked.

Miss Stone pointed to the list. "It says women may take two dresses. Two." She stared into her friend's eyes. "And woolen at that."

"Well now, that's not chiseled in stone," Rob said, "though you do want to keep your wagon as light as possible. Woolen material holds up well, and the nights will be cold."

Miss Finster cleared her throat. "Since we won't have any furniture or a plow in our wagon, perhaps we'll be able to expand the wardrobe option a bit." She and Miss Stone continued to study the list.

Eb turned away, unable to stay put until they read the underwear allowance and howled in protest. Those ladies would probably bring an extra wagon along just to hold their extra petticoats.

As he walked away toward where he'd left Speck, he heard Miss Stone tell Rob solemnly, "I assure you, Mr. Whistler, we shall succeed in being good travelers, and we won't slow down the wagon train."

Eb scooped up his horse's reins and hopped into the saddle, not sure where he was going. Anyplace where those refined, would-be pioneer ladies couldn't see him steam.

He headed for the path that led to the creek. Before he entered the scattering of trees, he looked back. Apparently Rob was done giving advice. Miss Finster urged the horse into a reluctant walk. The buggy made a wide turn and nearly clipped one of the wagons before they were headed back toward Independence.

Eb shook his head. "Come on, Speck. Let's get you a drink." More than ever, he wished he'd stayed in Oregon on his little ranch. But he was in it now.

Rob found him a quarter of an hour later, helping a family completely repack their wagon. The greenhorns had no idea of how to go about it. Heaviest stuff on the bottom, along with the bacon and other food supplies that needed to stay as cool as possible. Lightweight stuff on top. Eb had tried to talk them out of taking a big cupboard, but the wife insisted it was going with her.

"My grandmother brought it from Cornwall," Mrs. Harkness declared. "If I can't take it to Oregon with me, I'm not going."

"Then lay it down in the wagon bed and fill it with your tools and other heavy stuff."

"Books?" Mr. Harkness asked.

"You're taking books?" Eb asked.

"Only one crate." Mr. Harkness touched the wooden box in question with the toe of his shoe.

"That's a big box."

"We have to have books." Mrs. Harkness's voice grew more shrill each time she spoke. "How will the children do their schooling without books?"

Eb was relieved to see Rob approaching. "Well, whyn't you ask the wagon master? You folks have three wagons, and you're loading them mighty heavy. Those river crossings and mountain passes will do you in."

"Eb's right," Rob said, as if he'd heard the entire conversation—but then, he had, a hundred times. "You'd do better to sell some things here and have the cash than to leave them beside the trail in the Rocky Mountains."

"Oh no, not the books." Mrs. Harkness put her foot up on the crate and folded her arms across her chest.

"All right then," Rob said. "Make sure your wagon box is watertight, and stow that crate low in the wagon, like Eb said."

They helped heft cargo for the Harknesses and walked away a half hour later, tired to the bone.

"Mr. Leonard's wagon is yonder," Rob said. "What say we get our bedrolls out and have something to eat?"

They walked to Abe Leonard's wagon and pulled out their bundles.

"Where you want to make camp?" Rob asked.

"I slept over there last night." Eb pointed. "Made a fire pit." As they walked toward it, he said, "You should have turned them down flat, you know."

"Who? The Harkness family?"

"No, the English ladies. They'll never make it to Oregon."

"If they hire a man to handle the livestock for them, I can't see why we should object to having them along."

"Oh, you don't, do you? Isn't it obvious that they've never done a lick of work in their lives? Those are highborn women, used to being waited on hand and foot."

"You don't know that."

"Oh don't I just?" They reached Eb's fire pit, and he kicked at the charcoal in the bottom. "They can't harness a team."

"Miss Stone said she'd been around horses."

"Oh sure. Likely riding sidesaddle in the park, wearing a fancy velvet habit. And you can bet your boots she had a groom tacking up the horse for her."

"Well, Eb, they're healthy women, and apparently they have the means to buy a stout rig. I won't deny them a place on the train, and I don't see why you're so upset about this."

"I'll tell you why. You've always insisted that the best way to get everyone through to Oregon is to not accept any weaklings in the first place. Those women are trouble. They'll mean more work for us and possibly tragic results. But that doesn't matter to you. Two pretty ladies smile at you and charm you with their cute accents, and you're falling over backward to accommodate them."

"I resent that."

"Sure you do. Dulcie would have your hide if she knew."

"Dulcie knows how hard the trail is, but she wouldn't deny those women a place in our company. Not if they obey the rules. I expect she'd cheer them on. And I might add, it's encouraging to me that you noticed how pretty they are. Maybe there's hope for you yet."

Eb scowled at him. "Just watch yourself, Robert."

Rob pulled his hat off and wiped his brow with his sleeve. "All right, Eb. Let's leave Dulcie out of this. My wife has nothing to worry about. And if those ladies come back without an able-bodied man, I won't let them go."

"Promise?"

"You have my word."

"All right, but when they need help hauling water or starting a fire or plucking one of their precious chickens, I won't be the one helping them, ya hear?"

"I hear you. Now, why don't you fetch us some kindling, and I'll set up to cook supper. Mrs. Libby gave me some dried apple pastries. Might be a while before we taste that kind of cooking again."

Eb went off to the edge of the field to look for some dry twigs. Within a couple of weeks, the area would be bare of anything burnable. People would have to buy firewood from enterprising locals who came around to peddle it while folks camped here and waited for their wagon trains to pull out.

He mulled over what Rob had said, and he still didn't like it. Not one bit.

But he wasn't in charge, and that was his choice. Eb didn't like being in charge because the wagon master had to deal with all the complaints and the people who broke the rules. The scout got to ride ahead and get away from the grumblers all day if he had a mind to. In order to hold that position, he had to let Rob be in charge.

CHAPTER 7

Elise opened one eye. Indirect sunlight seeped through the thin muslin curtain at the window and filled the room. She sat up cautiously so as not to fall off the edge of the narrow bed. All night she'd kept as far over as she could, trying to avoid touching her mistress.

Lady Anne rolled over with a little moan and opened her lovely brown eyes. "Is it morning?"

"Yes, my dear. I'm afraid you haven't slept well, and I apologize."

"For what?"

Elise grimaced. "For having to share a bed with you, and such a small one at that."

Lady Anne sat up and shoved the blanket aside. "It's not your fault."

"This room isn't fit for a lady of consequence."

Her mistress chuckled. "I'm afraid any 'consequence' I once had is gone, Elise. And I chose to come to this wild place, remember? I intend to show you and those—those frontiersmen that I'm made of as stern stuff as the American women."

"Frontiersmen? Oh, you mean Mr. Whistler and Mr. Bentley."

"Yes, those two. They seem to think we're made of glass. That Eb Bentley has taken a notion that we can't either one of us cook or drive a wagon or do anything else useful."

"Well. . ." Elise swallowed hard. "I must admit that cooking is not my strongest talent. I can make tea and scones and boil an egg. That's about it."

"It's more than I can do." Lady Anne blinked at her. "Do you think he's right? Are we useless?"

"Not at all. Because we can learn. When we go to the general store today, I shall ask if they have a cookery book. One that tells

73

you how to make meals over an open fire." She rubbed her sore arms and forbore to mention her newly acquired driving skills.

"That's a good idea." Lady Anne scooted to the edge of the bed and swung her legs down. "Oh Elise, we've got to fit our trunks in."

"Never fear, my dear. We shall have our fripperies and enough foodstuffs to get us across the continent. I'm not sure about chickens though. Mr. Bentley might have a point there."

"Nonsense," Anne said. "We just need to find a man who can butcher *and* drive mules. Surely that's not too much to ask."

"Perhaps you're right. But we need to find someone today. We've only four days to prepare, and one of those is the Lord's Day."

The hotel served a sketchy breakfast of pancakes, sausage, and coffee. Elise choked down half a sausage patty and left the rest on her plate, instead filling her stomach with the bland pancakes. Lady Anne delicately spooned applesauce over her pancake, something she would never have done in the breakfast room at Stoneford, and poured a generous dollop of milk into her mug of coffee. Elise only hoped they could find better fare somewhere else at lunchtime.

They headed for the livery stable first, but Elise wondered if Mr. Pottle was the man they ought to buy from. Mr. Whistler had said there were other places in town. It might be worth their while to seek them out.

"I believe we should continue to keep my connections quiet," Anne said as they walked.

"You mean—"

"I mean that I shall continue to be plain 'Miss Stone.' It's served us well so far, and we don't want to appear pretentious. If the tradesmen knew my father was an earl, they would probably ask more for everything."

"I agree with you there."

"And on the wagon train," Lady Anne persisted. "This man we're about to hire, for instance. He mustn't know."

"Agreed." Elise wrinkled her nose. "It's bad enough that Eb Bentley thinks we're helpless. But if everyone on the wagon train thinks we are *rich* and helpless, that will be even worse."

"Yes. The other emigrants will be our neighbors for the next few months. We need to be friendly and make sure they see us doing our share of the chores. And you must always call me Anne, as you have been, never using my title."

Though Elise had played down their relationship since they boarded the ship in England, she didn't approve of familiarity between a domestic and her mistress.

"It's difficult sometimes to remember."

"We must," Anne said. "Imagine how they'd sneer at us if they thought we—that is I—was putting on airs. There is no aristocracy here, and I'm sure Americans disdain anyone who claims to be above them in any way."

"But you're not like that," Elise protested. "You're the kindest, most compassionate girl I know. Woman, that is. I'm proud of the way you've grown up, my lady."

"Thank you, but you must never say those words again, so long as we are in America. I am no longer your lady, and you are not my maid. You are my friend and a bit of a mentor/chaperone, I think. And I am very fond of you. That is no pretense."

"And I of you," Elise said. "I shall do my best not to betray the secret of your birth."

Lady Anne presented such a charming picture of an English lady, one born to the manor and reared in luxury, though not always conscious of it. Could anyone possibly think she was anything else?

"Perhaps we should go into the emporium on the way to the livery and speak for our supplies."

"I thought I would go by myself this afternoon while you rest," Elise said. "I'm sure it will be tedious, my—my dear." Lady Anne had never bargained with a tradesman in her life, and Elise would feel freer to dicker without her elegantly gowned mistress standing beside her.

"I think we should stay together. This town has such a ragtag bunch of people, I worry when you go out alone. Men wearing guns, and people flying out of saloons on every corner."

Anne had a point. There was a measure of safety in numbers,

and they had no time to waste. If they spoke for their equipment now, it would perhaps save a trip later in the day. "All right."

Ingram's general store was smaller and less organized than the one they'd patronized in St. Louis. Sacks of provisions were stacked nearly to the ceiling. Boots and iron kettles lay in jumbled heaps. Every square inch of wall and rafter was hung with harness, tools, and cooking implements.

Elise took out the list of supplies they needed and approached a man who stood on a ladder placing canned goods on a high shelf.

"Excuse me, sir. I'm told you sell lots of supplies for emigrants."

"That's right." He looked down at her. His jaw dropped as he stared for a moment. He came down the two steps to the floor and brushed his hands on the front of his apron. "You can't mean you ladies are joining one of the wagon trains?"

"Yes, we are." Elise raised her chin. "Why not, sir?"

"Well, it's just. . .you're just so. . .so. . . You don't look like most of the women heading west, that's all."

Elise glared at him. "What business is that of yours?"

Anne cleared her throat. "We have a list."

Her soft-spoken words reminded Elise that efficiency was more important than respect at the moment. She lowered her lashes. "Yes, and your establishment was recommended to us by the wagon master, Mr. Whistler."

The man eyed her for a moment then nodded. "Rob Whistler sends folks my way. He's an honest man. I guess if anyone can get you to Oregon, he can." He ignored the list Elise held out and turned to the counter. "Here's my usual outfit for a wagon. For each extra person, I'll add on these extra supplies." He pointed as he spoke to a notice tacked to the front edge of the counter.

"I'm sure that's fine," Anne said, looking uncertainly at Elise.

Elise hesitated. "We have yet to procure our team and wagon, but we won't need anything besides the basics."

"I'll set everything out on the back porch. You can pick it up there, and if there's anything you don't want, you can tell me then and I'll deduct it."

His plan sounded reasonable, and Elise nodded. "Fine. And we're thinking of taking a few laying hens."

"I haven't got any of those, ma'am. I can pack some eggs in a bucket of lard for you. They'll keep fresh a long time."

"Well. . ." Elise knew Anne had hoped for fresh fowl along the way. "I suppose that's the best we can do on short notice. We've no time to track down a farmer who can sell us chickens."

Thomas Costigan ducked inside the general store and peered around. The two Englishwomen were talking to the storekeeper. He gravitated toward the stove, though the day was fairly warm. An elderly man with a flowing white beard sat near it with a checkerboard set up on top of a nail keg.

"Hey there, young feller. Feel like a game?"

"Sure." Thomas sat down opposite him and cocked one ear toward the two ladies.

"All right, provisions for two adults," the storekeeper said to the English ladies.

"No, three," said Miss Finster. "We'll be hiring someone to tend our livestock for us."

The younger woman—Miss Stone—spoke up. "You don't know anyone, do you, sir? A healthy, honest man who'd like to work his way west?"

It was all Thomas could do not to turn and gape at them. They were heading farther west? Those two prim and proper ladies?

"Your turn," the old man said.

Thomas shoved a checker forward with his index finger.

"Lots of folks want to go west," the storekeeper said. "You might ask at the saloons. They tend to hang about there, waiting for someone to come in and ask."

"We will not be entering a saloon," Miss Finster said firmly.

"Oh, well then, you might check the porch posts outside. Some folks post notices out front here, or in front of the saloons, or at the post office."

"The post office. We'll try there." Miss Finster sounded as

though she was drowning and lunging for a piece of flotsam. "When will our order to be ready?"

"Well now, that depends." The storekeeper scratched his head and eyed their list. "You said you want triple everything on food?"

The two women looked at each other.

"I doubt we'll need that much bacon," Miss Stone said.

"Is there anything we can substitute for bacon?" asked Miss Finster.

"You have to understand, ma'am, the things the wagon masters recommend are things that won't spoil quickly."

"Well, yes. There is that. But my friend is not fond of bacon. We'd like a little more variety, if possible."

"I could give you some dried beef. And how about some dried peas? They're not on the list."

Miss Finster said something Thomas couldn't catch, but the storekeeper responded with, "Canned food? Well, yes, we've got oysters and some soup. I've had peaches and a few vegetables before, but they're expensive compared to dried foods, and of course, they weigh more. Some folks are leery of them."

"May we see what you have?"

During the next ten minutes, the ladies examined various wares and discussed the safety, reliability, and price of tinned foods. Thomas kept the checker game moving and listened with half an ear. At last, Miss Finster said, "We'll take all of those you have."

"Yes, ma'am." The storekeeper's tone revealed his pleasure in the transaction. Thomas wondered how long those tinned oysters had sat on his shelf.

"And more tea than it says here. Double, if you please. Instead of the coffee."

"Our hired man might like coffee better," Miss Stone said.

Miss Finster nodded. "You're right. I suppose we'll need both. Now about the tea. Do you have good quality black tea from India? What we had at our hotel this morning was abominable."

Thomas chuckled.

The old man sitting opposite him smiled. "Those ladies are a bit

finicky, wouldn't you say?"

"Just a tad." Thomas made his next move.

By the time the ladies had worked their way down the entire list, questioning the quality, price, and need for every item, several more customers were waiting in line behind them. Some didn't trouble to conceal their impatience. Finally the storekeeper excused himself, went through a doorway, and returned a minute later with a woman whom Thomas supposed was his wife. He went back to total up the English ladies' order and sent the woman to deal with the other patrons.

At last Miss Stone and Miss Finster left the general store.

Thomas stood and handed the old man a nickel. "Looks like you're winning this round, and I need to get going. Buy yourself a bun or something."

"Thanks, young fella."

The women were still visible down the street, and Thomas ambled after them. They turned at the corner. He followed at a leisurely pace. He had a feeling he knew where they were headed.

Sure enough, they wended their way to the livery stable where they'd rented their rig the day before. Thomas leaned against the side of a barbershop half a block away and crossed his arms. The nebulous plan that had begun forming in his mind was beginning to crystallize. If it worked, he'd have to get word to Peterson.

CHAPTER 8

The big barn door of the livery stable stood open, and two men worked inside. The bearded owner leaned on a paddock fence outside, talking to another man. He looked up as they approached and swept off his hat.

"Good morning, ladies."

"Good morning, Mr. Pottle," Elise said.

"Do you need a rig again today?"

"No, thank you, sir. We're here to purchase."

"Oh?" Pottle straightened and eyed her thoughtfully. "And what are you purchasing, ma'am?"

"A team of stout mules, please."

He let out a guffaw and tried too late to swallow it. "Pardon me, ma'am, but you wish to buy a span of mules?"

"However many it takes to pull a wagon over the plains to Oregon."

Pottle stared at her.

"Well, I never," said his companion.

"Let me get this straight." Pottle stepped toward her, frowning. "You ladies intend to take the Oregon Trail."

"Indeed we do, sir."

"Well now." Pottle shook his head.

"Oxen," said the other man. "That's what you want. Easy keepers, and if things go wrong, you can eat 'em."

"Oh, hush, Newt. Don't go scaring the ladies. H'ain't nothing going to go wrong for them. I expect they'll have a nice trip."

"In a pig's eye," his friend said. "My cousin went on a wagon train two years ago. The Injuns ran off their herd of milk cows, and they lost one of their kids crossing the Platte."

"Would you hush?" Pottle glared at him.

"Sure. I'll talk to you later, Ralph," the other man said. "Sounds like you've got some business to do." As he walked away, he said, "Wait till the boys hear this."

Elise gritted her teeth, suspecting that she and Lady Anne were about to become the subject of conversation in the nearest saloon.

"If you please, Mr. Pottle, we've been advised that mules will do us nicely. Since we have more experience with horses than cattle, we thought mules might be best. We intend to hire a driver, but we realize we may need to handle the animals in an emergency ourselves."

"Makes sense to me." Pottle walked over to the open barn door and called, "Benjy, bring those mules up from the lower pen. I've got a wagon train customer here."

He turned and smiled at Elise. "Now, these here are Missouri mules, ma'am. They're strong and they're tough. Tougher than most. They'll take you across the plains slicker'n greased lightning."

"How many mules do we need?" Elise asked.

"I'm thinking eight, ma'am."

"So many?"

"Well, you could haul your wagon with less, but if they get tired out, or if you need replacements. . .and of course, you could always sell one or two to someone less fortunate than yourselves, if'n theirs give out and they didn't bring any extry."

"I'm not sure we need so many," Elise said.

"Suit yourself. Come on through the barn, if you will, and have a look at 'em. Oh, watch your step there."

Elise hopped to one side and avoided a pile of fresh manure, but Lady Anne was not so fortunate. She stepped squarely in it and stopped, holding up her skirt and staring down at the mess surrounding her calfskin shoe. Her face turned a garish green.

"Quick, my—Anne! Come over here, my dear." Elise grabbed her mistress's wrist and all but yanked her to one side. "Now wipe your shoe on that straw." Glaring at the liveryman, she snapped, "What's the matter with you? Get a rag and clean off my lady's shoe."

"Oh, a little of that won't hurt her none," Pottle said. "If'n you ladies are serious about crossing the plains, you'd better get over lettin' a little horse manure frazzle you. Now these mules are the best you'll find in Independence. . . ."

Elise stared after him but didn't follow. "Are you all right?"

Anne's face was still pale, but she diligently rubbed her foot in the straw, trying to scrape off the manure. "He's right, you know. I've got to toughen up, like those mules of his, if I want to make it to Oregon."

"Well, you don't have to do it all in five minutes." Elise pulled out her handkerchief and knelt in the straw.

"Oh, don't," Anne cried. "You'll ruin it. I'll have my shoes cleaned tonight at the hotel. I can stand it until then."

Elise gave in and stood, but privately she doubted their spartan hotel offered niceties like shining shoes.

They caught up with Pottle outside the back door. The mules his hired men were herding into the small corral from a larger pasture looked enormous.

"They can pull all day," Pottle said with evident pride. "You give them a little grain when you stop for nooning of course."

"Ah, of course." Elise studied his face but couldn't read his expression through his bushy beard. "Mr. Pottle, if I may be so bold, how much are these mules?"

"A hunnerd dollars each, ma'am, and that's a bargain."

"A hundred?" Elise stared at him, outraged.

"Perhaps we should buy the oxen instead," Anne murmured.

"Oxen? Oh no, you ladies don't want oxen," Pottle said.

"Why not?" Elise asked, hiking her chin up a half inch. She suspected that Mr. Pottle didn't deal in oxen and didn't want to lose the sale of his high-priced Missouri mules.

"These mules are much better for your purposes," he said.

"Morning, Pottle. Ladies."

Elise whirled at the sound of the lazy voice. Eb Bentley touched his hat brim as he emerged from the back door of the livery stable.

"Mr. Bentley!" For some reason she couldn't fathom, Elise felt

both chagrin and relief at his appearance.

"Eb," said Mr. Pottle with a nod.

"Buying some livestock, are you?" Eb asked in Elise and Anne's general direction.

"Yes, they are," Pottle said, "and if you don't mind, we're in the middle of a transaction."

"Mr. Bentley." Anne reached for his arm and gazed up at him with her huge brown eyes. "Sir, was I mistaken, or did Mr. Whistler tell me a good mule would cost us around seventy-five dollars?"

Elise schooled her features not to show her feelings. Anne would do much better not to get too close to the rough-and-ready scout. On the other hand, perhaps she should take a lesson from Anne. In this situation, Eb Bentley might take their side, and right about now, she and Anne could use an ally.

"I believe he said something along those lines, miss." Eb's color heightened as he looked down at the beautiful young woman.

"That's what I thought." Anne turned her sweet smile on Pottle. "Could you show us some of those seventy-five-dollar mules, please, Mr. Pottle?"

The owner's face clouded.

Elise mustered her courage and stepped closer to Eb. "Mr. Bentley, I know that Mr. Whistler said horses aren't as hardy as mules, but Miss Stone and I would both feel more at home with horses, I'm sure. Even those big draft horses—they're quite gentle, aren't they?"

"Yes, ma'am," Eb said, "but they'd eat you out of house and home. There's no guarantee of good grazing along the way, and horses have to eat often. You'd need to carry a wagon full of feed just for them. It's not practical."

Elise sighed. "Then mules it is, I guess." She turned back to Pottle. "I believe you said we need eight?"

"Eight mules?" Eb asked. "Four will pull a regular wagon just fine. You might want to get a couple of spares though, and have the drovers bring them along with the other loose livestock."

Elise arched her eyebrows at Mr. Pottle. "Is that right?"

"Oh, well, I thought you was pulling a Conestoga wagon, miss. It's an honest mistake."

Scowling, Eb stepped toward the livery owner. "You use these ladies right, Pottle. You're not the only horse-and-mule trader in town. If you can't find them a team of six good, strong mules for four hundred dollars, I'll take them over to Parley Rider's place."

"Four—that's way too cheap." Pottle glowered at him. "I have to make a living, you know, Bentley."

"I'm sure Rider can make that deal for my friends. And if you've got a set of harness, add another hundred, but if you try to cheat these ladies, you'll have to answer to me." Eb looked toward the mules milling in the nearest corral. "Those look sound from here. Do I need to climb in through the fence and check their teeth?"

"No," Pottle nearly snarled.

"Good. Because Rob Whistler and I have sent you a lot of trade lately. You treat our people right if you expect it to continue." He turned and said to Anne, "Have you bought your wagon yet, ma'am?"

"No, we haven't."

He nodded. "Well, there's a woman over at a boardinghouse on Mill Street who has one for sale. She was going to go with us, but her husband died suddenly. She's already sold her ox team, but I told her to hold the wagon for an hour in case you wanted it."

"That's kind of you," Anne said.

He shrugged. "Make sure you don't pay more than seventy-five dollars for it. That's a fair price for a good, sturdy wagon with a watertight bed and bows to hold the canvas. And make sure you buy an extra canvas cover at the store. I don't think she has but one."

"We surely will," Anne said.

It dawned on Elise that he was not only ignoring her—he knew that Anne was the one holding the purse strings. Even though Elise had done most of the negotiating throughout their trip and tried to protect Lady Anne from having to deal with coarse tradesmen, Eb had somehow discerned that Anne would pay for their wagon and team. She wasn't sure whether to be apprehensive or to respect his acumen.

He lifted his hat and included her in his parting words. "Good day, ladies."

"Thank you, Mr. Bentley," Anne said with a smile.

"We'll see you in a day or two," Elise added.

"Looks that way." Eb glanced at the mules once more. "Pottle, don't give them that one with the notched ear. He's favoring his off hind foot." He strode away through the barn.

Elise stared after him, watching his tall, straight form as he moved through the shadowy stable and out into the sunlit street beyond.

"What are you thinking?" Anne asked softly.

"I'm wondering what he came here for."

"To tell us about the wagon?"

Elise frowned. "How did he know where to find us?"

"I'm sure I don't know. But let's finish our business with Mr. Pottle and get over to the widow's boardinghouse."

They walked together to the corral fence. Mr. Pottle was inside with the mules.

"All right, ladies, I've picked out six of the best for you. If you want the harness and collars with them, that'll be five hundred dollars cash."

"Is the harness in good repair?" Elise asked.

He hesitated. "Sure it is."

"Perhaps we should purchase a new set at the emporium," Anne said.

"No, no, I'll make sure it's ready for the trail." Pottle scratched his chin through his beard and waited for her verdict.

"All right then." Anne turned away and removed her chain-link purse from her skirt pocket and counted out the odd-looking American bills. With what they'd paid the emporium's owner, their bankroll looked very small.

"Are we doing all right?" Elise murmured.

"I believe so."

Five minutes later they left, with an understanding that they would be back for their new team and harness later. As they walked toward Mill Street, Anne said, "Seventy-five dollars seems like a huge price for a wagon. What is that in pounds?"

Elise quickly figured the price. "Mr. Bentley said it's fair."

"But you don't trust him."

Elise ruefully shook her head. "Isn't it funny how things change? Compared to Mr. Pottle, I'd trust Mr. Bentley with my life. But next to your father? No. I'd take one Stone man for ten Eb Bentleys any day of the week."

CHAPTER 9

Thomas followed the two women as they left the livery stable. He'd had to scramble for cover in the shadowy barn when the man from the wagon train came through and helped the women with their dealing, but he was pretty sure the scout hadn't seen him. He tailed the women out to the street and waited until they were out of sight of the establishment. He caught up to them on the sidewalk.

"Pardon me, ma'am," he said when he was within a couple of steps of their swaying skirts.

The two women spun around in a flurry of colliding crinolines.

"Yes, sir?" asked the older one, looking down her nose just a bit.

Thomas supposed he looked a bit shopworn to the meticulously gowned and coiffed ladies. He straightened his shoulders and cleared his throat.

"I ran into that fella from the wagon train a few minutes ago, and he said you were looking for someone to drive your team when you take to the trail."

"Do you mean Mr. Bentley?" the woman asked.

"Sure. He told me that if I was to ask, you might hire me. See, I want to go to Oregon, but I don't have the money for my own rig. I'm a hard worker. If you was to take me along and stake me for my grub, I could hitch up for you every day and drive if you need me to, and I could help you load and unload things and haul water—things like that."

The two women looked at each other.

"What is your name, sir?" asked the younger one. She was a regular stunner.

"Thomas G. Costigan, at your service." He doffed his hat and gave a little bow.

"I am Miss Finster," said the older one, "and this is Miss Stone.

We are on our way to see about a wagon now. Could you begin work today?"

"Oh yes, ma'am, I surely could."

"And where would you sleep?" she asked.

"Oh, I'd bed down with the herdsmen, I suppose. Most wagon trains have a herd of extra animals—milk cows and extra horses and mules and oxen—and they have men to herd them along behind the wagons. I could spread my bedroll with them."

The woman still seemed undecided.

"Excuse us a moment, won't you?" Miss Finster asked.

"Of course."

The two women stepped to one side and conferred in low tones. Thomas caught only a few words—"recommended," "proper," and something that might have been "scruffy."

Miss Finster turned back toward him after a few minutes. "Mr. Costigan, we have agreed to give you a trial. We hope to have a wagon to collect and load today. If you do well with that job, we'll hire you. In any case, we'll pay you for your time."

Thomas smiled and ducked his head. "Why, thank you, ma'am. That sounds fair and reasonable."

"And where shall we find you if we buy the wagon?" Miss Finster asked.

"How about at the livery, ma'am? You'll have to fetch your team."

Her eyebrows shot up. "Our team?"

"Uh. . .well. . .I assumed. . .uh. . .you said you were on your way to buy a wagon. I assumed you'd get mules. . .or, uh, oxen. . .from the . . .uh. . .unless the wagon owner is selling you his team, too."

She appraised him coolly for a long moment. "At Pottle's livery stable, then. In three hours."

"Very good, ma'am." He touched his forelock and backed away, bowing and trying not to fall off the edge of the boardwalk. He'd almost botched that interview—which would have ruined his entire plan.

The ladies walked away. He ducked into a doorway and watched surreptitiously. Sure enough, Miss Finster looked back at the edge of the block. He pulled back before she saw him and counted to

ten. When he peered out again, they were gone. He ran down the boardwalk and halted at the corner. He looked ahead, then left, then right. There they were. Those huge skirts were hard to miss. Men were dodging into the rutted street to keep out of their way.

Thomas turned and made a beeline for the nearest saloon. They were headed for the place the scout had mentioned. He needed to get word to Peterson and make sure the man wanted him to do this. So long as the ladies hired him, he'd be set for the next few months, but he'd ask Peterson for advance pay and have a free trip west. Thanks to the wagon master, who was a bit of a stickler, things looked pretty good on that front. Just to be sure the women had no complaints, he would limit himself to one drink and make sure he turned up a few minutes early at the livery. Thomas G. Costigan believed in covering all contingencies.

Elise and Anne located a ROOMS TO LET sign in the yard of a substantial wood-frame house. A woman of about fifty opened the door and showed them to a small but clean parlor. When she'd left them, Anne sat down on a threadbare settee, and Elise took a straight chair by the window.

A few minutes later, a thin young woman entered, holding a wailing bundle on her shoulder. A toddler clutched a handful of her skirt and, when she stopped walking, wrapped his little arms around her legs. The woman's dress was a nondescript cotton that hung limp on her frame. Her hair and her tanned skin were almost the same color as the dress. The only splash of color was the small pieced quilt she held close about the crying baby.

"You're here about the wagon?" she asked.

"Yes." Elise stood and spoke loudly over the baby's cries. "I'm Miss Finster."

The young woman nodded. "Sallie Deaver. Eb Bentley said you folks need a wagon."

"That's right. We're joining the wagon train."

Sallie patted the baby and shook her head. "We was, too, but

Ronny up and got himself killed yesterday."

Anne came and stood beside Elise. "I'm so sorry, Mrs. Deaver."

Sallie shrugged. "I'm going back to my folks in Connecticut. I sold the team already."

"Yes, it's just the wagon we're interested in," Elise said.

"You can have it for a hunnert. I advise you to be careful packing it. Ronny fell off and busted his neck."

"I see." Elise shot a quick glance at Anne, who was frowning at her. It was a ladylike frown, but still an indicator of her displeasure. Elise drew in a deep breath. "Well, Mr. Bentley told us it was worth seventy-five dollars. I assumed you'd sell it for that."

"I need money to get home."

"I'm sure you do. . . ." Elise glanced at Anne, who gave the tiniest of shrugs. If she didn't close the deal quickly, Elise was afraid her tenderhearted mistress would give away money they would need on the journey. "Seventy-five is all we have laid aside for this purchase, Mrs. Deaver. If that's not agreeable to you, I'm sorry we've bothered you."

Elise turned to her chair, where she'd laid off her cloak.

"Don't be so hasty, now." The baby gave a belch, and Sallie stopped patting him. "I'll take eighty-five."

Elise smiled, but not too congenially. "I'm sure we can buy a new one for less than that."

Sallie's mouth drooped. "You ladies have got them fancy clothes. I'm sure you can afford a few extra bucks. Me, I've got this dress and one other to my name, and this is the best one."

Elise eyed her thoughtfully. "Would you excuse us just a moment? I'd like to speak to Miss Stone privately."

Anne followed her into the hall, and Elise shut the door. "My lady, she might take a dress instead of the extra money. I'd offer one of my own, but she's so thin, I doubt mine would fit her."

Anne's face lit up. "Why didn't I think of that? I've got trunks full of dresses!"

"Yes. One of your morning dresses, perhaps. A simple style."

"There's that sprigged muslin that I only wear at Stoneford when we've no company."

"Perfect. I'll make the offer."

They returned to the parlor. Sallie was sitting on the settee with the baby in her arms and the toddler curled up beside her.

"Mrs. Deaver, you're right that we have been blessed with more clothing than you. Would you take seventy-five dollars and one good day dress for the wagon?"

Sallie eyes widened. "I might. Something pretty?"

"Oh yes. It's one that suits Miss Stone admirably, and it has a lot of wear left in it."

"And gloves?" Sallie asked, gazing pointedly at Elise's delicate crocheted pair. "I want to look proper when I go to Connecticut."

"Certainly." Elise didn't bother to check with Anne. She had a dozen pairs in her own trunk, and Anne had two or three times as many.

Sallie stood. "All right then. Do you have the money on you?"

"Yes," Elise said. "We'll bring the dress and gloves later today, when we come with our mule team to get the wagon."

"Fine by me."

Anne opened her purse and counted out the money. "I wish you well, Mrs. Deaver."

They left the boardinghouse and walked toward the hotel.

"Are you all right?" Elise asked.

"I'm fine," Anne said. "I'm glad things are working out for the journey. I feel sure God will bless us and we'll find Uncle David."

"I pray you are right."

Though their steps dragged, Elise wouldn't ask for a hackney unless Anne showed great fatigue. Anne had obtained her complete allowance for the remainder of the year from Mr. Conrad, and that would have to last them. Elise carried a portion pinned into her corset cover, and her mistress did the same, with enough to carry out today's transactions in her reticule. Elise kept reminding herself that they must keep back enough for a return trip, either by wagon or by ship. She refused to think about how long the overland trip would take. At least their transportation to Oregon was paid for, along with the supplies they would need along the way.

They stopped to dine at a rough eatery on the way. The plain food filled them up, but Elise wondered how Lady Anne would do when forced to eat their trail rations for months.

Back in the cramped hotel room, Anne lay down on the bed. Elise removed her outer skirt and her top petticoat, with its stiff whalebone hoop in the hem, and sat down to write to her sister in Germany:

> *Dear Gretl,*
>
> *I am about to set out on an adventure unlike anything I've ever done. My mistress and I have traveled from New York, where I last wrote to you, and come westward. We stopped in the city of St. Louis for a week, but now have come even farther, to a smaller, wilder town called Independence. Lady Anne and I have come to a momentous decision: we will push on to the Pacific in search of her uncle.*
>
> *I know this is shocking. The two of us would never under ordinary circumstances consider throwing aside the comforts and security of polite society. My mistress, however, is determined to locate her uncle, inform him of her father's passing, and persuade him to claim his title and estate in England.*
>
> *But alas! David Stone is reported to have gone to Oregon Territory. Because communication is so fractured here in America, she has no recourse but to go in search of him. Letters have not reached him, and we've not found a trustworthy way to get him word, so we shall carry it ourselves.*

Elise went on to describe the arrangements they had made, and even their dickering session with Sallie Deaver. She hoped her family would see the humor of the situation, though it might lose some of that as she translated her thoughts into German. Unfortunately, over the last twenty years, her English had become stronger than her command of her native tongue. It took her nearly an hour to compose the letter. She hadn't seen her sister in

six years. Would she ever see her again?

She closed the letter by admitting that she was a bit frightened by what lay ahead, yet excited about the possibilities. What she didn't express was the weight of responsibility she felt. Lady Anne's well-being lay squarely on her shoulders.

Had she made a mistake by falling in with Lady Anne's whim? No, she couldn't think that. The young woman was determined to find her uncle. If Elise had refused to go with her, Anne would have found another companion.

The scout's bluntness and the daunting list of provisions had nearly overwhelmed her, and she couldn't imagine how they'd have come through bargaining for a team and wagon had Eb Bentley not stepped in. There was no turning back now. Lady Anne was set on finding the new earl of Stoneford. And if that proved impossible, she would need someone there to comfort her at the end of the trail.

Anne stirred and sat up, stretching her creamy white arms.

"Feel better, my lady?" Elise asked.

"A bit. But you must stop calling me that, even in private. Sometime you'll slip in front of people."

"I'll try. And now I'll get the dress you're giving to Mrs. Deaver. It's nearly time for us to go and meet Mr. Costigan."

Elise opened the trunk that she thought held the dress in question. One of Lady Anne's finest ball gowns was folded in a sheet on top.

"Elise, why did I bring so many fancy dresses?" Anne asked, watching from her seat on the edge of the bed.

"I believe the logic was that one never knows whom one will meet aboard ship—or in New York or St. Louis."

Anne chuckled. "Well, Mrs. Deaver can't use a watered silk ball gown."

"This is the one I was thinking of." Elise pulled out the white muslin dress sprigged with embroidered pink flowers. The summer-weight dress looked darling on Anne, and Elise hesitated. "I hate to give it to her, you look so well in it."

"Perhaps I should save my plainest dresses to wear on the wagon train." Anne reached out and fingered the snowy material. "This one wouldn't be very useful though. In one day it would be ruined."

"Your woolen dresses will hold up better, as Mr. Whistler said."

"I suppose you're right. Let's give her the muslin. Or do you think—I did bring one mourning costume."

"No, she wants something pretty. I'll contribute a pair of my cotton gloves." Elise draped the dress over her arm and closed Anne's trunk.

"I've thought of another way we could save money." Anne's voice was a bit timid, and Elise turned to observe her face.

"I've thought along those lines, too. We mustn't spend all you have getting to Oregon, or we shan't be able to come back."

"Yes. So I thought that after Mr. Costigan loads our wagon today, we could move out to the field with the other emigrants. That way, we wouldn't have to spend any more for the hotel room."

"Such as it is. This room probably isn't much more comfortable than our beds in the wagon will be," Elise said. "But we'd be outside of town. Do you really want to be away from the shops and other conveniences?"

Anne shrugged. "It would help prepare us for what's ahead."

"I suppose that's true, though I hate to take you away from comparative ease. You do realize we'll have to cook for ourselves once we leave here?"

Anne gritted her teeth. "That's true. But it might be shrewd to discover our shortcomings before we're too far from civilization."

"Let's think about it and see how Mr. Costigan does." Elise didn't mention it, but she also had concerns about the security of their belongings once they were loaded in the wagon. Could they trust Costigan to guard it for them?

Costigan sat on a barrel outside the livery stable as the two ladies approached. Elise was glad, though she'd half expected him not to show up, and something perverse in her nature would have been gratified to know her suspicions were founded.

She caught Anne's eye. "Well, he's here."

"Yes. That's a good omen."

He hopped down when he saw them and tipped his hat. "Afternoon, ladies. Pottle's out back, rounding up your mules. He says you bought six stout ones."

"That's right," Elise said. "Can you drive them for us to the place where we'll get our wagon?"

"Yes'm. How far is it?"

"About half a mile."

"Then I'll just hitch 'em up and ground drive 'em over there. If you want, you can just tell me where it is, and I'll go fetch the wagon and bring it to your lodgings so we can load it."

"Well. . ." Elise hesitated. To outward appearances, Costigan wanted to please and was willing to work hard. Why couldn't she just trust him? Was it because he'd been recommended by Eb Bentley? Or was it her conservative, cautious nature and her compulsion to keep Lady Anne safe?

"We need to deliver the bundle to Mrs. Deaver," Anne said, nodding toward the package Elise carried.

"That is correct." Elise was a bit relieved for the excuse to go along and observe Costigan's behavior. "Let me speak to Mr. Pottle. He can help you harness the team, and Miss Stone and I will set out for the boardinghouse on Mill Street and deliver the package. When you have the team hitched, drive over, and we'll see you there."

The sun shone brightly, and a light breeze blew as she and Anne walked toward Mrs. Deaver's lodgings. Perfect weather for drying up mud and making grass grow. Elise felt stirrings of wanderlust. This journey could be the best time of her life, if she'd let it. She must help Anne see it that way, too.

She remembered the countless outings she'd taken Anne on when her mistress was a child. She'd tried to approach each day as an adventure and an opportunity to learn. Was this any different? They would see sights most Englishwomen couldn't imagine.

"You must make sketches of our journey," she said to Anne. "You draw so beautifully."

"Thank you. I believe I'll do that. I bought a new sketchbook in St. Louis for the purpose. It will help me remember the places we see." Anne tipped her head and looked at Elise from beneath the brim of her hat. "What do you think of Mr. Costigan now?"

"Still undecided," Elise admitted.

"I think he knows what he's doing," Anne said. "We're fortunate to have found a man so knowledgeable about horses and willing to go for low wages."

"We shall see."

The landlady admitted them to her parlor and went to fetch Sallie. The young woman entered a few minutes later with her little boy clinging to her hand. *The baby must be sleeping,* Elise thought. At least they didn't have to put up with the infant's wails again.

Anne stood and held out the package. "Here are the dress and gloves we promised you, Mrs. Deaver. I hope they please you."

Sallie sat down on the settee, and Anne placed the package in her lap. Sallie laid back the edge of the wrapping paper and gasped. Elise feared at first that she would say the dress wasn't suitable.

Sallie fingered the soft muslin folds. Her lips trembled.

"It's prettier'n anything I've ever owned." She looked up at Anne. "Thank you, but you could have given me something plainer."

Elise smiled wryly, thinking, *No, Sallie, she couldn't.*

"If it doesn't suit you, they have some ready-made dresses in Ingram's store," Anne said.

"Oh no." Sallie hugged the dress to her bosom. "This is the beatingest dress I ever saw. I can wear it when I get off the train in Hartford. Maybe my folks will quit saying that Ronny didn't take good care of me."

Elise forbore commenting on the skewed logic of her statement. Instead she slid the white gloves out from between the folds of the skirt. "Here are your gloves, Sallie."

"Oh my! They look brand new."

Elise cleared her throat. "Our driver will be here soon with the mule team. We'd like him to hitch up the wagon and take it to our hotel. Is there anything else you need from us?"

"I don't think so. I'm leaving for Connecticut tomorrow."

"We wish you a safe journey," Anne said.

They left Sallie to admire her new dress and headed back up the street. At the corner, they met Thomas Costigan, who was driving the team down the street, walking about six feet behind the last two mules and holding the long leather lines. The mules' feet and Thomas's boots squelched in mud with every step.

"How do, ladies!" He shuffled the reins and lifted his hat for a moment and then dropped it back onto his brow.

"Good day, Mr. Costigan," Elise called. "We shall be at the Kenton House Hotel. Mrs. Deaver and her landlady know you're coming."

He nodded.

"There now," Anne said as they resumed their walk. "If he's not dependable, I don't know what is."

Elise smiled. "Yes, it seems we've got the beatingest hired man in Missouri."

The ladies spent the next hour repacking their belongings and deciding what to keep in their satchels so that they'd have all essentials accessible. Thomas arrived with the wagon, and they went out to inspect it. Elise was impressed by the solid look of it, but Anne bemoaned the lack of space inside.

"How shall we get everything from the store in and still live in there?"

"Most folks take a tent and sleep in that," Thomas said. "Of course, you'll use your foodstuffs on the way, and you'll gain space every time you eat something."

The bows were in place above the wagon bed. With a little assistance out of Anne's reticule, Thomas found a couple of lads to help him carry the trunks down the stairs of the hotel and load them into the wagon. Then they spread the canvas top over the bows and tied it down.

"Well," Anne said dubiously, "there is our home on wheels."

"Yes. Are you sure you don't want to stay at the hotel one more night?" Elise expected her to vacillate, but Anne shook her head vigorously.

"No, I think we should move right to the field. We can get to know the other travelers sooner if we do. And as you said yesterday, if we've forgotten anything, we'll soon find out. Better now than a hundred miles out on the trail."

"All right, Thomas," Elise said. "We'll go pay the hotel bill, and you can bring out the last bits of our luggage. Are you prepared to stay at the field with the team tonight?"

"Yes, ma'am. I'll fetch my bedroll after we go to the store for your supplies."

Loading the provisions they'd purchased at the emporium took another two hours. They added a tent and a second wagon cover, along with a few sundries the ladies thought might be useful. For some reason, Thomas kept putting items in the wagon, taking them out, and rearranging them. Elise gathered it had something to do with the balance of the load. That and her occasional protests that some item or other had to travel where she and Anne could reach it easily.

"We can't be pawing through a ton of crates and bundles to find our cooking utensils," she told him at one point.

"No, ma'am, you can't." He hauled out the box of pans, ladles, and spatulas and positioned it on top of one of the trunks. "Now, where's your tinderbox? We may as well put that in with the cooking gear."

Elise gulped. She'd never mastered the art of fire building. There was so much she had yet to learn. Perhaps Thomas could tutor her and Anne in the fine points of trail living. They must become self-sufficient if they intended to survive this jaunt.

CHAPTER 10

Elise awoke for the twentieth time to find that at last the walls of their canvas tent were growing lighter. The sun must be rising. Unable to stand another moment on the hard, damp ground inside the tent, she sat up and rubbed her hip.

Shivering, she hauled her satchel onto her lap and groped inside for her clothing.

Anne rolled over and pulled the blanket close to her chin. "It's freezing!"

"Just about." Elise's teeth chattered as she fumbled with her clean stockings. Her fingers ached. The storekeeper had included two wool blankets in their kit—Thomas had declined one, saying he had his own bedroll. They had proven far from adequate for the cold night air. The women ended up adding extra flannel petticoats beneath their nightdresses. They laid one blanket beneath them and spread the second one over them and huddled together like children in an ice-cold nursery.

"We'll need to go back for more blankets." Anne tucked in the edges of the top one, now that Elise was out from under it.

"Yes, and a couple of feather ticks if you think we can stuff them into that wagon."

"I'm sure there's some reason why they didn't include proper bedding in our list of supplies." Anne's voice was muffled by the blanket.

Elise sighed as she tried to figure out which side of her corset went where in the semidarkness. "Men. They always think they have a good reason for everything." Immediately she felt guilty. "I'm sorry, my dear. I shouldn't complain. This is exactly why you wanted to come out here yesterday, and it's a good thing we did. We've already learned a great deal."

Anne poked her nose out of the blanket nest. "Yes. We learned that we have no hope of raising this tent without Thomas, and that there's not enough room for us to sleep in the wagon, even after we take out the tent and blankets. And that apparently western people don't use sheets. Or do you think Mr. Ingram just forgot to put them in?"

"No. I think they consider sheets to be superfluous on the trail."

Anne sat up, clutching the blanket about her. "Are they really so vulgar? These wool blankets are itchy."

"I'm so sorry, my dear. Of course they've irritated your sensitive skin all night long. We've simply got to find a solution to this bedding problem today." At last her corset seemed to be in place. "Forgive my asking, but could you. . . ?"

"Of course." Anne let go of the blanket and pulled Elise's corset strings. "It's hard to get it tight when my hands are cold."

"I believe I'll wear a dress that doesn't require hoop petticoats today," Elise said. "But of course, the one I want is in the wagon."

"I think I'll wear my cashmere since it's so cold," Anne said. "But none of the women in the encampment seem to be wearing wide skirts. Do you think we should forgo our crinolines altogether? It seems scandalous, but. . ."

"But I had the distinct impression yesterday that we were being sneered at," Elise finished for her. "Are we insane to carry fashionable clothing across the plains?"

"But what if we got to Oregon and found that everyone was wearing crinolines?"

"I don't know. From what I'm hearing, we'll spend a lot of time walking, and it will be dusty and dirty. We'll be doing our own laundry and cooking. We can't wear our good quality clothing for that." Enough light came into the tent now that she could see Anne's troubled face. "Perhaps we need some plain dresses in calico or printed muslin."

Anne sighed. "Like the one I gave away yesterday."

"No, not white. I think we should look carefully at what the other women on the wagon train are wearing. Most seem to favor a

full skirt with a basque that buttons up the front."

"I'm not sure I'm ready to give up my crinolines," Anne said.

"Well, I'm going to go and root through my trunk for something more suitable, and then I'll start breakfast." Elise patted about in search of her shoes.

"I shall help you." Anne crawled out of the blankets. "Brrr. But if I'm going to be a true pioneer woman, I need to brave the cold and learn to cook."

"Call to me when you're ready for me to help you with your corset."

Elise crawled out of the tent, stood up, and lowered the flap. She looked around at the camp. Every wagon but theirs had a fire burning near it, and women hovered over them. Children scampered about, and dogs woofed. Men walked purposefully with buckets of water and armloads of firewood.

"Morning, ma'am."

Elise turned and found herself face-to-face with Thomas. "Hello. Early risers here, aren't they?"

He chuckled. "That's the usual, ma'am. Once we're on the trail, we'll get up even earlier than this. We'll most likely pull out at sunup every day. That means we've got to have breakfast over with and the dishes packed up and the team harnessed and ready to move."

Elise eyed him with wonder. "Indeed."

With new determination, she found the dress she'd all but ruined on the ship coming over. She'd mended a tear, but the stains from food and tea spilled during a storm had refused to come out. She'd almost discarded it after they landed, but kept it, thinking she might be able to salvage the material. Out here, no one would care about stains, and the huge apron she'd purchased at the emporium would engulf her, covering most of them.

She changed in the wagon, donning the old dress, and climbed down. The final step was a good eighteen inches, and she plunged to earth and staggered. Thomas was lighting the fire and didn't seem to notice. After she caught her breath, she hurried to the tent door.

"Anne? Do you need my assistance?"

"Yes please."

Anne had on her stockings and cotton drawers. Elise helped her mistress get into her garters and chemise. Next came the corset. She fastened it in front then turned Anne around so she could pull the strings tight.

"Do you want your petticoat with the smaller hoop in the hem today?" Elise whispered.

Anne looked over the streamlined silhouette Elise had chosen. "Yes, I think so. I'm sure we'll be less of a curiosity if we leave off our wide hoops."

Lady Anne's plainest walking costume was still much more elegant than anything the other women wore. Elise helped her adjust the bodice and skirt.

"Where's my hat?" Anne asked.

Elise hesitated. The hat that matched the costume was very ornate, suitable for a promenade in Hyde Park.

"I thought perhaps we'd wear bonnets today. You have a lovely blue-and-white one that will shade your face from the sun."

"Oh. All right, if you think it best. I don't suppose I'll meet any dowagers of the ton today."

"My thought precisely. Fashion might not be an asset on the wagon train."

Cooking breakfast was an ordeal, especially with Thomas lingering about, looking ravenous.

Elise cut several slabs of bacon and put them in the cast-iron skillet. It had little legs that allowed her to set it over the fire, but the pan was extremely heavy.

"I can watch the bacon," Anne said. "How hard can it be?"

Elise handed her a long-handled fork. "Just be careful your skirt doesn't come near the fire." She got out the cookery book and ingredients for what the Americans called "biscuits." The biscuits Elise knew were small, shaped sweets, but the waiter in St. Louis had informed her that those were known in this country as "cookies." Their biscuits were more like round, flaky scones. Prepared well, they were very tasty, and Elise wanted to learn to make what seemed to

be a staple of the American diet.

She read through the recipe, feeling increasingly helpless. Cut lard into flour. How did one do that? With a knife? She could make scones—maybe she'd better stick to those. But there was no recipe for scones in the book, and she didn't think she could do it from memory. She drew in a deep breath and measured out the flour for a batch of biscuits. From a small keg, she scooped a blob of lard into her pottery bowl with the flour. Next she took a knife and fork and carved at the lard over and over, pressing the small pieces into the flour.

She was still at it when Rob Whistler came by ten minutes later. He greeted Anne first.

"Looks like your fire's getting low, ma'am. Would you like me to add some wood?"

"Oh, thank you." Anne stepped aside and watched him work.

Mr. Whistler lifted the spider off the coals with ease, added three short sticks of wood, then replaced the spider. He stood and brushed off his hands.

"How are you ladies getting along?"

"Fine, thank you," Anne said.

"Miss Finster?" he asked.

"I. . .uh. . .I'm cooking biscuits."

He nodded. "Most of the ladies make a big batch whenever they cook on the trail. That way, you have enough for a cold meal at nooning."

"That's good to know." Elise looked down at her bowl. "I'm not sure I'm doing this correctly. American cooking seems to be different from English, and so many things go by different names."

Whistler smiled. "I'm sure you'll get the hang of it. And Mrs. Harkness, over yonder"—he pointed across the encampment to where three wagons were drawn close together—"makes fine biscuits. She gave a few to Eb and me last night. I'm sure she'd be happy to give you some pointers."

"Thank you." Elise's independent streak vied with a rush of relief. Perhaps the other women on the wagon train would offer assistance, and even friendship, to her and Anne.

"How's that hired man working out?" Whistler asked.

"Fine. He brought us firewood this morning."

"Well, let me know if you need anything." Whistler nodded at her and Anne and strode off toward the next wagon.

"He's such a nice man," Anne said. "I think he likes you."

"Nonsense," Elise said. "He's only trying to enhance our chances of completing the trip successfully in order to save face with Eb Bentley."

"Whatever do you mean?" Anne stepped closer, her face troubled.

"Isn't it obvious? Mr. Bentley never wanted us along. He's sure we'll drop out or at best slow down the caravan. He probably thinks we'll die along the trail because we're so inept. Well, I intend to prove him wrong."

"Oh, I see." Anne nodded, still watching Elise's face.

Whatever was she hinting at?

A sudden crackling behind Anne drew Elise's attention. The flames of the campfire leaped high, and black smoke roiled skyward.

"Oh! The bacon!" Elise ran to the fire and grabbed the pot holder Anne had left on one of the rocks of their fire ring. When she reached for the spider's handle, the huge flames drove her back. She lunged in again, grabbed the handle, and tried to drag the heavy spider off the fire. She only succeeded in tipping it.

Hot grease spilled over onto the flames, and the fire roared higher.

Someone grabbed her from behind and yanked her back. Elise tumbled to the ground and gasped.

"You want to catch your clothes on fire?"

She looked up into the irate face of Eb Bentley.

Eb stomped on the smoldering edge of the Finster woman's hem and glared down at her. How ignorant could an obviously intelligent woman possibly be?

She sat up, patting vaguely at her skirt, and looked from him to the fire pit, where the blaze still roared. Miss Stone stood by staring, her face pale, with one hand clapped to her mouth.

"I suppose I should thank you," Miss Finster said doubtfully.

Eb sighed and offered his hand to help her up. She grasped it firmly and rose, batting at her ridiculous dress.

"Fires and full skirts don't mix, ma'am," he said. "Especially when you throw a pint of grease on the fire."

Her eyes blazed. "What do you know about it?"

"I know how to cook bacon."

She huffed out a breath and flounced away from him, toward the fire.

"I'd let that burn down and then start over," Eb called after her.

Miss Stone seemed to have found her wits at last. "Thomas's breakfast is ruined, and it's my fault. I suppose we'll need a new spider."

"Nah," Eb said. "Just take it to the creek and scrub it out good. But don't try to take it out of the fire until it's cooled down. And I suggest you give your hired man a cold breakfast this morning."

Miss Finster looked over her shoulder at him. "But I have the dough for the scones nearly mixed. Biscuits, that is."

Eb shook his head. "Whyn't you ask Mrs. Harkness yonder if she'll let you bake them over there? Her fire's down to coals. I expect they ate breakfast an hour ago."

Miss Finster's cheeks went red. "For your information, that fire was fine until your boss came along a few minutes ago and put more wood on it."

"My boss? Oh, you mean Rob?" Eb chuckled. "He's not my boss. Nobody's my boss, lady."

Her jaw tightened. "I beg your pardon. That should have been obvious." She marched to the back of the wagon, where she'd set out her cooking things, and began working furiously at some mixture she had in a pottery bowl.

Eb looked over at Miss Stone and shrugged.

"Thank you for your assistance, Mr. Bentley," the young woman said earnestly. "I'm sure that when the shock has passed, Miss Finster will realize how opportune your intervention was."

Eb stared at her for a moment and decided she wasn't poking fun at him. "Think nothing of it, miss. But I would get rid of those high-toned fashions if I were you. Hard enough getting in and out of a wagon in a dress, or so I imagine, but cooking around an open fire—well, you're just asking for trouble."

"Perhaps you're right. My friend and I will discuss it. Thank you very much."

Eb nodded and glanced at Miss Finster. She ignored him as she pored over a cookery book—or maybe the recipe really fascinated her. Eb touched his hat brim in Miss Stone's direction and ambled on toward the next wagon.

Daniel Adams, the owner, was loading a wooden box of pans into the back of his rig.

"Morning, Dan."

"Hey, Eb. Everything all right with the English ladies?"

"Oh, yeah. They just don't have much experience camping." Eb chatted for a moment then went on to the wagon belonging to Dan's brother. Hector was seated on a small keg, braiding some strands of twine together. Eb was about to speak to him when he noticed Costigan coming along the path from the creek that flowed into the Missouri River.

"Hey."

Costigan looked toward him and shifted his pail of water to his other hand.

"Yeah?"

"Your employers had a scare with their fire. You might want to help the ladies clean up the mess and teach them how to lay a fire that will give them some good coals for cooking."

Costigan frowned. "The fire was fine when I left to get the water."

"Took you long enough to fetch it," Eb noted.

Costigan said nothing but lurched on toward the women's wagon. Eb wondered how he'd react when he learned the ladies had

nothing prepared for him to eat.

He walked back to where he and Rob had spread their bedrolls the night before. Rob was saddling his horse.

"Heading into town?" Eb asked.

"Yeah, there's always a few last-minute folks who want to join up. I reckon we could take two or three more families. Need anything from town?"

"Nope. But I wish you'd turned those Englishwomen out."

"What do you mean? Throw them off the train? Why?"

"That Miss Finster almost burnt herself up this morning. If I hadn't happened along at the right moment, she'd have gone up in flames."

Rob frowned. "I was by their camp a little while ago and added a couple of sticks to their fire, but it wasn't out of control."

"Oh, she's blaming you for the incident. I don't know what happened for sure, but she managed to tip the spider over and dump the bacon grease on the fire. Her skirt was starting to catch when I grabbed her away."

Rob shook his head. "They just need to get their trail legs, so to speak. Good thing you came along."

"Ha!" Eb leaned toward his friend. "I almost wish I hadn't saved her. If she'd burnt herself to a crisp, we wouldn't have to stop along the way long enough to bury her."

"You don't mean that." Rob looked rather shocked at his bald statement.

Eb rubbed the back of his neck. "No, of course I don't. But, Rob, you've got to tell them they can't go."

"On what grounds?"

"They're. . .they're. . . Oh, you know! They're *ladies*."

Rob laughed. "Is that the worst thing you can say about them?"

"You know what I mean. They're the sort of ladies who haven't a notion of how to do for themselves. That means trouble on a wagon train. Sooner or later—and probably sooner—there's going to be an accident, and someone's going to get hurt."

"Settle down. I'll ask Mrs. Harkness to stop by and see if she can help them with their cooking setup. Miss Finster and Miss Stone could have stayed at the hotel until Sunday, Eb, but they didn't. They want to learn how to live out of a wagon before they hit the trail, and I have to admire them for that. They're *trying*."

Eb slapped his hat against his thigh. "Oh, they're trying, all right. Trying my patience."

CHAPTER 11

Mrs. Harkness looked up from her sewing as Elise and Anne approached the large family's encampment.

"Well, hello, ladies! I was thinking of coming over to meet you later. I'm Rebecca." She stuck her needle into her project and rose from the rocking chair that sat on the ground beside one of the wagons.

Elise introduced herself and Anne. "We wondered if you might be willing to help us. . . ." She stopped, embarrassed to admit their shortcomings. "Well, you see, neither one of us has ever had much instruction on cooking, particularly over an open fire."

Mrs. Harkness eyed her dubiously. "Surely you ladies have baked bread before?"

"Actually, we haven't."

The older woman made a *tsk* sound. "Your mothers didn't teach you?"

Elise felt her cheeks flush. "Miss Stone's mother died several years ago, and I. . .well, I began earning my living when I was quite young, and cooking was not one of my duties."

"Oh my."

"I can do passably well on a stove," Elise added hastily. "Basic meals and refreshments. But this is a new experience, working over the open flames and having a hungry hired man to feed. We thought you might be able to share your knowledge with us."

"I'd be happy to. Would you like me to come over to your wagon? It might be best if you learned using your own dishes and such."

"That sounds reasonable," Elise said.

"And most kind of you," Anne added.

Rebecca's cordial reception encouraged Elise, and she was able to overlook any differences between them. Fashion and "station" didn't matter as they went about the task of preparing a cook fire for baking.

Only an hour had passed since Eb Bentley had jerked her so rudely away from her fireside. Elise was still angry at him, though the sight of her singed hem had tempered her ire. That dress was ruined—unless she decided to shorten it. She had put it away in her trunk, out of sight until she had time to think about it.

First Mrs. Harkness showed them how to mix a simple batter for cornbread, or "johnnycake" as she called it. That was easier and quicker to prepare than biscuits, she pointed out. The ladies could always fall back on it when time was short, though it took an egg. Elise assured her they had several dozen among their stores, preserved in lard.

Baking the johnnycake in the dutch oven over the coals proved to be tricky. Mrs. Harkness had mastered the process from forty years or so of practice. She showed Elise and Anne how to situate the cast-iron pot on a bed of coals and then shovel more coals on top of the lid.

"But how do you know when the coals are ready—not too hot, but still hot enough?" Anne asked.

"They just look right," Rebecca said with a frown. "Dear me, I don't know."

They left the johnnycake to bake slowly while she showed them how to prepare passable biscuit dough. Anne insisted on learning, too. Elise was gratified to see that for the most part, she'd made her dough correctly. Their teacher pointed out that biscuits had the advantage of not needing eggs.

Again, the baking was the difficult part. They'd made four batches before Mrs. Harkness pronounced them "proper" biscuits. Elise was going to throw out the first three batches, but Mrs. Harkness protested.

"You're going to throw them away? That's scandalous! Even the ones you blackened, the oxen will eat. And I daresay that hired man of yours can stomach the others."

When they were alone, Elise and Anne agreed to give Thomas

the best biscuits and eat the trial batches themselves. It was a type of frontier penance, Elise supposed. And as Mrs. Harkness had reminded them, "Waste not, want not."

They parted cheerfully at the end of the lesson, and Rebecca offered to send her "big girl," Lavinia, over in the morning if they needed help at breakfast time, but Elise was now so confident that she was certain they wouldn't need Lavinia's assistance. And she most assuredly would not need Eb Bentley's aid.

On Saturday morning, Elise awoke while it was still dark. She lay in the tent listening for sounds of activity. Soon she caught faint rustles and a thud as one of the Adams brothers lowered the hinged back of his wagon. She sat up and groped for the clothing she'd carefully set out the night before, close at hand so she could find it easily. The dress was one of her plainer ones. She'd spent the previous afternoon taking in the skirt and shortening the hem so that she could wear it without hoops and full underskirts and yet not have it dragging on the ground. Even so, it hung longer than most of the emigrant women wore their dresses.

She emerged from the tent to the first birdcalls of dawn. Already wood smoke hung in the air. The glow of four campfires was visible from where she stood.

It's simply a matter of adapting to the schedule, she told herself. Breakfast at daybreak, bedtime at sundown or shortly after. She could make that adjustment and thrive on it.

Poor Anne found everything about the trip more daunting than Elise did. Elise felt they could overcome each difficulty, one task at a time. But for Anne, life in the encampment was completely foreign. Tending the fire, preparing meals, keeping their clothing clean and in good repair, not to mention the dirt, the smoke, and the drudgery of it all—these were things she'd never been asked to deal with before. Servants performed the menial labor, and her family and Elise had shrouded her from all unpleasantness. She'd put on a brave front during their entire trip, but at several points yesterday, Elise could tell she was on the verge of tears. Perhaps she was reconsidering her decision to find her uncle, no matter how hard the quest.

But just as Anne started to realize the sheer enormity of their undertaking, Elise began to revel in it. They would have to make changes. They must cast aside many assumptions and embrace the more casual ways of America—in short, the freedom. If they could do that, they could enjoy this new life. She would try to help Anne come to that point of view. Giving up the journey now was unthinkable.

In the gray morning light, Elise hurried to the wagon and took out the box she'd stocked the evening before with the utensils she would need for making breakfast, as well as the leftover biscuits they'd deemed edible. She resolved to cook bacon this morning without burning it or spilling the grease into the fire, and to fry a few eggs for Thomas out of those the storekeeper had packed so carefully for them a few days back. She hoped the eggs would mollify Thomas enough that he wouldn't notice their biscuits' imperfections.

As she stirred the ashes of last night's fire, she wondered how she would ever get the blaze going. Mrs. Harkness had told her to cover the live coals with ashes at night, to "bank" the fire. Elise had done that, but now there seemed to be only a few tiny orange coals left in the mess. She took a couple of sticks off the wood pile, but she didn't think they'd catch from the meager embers. She wished she had some paper to burn.

Where was Thomas, anyway? Maybe he'd gotten used to the idea that she wouldn't get up until the sun was high above the horizon and figured there was no sense building the fire too early.

She knelt and blew on the pile but only succeeded in blowing ashes over her precious coals. She brushed them away and blew again. The coals shone brightly while her breath lasted, but the large sticks showed no disposition to catching fire.

Eb Bentley came around the end of the wagon, strolling as though he had not a care in the world.

"Morning, miss. Let me make that up for you?"

Elise clenched her teeth. Why did it have to be him? And if he disdained her and Anne so much, why was he offering to do this for her? Wouldn't he rather see her fail and give up?

She rose and brushed off her skirt, resolved to learn to cope, no matter who the instructor. "Thank you, Mr. Bentley. Could you please show me how it's done? I'd like to become proficient at this, but there don't seem to be many live coals left."

"Oh, they're in there, miss. You've got to stir around in the ashes and pull together any little bits that glow."

He reached down and removed the large sticks she'd set in the fireplace. Tapping them together, he let the ashes fall off them into the pit.

"And you need some tinder—anything small that will burn well." He looked toward the edge of the field. "Anytime you're near pine trees, you can usually find little twigs underneath the overhanging branches. They're small enough to light from a match, and they usually keep dry, even when it's wet out." He strode purposefully toward the trees.

Elise placed her hands on her hips and gazed after him. Should she have offered to go? She probably wouldn't have been able to find the right twigs.

She wanted to. She wanted to know exactly what to use. This would make her and Anne more independent. She hurried after him, holding her skirt up and hoping he didn't turn and see her engaging in such unladylike behavior.

He reached a pine tree on the edge of the sparse woods. The emigrants were forbidden to cut down the trees. If they did, the man who owned the land would make them leave and would never allow another wagon train to form there. Anne had paid for enough split wood in town to give them a small woodpile. Once they hit the trail, Elise had no idea how they would find more, but they couldn't haul enough to feed their cook fires all the way to Oregon.

Eb lifted a low-hanging pine branch and ducked beneath it. Elise came up behind him.

"Will any pine tree do?"

He looked up with a flicker of surprise on his face. "Unless someone else beat you to it. See here?" He pointed to some small twigs sticking out from the trunk—smaller around than her knitting needles. "A handful of those will work."

"What about pine needles?"

He shrugged. "If they're dry, they'll catch fast, but they'll burn quick, too. Maybe quicker than you want them to. Get a bunch of these twigs, and then something a little bigger—that's your kindling—and put your fuel wood on last, once the little stuff is burning."

She nodded, hoping she could remember the steps. She would *not* call him back to demonstrate again. He gathered a few small branches off the ground inside the tree line, passed them to her, and then broke a few more dry twigs off the bole of another pine tree.

"All right, that should be enough."

She tried to match his long strides as they walked back to the wagon. He set down his load and picked up the crooked stick she'd used to stir the fire. Kneeling before the stone circle, he used the stick to probe the ashes until he found the little embers and herded them together. In a couple of minutes, he had a small cluster of them.

"Tinder." He held up his hand.

Elise placed a clump of the pine twigs in it. Eb bent and put them on top of the coals, heaped up above them in a loose bunch.

"More."

When he'd used all the little twigs, he took the larger dead branches, broke them in short lengths, and stood them up in a little pyramid over the pile, like the frames the gardener at Stoneford used to make over the bean plants. Eb stooped low and blew gently on the embers.

Nothing happened at first. Elise was disappointed. Apparently Eb didn't have the secret down as well as he thought.

Suddenly a flame shot up and licked the twigs. Eb kept blowing softly until the whole thing caught. He sat up and watched the kindling begin to burn.

Elise laughed. "I'm sure I would have given up."

"Are you carrying any matches?"

"Yes, we have a few, and a flint and steel."

He reached for some larger sticks from her woodpile. "You never need to be without fire, then. If you've got no coals, just set it up and light a match."

"Thank you."

"Not much to it. You'll be an expert inside a week."

"Maybe. I do want to learn how to do things for myself."

He nodded. "I see that. It's a commendable attitude." He added a few more sticks. "Let that burn down some before you try to cook. You don't want to put your pots over high flames like that. Wait until it's settled down and you have a bed of coals."

"Yes. Rebecca Harkness showed us what to look for yesterday." Though Elise still wasn't completely sure she'd know the exact moment to begin her cooking.

He stood and glanced toward her wagon. "Do you have a grate?"

"I. . .don't think so. Should I?"

"It'd make things easier. You can put it on top of the stones if you shape your fireplace right, and your pots will sit up above the fire. That's good for frying things."

She nodded. "I guess we could get one at the general store."

"Could be."

Anne poked her head out of the tent. "Good morning, Mr. Bentley."

He turned toward her and smiled. "Morning, Miss Stone. Miss Finster's going to have your coffee ready in two shakes."

"Oh, Miss Stone prefers tea," Elise said.

"Your tea, then." Eb looked at Elise. "You can set your pot of water in there. Can't burn water. And while it heats and the fire burns down to where you can cook over it, maybe I can give your wagon a last once-over."

"I beg your pardon?" Elise's urge to defend herself and point out that she was not the one who burned the bacon yesterday dissipated as she took in his last remark. "You intend to look into our wagon?"

"Yes, ma'am. Rob and I will inspect all the wagons today and tomorrow. We don't want anyone setting out unprepared."

"I assure you, we have all the equipment specified on the list."

"I'm sure you do," Eb said. "And I saw your wagon before you bought it, so I know it's in good shape. But have you loaded your goods to advantage?"

She wasn't sure what he meant by that last question, but Thomas had seemed to know how to load a wagon, so she looked him in the eye and said, "I believe we have."

"Good. Let's take a look."

He walked to the back of their wagon and stood expectantly, waiting for Elise to open up the rear flap. Elise glanced at Anne.

Anne shrugged. "If they're doing this to everyone. . .I mean, it's better to know now if we need to buy anything else. Isn't it?"

Elise tried to keep a neutral expression as she tied the flap back and lowered the tailboard of the wagon.

Eb peered inside then climbed up and began poking about.

Anne came to stand by Elise. "He's not opening our chests, is he?"

"No. If he did, I should protest loudly."

"I wish we could know that this is worth it—that we'll find Uncle David in Oregon."

"There are no guarantees."

Anne let out a sigh. "I suppose not. But it will take us months to make ourselves presentable again when we go back to England. I've already broken most of my nails, and I despair of ever feeling truly clean again. And we've not even set out yet!"

Elise slipped her arm around the girl—for Anne did seem like a girl to her still. Most days she kept her "mature young woman" mask in place, but Elise knew the child within.

"My dear, we can't turn back now. Think of the regret you'd suffer and the renewed agony of not knowing what became of David."

"Yes, you're right."

Eb climbed out at the front of the wagon and walked slowly to them, eyeing the buckets and tools they had tied to the side of the wagon.

When he reached them, he nodded soberly. "You ladies seem to have everything necessary for supplies. I suggest you lighten the load a bit. You're using mules, and they can only pull so much weight up the mountains."

"Lighten the load?" Anne stared at him with round eyes.

"Yes, miss. If I were you, I'd toss out a couple of those heavy trunks."

Outrage welled in Elise's breast. "Those trunks hold Lady—" She stopped short as she realized her mistake. Blood rushed to her cheeks, and her face felt like it was on fire. "I wouldn't think of asking Miss Stone to appear in Oregon City society, however provincial it may be, without a proper wardrobe, sir. You don't know what you're asking."

He shot her a keen glance then addressed Anne.

"I'm not saying you should get rid of everything, miss, but if you want to get to Oregon without killing those mules of yours, you'd do well to reduce your load."

Anne swallowed hard and turned to Elise. "Perhaps we should sell some of my clothing and buy plain calico dresses like the other women are wearing. We've talked about it. . . ."

"Yes, we have." Elise shuddered at the thought of Lady Anne in such drab dresses, but she could see the practicality of getting rid of the laces and flounces. In addition to blending in better with the farmers' wives, they'd be able to cook and tend livestock more safely in plain clothing. "I suppose we might be able to do with a bit less, and we could buy more once we arrived."

"Certainly." Anne's face brightened.

"Besides," Eb said drily, "Oregon City society may not be all you're thinking it is."

CHAPTER 12

Elise and Anne went about breakfast preparation with grim resolution. In only an hour, they were able to present Thomas with a plate full of biscuits (left from their lesson the day before), bacon (not burned), and eggs (cooked carefully by Anne in the bacon grease and only a little browned). While Elise took the dishes to the creek to wash them, Anne supervised the unloading of two of her trunks.

The rest of their morning was occupied in sorting through both women's gowns. After much deliberation, Anne closed the hasps on the smallest of her three trunks.

"I suppose if we're going to try this, we need to do it this afternoon. Tomorrow is the Lord's Day, and we can't be transacting business then."

Elise nodded. She wished they could have thinned their wardrobes even more. Most of the items they'd agreed to dispose of belonged to her mistress, but she'd added a dress from her own collection that required several petticoats to support it. Anne was giving up five gowns. Between them, they would relieve the mule team of more than fifty pounds of goods to haul, including the weight of the chest.

"Wilbur Harkness says he'll take us to town with it in his farm wagon," Elise said.

"Should we post a letter to Mr. Conrad or Cousin Randolph?" Anne asked.

"What for? We've nothing to tell them."

Anne nodded, but her brow puckered. "I felt a bit guilty not revealing our plans to Randolph before we left."

"You told Mr. Conrad. That's enough."

Elise had felt it needful for someone in England to know where they'd gone, in case tragedy befell them during their travels. But

Anne hadn't wanted to broadcast her plans to the world, and so they'd left England quietly. Elise hoped they could complete their mission and return in triumph.

The Harkness family had two wagons covered with canvas and stuffed with their goods, but Wilbur, the couple's eldest son of twenty-two years, had convinced his father to hold off on covering the smaller farm wagon.

"He told his pa they should put the canvas on last thing, and stow the tools and animal feed in it," Rebecca confided to Elise as they watched Wilbur and his younger brother load Anne's trunk. "That way we've been able to keep using the small wagon to fetch stuff."

"That's been a blessing to others," Elise said.

"Oh yes. Several families have needed to go into town for some last-minute business and found it very helpful not to have to take their ox teams and covered wagons."

Elise determined to pay Wilbur something and not take advantage of the family's generosity, but he wouldn't hear of it.

"We're neighbors for the next five or six months, ma'am. I wouldn't think of charging a neighbor when I'm going into town anyway."

It was more than most people would do, Elise was sure. Wilbur's mother and her two eldest daughters, Lavinia and fourteen-year-old Abby, rode with them and the trunk. Wilbur exhibited his courtliest manners, especially when Anne was close by.

At the general store, the owner reluctantly came out to inspect the merchandise they offered. He shook his head as Elise held up one gown after another.

"I dunno, ladies. I can't imagine the women of this town buying such fancy duds. And women going west sure won't want 'em. I get a lot of stuff people can't take with 'em, but I don't know if I can take these. The trunk, maybe, if you want to empty it out."

"Why would we want to sell you a trunk and keep the things in it?" Elise placed her hands on her hips and scowled at him.

He shrugged. "You could set up on the corner and ask folks if they'd like to buy, I s'pose. 'Scuse me, I got payin' customers inside." He ambled into his store.

Anne's eyes glimmered with unshed tears. "What shall we do now?"

"I could ask him if he'd trade these gowns for cotton and woolen dress goods," Elise suggested.

"Didn't sound hopeful." Lavinia grimaced in sympathy.

"You could try doing what he said," Mrs. Harkness told Elise. "Set the trunk down on the boardwalk here and sell to people going into the store."

"Ma, I like that lilac dress," Lavinia said, leaning over the open trunk. "Do you think we could buy it?"

"Don't talk nonsense, child. We don't have a spare nickel. Your father would rant from here to Sunday if we came back with a fancy dress like that."

"But Mr. Whistler said maybe there'll be dancing some nights— especially when we get to Independence Rock."

"And you'll wear your green cotton, not some outlandish fashion from Europe." Mrs. Harkness gathered her skirt and lifted it slightly. "I wish you good fortune, ladies. Come, Lavinia. Abby. Let's go get those things we came to get." They went into the store.

Wilbur, who'd stood by in silence during this exchange, said, "I've got to get over to the wainwright's and pick up our extra wagon rims. Do you ladies want me to hoist that chest out onto the sidewalk for you?"

"I suppose we've no other option," Elise said. At least the store owner had given tacit permission for them to set up their clothing business outside his establishment.

A few minutes later, two women who were walking toward the general store diverted their steps to see what the finely groomed ladies were offering out of a steamer trunk.

"Oh, how lovely," one of them said, her eyes softening. She fingered the folds of the golden satin gown Anne had worn to Lady Erskine's ball the previous spring. "So impractical though."

Her companion's lip curled. "Where would you ever wear it, Mary?"

"You never spoke a truer word."

The two women turned away.

A man and his wife slowed to take a quick look.

"Imagine spending good money on something like that," the man said. "You can't wear that to the chicken coop."

One somber woman turned up her nose and muttered, "The idea. Women out peddling their clothing on the street. It isn't proper."

Anne had again reached the verge of tears. Elise handed her a lace-edged lawn handkerchief. "There, my dear. Don't be discouraged. If no one wants them, you'll get to keep them—there's always a bright side."

"Oh Elise, you always say the right thing." Anne gave her a watery smile.

"Well, maybe I haven't said the right thing all day." Elise squeezed her arm. "I should have suggested that we pray about this venture before we ever set out on it. If the Lord wants us to sell dresses, He'll bring along buyers, now won't He?"

"Afternoon, ladies."

They looked up into the face of a cheerful young man in overalls. He smiled broadly through his russet beard. "Whatcha sellin'?"

Was this the answer to the prayers they had not yet voiced? Elise said, "Only the finest gowns you'll see this side of London. They were made by a fine seamstress there, sir. You must have a lady in your life who'd like to wear a dress of the best quality—something she couldn't find out here on the frontier."

He gulped and stole a glance at Anne then looked at the trunk. "Well, I do have someone, ma'am, but she's back in Boston. I had to leave her there while I came out to Missouri to start my farm. But I'm ready to go back and claim her now."

"How sweet," Elise said. "And she's been waiting for you."

"Yes'm. Two years. I reckon I'm ready to bring her out here now. We've set the wedding for June the twelfth, and I'm leaving as soon as I get my crop in the ground."

"Oh sir," Anne said, reaching into the trunk, "wouldn't your young lady like to have a pure silk gown? She could wear it when you take her to church in Boston."

"Or at the fete her parents throw before the wedding," Elise said. "Tell me, is she slender like my friend? Anne has the most beautiful gown in there that's gathered and flounced. The slate-blue one, Anne."

"Yes, ma'am, she's about the size of this young lady."

Anne delved into the trunk and brought out the gown Elise had mentioned.

"I could picture her in a dress like that."

"Are they wearing hoop petticoats in Boston?" Elise asked.

The young man's face went scarlet. "I'm sure I don't know."

"It's the height of fashion in London."

Five minutes later, the man carried Anne's gown and crinoline to his wagon, and she tucked the money he'd parted with into her reticule.

"I'm not used to the mathematics of the currency yet," Anne said, "but I don't think we got a quarter of what that gown cost new."

Elise smiled serenely. "You didn't, but you got some good wear out of it, and it's for a good cause. You know Mr. Bentley won't let us start out with an overloaded wagon."

"True. And we might need the money desperately before our journey is done."

"Let us give thanks," Elise said.

When Rebecca Harkness and her daughters returned, Lavinia carried a small bundle wrapped in brown paper.

"Sold anything?" she asked.

"One gown," Anne said.

Lavinia shrugged. "Better than nothing."

"Here comes Wilbur," her mother said. "Are you ladies ready to go back to the field?"

Elise looked at Anne. "It's getting late."

Anne glanced anxiously toward the door of the general store.

"Yes, and we hoped to have time to buy some suitable ready-made travel dresses to replace these. Perhaps we should ask the store owner again if he'd take the rest of the gowns. . .for a very small price."

"I saw a dressmaker's sign down the street," Lavinia said.

Elise looked where she pointed. "That's a thought. She may have customers who would buy our things."

"If you ladies want to go talk to her, I'll tell Wilbur," Rebecca said. "We can wait a few minutes."

"I'll show you where it is," Lavinia offered.

Elise smiled at Anne. "Why don't you stay here with Mrs. Harkness and Abby. I'll go with Lavinia and see if I can convince the seamstress to come look at the dresses."

"Maybe Miss Anne would like to go into the general store and look over the dresses they've got," Rebecca said. "If you're getting rid of your finery, you'll want something plain to wear on the trail."

Anne looked relieved. "I could go in and see what's available."

"That's probably a good idea," Elise said.

"Yes, and with Rebecca here to advise me, I'm sure I wouldn't purchase the wrong thing."

Mrs. Harkness's tanned face split in a big smile at Anne's expression of trust.

Lavinia led Elise down the street to a house with a modest sign out front. They found the gray-haired seamstress in the front room, where she apparently did most of her work. A rocking chair sat by the window with a work basket nearby, and a low table covered with folded lengths of fabric and pattern pieces cut from newspapers.

"Don't know if I can use any ready-mades." She peered at Elise and Lavinia through small, oval spectacles.

Before Elise could speak, Lavinia jumped in. "Oh ma'am, you've got to see them. These aren't any common dresses. They're beautiful ball gowns. Some famous tailor in England made 'em."

"Seamstress," Elise said gently. "But yes, we have a satin ball gown, and a couple of day dresses that any lady would be proud to wear to church, or to a wedding, or some other event. They're extremely well made. We wouldn't be selling them, except that my friend and I are heading for Oregon, and the wagon master says we must reduce our load before we set out."

"Hmm." The woman frowned. "I guess I can look 'em over. Can you bring 'em here? I've got a customer coming for a fitting any minute."

"Oh, well—"

"Of course we can," Lavinia said.

Elise arched her eyebrows.

"I'll make my brother drive the wagon down here with the trunk in it."

"All right, just be quick." The seamstress all but pushed them out the door.

They bustled down the sidewalk to the general store. Rebecca was unsuccessfully declaring the merits of Elise's promenade dress to two women who shook their heads and walked away as Lavinia and Elise approached.

"Pack them in the trunk, Ma," Lavinia called. "Wilbur, load it in the wagon. If we take these things to the seamstress's door, I think she'll buy them."

"Abigail, quick," Rebecca told her younger daughter. "Run into the store and tell Miss Anne." She and Elise hastily folded the gowns into the chest and closed it.

A moment later, as Wilbur tugged the trunk toward the rear of the wagon, Anne emerged from the store with an armful of calico. She lifted a questioning gaze to Elise.

"Don't count your shillings yet," Elise said, "but it's a possibility the seamstress with oblige us."

Wilbur called, "Come on, Liv, get on the other end."

Lavinia took one handle and helped Wilbur hoist it onto the wagon bed. A few minutes later, Elise knocked again on the seamstress's door.

"My customer is here." She glanced over her shoulder. "I told her I had someone bringing a few things to sell, and she said she'd wait. Bring them in. It's possible she might be interested in something."

Elise hurried back to the wagon, where Wilbur had already set the trunk onto the sidewalk.

"We're to take them in. Shall I help?"

Wilbur shook his head. "I think I can get it, if you hold the door."

Anne hopped out of the wagon and followed him up the steps. He set the trunk down just inside the threshold. "I'll wait for you."

Elise nodded and turned toward the seamstress. Anne closed the door discreetly behind them.

"Well, let's see what you got," the woman said.

Anne bent to undo the hasp. Elise glanced beyond the mistress of the house, curious about the customer who might buy the dresses. At once she averted her gaze. The woman standing in the far corner wore an extremely short red dress with a neckline cut so low Elise felt the blood rush to her cheeks. She was thankful that Wilbur had not ventured farther into the room. She helped Anne take out her satin ball gown first.

The seamstress bent close and fingered the material. "Hmm. Let me examine the stitching."

Elise helped her carry the mound of slippery material over to the window. The seamstress sat down and adjusted her spectacles. She proceeded to turn the bodice inside out and peer at the seams. She let go and pulled up the skirt until she found the hem and turned it for a critical look.

The woman in the corner stepped forward. "Now, that looks like high-toned cloth, don't it?"

Elise had to force herself to keep from staring at the customer's heavily powdered and rouged face. She looked over at Anne, but her mistress was delving into the trunk for another dress.

"I don't mean to hurry you, ma'am," Anne said, "but our driver is waiting. This lovely promenade gown belongs to Miss Finster, so it's a little longer than the others. It's a fine silk and woolen blend. I recollect her wearing it when we attended the Great Exhibition in London."

The seamstress grunted, but the other woman hung on Anne's every word, her lips parted and her eyes round.

"It were something special?"

"Oh yes," Anne said. "The Crystal Palace was a wonder on its own, but the exhibits and vendors from all around the world—it was truly amazing."

The woman sighed.

"And this was one of my day dresses." Anne pulled out their final offering. The customer's eyes gleamed when she saw the rich plum-colored fabric and silver braid.

"How much you want for these?" the seamstress asked.

Elise named a rather high price, she thought, in American dollars.

The seamstress scowled. "That's too much."

"Take them," said the customer. "Take them all, if you think you can let out that satin enough to fit me. In fact, if you can't, that's all right. I'm sure it would fit Velvet. She's scrawny as a stray cat." She stepped forward and touched the plum dress. "You'll have to alter this one, but I expect you won't have any trouble taking out a bit around the neck."

Anne gulped and turned a helpless expression Elise's way.

Elise reached out and patted her shoulder. "We are agreed, then."

The seamstress got up, still scowling, and folded the dress she held back into the trunk.

"And did you want the trunk as well?" Elise dared to ask.

The old woman squinted at her. "How much?"

Anne said, "Two dollars."

Muttering, the seamstress hobbled out of the room.

"It is a lot for the dresses," the customer said, "but I'm sure you ladies wouldn't cheat that old woman."

Anne's face flushed at the very suggestion.

"Certainly not," Elise said. "The price we're asking isn't half what Miss Stone paid in England."

"Yes, I can see it's all quality goods."

The seamstress came back and handed Elise a gold coin and several paper bills. "There. That'll buy you some cornmeal and bacon."

"Do you have any more?" the customer asked.

"Uh. . .nothing else for sale." Elise glanced at Anne, who shook her head vigorously.

They thanked the women and hurried outside. The sun had set, and the air was noticeably cooler.

"Well, now. Success?" Rebecca asked.

"Yes, thank you," Elise said. "And thank you, Wilbur, for waiting." She climbed into the back of the wagon with a little help from Lavinia. They each tugged at one of Anne's arms and got her up with them.

"There be a rug or two back there," Rebecca called from the seat beside her son as he flicked the reins and signaled the mules to move out.

"Elise," Anne whispered as Lavinia unfolded the thick wool blankets for them. "That woman. . ."

"Yes?"

"Was she. . .an actress?"

"Best not to ask, I felt. After all, does it really matter who wears our dresses?"

"Last chance to go to church for a long time, ladies." Wilbur Harkness grinned at them. "We've got room in the wagon for you—just."

Anne looked at Elise with longing. "I know God will go with us, but I shall miss being able to attend worship."

"Of course we'll go," Elise said.

That morning they'd donned their new calico dresses. The light material swirled about their legs. It felt odd, with only one petticoat and a pair of pantalets beneath it. Rebecca had warned them that the thin cotton wouldn't be enough to shield them from the sun in midsummer, but for now Elise reveled in the ease of movement the light garments gave her.

"Should we wear these dresses?" she asked Anne when Wilbur had left.

"I hardly think so." Anne's face looked pained. "Last week we attended services at the Episcopal church, and I didn't think our costumes were out of place."

"That is true." Elise reached for her satchel.

The Harkness family planned to attend the Methodist church, but Wilbur assured them that they could drop the ladies in front of the towering Episcopal building. As they left the field that now bulged with canvas-topped wagons, Elise spotted Eb Bentley saddling his horse. He looked a bit more dapper than usual, and she wondered if he was also headed into town to worship.

At noon, as the Episcopal church's bells rang the end of services, the two ladies emerged and stood on the sidewalk while the congregants dispersed.

"Wilbur said it will probably be twenty minutes or so," Elise said.

"Yes. I'm glad it's not so cold today."

Elise reached over and adjusted the soft muffler Lady Anne had tucked about her neck. She mustn't allow her mistress to become ill now. Taking care of Anne on the ship or in a hotel had been difficult enough, but she couldn't ask her to endure sickness in the discomfort of a covered wagon.

At last the Harkness family arrived. Wilbur and his father hopped down and assisted the ladies into the wagon. Even though they'd given up the broadest of their fashionable skirts, the women's dresses took up a large share of the wagon bed. The younger children crowded against the sideboards to give them space.

Mr. Harkness drove them down one of the less desirable streets of Independence, in a direct line toward the rendezvous field. To Elise's horror, the saloons that had been quiet when they arrived that morning were now open, and a few men drifted toward their doors.

Anne caught her eye and made a face. "It's Sunday," she hissed.

Elise nodded. Unthinkable—and yet, there it was. Apparently a large contingent of Americans did not observe the Lord's Day.

The door of a rundown establishment opened wide as they passed, and a woman minced out onto the boardwalk before it. Elise sucked in a breath. The dress the woman wore was of the same deep gold satin as Anne's ball gown—the one they'd sold yesterday. But the neckline of this dress plunged indecently, and the skirt was caught up with rosettes, exposing the woman's lower limbs and the edge of a black net petticoat.

Elise looked over at her companion. Anne's face had gone a

stark white. She stared at the woman until they reached the corner and Mr. Harkness drove the wagon into another street.

Anne turned around slowly and sank down into a heap.

"Are you all right?" Elise whispered.

Anne nodded, but her breathing was shallow, and she closed her eyes.

A few minutes later, after they'd entered a more respectable neighborhood, Elise realized they were drawing near the hotel where they'd stayed on their arrival in Independence. "Perhaps we could stay in town tonight," she said softly. "You could sleep in a real bed one last time." *And have less chance of becoming ill on the eve of our journey,* she thought.

Anne obviously wavered at the suggestion. The whole scheme of toughening up for the trip had worked to a point; they now knew better what to expect in their daily routine and the hardships of keeping food prepared and their clothing cared for. But roughing it might be better faced tomorrow morning if they'd had a good night's sleep.

"We might even get a hot bath," Elise said.

Anne smiled. "I suppose so. We'd have to rise terribly early to get to the field on time though."

Elise didn't bother to debate that. She called to Mr. Harkness, "Would you mind stopping at the hotel up ahead? I'd like to see if Miss Stone and I could stay there tonight."

"Oh, you'd miss the forming of the train," Rebecca said with a frown.

"I think we could rise early enough," Elise said. "Our hired man could hitch the team and get it into line for us."

Mr. Harkness pulled his wagon up before the hotel, and Elise climbed down and hurried inside. Knots of people, mostly men, stood about talking to each other. She excused herself repeatedly until they cleared a path for her. Again she was struck by how primitive the establishment was. Why exactly did she think this would be more comfortable than their bedrolls in the tent at the field? And there seemed to be far more patrons now than there had been a few days ago.

The landlord came from another room with an armful of blankets.

"Mr. Lewis," Elise called. "Would you have a room for Miss Stone and me tonight?"

"Oh Miss Finster. I'm sorry. You two were very nice customers, but, ma'am, we're full to bursting. Folks have started cramming into town for the emigrant trains. I reckon yours will be the first out, but I've got at least four people in every room right now, and gents sleeping on the floor down here."

Elise turned away disappointed yet with a sense of rightness. *This is Your will, Lord,* she prayed. *Thank You for giving us this clear direction. We'll stay with the wagon tonight.*

"Oh ma'am," Lewis called before she could reach the door.

Elise paused and looked back. "Yes?"

"You might want to meet this gentleman." He gestured toward a tall, shaggy-looking man coming down the stairs. "Mr. Hoyle is the captain of a train leaving next week. I know you like to talk to everyone you can who's been out West, about that fella you're looking for."

"Why yes. Thank you."

The man had heard the landlord's comment and eyed Elise curiously as he finished his descent. He walked over to her and bowed his head slightly.

"Ma'am. I'm Ted Hoyle. Can I help you?" His gaze roved briefly over her, and Elise guessed he was weighing her station, income, age, and stamina.

"I'm searching for a man I believe may have gone west a few years ago—David Stone. He formerly resided in St. Louis, and he then came here. We've lost track of him, and his family in England would like very much to locate Mr. Stone."

"Stone, eh?" Hoyle rubbed his bristly jaw. "Sure, I remember him."

CHAPTER 13

Elise's heart raced, and she felt a little giddy. "You say you knew Mr. Stone?"

"There was a man a few years back," Ted Hoyle said. "An Englishman, that is. He took three wagons. Said he was going to open a haberdashery."

Elise caught her breath. "Are you sure it was David Stone?"

"I think that was his name. Let's see, it would have been '51 . . .no, '50. That's it. The spring of 1850. He joined my outfit for California."

"California?" Elise let that sink in. "Then we're joining the wrong expedition."

"Where you headed?" Hoyle's brow furrowed as he again eyed the gown, hat, and coat she'd worn to church.

"Oregon."

"Well then, you're headed to the right place. See, the trails are the same for a while. A good while. And besides, unless I'm mistaken, that fella didn't go all the way to the coast with me."

"He didn't? What happened?"

"Changed his mind somewhere along the way. Split off when we got to the cutoff and went with another train headed for Oregon." Hoyle rubbed his chin again as if that would improve his memory. "Yes, I'm sure that's what he did. I talked to him a few times while we were crossing the plains. Said he'd tried farming for a while, but he wasn't very good at it. I guess he'd had a store before that—"

"Yes, he did," Elise said. "In St. Louis."

"Well, I guess he thought he was a better shopkeeper than he was a farmer."

"I don't suppose you know where in Oregon he planned to settle?"

"No, I don't, ma'am. Sorry."

"That's all right. You've been very helpful."

Elise rushed out to the wagon and called to Anne, "You'll never guess! I've got some solid word on your uncle at last."

Anne rose to her knees and clutched the wagon's sideboard. "No! Really?"

Elise nodded and lifted her skirt in preparation for climbing in at the back of the wagon. Abby and Ben, the brother between Wilbur and Lavinia in age, reached for her arms and hoisted her up.

"This gentleman is another wagon master, and he says David went with him on a train five years ago, headed for Oregon. We're on the right trail, Anne!"

"Well now," Rebecca said with a nod. "Your persistence paid off."

"Finally." Anne sank back and stared at Elise with wide eyes. "But. . .five years ago?"

"That's what the gentleman said, and he seemed quite certain. He thought David had been farming for a few years before he joined the wagon train."

"Well, think of that," said Rebecca.

"Are you staying here tonight?" Mr. Harkness asked.

"Oh. No, we're not. I'm sorry—I should have told you that at once. The hotel is full." Elise smoothed her skirt as the wagon lurched forward. Somehow beds and baths didn't matter anymore. They'd had word of David, and they would find him.

The night was still inky black when a piercing horn sounded across the field, signaling that it was time to rise and prepare to move out.

Eb was already poking at the embers in the rock fireplace where he and Rob cooked their meals when they weren't invited to share with one of the emigrant families. Rob came back from the center of the camp, where he'd blown the alert, smiling and polishing the bugle with his sleeve.

"You like that thing entirely too much," Eb said.

"It is a beauty. Traded a pair of beaded Blackfoot moccasins for it."

"You've told me that story a thousand times."

Rob sighed and stooped to tuck the bugle into one of his saddlebags. "It feels good to be getting onto the trail again."

Eb grunted and reached for the battered coffeepot. He'd feel a lot better when they reached Oregon. "I'll fetch some water."

"Got some yonder." Rob nodded toward where a galvanized bucket stood with a feed sack draped over it.

By the time Eb had the coffee on, Rob had four eggs, a slab of bacon, a frying pan, and some stale johnnycake laid out.

"May as well use the last of the eggs."

Eb frowned. "Guess we forgot to get more. Only a couple of people have laying hens along."

"We'll live." Rob squatted before the fire and fed two more sticks onto it. "I can tend breakfast if you want to make sure the drovers are rounding up the mules and oxen."

Eb walked out to the corral where they'd penned the animals the night before. Farmers and hired hands were sorting out the teams for each wagon. On the trail, they'd have to use the wagons themselves to form an enclosure for the stock, but here at the departure place they had the luxury of a separate fenced area. Mules neighed and shifted about inside. A horse nickered, and oxen lowed. The sprinkling of cows mooed to let their owners know they were ready to be milked. The men dodged about among the animals.

"Everything going all right?" Eb called to Abe Leonard.

"We'll figure it out."

Eb smiled and went back to the campfire.

"That was quick," Rob said. "I haven't even cooked the eggs yet."

"I'll go back in a few minutes if they haven't started to bring the teams in and hitch up. Looked like they had enough men out there in the dark."

"The sun'll be up before you know it," Rob said.

Eb squinted eastward, toward the river. He could discern a lighter gray band of sky on the horizon. "Wonder how Miss Finster and her young friend are doing."

As soon as he'd spoken, he wished he hadn't. Rob already ragged him mercilessly about the Englishwomen, teasing him about what he perceived as Eb's regard for Miss Finster.

"I'm sure the ladies will be fine," Rob said. "I haven't talked much with the man they hired, but he seems capable."

"I'll go by their wagon later," Eb said. He thought about shaving. He usually let his beard grow while they were on the trail. Maybe he'd start it today. Or maybe not.

He walked over to his pile of gear and pulled out his soap and razor.

"You can handle it," Peterson said. He passed Costigan a handful of bills. "You know people all the way along the trail from here to Oregon. I'm sure you can get word of this man. Just make sure you know where he is before his relatives do, and get the job done."

Thomas tried to count the money in the semidarkness.

"That's all you'll get until you report something definite," Peterson said. "Send word as quick as you can, so the boss knows."

Thomas gave up trying to see the denominations. It looked like enough, seeing as how his food and a small salary were being paid by the ladies. He'd never before heard of a job where you got paid twice. He shoved the money in his pocket and looked anxiously toward the road.

"I've got to get back there. Whistler's horn blew ten minutes ago. If I don't get the mule team up, he'll be suspicious and the ladies will be out of sorts."

"Go. Just don't forget to send word along the way, as often as you can without making it noticeable."

Peterson mounted his horse and trotted off toward Independence.

"What shall we do?" Anne wrung her hands as she paced beside the wagon, looking toward the corral.

The men of the company had driven most of the pulling teams into the encampment and were busy hitching them to their wagons.

Anne and Elise had eaten and cleaned up afterward. Elise had held back a plate for Thomas and couldn't pack the dish box away until his cup, plate, and fork were in it. The coffeepot still steamed over the dying fire, and the grate was cooling so they could pack it.

But Thomas Costigan had not shown his face that morning. The sun was rising, and everyone else seemed nearly ready to pull out, but their mule team was still in the corral with the extra livestock.

"I suppose we'd better go find those mules." Elise made the decision as she spoke. She hitched up her skirt. "We can't let everyone else be ready before us. We told Mr. Whistler and Mr. Bentley we wouldn't slow them down."

"That's true. And we wanted to come without hiring a man, so even without Thomas, we should be ready when the others are." Anne tied her shawl about her shoulders so she could use both hands to work. "Let's go."

They set off briskly to the corral. Nick Foster, the fifteen-year-old son of a farmer, was milking his family's cow just inside the gate.

"Good morning, Nicholas," Elise said. "We need to get our mules. I wonder if you could tend the gate for us."

"Surely, ma'am. One moment while I finish here."

"Perhaps we can go locate the team while you do that," Anne said.

Elise walked to the gate. It was fastened with a simple loop of twine over both the gatepost and an upright pole on the gate. She lifted the loop and swung the gate open.

"Careful," Nick called. "Don't let the other cattle out."

Elise quickly drew the gate back until it was open only far enough for her to step inside. She and Anne squeezed into the corral, and she turned to replace the twine.

Anne's sharp intake of breath made her whirl around. A huge ox ambled toward them, his head wagging from side to side. Anne clutched Elise's arm.

"Will he hurt us?"

135

"I don't think so." Elise's pulse roared as the ox came closer. Her mouth went dry, and her stomach flipped. "Nicholas?"

Nick called, "Oh, don't worry about him. That's just Bright. He's one of my father's extra oxen."

Even though all the other teams had been removed, a large herd of animals remained in the pen. Elise tried to ignore Bright, who now stood solidly a yard in front of her.

"Do you see our mules?"

"I'm not sure I'd know them from anyone else's." Anne's voice had a pronounced tremor.

"I believe Mr. Costigan marked the straps on their halters," Elise ventured. She should have paid more attention to the livestock question, but she'd gladly given the matter over to Thomas.

She grasped Anne's hand and led her cautiously around Bright. The big ox lowered his head and let out a thunderous bellow. Anne yelped.

"Nicholas," Elise shouted.

He strode quickly into the pen with something that looked suspiciously like a smirk on his lips.

"I'm here, ma'am. How can I help you?"

"We. . .need to locate our mules."

"Yes'm. How many you got?"

"Six," Elise said, "but we only want to hitch up four of them."

Nick nodded and set off across the corral.

Elise held her skirt up and followed. "Watch your step, Anne."

"This one's yours," Nick called, and Elise hurried toward him.

"Can you take two at a time?" he asked.

"Umm. . ."

The young man shook his head as though she were helpless. Elise hated the feeling of inadequacy. They hadn't even started the journey, and already she'd proven incompetent.

"Take this one. I'll bring two. Miss Stone, can you take one?"

"I think so." Anne sounded hesitant.

"Lead him over to the gate," Nick said to Elise. "If you don't think you can get him to your wagon, I'll come back. You didn't

bring any lead ropes, did you?"

"No," Elise said.

"All right. I'll grab those two mules over there. Let's go."

Leading the mule to the camp was terrifying yet exhilarating. Elise flinched every time the beast moved his head, afraid she'd lose her hold on the halter. The path seemed much longer than it had when they'd approached the corral, but at last she and the mule, whom she'd mentally nicknamed Challenger, arrived at the wagon.

"You present a challenge," she said softly to the big mule. "If I can't meet it, I shall have failed Anne and debased the purpose of our journey. Therefore, I shall face this challenge, and I shall win."

There were the lead ropes she and Anne should have taken, hanging from the back of the wagon. She held firmly to Challenger's halter. Anne had fallen back about ten yards and seemed to be struggling with the mule she led. Elise grabbed a rope, hooked it to Challenger's halter, tied the other end to an iron ring on the frame of the wagon, and grabbed a second rope. She hurried back to help Anne.

"Here we go." She clipped the rope to the smaller brown mule's halter. "I'll take him."

Anne let go of the strap and stepped back with a sigh. "Thank you. He stepped on my foot twice."

Nick passed her, leading two more mules.

"There are ropes at the back of the wagon," Elise called.

"Where's your harness?"

"Oh. In the wagon."

"Best get it out," Nick said.

Grateful beyond words, Elise decided the best way to thank him would be to secure Anne's beast and get the harness ready. She found it easily, in a large wooden crate inside the wagon, near the back opening.

"Anne," she called out through the gap in the canvas.

"I'm here." Anne stepped up close to the tailboard.

"Let me hand down the collars to you, and I'll try to get the harness."

Elise passed two of the padded leather collars out.

"Wait," Anne said. "I don't think I can carry any more." She disappeared.

Elise set the others out, ready to pass down on Anne's return. She reached into the crate for the huge mass of straps and buckles that was the harness. Long sticks with brass knobs on the end seemed to be a part of it. What were those things called? Perhaps Nick could tell her. She tugged at a wide leather strap, but it all seemed connected.

"Ready for more," Anne called from outside.

"Oh, here." Elise handed her the other two collars. "I'm not sure I can get the harness out by myself."

"I'll be right back."

A minute later, Anne clambered in at the front of the wagon and crawled over their trunks, sacks, and bundles to where Elise was working. Together they managed to haul the harness out of the crate and tip it out the back of the wagon into a heap on the trampled grass.

"Which two mules are the wheelers?" Nick yelled from the front of the wagon.

"I. . .have no idea," Elise confessed.

"We'll put the biggest ones at the back, then."

"Nicholas!" The strident female voice reached them from halfway across the bustling encampment.

Nick turned toward it, shielding his eyes. "Yeah, Ma?"

"Where's the milk?"

"Down to the corral. I had to help these ladies get their team up."

"Well, you go get it, young man! The idea! You need to do for your own family this morning, not those fancy ladies."

"All right, Ma."

Nick turned back to Elise with gritted teeth. "Sorry."

"It's all right," Elise said. "You go and do as your mother says. We can do the rest."

It was a gross overstatement, as Elise knew, but Nick hurried away toward the pen.

Anne's lips trembled, and Elise wondered if they had the same

thought. The way Mrs. Foster said "fancy ladies" sounded vulgar. Could she possibly be casting aspersions on their morals? The American women didn't seem to know what to make of them. Their accents and clothing set them apart. Mrs. Foster and the other forty or so women on the wagon train were trying to classify them.

She drew in a deep breath. "All right, Anne. Let's see if we can separate the harnesses and lay them out in one pile for each mule."

Anne seemed relieved to be given a task that didn't involve touching the animals again. It took them ten minutes to figure out that they had six sets of harness in the mound, not four.

"That's right," Anne said meekly. "Mr. Pottle insisted we might need to harness all six when we reach the mountains."

Elise removed two complete sets—as nearly as she could tell—and put them back in the crate. They laid out one set on the ground. Elise looked from Challenger to the harness and back.

"I think this is the front," she said at last.

"Need some help, ma'am?"

Elise's heart sank. Of all the people she did *not* want to see her in this weak position, Eb Bentley had to come along. On the other hand, just seeing the man's rugged face at this trying moment sent a wave of relief cascading over her.

Anne jumped in and saved Elise the embarrassment of admitting their predicament.

"Oh Mr. Bentley, that's very kind of you. I'm afraid our hired man has been delayed. . .somewhere. Miss Finster and I are trying to make sense of all this harness. Perhaps you would be so kind. . ." She smiled up at the scout.

Apparently her hopeful face was enough to sway Eb. "Sure, I'll help you. We need to get this train moving. But you know you need your man along."

Elise cleared her throat. "Yes, sir, we understand. We're hoping he'll arrive at any moment. I can't understand why he's not here this morning."

"Perhaps he mistook the day," Anne said.

"Perhaps." Elise was certain Thomas knew what day it was and that the wagon train was supposed to have moved out at daybreak. What if he'd decided to take the small advance payment they'd given him and desert them?

Across the field, Rob Whistler yelled, "Put your wagon next in line, Mr. Clark. Then you, Binchley."

"Here," Eb said. "This set of harness looks to be adjusted the longest on the sides. We'll put it on the big fella there."

He set about tossing the bundle of leather over Challenger's back, and miraculously, the straps fell into place on the mule's body. Eb quickly fastened a couple of buckles.

"Ever harnessed a horse?" he asked.

"No, but I'll try," Elise said.

He pointed to another mule, almost as large as Challenger. "Do him next."

Elise picked up another set of harness. She could barely lift it as high as the mule's back.

Anne came and stood beside her. "How can I help?"

"Let's see. . ." Elise looked over at the harness on Challenger to see how Eb had positioned it. "I'm not sure where this buckle goes. Can you go around and look on the other side and try to find where Mr. Bentley put it?"

Anne was gone for a minute, and Elise struggled to find a spot to attach every free end of leather. Anne came back carrying two of the wooden pieces with round brass balls on the ends.

"He says these are hames and they go on each side of the collar. The tugs hitch to them."

Elise hadn't expected that. She looked under her mule's neck and over at Challenger. Did she need to remove the collar? By this time Eb was putting on the big mule's bridle.

She tiptoed over and peered closely at the collar and hames.

"Got it?" Eb asked.

"I think so." She went back to Challenger and fumbled about until she felt that part was right. Now to fix the straps of the harness to the hames. By the time she had most of it done, Eb had harnessed mule number three and positioned him in front of Challenger.

"What's this?" Anne held up a rounded piece of leather. Straps with buckles hung from it, but Elise couldn't imagine where it should go.

"I'm not sure." Elise scrutinized Eb's work again but couldn't spot a piece similar to Anne's. She took it and held it up, frowning.

"That's the crupper, ma'am."

Elise jumped and looked up into Eb's face. He was closer than she'd thought, and she stepped away, bumping the mule's flank. The animal let out a snort of protest.

"The what?" she asked.

"The crupper. It goes under his tail."

Elise glanced toward the mule's rear end. With a grimace she headed back there. Eb seemed amused. He walked to the harness they'd left on the grass and picked up the last bundle.

She could see now one tab of leather on the mule's near side that must attach to this buckle. But how did one get the tail to lie over the crupper? She stared at Challenger's rump, frowning.

Suddenly Eb was beside her again.

"Allow me, ma'am." As he took the offending piece of leather from her, his large, tanned hand touched her fingers. Elise relinquished the crupper as if it had burned her.

"Thank you."

"Maybe you can bring up the last mule from the back of the wagon."

Five minutes later, they had all four mules in place, and Eb was making a final check of all the harness connections. Rob Whistler rode up on his horse.

"Eb, where you been?"

"More like where's their hired man been."

Eb definitely sounded grumpy. Elise exchanged a look with Anne.

"Costigan's not here?" Rob asked. "We're supposed to have pulled out half an hour ago."

"I know it," Eb said. "Can't be helped."

"Well, it's often this way on the first day." Whistler smiled down at Elise and Anne.

"I don't know about that fella," Eb said. "I asked about him at the livery. Pottle didn't seem to think much of him."

Anne's eyes widened. "Do you mean Mr. Costigan?"

"He's the one." Eb straightened and slapped the near lead mule on the shoulder. "You're all set, if you have a driver."

"But. . .you recommended Mr. Costigan," Anne said.

"Me?" Eb swung around to look at her. "I never did. In fact, I never saw him before he showed up with your wagon a few days ago."

Anne looked helplessly at her, and Elise hauled in a deep breath.

"I believe what he actually said the day we met him was, 'that wagon train fella' had told him we needed a man to go with us on the journey. He asked for the job."

Eb pursed his lips then glanced up at Whistler. "Did you talk to him, Rob?"

"I never. Not before he was hired."

Eb's eyebrows drew together. "Well, lookee yonder."

They all turned toward the road. Thomas Costigan walked quickly toward them.

"I reckon your driver's here," Eb said. "But I'll be watching him."

Rob nodded. "Me, too. Come on, Eb. We need to finish setting the lineup. Miss Finster, have Costigan put your wagon last in line. After we stop at nooning, you'll move up." He touched his hat brim and rode off.

"I'll check in on you later, ladies," Eb said. He didn't wait for Thomas to get there but strode away instead.

Elise clenched her jaw. Eb had neglected his usual duties to help them. They'd fulfilled his dire predictions about them—the ones she'd vowed would not come true. She and Anne had delayed the starting of the train and made extra work for the scout. Those reflections did not put her in a kindly mood toward Thomas.

"Mr. Costigan." She stood in his path with her hands on her hips. "We needed you, and you weren't here."

"I'm sorry, ma'am. I got called away last night, and I thought

142

I'd be back before—"

"Called away? By whom? We have a business agreement." *At least he's sober,* Elise told herself, but she wasn't going to let him off too easy.

"Sorry, ma'am." His confident tone had sunk to a mumble. He shot a glance in Anne's direction. "I couldn't help it, but I'm ready to go now."

"I should hope so," Elise said. "We have four of the mules hitched, as you can see. I wasn't sure which two you wanted to keep in reserve."

Thomas did a quick survey of the team. "This will do, except I put Bumper there in as a leader, him being so independent and all."

"Bumper?" Elise asked.

He slapped the near wheeler on the withers. "This one right here." He looked over the mules' backs toward where the lead wagons were rolling out onto the road westward. "No time to switch them now. Probably won't matter."

Elise made a mental note to learn the peculiarities of all their mules soon, in case Thomas proved unreliable again.

"Your breakfast is cold, but it's waiting for you on the other side of the wagon. As soon as you get your coffee, I'll pack up the coffeepot."

"Thank you, ma'am."

Anne sidled up to her as Thomas disappeared around the wagon. "He seems contrite enough."

"Yes." Elise frowned. "I don't know what to think. It's too late to change our plans and find another man, but we'd best learn all we can about caring for mules."

"Yes, and I'd like to learn to drive," Anne said.

"Excellent idea."

More than half the wagons had lumbered out of the field onto the roadway. Rob Whistler cantered toward them on his chestnut horse.

"You ready?"

"Next to it."

"Where's Costigan?"

Thomas came around the back of the wagon carrying his tin plate and cup. "I'm here."

"Get your wagon into the last place in line. Let's not have any stragglers the first day."

Thomas shoved his empty plate into Elise's hands. "Thanks, ma'am. Not half-bad this morning."

Elise supposed that was a compliment. "Just don't be tardy again." She hurried to put the dirty dishes away. No time to clean them now. They'd have to do them at noon, and she hoped the egg wouldn't stick too badly.

To her surprise, Anne was dumping the dregs of the coffee onto the smoldering remains of their campfire.

"Is there anything else?" she asked.

"Just that box. I hung the grate on the wagon."

Elise flung the dish box in over the tailboard as the mules leaned into their collars and pulled. The two women stood for a moment catching their breath and watching their wagon pull away from them.

"Oh." Anne looked down at the coffeepot in her hand.

"Come on," Elise said. "I don't suppose it will take us ten seconds to catch up."

They set out on their first day on the Oregon Trail, walking fifty feet behind the last wagon.

Elise heard a commotion behind, and she swung around.

"Oh my! Hurry, Anne."

The herd of milk cows and extra oxen and mules surged up the trail from the corral. Elise and Anne turned and ran for the back of their wagon.

CHAPTER 14

Elise sat on the wagon tongue, finishing her sewing before the last rays of daylight faded. They'd been on the trail three days, and she was weary beyond expression. Anne had already retired inside their tent.

"Everything all right over here?"

She looked up to see Rebecca Harkness approaching with Mrs. Legity, a widow traveling with her daughter, son-in-law, and their three children.

"Yes, thank you," Elise said.

Rebecca nodded. "Thought I smelt something burning over here earlier."

"Oh, well. . ." Heat rushed to Elise's cheeks. "Miss Stone and I are still learning to use the dutch oven to good advantage."

Rebecca smiled, and it transformed her careworn, critical visage into the pleasant face of a friend. "Would you like another lesson? Tomorrow evening if we stop in good time, perhaps we could bake gingerbread after supper."

"That sounds lovely."

Mrs. Legity snorted. "Don't know why you two thought you could head out for parts unknown without knowing so much as how to bake biscuits."

"There now, Agnes, likely these ladies had people to do for them back in England."

Elise swallowed hard. She didn't want to go into their former situation. "We would both like to increase our knowledge of household tasks."

Mrs. Legity snorted again, but Rebecca smiled.

"There now. When you talk, Miss Finster, it's like music. And Miss Stone—why, her voice is like honey."

"She is sweet," Elise said.

"Yes, and Wilbur's like a bee drawn to her," Mrs. Legity said.

Elise stared at her for a moment then averted her gaze. "Wilbur has been nothing but courteous in our presence."

"That's good to hear," Rebecca said. "I'm sure Miss Stone does seem like an angel to him. She's so pretty and dainty."

"She'll never make a farm wife."

Mrs. Legity's sour comments hurt, but Elise knew better than to show her reaction. In England, she'd have given any woman who spoke so a proper set-down. But these women, rough and dour as they were, held a trove of wisdom Elise envied. She had to live with them for the next five or six months, and she could either learn from them or turn up her nose and be snubbed. She chose to make friends.

"Mrs. Legity, I admire the fine stitching on your buttonholes. Did you make them yourself?"

"Aye. And I see you've been sewing this evening."

Elise nodded. "A small mending job. I tore a sleeve yesterday."

"You'd do well to take up your skirts while you're at it."

Elise hesitated, unsure how to respond. The pioneer women all seemed to wear their skirts scandalously short, exposing their ankles. Lavinia Harkness's were among the worst, but her mother didn't seem to care that Lavinia and her sisters sometimes showed the edges of their petticoats and even a bit of stocking.

"The fashions do change," she murmured.

"It's nothing to do with fashion," Mrs. Legity said. "If you're going to walk miles every day and cook over an open fire, you'd best have skirts that won't get in your way."

Elise recalled her near accident with the fire the week before, and the way Eb Bentley had hauled her away from the blaze with his well-muscled arms. Her face flushed anew.

"Perhaps you are right." Climbing in and out of the wagon was another activity where full skirts hindered her, and she'd noticed Anne impatiently yanking hers upward before she mounted the wagon step. A couple of inches off the hemline might in reality

allow them more modesty if it meant less hiking up their skirts. "I shall speak to Anne about it tomorrow."

Rebecca nodded. "That's the spirit."

Mrs. Legity had found the charred pot Elise had set aside. She'd hoped Thomas would carry the heavy iron kettle to the stream and scour it out with sand, but Thomas had disappeared as soon as he'd eaten. That seemed to be his pattern, and Elise had mulled how to keep him around camp for a few chores each evening, but she hadn't worked up her courage to speak to him about it yet.

Now Mrs. Legity peered into the dutch oven and wrinkled her nose. Elise felt compelled to say something.

"I hoped to take care of that earlier, but I needed to use the daylight for my sewing."

"Have you plenty of water?" Rebecca looked pointedly at the nearly empty bucket by the wagon's rear wheel.

"Uh. . .Mr. Costigan. . ." Elise glanced about, but Thomas was still absent.

"Don't go to fetch water by yourself," Mrs. Legity said darkly.

"Do you suppose we'll be able to do a washing soon?" Elise asked.

"It might be weeks afore we do," Mrs. Legity said.

Rebecca shrugged. "Mr. Whistler won't want to stop long enough for that until we get to Fort Kearny, I'll wager."

"Oh." Elise didn't consider herself overly fastidious, but already she was running out of clean stockings and underthings. Lady Anne had certainly never been so long without a bath.

"Well, we'd best get back to our wagons," Rebecca said. "Take care, Miss Finster, and do come by tomorrow evening if you're not too busy. We'll do a baking."

"Thank you, and perhaps you can share that knitting pattern you mentioned to me."

"I'd be happy to."

As the two women turned away, Elise caught an incredulous glance from Mrs. Legity. Probably she couldn't believe Elise actually knew how to knit, though it was something she'd learned in childhood.

Mrs. Legity offered not so much as a farewell, and the two walked away in the twilight. Elise sat down again and took up her needle, but it was so dark she couldn't see the thread against the fabric. With a sigh, she stuck the needle through the cloth, rose, and tucked the dress inside the wagon.

The next morning Thomas brought up the two mules that pulled in the wheel position while Elise stood over the bacon and Anne set out the dishes.

"Thomas, we'll need more water," Elise called.

"Got to get these mules hitched."

"But toting wood and water is part of your job."

Thomas frowned. "Don't remember that."

Elise gritted her teeth. No use asking him to clean the burned-on dutch oven. He would surely balk at that. "It is indeed part of the job, and if you need to rise earlier to do those chores, then so be it, but I'm sure you could bring a little extra fuel and water in the evening."

He tied the two mules to the wagon frame and walked out into the center of the camp again, where the loose livestock were confined at night.

"That man is starting to irritate me," Elise said to Anne.

"I understand, but here's the rub—he's the only man we've got or are able to have at this point."

"Yes. I'm beginning to feel he's taken advantage of us. He does hitch the team each morning—aside from that first day—and he drives all day, sitting on the wagon seat, while we have to walk. Then he unhitches at night, eats his supper, and disappears."

Anne carefully removed the coffeepot from the fire. She set it down on top of the dish crate and turned to Elise.

"We must learn to drive well. Both of us."

"I've been thinking the same." So far Anne had not asked Thomas to teach her, and neither of the ladies had taken the reins of the mule team. "It would be wise of us to master the skill—and

any others we might have to perform if our hired man abandons us along the way."

Anne's forehead wrinkled. "Where would he go? We've passed a few farms and that one little village yesterday, but I believe we're quite beyond civilization now."

"He says he knows people along the trail. There must be trading stations. And—and forts."

Anne nodded. "I did hear Mr. Whistler mention some forts. He said our first major destination is Fort Kearny. We'll stop there a few days to rest and trade, he said."

"Ma'am?"

Elise whirled to find Thomas standing behind her. With each hand he held the halter of another mule. His shirt was fastened by the two top buttons but hung open below them.

"Really, Thomas, your shirt," Elise said.

"Yes'm. Bumper here took off a couple of buttons. Thought maybe you could help me out."

"Do you have the buttons?"

He shook his head. "No chance to look for 'em."

Elise sighed. The buttons in her limited sewing kit were mostly small mother-of-pearl disks for mending her own clothing and Anne's. She also had a few cloth-covered ones that matched some of their dresses.

"Change your shirt after you hitch the mules. I'll see what I can come up with."

When he was out of earshot, Anne said, "I think he's only got two shirts to his name."

"And I've no masculine shirt buttons."

"Perhaps Mrs. Harkness would trade for something," Anne suggested. "She has several men to sew and mend for."

"That's good thinking. What shall I offer in trade?"

Anne smiled. "A yard of lace to put about the neck and sleeves of one of her dresses. She may fuss about fripperies, but I daresay she'd love to have some."

"Perhaps you're right. If that doesn't do the trick, I'll see if she has plenty of spices. I really think we purchased more than we'll use between here and Oregon."

"Yes, but if we're going to trade our supplies for Thomas's upkeep, we need to come to an understanding with him."

"True." Elise looked toward where he was fitting Challenger's collar over the mule's head. "I believe I can do that now. Mending wasn't mentioned when we hired him. But I shall be glad to do it— after I see a full water pail and a good-sized woodpile this evening." She turned over a slice of bacon. "I'm getting the knack for this, Anne."

"Wonderful! And I believe we should use our bargaining position to make Thomas agree to driving lessons as well."

"Hmm." Elise turned another piece of bacon. It looked quite appetizing, and the smell of it cooking made her stomach rumble. "Perhaps the time to broach that subject is when we present him with a large slice of hot gingerbread."

"My dears, I'm so worn out, I've got to go to bed after this batch is done baking, whether it's edible or not." Rebecca eyed the dutch oven doubtfully.

"I'm so sorry I ruined the last batch," Anne said contritely.

"There, there, it wasn't your fault." Rebecca patted her shoulder.

"That's right. Anyone might mistake saleratus for salt," Lavinia said stoutly, though Elise didn't see how that could be true. Still, she admired Lavinia for sticking up for Anne. The poor young lady's confidence was now lower than Bumper's shoe nails.

"We wanted a good batch tonight, so we could bribe Thomas," Anne confessed, "but he's probably asleep by now."

Rebecca laughed. "So that's why the baking lesson was so important. Well, it's a shame you ruined two cakes' worth of supplies, but I do believe this one will turn out all right. If he's gone to bed, you can give it to him at nooning tomorrow. He'll be surprised, you can be certain of that."

"That should work fine," Elise said, though she and Anne had

hoped to extract a good amount of wood and water out of Thomas before then. "We're grateful to you for your patience, Rebecca. I know you're tired." She finished the row she was knitting, turned the beginnings of a sock, and started on the next row. Perhaps a pair of woolen socks would help win Thomas over as well.

"It's not as though we're completely helpless," Anne said with a stubborn lift of her aristocratic chin. "I'm sure Elise could cook fine if she had a stove."

"Maybe," Elise said. *A stove and a couple of kitchen maids.*

"I do believe it may be ready." Rebecca handed Anne her cooking paddle. "Scrape off the coals, dearie, and make sure you don't dump any ashes on your gingerbread when you take the lid off."

"You're lucky to have enough wood tonight," Lavinia said.

If you only knew, Elise thought. She'd bargained with Thomas for replacing his buttons, and he'd grudgingly gone for more sticks.

"Yes, we'll soon have to start gathering buffalo chips, they tell me," Rebecca said.

"Buffalo chips?" Elise didn't like the sound of that.

"Is it wood chips?" Anne asked.

Rebecca and Lavinia laughed. "No, my dear, it's not, but it will burn clean if you get nice, dry ones. They say the buffalo aren't as plentiful as they used to be, but I expect, since we're one of the first trains this year, we'll find enough of their leavings."

Anne's mouth skewed. "You mean—oh, I say."

"Yes, that's what I mean." Rebecca passed her a pot holder. "All right, let's see if your gingerbread is edible."

"Mr. Whistler says we'll get to Fort Kearny tomorrow," Lavinia said on the first day of May, as she and Elise walked along beside the Harknesses' wagons. "That means we'll rest a couple of days and do a big washing and visit the trading post and dance in the evening."

"We're all looking forward to it," Elise said. They'd been on the trail more than a month and had come three hundred miles from

Independence. Elise was content with the life they now lived, if not always comfortable.

The warm winds already carried the dust stirred up by the wagons. She hadn't expected that until high summer. The dust sifted into the wagons no matter how tightly they tied the flaps down. Everything bore a coating of dust, and it sometimes blew so thick that they could barely see the wagons ahead of them.

Elise and Anne, along with the other women, had found that walking a few yards off the trail, to the side of the line of wagons, made it easier to breathe. It also afforded them a chance to pick up fuel.

The Harkness family carried a small barrow in one of their wagons. It was up to Lavinia and her younger siblings to fill the barrow twice a day and stow the dried buffalo chips they collected in the family's third wagon—the one that carried tools and animal feed. Once the two wheelbarrows full were stashed, the children could explore and play, so long as they stayed within calling distance of the wagons.

This afternoon, Anne was having a driving lesson from Thomas, and therefore had the luxury of riding on the wagon seat. Elise and Anne had taken turns over the last few weeks, and both were becoming fair drivers. Elise could now harness a mule in less than five minutes, and she was perhaps inordinately proud of that accomplishment.

"I can't wait to see what you and Miss Anne wear to the dance." Lavinia smiled as she trudged along.

"What will *you* wear?" Elise asked.

Lavinia laughed. "I've only this or my brown dress."

Elise found that tragic—that a girl of seventeen should have such a limited wardrobe. Even though she and Anne had eliminated one trunk back in Independence, they still had an extensive wardrobe stowed in their wagon. She almost opened her mouth to offer Lavinia the use of one of their gowns but stopped. Rebecca might not approve. And would such an act cause problems among the other women of the wagon train? She didn't want to prompt any

jealousies. She and Anne were snubbed already, apparently because their clothes were finer than the others' and because they had more of them. Even Rebecca, who had befriended them from the beginning, laughed at their continued use of parasols and gloves.

"A woman expects her face and hands to be tanned when she crosses the plains," Rebecca had said, "and carrying a parasol—well, that just means you're using your hands to carry something frivolous, instead of to work."

Elise didn't see it that way. Safeguarding her mistress's complexion—and her own of course—was an important part of a lady's maid's duties. In England they'd haunted London's exclusive shops for Lady Anne's cosmetics, and Elise had prepared lotions and emollients from recipes guarded closely among personal servants.

Out here there was nothing to work with, and she could only hope the cosmetics they'd brought with them would last throughout the journey. As a precaution, she'd picked up a few extra items before they left St. Louis, but she hadn't been able to obtain the high quality products available in London. If only she'd realized in New York how long their journey would last and that it would take them into the wilderness.

She sighed heavily. No use regretting such things at this point. Instead she would have to make the supplies they had last and find substitutes for those that gave out. Lavinia used lard to keep her lips from cracking. The idea of Lady Anne smearing lard on her lips repelled Elise. She was grateful that she had a good supply of the beeswax and rosewater concoction she and Anne preferred.

"Will you wear one of your Paris gowns?" Lavinia asked. "Miss Anne told me some of her dresses were made there."

"I expect that would make us complete outcasts," Elise said.

"Oh no, why should it? We'd all love to see them. I heard you have three trunks bursting with gowns."

"Mr. Bentley was probably right to advise us to get rid of most of it."

"As you've told me more than once, there's no telling whom

one will meet in Oregon City. Why, even at Fort Kearny there'll be army officers and their wives, and other folks who are traveling." Lavinia glanced at Elise's dress. "Even your calicos that you and Miss Anne bought in Independence are much prettier than what Ma and I have."

Elise put a hand up to the ribbon at the neckline of her bodice. After hard use on the trail, the dress was showing wear, but she knew Lavinia was right. She and Anne had bought the best quality they could find in Independence—sturdy fabrics with tight stitching, and in cheerful colors. By comparison, some of the emigrant women wore drab, shapeless garments that were heavily mended and wearing thin.

"Here comes Mr. Bentley," Lavinia said.

Elise kept her head down and refused to follow the natural inclination to look. Eb Bentley had become the bane of her life, second only to Thomas Costigan. Thomas was lazy, she'd concluded weeks ago. He refused to gather chips once they were beyond accessible wood, and he hauled water only if she bullied him mercilessly. That was too tiring. Her attempts at bribing him produced limited results. He still went off with the other single men whenever he got a chance and left the women to their own devices. Usually he showed up for meals, but sometimes he didn't. Elise concluded that he found sustenance at other campfires on those occasions, though once or twice she was certain their cache of leftovers had been plundered during the confusion of the early morning time when the team was hitched.

Elise had discussed the situation with Anne, but so far they'd kept their suspicions and their difficulties in dealing with Thomas to themselves.

Eb Bentley was another case entirely. He seemed to know everything about traveling overland in the American West, and his very omniscience on the topic annoyed her. Even worse, he seemed to show up just at the moment she exhibited her own ignorance. He'd ridden by on that oddly colored horse yesterday morning as Elise was scraping out yet another burned meal—her attempt at

flapjacks for breakfast. He'd shaken his head sadly and moved on without comment, but the incident had blackened Elise's day.

Now he rode along on his horse—white with large, reddish-brown spots—inspecting each wagon as he passed. Eb Bentley's eyes saw everything. If an ox limped even slightly, Eb spoke to the driver. If a strap hung loose on a mule's harness, he let the owner know. If a wheel squeaked too loudly or a bundle hung precariously on the side of a wagon, Eb brought it to the guilty party's attention.

Elise supposed that was his duty, and he was good at it. But she always felt like a naughty schoolchild when he came around, because she was sure he'd find several things amiss with the wagon she and Anne owned.

To her horror, he turned aside from the line of wagons and headed toward her and Lavinia.

"Afternoon, ladies." He tugged at his hat brim.

"Hello, Mr. Bentley," Lavinia called gaily.

"Good afternoon, sir." Elise wanted to admire the rugged figure he cut on horseback. His worn clothing—dark trousers and a blue shirt, with a soft leather vest over it, and that droopy, grayish hat he always wore low over his brow—enhanced that image. But she wouldn't allow herself to admire such a man. It was unthinkable. His long legs hung comfortably against the horse's sides, ending in well-worn leather boots coated with trail dust.

"You ladies doing all right?"

"Quite well, thank you," Elise said.

"Don't forget to drink something every now and again."

He smiled down at her and Lavinia, and Elise almost gave in. It was hard not to admire a man who stopped to see if you were comfortable, especially one with a smile like that. Eb's smile rarely saw daylight, but when it did, he very nearly inspired confidence in her. Was that admiration? He was a good man, and he only wanted the best for the people on the wagon train. Of that she was sure. So why did she dislike him?

Was it because he made her feel incompetent? Because she still felt he barely tolerated her presence and Anne's and was certain they'd fall by the wayside before they crossed the mountains ahead? Or was it because he was so different from David Stone?

That thought alarmed her, and she quickly shoved it down and smothered it. She'd tried not to dwell on thoughts of David these past few weeks. Besides, her reaction to Eb Bentley had nothing to do with her esteem for David Stone.

"We will," Lavinia said. "Thank you, Mr. Bentley."

He touched his hat brim again, his gaze lingering on Elise for a moment. She peered up at him from beneath the edge of her silk parasol.

"I'm surprised the wind hasn't grabbed that little thing away from you."

It took Elise a moment to realize he was teasing. Was this the frontier version of flirtation?

"I have a death grip on the handle," she said.

Eb laughed. "Well, if the wind gets to be too much, you might have to start wearing a poke bonnet like Miss Lavinia here."

Elise raised her chin. The limp, wide-brimmed bonnets the emigrant women had adopted were, in her opinion, the most unbecoming headgear she'd ever seen. Her London-bought chapeaus might be out of place on the plains, but she would never submit to a fashion as ugly as the poke bonnet.

Eb nodded, rather grimly this time. "I suspect you've got a death grip on your dignity, too, ma'am."

He rode off before Elise could think of a suitable retort.

"Of all the nerve," she said.

Lavinia giggled. "I think Mr. Bentley's funny. He doesn't usually say much, but when he does, it's anything but usual."

Elise cocked her head to one side and surveyed her young friend. "Lavinia, I expect you'd cause a sensation if you attended an assembly in London."

"What's that?"

"It's a social gathering."

"Hmm." Lavinia shrugged. "The most social gatherings I'll ever see will probably be at the forts or the dancing we have when we get

to Independence Rock. You and Miss Anne will dance, won't you?"

"I haven't given it much thought."

"If you do, I'll bet Mr. Bentley will ask you to dance with him."

Elise stared at her for a moment then turned and looked down the line of wagons again. Eb's spotted horse was clearly visible—the patches on its rump made it stand out even at a distance. She had danced with gentlemen—even an earl once—at Almack's Assembly Rooms when she'd accompanied Lady Elizabeth Stone. What would it be like to dance with a man who worked for a living? A wild, western scout like Eb Bentley?

She realized Lavinia was waiting for a response.

"Indeed. We'll see about that."

"Yes," said Lavinia. "I expect we will."

CHAPTER 15

When the wagons formed their circle that night, the livestock was again turned loose inside. The women would do their cooking and set up their tent just outside the circle. Elise never felt truly secure out there, especially as they were now within Indian Territory, though she'd only seen a few of the native people in the distance. Guards patrolled the camp all night, but even so, she longed for the day they'd used enough mule feed and cornmeal to make space for sleeping in the wagon.

"I'll be glad when we get to the fort," Anne said as they got out their dishes and foodstuffs for supper.

"Yes. I'm told they have good grazing there, and the herdsmen can keep the animals away from the wagons."

"That will be wonderful," Anne said. "The lowing and snorting keep me awake at night." She took the pottery bowl from the dish crate. "So. . .biscuits tonight?"

"I suppose so, and let's use a can of peaches." Elise took the tinderbox to the spot they'd decided to have their fire. For once, Thomas had arranged a fire pit without being told. Rocks were scarce on the grassy prairie, so he used the shovel to dig away the grass in a small area. His ministrations didn't extend to making the fire, so Elise prepared to do that. She headed back to the wagon for some tinder and the sack of buffalo chips she'd gathered earlier.

A sharp scream from Anne made her heart pound.

"What is it?" Elise dashed to the tailboard. "Anne? What happened?"

Anne appeared, white faced, at the canvas flap. "Bugs. Worms."

"Where?"

"In the flour."

"Oh." Elise had hoped they'd avoided that complication by

storing their food in tin boxes and small kegs, but apparently not. "Why don't you make the fire, and I'll sift them out?"

Anne climbed down shakily, and Elise took over the unpleasant task. The flour keg seemed to be thoroughly infested. Her inclination was to throw out the flour, but in the last month, she'd learned better.

"That's what we have sifters for," Rebecca had told her with a shrug. "You can't keep them out, try as you might, so you sift before you bake."

So far, Elise's vigilance had seemed to be working, but that was past. She steeled herself for the chore. If she could only see it as one more task, and not as the removal of vermin from the food she would eat an hour hence, it would help. Even so, her stomach roiled as she peered into the flour keg.

She scooped the bowl half-full of wriggling flour and backed out of the wagon.

"Where's our sifter?" she called to Anne, who was struggling with the tinderbox.

"I'm not sure we have one."

"What? Wasn't it on the list?"

"I looked for one when we first started making biscuits, but I didn't see one. The flour seemed to work without being sifted, so I didn't worry about it."

Elise sighed. "Perhaps I can borrow Rebecca's."

"Must we?" Anne asked. "After an entire month on the road, I hate appearing ignorant."

Elise knew that exact feeling. "Well. . .do we have something else we could use? Some sort of screen or. . ."

"Or netting?" Anne asked.

"Yes, that might do, if we stretched it over a bowl. Have we any in the sewing basket?"

"I don't know." Anne started to rise.

"No, keep on with the fire. We need that. I'll go and look for something."

Eb made his rounds at a leisurely pace. Rob had started in the opposite direction. They would visit each wagon with instructions on getting the water each family needed for the night, and they'd meet halfway around the circle and go back to their campfire spot for supper.

As he approached the Englishwomen's wagon, he paused for a moment and admired the view. Miss Stone, in her red calico dress, knelt on the turf and was industriously trying to build a campfire. As he watched, she succeeded in getting sparks from the flint and steel she held and blew them gently into a small blaze. These ladies had come a long way since Independence, and he didn't mean in miles.

Miss Finster, wearing an eye-pleasing plaid dress, sat on a box sifting flour. As Eb watched, he noticed the rather curious apparatus she used and stepped closer so he could see it better.

Miss Finster glanced up as his shadow fell across her work and flinched.

"Mr. Bentley."

"Good evening, ma'am. That's quite a fancy sifter you have there."

She glanced down at the black netting edged with jet beads. It was stretched over the lip of a large bowl, held in place with clothespins.

"Well, yes, we've had to improvise."

"May I ask. . . ?"

She sighed and let her shoulders slump. "It's the veil off Miss Stone's mourning hat."

"Mourning?"

Miss Finster shot a quick glance toward her friend, but Miss Stone was absorbed in building the fire bigger. "Her father died last fall. She put aside her mourning attire when we left England."

Eb gazed at the dark-haired young woman. "I'm sorry. I didn't know."

"She didn't want people to know. But she brought a complete outfit along, in case. . .well, her uncle. . ."

Eb nodded. "She's got spunk."

"Yes. I'm glad you realize that." Miss Finster looked up into his

eyes, and Eb's stomach did a somersault.

"You've both done well on this undertaking."

She smiled faintly. "Better than you expected?"

"Yes, I'll admit it."

She picked up the bowl, tipped it, and brushed a few worms off the net onto the ground. "I believe it's done us both good."

"I expect you're right." Eb cleared his throat. "We've sent four men with a wagon to haul some water tonight. They'll bring it in barrels, and everyone can go and get a bucketful."

"What about the livestock?"

"The drovers took them to a spot on the river about half a mile from here. But the water's pretty muddy, and Rob and I thought it would be better to bring some from a creek a couple of miles away for drinking."

"That's very kind of you gentlemen," Miss Finster said.

"Just trying to keep everyone healthy."

Eb touched his hat brim and turned away. Miss Stone was now putting a large, flaky buffalo chip on her fire. She stepped back and wiped her hands on her apron.

"Evening, Mr. Bentley."

"Miss Stone."

He nodded and walked on. Yes, they'd come a long way.

Outside Fort Kearny, the wagon train formed a wider circle than nights on the trail. The drovers moved the herd of livestock a distance away, where new grass was available. Since Whistler's train was one of the first to go through that spring, the emigrants were able to graze their animals within a mile of the fort without having to fight for the right to forage. They'd stay two days to bake, wash, and visit the fort. For the men, it would be a reprieve. For the women, it meant more work than usual, but they didn't mind. They'd anticipated this stop for weeks.

Wood was at a premium, as the fort's detachment and settlers and Indians in the vicinity had long since stripped the area of easily available fuel. On the morning after their arrival, Rob and Eb consulted with the men heading each family, reporting to them the advice of the fort's commanding officer. They drew lots for a detail of six men to cut wood in the hills a few miles away, and Rob sent them off with an empty wagon. Clean water was available from the well at the fort.

The women soon put their camps to rights and prepared to descend on the trading post. Eb and two of the Harkness boys were assigned to patrol the camp while the others were gone, so that nothing would be pilfered by the Indians that congregated to stare at the newcomers.

Elise and Anne were as eager to visit the post as the other women.

"I hope we can learn something about Uncle David here," Anne said as they dressed their hair in the tent, out of view of the curious.

"I hope so, too, but we have to keep in mind that this fort was built since your Uncle David came this way. Still, there's a chance one of the officers posted here met him in his travels." Elise coiled Anne's dark hair and pinned it firmly at the back of her head.

"What shall we wear?" Anne asked. "Should we get out better dresses than we've been wearing every day?"

"That would make us stand out. Do we want that?"

"Hmm. Perhaps not. The Indians are already quite bold. Rebecca said they wanted to touch her little Dorothy's hair." Anne shivered. "I hoped to shop for a new hat, but Mr. Whistler says the trader won't likely have anything like that. Staples and goods to trade to the Indians, that's what he said to expect."

"My dear, why do you need a new hat?" Surely Anne didn't want to replace the mourning bonnet she'd dismantled for the netting.

"The other women seem to take offense at our hats from the Bond Street milliner. Perhaps a straw hat or a poke bonnet would make them more accepting of us."

"Not a poke bonnet!" Elise moved around to where she could see Anne's face. "You wouldn't, my lady!"

"Hush, now," Anne whispered. "These tent walls are thin."

Elise nodded, ashamed of her lapse. Weeks had passed since she'd addressed Anne as her mistress.

"Pardon me. But really—one of those awful bonnets that hide the face?"

"But that's the idea—to hide it from the sun and this ceaseless wind. I fear my cheeks are chapping, despite my parasol and the lotion we brought, and my lips peel even if I use the emollient salve twenty times a day."

"I know," Elise said. "It's distressing, but I believe our remedies are better than what anyone else we're traveling with can offer."

"Perhaps the trader has something."

Thomas crouched behind the wagon wheel, listening. He could hear the women's conversation plainly. "My lady," indeed. He wasn't sure what to make of that exchange. Was the girl, Anne, some sort of upper crust? Both the women were high class, but now that he thought of it, Miss Finster seemed always to defer to Miss Stone. He'd thought it was because Miss Stone wasn't as strong as the older woman. But she was stouter now than when they'd left Independence. Walking all day beside the wagon train for more than a month had forced her to find a little stamina.

Once the ladies headed out for the fort, they'd be gone for hours. That was what he'd been waiting for—the time Peterson had told him to watch for. He'd been patient. With any luck, he'd have something to put in the report he'd send back East from the fort tomorrow. Troopers would take the mail out. Couldn't ask for better delivery service than that.

"Do you want your gray shawl?" Miss Finster said. "I'll fetch it for you when I get my reticule from the wagon."

Thomas dodged back and stood. Time to make himself scarce. If Miss Finster saw him, she'd order him to do some chores while they were gone. When he was sure they'd left, he'd come back. At least he hadn't been picked for the firewood detail. He'd have to watch out for Bentley and the Harkness boys, though. They'd be on guard. That was well and good—you needed a guard around Fort Kearny, especially since the Indian village seemed extra large this spring. Some of those braves had no conscience when it came to other folks' belongings.

He ambled off toward the barracks. The fort had a small garrison, but there was bound to be a card game later. He could line up some amusement for tonight and then come back to carry out his plan.

Elise hurried back to the encampment. She'd left Anne at the trading post with Rebecca Harkness, Lavinia, and Abby. Elise was determined to get some laundry done today, and Anne would be in good hands. The trader's prices had shocked her so much that Elise doubted she'd buy anything.

In an empty sugar sack, she carried her prize—two cans of beef stew. Anne didn't know of her purchase—she'd save it until they'd been out on the trail again for several days. When they were tired to death of bacon and the oysters were nearly gone, then she would open the first can of stew.

Now—where was Thomas? He'd disappeared this morning before she could ask him to fetch enough water to fill her big kettle and the washtub. She was determined to get this washing done, even if she had to haul the water herself—but that would be her last resort. Perhaps the promise of clean clothing for himself would be enough to motivate Thomas to haul the water.

As she came around Mr. Leonard's wagon and faced the small tent, she stopped short. The tent flap was loose. She and Anne had fastened it securely when they'd left camp an hour ago. She tiptoed forward and lifted the edge of the flap. Peering into the dim corners, she tried to determine if anything was missing or out of place. Their bedrolls and baggage inside looked undisturbed.

A rustling sound came from behind her. She turned toward the wagon. Had one of the Indians sneaked inside? Eb and Rob had warned all the travelers about the Indians—thieving savages, according to Thomas. The wagon master had set a guard. Still, with

fifty wagons to watch, those men couldn't see everything at once.

The rustle came again, followed by a muffled thump. Elise shivered. Should she go for one of the guards or investigate herself? If she went for help, the thief might escape with his plunder. She looked around and saw Eb strolling just inside the perimeter of the loose wagon circle a hundred yards away. If she screamed, he would hear her. She decided to confront the intruder herself and get a good look at him.

She walked stealthily to the back of the wagon. The canvas flap was down, but it hung loose at one edge. Her hand trembled as she reached for it. Was she insane to do this? Whoever was in there might be armed.

She looked about for anything with which she could defend herself. The wooden paddle with which she stirred laundry leaned against the side of the wagon. She hefted it and rested it on one shoulder. Now, if she could just fling the canvas back and grip the paddle before the thief leaped on her.

The flap drew aside before she could touch it, and she found herself face-to-face with Thomas. He was stooped over, his head only inches above hers. He stared into her eyes for a moment. She wondered if he would simply let the curtain fall and hope she would go away.

Elise choked back the laughter that threatened. This situation was not amusing.

"Thomas."

"Miss Finster."

"You frightened me."

"Oh? I'm sorry."

"I thought an Indian was rifling our supplies."

He smiled and straightened a little. "Not at all, ma'am."

They stood gazing at each other for a long moment. Thomas's smile gradually faded and became more of an appraisal.

"What are you doing?" she asked at last.

"Well, I thought you'd want to do some wash today, ma'am. I was going to get things ready for you."

"The washtub is already out."

"Oh. Is it?"

"It is. There's nothing else in the wagon for you to get."

His eyes narrowed to slits. "My stuff is in here. Surely I have a right to get something out of my own pack."

"That's not what you said you were doing."

Thomas raised his chin. Footsteps claimed Elise's attention. Eb Bentley was nearly to their wagon. Should she tell him about the incident? Better to consult Anne first.

"I shall require a great deal of water for my washing."

"Oh yes, ma'am." Thomas climbed down from the wagon.

"Good morning, Miss Finster."

Elise managed a smile for Eb. "Mr. Bentley."

"Been to the fort?" he asked.

"Yes, but I'm about to begin my wash day."

"Very industrious of you." He eyed Thomas. "Costigan."

Thomas nodded to him and went to the side of the wagon where their buckets hung. "I'll bring all the water you need, Miss Finster." He walked off toward the well.

"Everything all right?" Eb asked quietly, after Thomas was out of earshot.

"I'm not certain. He gives me pause."

"Aha." Eb pressed his lips together and watched Thomas's retreating figure. "Don't hesitate to tell me or Rob if there's a problem."

"Thank you. He was rummaging about in the wagon, and I surprised him. It could be nothing, but I'll speak to Anne later. If she feels unsafe, we'll come to you."

"Do that."

Eb shouldered his rifle and strolled toward the next wagon.

CHAPTER 16

W e certainly can't trust him," Anne said as they gathered in the last of the clean clothes that evening. "I can't see that anything is missing from the baggage though."

"Nor I." Elise quickened her steps as an Indian woman moved stealthily toward the farthest of their clothing. "Here! Leave that alone, you!" She ran and snatched the linen towel from the grass and walked back toward Anne, picking up Thomas's spare shirt and one of Anne's woolen petticoats as she went.

"Is that all of it?" Anne asked.

"I think so. Some of the woolens are still damp, but we'll lose them if we don't take them in now." Elise had stood guard over the laundry most of the afternoon. With only a short clothesline rigged between their wagon and Mr. Leonard's, she'd had to resort to laying out the rest of the items on the grass to dry. Within an hour, Indian women and children were hedging about the camp. A squeal from Lavinia had alerted the rest to beware of pilfering. Eb and several other men made continuous rounds, but they couldn't cover the whole perimeter of the camp at once.

"You look exhausted," Anne said, "and Mr. Whistler wants to move on tomorrow."

"I thought we were taking another day to rest."

"Apparently not. He says we should take advantage of the fine weather."

Elise let out a deep sigh.

"There'll be dancing tonight in the fort," Anne said.

"I'm too tired to dance."

"So am I."

"Wilbur Harkness will be disappointed, not to mention every other single man in our company and a fort full of soldiers."

Anne smiled. "They'll survive. But what shall we do about Thomas?"

"I'm certain he went through our bags."

"So am I."

"Let me think about it," Elise said. "He behaved very well for the rest of the day and hauled plenty of water. I even gave a bucket to Mrs. Libby."

They stopped beside their wagon, where they used the tailboard and an upended crate as work surfaces. "Let's fold these clothes and get supper started. I've had a pot of dry beans simmering all day." On most days they didn't keep a fire going long enough to cook beans, so this would be a change of diet.

"Here comes Mr. Bentley," Anne said.

The paint horse cantered toward them. Elise no longer felt apprehensive or annoyed at the sight of Eb Bentley. When had that happened?

He pulled up next to them in a small puff of dust and tugged at his hat brim. "Ladies."

"Oh," Anne gasped. "What is that?"

Elise noticed then that Eb had an animal carcass slung behind his saddle.

"I shot a pronghorn while I was scouting the back trail to see how far behind us the next train is. Would you ladies like a piece of venison after I butcher it?"

"That would be very nice," Elise said. Anne was still eyeing the dead animal with distaste. She would change her mind when she took her first bite, Elise was sure.

"I'll bring it by a little later."

"Thank you. And how far back *is* the next caravan?" Elise asked.

"If they push hard, they'll be here tomorrow night—they're camping where we were two nights ago." Eb touched his hat brim and trotted off.

"So that's why Mr. Whistler wants to pull out in the morning," Elise said. "He suspected another train was close behind us."

"Oh well. I suppose we're better off to stay ahead. The fresh

meat will be a nice change," Anne said doubtfully. "As grateful as I am for the canned oysters, I admit I'm a bit tired of them."

Elise smiled, imagining how happy Anne would be next week when she produced her tinned stew. The oysters and bacon, along with cornbread and biscuits, had been their staple foods for more than a month. They'd rationed out the dried fruit and rice, but their few root vegetables, eggs, and canned soups were now gone.

"I was able to get two tins of peaches at the fort," Anne said, her head tilted down.

Elise arched her eyebrows. "I thought we agreed that prices were too high."

"I know, but when I heard the word *peaches*, I was suddenly ravenous. If I'd known Mr. Bentley would give us some of his game, I'd have held back."

"Why don't we save the peaches for when you get that feeling again and just enjoy the venison tonight?"

"That's reasonable. Spread out our treats." Anne chuckled. "Odd, isn't it? Three months ago we'd hardly consider tinned peaches a delicacy."

"It was very nice of Mr. Bentley to offer us part of his meat," Elise said. "It looked to be quite a small animal. There wouldn't be enough for everyone."

"He's sweet on you," Anne said. "One of many heartsick men on this wagon train."

"Oh stop."

While Anne put away their clean clothes, Elise set about preparing a double batch of biscuits so they'd have plenty for the next day. She'd just put the lid on the dutch oven when Eb returned with a sizable chunk of meat in a sack.

"I reckon you can roast it or stew it, whichever you please," he said.

"Thank you very much, Mr. Bentley." Anne expressed her gratitude but stood back and let Elise accept the gift.

"Oh, and I . . ." Eb shifted on his feet and scrunched up his face for a moment. "I saw this at the trading post and thought you might be able to use it."

From the crook of his arm he produced a flour sifter and held it out to Elise.

"Oh! How wonderful!" She laughed aloud and reached for it. Her gaze met Eb's, and suddenly she felt self-conscious. "I'm sure that trader charged you a pretty penny. Let me—"

"It's a gift," he said quickly.

Elise hesitated, uncertain what the social standard was for presents from frontier scouts. The venison she had no problem with—many of the wagon train families shared small portions of supplies with each other. But the sifter fell into a different category—Eb had spent money for it.

"Thank you," she said softly. "Perhaps I can salvage Miss Stone's veil." She glanced about, but Anne had disappeared.

"Would you ladies be going to the dancing tonight?" Eb asked.

"Oh, well. . .we thought not, since we're rolling out at dawn."

He nodded. "I'm not much of a dancer myself."

"Mr. Bentley. . ."

"Yes'm?"

It was on the tip of her tongue to invite Eb to eat supper with them, but what was she thinking? She'd never in her life been that bold with a man. Now, if David Stone stood before her, it might be different.

And how would Eb take it if she invited him? And what would their neighbors in the other forty-nine wagons think? They had at least four months of trail before them. She'd hate for Eb to think she liked him in *that* way and have to spend the entire summer correcting the notion.

"I wondered if you and Mr. Whistler could use a dozen biscuits. Thomas finds them quite palatable now."

"That'd be fine, ma'am. Thank you."

"Independence Rock." Anne picked up her pace as they walked between the wagons and the low, muddy river.

"Yes, we're halfway now." Elise smiled. Both she and Anne could be proud of this accomplishment, and what tales they would have to tell when they returned to England.

Lavinia, Rebecca, and Abby walked with them today.

"We'll dance again tonight," Lavinia said eagerly. Her parents had allowed her to attend the revels at Fort Laramie, the second fort on the trail. Rebecca wouldn't permit her daughter to try on Anne's gowns, but she'd allowed the loan of a gauzy shawl from India, and Lavinia had gone to the dance walking as tall as a princess. Anne had worn a dress that wasn't a ball gown at all, but one she might wear to a country house dinner party. Even in that, a modest gray skirt and bodice, she'd caused a sensation at the fort.

Their friends in England would swoon from shock if they saw her now. Both Anne and Elise had lost weight, but they'd gained muscle and stamina. Despite their precautions, their faces had tanned. Their lips were chapped by the constant wind, and their hands had grown rough from hard labor. Even so, when Elise looked at Anne objectively, she thought her mistress was more beautiful than ever.

So, apparently, had the soldiers at Fort Laramie. Lavinia had coaxed the ladies into attending the dance. It was the first time Elise had danced in nearly a year, though Lady Anne had attended many parties and balls in last year's season. Elise accompanied her to most of them but did not always join in the dancing. Neither woman had found herself without partners all evening at Fort Laramie, however. Elise would recall the commanding officer's charming words to her for many a year.

"We get a lot of women traveling along the trail," he'd said as they waltzed about the parade ground in the moonlight and the regimental band played. "But we seldom see such beauties as we have here tonight." He'd gazed directly into her eyes as he spoke, and Elise had found herself blushing. Surely that statement was a bit bold for a man who had a wife present. But the commander's lady was off dancing with Rob Whistler and some of the higher-ranking officers. Elise decided to take it impersonally. "Yes, we've some lovely young ladies in the wagon train," she said.

Anne had been the center of a flock of officers and pioneer men. They cut in on each other furiously, and the poor girl had probably danced with more than fifty men. She returned to the camp exhausted but pleased that she had brought a bit of color into their lives. The only thing that could have made the evening better, Elise reflected, was if Thomas had stayed sober. He'd come and claimed her hand near midnight, and the whiskey on his breath was overpowering.

Eb Bentley hadn't danced, but he'd warned her that he didn't dance much. He was off guarding the wagons and livestock, a necessary precaution in view of the sizable Indian camp just outside the fort grounds. Eb always seemed to have guard duty when the musicians tuned up. Elise began to think it was his design. But what did it matter? He was only the scout, and his absence didn't disappoint her in the least.

They camped beneath the mammoth rock on the plains the last afternoon of June. Elise and Anne quickly raised their tent while Thomas unhitched the mules. They no longer expected him to put it up for them. What had once been a complicated and frustrating task was now another ten-minute chore.

Since they'd formed the wagon circle early, they had time to bake. Several of the men had gone hunting, and they rode into camp bringing quarters of buffalo and tales of the hunt. By the time Elise had built a fire, they were parting out chunks of meat to each family.

"What are you wearing tonight?" Anne asked as she filled the coffeepot.

Elise shrugged. "This dress. I promised Lavinia I'd fix her hair. By the time we're done with supper and cleaning up, I won't have time to change my clothes. But I'll help you dress if you wish to wear a gown."

"I thought perhaps my green promenade dress," Anne said, "but the evenings have been so warm of late that perhaps I'll wear the one I wore at Fort Laramie."

"It made a sensation with the soldiers," Elise said. "I'm sure

everyone here would love to see it again—it's a beautiful dress."

"Funny how we're keeping our fanciest gowns in reserve," Anne noted.

Elise smiled. "I fear we'd be snubbed again if they saw you in your full finery, my dear. They'd all think we imagined ourselves above them."

"They already think that."

"Several of the ladies act friendly to us now." Elise didn't add that nearly all the gentlemen seemed to find excuses to help them out. When Thomas wasn't about, it didn't seem to matter anymore. Bachelors like the Adams brothers and Wilbur Harkness happened by their campfire morning and evening to ask whether the ladies had plenty of water and fuel. Most of them lingered to gaze at Anne as long as they could get away with it.

"Mr. Whistler promised us two days of rest," Anne said, "though I wouldn't exactly call laundry and baking rest."

Elise smiled at her. "I suspect he was referring to the livestock getting the rest. We'll work all day, for certain."

"At least we're capable of putting in two days of demanding labor now. I'd never have imagined it." Anne clamped the top on the coffeepot and brought it to the fire pit. "Shall I put the grate on now?"

"Yes, and I'll set the stew on that. Too bad we've no potatoes."

"No, but the dumplings Rebecca taught you to make are almost as good."

Elise heard a distant shout. She shielded her eyes and looked upward. "The boys are climbing the rock."

Anne stood beside her. "Do you want to go up?"

"I think not. I'll save my strength for this evening."

That night's gathering was held outside the wagon corral. The leaders felt there was little danger, but nevertheless three men were detailed to guard the encampment and make sure the livestock remained calm.

Elise and Anne walked to the bonfire with the Harkness family. The Adams brothers joined them, and Elise took note that Anne crossed the distance with Wilbur on her right and quiet Daniel Adams on her left. Lavinia had her own followers. Several of the young men watched her as the group neared the grassy expanse near the bonfire. As soon as the fiddler and the accordionist began to play, a fellow of about eighteen came to claim Lavinia. Wilbur took Anne's hand and swept her away, much to Daniel's chagrin. He wandered off toward a cluster of other single men. Mrs. Legity and Mrs. Libby came over to stand with Rebecca and Elise.

"That's Johnny Klein with Lavinia," Rebecca said. "He spends most days back with the herd, but he manages to see my Lavinia at least once a day. Wouldn't surprise me if she heard a proposal before this journey's over."

Mrs. Legity's lip curled. "So long as it's not that Daniel Adams. He's twice her age."

"I doubt he's much over thirty," Rebecca said placidly. "Besides, he'd probably be in a better position to take care of her than one of these young pups would. He seems like a steady man, and he and his brother have the wherewithal to set up a prosperous farm."

Rob Whistler, wearing a pale shirt that looked clean in the moonlight, strolled over to them. "Mrs. Legity, would you care to dance?"

The widow shed her arrogance and held out her hand. "Why, Mr. Whistler, it would be my pleasure."

"Rob's a good man," Rebecca said. "Always dances with the widows first."

Elise hadn't thought about it, but she saw that Rebecca was right.

"Agnes Legity was in a snit earlier, going on about how Rob shouldn't dance, since his wife isn't here." Rebecca smiled and shook her head. "She doesn't seem to think that matters now."

"Mr. Whistler is a man who can be trusted, I'm sure," Elise said.

"Yes, I'd say so. Now Eb, he's a different sort."

"What do you mean?" Elise wasn't sure whether to be shocked or not.

"Oh, not that he can't be trusted. He can. You won't likely see

him out to dance though. That's all I meant. But he'll be right there in the morning, making sure everyone's got what they need. And while we mend our wagons and do our washing, he'll scout ahead for the next campsite and make sure the trail's safe for us."

"Well, Mrs. Harkness!"

Elise and Rebecca turned at the cheerful voice. Rebecca's husband, Orrin, had come up behind them.

"Be you looking for a dance partner?" he asked.

"Don't mind if I do since there aren't any army officers about to dance with."

Rebecca smiled at Elise and took Orrin's hand. Elise stood alone for only a moment before Hector Adams approached her with a shy smile.

"Miss Finster?"

"Yes, sir?"

"May I?"

"Delighted." She took his hand and stepped out with him in time to the music.

Eb walked slowly about the encampment, just within the circle of wagons. The oxen and mules were quiet tonight. Maybe the music coming from over near the bonfire soothed them. They'd made a big corral this time, with ropes tied between the wagons and boxes and gear piled up to discourage the animals from trying to get out.

Very few folks had stayed in camp. Even the young children were allowed to go over to watch the dancing for a while. Their parents would carry them back to their tents when they fell asleep.

Eb didn't mind watching the other folks' stuff while they played. He and Rob had a good company this time, and only a few troubles had beset them—small ones at that. A broken wheel, a child who burned his hand, a few cattle that wandered off but were soon recovered. But no one had complained about the rules, and all the heads of household cooperated with taking their turns in the lineup and participating in chores that benefited the entire outfit. He hoped the rest of the trip went as well.

Several times in his rounds, he crossed paths with Abe Leonard and Thomas Costigan, the other two guards. He wasn't sure Thomas was the best pick for the job, but he seemed alert each time Eb saw him. If he sneaked off and shirked his duty, Eb would make a note of it.

Two hours had passed when Rob entered the circle between two wagons and strolled toward Eb.

"They're winding down the party. You want to go have a dance or two?"

"Nah," Eb said.

"Aw, why not? I'll bet the ladies are disappointed." Rob laughed. "I had a turn earlier with Miss Finster, but I couldn't get near Miss Stone. The boys are lined up six deep every time the music changes."

"That right?"

"Yes. They all think she's unapproachable by daylight, but the moon and music give them courage."

"Hmm." Eb rested his rifle on his shoulder as Rob fell into pace with him.

"Whyn't you go over for a while?" Rob said.

Eb thought about it as they ambled past four more wagons. The moon was just past full, and it shed plenty of light on the enclosure. A rangy mule stood in their path, cropping what was left of the buffalo grass. Eb slapped it on the rump to make it get out of their way.

"Howdy," Abe called from up ahead.

"All quiet?" Eb asked.

Abe waved in assent. "How's the dancing going?"

"Fine and dandy," Rob said. "You want to go over? I'm trying to convince Eb, but he won't go."

"Oh, you ought to," Abe said. "A young feller like you should be dancing."

Eb laughed. True, Abe was ten years or so older, but Eb didn't consider himself a "young feller."

"Go on," Rob said. "Give me your gun and go kick up your heels."

Reluctantly, Eb surrendered the rifle. There was no reconsidering after that, but he felt exposed.

Rob scowled at him. "Git going!"

Eb slipped under the rope barrier between two wagons. In the dark expanse between the bonfire and the wagons, he walked alone. The warm breeze caressed his face. He'd kept shaving for three solid months on the trail. Didn't know why exactly. Maybe he'd skip it tomorrow. It would save time, and there wasn't any reason to keep on shaving.

The closer he got to the bonfire, the more alien he felt. The fiddle and the accordion blasted out a polka, and he hung back. He certainly wasn't going to make a fool of himself to that music. He stood in the shadows and looked over the twenty couples whirling about in the firelight. Miss Stone was dancing with Will Strother, a lad of about sixteen. They looked as though they were having fun. The Harkness sisters, Lavinia and Abigail, were out there with a couple of the Foster boys.

It took only half a minute to realize the one person he was looking for wasn't dancing. Eb looked about the edges of the circle. There she was, talking to Rebecca Harkness and "Ma" Foster. He edged toward them, staying behind the circle of watchers so he wouldn't catch their attention and have to stop and chat.

The riotous music ended, and the dancers caught their breath and swapped partners for another round. The musicians launched into "Jeanie with the Light Brown Hair," and some of the older men moved into the circle with their wives.

Now or never, Eb thought. His legs felt like sticks of firewood as he propelled himself toward her. Orrin Harkness had claimed his wife's hand, but Mrs. Foster still stood with Miss Finster, and Mrs. Libby had joined them. Eb took another step so that he was beside them and cleared his throat.

All three women looked over at him.

"Evening," Eb said. The music swelled.

"Well, hello, Mr. Bentley." Miss Finster sounded charmed to see him, which made his heart thrum annoyingly fast.

"Howdy, Eb," said Mrs. Foster.

Mrs. Libby just nodded, her eyebrows raised in apparent shock at seeing him.

"I wondered. . .well. . .uh. . .Miss Finster, you know I'm not much of a dancer, but. . .uh. . .well, if you'd care to. . ."

"Why, thank you. I'd be pleased." She put her hand in his.

Eb was surprised to find she wore gloves. Not knitted, keep-me-warm-in-January gloves, but soft, white cotton, I'm-a-lady gloves. He held her hand tenderly and placed his other hand tentatively on her waist. She smiled up at him and laid her left hand on his shoulder. Moonlight softened her features, and he could have believed she was in her twenties at that moment. Why didn't the men swarm her the way they did Miss Stone? They were crazy not to. Eb swallowed hard and made himself step in time to the music.

As they moved away from the older women, he was sure he heard Mrs. Libby say, "Well, did you ever?"

To which Mrs. Foster replied, "No, I never."

Elise knew her face was red, but she hoped no one could see that in the darkness. Of course, that almost-full cheese of a moon didn't aid her cause. It cast shadows almost as sharp as daytime ones.

Since her dance with Eb Bentley turned out to be the last of the evening, he'd been on hand to walk her back to the wagons. On her other side, Anne strolled along with Wilbur Harkness, who had vied with several other young men for the privilege. Anne kept up a bright chatter with Wilbur, which seemed to please him to no end. She described their panic as they tried to harness the mule team their first morning on the trail, making a comical anecdote out of it. Wilbur laughed so hard, Elise knew his heart was long gone.

She looked up at Eb's face. He was watching her, and his lips twitched when their gazes met.

"Nice evening," Eb said.

"Yes, I think everyone enjoyed it immensely."

He nodded slowly.

"You ought to be the hero of that story Anne's telling," Elise said.

"Oh, she just hasn't gotten to that part yet."

Elise smiled. Should she tuck her hand in his elbow? He hadn't offered his arm. She walked beside him, careful not to brush against his sleeve. Perhaps Eb was only seeing her "home" because he perceived it as his duty.

The white mounds of the wagon tops rested like puffs of cotton around the field. The little tent she shared with Anne stood pale against the grass. They'd left a path of about six feet between it and the wagon and built their fire to one side. The two couples stopped in the space between the prairie schooner and the tent, suspended between the bustle of the encampment and the vast quiet of the prairie. Eb seemed to feel it, too. Was he wishing for the ranch he owned? Rob had said this was Eb's last trip east. He wanted to stay on his land and not make another long trek. She could understand that. A cozy home waiting at the end of the trail. If only she and Anne could look forward to that.

"I guess you're glad we're halfway," she said.

Eb nodded. "I am. We've made good time and had few troubles. Though I can picture what you ladies are facing—staying in Oregon a short time and heading on back next spring."

Next spring. Elise hadn't allowed herself to contemplate it, but he was right—they'd have to spend the winter in Oregon. Maybe by spring they'd be ready to explore the option of sailing home. Wasn't a railroad being built across Panama? If they didn't have to sail around Cape Horn, the ocean journey might not be too arduous. She refused to even think about Anne's seasickness.

"Yes," she managed. "As soon as we locate Mr. Stone, I'm sure we'll be ready to turn homeward."

"Unless you fall in love with Oregon."

Her heart thudded. "Is it really as beautiful as they say?"

"You can't imagine, ma'am. You might not think much of it this winter—it rains a lot, at least where my ranch is. But come spring . . .well, it's about the prettiest place you'll ever see. It sets on the river, and there's mountains in the distance. Got some woods on my spread, but mostly it's open, and I'm going to run cattle on it."

"It sounds lovely." In a corner of her mind, she pictured a little cottage in a valley full of flowers—a place she and Anne could stay together comfortably, away from the constraints of England's society. She'd think about that. When they reached Oregon, if Anne seemed taken by the place, perhaps she'd suggest it—though at this point she was sure Anne had no plans beyond finding her uncle and returning with him to England. But if they couldn't find David. . .

A few steps away, Wilbur was saying, "Well, good night, Miss Anne. I sure did have fun."

"So did I, Wilbur. And thank you for walking me home."

Eb smiled at Elise, as though they were indulgent parents to the pair of energetic young people.

"Reckon I'd better go find Rob. Looks like things stayed quiet in camp though."

"Good night, all," Wilbur said. He turned and walked away.

Elise opened her mouth to bid Eb a good evening when a sharp cry came from Anne.

"Elise! Look. Someone's been in our tent."

CHAPTER 17

Eb and Miss Finster hurried over to the tent. Eb eyed the little canvas structure closely. Miss Stone had already untied one side of the front door flap and raised it, but she had no illumination other than the moonlight. It shone bright, more than halfway across the sky in its circuit, but even so, the interior of the tent lay in darkness.

"How can you tell?" he asked.

"There's a clod of dirt on my bed, and the blanket is mussed."

Eb stooped and peered inside, careful not to block the moonlight. The two bedrolls in the tent were smoothed over, except for a couple of depressions on one, as if someone had knelt on the blankets. He could plainly see the clump of dirt she'd mentioned, too, on the foot end of the bedroll, near the opening.

"Anything else out of place?" he asked.

Miss Stone frowned and studied the dim interior. "Not that I can see."

Eb straightened. "Miss Finster, want to take a look?"

Miss Stone stood back and let her friend move closer. Miss Finster went to her knees at the tent door and sat motionless for a long moment. She turned her head and looked up at him.

"Anne's satchel has been moved. I tidied up before we left camp, and I'm sure it wasn't crooked like it is now."

Eb nodded. "Do you want to light a lantern and look through your things tonight?"

Miss Finster looked to Miss Stone for the decision.

"Yes," the young woman said. "This makes me cross. I wouldn't be able to sleep, wondering if anything's been taken."

"We've a small lantern in the tent," Miss Finster said. "There's another in the wagon."

"Let me get the one from the wagon," Eb said. "That way you'll

181

be able to see everything without having to make a disturbance while you get the lantern." As an afterthought, he said, "Perhaps you'd best check the wagon, too, and see if it looks ransacked."

The women walked with him to the back of their wagon. A lantern hung just inside the back bow, and Eb took it out and lit it. He held it up so they could look inside. Miss Stone climbed up and surveyed the contents of the wagon for a minute.

"I think it's all right," she said.

Miss Finster gave her a hand, and she hopped down. Eb carried the lantern back to their tent.

Miss Finster crawled inside then turned and took the lantern from him. After a minute, she came back to the flap.

"I think both our satchels were gone through. I checked mine, and everything seems to be intact. Anne, here's yours."

She passed a large leather carryall through the opening. Eb took it and set it on the ground. He held the lantern while Miss Finster came out of the tent and Miss Stone opened the satchel.

After thoroughly inspecting the contents of the bag, which Eb decided he'd better not observe too closely, she caught her breath.

"The letter."

"Letter?" Eb asked.

"The last letter my uncle David sent from St. Louis. It's missing."

Eb thought about that. "Anything else?"

"No."

"Your marcasite necklace?" Miss Finster whispered.

"It's here."

Miss Finster turned to him. "She left most of her jewelry in a vault in England, but she brought a few less valuable pieces. The garnet necklace she's wearing is one. The marcasite pendant should have been attractive to a thief. I think that tells us something about him."

"What?" Miss Stone asked.

"He's more interested in your uncle than he is in your jewelry," Eb said.

Miss Finster nodded. "Precisely."

So many thoughts pummeled Eb's brain that he wanted to get away, off by himself under the stars, to think. Miss Stone had valuable jewels in England. Miss Finster apparently had none. Somehow that fit with the protective manner he'd observed in the older woman taking care of the younger. But it also reinforced little things he'd observed—Miss Stone held the purse strings on this expedition. Miss Finster might make most of the practical, everyday decisions, but the important questions rested with Miss Stone. And this missing uncle—who was he? Why would anyone outside his family care whether or not the ladies were able to locate him?

It was none of Eb's business of course. But thievery on the wagon train *was* his business—his and Rob's.

"I'd like to fetch Rob Whistler and discuss this with him, if you ladies don't mind."

As he'd half expected, Miss Finster looked to Miss Stone, who pressed her lips together, frowning. After a moment, she nodded.

"That's fine," Miss Finster said. "We'll wait here while you get him."

Eb strode toward his and Rob's campsite. Rob was spreading his bedroll a few feet from the fire ring.

"I need to talk to you," Eb said.

Rob looked up at him. He dropped the edge of the blankets and stood straight. "What is it?"

"Trouble at the English ladies' camp. Someone went in their tent while they were gone and took something."

"What?" Rob asked.

"You know that famous uncle of Miss Stone's that they're looking for?"

"Well, I dunno how famous he is," Rob said with a hint of a smile.

"He's famous enough that someone stole his letter out of Miss Stone's bag."

Rob whistled softly. "They're sure?"

"Yeah. I could see someone had been in there. Those ladies are neater than a pin, and their bedrolls were mussed a little. Miss Finster said her stuff had been looked through, too, but she didn't think anything was missing. I expect they fold every piece of ribbon just so, and they'd know if someone pawed through their baggage."

Rob nodded. "So. . .this letter. Why would someone take it?"

"I don't know, but I'm thinking we should take the ladies off a little ways, where no one else can hear us talking, and get the full story. Because there's more to it than we know."

"All right." Rob looked around. "I reckon we can go over near the bonfire. Most everybody's left there."

Eb could see that the big fire had burned down to embers just about right for roasting a prairie chicken, if anybody had one to roast.

"There's still enough firelight that everyone would see us."

"You think it's that important?"

"I do," Eb said. "We don't want to draw much attention to this."

"All right. I'll go out a hundred yards toward the river from their tent. You get them and meet me out there. Should I put another guard on to watch their camp?"

"Whoever did it got what he wanted."

"Right." Rob settled his hat more firmly and headed out onto the grassy expanse toward the river.

Eb hurried back to the ladies and led them to the meeting place. With the moon still high and bright, Rob's pale shirt made him easily visible if anyone was looking. The ladies' dresses were darker, and Eb had his leather vest over a chambray shirt. He placed himself between Rob and the wagons as a minor precaution.

"Evening, ladies," Rob said softly. "Eb's told me what happened. We thought maybe it's time we knew more about your uncle, Miss Stone, and why this letter would be valuable to someone outside your family."

Miss Stone looked at Miss Finster—an instinctive movement, Eb realized. She looked to her friend for advice, and Miss Finster looked to her for authority.

"First off," Eb said, "I don't mean any offense, but it might help us if we clear one thing up right now. You two aren't just friends, are you?"

After a pause during which those significant looks again cut the air, Miss Finster turned to face him squarely. "That is correct, Mr. Bentley. Miss Stone is my employer."

Eb nodded. He'd guessed it, but how many other people had? Not Rob, that was certain. He stood there staring at Miss Finster like a thunderstruck buffalo calf.

"Your employer?"

"That's right, Mr. Whistler," Miss Finster said. "I've worked for the Stone family for more than twenty years. First I was a housemaid at the earl of Stoneford's home. Then I was elevated to the position of lady's maid for the countess."

"Countess?" Rob's idiot expression grew more pronounced.

Miss Finster nodded toward Miss Stone. "Yes. Lady Anne's mother."

"Lady—" Rob caught a quick breath and whipped around to stare at Eb now. "You knew this?"

"Nope."

Miss Stone smiled and held out her hand in supplication. "Please, gentlemen, don't be concerned about that. This is exactly why we've kept quiet about my. . .connections."

"But why—I mean—they let you just—" Rob broke off and shook his head in bewilderment.

Miss Finster touched his sleeve and said softly, "Lady Anne's father passed away last October, and he had no male offspring to inherit his title. Lady Anne has no brothers, you see. But the earl did."

Miss Stone's sad smile was tragic in the moonlight. "That's correct. My father had two brothers, but one of them predeceased him. That leaves only Uncle David."

"And Uncle David is the new earl," Eb said slowly, thinking it out as he went.

"Yes, if we can find him," Miss Finster said. "He has to return to England to claim his title and Anne's father's estate."

Rob blew out a long breath. "I'm guessing this estate would be worth claiming."

"Oh yes."

The two ladies stood in silence while Eb and Rob absorbed the information.

"Do you have any idea who might have done this?" Rob asked at last.

"I have an idea," Miss Finster said. "I caught our hired man poking about in the wagon another time, and he claimed he was only getting something from his own bundle, but he'd changed his story, and I thought at the time he looked guilty."

"I remember," Eb said. "You've had some trouble with him shirking his chores, too, haven't you?"

"Some."

"What do you think we should do?" Rob asked Eb.

Eb thought for a moment. "Search him." It might cause trouble in the train if nothing turned up, but he didn't like the idea of a ne'er-do-well skulking about the ladies' camp.

"I'll do it," Rob said. "Where does he keep his bedroll?"

"In the back of our wagon," Miss Finster said. "I think he usually sleeps near the men who are tending the livestock."

"You ladies can retire," Eb said. "We'll make sure the guards pay close attention to your camp tonight."

"Thank you," Miss Stone said. "That will be a comfort."

She and Miss Finster headed off across the grass toward the encampment.

"Let me get Costigan," Eb said.

"No." Rob started walking.

It didn't take Eb long to catch up. "Why not?"

"You've got it in for him. If he's not forthcoming, I'll get one of the other men, and we'll search his person, like you said. But check his bedroll first, and any other gear he has. I don't want this to get personal."

"Why would it?" Eb growled.

"You tell me."

Eb grabbed his arm and stopped. "What are you talking about?"

Rob dropped his voice to a whisper. "Come on, Eb, you know

you've got it bad for Miss Finster. I don't want you giving Costigan a reason to hold a grudge. Don't worry—if he's got that letter, we'll get it. But if it's on him, I don't want you to be the one to take it off him."

Eb's jaw worked as he tried to decide whether to laugh or yell at his friend.

Rob laid a hand on his shoulder. "Take it easy. It's all right."

"Take back what you said."

Rob's face puckered in a frown. "What? That you like her? Don't be ridiculous. It's obvious."

"I don't treat her any different than I do the other ladies."

"Oh sure. Back in Independence, you wanted me to refuse to let them join us. You were positive those two would cause trouble. Well, guess what? They're not the ones causing trouble. I can't see that they've held us up any either—except maybe that first morning. But the first day is always chaos. And now, every night when you come in from scouting, you stop by their wagon to see if they're doing all right or if they need something. It's fine, Eb, but you might as well quit denying that you like her."

Eb had no reply. He glowered at Rob for a moment then turned on his heel.

Thomas tossed down his poker hand in disgust. He'd lost almost a dollar, and he'd only been playing for half an hour. This just wasn't his night.

"Costigan."

He glanced up. Rob Whistler was standing just outside their little circle of five. This couldn't be good. Probably he'd get ragged on for gambling with the boys. Some of the parents took exception to their kids playing cards.

"Yeah?" It was hard to stare Whistler down when you were sitting on the ground, so Thomas stood.

"Word with you," Whistler said and walked away.

Thomas sighed. "Deal me out, boys."

He followed the wagon master away from the drovers' camp. Whistler stopped and waited for him.

"What do you want?" Thomas asked.

"When you were on guard duty, did you see anything unusual?"

Thomas squinted at him. "No. Something happen?"

"Miss Stone says someone took something from a bag in her tent."

Not what he'd expected. Those English dames were sharper than he'd thought. He'd figured she might notice it tomorrow or the next day.

"I didn't see anyone nosing around."

Whistler held his gaze for a long moment. "In light of some other things that have happened, we'll need to check through your stuff."

"What things? You got no right."

"Yes, I do, Costigan. We've got no law out here except me. You and all the others agreed before we left Independence that what I say goes. Now, Miss Finster says you were snooping around in their wagon a while back."

"I was looking for her washtub. I didn't know she'd already set it out. Oh, good night!" He turned away.

"If I were you, I wouldn't make this difficult." Whistler's tone was icy. Funny, Thomas had always figured Bentley for the tough guy of the duo. Where was Bentley, anyhow?

"I'm telling you I didn't take anything of theirs."

"Then you don't mind us searching your stuff."

"Yes, I do mind. When those women hired me, I didn't expect to be accused of stealing. Listen, I put up with late meals—and burnt half the time at that—and those two not knowing a linchpin from a rattlesnake. If you think I'm going to stand for this—"

"You will stand for it if you want to stay with us," Whistler said.

"Rob!"

Thomas looked toward the voice. Eb Bentley and Wilbur Harkness were coming toward them from the drovers' campsite. Bentley waved something small and white in the moonlight. Thomas clenched his teeth.

"What have you got?" Whistler asked as they drew nearer.

"It's a letter addressed to Miss Stone's father, in England."

Whistler eyed Thomas narrowly. "Now isn't that a coincidence. That's the exact item Miss Stone told us was taken from her bag."

"You planted that," Thomas said to Bentley. "You haven't liked me since that first day, when I was late. That couldn't be helped, but you've held it against me ever since. You filched that while we were on watch, and now you're using it as an excuse to get me in trouble."

"Oh, be quiet," Bentley said.

Thomas turned to Whistler. "I'll bet those women don't want to pay me, that's it."

Whistler asked Bentley, "You got a witness?"

"Yes. Wilbur went with me to where Costigan's bedroll was stashed. He watched me go through his bundle."

"That's right," Wilbur said. "Eb found the letter rolled up inside a shirt."

"What's your interest in this letter?" Whistler asked Thomas.

"Nothing. I didn't take it."

Whistler shook his head. "You can't bluff your way out of this. I'll advise Miss Finster to pay you off, and you'll be leaving us at the next civilized place we come to. I reckon that'll be Schwartzburg. We'll be there in a few days. It's not much, but you'll be safe there until another train comes along, or you can go back East if you want. Now, I'm not going to do anything to you, so long as you behave yourself. One more stunt like this, and we'll confine you until we get to a place where we can turn you over to the authorities."

Thomas knew he was beat. He'd just have to send word to Peterson that he'd failed. He didn't like that idea. Maybe he could figure out a way around it. No time to think now. Whistler was jawing again.

"On second thought, I'll get your pay from the ladies and bring it to you. You keep clear of them while you're with us, you hear me, Costigan? Them and their belongings and their livestock."

"Oh, I hear you all right." Thomas walked away before he could say more.

CHAPTER 18

The next morning, the ladies dressed in the dark tent and stepped into the cool daybreak in the shadow of the great rock.

"Our laundry is done up," Anne observed. "What have you planned for today?"

Elise walked toward the back of the wagon. "Baking. I want plenty ahead—maybe enough to last us all week. Although we won't need so much, since we're not feeding Thomas anymore."

"Yes. I won't be sorry to see him leave the company." Anne threw her a worried glance. "You don't think he'll bother us again, will he? Out of spite, I mean?"

"I hope not. We shall miss him when it's time to lug water."

"Perhaps someone else will help us."

Elise shrugged and reached into the wagon for her crate of pans and utensils. "We can survive on our own. We've proven that. But I shan't say no if Wilbur or one of the Adams brothers offers to help us."

"I wouldn't look for Daniel to come around," Anne said.

"Oh? Why's that?"

"I turned him down last night."

Elise paused with the crate in her arms. "Do you mean. . .for a dance, or. . ."

"He asked me to marry him."

As the sun sent its first rays over the prairie, the other travelers began to stir. Oxen lowed, and a man called to his son. Elise couldn't move. She just stared at Anne.

"When did this happen?"

"While we waltzed." Anne chuckled. "Oh Elise, don't look so stricken. I told him that I had no plans beyond finding Uncle David and returning to England. He asked if there was anything he could

do to change my mind. I tried to let him down gently."

Elise sighed and set the crate on the ground. "Well, he's been pining over you for a month. I suppose I should have expected it. We're usually right ahead of them in line, except when we change to the back, and we see more of him and Hector than we do of a lot of others. And, Anne dear, he *is* a nice young man."

"But I don't think I wish to spend the rest of my life on a wheat farm. That's what he hopes to do, you know—raise wheat."

"It does sound a bit bland, yet—don't you think there's something appealing about it? A secure place with a man who adores you? Of course he wouldn't be able to afford a cook or a housemaid, I'm sure."

"I don't know if I'd care, if I met the right man," Anne said.

"Dan Adams isn't the one though?"

"That's right." Anne took the tinderbox from the crate.

The livestock in the wagon circle stirred and shifted. A horse snorted, and Elise looked toward the sound. Eb Bentley was slipping a headstall over his paint gelding's poll.

"Odd how the idea of marrying a commoner isn't nearly as repulsive as it was three months ago." Anne bunched up a handful of wood shavings and dry grass.

"It's because you're not in England now," Elise said.

Anne shook her head. "I even feel a bit guilty nowadays, knowing I would have thought of people like Rebecca Harkness and the Adams boys as beneath my notice." She hit the flint and steel together and blew on the sparks.

"I agree with you," Elise said. "When you get to know some of these folks, you realize they've a bit of regality about them."

Anne reached for the small store of kindling Thomas had left by the fireplace last night.

Elise ruminated on their change of perspective as she got out her butcher knife and sliced off a small bit of bacon fat to grease the spider with. Anyone in England who knew Lady Anne would be shocked to learn she would even consider marrying a plain American and living in what they would call obscure poverty. She tried to picture Anne visiting someone like the Blithes or the Cranfords and taking Dan Adams along to a dinner party. It wouldn't do at all. Anne would be snubbed in rare form. Yet she *could* picture Anne and Daniel living in quiet contentment if only Anne were bitten by love. *If I fell truly in love, class wouldn't matter one whit.*

Eb led his paint out of the corral between their wagon and Abe Leonard's and stopped to give the saddle's cinch strap one last tug. He looked over and nodded at them.

"Morning, ladies."

"Good morning, Mr. Bentley," Elise said. She couldn't seem to look away from him. His dusty hat, so worn and comfortable looking, was the perfect complement to his rugged features. It was an honest hat. And she believed he'd shaved this morning. How had he managed that before the sun was fully up? A man of unexpected talents.

"Lovely day," Anne sang out.

"Yes, it is." He hesitated a moment then led his horse closer to Elise. "I have to admit, you ladies have surprised me. I know you're going to have it rougher in some ways without Costigan, but I think you can make it."

"Why thank you, sir." Elise marveled at the warmth in her heart. "Coming from you, that is praise indeed."

"Well, if you need anything, you tell me or Rob. We'll see that you're taken care of."

"We'll do our best not to call on you too often."

He nodded, gazing at her with thoughtful brown eyes. "I reckon you will."

Elise resolved anew to prove that his faith in her and Anne was not misplaced.

Eb smiled and swung into the saddle. "Up, Speck." He touched his hat brim and trotted off to the west.

"Nothing common about that man," Anne said.

The next morning Rob Whistler blew his horn from the center of

the wagon circle before it was light enough to see more than the snowy wagon covers. Elise and Anne were already dressed. They hurried out into the central corral to separate their mules from the other livestock. Elise nearly bumped into Nick Foster.

"I've got one of your wheelers here, ma'am."

"Thank you, Nick!" Elise took Challenger's halter from him and tugged the big mule toward her wagon. She tied him up and went back for another mule. Anne passed her, leading Chick, one of their leaders.

"Get the harness out," Elise called to her. "I'll bring Bumper and Blackie."

They had come nine hundred miles from Independence, Missouri, but the mules looked to be in good flesh to her untrained eye. The two days of leisure at Independence Rock had left them well rested. The men had taken the stock out of the camp during the day to let them graze along the river, and all of the animals seemed to have benefited from it. Bumper, at least, exhibited high spirits this morning, kicking out at another mule they passed.

They were ready to move out when the horn sounded again, and Elise took the reins. Anne sat beside her on the seat. They'd used enough provisions to more than offset her weight. Elise directed the four mules to move into line behind Mr. Leonard's wagon, with the Adams brothers behind them. She felt rather powerful, sitting up on the seat. An hour of staring at the mules' hindquarters and the water barrel fixed on the back of Mr. Leonard's wagon lessened that impression. After two hours, Anne climbed down to walk for a while with some of the other women and gather buffalo chips for their evening fire. Toward noon, she returned and clambered up beside Elise again.

"Would you like me to drive for a while?"

"That would be nice. My shoulders are tired."

Anne stood and braced herself while Elise slid over on the seat.

"The clouds look ominous," Anne observed as she took the reins.

Now that she was on the other side, Elise could see farther westward beyond the wagon ahead. The overcast sky had gone nearly black, and the clouds were low enough to obscure the distant mountains.

"I'd say we're in for a storm."

Experience as they'd crossed the Nebraska prairie had taught them how violent a thunderstorm could be out here, with no trees to break the wind.

The wind picked up, tossing whirlwinds of dust high. Some of the drivers took their wagons to one side of the rutted trail so they wouldn't breathe so much of the roiling dust. Gusts tore at Elise's skirt and made the canvas wagon cover pop. The tall prairie grasses rippled like sea waves. Thunder rumbled over them, and lightning crackled in the distance.

Rob cantered his chestnut along the line as the first raindrops spattered down.

"Circle the wagons," he shouted. "Hobble your teams if you can and turn them loose in the middle. Circle now so the drovers can drive the loose herd inside. Storm's a-coming!" Elise's heart caught then raced. They'd never hobbled the mules without Thomas. She doubted they could unhitch and hobble them all in time. Anne thrust the reins into her hands, slapping them against the wheelers' haunches. "Get up, Bumper! Up, Challenger!"

Anne clung to the edge of the wagon seat, but Elise had to brace herself with her feet as the mules followed Mr. Leonard's wagon. They lurched out of the rutted trail into the tall grass, plowing it down as they went.

As the rain increased to a downpour, the wagon ahead stopped. Others had lumbered into a lopsided oval. Elise hauled back on the reins, and the mules stopped just behind Abe's water barrel.

"Quick, Anne! The hobbles."

Elise leaped down into the wet grass as Anne dove into the wagon. Every traveler dreaded a stampede, and the storm could be more than enough to set one off.

Elise's fingers fumbled as she worked to unhitch the leather traces from the whiffletrees near the wagon tongue. Anne appeared, carrying an armful of short leather straps. Her calico dress was already soaked and clung to her frame. Elise decided to try to hobble the mules first then unhitch them.

"Work on Blackie first," she yelled over the wind. Blackie, the near leader, was the most placid of their mules and would probably allow Anne to work on his legs without a fuss. Challenger, on the other hand, pawed at the ground, throwing his head and snorting. "Oh, you'd love to get loose, wouldn't you?" Elise muttered.

Each rawhide strap had a loop in one end. This had to be slipped over the mule's elevated foot and pulled tight. The other end was then buckled around the other front leg. With great difficulty, she got the loop around his right cannon. She wasn't sure she could hook the other end around his left leg. Still in harness, Challenger was bound to Bumper, and she couldn't get between them.

"Let me help."

She looked up into Eb Bentley's brown eyes. His hat was pulled low over his brow, and his clothes were drenched, too. The rain pummeled them mercilessly.

Elise surrendered the end of the hobble to him.

"Unhook him from the wagon," Eb yelled.

She managed it at last. Eb had the strap in place by the time she released the toggle. Eb unbuckled him from the rest of the team. Still in his collar and harness, Challenger crow-hopped away from his teammates into the center of the circle.

Out of nowhere, Dan Adams appeared. "Give me some of the hobbles. Get under the wagon."

She'd expected him to say "in the wagon," but as she processed his command and handed over the remaining hobbles, she realized that hailstones the size of peas, and some as large as grapes, now pelted them. She ran to the side of the wagon and threw herself down, rolling the grass flat as she gained the shelter beneath the wagon bed. She stretched out, parallel to the box above her. If the mules still hitched should begin to move, she didn't want to be run over.

A moment later, Anne joined her, wild eyed and shivering. "The cattle are panicking. The men are trying to close the gaps between the wagons."

Elise crawled to the front of the wagon and peered out. All

of their mules were unhitched. She could see the wheels of Abe Leonard's wagon thirty feet away. Over the wind, the noise of hailstones hitting the ground rivaled the thunder. She could hear the screams of mules and urgent lowing of the oxen. Animals shifted about and bumped the side of the wagon. Outside their shelter, everything moved and roared.

Anne lay on the ground and covered her head with her arms. Elise moved closer and wrapped an arm around her. Anne's body convulsed with shivering.

"So c–cold," she cried.

Between the rear wheels, Elise saw someone's feet. A big wooden box plopped down on the sodden grass and accumulation of ice balls. Still the man kept working. *He's tying ropes between the wagons to keep the animals in,* she thought. *Dear God, help them!*

A fearsome ripping came from above them. Anne jerked her chin up and stared at Elise.

"The wagon cover," Elise said. Everything in the wagon would get soaked.

Anne threw her arms around Elise's neck and clung to her. Elise held her and stroked her back and shoulders. It reminded her of the night Anne's mother had died. The girl had wept for hours, inconsolable.

At last the roaring lessened. Elise relaxed her hold on Anne and crept to the edge of the wagon. Rain still fell, but softly now. The hail had collected in rows along the ground beside the wagons. Some of the stones were as large as eggs. Many of the canvas tops had split or shredded. Men moved slowly among the herd of livestock, speaking quietly to the animals. Others stood in gaps between wagons with sticks or guns in their hands, ready to drive back a mule or ox that wanted to escape.

How badly damaged was their own wagon? They had a spare cover. If only she could get at it now and spread it over the bows before all their foodstuffs were ruined.

Eb Bentley came and hunkered down next to the wagon. "You ladies all right?"

"Yes. But our wagon top is torn, isn't it?"

"Not as bad as some," Eb said. "And we've lost a few animals."

"Lost them?"

"Two are dead from the hailstones. Half a dozen more got past us and ran off."

"Are any people hurt?" she asked.

"Nothing serious. I think all your mules are safe, but I'm not sure. We'll stay here until tomorrow. The stock needs to calm down and warm up again. Some of them were so shocked by the storm and the cold that they could die just from that."

"Really?"

He nodded. "I've seen it before. We'll build fires as soon as we can, just to take the chill off. If I hitch your mules to the side of your wagon, can you rub them all over with a sack or something?"

"Yes, I can do that."

"That'll help warm them up. Tell me where your coat is in the wagon, and I'll try to get it out for you."

Anne poked her head out beside Elise. Her face was streaked with tears. "I can help, too, Mr. Bentley."

He eyed her for a moment then nodded. "We can use you."

Elise thought her arms would drop off before she stopped rubbing the mules. Eb and Daniel found all six of their team—the four they'd released and their two spares in the loose herd. They rotated the ones they rested, and this morning Prince and Zee had been left in the drovers' care. Those two seemed less traumatized than the others. Chick and Blackie were the worst. They stood trembling while Elise and Anne brushed them and rubbed them with the sacks.

At last the sun peeked through holes in the clouds. When the mules' hair was dry, Elise threw down her gunnysack. Eb had used the dry chips they'd collected yesterday and started a fire. She filled the coffeepot from the small rain barrel on the side of the wagon.

"There's still a little ice inside the wagon," Anne said. "If you think the mules are all right now, I'll toss the ice in a bucket and see what needs to be aired."

"Good. I expect some of those men could use a cup of coffee."

Elise found on a quick inspection that their food containers were unharmed. Some of their bedding was sodden with rainwater and melted hailstones, and the extra harnesses should probably be taken out and oiled. Most other things would survive the wetting.

A half hour later, when Dan Adams came over and asked if they had an extra wagon cover to replace their torn one, she held up the steaming coffeepot.

"We do, sir, and we have hot coffee. Are you interested?"

"Oh Miss Finster." Dan grinned at her, his teeth gleaming in his mud-streaked face. "If you give me a cup of hot brew, I reckon I'll feel fit enough to put your new wagon cover on all by myself."

"That's impressive, sir, but you needn't. Miss Stone and I will be happy to help. But drink your coffee first."

Other men appeared as if by magic—Dan's brother Hector, Abe Leonard, and even young Nick Foster. Elise kept an eye on Anne as she moved among them, smiling equally on them all. No trace of tears remained on her flushed cheeks. Dan watched the lovely dark-haired girl with a mournful gaze but managed a smile when Anne offered him a cold biscuit.

Eb arrived at last, trudging slowly with his chin low on his chest. Elise went to the fire and lifted the coffeepot.

"I've about one cup of coffee left in this pot, Mr. Bentley," she called to him. "I can't guarantee you won't get some grounds."

"I don't care if I have to chew it to swallow it," he said.

She smiled and poured the dregs into the tin cup Nick had emptied.

Anne took the pot from her. "I'll start a new batch."

Eb took a long sip and sighed. "Thank you kindly, ma'am. That hits the spot." He eyed her over the rim as he took another drink. "I've got some news for you," he said a moment later.

Elise's stomach clenched. "What sort of news?"

"Costigan's gone."

"Gone?" She stared at him. "How do you mean?"

"He lit out this morning, shortly after we broke camp. One of

the drovers told me. He took Rob's extra saddle horse."

Elise had to concentrate to keep her jaw from dropping. "He stole Mr. Whistler's horse?"

"That's the word. Ralph Libby saw him leading the mare out. He said Costigan claimed Rob told him he could use the mare today to do some hunting. But he had his bedroll with him."

"And Mr. Whistler knew nothing of it."

Eb shook his head.

"I'm so sorry."

"Not your fault."

"Perhaps not, but Anne will feel responsible. If she hadn't told you about the letter—"

"We're better off without him," Eb said.

"Anne will want to reimburse Mr. Whistler for the horse."

Eb shook his head. "Don't even suggest it. Rob wouldn't hear of it, and there's no need to cause Miss Stone more distress. I'm just surprised he didn't take my other mount. Anyway, we'll report him as a horse thief to the authorities the next time we have a chance. If some troopers pass us, Rob will send a letter back to Fort Laramie to alert them."

"It's so evil. Anne paid him every cent she'd promised him, even though he'd only gone halfway with us."

"I figured." Eb sipped his coffee.

"She wanted to be sure he wouldn't be stranded out here. Do you think he'll make it to Schwartzburg on his own?"

"Likely, unless this storm caught him bad."

"He's obviously resourceful," Elise mused.

"That's one way of putting it. He knows the country, and we're only a day's ride out from the trading post at Schwartzburg. Oh, it'll take the wagons four or five days more, but he'll be there tomorrow, I reckon, if he keeps moving."

Elise let out a long breath. "So."

Anne came back with the coffeepot. "I'll put this on the fire. You gentlemen come back in a while, and we'll give you another round." She came over to stand beside Elise. "Dan's looking over our wagon cover."

Eb handed Elise his empty cup. "I'm heading out with a couple of men to look for the missing stock. Dan will take care of you though."

Elise went to the front of the wagon, where Daniel was standing on the seat, peering over the wagon top.

"How bad is the damage?" she called up to him.

"Could be worse. It's mostly the front end that tore. I'm thinking if your extra cover will fit, we could put it right over this one. That would give you extra strength on the part that's still good, and it would be less work in the long run."

Anne came to stand beside Elise. They looked up into the front opening and could see the sky through the large gashes in their "roof."

"Do you think we could mend this one?" Anne asked. "If so, maybe we should take it off now and work on it in the evenings."

Dan shook his head doubtfully. "It's pretty extensive. I think I'd leave it on. You can baste some of the tears together from inside at your leisure."

"How is your wagon, and Hector's?" Elise asked.

"Hec's is all right. Mine's got one rip. For some reason, we didn't get it as bad as you did—or maybe our cloth was stronger, I don't know." Dan hopped down beside them.

"I'd be happy to stitch yours up this evening," Elise said. "Maybe we can take a piece off this one where it's torn worst and use it for a patch."

"You don't need to do that," Dan said.

"You've helped us a lot. I'd be glad to do something for you."

Daniel nodded. "All right. Now, let's get your extra cover out."

"I know right where it is," Anne said. She and Dan walked to the back of the wagon. Elise decided to leave them alone to do it. If anything needed to be said between them, she didn't want to hinder them by her presence.

"Miss Finster."

She whirled and smiled as Rob approached her. "Hello, Mr. Whistler. I'm so sorry about your horse."

"Don't fret about it, ma'am. How are you and Miss Stone faring?"

"Well, thanks to the gentlemen of this company. Daniel Adams is helping Anne get out our spare wagon cover now."

Rob looked up at the still-damp canvas. Ragged edges fluttered in the breeze.

"Good. We're going to stay right here until morning. The stock needs time to settle down. We're a ways from water, but most folks have enough to last a day."

"We can all use the afternoon to make repairs and dry out, I expect."

He nodded. "And at daybreak, we'll move on."

"I wish we could do something about your horse," Elise said.

Rob pushed his hat back and squinted up at the sky. The clouds were higher and sparser now, and the wind carried them along eastward.

"Well, she was a good mare, but. . .I hope we've seen the last of Costigan."

Elise had hoped for a town or at least a small settlement at Schwartzburg. What she got was a small trading post and livestock dealer. Schwartz had begun the post where a large creek flowed into the Platte, as a place to capitalize on the trade with wagon trains and Indians. He also collected horses and mules, which he traded to the army. Wagon trains were not allowed to camp within two miles of the post so that Schwartz's livestock could have the grass within that distance.

Whistler's company, as they were known along the way, camped just after noon as close as they could—two miles east of the post, where the grass grew lush and a line of elm trees edged the river. The Harkness men emptied their farm wagon and offered to drive up to a dozen ladies to the trading post so they could shop.

"You go ahead," Elise told Anne. "There's no need for us both to go, and I'll catch up on things here."

"If you're sure."

Elise smiled. "I am. Mr. Whistler says prices are exorbitant here, and I doubt there's anything I'd want to purchase."

"All right." Anne opened her purse and took out a roll of American bills. "Here, I'll leave this with you so I won't be tempted. If it can't be bought for a few coins, we'll do without it."

Elise tucked the money deep in her pocket and looked around to check if anyone was watching. With Thomas gone, they were probably safe. No more problems had surfaced in the last few days beyond weary livestock and leaking wagons. Some of their fellow travelers had seen their osnaburg or canvas coverings damaged beyond easy repair in the hailstorm and hoped to buy more fabric at Schwartzburg.

Elise busied herself with baking gingerbread by Rebecca's recipe, mending, and washing out a few underthings. She felt quite domestic. Perhaps there was hope for her as a housewife someday. Several men in their company had taken to coming 'round in the evening and chatting with the ladies, and not all of them goggled at Anne. Their attention made Elise feel feminine, and she longed to wear a pretty gown again. Her two calico dresses had faded and hung shapelessly.

There was talk of dancing that evening. On a whim, she opened Anne's largest trunk and looked over her mistress's gowns. If they didn't overdo it, perhaps they could wear something a little dressier this evening than they had since Independence. If she could persuade Anne, the battle was won. She laid out a modest brown plaid walking dress with an ecru underskirt for her mistress and opened her own trunk to find something suitable for herself.

She took the gingerbread out of the dutch oven at the perfect moment. Now for some biscuits. As she worked the handle of her sifter, she thought about Eb Bentley. He was nothing like David Stone, yet he embodied many of the qualities she'd always considered essential in a man—in a husband. There. How shocking was this admission? She peered into the sifter and found only a small mound

of worms and a couple of beetles. She tipped them into the fire and scooped another pint of flour into the sifter.

"Elise!"

Her name came from a distance, borne by the wind, but it was Anne's voice that called. She squinted westward. Eb's pinto pounded toward her along the trail from Schwartzburg and—could it be? Anne was perched behind the saddle, peeking around Eb's shoulder and waving her handkerchief, her skirts billowing above her knees.

Elise plunked the sifter down beside the bowl of flour, lifted her skirt, and ran to meet them.

Eb stopped the pinto so quickly that Speck almost sat down on the trail. Anne slid off the horse's rump and was standing up beside Elise before Speck got his feet under him again, as though Anne and Eb had practiced the maneuver and performed it on purpose.

"Elise! There's news!"

By now alarm had seized Elise. When Anne threw herself into her arms, Elise clutched her fiercely. A quick glance up at Eb's face revealed nothing.

"What is it? Tell me."

Anne sobbed. "Uncle David. They say he's buried in the graveyard near the trading post."

CHAPTER 19

Anne collapsed in Elise's arms. Eb jumped off the pinto's back as she swooned and helped Elise lower her gently to the grass beside the dusty trail.

"Anne? Anne, my dear." Elise patted the girl's face. She hadn't any smelling salts nearby, though there was a vial buried deep in one of Anne's trunks. They hadn't needed them since St. Louis.

"It's a shock," Eb said. "I could see she was stunned when she heard it, and I told her she should wait for you to come. She insisted on telling you herself, so I brought her back here."

"Thank you," Elise said. "I'm not sure what to do."

"I can carry her to your tent."

His intent eyes and evident concern made her heart clutch for an instant. "Perhaps that's best. We've smelling salts, and I'll make her a strong cup of tea."

Anne's eyelids fluttered, and she blinked up at them. "Oh dear. Have I swooned?"

"Yes, but don't distress yourself. You'll be fine." Elise brushed a tendril of fine, dark hair back beneath Anne's hat brim. If Eb weren't hovering, she'd loosen the poor thing's corset strings.

"The trader," Anne said faintly. "He's German."

Elise wondered if Anne had temporarily lost her senses. Of course the trader was German, with a name like Schwartz. Anne's eyes widened suddenly and focused on Elise once more. "Uncle David. He died here. The trader said so."

Elise frowned. "Did he say when? Or how it happened?"

"A few years ago. He wasn't just sure when, but he was certain it was Uncle David. He says there's a marker in the cemetery." Anne sat up and grasped Elise's wrist. "We have to go and see it."

"Of course." Elise glanced at Eb. "I hate to ask, but would

204

you go with us?"

"Sure. I'll get my other horse. Can one of your mules go under saddle?"

"I believe Thomas rode Chick a few times."

He nodded. "I'll see if I can borrow a couple of saddles."

Elise almost insisted on sidesaddles, but that might be a bit optimistic.

Eb stood. "Miss Stone, may I carry you to the camp?"

"I should say not. I'm perfectly capable of walking." Anne reached for Elise, and together they rose. Anne inhaled deeply and straightened her shoulders. "I shall be fine."

Elise smiled at Eb. Anne's spirits were back to what they should be.

"At least let me put you up on Speck, and I'll lead him," Eb said.

Anne consented and let him boost her into the saddle. When they reached camp, she slid down with a steadying hand from Eb. She looked into the tent and stopped halfway under the flap.

The dresses, Elise thought. She'd left them laid out on their bedrolls.

"I don't believe I shall dance tonight," Anne said.

Elise feared Anne would faint again. "I'm sorry, dear. It was presumptuous of me."

"You didn't know about—" Anne sobbed.

Elise looked over her shoulder at Eb. "Give us a few minutes."

He nodded. "I'll get the other mounts."

An hour later, they rode toward the trading post together. Eb had scrounged up one sidesaddle without Elise mentioning it. Mrs. Libby, who was past sixty, had come up with it. Anne insisted Elise use it on Eb's spare horse, a solid brown gelding that Eb inexplicably called "Pink." Anne rode Chick astride, with the voluminous skirt of her riding habit cascading about the mule's flanks in waves of blue velvet. It held enough yardage to cover her ankles, to Elise's relief. The last thing they needed was trappers and Indians ogling her ladyship's limbs.

Elise had only ridden a few times, and for the first mile she was too terrified to think of anything but maintaining her balance and gripping the pommels between her knees. By the time they could see the buildings, her confidence had marginally returned. Although Eb claimed he hadn't ridden Pink for a couple of days, the gelding moved calmly and seemed willing to follow Speck anywhere.

The trading post was made of mud brick—adobe, Eb called it. "Those walls are a couple of feet thick," he told them. "They'll stop a lot of bullets."

"Is there need for such protection?" Elise asked.

"Oh yeah. Schwartz sells livestock to the army. The Indians will try to run off the herd every chance they get."

Anne seemed lost in her own thoughts, paying no attention to the conversation.

"Now remember, Schwartz is a shrewd one," Eb said as they tied up the horses. "He'll squeeze the last penny out of a traveler."

"He's dishonest?" Elise asked.

"Hasn't been proven, but likely. Last summer when we got here, another wagon train had lost thirty head of livestock while they camped nearby. The wagon master said it wasn't Indians that stampeded their herd, but Schwartz denied any knowledge of it."

Elise patted her pocket where Anne's hoard of money still lay. She fully intended to return to camp without parting with a cent.

"Now, I see Rob's horse, Bailey, tied up yonder," Eb said. "Whyn't I go in and see if he's inside? I'll tell him what's up, and he can go with us, too."

Eb must distrust the trader deeply to want his friend's support for something as innocuous as a visit to the graveyard. Elise nodded. "We'll wait here for you."

He went into the building. Elise and Anne walked over and stood in the shadow of the eaves. The heat was oppressive, but at least they were out of the direct rays of the sun. A couple of other buildings sat nearby—one no more than a hovel, which Elise hoped was a storage shed, not a dwelling. The larger structure appeared to be a barn, and she could see several men moving between it and a

fenced pasture east of it.

A cluster of people from the wagon train came out of the trading post.

"Hello," Mrs. Legity called. "You been inside yet?"

Elise shook her head. "No. Did you find any bargains?"

Mrs. Legity snorted. "Not what I'd call bargains." She pulled up suddenly and looked Anne over from head to toe. "That outfit looks a mite hot for this weather."

"Perhaps you're right," Anne said with a sweet smile.

Elise noted the beads of perspiration on her mistress's brow. As soon as the others had walked on toward the Harkness wagon, she pulled out a handkerchief.

"Allow me." She patted at Anne's forehead. "I'm so sorry. Mrs. Legity is right—that habit is far too heavy for this sun."

"It was a choice between modesty and comfort, I fear. For once, I wish I'd been less proper."

Elise held back a laugh. "My dear, if your friends knew all the rules of propriety you've broken in the last three months, they would never receive you again. I can only hope that you don't suffer heatstroke for the sake of convention."

"Yes. I should have just leaped on the mule wearing my calico. Lavinia would have done it."

"I daresay she would." Elise was glad Anne could laugh about the wardrobe situation, but would she go back to her mourning weeds soon?

The door to the trading post opened, and Rob and Eb came out together.

"What's this all about?" Rob asked the scout. Eb quickly told him about Anne's earlier visit to the trading post and what Schwartz had told her.

"There's another fellow behind the counter now," Eb told the ladies. "He says Schwartz is out at the corral. Binchley hoped to trade in his oxen here for some better ones, and Schwartz is showing him what he's got."

"Shall we go out there and speak to him?" Anne asked.

Rob offered Anne his arm. "Let me escort you, Miss Stone. We'll find out where this graveyard is."

Elise walked beside Eb in their wake. The enormity of Anne's news hit her. If David was dead, their mission was ended. She would never again see the man whose memory she'd treasured all these years. They could return to Fort Laramie with the next cavalry detachment or train of freighters' wagons that came through heading eastward—and thence on to Independence and eventually New York and London. Was she ready to return home?

More important, perhaps, was the question of the earldom. Would the authorities in England accept whatever evidence they could collect? Elise doubted a death certificate existed.

Schwartz greeted them and left Mr. Binchley with instruction to think over his offer.

"I'm so sorry that I had to bear you such sad news, miss," he said to Anne in heavily accented English. He glanced at Elise, Eb, and Rob. "I see you've brought your friends to support you. You'd like to see Mr. Stone's grave of course."

"Yes, sir, I would. At once, please."

Rob patted Anne's hand and addressed the trader. "Where is this graveyard of yours, Schwartz? We'll take Miss Stone there to view her uncle's grave."

"I'll show you. It's beyond that grove yonder." He pointed toward a distant clump of trees.

Rob frowned down at Anne. "Shall we get the horses? Or perhaps we can borrow the Harknesses' wagon."

Eb looked toward the road. "Wilbur's left to go back to camp."

"I can walk that far," Anne said.

It was a stroll of a quarter mile, and had their purpose been less grim and the sun's rays less intense, it might have proved a pleasant stroll. Though the path was not well worn, someone had recently gone before them through the grass that nearly reached Elise's waist.

In a few minutes, they arrived beneath several spreading willows, which gave a welcome respite from the sun. Schwartz paused in the shade and pointed to where the path continued.

"It's just down there a few steps more. Mr. Stone is buried on the left side of the lot. It's marked with a wooden cross, as are most of the graves."

"His name is on it?" Eb asked.

"Oh yes."

"We'll find it."

Schwartz gazed at Anne for a moment. "An Englishman, wasn't he?"

She nodded. "My father's brother."

"I am sorry."

"Can you tell me how it happened?" she asked.

Schwartz inhaled deeply and looked toward the river. "He came by with a company of other travelers in the summer. This time of year or a bit later."

"How did the man die?" Eb's gaze bore into the German.

"He was sick when he got here. Asked if he could lay up a few days and then catch up to the others. I let him sleep in the cabin with my men—wish I hadn't though. He got worse, and they were all afraid they'd catch his disease. It wasn't cholera though. I made sure of that before I let him stay on. He died the third day, I think it was."

"What about his things?" Eb asked. "His wagons, saddle horse, and any personal effects."

"Wagons?" Schwartz seemed surprised at that.

"We were told he took three wagons full of goods," Anne said. "He planned to open a store in Oregon."

Schwartz stroked his beard. "I didn't know that. I suppose he had other men driving the wagons for him. The captain of the company left him here with a horse, saddle, and bedroll. That's all I know about."

"And what became of those?" Eb asked.

Schwartz spread his hands in supplication. "We had no way of knowing whom to contact, and I kept the horse as payment for the care he received. There was nothing else."

"Nothing?" Anne asked bleakly.

"I think not."

"Surely the wagon master gave you a way to contact him or Stone's drivers," Rob said.

"No, sir." Schwartz glanced toward the trading post. "I left my nephew in the store, and his English is not so good. I should go and check on him."

Rob and Eb exchanged a dark glance. "You must compensate Miss Stone for her uncle's horse, saddle, and other gear," Rob said.

Schwartz glowered at him. "I told you—"

"We know what you said," Rob replied. "It didn't sound as though he received much care. A horse and saddle is too much payment for digging a grave. I don't expect the man stayed without some cash in his pockets either."

"He had no valuables on him when he came here." Schwartz's harsh tone softened when he glanced at Anne again. "Of course we had to burn his bedroll. You understand. The sickness. . ."

"Leave us," Eb said.

Schwartz nodded and strode quickly toward the trading post.

Anne raised a gloved hand to her lips and closed her eyes. Elise put an arm around her.

"Are you all right, my dear?"

Anne nodded. "Let us go on."

They stepped out of the copse into the harsh sunlight. A short distance away, several weathered crosses stuck up out of the tall grass. Rob took Anne's hand and threaded it through the crook of his arm again.

"The left side," Anne said softly. The grass was bent over in several paths among the markers, and they veered to the left edge of the little cemetery.

A moment later they located the cross made of two short boards nailed together. DAVID STONE was carved rudely into the horizontal piece. They all stood gazing at it for a moment.

Anne sobbed. "It's too awful." She wiped tears from her pale cheeks with her delicate white handkerchief.

"I know." Elise stepped closer to her, on the other side from Rob.

Tears flooded her eyes. "But if you hadn't inquired at the trading post, we might never have known of this. We might have passed by and never learned his fate."

"Yes. We could have gone all the way to Oregon on a fruitless errand."

"I wonder what became of his wagons full of goods," Elise said.

Rob looked over Anne's head at her. "Shall we say a few words?"

"I would like that," Anne said.

"Is the Twenty-Third Psalm all right?"

"Yes."

Rob started to recite the psalm, and Elise took Anne's hand. Together they whispered the words in unison with Rob. From behind them, Eb's quiet voice joined in.

"'...And I will dwell in the house of the Lord for ever. Amen.'"

After a moment's silence, Rob began to pray. "Dear heavenly Father, we ask that You would comfort Miss Stone's heart. We pray also that You would give her wisdom and guide her footsteps as she has some decisions ahead of her. For David Stone, we thank You for his time on this earth, and that he was a man people loved and respected. Please comfort his family in England when they receive this news. Amen."

Elise opened her tear-filled eyes. This crude resting place was completely inadequate for David.

Eb cleared his throat. "The inscription looks mighty fresh."

Elise stared at the boards for a moment before his words penetrated her numbness. The cross of wind- and rain-battered boards looked as though it might well have stood there for several years, but the letters on the crosspiece left yellowish wood exposed.

"Yes, it does," she said.

Eb walked around them and bent over the marker. "No dates, just the name. What do you think, Rob?"

"I'm not sure." Rob looked about. "It's a mite trampled here, wouldn't you say?"

Eb surveyed the grass around the grave. He went to his knees and spread back the stalks at the base of the cross. He picked up something small between his fingertips and held it close to his eyes. He held it out to Rob and dropped it into his hand then burrowed into the grass again, searching carefully.

"What is it?" Elise asked.

Rob held out his palm. "A wood shaving. A fresh one."

Eb rocked back on his knees and held out more.

"Looks like we need to talk to Mr. Schwartz again," Rob said.

Eb stood. "No need for you ladies to get into it. We'll get the truth out of him."

"But I don't understand," Anne said. "Why would he lie about a grave?"

"Maybe he's not telling the truth about how Mr. Stone died," Rob said.

Eb shook his head. "In that case, why did he even offer the information that there was a grave here? When Miss Stone asked at the trading post, he could have simply said he'd never heard of the man."

"And why carve his name on the cross now?" Elise asked.

Rob frowned. "Maybe to make it look as though they took better care of him than they really did?"

A thought leaped to Elise's mind. "Mr. Hoyle."

"Who?" Eb asked.

"A man I met in Independence. He was forming a wagon train. He's the one who told us David Stone traveled west with him in 1850. And also the one who mentioned the three wagons full of merchandise."

"What else did he say?" Eb asked.

Elise frowned in concentration. "He said David originally planned to move to California, but on the trail he changed his mind. He went to Oregon instead. At least, Mr. Hoyle said he left their company with a group of other wagons at the cutoff."

Eb looked at Rob. "If he stuck with them to the cutoff, he would have been alive when they passed here."

"Yup."

Anne looked from Rob to Eb and back again. "So either Mr.

Hoyle or Mr. Schwartz lied. How do we know which?"

Rob pushed his hat back. "I've known Ted Hoyle for at least three years. Never heard anything bad about him. He's generally considered reliable. But Schwartz. . ." He shook his head.

"Sounds like we'd better have that talk with the trader," Eb said.

Rob nodded. "You ladies go back to the trading post and wait for us. Eb and I will see if Schwartz is out near the barn again."

Elise took Anne's elbow. "Come. These two gentlemen will get to the bottom of this."

Anne sniffed and wiped her damp eyes with her handkerchief. "Yes, I trust Mr. Whistler and Mr. Bentley implicitly."

They walked back through the willows and toward the buildings. Elise steered Anne away from the barnyard to avoid the men working there. They neared the trading post from the back.

"If we wait here, we can see when Mr. Bentley and Mr. Whistler leave the barn," Elise said. "I'd just as soon be out of sight of the wagon train people entering and leaving the post, too."

Anne concurred, and they stood quietly beneath the eaves. A back door was open, and somewhere inside, two men were talking. Elise pricked up her ears and leaned toward the open doorway.

"Elise. . ."

Anne stopped speaking when Elise held up an urgent hand. She was almost certain. . . Yes, it was true.

"One of the men inside is speaking German," she whispered to Anne.

"It must be Mr. Schwartz, but to whom is he speaking?"

"I don't know. None of the other folks in our company speak German that I know of." Elise tiptoed closer to the doorway.

One man said quite clearly in German, "I think they're buying it."

She held her breath. It had been so long since she'd had a conversation in her native tongue, she had to listen closely. Although she disliked Schwartz based on what Eb and Rob had said, she would find it satisfying to go around to the front room of the trading post and have a chance to speak to him in German.

As this flashed through her mind, the second man laughed. "That's good, if they believe you. Amazing how trusting some people are."

Elise frowned. What were they talking about? Not a literal transaction, it seemed. Anne was waiting a few steps away, eyeing her curiously. Elise put a finger to her lips, and Anne nodded.

". . .The young woman, she is distraught, but what can I say? If we can fool her, we will get a good payoff. That and the livestock will make this a profitable encounter, I think."

The other man laughed. "They'll never be able to prove it wasn't Indians, not with the evidence we'll give them."

"Enough," Schwartz said, louder than before. "Now go back to work."

Elise stepped quickly away from the door, grabbed Anne's wrist, and pulled her around the corner of the building.

"What's going on?" Anne hissed.

"A good question." Elise held her close to the side wall as footsteps clumped out into the cleared area behind the post. A moment later Schwartz came into view, walking away from them. He headed straight for the barn and corral without looking back. Elise exhaled.

"There are Mr. Bentley and Mr. Whistler." Anne nodded toward the barn. Apparently Eb and Rob had unsuccessfully searched for Schwartz in the outbuildings. They now met him outside near the corral and stood talking for a minute.

"What I heard sounded suspicious," Elise said softly. "I want to tell those two gentlemen and see what they say—but definitely not in front of the trader."

CHAPTER 20

"Do you have witnesses?" Eb asked Schwartz.

"Witnesses?" The big man repeated. "To Stone's death, you mean?"

"Yes." Eb didn't blink.

Schwartz shrugged. "My hired men. Let's see. . .one of them is dead now. Drowned crossing the river. Another went hunting last fall and never returned. My hired hands come and go. I'm not sure I can produce anyone else who was here when this regrettable incident happened."

"I'll just bet," Eb said.

Schwartz's eyes narrowed. "What are you driving at?"

Rob stepped forward. "Here, now, gentlemen, no need to get upset. Mr. Schwartz, is there anything else you can tell us about Mr. Stone's final days? For instance, who was captain of the wagon train he traveled with?"

Schwartz spread his hands, palms up. "You ask me to remember, after so long a time?"

"If it was someone you knew. . .someone you'd dealt with before. . ." Rob eyed him closely.

"I think the emigrants had elected a captain from their company. They were traveling by the book, as we say. Using one of those handbooks that tell you where the next watering place is."

Rob glanced at Eb. They both knew better than to suggest Ted Hoyle had captained Stone's train.

"We'll bring Miss Stone into the store in a few minutes," Rob said. "I expect you to give her a hundred dollars for the horse and saddle."

"A hundred dollars?" Schwartz stared at him. "You want to drive me out of business, is that it? I hardly make a penny on the supplies

215

I sell here. Every grain of corn must be hauled across the plains. I can't pay her a hundred dollars."

Eb opened his mouth and closed it again. He was going to ask why Schwartz had altered the grave marker, but he already knew something wasn't right. The whole business stank. If he'd lied about the grave, he'd probably lied about the rest, too. Maybe he'd laid claim to all of David Stone's goods—wagons, merchandise, livestock, and all.

"I think that would be the least you could do," Rob said. "I'll bring her in shortly." He nodded to Eb, and Eb followed him toward the trading post.

"I don't like it," Rob said.

"Me either." Eb nudged him. "The ladies are waiting for us. Miss Finster looks fit to tear into somebody."

Rob doffed his hat as they approached the women. "Well, ladies, I'm not thoroughly satisfied with the outcome, but I told Schwartz I'd take Miss Stone into the store, and that I expected him to compensate her. We'll see what happens."

"Do you think he really got Uncle David's horse?" Miss Stone asked. "I don't believe he's telling us the whole truth, but if he's a liar, why not lie about that?"

"I'm not sure what he's up to, but the scoundrel ought to at least feel it a little in his pocketbook." Rob looked over his shoulder. "He's coming up from the barn. Do you feel ready to face him again, Miss Stone?"

"I suppose so, but I'm not sure it would be right for me to take money from him."

"You go on," Miss Finster said. "Trust Mr. Whistler's judgment. Meanwhile, I'll speak to Mr. Bentley about what I heard just now."

Eb studied her face. "What's that?"

"Elise heard Herr Schwartz talking to someone in German a few moments ago," Miss Stone said.

Miss Finster flushed and looked down. "It may be nothing, but I thought I should tell you."

"Perhaps I should hear it before we go inside," Rob said.

"All right."

Eb glanced around and saw that Schwartz had veered off toward the back of the building. Miss Finster waited until he was out of sight. She lowered her voice and stepped closer to Eb and Rob than she normally would, and Eb felt her sense of urgency.

"He told the other person—and I've no idea who that may be, except it seemed to be someone working for him—that 'the young woman is distraught.' I wondered if he might be speaking about Anne. Then he said that if they can fool her, they will be paid well. What was I to think, other than that he must be lying to us about David's death? Though how on earth he could profit from that, I have no idea."

Rob's face wrinkled as he thought about it. "If he's lying, he certainly won't want to part with a hundred dollars for a horse he never took possession of."

"That's true," Eb said. "On the other hand, if he does agree to pay Miss Stone, that wouldn't necessarily mean he's telling the truth. It might be a sign that he's deep into it for something. The question is, what?"

"Do you really think my uncle survived the trip west?" Miss Stone asked. Her tear-streaked face and reddened eyes presented a pathetic picture, and Eb wanted badly to comfort the young woman.

"I wish I could tell you what all of this means, miss. Personally, I'm leaning toward thinking that grave yonder is a fake—or else it belongs to someone else. Seems to me Schwartz or one of his cronies carved the name on the cross today because they saw that it might benefit them. Whether your uncle is actually resting in that plot is questionable."

"Let's go in and see what he says to you," Rob suggested.

Miss Finster nodded. "Go, Anne. I'll wait out here with Mr. Bentley."

Rob and Miss Stone walked toward the front of the trading post. As soon as they rounded the corner, Miss Finster looked up at Eb.

"There was more I didn't want to tell you in front of Anne.

I don't think it will affect Mr. Whistler's conversation with the trader—in fact, it may be better that he doesn't know it yet, so he won't inadvertently give away anything."

"Oh? What's up?"

She inhaled sharply and glanced toward the barn as though marshaling her thoughts. Eb couldn't help noticing how pretty she looked. She wore a fetching brown hat he didn't believe he'd ever seen before, and her golden hair just showed around her forehead and ears. Her skin glowed with good health, and she looked less fragile than she had when they'd set out in April. Not that she and Miss Stone were ever sickly, but they'd both grown stronger on the trail.

"He said something about livestock to the other man. I didn't hear much, but when he mentioned Anne—that is, the 'young woman'—he said something about how some people are so trusting, in a detrimental way."

Eb frowned. He thought he understood what that meant—just.

"And then he said what I told you before about being well paid if they could fool her. But it was what he said next that really caught my attention."

"Which was?"

"He said—in German, you understand—that between that and the livestock, this should be a profitable encounter, and the other man said 'they'll blame it on Indians.' He mentioned leaving some evidence."

"What did you take that to mean?" Eb asked. "What encounter was he talking about?"

"I thought at first he meant with Anne. But Anne hasn't anything to do with livestock, except our poor little team of six mules. Unless he meant her uncle's livestock, that pulled his three wagons. But that was years ago, so why would he refer to it in the same breath as 'this encounter'? Or 'this meeting'?" She sighed and touched his sleeve lightly. "Mr. Bentley, I'm of German birth, but I've lived in England since I was sixteen."

"I never would have guessed. You speak English just about perfectly, ma'am."

"Thank you."

"In fact, I was surprised when you said you could speak German. I thought you were English all this time."

She smiled. "My name should have given me away. *Finster* means 'dark or brooding' in German."

He appraised her for a moment and then shook his head. "You're not like that."

"That's kind of you. My point is, it's been decades since I regularly conversed in the German language. But I'm wondering if perhaps he meant this encounter with our wagon train."

Eb inhaled slowly through his nose. "Our herd."

"Yes. When he said that about Indians. . ." She frowned and nodded slowly. "Yes, I'm certain that is what he said. They would leave evidence, and we would blame the Indians."

He huffed out his breath. "We'll increase our guard tonight."

"A wise precaution, I'd say."

"Yes. But will it be enough?" Eb took a few steps away from the adobe building, and Miss Finster walked with him, her face anxious. "What would his thieving ways have to do with Miss Stone?" he asked. "Why bother to fool her into thinking her uncle died here if he didn't? And if he did, why go to the trouble of carving the name on the cross all of a sudden?"

"And why would Mr. Hoyle say David continued with his company to the cutoff for Oregon? He seemed to remember Mr. Stone perfectly. I believe he liked him, and it sounded as though they got to be friends. I don't think he was mistaken."

Eb nodded. "Ted Hoyle's a sharp customer. He wouldn't have told you all that if it wasn't true."

"What can we do, then? Is there any way to prove whether or not that is truly David Stone's grave?"

"Short of digging him up, I don't see how. And even that might not prove anything. Could be someone's buried there, and they stuck the marker with Stone's name on it over the remains. Unless there was something in the grave that would positively identify the body. . ." He shook his head. "Not worth distressing

Miss Stone further, I'm thinking."

"But if the grave were empty. . ." Miss Finster looked up at him so hopefully Eb wanted it to be true and to prove it to her instantly.

"I doubt Schwartz would chance it. And he had plenty of old graves to choose from."

"I suppose you're right. But I have another question."

Eb's heart stirred, and not only for Miss Stone's predicament. For some ridiculous reason, he wondered how many becoming hats Miss Finster had in her wagon. "Yes, ma'am?" he managed.

"If Schwartz is lying, how did he know about David Stone?"

"That's easy. Miss Stone told him herself when she went into the trading post this morning. She showed him that portrait of her uncle that she carries around in her handbag."

Miss Finster nodded. "I'm sure she did. She inquires of everyone we meet. But still. . .assuming Schwartz thought quickly and concocted this story of David's illness while she stood there, do you think he'd have time to prepare the grave marker?"

Eb scratched his chin. "It took more than an hour for me to take her back to camp, get the horses ready, and fetch you two back here. He or one of his men could have done it in that amount of time. I think the shavings prove it was done recently. Very recently. And it points to someone standing there in the cemetery to do the carving, not preparing the cross in the barn or someplace else. A quick job on a marker that was already in place, if you ask me."

"I suppose you're right. But I still wonder if he only learned it when Anne inquired."

"He's shrewd. When a company of people comes to his store, he'll spot someone who might be easy to trick, and then he'll figure how to get that person's money. I was in the post when Miss Stone asked about her uncle. She reacted so strongly—he might have conceived the whole plan right then and there."

"How did he react to her distress?"

Eb shrugged. "He seemed concerned, but I wasn't really watching him closely. Maybe I should have, but I was more worried about her. Mrs. Harkness and I took her outside for some fresh air,

and Miss Stone asked me to take her back to the wagons so she could tell you."

"Here they come." Miss Finster moved her chin just a bit in the direction of the trading post.

Eb waited until Rob and Miss Stone reached them. "What happened in there?"

"Not much," Rob said. "Schwartz refused to pay Miss Stone anything. I asked if he'd sign a statement saying David Stone had died here and when, but he wouldn't. He said he didn't personally witness the death, and he didn't want to get in trouble."

Eb grimaced. "Getting awfully honest all of sudden, isn't he?"

"Seems like it. Finally he offered Miss Stone a few groceries," Rob said.

"I wasn't sure I wanted to take them." Miss Stone's pert chin rose in defiance. "Wouldn't that be like admitting he's telling the truth?"

Rob smiled. "I told him she'd think on it, and we'd come back later if she wanted the things."

"How much did he offer?"

"Ten dollars' worth of goods, but at his prices that wouldn't amount to much."

"Elise, he wants a dollar a pound for flour. And they have a few fresh eggs—at two dollars apiece. Can you imagine?" The young woman's brown eyes fairly sparked.

"No, I can't," Miss Finster said. "Shall we go back to camp?"

Elise tossed and turned that night, hearing the guards every time they passed the tent on their rounds. Rob and Eb had met with the men of the company and told them they suspected the camp might be raided, emphasizing the need for watchfulness. They'd tightened the wagon circle before sunset and made certain every mule, ox, milk cow, and saddle horse was safe inside. Because of the tight quarters and shortage of grass, the animals were fretful all night. Frequent bouts of kicking, squealing, braying, and snorting kept the travelers in a restless, intermittent doze.

An hour before dawn the camp began to quicken. The guards woke the men who were to relieve them.

"Mr. Whistler insisted on keeping a double guard while we break camp," Anne remarked as she led Chick over to be harnessed. "So far everything is going smoothly."

"Yes, almost too well," Elise said. "Maybe there was no danger after all."

"Or maybe they saw our vigilance and decided not to risk a raid."

As they worked together to get the mules harnessed, Eb rode up on Pink and dismounted near them.

"You ladies all right this morning? Need anything?"

"We're fine, thank you," Elise said. She was glad they had the wheelers already hitched and were nearly done with the leaders. "We'll be ready to pull out in five minutes."

"Great. We're not far from where the Sweetwater flows into the Platte. I think you'll find the change in terrain pleasant, but we will be climbing steadily now." Eb cast an appraising eye over their two near mules. "Your team looks in pretty good shape. Better than some."

"Thank you," Elise said. "We pamper them a bit, I'm told, but I think men and animals work better when they're well fed."

He smiled. "You've done well. A lot of folks have run out of grain."

Anne's head popped up over Blackie's back, from where she'd been fastening a buckle on the other side. "We determined at the outset to bring plenty of oats for them. I can't stand to see a hungry animal."

Elise said, "She'd pick up stray cats, too, if there were any out here."

Eb chuckled and laid a hand on Chick's withers. "I don't know how you ladies do it, but you have the smartest wardrobes and the fittest livestock of the company."

"Thank you." Elise dropped her voice. "I guess we worried for nothing yesterday."

"I'm not so sure," Eb said. "We'll keep a double guard again tonight."

"You think they might follow us, then?" Elise glanced Anne's way, but she was busy with Blackie's harness.

"You may have mistaken their intentions," Eb conceded. "But Rob and I would rather be safe than sorry."

"I admit I'll feel better when we have another day's journey between us and Herr Schwartz."

"Yes. This morning I'll ride ahead and scout our stopping place for nooning, and after that I'll scout our back trail, rather than farther ahead of us."

"Probably wise."

Eb smiled at her. "Don't fret, Miss Finster. We'll soon be out of Schwartz's territory."

Beyond the river, the banks rose in bluffs that cut off their view, but on the other side, they could see a fair distance. The mountains loomed, snowcapped and daunting. Every time Elise surveyed the rugged peaks, her chest ached. Nothing like this could be found in England. She must encourage Anne to make more drawings. Since Thomas left them and their labor had increased, Anne hadn't taken out her sketchbook.

"If you hadn't told me we can cross this mountain range fairly easily, I'd never believe it," Elise said.

Eb grimaced slightly. "I didn't mean to give you the impression that it will be simple. It's a rough road, and up north in the Oregon Territory it can be even rougher. But a lot of people have gone before us and improved the road. I think you and Miss Stone will do just fine. Mrs. Harkness, on the other hand, may have to part with some furniture and books."

Elise drove most of the morning, with Anne beside her on the seat. Rob had warned all of the travelers to stay close together.

"We don't want any stragglers today. I'll have the drovers keep the herd of loose stock within sight of the last wagons, too."

The herdsmen wouldn't like that. They ate enough dust when they kept the animals back half a mile or so. But for one day, they could stand it, Elise supposed.

Everyone seemed a little on edge. Abe Leonard barked at his oxen more sharply than usual, and the Adams brothers hadn't stopped by to offer their assistance in the morning. When her son-in-law didn't bring water quickly enough, Mrs. Legity had railed at him so loudly that the entire camp heard every word.

Elise fretted at the slowness of their pace. Her mules could outdistance the ox teams in short order, but they had to keep their place in line. Where the terrain allowed it, they could spread out in several columns, but when they had to go single file, they still had to resume their assigned position.

They rode the two miles to the trading post and crawled past it at the oxen's gait. A few people stopped to buy one or two items they'd decided they needed no matter what the price, but most of the wagons plodded steadily on.

After another hour on the trail, Elise handed the reins to Anne and got out her knitting bag. She was determined to master Rebecca Harkness's sock pattern before they reached Oregon, and her third attempt looked promising.

She peeled off her gloves. Already her hands were sweating. This would be a searing hot day unless she was mistaken. She patted her forehead with a handkerchief and picked up her partly made sock.

"Do you think we're doing the right thing?" Anne asked a minute later.

Elise stopped stitching and looked over at her. Anne's wide-brimmed hat shadowed her sober face.

"How do you mean that?"

Anne gave a half shrug, keeping her gloved hands and the lines steady. "Going on."

"As opposed to turning back?" Elise asked.

"Yes. I can't help thinking that perhaps Uncle David *is* buried back there at Schwartzburg, and we're going farther and farther from him and home."

"Herr Schwartz was lying. We all agreed on that."

"Yes, but what if he wasn't lying about all of it? What if the

grave part is real?" Anne looked at her anxiously.

"I don't see how it can be," Elise said. "And I don't trust that man any further than I could throw an ox. You must keep your faith strong. God will bring this odyssey to the conclusion that pleases Him, and I trust Him."

"I know you're right. And with that aside, part of me keeps saying, 'We can't leave the wagon train now.' Tearing ourselves away from this company would be traumatic, don't you think?"

"Well, yes." Elise began to knit again. "It's come to seem a bit like a family, hasn't it? But we'll all part when we reach Oregon."

"Oh, I know that day is coming. But it seems to me we've got unfinished business now, beyond finding Uncle David."

"Whatever are you talking about?"

Anne smiled. "This is as much about your future as it is about mine."

"Dear Anne, I'm sure we can build a future together, whatever happens."

"That's not the future I'm talking about."

"Then whatever *are* you talking about?"

"Why, you and Mr. Bentley of course."

The blood rushed to Elise's cheeks, and she put her hands to her face. "Oh dear."

"Yes," Anne said. "You care for him."

"You know me so well, I can't deny it. I suppose I do care, but that doesn't mean anything will ever come of it." Elise lowered her hands and stared piteously at Anne. "He's not at all what I imagined in a. . .in a husband."

"No, I expect not. Yet doesn't he embody everything a woman desires? Everything she needs in a man?"

Elise's embarrassment climbed even higher at Anne's intimate, wistful tone.

"Please, I. . ."

"What? You mean to say you don't think about it?"

"About what?"

"Marrying him of course."

"No. Yes. I mean, it's out of the question."

"That depends on what the question is."

They rode in silence for several minutes.

"Besides," Elise said, as though their conversation had not lapsed. "I wouldn't leave you now. Not when you need me so much."

"Thank you, my dear friend. But once this journey is over—when we've found Uncle David—though I love you, I shan't need you so much. If an opportunity arose. . ."

Elise shook her head. "Put that notion aside, my dear. Eb Bentley has shown no indication of such a possibility. He's an independent man. I've heard him mention his ranch in Oregon, and he wants to get back to it and stock it with cattle. He never intends to leave Oregon again."

"That doesn't mean he wouldn't take a wife to share that life with him."

"I have no hope of it. Just because a man treats you civilly doesn't mean he has matrimonial designs on you."

"Mr. Whistler has a wife, you know."

"I've heard him mention her."

"Yes, and he thinks his best friend would be much happier if he had one, too. He told me so." Anne drove along placidly, adjusting the reins when needed and calling to the mules now and then. Elise knit half a sock while her thoughts soared over the plains to Oregon.

CHAPTER 21

Eb rode slowly back to meet the wagon train. It was too hot to ask Pink to go any faster. He would switch his saddle over after eating and ride Speck this afternoon. He spotted the dust of the train long before he could see the lead wagons. They'd only made about four miles. He hated to suggest it to Rob, but if they took a long nooning, the animals would be fresher in the evening, when the sun headed down and the earth cooled.

Rob rode up to the head of the column to meet him.

"Everything quiet?" Eb asked.

"So far."

Eb turned Pink and rode alongside Rob, heading west again. It was the best way to let Rob catch him up on the train's progress that morning without being overheard by any of the others.

"You still planning to ride back to Schwartzburg when we stop?" Rob asked.

"I don't suppose it would do any good."

Rob turned in the saddle and looked back through the sea of dust, at the long line of wagons. "I don't like the idea of you going back."

"It'll only be four or five miles."

"I know. But you're likely to get in a tight spot if you go nosing around."

"Nah," Eb said. "There's another wagon train close behind us. Likely they'll reach Schwartzburg today. I can mingle with their people."

"Yes, but if Schwartz spots you, he'll figure something's up. I think you should stay clear of the place."

"All right, I won't go. But I'd still like to scout the trail behind us a ways."

"If you think it will help. We've an invitation to eat supper tonight with Miss Finster and Miss Stone if we've a mind to."

"I was thinking we ought to take a long nooning and move on in the evening. Let the stock rest while it's hottest and move out once the sun's mostly down."

Rob nodded. "I expect that would be a good plan today. I hoped we'd be farther from Schwartzburg when we stopped though."

"So did I." Eb looked ahead at the road he'd ridden that morning. "It's almost two miles to the spot where I thought we'd stop. Think they can go on that long?"

"Probably. Binchley's got an ox that's about done in. He really should have traded with Schwartz, but he said he didn't have enough cash."

Eb sighed. "We'll probably get some tough, stringy beef tomorrow."

"Yeah. Well, we may as well push on. You talking about that spot with the trees and grass down in the bottom?"

"That's the one."

"They'll make it that far. Especially if we tell everybody we'll take a long rest once we get there."

"All right. It's a good spot to water the livestock after folks draw the water they want to use."

"I remember it. Let's spread the word." Rob turned Bailey around but paused. "Shall I tell the ladies we'll eat supper with them?"

"Do you want to?" Eb asked.

"Of course. They're not the best cooks on the train, but the company can't be beat. And it'll give you a good chance to get better acquainted with Miss Finster's sterling qualities."

"Oh, you know so much about her?" Eb eyed his friend skeptically.

"I know it's time you got married again, and I haven't seen a prospect as pleasing for many a year."

"Get off that hobby horse, Rob."

"Not until you're married."

Rob urged Bailey into a trot. They rode back to the wagons, and

Rob told the first driver to stop when he got to the place Eb had described. Together they rode back along the lines, telling families to expect a long nooning. Most of the people expressed gratitude.

Eb smiled when he came in sight of the Englishwomen's wagon. Miss Stone sat straight as a flagpole on the seat, holding the lines like they were made of spun sugar. Miss Finster sat beside her, wearing a wide-brimmed straw hat with a cluster of pheasant feathers and knitting away lickety-split. They made a charming picture of both competence and domesticity—and beauty, though Eb wasn't much to comment on that, especially with Rob watching like a hawk for something to tease him about.

He rode up close and doffed his hat. "Long nooning today. We'll set out again when the sun's past its hottest."

"That sounds good, Mr. Bentley," Miss Stone called with a smile.

Miss Finster nodded. "Please God there'll be some shade where we stop."

"There's a few willows near the river, ma'am."

"Good. Will you and Mr. Whistler eat with us? If we're having a long rest stop, we'll prepare our big meal then, instead of in the evening."

Eb turned Pink around, so the horse moved along beside the wagon at the mules' pace. "That would be a pleasure, ma'am."

"We'll be pleased, Mr. Bentley," Miss Stone called over the clopping of hooves and the creaking of harness. She smiled so large Eb wondered if he'd made a mistake in accepting the invitation. Between Rob and Miss Stone, he felt like a rabbit with its neck in a snare.

Later, when they sat in the meager shade, it didn't seem like such a bad idea. The ladies served their plain dinner graciously, and Eb couldn't think of any other wagonside he'd rather eat at. The wagons were loosely circled, with the livestock in the middle as usual, but they constantly tried to stray out through the gaps. The ten men on guard spent as much energy keeping the livestock in as they did watching for intruders. Miss Finster had tied her clothesline in two passes at knee and waist height between her wagon and Abe

Leonard's, and Dan Adams had rigged a similar arrangement with his wagon, behind the ladies', so while they ate their dinner no oxen nosed out into their eating area.

Both ladies wore dresses that looked fine enough for a fancy funeral. They hadn't ever given in to the droopy bonnets most of the women wore out here, even when the wind blew strong across the prairie. That suited Eb just fine—he liked the way Miss Finster's elegant hats framed her face. And Miss Stone would look good in anything, with her youth and beauty. She looked healthy now, much healthier than she had in St. Louis. He was glad she was smiling again. Seeing her weep yesterday when she stood at the grave was hard—but her spirits seemed to have lifted.

The biscuits were a little tough, but Miss Finster had cooked the bacon to perfection, and Miss Stone had baked a cake of sorts. It was doughy and sweet, and chunks of tinned peaches hid in its depths.

"Miss Anne, I don't know if I've ever had anything that hit the spot like this," Rob said. He sat on the ground with his long legs stretched out before him and his back to their rear wagon wheel.

"It's tasty, all right," Eb said.

"Why, thank you, gentlemen," Miss Stone said. "I modified Mrs. Harkness's cobbler recipe. Elise thought we'd best use up most of our canned goods before we go much farther."

"They're heavy," Miss Finster said, and the two men nodded.

"Now's the time to use up anything you won't need later on," Rob said.

"Has Orrin thrown out that big cupboard yet?" Eb asked.

"Nope. Rebecca says she won't go to Oregon without it. I reckon she'll toss the schoolbooks first."

Miss Finster rose and took the coffeepot off the fire grate. "Gentlemen?"

"Thank you." Rob held out his cup. The ladies had four china cups with saucers, unlike the tin cups most of the people carried. They didn't seem to mind having cups that were a little heavier and a little more fragile.

She filled Rob's cup and came over to Eb. He held his out for her. Nice, how the handle didn't get hot when she poured the steaming brew into it.

He took a cautious sip. It was hot all right, but he also knew by now that Miss Finster's coffee was a bit hit-or-miss.

She looked anxiously from him to Rob. "Well? Have I poisoned you?"

"Mighty good," Rob said.

Eb had to agree. She'd hit it right. Either she was getting better at cooking on the trail or today was an exceptionally good random draw. He nodded at her.

"Well, good." She took the pot back to the fire and lifted a small, steaming kettle. "The tea water is hot, Anne."

Miss Stone got up and fussed around for a minute or two, measuring tea leaves into a round, pierced tea ball. The ladies carried a teapot. The first time Eb had seen it, he'd laughed aloud. Now he thought it was nice. They'd come a thousand miles and hadn't busted it. He guessed they'd proven their right to make tea the way they wanted it.

Miss Finster poured the pot of hot water into the teapot. "Too bad we haven't any milk." She glanced toward the wagon. "I guess I'd better fetch another bucket of water, or we won't be washing dishes."

"Let me get it for you." Eb set his cup and saucer on the ground and pushed himself to his feet.

"No need," Miss Finster said. "I wasn't hinting."

Still trying to prove her competence.

"I know." He looked her straight in the jay-blue eyes, something he'd avoided doing too often. "I'd like to get it for you."

She hesitated then handed over the wooden bucket. "If you've no objection, I'll bring the small pail and fill it, too."

Eb could have carried them both without breaking a sweat, but something kept him from protesting. He just nodded. His face felt like it was on fire.

"We shan't be five minutes, Anne," Miss Finster said.

"Take your time." Miss Stone poured a little of the tea from

231

the teapot into her cup and eyed it critically then set the pot down. "You'll keep a close eye on her, won't you, Mr. Bentley?"

"Aw, call me Eb. And yes, of course I will." It came out a bit gruffly, but Miss Stone's smile told him she forgave any shortness on his behalf. Rob just leaned back against the wagon wheel and sipped his coffee, not looking at him, but Eb suspected he was smirking behind that cup.

Next thing Eb knew, they were walking away from the wagon circle, toward the river. The cattle had stirred up the already muddy river at the most accessible place, but there was a path a little way upstream, and Eb led her there. Miss Finster peered up at him from under that outlandish hat. How did she keep it from crushing in the wagon, anyway?

"I thought Miss Anne looked happier today," he said.

"Yes. We talked this morning. She wants to go on. She and I both trust your instincts—yours and Mr. Whistler's."

"About Schwartz, you mean?"

"Yes. I've no doubt he lied to us. It was hard for Anne to leave, wondering if her uncle was really buried there, but she's decided to believe he's not and to trust God to see us through to the end of our journey."

"That's the right way to think."

"I believe Anne has handled this entire thing well." She smiled, and he thought again what a picture she made—a refined lady out here in the wilderness, keeping her dignity and her daintiness, but not afraid to pitch in and do the heavy work herself.

Eb paused where the path led down the riverbank. "I think you're a lot like Miss Anne yourself. And I daresay you've helped her along on her journey."

She gazed up into his eyes. "Thank you, Mr. Bentley."

Should he offer his hand to assist her down the few steep steps? "I don't suppose you could call me Eb?"

She glanced away, down at her bucket first and then toward the river. "Habits are difficult to break, but I shall try. My given name is Elise."

He shifted his bucket to the other hand and reached out to her. "May I help you down this spot in the path, Miss Elise?"

Her dainty fingers grasped his rough hand with a surprisingly strong grip.

On the way back to the campsite, Elise wondered how she'd gotten herself into this situation. She'd willingly agreed—no, if the truth be told, she had initiated—going on this walk to the river along a secluded path with a man she knew only superficially.

Even as she thought how improperly she was behaving, she knew that was silly. Rules from British high society did not apply here.

The quiet scout walking beside her carried both pails of water. He wouldn't give up the smaller one, though she'd protested. There came a point where she could see that his pride would be hurt if she persisted, and so she gave up.

Edwin Bentley—Eb—had become a bigger distraction than the snowcapped mountains looming before them or the vague fear that a band of wild Indians would suddenly appear over a ridge. She couldn't hold one rational thought in her head with him walking beside her.

"I expect we should let the livestock loose to graze," he said. "There's not enough grass in the wagon circle to last them long."

"We don't want to take any chances this close to Schwartzburg."

He nodded. "Probably I'm overly suspicious. I just can't help thinking Schwartz was up to something. And what you heard about them blaming the Indians. . .well, that can't be good."

"I didn't see many Indians around his place."

"There were a few in the trading post when I went in yesterday morning. Not many. They're mostly out hunting buffalo now, I reckon."

As Elise looked up at his resolute profile, she knew he would give his life to protect the people in the wagon train. Eb Bentley was a man she could trust, and one she could admire without regret.

"Anne asked me today if we were right to go on," she said.

Eb paused on the path and looked down at her. "What do you think?"

"I should hate to wait at Schwartzburg for a company heading east. But beyond that, yes. I think we should continue our search."

"So do I."

Her heart swelled. "Thank you. It helps to have a rational man support our decision. I admit I had second thoughts."

Eb studied her for a moment. "What will you do if you get to Oregon and don't find him?"

"I suppose we'll go home. Though Anne will be crushed."

"I suppose her family wants her back. They must be worried about the two of you."

Elise gave him a wry smile. "Her family is small—smaller than it used to be. Those remaining are not so doting as you might suppose."

"Her friends. . . ?"

"Yes. Well, you see, friends aren't always faithful. Anne has had a comedown in position since her father died. Her loss of fortune. . . I'm sure some of her friends truly care about her, but right now she is depending very much upon finding her uncle so that he can set things to rights for her. If that doesn't happen. . ."

"Does she have a plan?"

"Oh yes." Elise looked away from his direct stare. "The two of us will probably settle in a quiet corner of England and live out our lives together. I will gladly serve her, though she treats me more as a friend than a servant."

"I haven't seen any hoity-toity ways from her since I've known her."

"No. She isn't like that. We decided to act as friends on this trip, and it has become true. She is my dearest friend now. If God wills us to live humbly together as spinsters for the rest of our lives, I shall not be discontent. Though I can't imagine that for Anne. With her beauty and her gentle spirit, even though she'll have only a meager allowance, I would think some fair-minded man would fall in love with her."

"Yes, one would think so. In fact, I'd say several have."

Elise smiled. "Yes, the young men in our company adore her. Several are head over heels, but she tells me she hasn't found one she can love with all her heart, and so she keeps them at arm's length. She tries to treat them all equally, and I think she's done a good job."

Eb cleared his throat. "And yourself? You wouldn't consider marrying unless she was settled?"

Elise glanced at him sharply. His open expression brought a flush to her cheeks. "I must think of her first. It is my duty to her and to her parents. But if she should find the protection of a good man she can love, I suppose anything is possible. With God, I mean. . ."

"Oh yes," Eb said. "Anything at all."

"Even at my age."

He chuckled, and she realized she'd said the words aloud. Her already warm cheeks flamed.

"Forgive me, Mr. Bentley—Eb. That was a private thought gone renegade."

He looked as though he would speak, but footsteps approaching from the encampment stopped him. They both looked up the path. Mrs. Legity and her son-in-law, Josiah Redman, approached carrying water pails.

Eb gestured for her to precede him, and Elise resumed walking.

Mrs. Legity came even with them, and Elise stepped out of the path for her.

"Miss Finster," Mrs. Legity said in a high-pitched tone that bespoke rampant speculation.

"Hello," Elise said as cheerfully as possible. She smiled at Josiah, who nodded.

"Mr. Bentley." Mrs. Legity drew out his name.

"Ma'am."

After the two had passed, Elise looked over her shoulder at Eb. He winked at her. Elise whirled toward camp in confusion, certain that her beet-red face would confirm any rumors Mrs. Legity fancied to start.

They set out as the sun threw its last rays from behind the mountains onto the wisps of cloud above. The array of color filled Elise's heart with a yearning she didn't understand.

"We need to hurry," Anne called over Bumper's withers. "We're leading tonight."

Holding first place in the line of wagons was an honor not to be taken lightly. They'd only had the privilege twice so far, and Elise was determined to be ready when the moment came to form up. For once she wouldn't be staring over the mules' ears at the back of Abe Leonard's wagon. Instead she'd see the vast openness before them, and perhaps Rob's back, or even Eb's if he didn't ride off miles ahead to scout. That prospect spurred her on as she tugged at the harness straps.

A moment later Anne again called her to earth with a low cry of distress.

"What's the matter?" Elise asked.

"There's a buckle missing from Bumper's breeching."

"Is the strap broken?"

"No, I don't think so. How could this have happened?"

"All too easily, I'm afraid. I'll look around in the wagon."

"I'll check here in the grass. Perhaps we dropped it when we unhitched." Anne knelt and began to pat the trampled stalks near the mules' feet.

Elise fumbled about in the empty crate where they kept the harness during their stops. It was empty. For the first time, they were hitching all six mules to the wagon. Hector Adams had come while they were packing up and told them Rob said they would have a harder pull than they'd yet experienced, and to put their full teams in the lineup.

Anne came to the back of the wagon. "Find anything?"

"No. I may need to light the lantern."

"I'll do it."

"Do we have any extra buckles?" Elise stuck her hand into a crack between the crate and the dish box and willed her fingers to find the missing item.

"Shoe buckles," Anne said with a laugh.

Elise frowned. "Get ready to drive, and make sure we haven't left anything out that should be packed. I'll see what I can find."

Ten minutes later they took their place at the front of the line with Elise driving. "Go straight on," Rob told her. "There's not much of a moon, but there's plenty of starlight tonight, and the road should be clear and obvious for the first hour or two." She slapped the reins on Challenger's and Blackie's hindquarters. With Zee and Prince in the swing position, between the leaders and the wheelers, the elongated team seemed to stretch for miles before her in the eerie starshine.

Anne sat beside her, gazing ahead as they rumbled into the foothills and left the river below them.

"Too bad we have to waste this romantic moonlit ride."

Elise laughed. "It won't be wasted if it brings us closer to South Pass."

They rode along peacefully, with Rob checking in on them every thirty minutes or so and reporting that all was calm in their wake. The temperature had cooled significantly, and with the ever-present breeze, the evening made for comfortable traveling.

Two hours into their trek, a lone horseman rode toward them out of the west. The mules were leaning into their collars and straining a bit as they climbed toward the pass.

Anne nudged Elise with her elbow. "Here comes Eb. He'll ride up and put a finger to his hat brim and say, 'Ladies.'"

Elise laughed. "Probably."

"Nice to have a dependable man around, isn't it?"

Before she could answer, Eb trotted up on Speck and touched his hat. "Ladies."

"Good evening, Eb," Elise said, quite loudly in hopes of covering Anne's unladylike giggle. "How does the road look ahead?"

He swung Speck around and let him walk slowly beside the

wagon. "Smooth as glass—uphill glass, that is. No trouble from behind, I take it."

"We've heard nothing untoward."

"Good. We'll stop and rest in a little while. Then we'll continue on for a ways. You'll come eventually to a highland meadow that will make good grazing for the stock. It's about three miles ahead. But I'll see you again before then." He nodded and wheeled the spotted horse away.

"Three miles ahead," Anne said. "So—another three or four hours at ox pace?"

"Maybe more, with this incline." Elise had barely spoken when they heard a shout behind them—not the usual shout of an ox driver to his team or a parent to a child. "What was that?"

In the distance a series of loud bangs erupted, followed by more shouting. Anne grabbed Elise's arm. "Gunfire. Should we stop? We can't circle the wagons here on this uphill grade."

Elise's stomach clenched. "Maybe that's what they planned on. Waiting for us to get into an indefensible position."

"Keep going, then," Anne said. "We should keep on unless Rob or Eb tells us otherwise."

Elise slapped the wheelers with the lines. "Up! Chick, Bumper, move along!" The mules perked up their ears and stepped a little faster.

A closer voice reached them, from two or three wagon lengths behind.

"Any men who can, ride back to the herd."

"Should I hop down and run back to ask Dan what's happening?" Anne asked.

"No! Don't you dare leave me up here alone."

After what seemed forever, they heard hoofbeats coming up the line fast.

"Keep going," Rob's steady voice shouted. "Keep your teams moving along."

"Is there trouble back there?" Dan Adams called.

"A bit. Eb and some others went back to help. The best thing we

can do is keep everyone moving until we get to a spot where we can circle. We're vulnerable all strung out like this."

Elise kept driving, but for the first time she wished she wasn't leading tonight. Driving in first position in daylight as they rolled across the empty prairie was one thing, but her heart seemed to have climbed into her throat and taken residence there.

"How far?" she asked as Rob cantered up alongside her perch.

"I believe there's a more level spot up ahead—perhaps a quarter mile. I'll go on and see, but I won't go too far."

He rode forward, and Elise flicked the reins again. "Keep going, boys! It's not far now."

"Thank God we've got all six of our mules hitched tonight," Anne said.

"Yes, they can pull harder."

"And we won't lose our reserves."

Minutes later, Rob cantered back down the trail and reined in next to Elise. "It's not far. Keep going up there about as far as you can see now, and the trail will open out in a grassy area. Pull off to the left and start the circle as best you can. I'll ride down the line now, but if possible I'll get back up there to guide you."

CHAPTER 22

He's not an Indian." Eb stared at the prisoner in the moonlight. Will Strother and Josiah Redman stood by, guarding the young man while the rest of the drovers tried to calm the livestock and move them up the trail behind the wagon train.

"Wish we coulda got them all," Will said. "They shot Nicky."

"I saw him," Eb said. "It's not serious. Nick's mama will fix him up in no time." He deliberately made light of Nick's wound to soothe the boy. Bad enough the Foster boy had been grazed by one of the raiders' bullets. He didn't need the rest of the young men getting all hotheaded and eager to retaliate. "What we need to do is get the wagons to where they can circle and run the rest of the stock inside. Then we'll see how many head are missing and decide what to do about this."

"We should maybe go after them now," Josiah said.

Eb shook his head. "We're in their territory. They have the advantage in the dark. Our top goal is safety. Recovering a few head of livestock isn't worth losing one of our people."

"All right, so what do we do with him?" Josiah jerked his head toward the young man who sat on the ground with his wrists and ankles bound. He watched them closely as they talked.

Eb lifted his right foot and nudged the prisoner's foot with his boot. "Who are you?"

The young man just blinked up at him.

"When he talks, it ain't English," Josiah said.

Eb nodded. "Schwartz's nephew, I'm thinking." He hunkered down next to the prisoner. "I got a feeling you understand more English than you let on. But that's all right. I've got someone who can speak your lingo."

He stood and looked at Josiah. "Abe Leonard's got the last

wagon in line tonight. Walk this fella up there and tell Abe I want him tied up in the back of the wagon. Then one of you ride along behind and make sure he stays in it. Once we get the wagons circled again, I'll deal with him."

"Yes, sir," Will said.

Josiah nodded.

Eb mounted Speck and rode to where James Binchley was overseeing the herdsmen.

"How you doing, James?"

"Good, considering. They came out of nowhere, Eb. Guess we'd let the herd lag behind a little too far, and they figured they could run off some stock before the rest of you would get down to help us."

"Yeah, that's what I figured. I guess moving after dark wasn't such a bright idea."

"Seemed logical, with it so hot in the daytime."

Eb nodded, appreciative of the man's support. "Live and learn."

"At least we had a double guard on the herd tonight." Binchley gave a short bark of a laugh. "Some of the boys complained. But you expect that from boys. They won't question the orders from here on."

"Not for a while, anyway. I'm sorry Nick Foster got hurt."

"Yeah, that's too bad. He's young and tough though. It hit his arm, but I don't think it broke the bone."

"Nope, it didn't."

"He's a lucky young man," Binchley said. "And so are we all—I don't think we lost more than six or eight mules. No cattle."

"We'll take a count as soon as we get camped."

"Hey, Eb!" Elijah Woolman, the eighteen-year-old son of a farmer, rode up holding out what looked at first like a stick. "Look at what we found!"

Eb took it from Elijah and studied it. "It's a Lakota arrow. Where'd you get it?"

"Down in the flat yonder. We think the thieves were hiding there in the brush by the river and rode out as we passed by. Mr. Clark and I went to look around and see if we could learn anything, and we found this lying on the ground."

Eb stuck the arrow into his scabbard, alongside his rifle. "They planted it to make us think Indians attacked."

He rode forward, up the gradual slope. When he reached Abe's wagon, he found Josiah Redman riding behind with his rifle across the pommel of his saddle.

"Prisoner's quiet so far," Josiah called with a casual salute.

Eb went on up the line until he found Rob at the small meadow, directing the first wagons into formation. He rode over and halted Speck next to Bailey.

"Everything all right yonder?" Rob asked.

"As well as you could expect, maybe better."

"Just the one kid hit?"

"Yup. He'll be fine. Keep him off herd duty for a week or two though. You know they caught one of the raiders?"

"Heard it but didn't know if it was true."

"It is. We've got him tied in Leonard's wagon at the end of the line."

"What are you going to do with him?"

"Thought I'd ask Miss Finster to talk to him."

Rob jerked his head around. "Are you crazy?"

"No. It's a white man, but he speaks another language. I figure it's German. Schwartz's nephew, maybe. I never saw him at the trading post, but. . ."

"I did. I'll come with you after we get the circle formed."

Elise wiped her brow with her sleeve. Uncouth, she thought, but she didn't bother to look for a handkerchief. She and Anne worked as quickly as they could to take the harness off the six mules. Rob had instructed them to unhitch, as they would wait for daylight to move on. The immediate goal was to pen all the livestock inside the wagon circle and wait for morning, with every able-bodied man armed and on watch.

She finally released the wheelers into the circle as Abe Leonard's wagon pulled into the spot ahead of hers. To her surprise, two

mounted men rode just behind Abe's wagon. The rearguard of the train, she supposed.

She walked over to them and recognized Josiah Redman, Mrs. Legity's son-in-law, as the closer rider.

"Shall we tie up our clothesline to the wagon and unpack boxes and such to fill the gap, Mr. Redman?" she asked.

Redman hesitated and measured the distance between her wagon and Leonard's with his eye. "Tie the clothesline on your end and bring me the other. And you don't need to pile up your bundles. We'll keep a couple of men here all night."

"Oh." That was odd, but Elise did as he'd said. She wasn't averse to having a couple of armed men close to her station, but she wasn't sure she and Anne would want to put up the tent and crawl inside. An air of expectancy hovered over the temporary camp.

As she finished tying the end of the rope through the iron ring at the front of the wagon bed, Eb rode up. She could tell it was him, though the moon had gone behind the clouds, because Speck's white patches stood out clearly.

He dismounted and walked over to her. "Miss Elise, I wondered if you'd do us all a favor."

"I? What could I possibly do for the company?"

"Come speak to the prisoner and see if he understands German."

"Prisoner?" She stared at him.

Quickly Eb sketched out for her what had happened on the trail behind them while she drove her team up the slope to the meadow.

"Are you willing?" he asked.

"Yes, I suppose so. Will I have to get into Mr. Leonard's wagon with him?"

"I'll have the boys bring him out."

A few minutes later a young man bound with ropes sat on the tongue of her wagon. Elise and Anne stood together next to the wagon, clutching hands.

"I had no idea," Anne whispered. "While we were tending to the team, they had him in there, just a few feet away."

"Yes." Elise swallowed hard. Why hadn't she asked Eb to take him somewhere else, where Anne didn't have to see him? "Stay back, my dear. I'm sure they've disarmed him, but it wouldn't do to draw the attention of an unsavory character to you."

Eb came over to her. "Are you ready?"

"What shall I say to him?" Elise asked.

"Don't tell him your name or anything else about you and Miss Anne. I think he speaks English, or at least understands it some, but he doesn't want us to know that. Just see if you can tell if he understands your lingo. If he does, you can ask him if he's one of Schwartz's men and what they were up to." He extended his hand to her.

Elise tried to quell her trembling as she placed her hand in his. Eb drew her over to where the prisoner sat. The men had brought a lantern, and she could see his face clearly. But if he was bluffing about his linguistic skills, how could she make him betray himself?

"You are right," she said in clear German, looking toward Eb. "I think your decision to hang him is the correct one." She turned back to watch the prisoner's face. "He is definitely one of the thieves and worthy of execution. As soon as possible."

The young man's face blanched. He stirred as though he would leap up, but his bonds held him in place.

"*Nein, frau!* Nein!" In German, he blurted, "What have I done to you? You mustn't let them kill me!"

She glared at him fiercely. "If you want to be spared, you had better tell these men what you were doing and who was involved. They would just as soon hang you as not. And you can stop pretending that you don't speak English."

He shook his head and raised his tied hands. "Please, madam," he said in German, "my English is not good. If you will tell them—please—I did not want to do anything to them. It was not my fault, but they made me go with them."

"Who?" she asked. "Who made you do this?"

His whole body wilted and his chin drooped. "Herr Schwartz."

"Your uncle?"

His head snapped up. "He is not kin to me. He brought a couple

of us over to work for him, and he tells people we are his family, but it isn't true."

Elise glanced at Eb. He was watching her keenly. "He says Schwartz was behind it all, and he forced his workers to take part in the raid. This man claims he's not related to Schwartz and didn't want to do it."

"How long has he been with Schwartz?"

Elise asked the man.

"A little more than a year. He said he couldn't trust the Americans he had working for him before. He brought me and Franz over last year. He paid our passage and said we could work it off in six months. But he doesn't treat us well. I've been saving my pay so that I can leave him and strike out on my own, but it's hard. He pays us next to nothing."

Elise relayed this information, and Eb directed her to ask what Schwartz would do with the livestock he had stolen.

When she did, the man replied, "He has a place to hide them for a while—a canyon in the rocks. He takes them feed. And after a while he will bring them out a few at a time and sell them."

"Can you show our men where it is?" Elise asked.

"No! He would certainly kill me."

Elise laughed and said harshly, "You care now who kills you? All right, it's your choice. I will tell these men to go ahead and do it."

"What's he saying?" Eb asked.

"He will tell you where Schwartz hides livestock he has stolen."

Eb gazed at Elise with new admiration. "I don't know what you told him, but thank you."

"Only that you would hang him at once if he didn't cooperate."

Eb suppressed a smile. "At dawn we'll take the wagons on to the place I originally planned for us to camp. There's better grazing and access to the river. Then we'll leave a dozen men with the camp. The rest of us will ride back to the trading post and settle things with Schwartz."

"What will you do with this man?" Elise asked.

"I don't know yet. Ask him where the hiding place is, please."

Elise turned back to the prisoner and spoke to him in German. Eb tried to pick out a word or two, but he couldn't. The young man seemed to understand perfectly, however. He grimaced and rattled off a lengthy explanation, during which Elise nodded periodically.

"*Danke,*" she said at last. She turned and took Eb's arm, leading him a short distance away.

"I'm sure he understands you, so be careful what you say in front of him. Tell your guards as well."

"All right."

"He says the animals will be in a canyon—a sort of ravine or steep valley, I take it, up Willow Creek."

"How far?"

"About two miles. The way is rocky at first, which hides their hoofprints. A large rock juts out over the water. If you go behind this rock, you should be able to locate the trail easily."

"We'll find it." Eb realized she still held on to his arm lightly. He dared to pat her fingers for a moment. "You've done well, ma'am. Danke."

She smiled and squeezed his arm just a little. "You're welcome. Need I remind you to be careful, whatever you do? Herr Schwartz is a rogue."

"That and a few other things." Reluctantly, Eb released her hand and walked over to Josiah. "Put him back in Leonard's wagon and tie him down. Keep at least two men guarding him all night."

He walked around the outside of the circle. Rob was helping Orrin Harkness and his boys close the gaps between the wagons in the barricade.

"We'll only stop here until sunup," Eb said.

"Yes, but we don't want to make it easy for them to start a stampede if they come back." Rob lifted his hat and wiped his brow. "What's going on in your head, Eb?"

"We take most of the men at daybreak and ride back to Schwartzburg. The prisoner says Schwartz forced his employees to

steal for him. Not sure I believe him about the coercion, but we need to meet him with a show of force and be ready for resistance."

"Spoken like an old soldier."

"Watch who you're calling old."

Rob smiled. "All right, you'll be in charge."

"I think you should stay here with the company," Eb said.

"Why?"

"If things don't go well, they'll need you."

Rob squinted at him in the near darkness. "How many men do you think Schwartz has?"

"Not that many, but he's foxy."

Wilbur, his father, and his younger brother Ben came over to stand beside them. "We going down and teach that trader a lesson?" Wilbur asked.

"Not until we move the wagons to a better place at daylight," Eb said. "Then we'll split up the men. Leave a dozen here. The rest will go with me."

"As near as we can tell, they only got about eight mules at the most," Orrin said.

"They would have gotten more if our men hadn't been on the lookout for them," Wilbur added.

"Well, eight is too many," Rob said. "But they're not worth killing over."

"I don't intend to kill anyone unless it's necessary." Eb gazed levelly into his eyes. "We'll be fine, Rob. I won't shame you."

"It's not you I'm worried about. Some of these young fellas are mad as sin."

When Elise awoke, the sun was beating mercilessly on the tent and the interior felt uncomfortably warm. She stirred to lift the tent flap a bit, hoping for a breeze off the river. Drumming hoofbeats grew louder. She listened for a moment. Shouts of exultation greeted the riders.

"Anne! Wake up, dear."

Anne stirred and blinked at her. Perspiration stood in beads on her forehead.

"The men are back," Elise said.

"Help me with my corset—quickly!"

A few minutes later, they crawled out of the tent and brushed their skirts down. The travelers had gathered near the Harkness wagons, so Elise and Anne made their way around the circle to stand on the fringe of the crowd. Eb stood on a crate between two of the wagons.

"Mr. Harkness has volunteered his smallest wagon for use as a temporary jail," Eb was saying to the listeners.

Elise peered around and spotted a group of men standing a ways off, holding four men at gunpoint. Among them was Schwartz.

"We'll keep the prisoners in there until we get to the next place that has some legal authorities," Eb said.

"Whyn't we send them back to Fort Laramie and be rid of them?" asked Mr. Libby.

"I'll let Mr. Whistler answer that."

Eb hopped down from the crate, and Rob climbed up to take his place. "If we sent off a detachment of our men to deliver these prisoners, we'd have to send quite a few, just to make sure our men were safe and couldn't be overpowered. That in turn would weaken our force with the wagons. I don't know about you, but with the rugged terrain ahead of us, not to mention possible trouble with the Indians north of here along the Snake, I don't like the idea of having fewer men where the women and children are."

"How long would it take 'em to ride back to Laramie?" Hector Adams called.

"Well, they'd need to take the wagon, unless you want to put the prisoners on horses, and that, to my way of thinking, is asking for trouble." Rob shook his head. "I think the safest way is to take them along with us."

"Did you recover all our livestock?" Mr. Binchley asked.

"I'm happy to say our delegation did that. However, they also found a few oxen and a couple of horses that didn't belong to our

company in the canyon. And of course, back at Schwartz's trading post, there was quite a bit of stock in his pens. We can't just leave all those animals with no one to care for them."

"So what are we going to do?" Abe asked.

"I'd buy one of the oxen," Binchley said.

"Who would you pay?" asked Nick Foster's father, James.

"You should just take it," Wilbur said. "They stole from us. That's restitution."

"Now, folks, let's not let go of our morals and common sense." Rob looked out over their heads. "Eb, can you speak to this issue, please?"

Rob got down, and Eb climbed back up on the box.

"We figure we'll release the first man we captured and leave him in charge of the trading post."

"But he's a thief," James Foster shouted.

Eb raised both hands. "Folks, hear me out. There are other wagon trains behind ours. One of them is camped two miles east of Schwartzburg. Their scout came to the trading post this morning while we were there. We told him what was going on and that we'd have someone there by noon to open the store for his people. He gave his word that they'd do things in an orderly manner. Now, that's a good thing. They could take advantage of this situation. But we're not that kind of people, and neither are they."

A murmur ran through the gathering, and Elise shivered.

"Hear me out," Eb said. Although he didn't shout, people quieted to listen. "The young man we caught last night is as close as we've got to an honest man from Schwartzburg. I believe that if we go with him today and open the store, he'll behave himself. Mr. Whistler will get behind the counter with him, and he'll sell goods and livestock to all of you at fair prices. I'm talking fair—enough to allow that young man to restock the trading post after we leave. We're not going to steal from him. And then the folks in the next wagon train can come in and buy from him."

"That sounds all right to me," Dan Adams called.

Eb nodded in his direction. "Thanks, Dan. Folks, as near as

I know, we're all Christian people. We don't want to turn around and steal from anyone. We'll see that Schwartz and the other three men who stood against us this morning are turned over to a marshal or an army officer, and we'll leave the young man who's in Abe Leonard's wagon to run the post. Rob and I will write out statements for him to keep by him in case the law wants proof later that he has a right to be there. And we'll also give statements when we turn the prisoners over, telling exactly what happened and how that one fellow helped us get back our own livestock."

He stood still for a moment while the people absorbed what he'd said.

"All right. Let's get the prisoners accommodated, and then anyone who wants to trade can ride back with us. Mr. Harkness won't be able to haul folks in his farm wagon like he's done before, so you'll have to ride or take another wagon, but I reckon we can get our business done by noon and leave Schwartzburg to the next company of emigrants. We'll get on our way this afternoon and push on into the evening."

He jumped to the ground before anyone could raise more questions.

Anne grabbed Elise's arm. "I'm going to see if I can use Mrs. Libby's saddle on Chick."

"You want to go back to Schwartzburg?"

"Yes! I'm going to get a few of those eggs if I have to raid the henhouse myself. I'll ask Eb how much it would be fair to pay for them."

She hurried away.

"Do you want to go back and trade?"

She whirled to find Eb at her elbow. "Oh, no thank you."

"This may be your last opportunity before we get to Oregon. It's chancy along the Snake these days."

Elise smiled. "Take Anne. She wants an egg or two. Since we're going to stay here several more hours, I think I'll do some baking."

"All right. We found Rob's horse in the canyon, you know."

She stared at him. "You mean. . ."

250

"Yes. The one Costigan stole."

"Thomas wasn't with them, was he?"

"No. I asked Schwartz, but he won't talk to me."

She thought about their options. "I'd like to know where he is."

"Me, too," Eb said. "Always better to know where your adversary is."

"I could ask the young man before you release him."

He nodded. "I was going to see if you'd talk to him anyway, so we'd be sure he understood what we're going to do. I want him to realize we're putting him in a position of trust. We'll give him papers, like I said, in case the law comes out here. But he'll be alone for a while. It could be dangerous for him. Indians or some other no-good like Schwartz could come and try to take over."

"He may not want to stay here alone."

"That's true. If he wants to go with us, he can, but that would mean abandoning the post and taking the extra stock with us. Still, I want him to know what he's up against if he stays. Maybe he can get someone to help him before too long. I just can't think of a better plan."

Neither could she.

"Eb, have you thought any more about digging up that grave?"

He hesitated. "I'll ask Miss Anne if she wants us to."

"Thank you."

Eb rode out to the cemetery with Hector Adams. He'd left Rob in the store with the young German man, who Elise had learned was named Georg Heinz.

"You think that young fella will be all right here?" Hector dismounted and unstrapped a shovel from his saddle.

"There'll be enough traffic along the trail for the next couple of months that he should be," Eb said. "If someone who wants a job comes by, he'll make out."

"If that someone is honest."

"Right." Eb let Speck's reins fall and reached for his own

shovel. "Let's get this done. I don't want to hold up the train, and I don't want to keep Miss Anne wondering any longer than needed." He looked back toward the buildings. "I was afraid she was going to insist on watching."

"Dan will take care of her while we do it. He'll make sure she stays up yonder."

Eb strode to the board cross marked DAVID STONE. He looked at it for a long moment. Hector gave a long sigh and removed his hat.

Eb took his hat off, too, and looked skyward. "Lord, we mean no disrespect. I'm asking that You let us know for sure if this grave belongs to Mr. Stone."

After a moment's silence, Hector said, "Amen."

Eb grasped the crossbar of the grave marker and pulled it from the ground. He laid it aside in the grass. Hector put the blade of his shovel to the earth and stepped down on it hard.

CHAPTER 23

Elise carried the two plates carefully, mindful of her calico skirt swirling in the wind. At least it wasn't so hot up here on the mountainside.

"What've you got there, Miss Finster?" called Charles Woolman, who had drawn one of the first watches over the prison wagon.

"Dinner for the prisoners. I've got two plates here, and I'll bring two more."

The second guard, Landon Clark, lowered his gun from his shoulder and walked toward her. "What are you giving them?"

"Mr. Whistler didn't say nothing about feeding them," Woolman said.

"It's very plain food. Just beans, cornbread, and a few dried apple slices."

"That's better'n what I'll likely get," Clark said.

Elise frowned at them. "You have to feed them. I wasn't sure the men had thought about it before they rode off, so I decided to provide their dinner today. Someone else can contribute at suppertime."

Woolman shook his head. "I'm not sure we can let you give that to 'em, Miss Finster."

"Why ever not? You've got to treat them humanely. We can't haul them all the way to Fort Dalles or someplace in between and hand them over malnourished."

Clark shrugged. "Don't see why not. They stole from us, and they'd have killed any one of us they had a chance to kill. They shot the Foster boy, you know."

Elise winced. "Yes, I know."

"I think we should hold off until the captain gets back." Woolman looked at Clark, and his companion nodded.

Elise hovered between tearing into them and retreating meekly. A shout from the other side of the camp drew her gaze.

Rebecca Harkness waved toward the trail. "They're coming back."

Elise hurried to her fireside and set down the two plates. She gathered her skirts and hurried to where Rebecca and several others had gathered to meet those returning from the trading post.

Anne rode in on Chick at Dan Adams's side. Elise waved, and they veered toward her.

Dan hopped to the ground, but before he could reach Chick's side, Anne had slid off the saddle, carefully balancing a small basket.

"Elise! It's not him."

"Not David?"

"No. It's someone else," Anne said.

Elise folded her into her embrace. Dan caught Chick's reins as Anne let go of them.

"I'll take care of the mule," he said.

Elise drew Anne toward their wagon. "Where are Rob and Eb?"

"They're talking to the leaders from the next train. They said there's at least two more companies behind them. Rob told that young German fellow to be polite and treat them fairly. He seemed to understand. Oh, and Rob made out a price list for him to use while he trades." Anne laughed. "You should have seen him, wearing an apron and measuring out groceries."

"Rob Whistler is a good man," Elise said.

"Yes, he is. He saved out half a dozen eggs for me. I paid a dollar for the lot." Anne held out her basket.

"How delightful! We can make a cake next time we stop if you'd like."

"Or feed them at breakfast time to the men who've helped us so much."

"Whatever you wish, my dear."

Anne's face sobered. "And Eb and Hector dug up the cemetery plot."

"What did they find?"

"They wouldn't tell me, but Eb says he's positive it's not Uncle David." Anne drew in a deep breath. "So. We're going onward, as we planned."

Elise squeezed her shoulders. "We'll trust God to bring us to David in Oregon."

Anne nodded and glanced about. "Oh, you have dinner ready."

Elise grimaced. "I made those plates for two of the prisoners."

"That was kind of you."

"The guards wouldn't let me give it to them."

"What? That's awful." Anne glowered toward the prison wagon. It was drawn apart from the circle, and the two guards stood talking near the tailboard. "Well, when Rob gets back, you take it up with him."

"I shall. I suppose you and I might as well eat in the meantime."

Elise fed Dan Adams, too. Afterward he hovered about Anne so closely as she washed the dishes that Elise decided he would soon wear out his welcome. She handed him a bucket and asked him to bring more water. Finally the wagon master rode up with Eb and Hector.

After a quick consultation with the guards, Rob came to Elise's fireside.

"I understand you're willing to feed the four prisoners."

"Yes, if Mr. Woolman and Mr. Clark will let me."

"That's good of you. Of course we have to meet the prisoners' basic needs until we turn them over to the law." Rob noticed Dan approaching with the water. "Dan, will you give me a hand, please? We'll get some of this food over to the prisoners."

Quickly Elise filled the plates she had. "We only have three," she explained. "I can borrow another, or they can take turns eating."

"I'll get you another one," Dan said.

He hurried off to his wagon and returned a moment later with a tin plate. Elise loaded on the beans and apples, and she added an extra slice of cornbread to each plate, partly out of spite to the two unsympathetic guards.

"I'll ask another family to pitch in tonight," Rob said. He and

Dan took the meals to the prison wagon.

As Elise began to wipe out the pans, Eb strolled over.

"Good day, Mr. Bentley," she said.

He eyed her for a moment, and she couldn't decipher the odd look on his face. At last he pushed back his hat and said, "Good day, *Miss Elise*."

Her cheeks grew warm. So that was it. She busied herself with rinsing out the bean pot. "Eb. I understand things went in Anne's favor at the cemetery."

"Yes. We've eliminated the possibility that her uncle is buried in that grave."

"Do I want to know how you are so certain?"

He hesitated. "Probably not."

"She said it was someone else." Elise glanced up at him. "So the grave wasn't empty?"

"Oh, it had an occupant, all right. But unless Mr. Stone was . . .shall we say, of unusually small stature. . .then it most certainly wasn't him."

"A child," Elise whispered, staring down at her hands.

"That or a small woman. The bits of clothing contribute to the evidence that the unfortunate soul was female."

She nodded. "Mr. Stone was as tall as yourself, sir. A well-proportioned man."

"You knew him well?" Eb asked.

Again she flushed. "Yes. As well as one might when working in his brother's home. I saw him frequently before he left England." She turned away and carried the pot to her dish crate.

Eb followed her. "I'm sorry we had to go through this, but it seemed to relieve Miss Anne's mind."

"It must have been a chilling experience for you and Hector. Thank you for doing it."

Eb nodded. "Elise. . ."

"Yes?" She wiped her hands on her apron and looked up at him.

He didn't say anything for a long moment. They stood looking at each other, and though she couldn't fathom why, she felt her

heart was near breaking.

"You think young Heinz will be all right?" she said at last, to break the silence.

"Yes, I do." Eb shifted and looked away. "Rob said there was a family in the next wagon train who'd been sick and were worn out. They wanted to rest for a while. Their captain suggested the man might work with Heinz for a while, to pay for their keep while they stay there, and they could move on with a later company when they were ready."

"That makes me feel a little better." She glanced toward the fire. "I've a bit of cornbread left. I'm afraid I gave away all the beans. I ought to have kept some over for you and Rob."

"No matter. I'll find something."

"And you've no more word on Thomas Costigan?"

"No. He's gone on, I'm guessing. We may hear of him farther along the trail. I'm glad Rob got his spare horse back. Binchley got a stout pair of oxen, too. We're in pretty good shape now, I think."

Elise pried the last pieces of cornbread from the pan. "Here. If you take this, it will save me putting it away."

"Much obliged."

He ambled away, chewing the meager offering. Elise hoped some other woman would take pity on him and give him something more substantial to eat.

He was back a half hour later, when Rob had blown the horn and passed the word to hitch up the teams.

"Can I help you ladies?"

"Thank you, but we're just about ready," Elise told him. She ran her hand over Zee's flanks as she visually checked all the straps and buckles on the near side of his harness.

"What's that?" Eb asked.

"Hmm?" She looked where he was pointing.

"That sparkly buckle."

Elise chuckled. As usual, he'd found her out, but this time she felt no embarrassment. "That, sir, is a buckle off a bejeweled evening purse. We were lacking one buckle when we needed to harness all six of our mules, and I found that amongst our things."

Eb shook his head. "I don't know how you do it—you and Miss Anne both. You seem to go at everything sideways, but it works." He bent over and peered more closely at the buckle.

"They're not real jewels, if that's what you're wondering."

"It did enter my mind. If I'd have known, I could have brought you a buckle from the trading post."

"Yes, or Anne could have, if she'd thought of it. Don't you worry, Eb. We'll get by."

He straightened and smiled at her. "Yes, I reckon you will."

Eb rode Pink ahead of the wagon company as far as South Pass. Their train had made good time since Schwartzburg, and none of the other groups had caught up to them. One band of freighters had passed them, and he'd seen a couple of Indians from a distance, but the trail seemed quiet compared to last year.

He sat for a while on his horse, scanning the western horizon. If only he were heading home to Jeanie.

He lifted his gaze to the cloudless sky. Up here, the breeze was cool. Tonight they'd need their wool blankets, even in mid-July.

Rob would need him today to encourage more folks to lighten their wagons, so he turned eastward. This slope was not the steepest they would encounter, but the long, steady climb would take its toll on the livestock. So far Elise and Anne's team seemed to be holding up well. Most of their heavy supply of feed was gone now, but the extra rations they'd used had stood them in good stead.

Odd how his thoughts could leap so quickly from Jeanie to Elise.

"Elise." He said the musical name aloud. He no longer felt guilty. That had to be good. Rob would think so.

He met Rob at the head of the company. So far they'd lost two wagons. One family had turned back early in the trek, and another had broken an axle beyond repair. The owners had no spare, so now the young couple rode muleback, with what little gear they'd kept on

their other two mules. They'd get to Oregon with a few threadbare clothes and little besides, but they were sturdy and hopeful. They'd make it.

Rob's first words confirmed Eb's feelings about the weight of some of the wagons.

"I've been working on the Harkness family, but Rebecca's stubborn. She won't give up the furniture. And now that their third wagon is hauling the prisoners, their tools are in the family wagons, too."

"They may want to take back their loan of the wagon," Eb said.

"I'm afraid they might."

"Well, we can make the prisoners walk more."

"I suppose it's fitting. I don't want to lose them, is all." Rob sighed and looked ahead. "How's the trail look?"

"Same as always at the pass. Not much traffic. There's nobody else at the camp spot."

"Good." Rob looked behind him. "There's a gap behind Binchley's wagon. Guess we'd better go see what's holding up the Fosters."

Most of the day, Rob persuaded folks to be reasonable while Eb and the Adams brothers helped unload heavy items. They sent the drovers with the herd of loose stock on ahead, to give the animals more time to graze. By sunset, all forty-eight wagons had topped the pass, albeit some with reluctant owners.

Eb followed the last wagon—Landon Clark's—over the almost imperceptible summit of the pass and found Elise standing alone at one side of the broad trail, gazing west.

Eb rode Pink up beside her and dismounted. "Long thoughts?"

"Yes. As long as the shadows. This is the watershed, isn't it?"

"Yes, ma'am. They call it the Great Divide. All the rivers from here on flow west."

She turned and looked back, but they were past the top, and you couldn't see far. She gave a great sigh and faced west again.

"Miss Anne must be driving."

"Yes. I told her I wanted to walk for a while."

"Don't blame you, but you don't want to linger back here alone. There's bears and cougars in these parts." He didn't mention that there might be two-legged vermin as well.

Elise began to walk slowly downhill. "I've been thinking about Rob Whistler's horse."

"Oh? Bailey's a good mount."

"Not Bailey," she said. "The other one."

"I see." And he should have. She was a thinker, and no doubt she'd been turning over the implications in her mind since he told her they'd found Rob's stolen horse.

"It was Thomas Costigan who told Schwartz about David Stone."

"That seems likely." He walked along beside her, leading Pink.

"He traded his horse at Schwartzburg."

"I expect he's gone on ahead of us now," Eb said.

She nodded. "Georg Heinz barely remembered his visit, but that's what he thought happened. I believed Georg when he said he didn't know anything about Mr. Stone though."

Eb considered that. He had only what Elise told him to go on so far as what the young German man had said.

"But for some reason," she continued, "Thomas thought it would be to his advantage to tell the trader about the Stone family. He either prepared that cross or had Schwartz do it."

They walked on for a minute, with only Pink's steps and the distant rumbling, creaking, and shouting from the wagon train breaking the silence.

"Has to be some money in it for him," Eb said at last. "Can't see it any other way."

"Yes. That means either he hopes to find David and get some money out of him—which doesn't make a lot of sense to me, since David hasn't claimed the estate of Stoneford yet—or someone else is paying him."

"Can't argue with you there."

"I think he hoped we'd give up and go back to England."

"Yes. But he went on."

"That troubles me," Elise said. "I must tell Anne."

"She may have thought it out."

Elise nodded. "She might have. She's an intelligent girl. I worry about her running headlong into something she doesn't understand."

"Like someone wanting to take advantage of her uncle?"

"Perhaps. I wish I knew."

"Elise." He stopped walking. Pink stopped, then Elise.

She turned to face him. "Yes?"

"If there's anything I can do to help you. . .you or Miss Anne. . . well, you can count on me. You know that, don't you?"

She smiled a bit sadly, and he thought it was a pity she had to know sadness and unease out here. She reached up hesitantly and touched his cheek. Warmth flowed through him. In that second, he wished he could find Thomas G. Costigan and thrash him—and set the world to rights for Elise.

"Yes, Eb," she said. "I know."

CHAPTER 24

Elise wandered farther from the wagons while Anne drove. Even buffalo chips were scarce now. Finding fuel grew harder each day. She could see wooded hills in the distance, but they were too far away to do her any good.

Lavinia walked toward her, pushing her chip barrow. Abby trailed her sister's steps.

"Find anything?" Lavinia called.

"No. Did you?"

"Just a little dried dung, but it's not buffalo. Ma won't be happy."

"Ma's never happy since she had to leave Great-Grandmother's cupboard," Abby said.

"I'm sorry." Elise had already expressed her sympathy to Rebecca, but the girls seemed to need a little extra encouragement. "It must have been hard for your mother to part with so many things that held memories for her."

"I know you're right." Lavinia fell into step with her.

Elise headed back toward the line of wagons on a diagonal course, watching the ground as she walked. The bunch grass was heading up, and it was hard to spot much that was useful down between the stalks.

"Maybe we'll have a cold dinner tonight." She gave the girls a rueful smile and patted her empty chip sack.

"And tomorrow night." Abby kicked at a tuft of milkweed. "We're running out of stuff we can eat without cooking it though."

"Ma says if we can get her enough fuel, she'll make a big batch of beans tonight, and biscuits, too," Lavinia said. "Enough to last three or four days. Of course, we'd have to give some of it to the prisoners."

"Wish we had some meat," Abby said.

"I believe some of the men went hunting." Elise determined to steer the conversation away from the prisoners. The Harkness family had given the most by providing the wagon. They also took a rotation for providing the men's meals. How deeply did Rebecca and the rest of the large family resent that? Eb had told Elise that they couldn't haul their heavy furniture over the Blue Mountains and the Cascades anyway, but the Harkness clan might not see it that way. "Didn't your brothers go off with Mr. Bentley this morning?"

"Yes," Lavinia said. "Wilbur and Ben both went. Pa wanted to go, but we needed him to drive."

As they neared the file of wagons, they came abreast of a small group of women who were walking together.

"Hello, ladies," Elise called. "Are you finding anything to burn?"

"Precious little," Agnes Legity said, "and it's our turn to feed the thieves."

"They should have hung 'em all back at Schwartzburg," Mrs. Strother said. "I told Mr. Whistler we have barely enough to get us through to Oregon without giving any of our food to those rascals."

Elise turned to Lavinia and touched her arm. "Let's take what you have to your mother, shall we?"

Lavinia and Abby seemed happy to leave the other women. Elise saw them to their family's place in line. Rebecca was walking near the wagon her husband drove, with one of the young children on each side of her. She shook her head when Lavinia showed her their meager findings.

"I don't know what's to do for fuel."

"Maybe we can twist up dry grass," Abby said. "I heard Ben say some people are trying to make little logs out of dried-up grass."

Rebecca frowned. "Wouldn't burn long. We'll see if the boys find anything. I told 'em when they rode out this morning to bring me anything that looks combustible."

Late in the afternoon after they'd formed their circle and released the teams, the hunters returned. Word spread quickly that they had killed two antelope. The animals weren't very large but would provide a taste for any families who wanted it.

"Perhaps we could get a soup bone," Anne said. "With rice and a bit of that dried corn, it would make a passable stew."

"We can ask," Elise said. The meat wouldn't stretch far among the company, and she knew several families were reaching the end of their supplies. Dan Adams had confided to Anne that he and Hector were down to beans and cornmeal. If they had no fire to cook it on, they'd go hungry.

Eb came by half an hour later carrying a haunch of fresh meat.

"Miss Anne, can I slice off a steak for you ladies?"

Anne, who would have cringed at the sight four months ago, fairly drooled over the raw meat. "That would be wonderful!"

"You're too generous," Elise said. "So many are hungrier than we are!"

Anne frowned. "She's right, and to be honest, we've nothing to cook it with."

"Tell you what. I'll give you a slice now, along with a few sticks I picked up this afternoon. Cook your supper and heat a kettle of water. After we're done with the butchering and rationing, I'll bring you some meaty bones you can stew. You can let it simmer over what's left of your fire. I believe you're in line to feed the prisoners tomorrow."

"That sounds good, but shouldn't you and the other hunters get a good share of the meat first?"

"Don't you worry about us. The Harkness family's got a whole quarter, and I left a good portion with Rob for him and me. Say—" He stopped as though a new idea had hit him. "What if we bring it over, and we have one cook fire tonight? If you'll cook for Rob and me, that'd give you extra wood for the stewing."

Anne grinned. "And maybe we could do a batch of biscuits. Sounds like a good bargain to me!"

"I can't say no," Elise said. "But, Eb, don't put it about that I'm making stew for the prisoners."

"Oh? I thought other ladies would be glad to hear you were doing it."

"Some of them resent those men eating at all." She told him of

the murmuring she'd heard earlier. "If their husbands feel the same way. . ."

Eb nodded. "It could get ugly. Guess I'll suggest to Rob that we double the guard on the prisoners tonight."

"Mr. Bentley. Eb."

Something nudged Eb's leg, and he sat up, reaching for his pistol.

"It's me, Eb."

"Miss Anne?" He squinted at her in the shadows. The camp was quiet but for the restless movement of the animals inside the wagon corral.

"Elise told me to get you. Some of the men are planning to attack the prison wagon."

Eb threw off his blanket and grabbed his left boot. "How do you know this?"

"We were baking extra johnnycake and Elise wanted to get more water."

"This late?" He frowned up at her as he tugged on the boot.

"Yes. We wanted plenty, and the coals were still hot. We might not have another chance to bake for days. Elise was going to see if any of the Harkness men would escort us to the creek. She overheard Mr. Foster and some of the others talking about rushing the wagon and—and getting the prisoners out. They want to kill them."

Eb pulled on the other boot and picked up his gun belt as he stood. "Where's Elise?"

"She went out to the prison wagon to tell the guards."

Eb gritted his teeth. Rob was out there with three other men that they'd judged could be trusted. What if one or more of them was in on this plot? He quickly ticked them off in his mind. Abe, Wilbur, and Dan. Shouldn't be any trouble there.

"Go back to your wagon and stay there," he said to Anne.

"What about Elise?"

"If she's still at the prison wagon, I'll make sure she gets back safely."

Anne lingered as he strapped on his holster and stooped to get his rifle. "You care about her, don't you, Eb?"

He jerked his chin up and eyed her cautiously. "I suppose I do."

"I suppose you more than suppose."

Eb grunted. "I'll take care of her."

Anne headed off toward the orange embers of her cook fire, and he strode toward the prison wagon. From twenty yards away he saw a wispy, pale figure to one side of the white-shrouded wagon. A few more steps and he could see that it was Elise, in a light-colored dress, talking to someone.

"Who's there?" Rob's shout didn't slow Eb down.

"It's me."

Abe Leonard stood beside Rob and Elise, with a long gun resting on his shoulder.

"We may have trouble," Rob said quietly. He was wearing his holstered pistol, and Eb was glad. Rob usually left it in his saddlebag.

"Miss Anne told me." Eb nodded at Elise. "You'd best get back to your camp, ma'am. May I escort you?"

Before Elise could answer, the tramp of many boots approaching reached them.

"Who's there?" Rob called.

"Charles Woolman."

Eb seized Elise's arm and drew her behind him.

Woolman and six other men walked over and stopped a few feet in front of Rob. Eb glanced around and saw Wilbur Harkness, one of the other guards on duty, peering around the edge of the prison wagon. Dan Adams must be somewhere nearby, too. Eb wanted to think Dan, Wilbur, and Abe would stand with him and Rob no matter what, but how could a man know for certain?

"What do you fellows want?" Rob asked.

"Thought we'd relieve the guard," Woolman said affably, but the tension in his companions' posture belied his tone. Eb shifted his rifle to his left hand and rested his right on the butt of his pistol.

"We've only been on duty an hour," Rob said.

Charles Woolman smiled. "We thought we'd lighten your duties some."

"I don't think so."

The smile disappeared. "Come on, Whistler," Woolman said. "You know those men will all hang if we get them to where there's law. All we aim to do is speed up the process and relieve the burden they're placing on this company."

"Forget it," Rob said.

"They're eating our food," James Foster said.

Eb looked over the small company of men. "Elijah, James, are you sure you want to be in on this? Josiah, I'm really surprised to see you here."

Josiah Redman's head drooped. "It's not my idea, Eb. But they've got a point."

"Oh, come on," Eb said. "Did your mother-in-law send you over here?"

Josiah glared at him.

Rob held up a hand. "All right, boys, just calm down. Charles, there's not going to be any violence done to these prisoners. You hear me?"

Woolman didn't answer but held Rob's stare in the starlight.

Dan Adams's deep voice came from behind Eb. "We've got five guns against you men, and all of them ready to fire. I suggest you go back to your wagons."

Eb wondered if Woolman or any of his friends had seen Elise. He didn't let his gaze waver from the group before him, but he wished he'd given her his pistol. Maybe Dan had pulled her back behind the wagon.

From inside the canvas cover came a guttural plea.

"Whistler! You won't let them harm us, will you?"

"Be quiet, Schwartz," Rob said. "Everything's under control."

"Are you sure about that?" James Foster took a step forward. "My boy was shot. He could have been killed. Now you're pampering those thugs. They eat better than the rest of us, and they only walk on the steepest parts of the trail. We're starving, Whistler."

"It may be weeks before we can turn them over to anyone," James Binchley said. "Think about it, Rob. We can't sustain them that long."

"It's not fair to expect us to," Woolman said.

Someone touched Eb's back lightly and he stiffened. A figure swished past him. He reached to stop her, but it was too late.

Elise planted herself nose to nose with Charles Woolman.

CHAPTER 25

"How dare you speak to the captain that way?" Elise could barely control the urge to slap him.

Woolman eyed her coolly. "Well, now. We've got lady guards, have we?"

Elise hiked her chin up. "You don't have to worry about your stash of dry beans, Mr. Woolman. Miss Stone and I will feed the prisoners from here on." She looked over the others in his little group. "Mr. Redman, Mr. Binchley, Mr. Foster. I thought better of you gentlemen. Don't tell me your wives want you here, because I don't believe it. You're all married to decent women."

She strode past them and made a beeline for her wagon. The absolute nerve of those men. She'd seen James Binchley dump a good forty pounds of bacon a week ago to lighten his wagon. Now he begrudged the prisoners a little food.

Anne met her at the edge of the glow cast by their dying fire.

"What happened? I was terrified, Elise."

"They're a bunch of bullies. I'm going straight to the Harknesses' wagons and tell Orrin what's going on. Wilbur's out there with Rob and Eb, along with Dan and Mr. Leonard, but they could use some reinforcements." She bunched up her skirt and prepared to go but turned back for a moment. "Oh, and I just told that horde of riffraff that we'd feed the prisoners from now on, so they don't have to give up their precious supplies."

Anne's jaw dropped. "Can we do that?"

"For a while." Remorse hit Elise, and she walked back to Anne and laid a hand on her sleeve. "I'm sorry. I shouldn't have said it without asking you."

"No, we'll get by." Anne smiled at her. "Look at the sacrifice Rebecca made. She gave up that furniture she loves so we'd have a prison wagon. We'll be fine."

Elise nodded and squeezed her arm gently. "Thank you." She hurried to the Harkness family's camp. Orrin sat by the smoldering remains of a very small fire.

"Mr. Harkness, there's trouble over the prisoners. Dan and Rob and the others may need help."

Orrin jumped up. "I was afraid something would happen, the way Woolman was talking." He reached into the nearest wagon and pulled out a rifle. He bent down and looked under the wagon. "Get up, Ben. Bring your shotgun."

Rebecca's head popped out between the flaps of a small tent nearby. She blinked. "Elise, is that you? What's happened?"

Orrin and Ben hurried off into the darkness, and Elise tiptoed closer to Rebecca. "I think things will be fine, but some of the men were making a fuss over the prisoners."

"Should we raise a few of the others?"

"I don't think it would hurt. Who else will support the wagon master?"

Rebecca crawled out of the tent. "Well, there's Mr. Libby. He's close by."

They thought of two other men who had always seemed fair minded. After alerting them, Rebecca walked Elise back to her wagon. Anne had poked up the coals enough to heat water for tea.

"I've heard them talking and arguing some"—Anne said, nodding in the direction of the prison wagon—"but nothing that sounded badly out of hand. And I saw your husband and Ben go by. I hope things will settle down soon." She smiled at Rebecca. "May I pour you some tea?"

"Land, if you ladies ain't the beatingest. You know I'll not turn down anything served in a china cup." Rebecca accepted her tea, and they sat down on boxes to talk quietly.

Elise limited herself to one cup of tea and took out her knitting. She'd gotten used to working in near darkness in the evenings, and the second sock was nearly finished.

Fifteen minutes later, Orrin, Ben, and Eb appeared out of the shadows.

"Come on, Becca," Orrin growled. "I reckon we can get some sleep now."

Rebecca stood and handed her cup and saucer to Elise. "Thank you, ladies. I had a delightful time."

"Good night," Elise and Anne called as the Harknesses left.

Eb lingered next to their wagon, and Elise turned to him for news.

"Things should be all right," he said softly.

Elise nodded. "Thank you."

"And you."

"I hope we've heard the last of their nonsense," Anne said. "Elise, I shall retire now."

"Good night, dear." Elise watched her go into the tent and looked back at Eb. "They backed down, then?"

"Right after you left, Josiah came over to our side. When Orrin and Ben showed up, I think that clinched it, but then we got Libby and Bishop, too. You must have told them."

She nodded.

"We owe you and Anne a great debt. Everything calmed down when Woolman and his bunch saw they were solidly outmanned."

"Good. Will you be able to rest tonight?"

"For a while. I'm scheduled to relieve one of the guards in a few hours."

"Go and sleep, then. Come by for breakfast if you can before we break camp."

Eb nodded gravely. "Thank you. And what about you? Will you be able to sleep?"

Elise sighed. "I think I will. I admit I was so worked up that I fretted a bit this evening. But I picked up my knitting while Rebecca was here, and I actually finished my project. Knitting is calming to the nerves."

"That so?" Eb's smile brought a vague yearning to her heart.

"Yes, it is, and I'd like to give you the result, if you're of a mind to take it."

He arched his eyebrows. She went to the rear of the wagon and reached inside for her knitting bag.

"Here you go. Gray woolen socks. They're not perfect, but they'll keep your feet warm in the mountains." She held them out, suddenly nervous. What if he read too much into the gesture—or not enough? She'd used the finest yarn she could find in St. Louis, and the finished product was nothing to be ashamed of. In fact, Anne and Rebecca had praised her work highly as they waited for the men to return.

"I hardly know what to say." Holding the socks close, he inspected them in the dimness. "I allow I could use some new socks. Thank you very much."

She let her breath out. "You're welcome. I was afraid—"

"What?"

"Nothing." Her face flushed, but she hoped he couldn't see it.

Eb smiled. "Good night, then."

They stood looking at each other for a long moment. At last he stirred and resettled his hat before turning away.

The wagons rattled on for the next few weeks as they headed north toward the Snake River. More trees lined the trail, and wild game increased. Between Eb and the Adams brothers, Elise and Anne had more meat in their stew pot than they'd had the first half of the journey. Several other families continued to contribute to the prisoners' meals, so Elise and Anne were not unduly burdened.

Eb came by nearly every morning to check on them before the wagons moved out. Sometimes he came early enough to help harness the mules. On other days, he stopped for a minute and spoke to them from the saddle before he rode out to scout. Elise treasured the moments he spent with her—even more those evenings when he sat by their campfire and shared their meal.

Sometimes Rob or Wilbur joined them, and now and again Dan Adams and his brother walked over, but Dan still seemed a bit wary around Anne. Elise wondered if he still hoped she'd change her mind and accept him as a suitor, or if he'd reconciled himself to the generous friendship Anne shared with all the young men. Even

Nick Foster, who was recovering from his wound, and Will Strother vied for the privilege of walking with Anne in the cool mornings, though she was several years older than they were.

Elise was happy with her one admirer. As the miles and the days passed, her heart became firmly attached to Eb Bentley. It worried her mildly, when she allowed herself to think about it. Mostly she told herself how blessed she was to have a dependable man like Eb for a friend.

They'd had the prisoners in custody for nearly three weeks when Eb rode back from scouting late one morning, accompanied by a dozen cavalry troopers. Word soon spread through the company that the troopers were headed for Fort Laramie and would take the prisoners.

Elise sought out Rob and took him aside.

"I've spoken to Anne and Rebecca. We'll collect cold food for a lunch for the prisoners and the troopers if you wish. Or if you want to stop longer, we'll prepare something hot."

"Well, we're trying to work out some details," Rob said. "I guess we should have taken enough mules from Shwartz's stock for the prisoners to ride on."

"Oh dear. I'd offer one of our mules, but Eb tells me we'll need them all in the Blue Mountains."

"You surely will. Don't worry—the lieutenant said he can offer compensation if Harkness will sell him the wagon and team. If not, they have a few packhorses along and may be able to redistribute their supplies. Or maybe some of our other folks will sell their extra mounts."

An hour later the cavalrymen were off with the prisoners riding two of their pack mules and two purchased from the company. The Adams brothers helped the Harkness men repack their three wagons, and Rob blew his horn to alert the travelers to prepare to move.

"I feel so free," Anne said as she hefted their dish box over the wagon's tailboard. "No more cooking for prisoners or worrying about their safety."

"Do you suppose we can remember how to cook for two?" Elise asked.

"Oh, some of the boys will still come around, I expect."

Elise smiled. "Yes, and often as not they bring us something for the kettle." She looked northward, over the beautiful hills. "We're not far from the Snake River. Just think, Anne. In a month, we'll be in Oregon City."

"And we'll find Uncle David."

Elise grasped her hand. "I pray it is so."

That evening Eb didn't get back to camp until dark, and he heard music from a mile away in the still night. As he drew closer, he could see couples dancing by firelight. He took care of Speck and washed his face and hands then wandered over to the revelry.

He sidled up to Hector Adams and watched the dancers bounding about to a lively tune. As usual, when the music stopped, Anne Stone was the center of a flurry of hopeful young men. Mr. Libby began to play another tune, and the couples reformed. The disappointed fellows looked about for available girls while Anne sprang off with Elijah Woolman.

Her choice of partners surprised Eb mildly, but then, Anne never did show partiality among the boys. He was glad she didn't hold it against Elijah that his father had led the men bent on a lynching a few weeks ago.

Hector glanced his way. "Howdy, Eb."

"Hec."

"She's yonder."

"Who?"

"Miss Finster," Hector said. "Who else?"

Eb tried not to smile, but he couldn't help it. He looked where Hector's chin was pointing and spotted Elise a third of the way around the circle of watchers.

"Much obliged." He left Hector and ambled slowly toward her. When he stepped up near her, he could smell her light fragrance.

She must have brought something with her that smelled good. Most days he didn't notice it—they all smelled of smoke and sun and perspiration. Couldn't help it. But sometimes of an evening, he caught a faint whiff of that scent. Lilacs, maybe? Something his mother had grown.

"Good evening, Eb."

"Hello."

She smiled large, and Eb's stomach clenched. Seemed like every night it was more and more important that he see her face.

"You're late getting back tonight," she said.

"I rode on to the river."

"Will we make it tomorrow?"

"The next day, I think."

She nodded, with the sweet smile still hovering on her lips. Should he ask her to dance? He'd like to hold on to her again, to feel her warmth and softness. Dancing allowed him to touch her. But it was so public.

"It's a fine night," she said.

"Yes."

They stood side by side, watching the movement of the dancers. Rob wasn't out there. He must be on guard. Dan Adams was dancing with Lavinia Harkness. She looked about to swoon, she was so happy. Her brother Wilbur cut in on Elijah Woolman and stole Anne right out of his arms.

Eb turned to Elise on impulse. "Would you walk with me?"

Her eyes widened, but she slipped her hand through the bend of his arm.

"I'd be delighted."

He led her quickly away from the circle and out away from the wagons, hoping no one had noticed. When they reached the trail, he slowed his steps and walked languidly with her northward.

After a hundred yards, he started to hear the crickets over the distant fiddling and the drumming of his heart. "I've been thinking a lot," he said.

She stopped walking. "Oh? What about?" The half-moon's light showed him her face, clear as day and dearer than life.

"You," he dared to say.

She caught her breath, and his heart tore off again, fast and loud. He felt it in his throat and wondered if she could feel it where she held his arm. He reached over and enclosed her fingers in his hand.

"Elise, I. . ."

She waited, expectant, maybe a little cautious.

"I sure do think a heap of you."

He saw the surprise in her eyes, quickly replaced by humor.

"That didn't come out very well, did it?" He cleared his throat. "What I mean is, I admire you. A great deal."

"Thank you, Eb. That means a lot to me."

Before he could think too deeply about it, he pulled her into his arms. She didn't resist but raised her hands to his collarbone and up around his neck. He didn't have to bend far to touch his lips to hers. How long had he craved this warm embrace? Since Jeanie died. He held her close, and she hung on to him, not a desperate clinging, but she rested in his arms as though this was her spot, and she belonged.

He released her with a sigh. The stars flared brighter, and the music swirled about them in a slow, dreamy melody.

"I love you," he said.

Her face glowed as she smiled up at him. "And I love you, Edwin Bentley."

He drew her toward him again. She kissed back, and he never wanted to let her go. Finally he lifted his head and held her close against his chest.

"I've got a ranch. It needs a lot of work, but I plan to tear into it this fall. If I thought you'd be there with me. . ."

She stirred and ran her hand lightly up and down his sleeve. Her warm touch tantalized him.

"I don't know what to say."

"Say you'll marry me, Elise. I'm not a wealthy man, but I can take care of you. We can have a good life together."

She exhaled deeply and rested her head against the front of his

shirt. They stood for a long time in silence with the crickets chirping. The fiddle broke into a riotous polka and people clapped in time.

"It sounds wonderful," she said at last. "I've always dreamed of having my own home."

"It's a pretty place. I bought the land the first time I made this journey. Didn't have the heart to live there alone at first. My. . .my wife died on the trail. Maybe you knew that."

"No, I didn't." Elise raised her head and looked up at him with glittering eyes.

"Long time ago." He touched her hair and gently pressed her head back onto his shoulder where it belonged now. "Anyway, the next year I built a small house and settled in there. Then I got the barn built. It just took me some time."

"It must have been hard to be alone like that."

"That's pretty much why I kept helping Rob with his business. He likes bringing people west. It gave me a chance to get away from. . .from the memories and the loneliness, I guess. But this is my last wagon train. I'm ready now, and I don't want to keep traveling. Rob's quitting, too. Dulcie wants him to stay put, and I don't blame her."

"I don't really have a choice," Elise said softly. "I'm sorry, Eb. I have an obligation to Anne."

"But once we get to Oregon. . ."

"I don't see how I could leave her until she's found her uncle."

Eb was quiet for a long time. The music stopped, and he could hear some loud talk. The party must be breaking up for the night.

"I pray she'll find David quickly," Elise said. "But until her quest is ended, I am bound to her. You do understand?"

Eb's chest hurt. Slowly he loosened his hold on her and stepped back.

"Sure. I understand."

CHAPTER 26

Eb didn't come by the wagon the next morning.

Elise went over their conversation in her mind a thousand times. He was hurting, she was sure. But her heart ached, too. That didn't mean she would avoid him.

She made extra coffee, hoping he'd show up before they broke camp, and ended up giving it to the Adams boys. Late that evening, she and Anne unhitched alone. Elise was exhausted from driving most of the day and walking the rest. Anne scrounged a few sticks and made them each a couple of flapjacks, but the fire wasn't hot enough and the cakes were pale and doughy.

"I'm sorry," Anne said. "I should have tried harder to find more wood."

"Never mind. I'm not very hungry."

"I haven't seen Eb all day. He was late last night, too."

"Yes," Elise said.

"But you saw him last night."

Elise pressed her lips together. She wished Anne wouldn't persist.

Wilbur, Ben, and Lavinia Harkness came over, laughing and swinging the family's buckets.

"We're going for some water," Wilbur said. "Want to come?"

Anne hurried to grab a pail. "Yes, thank you. Elise? Coming?"

Elise shook her head. "I'll stay."

"Want your knitting bag?" Anne asked.

"No. I think I'll retire early tonight."

"All right." Anne hesitated. "I'll see you later."

As the young people walked away, Lavinia said, "Is Miss Elise feeling poorly?"

"I think she's just tired," Anne said.

Elise sat in the flickering shadows for a full ten minutes. If she moved, her heart would shatter. At last she forced herself to stand and rake the embers together then cover them with ashes. She glanced around the little camp. The coffeepot sat on a rock by the fire, where she'd left it when Hector brought it back. Other than that, all their belongings were in the wagon or the tent.

She went to the little tent and crawled inside. In the pitch darkness, she removed her dress, stockings, and corset. She took down her hair and lay down on her bedroll.

What had she done?

Eb was a good, kind man, and she loved him. Had she flung away her one chance at a happy life?

No, she told herself. *I can be happy with Anne.*

Tears rolled down her cheeks. She scrubbed them away with the backs of her hands. She closed her eyes and sobbed.

Lord, I love him. I can't stop. So is this the way I'll feel for the rest of my life? Please take away the hurt. I'd rather not have loved him than to feel this way.

She remembered his kisses. Putting a finger to her lips, she knew the pain was worth it. And yet. . . She buried her damp face in the pillow slip and hoped her spasms of weeping would pass before Anne returned.

"Send it by ship," said the quartermaster at Fort Dalles. "That's the surest way this time of year."

Thomas G. Costigan scowled at him. "By ship? That will take months. And what if the ship goes down?"

The quartermaster shrugged. "If you send it overland, it won't reach New York until next spring. Maybe high summer. And the shipping route is quite reliable now. If it's a really important message, you might want to do both. One is bound to get through."

"That would be expensive." Thomas considered his limited resources. How important was it that he get a message to Peterson, anyway? He supposed he wouldn't be paid until he got back East.

Why not just go on to the Willamette Valley, finish the job, and then report in person? He could hop a ship as fast as he could put a letter on one.

He slapped the desk and straightened.

"Well?" asked the quartermaster.

"Changed my mind. Thank you."

Thomas walked out onto the parade ground and looked over the town below him and the Columbia River beyond. He didn't need any more instruction or communication. It didn't matter whether the two women had given up or continued their journey. He just needed to get on down to Oregon City before Rob Whistler's wagon train came through and make sure David Stone was dead—one way or another.

For nearly two weeks, the company progressed slowly to the Snake River and then along its winding banks. Eb never came to their wagon. Most days, he was gone as long as the daylight lasted. Any news was relayed by Rob.

Anne confronted Elise one morning as they moved into line behind Abe Leonard.

"What happened between you and Eb?"

"Why do you think anything did?" Elise asked. She'd begun knitting again, but not socks this time. She was determined to produce a knitted jumper for the baby Josiah Redman's wife was expecting.

"I haven't seen him in ages. Up, you!" Anne slapped Bumper and Challenger with the reins then turned to gaze at Elise. "I thought he liked us, and I know *I* didn't quarrel with him."

Elise's cheeks grew warm. "We didn't quarrel."

"Then what?"

After several seconds of silence, Anne reached over and clasped one of Elise's hands. "Tell me, dear. I know you care for him, and you've been dragging around camp for a fortnight. It's depressing to see you so unhappy."

Elise gasped an involuntary sob. Tears sprang into her eyes.

"Oh dear." Anne produced a fine handkerchief, still pretty and soft despite their harsh laundry conditions.

Elise dabbed at her eyes. "Thank you. I daresay it won't seem like much to you, since you've had so many marriage proposals—"

"Only four," Anne said. "Well, five if you count Wilbur's second one. But from four gentlemen."

Elise smiled though she didn't feel like it. "Darling, that's splendid. Haven't you given any of them serious consideration?"

"I don't see how I could, not knowing what my future holds. Do you?"

"No." Elise faltered and gazed down at the ball of wool in her lap. "No, I don't. And that's just what I told Eb."

"You told—oh Elise." Anne lowered her hands and the reins. Her shoulders sagged.

"Here now, you're letting the mules slow down." Elise reached for the whip.

Anne sat up and adjusted the reins. She took the whip from Elise but didn't use it.

"So, he proposed to you."

Elise nodded.

"The night of the last dancing?"

"Yes."

"I was so happy for you that night. He kept you out late, walking in the moonlight."

Elise sighed. "It started out a happy time. But I had to tell him."

"Tell him what?"

"That I couldn't."

Anne was quiet for a minute, watching the mules. "You wanted to say yes."

Elise's lips trembled so that she couldn't answer. She sniffed and raised the handkerchief to her eyes.

Anne looked over at her. "My dearest Elise, I'm so sorry! You must tell him you were mistaken."

"How can I?"

"You mean because he's nowhere to be found, or because you were not mistaken?"

For some reason, this question made Elise's tears spill faster. To her surprise, she saw that Anne was crying, too.

"Anne, do you think you could love Dan Adams?"

Anne arched her eyebrows then shook her head. "I...don't think so. Not that way, though he's a very good man. And Wilbur is a dear. But no, I don't think I want to marry either of them. Wilbur's not settled enough in his character. And as to the others, why Mr. Shelley is too old, and Wally is just a boy."

Elise managed a watery smile. "You've quite a litany of suitors. But I agree on all of them, except possibly Dan."

"Perhaps if things were different. With Uncle David, I mean. But I never aspired to marry a farmer, you know."

"Yes, I know." Though a quiet farm life sounded alluring to Elise, Anne had become quite adventurous, and her youthful spirit would want variety and a bit of unpredictability. "This trip should have soured you on travel and adventure, but I can't see that it has."

"Quite the opposite," Anne said. "I'm ready to dive into it with Uncle David, if he's willing."

Elise nodded. "That would be lovely for you. You'd have his protection."

"And you could marry Eb and go off to become ranchers."

Anne's eager smile almost drew Elise into her fairy tale, but she knew it couldn't be. "We must find your uncle." *And by then, Eb will have forgotten me,* she thought.

"You mustn't throw away what he's offering because of me," Anne said earnestly.

Elise feared no answer would satisfy her. As she tried to find an explanation that could not be argued against, Rob cantered up on Bailey and slowed to pace the horse with Elise's mules. They had veered off westward from the Snake, where a sweeping bend curved the river northward.

"Say good-bye to the Snake, Miss Elise. That's the Farewell Bend. We'll see it no more."

"So we're heading into the mountains now."

"Yes. The Blue Mountains. Beautiful, but treacherous."

He cantered off up the line. Elise gazed over at the winding river.

"We're nearing the end of the trail," Anne said.

"Yes. But they say the hardest part is yet to come." They rode on in silence, each deep in her own thoughts. Parting from Eb would be the most difficult part of this entire adventure, Elise mused. But he had already begun the separation. Could it be any worse than this? Anne might open the subject again if she looked at her, and so when Elise could no longer see the river, she looked straight ahead.

The Blue Mountains proved worthy of their reputation. Eb stayed with the company more, as the people worked together to get every wagon up each brutal slope and down the other side. Some families combined the strength of their livestock, double-teaming and even triple-teaming their wagons upward.

Elise and Anne's six mules managed, after they'd jettisoned another of Anne's trunks, a few more clothes, three books they'd both read several times, and one of their kettles. They took turns walking up the inclines, so that the team had only one of them to pull.

Eb and Rob seemed to be everywhere, giving advice, throwing their shoulders to the load when needed, and helping repair wagons that were damaged in the cruel passage.

And yet Eb never came near. Elise saw him at dawn one morning with Anne, carrying an armful of wood for her. But he stopped and passed the bundle to Anne before they came within hailing distance. He wouldn't place himself where Elise could speak to him, or where he couldn't avoid greeting her without being rude. Her chest tightened and she clenched her teeth. She turned her back as Anne approached with the wood and prayed for grace.

Anne dropped the sticks and began to build up the fire. Elise filled the kettle with water, not speaking. She got out dishes and bacon and cornmeal for mush.

"I saw Eb," Anne said when she took the kettle from the grate fifteen minutes later.

"Did you?" No matter how she tried, Elise couldn't feign disinterest with Anne.

"I asked him plainly why he stays away."

"Oh."

Anne turned and faced her with brooding brown eyes. "He said you wouldn't have him, and he doesn't wish to distress you by hanging about."

"Hanging about?" Elise set the kettle down with a thump that slopped a little hot water. "Is that what he calls it? I'd thought he was courting me." She sobbed and realized how ridiculous that sounded, when she had abruptly ended the courtship. Hanging about indeed.

"Well, yes." Anne had tears in her eyes as she walked to Elise and placed her arms around her. "Dear Elise. I know you love him."

"So does he. I told him so." Elise sniffed and pulled away. "Excuse me."

She went to the tent and blew her nose. Hastily she rolled up their bedding and set it and their satchels outside.

Anne had their breakfast plates ready, and Elise accepted hers.

"Thank you. We can strike the tent as soon as we finish."

The journey to the Columbia and Fort Dalles stretched out, uneventful yet full of everyday crises. Elise did what she did best— she coped. Scorched food could be salvaged, torn clothing mended, and broken straps could be sewn. Her heart was another matter. She'd pined over David Stone for many years, imagining herself heartbroken, but she had never imagined the pain she felt now.

When they struck the river, ten wagons left them. The owners had decided to ferry down the Columbia to Vancouver. The rest were bound for Oregon City by way of the Mount Hood Toll Road, Barlow's route. Rob's tales of the dangers to come scared Elise a bit. Yet they'd come through so much she felt she ought to have more confidence. They were tough now. They could deal with what lay ahead.

Eb stood at the edge of Summit Meadows, his head bowed and his hat in his hand. After several minutes, he went to his knees in the long grass. He prayed silently, tears running down his cheeks and into his beard stubble. The wind blowing through the pass had a bite to it. He hoped snow wouldn't arrive before the wagon train.

After a long time, he got up and went to where he'd tied Speck. He took his coat from the back of the saddle and pulled it on. He would camp tonight near Jeanie's grave. He always did when he came across the Barlow Road. It had cost him a dollar to ride through with Speck. The wagons' owners would pay five dollars each. It was worth it though, to avoid the perils of the Columbia in autumn. So long as the wagons didn't crash, that was.

He inhaled carefully and tried not to think about the chute on Laurel Hill. Every year he dreaded going there. He hated snubbing wagons down the chute. Every year he told Rob he wouldn't do it again. Rob could go without him. But he'd only stayed away one year—that first year after he lost Jeanie.

One thing was for certain—if Elise's wagon was going down Laurel Hill, he'd be there to make sure it landed safely at the bottom. He fumbled in his saddle bag with chilled hands for his gloves and pulled out the socks she'd knitted for him. He stared down at them. This would be a good time to start wearing them.

He carried his gloves and the gray woolen socks to a stump and sat down. He used the toe of his right boot to lever off the left one. Peeling down his worn sock, he scowled at the hole in the heel. The new ones were so fine, he almost hated putting them on.

"Hey!"

He jerked his head up and listened. Was it just the wind, or had he really heard a shout?

Nothing. Maybe it wasn't a human shout. Maybe there was a catamount in these parts.

He put the boot back on and pulled off the right one. He'd just got it back in place, solidly on his foot, and picked up the ragged socks he'd discarded when he heard it again.

"Help!"

Now, that was human.

He dropped the socks and hurried toward the trail, where he stopped and listened.

"Hello," he shouted.

"Hey!"

It wasn't very loud, but it came from the other side of the trail, where the ground dropped off perilously. He hurried over the wagon ruts and through the tall weeds. At the edge of the precipice, he looked down.

"Anybody down there?"

"Help me!"

"Where are you?" he called, scanning the rocks and brush below.

"Here!"

A bush moved, off to his right and at least fifty feet down. Eb caught his breath. A buckskin horse was lying motionless on its side near the sheer wall, about five yards from the bushes. It would be a difficult climb down. How on earth would he get the fellow up?

"I need to find a path down."

The bush moved again, but the man didn't reply.

Eb dashed back to Speck and took his rope from the saddle. He wasn't sure it was long enough to get him over the cliff, and he surely couldn't carry a man up a rope. He led Speck across the meadow.

"Come on, boy. We've got to find a safe way down that drop."

It took him twenty minutes to find a place where he was certain he could get down without losing his footing. He tied Speck at the top and shouldered the coil of rope and his canteen. He checked his revolver and knife and headed down.

A harrowing climb down brought him into the ravine he'd surveyed. He picked his way over rocks, brush, and debris toward where he thought the man lay.

He spotted the dead horse first and headed for the bushes nearby.

"I'm here."

A bush shimmied, and Eb walked forward.

"You hurt bad?" He drew his pistol, just on principle.

"My leg's busted," the man gasped. "Can you get me out of here? I've been down here three days. Maybe four."

"I'll sure try." Eb parted the bushes and stared down into the strained face of Thomas G. Costigan.

CHAPTER 27

Elise drove when they left Fort Dalles, and Anne walked most of the morning with some of the other women. The desolate, arid land they crossed held no appeal for the emigrants. All were eager to push on to the lush Willamette Valley they'd heard so much about.

Rob's horse came trotting along the line, and Elise seized the rare chance to speak privately with the wagon master.

"Mr. Whistler!"

"Yes, ma'am."

"I haven't seen Eb for several days now."

Rob's face fell into grave lines. "No, he's gone on ahead."

"Doesn't he every day?"

"Mostly, but we won't see him for a while now."

"I don't understand," she said.

Rob pulled his hat off, wiped his brow, and settled the hat on his head again. "We're nearing the place where Jeanie died."

"Ah."

Jeanie. Elise had never heard her name before, but she didn't have to ask who Jeanie was. Even Rob spoke the name with reverence.

"What happened to her, if I may ask?"

"You may. There's a place coming up. Not for a few days, but it's a very steep grade going down a mountain. We'll have to snub the wagon wheels to trees and lower them with ropes down a chute of sorts."

Elise stared at him. "You mean—?"

"Eb didn't want her to drive, but she insisted she could do it if he and the other men tended the ropes." Rob shook his head. "The rope gave way, and their wagon crashed on down the slope. Jeanie . . .Jeanie was killed instantly. At least she didn't suffer."

"He told me she died on the trail, but I had no idea."

"It was pretty bad," Rob said.

"And they were so close to their destination."

"Yes." He sighed. "We don't try to drive wagons down there anymore. It's one of my rules. We rope them all down, with no people inside." He looked ahead toward the mountains. "Eb will be there when we need him. But every trip he goes on alone and camps near that place. I expect he spends some time at her graveside."

Elise drew in a shaky breath. What had she done to Eb, turning him down when he was so near this emotion-filled place? It must have taken great courage for him to declare himself to her, knowing he'd have to pass his wife's grave soon.

"Oh dear," she whispered.

Rob eyed her keenly. "Are you all right, Miss Elise?"

She couldn't lie, but if she said no, he would feel he needed to do something to help her. She gazed at him, unable to speak.

"He told me about your conversation the night of the dancing," Rob said quietly.

Elise looked down at her hands, holding the reins. "I've been cruel to him."

"That's not the way he sees it. He said you were being kind to Anne—being a mother when she has none of her own. He thought that was upstanding of you."

"Did he?" Her voice caught. "I thought he was angry with me."

"No, ma'am. Don't think that. He is grieving a bit though. For you, I mean."

They rode along, and Rob didn't flit off to check on another wagon. Elise decided he had more on his mind, and she was right.

"This is the first time I've seen him take to a woman since Jeanie died," Rob said. "I had hopes that you'd marry him. Eb needs a good woman by his side."

Her cheeks felt warmer than the cool sun of September warranted. "I also had hopes, sir. And yet, I can't help feeling it was wrong of me to raise his expectations."

"Now don't go all guilt ridden on us. You know where God wants you. Right now, it's on this wagon train. And if we get to the end of the trail and you feel He still wants you with Miss Anne, then that's where you should be. Neither Eb nor I would fault you for that."

"But I've disappointed him horribly."

"Yes."

She wished he hadn't agreed so readily. The heaviness that had plagued her since she'd rejected Eb pushed down on her now, so weighty she thought it might crush her lungs.

"Let the Lord work things out," Rob said.

"That's sound advice."

He nodded and touched his hat brim. "Good day, Miss Elise." He urged his mare into a trot and rode up the line of wagons. Elise settled in to watch the mules. They were climbing, and ahead lay the forested slopes of the Cascades.

"Dear God, whatever You want for me, I'll accept," she whispered. "Just please, don't let me be the one to leave Eb heartbroken by the trail again."

Thomas was hanging over a cliff, tied to a framework of tree limbs. Eb Bentley thought he could get him up over the rim of the drop-off by having his horse pull the travois contraption up. It had seemed like a reasonable idea at the time, but now it seemed insane. Every step that horse took raised him higher off the bottom of the ravine and shook the travois until Thomas was sure it would go to pieces. Pain lanced through his leg and up his entire body.

They must be almost to the top. He could hear Eb talking to the horse.

"Easy, Speck. Just a little more."

The strain on the rope increased, pulling the branches up and away from the edge. Thomas ground his teeth together to keep from screaming. He was helpless, strapped to this thing. A moan escaped through his teeth.

Eb said something low to the horse. All movement stopped, with Thomas suspended vertically over the edge, fifty feet above his dead horse.

"You all right, Costigan?" Eb yelled.

"Yeah. Just get on with it."

Eb's horse snuffled, and the frame shivered again. It inched upward, a bit at a time, then a big jump. At last it crashed backward, and Thomas was lying on his aching back, staring up at the sky and gasping for breath. The pain in his leg nauseated him.

"Good boy." Footsteps approached and then Eb was beside him. "Costigan? You with me?"

"Yeah. Lost my hat."

"I ain't going to get it."

"Didn't think you would. Just get me off these sticks."

"I'll have Speck pull you over to my camp spot first."

Thomas swore. Eb had used another short rope, his dead horse's reins, and both their belts to secure him to the travois, and he wanted nothing better than to have the straps removed.

Eb walked away and made some adjustments to the rope. He lifted the ends of the branches so that Thomas's head was higher than his feet. Excruciating pain washed over him.

"My leg!"

Eb lowered the travois to the ground. "Sorry about that. We'll have to drag you over the ground. That'll be rough."

"Can't you just camp here?"

"Too close to the edge."

Before they'd gone ten yards, Thomas let himself fall into blackness.

When he woke up, stars shone overhead. He heard snapping and turned his head. Eb was crouched near a small campfire.

"Musta passed out," Thomas muttered.

"Good thing we splinted your leg before I moved you, I reckon." Eb raked at his fire and set a small coffeepot on the coals. "If nobody comes along by morning, I'll take you down off this mountain. Don't want to, but I will if I have to."

Costigan grunted. How long would it take to get him to the nearest house? He was sure Eb wouldn't take him farther than that.

"You still with the wagon train?" Thomas asked.

"Yup. They'll be here day after tomorrow."

"Whyn't you just keep me here until they come?"

"Oh no." Eb opened a little cloth bag and peered into it. Coffee, Thomas surmised. "Your leg's bad. I looked at it while you were unconscious. Other than that, I'd say it's mostly bruises. But you need to see a doctor—someone who can set it right, or you might never walk on it again."

Thomas grimaced.

"Be thankful you didn't break your neck," Eb said. "Look, I've got jerky and some crackers and a couple of biscuits. I'll make us some coffee. Wish I had something to kill the pain for you, but I don't."

Thomas nodded. "I appreciate it, Bentley." A cool breeze blew over him and he shivered. "You got a blanket?"

"Yeah. I brought your bedroll and saddlebags up earlier." He walked out of the small circle of firelight and returned a moment later with a dark wool blanket. He draped it gently over Thomas.

"All right?"

"Yup." Thomas didn't tell him how even the weight of the blanket made his leg scream with pain. What was the use?

"I'll tell you now," Eb said, "I'm turning you over to the law."

"What for?" Thomas knew he was at Eb's mercy, but it didn't seem fair.

"Where should I start? Horse stealing?"

Thomas said nothing.

"And then there's the little matter of Mr. Stone."

"What about him?"

"I figure you heard about him in Independence from conversations between Miss Stone and Miss Finster. Just bits and pieces, but everywhere they went, they were asking about him. You got curious and followed them. You signed on with them under false pretenses—told them I'd recommended you, but I hadn't. And somehow you came to understand that Miss Anne's uncle might be worth some money. You stole her letter to see if you could piece together the story."

Well, he had it partly right. Thomas closed his eyes and tried not to think about the pain.

"At first I thought you were just a petty thief looking for an opportunity. But you made a mistake at Schwartzburg."

"What was that?" Thomas asked.

"More than one mistake, actually. First, you told Schwartz about Miss Stone. Bad business. Schwartz is slipperier than a greased eel. Then you got him to help you try to convince Miss Anne her uncle was dead. You hoped she'd turn back so you could find David Stone on your own."

He was close to the truth. But Bentley thought he was on his own mission and had no clue about Peterson.

"Then there's Rob's horse. Taking that mare was a big mistake. We might have overlooked it if you'd stolen a mule. Not one of the wagon master's horses." Eb came over and held out a piece of jerky. "Can you eat?"

"I'm starving." Thomas took the jerky and held it to his mouth. He wasn't sure he had the strength to take a bite.

Eb sat down and chomped off a piece of his own strip. He chewed for a minute. "You wanted to get to Stone before anybody else did. I'm not sure how that would help you. Not yet, but I'll figure it out. I mean, David Stone doesn't have any money to speak of. Not now."

Thomas chewed on the tough jerky until it began to soften. Just let him talk. Maybe he'd reveal something useful.

Eb froze with his strip of meat partway to his mouth. He sat perfectly still for a moment then scowled down at Thomas.

"You were going to kill him, weren't you? Because he might not be worth anything right now, but to somebody he's worth a whole lot if he's dead."

CHAPTER 28

Eb stood on the mountainside, watching the wagon train approach. The sun was still low behind them, barely peeking over the next row of hills. The oxen looked as small as mice. He could easily pick out Elise and Anne's wagon by ticking off the teams in the order they always used, minus the families who had left them at The Dalles. Between Abe Leonard, with his ox team, and the Adams boys with their two wagons, were the ladies and their six-mule team.

It was going to be hard seeing her again, but he wouldn't let anyone else take her over this mountain. He thought about riding down to meet them, but he hated to make Speck climb back up here again.

Instead he walked back to his camping spot. Speck grazed in the meadow. The pinto had had a good rest and plenty to eat the last few days, without having to fight for it. Eb went to the fire pit and poured the bottom half of his morning coffee into his tin cup. He'd cut it close on provisions. Hadn't counted on having to feed Costigan for a day. But he'd have something good tonight, he was sure. The ladies on the first few wagons down the chute would start baking for the men who would work long into the night.

He felled a couple of medium-sized trees at the top of chute to use as drag anchors behind the wagons and hiked back to his lookout. The wagons were much closer now, nearly to the steepest part of the upgrade. He left his gear at the campsite and headed down the mountain, carrying only his rifle.

Rob spotted him and waved his hat. Eb raised his hand and went on down. Landon Clark's wagon was first in line, with a double team of oxen. Rob was checking over the wheel hubs and fittings as Eb approached.

"I think you'll be all right, Landon. We'll get you up, let all the cattle rest awhile, then bring them back down to take the Binchleys' wagon up."

"Where do you need me most?" Eb asked.

"I'm still trying to convince Mrs. Libby to lighten her load. And Dan and Hector won't give up any of their tools. They're both planning to pack a few loads up on their backs, but still. . ."

"We could use them better to help other people."

"I know, but they think they've pared down to the barest necessities. Oh, and the Redmans and Strothers are going to double up their teams. They might need help."

Eb gazed down the line of wagons and nodded.

"They're number twelve today," Rob said.

Eb didn't have to ask who. He'd already figured that out from his lookout. He'd have to pass Elise and Anne's wagon to get to Josiah Redman's.

Anne was inside the wagon, handing a wooden box down to Elise. Eb sprang forward and took it from her.

Elise stared at him with eyes big and round. They were bluer than the tranquil sky above. He couldn't look away.

"Eb."

"Elise."

"We missed you." She looked down then, her coral lips pressed into a thin line.

"Thanks. Where do you want this stuff?"

"Anywhere. We'll likely leave it."

He glanced at the contents. Another kettle, four china cups and saucers, two more books, five pounds or so of bacon, and something made of green cloth.

"I'm sorry."

She shrugged. "We cooked up a lot of bacon last night and gave away most of it."

"Wish I'd had some yesterday."

She smiled at that. "I'm glad you're back."

With the six mules pulling and Anne driving, Elise got behind the wagon and pushed, with four strong men helping.

"Go on, Miss Elise," Hector Adams said, scowling at her as he shoved his shoulder against the frame below the tailboard.

"I'll do my bit, so long as I'm able."

They'd agreed that morning—Elise would drive up the first part of the slope, and Anne would walk. Anne took the reins halfway up. It took three hours in all to get up the mountain. When they finally reached the crest, Elise flopped against a tall fir near the trail and panted, not caring if she ever stood again.

"Elise, dear, eat this."

She opened her eyes. Anne hovered over her with a cup of water and a slab of johnnycake.

"Have you looked down the chute?" Elise asked.

"Not yet." Anne's face betrayed her anxiety.

Elise took the cup and the cornbread. "Thank you. Get some for yourself."

Eb found them a few minutes later. He hunkered down beside them and cast a critical eye over both women. "We'll take your wagon down in about ten minutes."

Elise set down her cup and arranged her skirts so she could rise modestly. "I'll help."

"No, the other men and I will take it down. There's a path you ladies can walk down that's away from where we'll be working. It's steep, but you should be all right if you go slow and help each other. You can take your tinderbox if you want and go down to the meadow and start a cook fire. When we bring you your wagon, you'll have a nice bed of coals ready for baking."

Elise met his gaze steadily. "What about the mules? I can drive the team down."

"You will not." He spoke quietly, but he stared down at her with eyes of steel.

Elise's heart tripped. Was this too much like the conversation he'd had with Jeanie a few years back? She drew in a deep breath. "All right."

He held the gaze a moment longer then nodded. "Thank you." He glanced over at Anne. "Might as well tell you ladies now. Some freighters came through here yesterday."

"They passed us on the trail," Anne said. "Seemed in a big hurry, and they muddied the water at the creek."

"They're a brash bunch," Eb said. "But they seemed like honest men. I. . .entrusted them with a man I'd found injured near the trail."

"An injured man?" Elise asked. "What happened?"

"His horse went off the edge of a bluff in the dark. His leg was broken." Eb hesitated and added, "It was Thomas G. Costigan."

Anne gasped.

"Thomas?" Elise eyed Eb closely.

"Yup. He said he'd been lying there three or four days when I came along. Heard him yelling. I got him up to my camp. Those freighters came the next day, and I asked them to get him to a doctor if they could. They had a ledger, and they let me use a sheet of paper from it to write out a letter to Marshal Nesmith in Oregon City. They'll give it to him when they get there. I put in it what I know about Costigan, and what I suspect."

"What do you suspect?" Elise asked.

Eb gritted his teeth and looked at Anne. "I believe he was out to murder your uncle."

"What?" Anne's face went white.

Elise reached for her hand. "Why would he do that?"

"Well, I don't like to say it or even think it, but you told me once that if David Stone was proved dead, somebody else in England would profit."

Elise and Anne stared at each other.

"It's true," Elise said. "But how—"

"I don't know how, but Costigan was going to get something out of it. He'd told Schwartz he'd get paid to fool you two into giving up hunting for Stone, didn't he?"

"Something along those lines."

Eb nodded. "I think someone paid Costigan to find out if Stone was still alive, and if so to. . .to change that."

"It makes me ill to think of it," Elise said.

"It makes *me* furious." Anne balled her hands into fists. "Are you sure he won't get away again?"

"His leg was busted up pretty bad, and I think infection had set in. But I put all I knew down on the paper and impressed on the freighting captain that it was vital to get that to the marshal."

"Thank you," Elise said.

"Just doing what seemed right. Maybe the marshal can make him tell who really employed him." Eb stood. "Now, let's get your wagon ready. We'll tie four ropes to the frame and loop them around trees. Four men will let the ropes out slow. Shouldn't be any problems."

Elise swallowed hard. Suddenly she was sure she didn't want to watch. She was glad Eb had given her other instructions.

"Let's get a few things out of the back, Anne. We'll go down and bake some biscuits."

After a harrowing descent along a rudely blazed path through the woods, they came into a pleasant meadow where the first eight wagons were already aligned to make the beginnings of a circle. Anne carried their tinderbox, mixing bowl, and a jar of sourdough starter in a bucket, while Elise brought the flour and other ingredients for their biscuits in a sack. They hurried to Mrs. Foster, who had a fire going.

"There's good water not far away, ladies," Mrs. Foster called.

They left their supplies near the Fosters' wagon and hurried along another path, to the little stream spilling down over the rocks.

"You need to speak to Eb tonight," Anne said as they started back to the camp.

"What about? Thomas?"

"No. About your future."

Elise pulled up and stared at her. "Whatever do you mean?"

"You need to tell him that you'll marry him as soon as we locate

Uncle David—which I've no doubt we'll do within a few days. Thanks to Thomas's accident, I expect we'll find him in good health."

"We've no assurance—"

Anne cut her off with a sweep of her hand. "No, we've none whatsoever, but if God wills, you and Eb Bentley can have a happy life together. The sooner you tell him that, the better."

"But, my dear! What will you do?"

"Do? Why, go back to Stoneford with Uncle David of course. While I shall miss you, my heart will warm each time I think of you and Eb on your ranch. And you will write me long, news-filled letters, telling me about the cattle and the weather and what you've baked for your husband's dinner."

"I can't just go and tell him. . .that."

"And why not? If you need a little assistance, I could tell him for you. Elise, you love him. This is your chance for happiness. Don't let him go off again without knowing you'll have him. Please don't do that to him."

Eb came into camp with the Harkness men, driving their last wagon—the small one that had been their prison wagon. Elise watched as they maneuvered into place and completed the circle. The boys who had been guarding the livestock bustled to help them close the gaps.

Anne came to stand beside her, holding Elise's shawl.

"Go tell him. I'll have a plate of hot beans and biscuits ready when you bring him here after."

"But—"

"No buts." Anne laid a hand on her arm. "Don't fail me, Elise."

Elise frowned at her. Their relationship had changed so drastically in the last six months that she knew she could argue with her mistress now, and she could probably browbeat Anne until she won. But she didn't want to.

She walked toward the Harkness camp, around the big circle. The men were still unhitching the teams.

"I've got everything ready," Rebecca shouted.

"Good, 'cause we're hungry," Orrin said.

Elise sneaked past him and Ben as they worked on the first team of mules. Wilbur saw her as she passed him and called, "Hello!"

Elise nodded to him but didn't stop. Eb was peeling the harness off the last team. She stood back for a moment, watching his swift, efficient movements. When he turned away with the harness in his arms, he spotted her and stopped in his tracks.

"Evening."

"Hello." She stepped forward. "May I speak to you?"

"Certainly." He took the harness to the wagon and bundled it inside. When he faced her, he offered his arm. "Shall I take you back to your wagon, or would you like to take a shortcut?"

She smiled at that. There was no shorter way to her wagon than the way she'd come, unless they went directly across the circle seething with oxen and mules.

"Is there such a thing as a long-cut?"

"I think we could find one."

They walked away from the wagons, toward the verge of the forest. She pulled her shawl close without releasing his arm. It felt good to be near him again, to be touching him and knowing he enjoyed it.

His pinto was picketed near the edge of the meadow. Nearby, a fire pit held cold ashes, and a small pile of gear lay tumbled on the grass.

"Rob and I are camping here. Care for a chair?"

Eb steered her toward a fallen log. She sat down, careful to leave him plenty of space, and he sat beside her.

"What can I do for you?"

She drew a deep breath and gazed out over the sloping meadow. "It's lovely here."

"That it is."

"I imagine it's even more beautiful in the valley." She sneaked a glance at him. Eb was watching her intently. "I want to stay here in Oregon, Eb." She held her breath.

His eyes widened, and he reached over to enclose her hand in both of his. "You mean that?"

"Yes."

He squeezed her hand.

"If you can just wait a little bit until I deliver Anne to Mr. Stone, why then. . ."

"You'll marry me?" he asked softly.

She nodded, unable to trust her voice.

"I know you can't leave her yet," he said.

"But you'll wait? You won't forget me or. . .or be angry?"

"The only thing I'll be is waiting. When you say the word, I'll be there."

"Oh Eb, I love you."

He pulled her into his embrace, and she squeezed him. He smelled of pitch and sweat and horses, but she didn't care.

"If it takes awhile, I'll be getting the ranch into shape," he said. "Just let me know."

"I will."

He kissed her, and Elise let him hold her for a long time before she remembered her instructions.

"Oh! Anne is fixing our dinner."

He didn't move. "There's one more thing."

"What?" She didn't want to leave their spot either, although she felt vaguely wicked for staying out here with Eb.

"What will you do if her uncle has passed away?"

Elise sighed. "I refuse to think about that."

"But you should."

She pulled away from him. "I don't know. I suppose I'll try to talk her into staying with us—if you're agreeable to that."

"I am."

She smiled. "Thank you. That means a lot."

He pulled her back against his shoulder. She rested her head against him for a moment.

"We really should go."

"Huh." Eb stroked her hair. "It's a tough choice. Of course, I haven't had much of a meal for three days now."

Elise laughed and stood, brushing her skirt into place. "Come, Mr. Bentley. You need to keep up your strength."

She took his arm and walked with him toward the wagons.

Eb sniffed. "Somebody's burning something."

"Likely it's Anne."

"I expect you're right."

CHAPTER 29

Oregon City knelt on the eastern bank of the Willamette River, beckoning to Elise's heart like paradise. After six months on the trail, sleeping in the little tent and eating the plainest of provisions, caring for their mules, and driving the wagon over every inch of the inhospitable trail, she and Anne had arrived.

"I can scarcely believe it," Anne said, clutching her hat with one hand as though it would fly off and sail onward to the Pacific. "We've done it, Elise!"

"Yes, we have. Now we've only one more task to accomplish."

They were twentieth in line, more than halfway back on their depleted train. Anne leaned out to the side, gulping in the sight of the businesses and solidly built houses that made up the town.

"Rob said this was the first city incorporated west of the Mississippi," Elise said.

"The Mississippi—that crossing seems like another life."

Elise smiled. "It was. We're pioneer women now, not the two fine ladies who left England last spring."

Anne's musical laugh burbled out, lifting Elise's spirits to new heights. "I wouldn't trade this journey for anything. When Uncle David and I get back to London, we'll be the most popular party guests in town."

"Everyone will want to hear your tales." Elise had let the team slow as she scanned the signboards on the shops. She snapped the reins on the wheelers' rumps to make them quicken their pace and close the distance between them and Mr. Leonard's wagon.

Eb rode up beside Elise. "The store Mr. Stone kept is on the next street. Turn right up yonder. Folks filing land claims will keep on going straight. I'll show you where you want to be though."

"Oh dear, I haven't said good-bye to everyone." Anne's stricken face mirrored Elise's confusion.

They'd camped ten miles out last night, and everyone had visited other people's campfires, jolly and hopeful for the morrow. Elise had learned how to send letters to families who had no address as yet. The Harknesses hoped to settle near Oregon City and would pick up mail sent to them there in care of general delivery. The Adams boys had plans for farming near Champoeg, twelve miles to the south. The Libbys hoped to join their son and his family up the Clackamas River.

But still, she'd expected somehow that they would all be together one last time, not flake off one by one as the train progressed.

"Where will you and Rob be?" she asked.

"I'll stick with you for a while," Eb said. "Rob will go as far as the land claims office to help anyone who needs it. After you ladies are settled, I'll go and find him and help out wherever I'm needed. But I hope to leave for my ranch by tomorrow."

Elise's heart dropped. Eb would leave them, and she and Anne would be alone again. Unless they found David. And then?

"You've got my instructions on how to find me," Eb said.

She nodded. His ranch was south of Oregon City, a few miles outside the flourishing town of Corvallis. He and Rob had both bought land there several years back. She could send Eb a message at Corvallis, or make her way up the river to that town. But the prospect of doing that alone after so long with the close-knit wagon company frightened her.

Eb's eyes narrowed. "You send me word, and I'll come back here for you."

She nodded, her mouth so dry she couldn't speak.

He reached out and touched her shoulder just for a moment. "All right, here's where you turn off. I'll go ahead and scout you a spot near the haberdashery—six mules and a schooner need space."

He and Speck trotted off and rounded the corner.

"Gee," Elise called. She tugged on the reins, pulling the mules' heads to the right. The leaders swung around, and the swing team and wheelers followed.

"Good-bye! Good-bye!" Anne shouted, leaning far out over the side of the seat, so she could wave to the Adams brothers. "Thank you! You, too!"

She settled back beside Elise and smoothed down her skirt. "I shall miss them."

"Yes." Elise glanced at her. Anne was dabbing at her eyes with a handkerchief. "Are you sorry you let Dan get away?"

"No. I don't think so." She sighed.

Buggies, farm wagons, pack mules, and saddle horses filled the street. Elise guided the mules while trying to keep track of Speck's brown-and-white rump ahead of them. Footsteps pounded up from behind, and Ben Harkness's head appeared on Anne's side of the wagon.

"Ma said to give you this!" He thrust something into Anne's hand.

"Oh, thank you," Anne said. "Give her my best."

"And remember, if you ladies need anything, we won't be far away."

"Bless you, Ben," Elise called.

Anne leaned out over the street again and waved. "Good-bye!"

Elise squinted ahead. "I've lost Eb."

"He can't be far." Anne unrolled the cloth Ben had given her. "Oh, look. It's one of Rebecca's knitted dishcloths."

Elise glanced over at it. "She was knitting that last night, bless her heart." Ahead, one of the larger buildings sported a sign reading VALLEY MERCANTILE.

"That must be it." As she spoke, she glimpsed Speck. Eb was still in the saddle, waving to her.

The mules lumbered past the store, which seemed to be a popular shopping place. Eb gestured for her to pull around to the far side of the building. Two minutes later, Elise and Anne stood on the front porch of the store. Elise's lungs burned. How must Anne be feeling now? She looked over her shoulder. Eb was right behind them.

"Are you ready, Miss Anne?" he asked.

Anne nodded. "Yes, though I wish I had changed into a promenade dress."

Elise smiled. Last night they'd discussed what they would wear on their arrival at Oregon City. They'd decided not to cast aside their calico dresses, out of deference to the many women in the company who had nothing better.

"You mean you've still got all your gowns?" Eb eyed her with amusement.

"Not all, but several, and not much else. We got rid of just about everything but the mules' rations, enough food to get us here, the harness, and our clothing. Our wagon is really quite empty," Anne said.

Unfortunately, her purse was, too, Elise knew. If David was inside this building, all would be well. If not. . .well, they could sell the team and wagon.

Anne squared her shoulders and stepped to the door. Eb held it for them, and the ladies entered the dim building.

A woman stood behind the counter. Anne walked directly to her.

"Excuse me. I'm looking for David Stone. Would he happen to be here?"

The woman looked at her for a moment then turned her head and yelled in a rusty screech, "Nathan!"

Elise jumped. Anne glanced at her and smiled. They waited in silence until a dark-haired man of about thirty, wearing a long, white apron, emerged from among the shelves of groceries.

"What is it, Nancy?"

Elise exhaled. She hadn't admitted how much she was counting on finding David—at once, while Eb was still at her side.

"This woman wants to find Mr. Stone. She talks like him."

The young man turned to Anne. His eyebrows lifted, and a gleam lit his eyes. "Well, now. Mr. Stone? Mr. David Stone?"

"Yes." Anne sounded a bit flustered. "Is he about?"

"No. I'm sorry, he's not."

"But. . ." Anne swung around with tears threatening to spill from her eyes and looked to Eb.

"David Stone used to own this store, I believe," Eb said gruffly.

"Yes, he did." The man smiled. "I'm Nathan Daley. I bought out Mr. Stone about a year ago."

"A year ago?" Anne sagged against her, and Elise slipped an arm about her.

"Do you know where he's gone?" Elise asked.

Daley shrugged. "It's my understanding he bought a spread down near Eugene. He sold out to me, lock, stock, and pickle barrel, you might say." He chuckled, but Elise couldn't raise a smile.

"Do you have an address or directions to his property?" she asked.

"Can't say as I do, but I expect you could reach him through the post office at Eugene. It's quite a ways south of here. . . ."

"I know where it is," Eb said.

Anne opened her handbag. "Just to be certain, this is a miniature of David Stone. It was made when he was about twenty."

Daley took it and carried over to the nearest window. "Yup, that's him." He turned and grinned at Anne. "He looked like you, miss."

"Yes." Anne took the picture back, somber faced. "As far as you know, then, he's in good health?"

"He was when he left here. I'm sorry I can't tell you anything more recent."

"It's all right."

Eb drew them aside. "What do you ladies want to do? Eugene is a far piece."

"Perhaps we should take rooms for the night," Anne said doubtfully.

Elise couldn't help noticing the bins of cabbages, carrots, beets, and other fresh vegetables at the front of the store.

"Should we buy a few supplies?"

"The sight of those cabbages makes my mouth water," Anne said. "But unless we have a place where we can cook. . . We don't want to go on camping, do we?"

Elise hesitated, not sure how much cash Anne had left.

"There's a boardinghouse or two," Eb said.

The door opened and a tall, thin man strode in, heading straight for the counter. Daley had gone to aid a customer, and the woman behind the counter eyed the newcomer.

"May I help you, sir?"

"Yes. I understand this establishment is owned by David Stone."

Elise grabbed Anne's arm. "It's the mustache man."

Anne caught her breath. "Are you sure?"

"Yes." Elise took Eb's arm and hustled the two of them behind a rack of harness. "Eb, that man was on our train out of New York, and our steamship across the Mississippi. Anne spotted him watching us near the dock in St. Louis."

"And you think he followed you all the way out here?" Eb's face looked less than credulous.

"I don't know how," Elise said, "but I'm sure it's him."

Eb walked to the end of the aisle and stood watching the man at the counter.

"Wonderful," the man said with great sarcasm. "And how far away is Eugene?"

"You'll have to ask Mr. Daley," the woman said. "He was just explaining it to someone else."

"Someone else?" the man asked. "Not a Mr. Thomas G. Costigan?"

"Why, no. I've never heard of that person. This was two women."

"Two women?" the man snapped. "Two *English* women?"

"Yes, I'd say so. Very pretty accents." The clerk nodded toward where they stood, partially concealed by the racks of merchandise. "They're still in the store."

As the man turned in their direction, Elise squeezed Eb's arm.

"Can you talk to him and detain him?" Eb whispered. "I'll go for the marshal."

Anne strode to the open area before the counter and planted herself before the man with the mustache.

"Who *are* you?"

"I beg your pardon." The man darted a glance toward the door as though looking for escape. Eb was just closing in behind him.

"You followed my companion and me halfway across this country to St. Louis," Anne said, "and now we arrive here in Oregon City after an arduous journey and find you here—inquiring for my uncle."

"Aha." The man gulped and looked her up and down.

Elise stepped up beside Anne and glared at him. "You'd best explain yourself, sir. Start with your name."

"I. . .er. . .Charles Peterson."

"And how did you get here?"

He seemed relieved at that question. "I came by ship. Most of the way, that is."

"Why?" Elise asked.

He hesitated then said with an air of confession, "I was employed to search for Mr. Stone."

"By whom?"

"That is a private matter."

"Is it?" Anne asked. "Because my family's solicitor told me the trustees of my father's estate would not spend any more money looking for my uncle. If they are not paying you, I demand to know who is."

"I am not at liberty to say, miss. Now, if you will excuse me—"

"No! I will not excuse you." Anne held his stare, and Elise slipped around the man and stood solidly in front of the door.

"Nathan," screeched the woman behind the counter.

Mr. Daley hurried toward her, wiping his hands on his apron. "What is it?" He looked at Anne and Peterson. "May I be of some assistance?"

"We would like the marshal to question this man," Anne said.

"Oh dear. The marshal? Whatever for?" Daley glanced at Nancy. "What's this about?"

"This man inquired about my uncle," Anne said. "In practically the same breath, he asked for a man we know is a criminal."

"What are you talking about?" Peterson asked. "I did no such thing."

"Yes, you did. Thomas G. Costigan is now in the marshal's

custody. If you're an acquaintance of his, then you should speak to the marshal as well."

"I don't know what you think you know, but I shan't be a part of this scandalous scene." Peterson backed toward the door and bumped into Elise. "Oh excuse me, ma'am." He looked at her and gave a start. "Oh, my."

"Yes," said Elise. "We'll all wait here until the marshal arrives."

Daley looked in dismay at the crowd of customers gathering to watch. "Please, ma'am, if you could just take this dispute elsewhere. . ."

"I'm afraid we can't," Elise said.

She felt a shove on the door behind her, and then someone knocked.

"It's Eb!" Anne was looking out the window. "He's got Rob and some of the boys with him."

Elise opened the door. Eb strode in and gave Peterson a stern look. "Stay where you are, mister. I've sent a young man to fetch the marshal. Dan, watch the door."

Dan Adams took up his place next to Elise. Hector Adams, along with Rob Whistler, Wilbur Harkness, and Eb, formed a ring around Peterson. The store seemed very small and crowded. Anne edged over to Elise and groped for her hand.

"I'm sorry for the inconvenience, folks," Mr. Daley called to his customers. "Just continue your shopping. I'm sure this misunderstanding will be clarified soon."

The shoppers drifted back to the displays of wares. Within minutes, Ben Harkness came to the door with another man.

"Here's Marshal Nesmith," Ben said.

The marshal nodded to Eb. "Bentley. That the fella?"

"Yes, sir."

The marshal walked over to Peterson. "Who are you?"

"The name is Peterson, sir. I just came by ship, all the way from New Orleans, and before that down the Mississippi."

"You know Thomas Costigan?"

"Well, I. . ."

"That's good enough for me." Nesmith nodded at Eb. "If you and Whistler say he's a bad'un, I'll take him in for questioning."

"I think that would be wise," Rob said.

They sent the Adams and Harkness brothers on their respective ways with hearty thanks. Rob treated the ladies to tea and a sandwich at a café while Eb accompanied Nesmith and Peterson to the marshal's office.

An hour later, Anne and Elise went to tell the marshal their story with only Eb and Rob present. Anne explained her family's situation in detail, and Elise added what she knew of Peterson's and Costigan's activities.

"Well, it's starting to add up," the marshal said. "Costigan's in a bad way. The doctor thinks he might not make it."

"Oh dear," Elise said. "It's that bad?"

"Well, his leg's infected, and he won't let the doc take it off. It might kill him. So I told him, whatever he knows, he'd best tell me. And he said this Peterson hired him in St. Louis just to follow the ladies around and see if they learned anything about David Stone's whereabouts. Costigan gathered that someone in England wanted to find the man and was hoping the ladies would lead him to Stone. When he heard them tell someone they had decided to join the wagon train, he told Peterson, and Peterson told him to hire on with them if he could, or to join the train some other way. Peterson offered him a lot of money to come overland with the ladies and see if they found Stone. What he didn't tell Costigan, it appears, is that he would set out by ship and try to get here first."

"I may be a little slow," Rob said, "but why do they want to find Miss Anne's uncle so badly?"

"He's the new earl," Eb said, "and he'll be worth millions if he claims the title."

"So they hoped to extort money from him?"

"The way I see it—" Eb glanced at Anne.

She nodded. "Go ahead, Mr. Bentley. Your theory makes as much sense as anything else I can think of, probably more."

"Peterson was going to kill David Stone," Eb said. "That way, if the concerned parties in England could get a valid death certificate proving Stone was deceased, the next in line could claim the estate. Be the new earl."

Anne sighed. "I'm afraid it's true. Thomas must have figured it out when he saw the letter addressed to my father—the earl of Stoneford. Marshal, will you prepare a letter to my family's solicitor, Andrew Conrad? He must learn of this as soon as possible. It will be months before it reaches him, I know, but action must be taken in England."

"Who is this person who would get your uncle's money and title?" Nesmith asked.

Anne put her hand to her forehead and drew in a deep breath. "I've no proof, but I fear my cousin is behind all of this. He's in line for the earldom, but he can't inherit a penny unless Uncle David's death is proven."

"I see. Once we sort this all out, I'll write that letter for you, ma'am."

"Thank you. I'll need to go to Eugene as soon as possible to find my uncle and tell him all that has happened."

"I have a man down there," the marshal said. "I'll send him word to look into Mr. Stone's whereabouts. I wouldn't want any more trouble out of this business."

"Miss Anne, you could go as far as Marysville with Eb and me," Rob said. "Corvallis, they call it now. You'd be more than halfway to Eugene, and we'd be happy to escort you that far."

"That's generous of you," Elise said.

Anne smiled at the two men. "It sounds wonderful."

They wrote out statements of the events leading up to their encounter with Peterson, and Rob and Eb took them to a boardinghouse.

"This place has a good reputation," Rob said. "If you want, you can keep your wagon and drive it to Corvallis. Or there's a stagecoach that takes mail that far."

"It would probably be more economical to drive ourselves, if you don't mind our slow pace," Elise said.

Rob nodded. "Fine with me. I was thinking you might want to send a letter right away. If Mr. Stone is set up in Eugene like Mr. Daley said, then you could go on down there. But if he's not, I'd hate to see you go all that way for nothing."

"That might be wise," Anne said.

Elise smiled up at Rob. "I regret that you've delayed getting home to Dulcie on our account."

"So do I," Eb said.

"She'll understand if I take another day or two." Rob eyed his friend for a moment. "So, you want to sleep in a bed here at the boardinghouse tonight?"

"I might get used to luxury then," Eb said.

"Fair enough. We'll camp by the boat landing." Rob said to Anne, "We'll help you get a letter on the steamer in the morning before we set out. If you tell your uncle to write to you at the post office in Corvallis, you might not have long to wait after you get there."

CHAPTER 30

Four days later, Elise and Anne were quite comfortable in their rooms at the City Hotel, a rambling, wood-frame building on the corner of Madison and Second Streets in the bustling town of Corvallis. Rob and Eb had left them two days earlier and returned to their ranches a few miles outside town.

Elise rose early on Monday and donned her best remaining morning dress and matching bonnet. The warm weather prompted her to choose a shawl instead of an overcoat, even though October was nearly upon them.

A light tap on her door announced Anne's arrival.

"Good morning! Ready for breakfast?"

They went down to the dining room, where Anne attacked the generous breakfast with relish. Elise also savored the food, thankful they could eat eggs and toast with jam and butter, and even more thankful that someone else had prepared it all. Immediately afterward they set out for their daily walk to the post office.

"Are you sure we can afford the hotel?" Elise asked, not for the first time.

"My dear, we've settled this," Anne said. "I have a bit left, though not a large bit. It's true that we'll be out of funds soon, no matter what happens. Until we know whether Uncle David is alive and able to help us, we have to live."

"Yes, but we could live more frugally."

"How? By camping in the wagon? No, I'm glad we sold it," Anne said. "The money from that will allow us to continue staying here several more weeks if we must, or to find transportation south to Eugene."

As they entered the post office, the postmaster looked up from his business of sorting mail.

"Ah, Miss Stone. Happy news, I hope." He held out an envelope.

"Oh, thank you!" Anne seized it. "God bless you, sir!"

She and Elise hurried outside and found seats on the front porch of a nearby store. Anne examined the front of the envelope. Her name and "General Delivery, Corvallis" were scrawled across it.

Elise could hardly breathe while she waited for Anne to remove the paper inside and unfold it. The young woman read the message silently then looked at her.

"Well?" Elise asked.

"It says, 'Come on to Eugene. David.' That's all."

"But it's enough," Elise said. "We must send word to the marshal."

"Yes. And to Eb. Elise, listen to me." Anne took her hand and looked earnestly into her eyes. "I want you to marry Eb now. I'll go up the river myself and find Uncle David. It's only two days' journey, or one if I press on at a good pace."

"It's almost fifty miles. You can't do that in one day, even with a good, fast horse and buggy."

"I think I could."

"Well, stop thinking it."

"You don't need to go with me."

Elise looked away. "David should come here to get you. I find it very odd that he didn't say more in his letter." Elise shook her head. "No, I can't let you go alone."

Anne glowered at her. "I should be perfectly safe. We're in civilized territory now."

"That is a matter of opinion."

"Well, let us send our messages and see what arrangements I can make for travel."

They stopped at a store, where Anne purchased several sheets of paper and two envelopes, and continued on to the post office. While she wrote a brief message to the marshal, Elise, at her insistence, penned a note to Eb:

Dear Eb,

We've heard from Anne's uncle and he urges her to go to Eugene. She insists she can travel alone, but I can't let her. I hope we shall make the journey in less than a week.

Elise reread what she had written and then, with blushing cheeks, added, "Surely within a week or two, my errand will be completed and I shall return to Corvallis."

"Don't seal Eb's letter yet," Anne said. "I want to write him a note as well."

"All right."

"Here, can you address this to the marshal for me?" Anne passed her the message she had written and grabbed another sheet of paper.

A minute later, Anne placed both their notes to Eb in an envelope, sealed it, and took their two letters to the counter.

"How long will the one to Mr. Bentley take?" she asked the postmaster.

He squinted down at the address. "Oh, it's only five miles or so out there. Somebody will take it today."

"Wonderful." Anne turned and took Elise's arm. "Come, my dear. Let's go and inquire about boats and buggies and all that sort of thing."

Eb hitched his horse outside the City Hotel and brushed off his clothes. He was wearing a new shirt, and he was careful not to let Speck slobber on it. The sun was sinking, and he hoped he'd find the ladies inside. If they'd headed out this morning, he would be hard pressed to catch them.

He walked into the lobby and ambled to the desk. "Howdy."

"Hello," said the clerk.

"I'm here to see Miss Finster and Miss Stone."

"I believe they're at supper." The clerk nodded to his left, and Eb headed in that direction. He came into a dining room with four long tables. Seated at one of them were Anne, Elise, and six men.

Anne saw him first. She nudged Elise and spoke in her ear. Elise looked up, and her face broke into a beautiful smile. She rose and came to meet him.

"Eb! How wonderful to see you. You didn't have to come."

"Didn't I? Miss Anne seemed to think I should."

"Really?" Elise looked back at Anne, but her friend was deep in conversation with two of the men seated at the table. "We're nearly done eating. Can I get you a cup of coffee? There's an unoccupied table over there—you see?"

She pointed to a smaller table in a corner.

"Sure."

He went to it, and a moment later Elise came over carrying two ironstone mugs.

"Is Miss Anne coming?" he asked.

"She says she will in a minute. One of the gentlemen is quizzing her about London."

Eb held Elise's chair while she slid into it. He sat down. For a moment, he stayed still, looking at her. She sipped her tea and watched him over the rim of her cup.

"You're a sight for sore eyes," Eb said.

"Thank you. I've missed you terribly."

"Have you?" Her words emboldened him to reach for her hand.

"Yes. How is everything at the ranch?"

"Not too bad. A bit overgrown. I've bought twenty head of stock. Planning to get some more next week. And I've. . .fixed up the house a little."

She smiled. "Anne's uncle answered her letter—a bit tersely, but he told her to come."

"So you said in your note."

Elise nodded. "So we're going. We hope to leave tomorrow morning." She lowered her voice. "If we go upstream a ways, we may be able to get a riverboat as far as Eugene."

"Oh, I don't know. It's pretty shallow above here."

"Well, if we must, we'll hire a wagon and horse."

"Elise, stay here."

"What? I can't."

Eb pulled in a deep breath and let it out again. "Anne says you can."

"She can't go by herself. I can't let her."

"Rob says you can, too."

"What?" She eyed him as if he were crazy. "What does Rob have to do with it?"

"He's coming in the morning. Him and Dulcie."

Elise brightened. "We'll get to meet Dulcie at last?"

"That's right. I showed her and Rob your letter and Anne's last night. They both want to come. Elise, they'll take Anne to Eugene."

"What? You're not serious."

"I'm dead serious. They want us to. . .well, you know. To be together. To get married. Now, while Anne's still here. And then they'll take her to Mr. Stone. It will be a nice outing for them, Dulcie says. Rob's been gone all year, and she's been stuck at home by herself. I'll take care of their livestock, and they'll get to have an adventure together. Dulcie's wild to do it."

She seemed to weigh his words carefully. "That's. . .wonderful of them to offer, but I feel obligated to finish what I started. When I've left Anne with David, I'll come back here."

Eb sank back in his chair. He didn't want her to go, but he didn't want to argue either. She was right about Anne—the girl was too young and pretty to travel alone in this country. Why had he let Anne get his hopes up with her silly message? *I think you should come to town now and marry Elise at once.* What did a girl like Anne know about marriage and obligations, anyway? She was only spinning dreams.

But what if they went off and something happened to keep Elise in Eugene? Supposing one of them got injured or became ill? And what about David Stone? Eb had the feeling there was something between him and Elise twenty years ago. She blushed every time his name came up. What if they saw each other again and Elise didn't *want* to come back to Corvallis?

"So. . .you don't know any more about Stone. Whether he's got

a family or anything?"

"No, we don't. The message was very short, but I suppose he was in a hurry to get it off quickly."

Eb thought about that. Maybe Elise was right to be cautious. But he hoped that once she met Dulcie, she'd give in. Everyone loved Dulcie, and she was so sensible and efficient. Elise couldn't say no to her. And Anne's suggestion in her letter of a wedding here in Corvallis before she parted from Elise could come true. That's all he had to do—bide his time. Tomorrow Elise would be his bride.

"Eb! How delightful." Anne stood beside him, beaming down at them.

Eb stood and greeted her. The supper crowd was thinning out.

"Won't you join us, Miss Anne?" he asked.

"Yes, thank you."

Eb pulled out a chair for her.

"I've been thinking," she said, smiling brightly at Elise. "Marshal Nesmith said he has a deputy in Eugene. If I go down there and find this deputy, he can go with me to Uncle David's property. I shall be perfectly safe."

"You don't need to worry about your safety," Eb said. "Rob and Dulcie will go with you."

"What?" Anne stared at him.

"They'll be here in the morning," Eb said. "They want to ride down to Eugene with you. Rob's bringing a wagon, and you can ride together. They'll take you safely to your uncle. Dulcie's looking forward to it."

Anne smiled in triumph at Elise. "It's perfect."

"It does sound. . .fortuitous." Elise shot Eb a glance that seemed almost shy for someone so self-sufficient.

"And you can have the wedding before we set out," Anne said.

Elise raised a hand. "I'm not sure. . . ."

"What?" Anne asked. "If the Whistlers will travel with me, we can have the ceremony right away. Come on, Elise. You can't disappoint me after all these months of planning."

"Who's been planning?" Elise asked.

"I have of course."

Eb swallowed hard. What if she said no again?

"Elise?" he asked softly.

She turned and looked at him with those blue eyes that melted him. "Will you?"

She hesitated a moment.

"I know the preacher pretty well," Eb said.

"This is so sudden."

"A mite, but. . ."

"But you both know you want to be married," Anne said.

Eb raised his eyebrows and waited, barely able to breathe.

Elise clasped his hand. "When will Rob and Dulcie get here?"

"In the morning. I could go around tonight and speak to the preacher."

She pressed her lips together and smiled, blushing to her hairline. "All right, I will."

Something tight let go in Eb's chest. If they'd been alone, he'd have kissed her for sure.

"My dear ladies!" The small, auburn-haired woman hopped down from the wagon before Rob could get around to help her. "I'm so thrilled to meet you. I'm Dulcie."

Elise warmed to her at once and drew her into an embrace. "We're pleased to meet you, too."

Anne kissed her cheek. "Your husband did so much for us on the trail. And now you're both going to help me get to Uncle David."

"I'm looking forward to it more than you can imagine."

"Well, hey there!"

At Rob's warm greeting, Elise looked toward the street. Eb was driving up in another wagon, and another man rode beside him on a chestnut horse.

"Anne," Elise said. "Anne! It's—"

Anne turned and stared. "Oh my." She walked over to the newcomers. "Dan? What are you doing here?"

Eb laughed. "I ran into him when I got into town. He was riding up Madison Street, looking lost."

Dan Adams dismounted and gazed longingly down at Anne. "I couldn't stop wondering if you'd found your uncle. Finally Hector got sick of it and told me to ride on down here and see. I figured if you'd left already, I could ask Mr. Whistler, and he'd know."

"Sure enough, I know!" Rob slapped Dan on the back. "You might as well come to the wedding, Dan."

"Wedding?"

"That's right. Eb and Miss Elise. We're about to walk over to the church. Come along."

On the way, Rob told Dan the details. Anne walked with Dulcie, chattering away about their upcoming trip, and Elise found herself behind them, with Eb at her side.

"Didn't get a chance to say hello, Miss Finster."

She eyed him cautiously. "Miss Finster, is it?"

"I won't get to call you that much longer."

She smiled and slipped her hand through his arm. "Hello, yourself."

"I don't believe I've seen you looking quite this beautiful before."

Elise felt she might explode into a million glittering shards. "Not even in St. Louis, before the wind and the mules and the campfire took their toll?"

He gazed down at her as they walked and squinted up the corners of his eyes. "Not even then. And you were a sight then."

They reached the church, and Dulcie waited for her at the door. "Here, dear Miss Elise. I nearly forgot to give you these." She folded back the muslin cover over a bundle she'd carried. In the crook of her arm lay a plump bouquet of hawkweed and black-eyed susans. "I don't have many tame flowers yet."

"These are lovely," Elise said.

Inside the church, the minister met them with his Bible in his hand.

"Morning, folks." He shook Eb's hand and Rob's.

Rob said, "You know Dulcie. This is the bride, Miss Elise

Finster. And this is her friend, Miss Anne Stone, and a friend of us all, Daniel Adams."

The minister greeted each one. "Are you ready to begin?"

Eb nodded.

"Reckon we should," Rob said. "We've got a trip ahead of us."

"Then come this way."

They followed the minister to the front of the little church. Eb and Elise stood before him, with Anne next to Elise and the others close in a half circle.

This is it, Elise thought. *I'm an American now. I shall never go back to England. I shall never see Stoneford again or wait on Lady Anne.*

She looked up at Eb. He must have seen some flicker in her expression. He took her hand and tucked it through his arm then stood facing the minister but caressing her hand.

She passed the wildflowers to Anne. The minister pronounced the vows, and she and Eb repeated them. When he asked for a ring, Rob surprised her by producing one from his pocket. She looked up at Eb, and he smiled at her. So he'd bought a ring yesterday, too. What else had he done while she basked in blissful ignorance with Anne last evening?

Whatever it was, she knew it was for her peace and comfort.

"I pronounce you man and wife," said the minister.

Eb bent to kiss her, and Elise clung to him for a moment.

Her girlhood dreams couldn't have conjured up this moment if she'd tried. Elise Finster, well-trained lady's maid, marrying a roughhewn rancher in the Oregon Territory.

Eb pulled away slightly and whispered, "Hello, Mrs. Bentley."

Elise smiled. God had reached across two continents to bring her and Eb together. She had never been so happy.

LADY ANNE'S QUEST

CHAPTER 1

October 1855

Halfway across the stream, the front wheel plummeted, and the wagon's whole front end jolted downward. Anne grabbed the edge of her seat and clung to it while trying to brace her feet against the footboard.

"I knew we should have gone to the ferry," her companion, Dulcie Whistler, cried.

Dulcie's husband, Rob, urged his saddle horse alongside them. "You all right?"

"Yes, but we seem to be stuck in a mud hole." Dulcie slapped the reins against the flanks of her team. The two mules leaned into their collars and strained to pull the farm wagon free of the muddy river bottom, to no avail.

"Miss Anne, you going to be all right?" Rob asked.

Anne gritted her teeth and nodded. "I can hold on for a while."

"Good, because the problem seems to be on that side, and I don't think I'd best go around there."

His chestnut horse, Bailey, splashed through the water to the head of Dulcie's off mule. Rob bent over and grabbed the cheek strap on the mule's bridle.

"Come on, Rufus! Pull!"

His urging wasn't enough. The two mules continued to struggle until Anne was afraid they would exhaust themselves.

"Hey, Dan!" Rob waved to the young man who had accompanied them on this journey. "Tell the others to wait. Unhitch Smith's team and bring them up here, but keep to the upstream side." He rode back closer to Dulcie. "Don't worry, sweetheart. We'll double-team you out of there. Triple team, if need be."

Dulcie shook her head. "At least it's so shallow we won't drown if we fall in. I told you we shouldn't have tried to ford here."

"I know, but Mr. Perkins insisted. I don't think he's got much money, and the ferry costs a dollar. This time of year, you can usually get across here with no trouble." Rob looked toward the shore behind them. "Dan's getting the other team ready. You holding on, Miss Anne, or do you want to climb off?"

Anne unclenched her teeth. "I'm not sure how long I can hang on." The wagon's corner sagged so steeply beneath her that her arm and leg muscles were already exhausted from clinging to the seat. And she'd thought her days of rough living on a wagon train had ended a week ago, when she'd rolled into Oregon City.

"Here comes Dan with the other team." Rob turned Bailey and splashed away from them, seeming to forget Anne's predicament.

"I'm sorry, dear," Dulcie said. "Can you hold on to me and pull yourself up higher on the seat?"

Anne grasped the offered arm and levered herself closer to Dulcie. Rob and his horse came even with them again.

"Dan's going to take you off," he told Anne. He went on with Mr. Smith following him and leading the second team of mules.

Dan brought his mount close to the wagon on Dulcie's side. "Can you climb into the wagon bed and get back here? If you get on behind my saddle, Star can carry us both."

Several thoughts flashed through Anne's mind, none of which could be expressed in a genteel manner. Dan thought like a farmer, with no concern for her feminine sensibilities. His very practicality irked her. That and the fact that the young man whose suit she'd rejected a couple of months ago had once more inserted himself into her life without cause.

Dan had invited himself on this trip of about fifty miles, and she knew it was only so he could be near her, a circumstance she'd as soon do without. She wouldn't even spare a thought for the unimaginative name he'd given his horse. The placid gelding had a splotch on his forehead that horsemen referred to as a star, though in shape

it was more of a blob. Now if he'd consulted Anne, she could have helped him think of a name with much more flair. Of course, flair would be wasted on a farmer.

Using all her remaining strength, she hauled herself up and over the back of the wagon seat, with a discreet push from Dulcie. All of her trunks had slid to the front of the tilted wagon box. She clambered over them, trying as best she could to keep her ankles hidden beneath the flounce of her skirt and to avoid Dulcie and Rob's one satchel, all of their bedrolls, a bundle of firewood, and the boxes of foodstuffs and cooking utensils. Once past the major obstacles, she clutched the side of the wagon and pulled herself precariously erect. Dan moved Star forward a step and reached for her. The wagon gave a sudden lurch, and Anne stumbled.

Dan caught her arm and steadied her. He looked forward and shouted, "Hold on, Rob! I'm taking Miss Stone off the wagon."

Too late. The combined teams of mules had thrown their weight into dragging the wagon free. Though Dan lunged to slide an arm around her waist and Anne leaped toward him, she tumbled into the foot-deep river.

She sat for a moment with the water swirling around her. Air ballooned her full calico skirt. It absorbed water and gradually sank to the surface, where the current tugged at it. Anne hastily clapped the sodden fabric against her legs and stared miserably up at Dan.

"Are you all right?" he asked with a grimace.

"I haven't broken anything, if that's what you mean." Anne regretted her curtness. Dan was a kindhearted soul, and her predicament wasn't his fault.

He started to swing his right leg over the saddle, but she shrieked, "Don't get down!"

"Why not?"

"The water will be over your boots. I'm all right." She scrambled to her feet to prove it and stumbled on the uneven river bottom. She was able to catch her balance, but her soaked dress clung to her in a mortifying manner, and the current continued to tug at her legs, skirt, and petticoats. Walking to shore would challenge her.

Dan settled back into the saddle and kicked off his left stirrup. "Well, at least let me pull you up and carry you to shore."

"No."

He frowned down at her. "Are you sure?"

"Positive." Anne could think of nothing that would induce her to give in. The thought of clawing up onto Star's back in her dripping costume made her shudder. The horse would hate having a wet bulk added to his load—and her drenched layers of clothing must weigh a great deal. Beyond that, the picture of herself holding on to Dan while the poor horse picked his way across the Long Tom only confirmed her instincts. With her eye, she measured the distance to the bank they'd left and then to the one ahead of them and set out for the far bank. Dulcie's wagon had nearly reached it, thanks to the extra team of mules.

Anne kept a little upstream, out of the mud the mules had churned up. The water deepened to mid-thigh, but the current wasn't too strong, and she waded against it, finally reaching shore.

"Sorry you took a dunking, Miss Anne," Rob shouted as she stumbled up the low incline.

Dan's horse lunged up the bank, and he dismounted and came to her side.

"I'm so sorry. I'll get a fire going straightaway."

Anne looked toward the wagon. "I need dry clothes."

"Of course." Dan's face flushed. "Mrs. Whistler will help you, I'm sure. We can hang a blanket. . . ."

They both fell silent and watched Dulcie drive the wagon up the slope. When it reached level ground, she called, "Whoa!" and the mules stopped, snorting and shivering.

"Good job," Rob told his wife. He turned his horse and trotted over to Anne and Daniel. "We may as well camp here. It will take several hours for the other five wagons get across on the ferry. Miss Anne, we'll get you dried out in no time."

Anne nodded. Her teeth had begun to chatter. Though the October afternoon wasn't too cold, the breeze cut through her drenched clothing.

Dulcie hopped down from the wagon, hiked up her skirt, and ran toward her. "Anne, you poor thing! Tell me what to get for you. Mr. Adams, get a move on. Start a fire over there, if you please." She pointed to a grassy clearing where others had camped recently.

"Yes, ma'am." Dan's chin sank nearly to his chest as he shuffled away, the picture of contrition.

Dulcie smiled at Anne. "Well, if he hopes to persuade you to marry him on this outing, he's not off to a very good start, is he?"

Anne grimaced. "He's a very nice man. I just—"

Dulcie patted her arm. "Don't fret about it, dear. He came at his own urging. Now, come over to the wagon, and I'll give you a blanket to put around you while I get your dry clothes out. Come. You're shaking."

Anne let Dulcie lead her to the side of the wagon. She'd traveled across the plains during the past six months on Rob Whistler's wagon train, but she'd only met Dulcie yesterday.

Yesterday—the turning point in Anne's life. She'd watched her best friend, Elise Finster, marry the wagon train's scout. Elise had been with her all of Anne's life. She'd helped care for her since birth, on Anne's father's estate in England. She'd even agreed to accompany her young mistress to America after Anne's father died.

Though she was glad Elise had found love on the journey, Anne now felt abandoned. Logic told her that was silly. After all, she had insisted Elise marry Eb Bentley without further delay—in fact, had practically bullied her into it. She hadn't anticipated the emptiness that would descend on her as she journeyed away from her closest friend and confidante.

"Here you go." Dulcie pulled a dry petticoat and stockings from Anne's leather satchel. "Now, for a dry dress. Should I open one of your trunks?"

By the time they'd found a suitable traveling dress and all the accessories Anne needed, Dan had a cheerful fire blazing. To her relief, he crossed the stream again and rode off with the other families to help them ferry their wagons across upstream. She suspected his embarrassment had sent him on the errand. Dulcie and Rob set up camp while Anne changed behind her makeshift screen and dried her hair near the campfire.

"I'm going to make lots of coffee and a big pot of stew," Dulcie said. "If anyone else gets wet, or if any of the other women are too tired to cook, I'll have something to share with them."

"That's kind of you," Anne said.

Dulcie shrugged. "Folks have it hard on the trail, but you know that. I'm sorry we changed your plans for you. You weren't banking on making this trip with five other families—and Dan."

"It's all right."

Anne was mildly surprised to find that she meant it. Mr. Smith had approached Rob in Corvallis. He'd heard the wagon master was going south to Eugene, and he led a small group of families who'd arrived on a wagon train just days after Whistler's had come in. These five families wanted to go to the Eugene area, and they hoped Mr. Whistler would grant them his protection and the benefit of his knowledge of the area by letting them join his party.

"Some of those folks need all the help they can get," Dulcie said.

Anne laughed. "I'm afraid that's true. They're blessed to have Rob leading them, even though they don't have any more big mountains or hostile Indians to face." Although the short trip to Eugene had been planned to help her, she couldn't begrudge the Whistlers' kindness to a few strangers. She pulled her hair back and tied it with a ribbon. "How can I help you?"

Dulcie smiled at her across the fire pit. "You could get out the coffeepot and coffee. Rob brought a couple of buckets of water while you were dressing. Can you make coffee?"

"It's one of the skills I acquired this summer." Anne laughed. "It took awhile to master. In fact, Dan Adams and your husband were the victims of a few of my less successful attempts."

"I just love the way you talk." Dulcie's eyes went all dreamy. "Hard to think I'm out here camping with a fine English lady."

"Oh, you mustn't say that!" Anne glanced about, but no one else was near. "Dan doesn't know about my father's title, and I'd just as soon he didn't."

"I suppose it would discourage him if he found out."

"It's not *that* I'm worried about." Anne realized her words must sound a bit crass. After all, she didn't want to hurt Dan. "It's just that people treat me differently if they know."

Dulcie nodded thoughtfully. "I'll try not to, Miss Anne."

"Just Anne is fine. And thank you. I like the way you and Rob treat me. Let's not allow words to make a difference." She went to the wagon and pulled the coffeepot from the box of pans and kettles. Dulcie's small sack of coffee was stashed inside a biscuit tin as a precaution against dampness, and she took the tin with her to the fireside. She measured the coffee carefully. Even though she would only be with these people another day or two, she did not want to bear their disdain for being a helpless lady who didn't know how to do anything useful. She'd had enough of that.

Dan stayed with the Perkins family as they waited for the ferry to return. Their wagon would be the last to cross the Long Tom River. After watching Dulcie's struggle, none of the others were willing to risk the ford. Loading each of the five wagons separately and waiting while they were deposited on the far bank took almost three hours. Dan regretted missing that time with Anne—yet he was glad to be out of her sight for a while.

He still couldn't believe he'd let her fall into the river. It wasn't truly his fault, but he still felt responsible. He should have told Rob he was about to transfer Anne to his horse. Before the incident, he'd already been low in her esteem. Now he'd sunk to the depths of a well, and the bottom felt mucky.

He should have stayed away.

He and his brother, Hector, had left the wagon train at Oregon City after claiming their land. They'd gone on to Champoeg and found their acreage. It was beautiful—just what they'd hoped for. Hector had plunged into making the open land into a farm. Dan worked beside him, but his heart had flown elsewhere.

After a week, Hector had told him as they nailed down shingles on the cabin's roof, "Daniel, you need to forget that woman."

His harsh tone hurt. "That woman" was Anne, the most beautiful, graceful creature on earth. Dan had lost his heart before they'd even left Independence. Anne seemed to like him. After months on the trail and making himself as agreeable as possible to her and her companion, Miss Finster, he'd put his future in Anne's hands.

Proposing to her scared him to death. He'd blurted it out while they were dancing one night by the flickering light of a bonfire. The stunned look on her face had told him what her answer would be before she uttered a word.

He'd known he wasn't good enough for her. She might as well have said that, but she was too polite. Her excuse was her uncle. Anne had made the journey to find him, not to settle in Oregon. Certainly not to marry a man who planned to farm in Oregon. Her goal was to locate her missing uncle and accompany him back to England, the land of her birth. Apparently Anne's father had died, and this elusive uncle was needed to head up the remaining family. Letters hadn't reached him, and Anne had undertaken the trip with a friend—an older woman who was also charming and ladylike—on a quest to find him. Without trying, Anne had captured and broken Dan's heart.

"I'm not sure I can forget her," he had confessed to Hector.

His brother sighed and laid down his hammer. "Then you'd best go after her."

Dan gaped at him. "What good would that do?"

"Maybe none at all. But if you declare yourself—"

"Did that."

"Again," Hector said testily. "If you lay it all out before her, and she still says no, well then, maybe you'll be able to settle down and work."

"I'm working."

Hector barked out a little laugh. "You've been pounding on the same shingle so long I'm surprised it hasn't splintered all to bits. That's the way it's been all week. Go on, Daniel. Marry her or get over it."

"I...don't know where she's got to now, Hec."

"You know she went as far as Corvallis with Rob and Eb. If she's gone on from there, they'll know where."

Dan swallowed hard. Star could take him to Corvallis in less than a day. "What about you?"

"I'll be fine while you're gone. I'll get this cabin watertight for the winter, and then I'll start breaking ground."

Daniel sat still on the roof with his hammer hanging loosely from his hand. Was there any hope? He didn't think so. Unless Anne had learned that her uncle was dead. That was what she'd feared most, she'd told him once. That Uncle David had passed away, and her arduous journey was for nothing.

She'd need some comfort if that happened. With a lot of prayer, maybe he could convince her that all was not lost—that God had brought her clear out here for another purpose, namely to become Mrs. Daniel Adams.

"You really think she'd listen to me?"

Hector shrugged and reached for another nail. "Maybe not. But if you don't go, you'll always wonder, won't you?"

"I suppose I will."

"Well, go on then. Come back here with Anne or ready to forget her and work harder than you ever have before."

Dan hoped he could find the drive and energy Hector wanted him to show on his return, because he wasn't optimistic about his chances with Anne. Why had he ever thought she might change her mind if she spent more time with him? So far, all he'd managed to do was ride Star along near the wagons and drop Anne in a freezing cold river.

As each wagon lumbered off the ferry, he instructed the driver to take it down to Rob's camp and set up for the night. By the time they got all of them across, darkness was falling. Dan's muscles ached, his belly growled, and he feared he was catching cold. Dulcie met him and the Perkins family with her full coffeepot in hand and invited them to come share the Whistlers' campfire and have supper. The savory beef stew helped take off some of the cold and the gnawing in his midsection, but watching Anne flit about the edge of the circle of firelight kept his stomach from settling.

She didn't ignore him; nor did she pay him special attention. Dan felt smaller and smaller as the others talked around him, planning tomorrow's travel.

"We should make Eugene by midafternoon," Rob said.

"We sure do appreciate your help getting down here safe," Mr. Smith said.

Rob shrugged. "Like I told you, I was coming anyway."

Dan finished his meal and handed Anne his empty plate. "Will you ladies need any more water or firewood tonight?"

"I believe Rob's taken care of everything," she said.

He nodded. "Well, thank you for the meal. It was delicious."

"You're welcome, but Dulcie made it."

Anne walked away with the dishes, and he watched her, an ache in his heart. If she didn't find this missing uncle of hers, she'd be all alone in the world. He'd heard her father had died a year ago. Her journey and the search for her uncle probably eased her grief, but how would she feel when it was over? She'd need something else to think about, that was sure.

He walked past Rob's wagon toward where he'd picketed Star. The bulk of Anne's steamer trunks rose dark in the wagon bed, and he smiled. How could a woman have so much baggage? His mother had owned three dresses: one for everyday, one for town, and one for church. Anne must come from a wealthy family back in England—she and her friend Elise both. Fine quality people, with enough clothes to outfit an entire normal school.

He scowled and turned away from the wagon. Maybe Anne would stay with Elise and Eb at their ranch if things didn't go well with her uncle. She'd certainly made it clear that she didn't want to become Mrs. Daniel Adams.

They broke camp early the next morning. Anne helped Dulcie with breakfast while Rob and Dan helped the other men hitch their teams. The sooner they took to the road, the better. Anne's hands

trembled as she measured out the coffee. She made herself stop hovering over the Whistlers and Dan while they ate, but she was eager to snatch their dishes so she could wash and pack them.

At last they set out southward once more. They rolled toward the hills all morning. When the sun was high overhead, Rob called an hour's stop for nooning, to let the livestock rest. Anne fidgeted until the wheels rolled onward once more.

They'd just reached the hamlet in the shadow of Skinner's Butte when a cry from one of the wagons caused Dulcie to halt her team. Anne looked back to see the men congregating about the Perkinses' wagon.

A couple of minutes later, Rob rode up on his horse.

"Their axle is busted clean through."

Dulcie sighed. "At least we're close. But I surely did hope we'd reach Mr. Stone's house before dark."

"Well, we can fix it, but we'll have to completely unload their wagon." Rob shook his head. "Miss Anne, I'm sorry I let these people talk me into letting them come along with us. I feel responsible to see them safely there."

"Couldn't Anne and I drive on ahead and inquire at the post office as to where her uncle lives?" Dulcie asked.

Rob hesitated. "I promised Miss Finster—that is, Mrs. Bentley—that I'd look after Anne. Besides, Eugene is a pretty tough place, I'm told. I'm not sure you ladies should go there without an escort."

"I hate to lose the daylight," Dulcie said. "Odd how her uncle didn't give her directions."

That very thing had troubled Anne, too. She'd written her letter carefully, telling Uncle David she had come all the way from England to find him. But on Elise's advice, she hadn't mentioned the main reason for her journey. *I'm told you've moved to a farm near the town of Eugene,* she'd written, *and I'd like to visit you. I haven't seen you since I was an infant, and I confess I can't remember you, but I'd be delighted to meet you again and catch you up on the family news. Please send your reply to me at General Delivery, Corvallis. Your loving niece, Anne Stone.*

His simple reply—*Come on to Eugene. David*—had thrilled her and troubled her at the same time. Her uncle was an intelligent, well-educated man. Why hadn't he offered to ride down the river fifty miles to see her? And why hadn't he at least written more than those five words? Was he shocked to hear she was nearby? Was he embarrassed at what she would find? No, if that were true, he could have simply ignored her note and let her think it had gone astray. She had spent eight months trying to find him, and now she was within a few miles of his residence. She felt she would suffocate if they didn't press onward and put an end to her anxiety.

"Let us go on," she said to Rob. "We're this close. We can head into town and wait for you at the post office."

Rob's face twitched and tensed and wriggled. At last he said, "What if I send Dan with you?"

"Yes," Dulcie said quickly. "Or send him with Anne in the wagon. You and I could catch up quickly on horseback, if he'll let me ride his Star."

"Hold on," Rob said. "I'll ask him."

He rode back to where the others had begun unloading the Perkins family's belongings.

"I hope Dan will go," Dulcie said. "You've waited long enough for this."

Anne tried to sit still and not let her face show her anxiety.

Dan cantered Star to where they waited. "Miss Anne, you want to go on ahead to town?"

"Yes, if you're willing, Daniel."

He nodded. "Mr. Whistler says if you want to ride, you can take Bailey. He'll drive Mrs. Whistler on in the wagon after they get the Perkinses squared away."

Anne looked to Dulcie. Would she be disappointed to be left behind while Anne completed her adventure?

"That makes sense," Dulcie said. "You have a riding habit in one of those steamer trunks, I dare say."

"Yes, I do," Anne said. "Would you mind horribly?"

"Of course not. Get your outfit, and I'll help Dan put my saddle on Bailey."

In less than ten minutes, Anne was ready to ride, though she had to call Dulcie behind the bushes to help fasten her bodice correctly. Even though she'd survived the half-year trek to Oregon, she still depended on another woman to help her dress. That bothered Anne. From now on, any clothing she purchased would close in the front, and she would learn to sew more than buttons if it bored her to tears. She settled the matching hat firmly on her head and secured it with two long hat pins. Soft leather gloves and a crop completed her costume.

Dulcie gathered the dress, shoes, and bonnet she had discarded. "Don't you look fine, Miss Anne."

"Why, thank you." Would the other women think she was putting on airs, donning a velvet habit for her entrance to Eugene? She decided not to make the rounds of the wagons to say goodbye. From a distance, they would have fewer details to criticize. She pulled Dulcie to her for a quick embrace. "Thank you for everything."

Dulcie waved a hand through the air. "I'll see you in an hour or two. Mind you stay close to Daniel."

"I will."

"Of course you will. And if you're going on to your uncle's before we get there, leave word for us, won't you? Rob thinks there's a boardinghouse in town, and we'll try to get lodging there tonight. If there isn't a decent place, leave us a note at the post office."

"That sounds like a good plan." Anne walked to where Dan held the two horses. "I'm ready."

Dan's eyes widened as he gazed at her, and his face went pink under his short beard. She hadn't considered the effect her change of attire would have on him. She'd worn the habit a couple of times during the wagon train journey, but she wasn't sure Dan had seen her in it.

She mounted quickly, before he could get ideas about helping her, and gathered the reins. "Shall we go?"

"Yes, ma'am. Rob says the town hasn't had a post office long, but there should be a sign up."

They rode along at a smart trot. Bailey behaved perfectly, and Star kept pace alongside, snorting occasionally. A hill rose sharply from the level ground before them, and at its feet she could see several substantial buildings. Anne's spirits rose. The golden sun shone on a wide, lush valley that promised abundance. Being mounted on a decent horse added a thrill of well-being. She'd always loved to ride, and her father had kept a stable of excellent hunters at Stoneford.

"Do you ever hunt?" she asked on impulse.

Dan frowned. "Well, sure. Hector and I plan to go after elk once we get our house tight."

Anne realized her foolish mistake. Of course he hunted game—several times he'd gone out with hunting parties from the wagon train. How could she think he'd understand she meant riding to hounds? She said, "Of course. How silly of me. I wish you success." She looked ahead to the cluster of houses and businesses that lined the main thoroughfare of the town. "Do you see the post office?"

Dan surveyed the street and pointed. "There." They rode to the small board structure, and Dan dismounted and came around to help Anne down from Bailey's back. He tied her mount to the hitching rail and offered Anne his arm.

Two men were leaning on the counter inside, deep in conversation with the bearded man on the other side. When Anne and Daniel entered, they fell silent and straightened, watching them. Heat flooded Anne's cheeks as she walked forward.

"You the postmaster?" Dan asked.

"Yes, sir. Postmaster, county clerk, and attorney at law. Help you?"

Dan said, "We're trying to locate a man named David Stone. I understand he lives near here."

The postmaster nodded slowly. "There's a fellow by that name south of here. Eight or ten miles, I'd say."

"Does he come in regular for his mail?" Dan asked.

"Haven't seen him for a while. I'd have to ask my wife if he's been in lately. I've been real busy, and a lot of days she's in here to wait on folks."

Dan nodded. "Well, if it's not too much trouble, could you please give us directions to his house?"

Anne felt a new glimmer of hope as the postmaster replied. She and Dan walked out to their horses.

"We can get there and back before nightfall," Dan said.

Anne cast an anxious glance down the street. "No sign of Rob and the others yet."

"That must be the boardinghouse." Dan pointed across the dusty street and down a few buildings. "We'll leave word there and speak for rooms."

"I may want to stay at Uncle David's house tonight," Anne said.

"That'll be fine, if things work out well. But we'd best reserve a place for you in case they don't."

They trotted along swiftly, mindful of the time. Anne made polite conversation so far as was necessary, but Dan was a quiet man, so their words were sparse. She felt sorry for him. He was obviously on edge. A muscle in his cheek twitched now and then, and he threw her frequent glances, part longing and part panic. She supposed he dreaded handing her over to Uncle David and returning to his farm alone. She wished she could soothe his heart, but she had no comfort that wouldn't encourage him to think things she didn't want him thinking.

Her muscles ached as Bailey trotted over the rutted road. Her six months on the trail had strengthened and hardened her, but she'd hardly ridden a horse at all—not since the trading post at Schwartzburg—and her spine now felt each jarring step Bailey took.

After half an hour, she took pity on Dan and threw out an innocuous prologue to conversation.

"I shall miss Elise sorely."

"Oh yes. I imagine you will."

She nodded. "We'd grown very close."

Dan rode in silence for the space of two minutes before he commented again. "I believe you said once that you'd been friends a long time."

"Yes. I've known Elise since I was born." Perhaps this line of talk wasn't so innocuous after all. Anne didn't care to have Dan know that Elise had been her employee—her lady's maid, to be exact. Elise had served her mother for many years, but for the last three, since her mother's death, Elise had been Anne's closest companion, chaperone, and advisor. "We were planning to take a little house together back in England if things didn't work out with Uncle David."

She glanced at Dan. Was she revealing too much? He looked pensive, and she knew he was a thinking man. She did miss having Elise along to discuss things with. Dulcie was a dear, but she was a new acquaintance, and her thoughts seemed to go no deeper than what Rob would like for supper. Rob adored her, it was plain to see, and Dulcie oozed kindness. But sometimes one liked to share one's deeper thoughts.

"And if they did work out? What did Miss Finster plan to do if everything went well? Before she met Eb, I mean."

"She'd have gone home—that is, back to England—with us," Anne said.

"And lived with you?"

"Oh yes." She almost added, "She's lived with my family more than twenty years," but decided that would require further explanations, and so she fell silent. The road had wound through a forest but now came out in open farmland. That was something she could safely discuss with Dan. "The soil seems very rich here."

"Yes." Dan's expression perked up a little as he looked over the fields they were passing. The dark brown earth had been plowed, planted, and harvested, by the look of it. "They say you can get forty bushels of wheat to an acre in this valley."

"That's good, I take it."

"That's very good."

"Then you and your brother should be happy here."

Dan smiled. "Hector will, anyway. He has a sweetheart back East. He hopes to bring her out here next year. But we have to get the house built and the farm producing first."

"Your brother has a sweetheart?" Anne stared at him in surprise.

"I never had an inkling."

"He's pretty tight-lipped about it. She's a schoolteacher. When he told her about his dream of owning a successful farm out here, she agreed to wait for him. Hector's strongly motivated to make the farm succeed, you might say."

"Well, yes." She eyed him thoughtfully. "You should be helping him."

Dan bit his upper lip but said nothing.

Anne looked away. Dan was counting on persuading her to marry him. She could feel it. To pursue that goal, he'd left his brother alone at their new farm. It would probably be kinder to state the truth baldly: she liked him, but she would never consent to marry him. Anne wanted a marriage based on something more than friendship. She wanted a love so deep she knew she couldn't be happy with any other man on earth. It wouldn't be fair to a man like Dan to marry him. He would be good to her, she was sure. He would provide for her to the best of his ability. If she lived on his farm, she would probably be able to see Elise several times a year. But she would never know what it was like to truly love a man.

"That must be the lane up there," Dan said.

Anne looked ahead and saw a road diverge from the more traveled way they followed. They turned the horses in, and she scanned the terrain as far as she could see. A few seconds later, she spotted a small, roughly framed, wooden house with several fenced enclosures around it. A few cattle grazed in one pen, and a thin roan horse trotted along the fence in another.

"Is this it?" she asked.

"I think so."

Anne frowned. The unpainted house looked run-down. She saw no evidence of a garden. A clothesline off to one side caught her eye.

"Dan?"

"What?"

She swallowed hard and pointed. On the clothesline, a man's shirt and trousers hung amid linens, a skirt, two aprons, and a petticoat.

"Oh." Dan glanced keenly at her. "Is he married?"

"That's what I'm wondering. He didn't say." At least no diapers or children's togs flapped in the breeze. "Maybe we've got the wrong house."

"Maybe," Dan said. "If so, whoever lives here should be able to tell us where his place is."

The horses trotted up to the front stoop and halted. Anne sat for a moment, gazing at the door. Dan dismounted and dropped Star's reins. The roan in the paddock whinnied and leaned its head over the fence toward them. Bailey snuffled.

Dan walked around Star and reached up to help Anne down. She touched the ground lightly and stepped away from him immediately. Though she was loath to approach the house, she didn't want Dan to think she enjoyed his touch excessively.

She was almost to the steps when the door opened inward. A stocky man filled the doorway, appraising her. His damp, straw-colored hair looked as though it had recently been in close contact with a pair of dull scissors. His beard was trimmed unevenly to about an inch in length. His waist was bigger around than his chest, and a pair of black suspenders supported his gray trousers. His shirt was a coarse, linen-and-cotton weave.

His calculating look spread into a broad smile. "Anne? Is that you? Why, h'aint you growed into a pretty thing?"

CHAPTER 2

Anne gulped. How could this man be her uncle? Impossible.

She sucked in a deep breath. Though he repelled her, she must use her manners and greet him warmly. He was now her closest living relative. Or was he? Could there possibly be two men named David Stone in the territory? Perhaps this was all a mistake.

Her stomach plummeted at the thought, but she pasted on a smile.

"Hello. I'm searching for Mr. David Stone. Would you happen to know where he lives?"

He laughed, a big, noisy guffaw. "Why, sweetheart, you're lookin' at him." He moved down onto the next step, and Anne backed away, into the solid bulk of Dan Adams.

"Daniel," she gasped.

Dan touched her back only for an instant, and she took comfort from that reassuring pat. He stepped around her, between her and the stranger.

"Howdy. Are you Mr. Stone?"

"Yes, I am," the other man said. He held out a meaty hand. "I'm this little gal's uncle. And who might you be, mister?"

"My name is Daniel Adams."

The man's eyes narrowed to slits as they shook hands, as though he was trying to categorize his guest, but Dan didn't offer more information.

Anne recovered at least a portion of her poise and moved up next to Dan. "I'm sorry, but you're not at all what I expected." She eyed the man. He was several inches taller than she was but not nearly as tall as Daniel. She gazed at his fleshy face, his flinty eyes, and his slicked-back, badly barbered hair.

She longed to bring out the miniature portrait in her handbag, but an inner restraint told her not to. This man could not be the same one who posed for the portrait twenty years ago. Or could he?

"You wrote that you wanted to see me and give me some news," the man said. "Come on in."

Anne looked at Dan. He arched his eyebrows, seeking her opinion.

"Well, I. . ."

"Come on." The man started up the steps again, beckoning with his beefy arm. "Millie's got supper ready."

Anne swallowed hard and looked to Dan again. He held out his crooked arm. She took it and walked with him up the steps and into the little house.

Her eyes took a moment to adjust to the dim interior. The house appeared to be divided into two rooms, and they had entered the kitchen. A cookstove stood to the right, with a stovepipe reaching up and bending to meet the chimney. A rough wooden table stood in the middle of the floor, and a woman came past it with her hands extended in greeting.

"So you're little Anne." She smiled broadly and seized both Anne's hands. "Oh my, what a lovely young woman you are." She threw the man a reproachful glance. "David, you should have told me."

He shrugged. "Didn't know. This here's Millie."

Anne found it hard to rip her gaze away from him and appraise Millie. The woman's thick auburn hair hung loose about her shoulders, and she wore lip rouge. Beyond that, the dim lighting left her in mystery, but her gathered and flounced dress looked to be of decent quality, unlike the man's clothing.

"Is this your husband?" Millie asked.

"No," Anne said quickly. "Dan is just a friend. He offered to ride down here with me, since I didn't want to travel alone." She eyed the stocky man as she spoke, hoping to shame him at least a little for not offering to go to Corvallis for her, but he only smiled and nodded.

"Well, let's sit down, folks. You must be hungry. Millie's been keeping a pot of stew simmering all day. We thought you might get here this afternoon."

344

Millie hurried to a bank of curtained shelves on the far wall and pushed the calico curtain aside. "I only set up for three, but you're welcome to join us, Mr. Adams." She turned with a tin plate and a thick china mug in her hands.

"Let me help you," Anne said.

"Oh no, that's all right. Sit right down." Quickly Millie laid another place setting for Dan. "Just grab that little bench by the window, Mr. Adams."

The four of them sat down at the table, and Millie began ladling out portions of stew. No one mentioned giving thanks for the food, which Anne found unsettling. The Stones had always been God-fearing Anglicans. She glanced at Dan, and he gritted his teeth then said, "Would you mind if I said grace?"

Their host stared blankly at him, but Millie said, "Go right ahead."

Anne closed her eyes. She'd never heard Dan pray before, but his quiet words soothed her.

"Dear Lord, we thank You for a safe journey and for the food we are about to receive. Amen."

"Amen," Anne whispered. She opened her eyes. Millie stood with the ladle in her hand, watching Dan as though waiting for a cue to continue serving.

"So you had a good trip down here from Corvallis?" the man asked.

"Well enough," Dan said.

He looked at Anne. "And did you come all the way across the country, or did you sail?"

"We came by wagon train," she said.

"Is that right?" He shook his head. His drying hair tumbled willy-nilly down his forehead. "Rough trip. Isn't that right, Millie?"

"It's bad enough." She handed him a bowl of stew. "Pass those biscuits around, David."

The food was more palatable than Anne had dared hope, and she ate two biscuits with apple butter and a large bowl of beef stew.

"Your stew is delicious," she said to Millie. "Thank you so much for feeding us."

"Yes," Dan said. "Mighty fine meal, ma'am."

"Oh, it's nothing." But Millie's smile said it was something. "What was the family news you hinted at in your letter to David, Miss Stone?"

"Oh." Anne hesitated, trying to recall the exact wording of her letter. "I assumed Uncle David would want to catch up on the family's doings. You see, my father passed away last year, about this time."

"Oh, that's a shame," Millie said.

"Your father?" the man asked.

"Yes. Your brother. He was—" Anne cleared her throat, uncertain as to how to approach the subject. "Well, as you know, he was the eldest, and he was. . .considered the head of the family."

"Mm." Her host's eyes narrowed, but he said nothing more.

Millie reached over and patted her hand. "There now, you must be feeling kind of blue."

"Yes, I do miss Father." Anne blinked back the threat of tears. "And then there was Uncle John. We tried to write to you, but the letter came back unopened."

"Uncle John?" Millie prodded.

"My father's brother," Anne said. "He was between Father and David in age."

"Oh, what a shame." Millie turned to David. "You've lost two brothers. What an awful blow."

"Yes." He swallowed hard and stared down at his bowl. "Well now. I guess that means some. . .some changes in the family."

"Indeed it does." Anne watched his face, waiting for him to ask about the peerage or the estate. Instead, he lifted his mug. "Got any more coffee over there, Millie?"

"Of course." Millie jumped up. "Miss Stone? Mr. Adams? Would you like more?"

"No, thank you," Anne said, but Dan handed her his mug with a grateful smile.

While Millie poured the coffee, Anne studied David. His gray eyes and blocky frame told her this couldn't be her uncle, but could she be sure? His shaggy beard meant nothing; his once-blond

346

hair could have darkened over time. He could have gained weight, but would he have completely lost his refined British accent? She doubted that, though twenty years among rough Americans might contribute to the effect. And if a man wanted to blend in with those around him, he might make a conscious effort to lose his accent. But still, a man like that would have to be intelligent. This one seemed a bit dense. And Uncle David had surely been intelligent. Elise had adored him, and she'd often said how bright and personable David was as a young man.

If this were the same man, why didn't he seem to care that his two brothers had died within the last year and a half? Why didn't he realize he was now in line for her father's title? He hadn't even asked if she had siblings or if John had married and produced an heir before his death—or even how he'd died, for that matter. It didn't seem natural. She sent up a silent prayer for wisdom.

She noted Millie watching her as she carried the cups to the table. The gleam in Millie's eyes sent a warning through Anne. This woman seemed to have the cleverness David lacked.

"There you go, Mr. Adams." Millie set Dan's cup down beside his plate, smiling down at him. "It surely was kind of you to bring Anne all this way to see her uncle. David tells me that when he last saw her, she was only a baby." She tossed David a sharp glance, and he nodded vigorously.

I did say that in my letter, Anne thought.

"Still in her cradle. Sweet little mite." David reached for his mug. As soon as Millie gave it to him, he took a sip, then drew back quickly from the cup and blew air rapidly in and out of his mouth. After a few seconds he swallowed with a grimace. "Hot."

"Of course it's hot." Millie's snarl softened to almost a purr as she turned back to the guests. "We're so sorry that your papa and his brother passed on. Now, tell me about the rest of the family."

"Oh. Well, my mother is gone as well. She. . ." Anne glanced at Dan, but he was no help. He watched her avidly, but he couldn't guess at her inner turmoil. Anne hoped the depth of her distress didn't show on her face.

"Aw, that's terrible," Millie said.

Anne gulped, hoping fervently that Millie was not her new aunt. "Thank you. It's been three years and more."

"And do you have brothers and sisters?" Millie asked.

"No."

"Oh, so you're all alone now. What a pity." Millie looked over at David, as though expecting him to say something.

"Sorry," David said. He worked his mouth for a moment, contorting his face. "Get me some water, Mill. I burnt my tongue."

Millie got up and went to her worktable, returning with another cup, this one filled with water. "So, Miss Stone, you made this journey all the way from England to Oregon to find David, or did you come for some other reason?" Millie asked.

"Well, I. . ." Anne hesitated. "There was the matter of. . ." She glanced at Dan. He didn't know the whole of her mission, and she wished she'd explained it all to him on the way. How could she get around this now without either lying or giving away too much? If this man was truly her uncle, he had a right to know his own situation. And yet, if he *was* her uncle, why hadn't he figured it out by himself? Her father had told her more than once that David had struck out for America because he was certain he'd never inherit—being the third son set you free from family responsibilities.

"Speak up, girl," Millie said with a smile that seemed to Anne a bit calculating. "We're all family here. Well, except Mr. Adams, that is."

Dan cleared his throat and looked at Anne. His cheeks reddened above his short beard.

"Oh, maybe that's only a matter of time." David guffawed. "Is that the way the wind blows?"

"No," Dan said. "I'm only a friend, as Miss Stone said."

"I see." David smiled knowingly and turned his attention back to Anne. "Go on then. What brought you thousands of miles to see me?"

Anne's stomach seemed to drop away. She clenched her hands in her lap. "When my father died—well, there's the matter of his estate—"

"His estate?" David reached for another biscuit. "Did he leave you much?"

"David, that's rude," Millie said.

"Well. . ." Anne gulped and looked helplessly at Dan.

"Perhaps that's a private matter," Dan suggested.

"Well, it would be, but. . .well, my income is separate from your inheritance. . . ."

David looked up from the biscuit he slathered with apple butter. "*My* inheritance?"

"David inherits something?" Millie asked.

Anne nodded.

Millie's smile blossomed. "Well, speak up. What does he inherit?"

CHAPTER 3

You mean my brother left me something in his will?" David grinned at Anne. "Now, isn't that the nicest thing you ever heard?"

"What is it?" Millie asked. "Money?"

Anne shrank in her chair. "Well, uh. . ." She looked to Dan again, as though casting about for a lifeline. What did she expect him to do? He had no idea what was going on.

Of course, there was that incident on the wagon train, where Anne's hired man had stolen a letter from her luggage. Wasn't it a letter from her missing uncle? And did that have anything to do with all of this?

"I'm sure the family's lawyer will contact you about it, now that Miss Stone has found you," he said.

Anne's look of gratitude made all of the heartache he'd endured in the last six months worthwhile. She smiled and caught her breath.

"That's right, Uncle David. Our solicitor tried to locate you in St. Louis—"

"St. Louie?"

"Yes," Anne said. "Your last letter to Father came from there."

"Oh, of course." David gave a little laugh. "Been a while since I was in St. Louie."

"Yes. More than ten years. We all wondered where you'd gone. If you were still alive, even." Anne stopped and pressed her lips together.

"Well, you've found him now," Millie said heartily. "So just what does this inheritance amount to?"

When Anne hesitated, Dan said, "I'm not sure she can tell you that, ma'am. Doesn't the lawyer have to send official notification or something?" He eyed Anne keenly, hoping she'd see that he was offering her a way out if she didn't want to disclose any further information.

Anne seized the opportunity. "That's right. I felt like traveling, so a friend and I decided to come to America and look you up." She smiled a little too brightly for the paleness of her face, Dan thought.

"This friend?" Millie gazed at Dan.

"Oh no. Not Daniel. It was Elise Finster. Do you remember Elise, Uncle David?"

"Hmm. . .Elise. . ." He frowned and shook his head. "Can't say as I do."

"She was my—" Anne faltered to a stop and swallowed hard. "She's a good friend. She sailed to New York with me, and we made the trip west together."

"Oh. So where is she now?" David sounded a little nervous, and he glanced toward the door as if more British people were about to invade his home.

"She stayed in Corvallis," Anne said. "But she'd be delighted to see you again, if you wish."

Dan noted that Anne didn't mention her friend's marriage. She seemed to have grown cagey and was trying to keep from letting go of any more information than was necessary now. Maybe this was the time to get her away and have a long talk.

He shifted, as though about to rise. "Well, this has been a pleasant visit, and I'm so glad I was able to help Anne find you. But if we wish to get back to Eugene before total dark, we need to be going."

"Eugene?" Millie asked, her dark eyebrows flying upward. "You can stay here. No need to ride all that way tonight."

"Oh no, we have friends expecting us," Anne said hastily.

Dan jumped up and pulled out her chair as she rose.

"Now, wait," David said. "This inheritance. What do I have to do to find out more?"

"Perhaps I can come back tomorrow." Anne threw Dan a worried glance. "I can't tell you figures or anything like that, but I can bring you the solicitor's address in England so you can write to him."

"You mean you ain't got it with you?" David asked.

"Why, I. . ."

"We left all our luggage with our friends," Dan said. He could hardly believe an English gentleman—even one who had been in America for twenty years—would address a lady in such a manner.

"That's right," Anne said. "In fact, I borrowed a horse from them so we could ride out here quickly. But we'll come back in the morning."

"I can't persuade you to stay?" Millie stepped close to Anne. "Honey, we can make you a bed near the stove just as cozy—"

"Oh no, thank you. We have rooms waiting for us in Eugene."

Millie's smile disappeared. "Fine. Let me get your things." She walked to the pegs where Dan's hat and Anne's jacket hung.

David was still gaping at Anne. "I certainly didn't expect to inherit anything from your father."

Anne's eyes narrowed. "You didn't?"

"Well, no. Why should I?"

"As I explained earlier, Uncle John is also deceased. He had no heirs."

"That was mighty nice of him, but how come you don't get it all?"

Anne drew in a deep breath but seemed unable to speak.

Millie came over and held out Dan's hat. Turning to Anne, she offered the velvet jacket of her habit. "Did your pa name David in his will and cut you out or what?"

Anne made a strangled sound.

"Nothing like that, I assure you," Dan said, taking Anne's jacket. He held it for her, determined to remove her from the house as swiftly as possible. "We promised our friends we'd get back before night, so we must go."

"Well, we'll be looking for you in the morning." Millie's voice had taken on a hard edge.

"Yeah, bring them papers with you. Address and such." David walked to the door with them and opened it.

Dusk had fallen over the valley. Dan led Anne to the horses and tightened Bailey's saddle cinch. As he untied the horse and turned the gelding toward Anne, her uncle followed them down the steps and grasped Anne's sleeve.

"There's more to this than you're saying, gal."

"Let go of me."

Anne's icy voice spurred Dan to action. He stepped up beside her and glared at her uncle. "Stand back, Stone. We'll bring everything necessary in the morning."

David glowered at him. "Make sure you do."

They cantered out of the dooryard and northward toward Eugene. Neither spoke until they'd gone nearly a mile. Anne slowed Bailey, and Dan let Star drop into a trot, too.

"Dan, I must apologize to you."

"Whatever for?" he asked. "Seems to me your uncle and aunt are the ones who need to apologize."

"I should have told you everything before we set out for this place. I deeply regret not doing so."

Dan's face softened. "Miss Anne, you have no obligation to me whatsoever."

She turned forward for a moment while she tried to collect herself. Her face burned. "That may have been true until today, but I owe you much for what you did in there."

Dan rode in silence for a moment, then said, "I'm glad I was along."

"So am I!" She looked at him in the twilight. "Daniel Adams, I can't imagine what would have become of me if I hadn't had you to lean on. At first, I thought it was just me. I was disappointed that my uncle wasn't all I'd expected him to be. Not just his appearance—though I'd imagined him to be taller, fairer, and more. . .shall we say, more fit? And his eyes. In the portraits we have of him, his eyes are quite blue."

"You might say they were blue," Dan said pensively. "Sort of grayish blue."

"Yes. Not at all the vivid blue in the paintings. I told myself, that is the painter's fancy. But I knew it wasn't. You see, my father's eyes were blue, and Uncle John's as well. At Stoneford there's a portrait of the three brothers. They sat for it when David was fourteen. And his eyes are the same shade as Father's and John's."

"Your eyes are brown," Dan pointed out.

"True. They say I favor my mother, which is a great compliment. Her hair was a rich brunette, and her eyes brown." Anne sighed. Now was not the time to get sidetracked in her memories. "But this man! He claims to be my uncle, but he can't be. His manner is vulgar, and his speech—what can I say? No Englishman of gentle birth would so forsake the language. It's not as though he hiked about the wilderness with trappers for twenty years. He ran a respectable business in St. Louis and then in Oregon City. People recalled his British accent."

Dan nodded soberly. "You believe this fellow is an impostor."

"Yes." Relieved to have said it, Anne huffed out a deep breath. "I see no other explanation. Add to that the fact that he knew nothing of the family's matters. He didn't ask after any family members, and he didn't seem to know the first thing about. . .well, about anything I hadn't put in my letter or mentioned after we arrived."

"I see what you mean. And that woman—she's a sly one."

"Isn't she?" Anne shuddered. "I can't bear to think of her presiding at Stoneford."

"This. . .Stoneford," Dan said. "That's your home in England?"

"Yes." She looked down at her hands, grasping Bailey's reins. The well-trained horse kept up his trot without urging from her. She'd given no thought to guiding him for the last mile. "Dan, I should have explained my family's situation to you. But you see, Elise and I had agreed before we left New York that it was best to keep it quiet. Other people didn't look at me the same way if they knew. . . ."

"It's all right," Dan said. "I believe in privacy."

"Yes, and I appreciate that. This wasn't really a secret, but it seemed more effective not to shout it about—sort of like your brother's fiancée. I'm sure if Hector had felt anyone needed to know, he'd have told them."

"Certainly he would."

b Anne nodded. "So I'm telling you. My uncle David—whether he is this man or not—and I highly doubt that he is—" She hesitated, knowing their relationship would change forever when she uttered her next few words.

"Yes?" Dan said gently.

"He inherits everything—Stoneford and all its lands, the family fortune, and the title."

"Title?"

Dan's frown for some reason tugged at her heart like an infant's cry. He was so innocent, so guileless.

She swallowed hard and forced herself to say it. "My father was the earl of Stoneford. The title and the estate are passed down to male heirs only under British law. I, being a female, do not inherit."

"I. . .see."

Darkness had cloaked them so that Anne could still see his face, but indistinctly. What was he thinking?

"I had no brothers," she added.

"So your father's brothers are next in line."

"Exactly. Uncle John was next. Unfortunately, he died in battle unmarried. Uncle David had no way of knowing that. But it's up to him now, him and his sons—if he has any." She thought of the man they'd just left at the little farmhouse and shivered again.

"If that man is your uncle, I'll eat my hat," Dan said.

She smiled at that. "Thank you! For that and so much else you've done today."

"I could see how uncomfortable you were, and I knew something wasn't right. At first I wondered how you could have such a crude relative. It didn't take me long to see that you wondered the same thing and were having doubts about coming here."

Anne nodded. "That's when I decided not to tell him about the earldom or give him details about how to claim his inheritance. I wish I hadn't said a word about it, but I had, so it's too late. I'll have to go back tomorrow."

"We'll tell Rob everything. He'll go with us."

"Yes." That thought buoyed her. "He's a very smart man, and he reads people well. I've another card to play, too."

"Oh?" Dan asked.

"You know I had some dealings with the marshal in Oregon City."

"Yes. That fellow Peterson was trying to hunt down your uncle. I'm beginning to understand why."

"My uncle—my real uncle, I should say—is worth a lot of money to some people. What worries me most is that to some he's worth more dead than alive."

Dan pulled back on Star's reins. Both horses stopped, and Dan peered at her in the darkness. "Is there another brother?"

"No. But there is a cousin. He can't inherit unless David is proven dead."

Dan let out a deep sigh. "Now it makes sense. Anne, I'm so sorry."

"So am I."

He nudged his horse closer to hers. "We'd best hurry back to Eugene."

"I agree. As I was about to tell you, the marshal has a deputy there. Perhaps he would come out here with us and Rob tomorrow. If we act cleverly, I'm sure we can expose this charlatan."

"Yes, but we need to make sure before we leave town tomorrow that the person who owns this farm is really your uncle. There could be two David Stones."

"Yes, there is that."

"Well, let's get a move on. I don't like to have you out here in the open like this, now that I know your story."

Anne chuckled. "I'm in no danger. And I have a rather large, armed escort along."

"Well thank you, ma'am," Dan said, "but I disagree. You are the messenger who wants to alert your uncle to his new position and wealth. Remember Peterson? There may be someone else out there who would like you to give up the search."

CHAPTER 4

The boarders had long since eaten their supper when Anne and Daniel rode into Eugene, but the landlady had graciously set out coffee, crackers, cheese, and cookies for them and the Whistlers in her parlor. Dulcie's reaction to Anne's story was as Dan would have expected—she gathered Anne to her bosom and assured her that Rob would get to the bottom of things. Dan fully anticipated Rob to continue wearing his captain's persona, willing to take charge and face down the imposter.

Rob, however, surprised him by going out immediately to fetch the deputy marshal. While he was gone, Dulcie told them of how they'd at last untangled themselves from the pioneer families. Rob had spent a good half hour at the post office, talking to Eugene Skinner, the postmaster and founder of the city. One of their numerous topics had been where Rob could locate the deputy marshal for Miss Stone, so that she could check in with him as Marshal Nesmith had instructed her in Oregon City.

Rob returned with "Bank" Raynor in tow. The deputy stood only a couple of inches taller than Anne, and thin as a sapling, but his face—the part that showed above his gray-streaked beard—looked like a tanned hide. As he entered the parlor, he snatched off a disreputable-looking felt hat. He wore tall boots over whip-cord breeches. A long hunting shirt hung down below his buckskin jacket. A sheathed hunting knife was mounted on his rawhide belt, and he wore a long-barreled pistol strapped to his side. Dan decided that Raynor was the man to have beside him if he ever came face-to-face with a grizzly.

After the introductions, Rob set a chair for the deputy strategically near the food, the fire, and Anne. It seemed prudent to Dan to keep in the background, so he eased around to the corner, where he leaned against the wall and listened to the conversation, but contributed only when asked a question.

Patiently, Anne told her story again, from the death of the earl back in England to the strange couple they'd found living at the farm south of Eugene City.

When she'd finished, Bank Raynor sat in silence for a long minute, gazing at her face. He'd downed a great quantity of cheese, at least half-a-dozen cookies, and two cups of coffee. Dan wondered if he was feeling sluggish, lulled by the warmth of the fire and Anne's musical voice.

"So, what should I call you?" he asked at last. "Are you 'your ladyship,' or 'countess,' or what?"

Anne smiled at him. "Miss Stone is fine, sir."

"And you can call me Bank."

"All right."

Bank moved slightly, making the smallest gesture with his coffee cup, and Dulcie jumped to refill it.

"So, Miss Stone, you have several indications that the man who claims to be your uncle is not really your uncle."

"That's right," Anne said.

"Is there any possibility that this is all a misunderstanding—that this is another individual with the same name? Stone is not that uncommon."

"I thought of that." Anne clasped her hands on her knees and leaned toward the deputy. Her earnest, beautiful face couldn't help but win him over, Dan thought. "If it were a mistake, surely he would have protested when he read my letter, saying I had arrived from England. Wouldn't he have written back asking questions? Suppose this other David Stone coincidentally had a niece in England, too. Wouldn't he balk when I told him his two brothers had died? I don't know as I mentioned my father's given name, Richard, to him, but I surely told him about my uncle John's death. I also spoke of my mother, and I mentioned a longtime family servant by name. Why didn't he raise questions?"

Bank shot a glance into the corner, surprising Dan. He'd almost

felt invisible. As the deputy addressed him, he straightened his shoulders.

"You agree with that, Adams?"

"Yes, sir. Miss Anne mentioned several things that would cause a complete stranger—one with any integrity, that is—to say, 'Hold on, miss, you must have made a mistake.' But this fellow never did that. And he kept trying to draw more information out of her."

Anne nodded. "His companion, too. Millie. She seemed especially anxious to learn more about my family and my father's will. I wish I'd never mentioned that, but on our arrival I was so confused I wasn't sure how to proceed. As it was, I at least had the presence of mind not to give them any details about the estate or Uncle David's inheritance. But I did let fall that an inheritance from my father would come to him. I shouldn't have done that, but there it is. I was still sorting the facts and realizing that this man knew nothing about how English inheritance law works."

Bank nodded, stroking his beard. "And you first made contact with this man when?"

"Last week. I wrote a brief letter from Corvallis as soon as we arrived overland."

"Right. But you didn't tell him in the letter about the earl dying or his inheritance."

"No, sir," Anne replied. "I wanted to break it to him in person. And so far as I know, he still doesn't realize that my father was an earl."

Dan folded his arms and leaned back into the corner again. He was beat, and Anne had dark shadows beneath her expressive brown eyes. He hadn't taken the time yet to work out the implications of all he'd learned that afternoon. The woman he loved was a true aristocrat. He'd always known Anne was quality, but the daughter of an earl! How could he ever have imagined she might accept his suit? He shook his head. He and Hector would have a good laugh someday over his audacity, but right now his heart ached too painfully for him to see it as humorous. Maybe one day, Uncle Dan would take his brother's kiddies on his knees when they asked him why he was still a bachelor and tell them the tale of "The Lady and the Farmer."

Rob set his coffee cup on the side table. "Sure wish I'd known about this before I met Mr. Skinner yesterday. He seemed to know who Mr. Stone was and think well of him. Said he last came in for his mail a few weeks ago." He shrugged. "Miss Anne, maybe there's a way you could test this fellow to find out for sure how much he knows."

Bank nodded. "I was thinking the same thing. Trap him somehow into showing he's no kin to you."

Anne opened her handbag and reached into it. "I agree. I'd like to show you the portrait I have of Uncle David. I've shown it to Mr. Whistler before, but I don't believe Mrs. Whistler or Mr. Adams has seen it." She took out the framed miniature she'd carried from England to Oregon, opened the case, and passed it to Bank. "He was the youngest of the three brothers. Of course I don't personally remember him, since he left England while I was a baby, but I'm told this is a good likeness of him at the age of twenty—that is, about twenty years ago."

Bank studied the picture and handed it to Dulcie.

"Oh, he's a gorgeous boy," Dulcie said. "Those eyes! And lashes as long as a girl's." She passed the miniature to Daniel.

He looked down at it. The blond young man in the portrait was indeed handsome, with wavy locks and vivid blue eyes. Any young woman would swoon over him. Dan glanced over at Anne and met her gaze. "He's as unlike the man we met today as a bluebird from a blue jay."

Anne smiled. "Yes. Alike in a few general characteristics, but very different. I might have accepted that he'd gained weight and coarsened his looks through drink and poor food, but his manner of speech and gaps in knowledge clinched it for me. He's not my uncle."

Dan passed the portrait back to her and resumed his place in the corner.

"Well, an obvious way to trick him would be to ask if he remembers something and make the details wrong," Rob said. "If he

agrees with you, he's lying."

Anne nodded. "Perhaps we can plan such a snare." She drew two envelopes from her handbag. "I also have the last letter my father received from him ten years ago. It's quite worn and tattered, I fear, but I ask you to put it next to this brief note I received in Corvallis and tell me whether the same person could possibly have written the two."

Bank carefully extracted the first letter and glanced at the flowing script that went on for two full pages.

"Is that the same one that was stolen from your luggage on the wagon train?" Rob asked.

"Yes, and I'm extremely thankful that you and the other men on the train were able to recover it for me."

Bank opened the second letter and grunted. After a moment, he held the two envelopes side by side. "Interesting. Not only are these addressed in different hands, but I submit that the person who addressed this second one is not the person who wrote the note inside it."

"I agree with you again," Anne said with a smile. "My guess is that David—or whatever his name really is—wrote the note, and Millie addressed it for him."

Bank passed the two letters to Dan, and he compared the handwriting, especially that on the two envelopes. "Something tells me that reading and writing are not his long suit."

"No. But my uncle David was an avid reader. In that letter to my father, he mentioned two books he had recently read." Anne placed the miniature back in her purse. "I should have seen it earlier. In fact, I did see it—or at least I saw clues that made me uneasy. But I didn't want to believe I was being deceived. I've looked so long and hard for him that I wanted it to be true. I wanted my search to have finally come to an end."

"Of course," Dulcie said. She reached over and patted Anne's shoulder. "I'm so sorry, my dear."

"Don't worry," Rob said. "We'll get the truth out of that scoundrel tomorrow."

Dan wondered whether they would. Maybe they could prove the man at Stone's farm was an imposter, but would that bring them any closer to finding Anne's uncle?

Anne rode in the wagon the next day, with Dan driving. Rob and Bank rode their horses just ahead of them. Much to Dulcie's chagrin, Rob had insisted she stay in Eugene City and make the acquaintance of Mrs. Skinner.

"We don't know what this fella will do when we confront him," he pointed out. "We know he's slippery. I figure having to protect Miss Anne is a big enough worry for the three of us, without you being there, too. And if it comes down to needing support in this town, we'll need the Skinners on our side."

Dulcie huffed and rolled her eyes, but in the end she persuaded the landlady to prepare a small cake for her to carry to the Skinner house after the others set out.

Anne rode first to the county courthouse, at Rob's suggestion. They all hoped the people and records there could shed some light on the situation. The clerk behind the desk produced a copy of the deed to Anne's uncle's property.

"I remember him," the clerk said. "Tall, fair man with a British accent."

"Yes," Anne said, delighted to hear this description that coincided with her expectations.

"You should talk to Mr. Skinner. He's the county clerk. I'm just an underling. He'll know more about it, I daresay."

"I was hoping Mr. Skinner would be here today," Bank said. "Would he be over at the post office?"

"He might. Some days he's off on business."

Bank nodded. "Come, Miss Stone, we can stop in at the post office. I doubt Mr. Skinner can take the time to ride out there with us, but it would be good to at least get his take on this."

Dan went into the post office and came out frowning. "He's gone for the day. Rode up the valley—something to do with cattle."

"All right then, we'll proceed as we planned last night," Bank said. "You ready, Miss Stone?"

"Yes." Anne didn't really feel ready to confront the man at Uncle David's farm again, but she was glad she had three stouthearted gentlemen with her this time.

A low ceiling above them threatened rain as they rode southward. Anne wore her woolen overcoat, warm wool gloves, and a floppy velvet bonnet that covered her ears. Dan turned up his collar and settled his hat low on his head. He had leather gloves, but Anne thought he might do well with a soft muffler. Perhaps she would knit him one to show her appreciation for his support in this venture. Elise had taught her to knit, and while she couldn't tackle anything with size yet, a muffler should be within her ability.

They arrived at the small house as the first raindrops splashed down. Dan helped Anne down from the wagon. Rob eyed the nearby barn and dismounted.

"Wonder if we can put the horses under cover."

"Let's see what we get for a reception," Bank said.

They walked to the door, and Dan knocked. A moment later, Millie opened it. She looked at him and Anne, then past them to Rob and the marshal. Her eyes flared, but she stood back and opened the door wider, her expression neutral.

"Good morning. I see you've brought some friends."

"Yes." Anne walked into the house and spotted David standing near the table.

His face clouded as the men entered behind her. "What's this?"

"Hello." Anne smiled. "I hope you don't mind. I brought along my dear friend Rob Whistler. I mentioned him to you yesterday." She gestured toward Rob. "And this is Deputy Marshal Bank Raynor."

"Marshal?" David scowled at Bank, then looked back at Anne. "What did you bring him for?"

Bank stepped forward. "My boss—him being Marshal Nesmith, up in Oregon City—asked me to ride out here with Miss Stone and make sure everything went all right. Seems she had a little trouble up north of here when she tried to find you."

"Is that right?" David looked back to Anne. "You didn't tell me."

Bank said, "Well, somebody didn't want her to find her uncle. That fella's in jail now, but the marshal asked me to see that there weren't any shenanigans today."

David stared at him uncertainly.

Millie stepped forward. "Well, isn't that thoughtful of you? We had no idea Anne had so much trouble. Won't you all sit down? I think we have enough seats. Let me see. . . ."

A few minutes later, Anne and Millie were seated at the table with David and Bank, while Rob and Dan stood back to listen.

"Now, Mr. Stone," Bank began, "it seems you've been named as an heir in the will of Miss Stone's father. You can understand why we want to be sure you're the right man before she gives the information on how to claim that inheritance."

"Well, uh, sure." David looked to Millie, but she said nothing.

"So, I have here some information. . ." Bank took a slip of paper from the pocket of his hunting shirt. On it, Anne had written a few facts about her family the evening before. "Now, can you just confirm for me, please, your date and place of birth?"

"Uh. . ." David swiveled his head and again looked at Millie.

She gave a slight nod without changing the tight set of her mouth.

"Let's see. . .I was born. . .uh, that would be May 16, 1824."

As he spoke, Anne watched Millie. She closed her eyes briefly but otherwise didn't move. Anne knew the date was off by nearly ten years but didn't speak up.

"And whereabouts was that?" Bank asked.

"Oh, in England," David said more confidently.

"Where in England?"

"Mm, outside of London."

"Could you name a town, sir? Or a county at least?"

"Uh. . .it's been a long time. I'm not sure I remember."

Bank grunted and looked down at the paper. "And could you name your four siblings for me?"

"Huh?" David stared at him blankly.

"Brothers and sisters," Millie said. "He wants to know the names

of your brothers and sisters."

"Oh." David ran a hand through his beard. "Well, uh, there was me and...me and Anne's father, and...hmm...well, there was John."

His gaze darted to Millie and then to Anne.

Anne tried to smile encouragingly.

"Uh, Millie, can you get me some coffee?" David asked.

"Certainly." Millie hurried to the stove and then bustled about between the cupboard and the table.

Anne rose. "May I help you, Millie?"

"Uh, sure. There's two more cups there. See if the other gents want coffee, would you?"

A few minutes later, David, Bank, and Rob sipped their coffee. Anne caught Dan's gaze as she resumed her seat. Dan nodded soberly.

"Well, then," Millie said, "maybe we can get on with the paperwork now. Is there something for David to sign?"

"Not just yet," Bank said. "Mr. Stone, it appears you don't know much about your family."

"Well, now, that's a fact." David smiled sheepishly. "You know, it's been a long time since I saw any of 'em."

"But still," Bank said. "You ought to know when you was born. Any man should know that."

"What'd I say?" David asked. "Don't tell me I gave you the date wrong."

"You certainly did."

"Well, what do you have? Maybe somebody copied it wrong."

Bank scowled at him. "I don't think so, but if you can tell me your mother's name—"

Millie shoved her chair back. "This is ridiculous. David's scatterbrained. So what? Does that mean he can't have what's rightfully his?"

"Not at all," Bank said. "I'm just not sure anything's rightfully his."

"Why, you!" Millie stood shaking and glowering at Bank. "It's not his fault that he's stupid."

"That's right," David said. "That old dun mare of mine kicked me in the head last fall. I can't remember half of nothing since then."

Anne managed to keep a straight face, but Bank let out a guffaw, and Rob barked a little laugh as well.

"Is that right, ma'am?" Bank asked Millie. "Did he take a kick to the head recently?"

Millie hiked her chin up. "Yes, he did. If I hadn't nursed him back to health, Miss Stone here wouldn't have an uncle to her name." She turned a malevolent glare on Anne.

"Well, then," Rob said with a deferential glance at Bank, "perhaps you could answer a few questions, ma'am. Maybe you can tell us the name of your mother-in-law."

"Well. . ." Millie's mouth twitched.

"Her mother-in-law?" David said.

"Yes, I asked your wife if she could tell me your mother's name," Rob said.

"She's not my wife," David said with an injured air.

"Oh, pardon me," Rob said.

Millie's face had gone crimson, though with mortification or rage, Anne couldn't tell.

"And just what is your relationship to this gentleman?" Bank asked.

"I don't see that that's any of your business," Millie replied.

Rob smiled apologetically. "So you can't help him with the necessary information? That's too bad, ma'am, because if he really is entitled to something, it'd be a shame if he couldn't claim it."

Millie didn't speak, but her face shivered and squirmed until Anne thought she would explode.

"Well then, I guess it's time for us to hit the road," Rob said. He stood and pulled out Anne's chair for her.

Anne rose and cleared her throat. "Well, I, uh. . .I guess we'll be going." This was where she would ordinarily thank her hostess and assure her that meeting her had been a pleasure. For once in her life, Anne's manners didn't help her.

Dan held up her coat. "Come on, Miss Anne."

Bank rose, turned, and took a step toward David until their noses

were only inches apart. "I don't suppose you want to tell us where the real David Stone is—the gentleman who owns this property?"

"I own it," their host said.

"Oh really? Can you show us a deed?"

"Well, uh. . ."

"You'd have to go to the county courthouse for that," Millie said. "He doesn't keep it in the house."

"Funny thing," Bank said. "We were there this morning. We saw the deed on file. And the man who owns this land was able to give them proof of his identity." He stretched up into David's face. "And he isn't you." He drew his pistol and poked it into the man's ribs. "You want to tell me who you really are?"

CHAPTER 5

He's David Stone." Millie's voice was like granite.

"Really?" Bank didn't bother to look her way but kept staring into the man's eyes. "Ma'am, did you know it's a crime to abet a criminal?" He prodded their host. "Put your hands up. I'm taking you back to town."

Slowly the man raised his hands. "I didn't do anything. Millie—"

"As far as I know, his name is David Stone," she said. "I haven't been here that long, but that's the only name I know him by."

"Millie—"

"Don't talk," she snarled. "Are you completely daft? If you want to go to prison, go, but you're not taking me with you." She strode to the door, snagging a shawl from a peg on her way out.

The door slammed shut behind her.

"You want me to stop her?" Dan asked.

"Not unless she's stealing one of our horses," Bank said.

Dan hurried outside, and Rob followed.

"Miss Stone," the deputy said, "I'm going to truss this fella up and put him in the back of the wagon. That all right with you? If you'd rather not ride with him, you can take my nag."

Anne looked down at her full-skirted traveling dress. She hadn't brought Dulcie's sidesaddle along today. "I'll be fine in the wagon, so long as you search him first for weapons."

"No fear."

Anne nodded and staggered out the door. Her legs felt like rubber. Dan met her on the steps and offered his arm.

"Where is she?" Anne asked.

"She went to the barn. Rob's keeping an eye on her."

"Mr. Raynor plans to take the man back to Eugene."

"Fine by me." Dan went with her to the wagon and gave her a hand up.

368

The barn door opened, and Millie rode out on a chestnut horse. She cantered toward the road without looking their way.

A few minutes later, they set out with Dan driving and the man who claimed to be David Stone tied up in the back. Bank and Rob rode close behind them, watching the prisoner every step of the way.

As they drove, Anne's mind whirled. Had she set out on a fool's errand last spring? She remembered the tip Elise had received in St. Louis that had sent them across the plains in Rob's wagon train. Had they chased a false clue all year long? They'd questioned hundreds of people, inquiring for David Stone. With persistence, they'd located a few who remembered an Englishman—the accent had made him stand out. People remembered that and his genteel manners. Obviously this was not the man to whom they'd referred. Maybe he really was named David Stone, but she doubted it. And where was her uncle?

She backtracked in her mind. Where had they lost the real David's trail?

"Oregon City," she said softly.

Dan looked over at her. "What?"

"People in Oregon City knew my uncle. Two years ago, he was there, and he had the British accent and the refined manners. Those who knew him by sight looked at the miniature and said it was him. That's where we lost the trail."

"How do you figure?" Dan asked.

"Someone told us David had bought some land near Eugene. I wrote to him in care of general delivery at the Eugene City Post Office. And I got back the note from this man and Millie. So was my uncle never here?"

"I'm pretty sure he was," Dan said. "From what the county clerk told us, the man who registered the deed to that land was the genuine article."

She sighed. "You're right. I was forgetting that. But if Uncle David bought the property, where is he now?"

"Maybe the marshal can get more out of the impostor when he's got him in the jail. Without Millie around to prompt him, he might actually say something relevant."

"True. Perhaps I should make another list of questions—like how long has this fellow been at the farm? And does he claim to own it outright? If so, how did he pay for it? We know Uncle David had means. He'd sold his business in Oregon City."

"And Mr. Skinner told Rob he knew Mr. Stone. I'm sure Bank can get Skinner to take a look at the prisoner once we get back to Eugene. That should settle it."

Dan had such a practical mind. That was a comfort. Anne settled more comfortably on the wagon seat. If she didn't look behind her on the way to town, she might be able to forget that they were transporting a prisoner who'd tried to claim her uncle's inheritance.

Millie Evans waited near the river for a good hour. Shouldn't take them longer than that to clear out. She let the bony mare graze and thought about her prospects.

If they'd left Sam alone, things would be fine. If they'd arrested him, she'd have to fend for herself—nothing new. But she'd want to get her stuff out of the house if she could and avail herself of any plunder she could carry. The rain had stopped, but not until she was thoroughly wet. She'd risk building a fire in the farm kitchen's stove and dry out.

When she judged enough time had passed, she put the bridle back on the mare and headed by farm lanes and wooded paths toward the Stone farm. She approached from the side and sat watching for a long time from beyond the corral before moving closer. The wagon and team were gone, and no saddle horses stood in the yard. Unless they'd hidden their mounts in the barn, the marshal and the rest were gone.

The cattle still grazed in the pasture. She'd expected Sam's horse to be missing, but the skinny blue roan cropped grass alongside the steers. They must have hauled Sam off in the wagon, she decided. That wasn't good. Not that she cared—much. But she could use his roan for a pack horse.

She approached the back door of the house cautiously, not seeing any flicker of movement in the one window on that side. The stillness was creepy. She dismounted and hitched the mare securely. All she needed was to have her horse light out on her.

The quiet of the house felt even eerier than that of the barnyard. She checked both rooms to be sure. She wouldn't dare sleep here. The marshal might come back. He would probably send someone to tend the livestock today or in the morning. He wouldn't leave the cattle there for someone to steal. Or, if he was that stupid, Miss Stone would do something about it. She was probably the tender-hearted type that would hand-feed an orphaned bear cub until it got big and killed her. And anyway, she'd no doubt lay claim to all of David Stone's property in the name of protecting the family's belongings.

Just how extensive were they, anyway? That mysterious estate in England must be worth a lot, or his niece wouldn't have come halfway around the world to tell David he'd inherited it. Too bad there wasn't a way to find out.

In the bedroom, she grabbed her extra dress and petticoat and her heavy winter coat off the pegs on the wall and emptied the dresser drawers into a sack. Too bad the little plan she and Sam had cooked up hadn't worked out. He'd invited her to come cook for him when his rich boss went off into the mountains. Millie had conceived an idea that when Stone returned, she might convince him to keep her around for more than her cooking. He obviously had money. He had big plans for this farm and the improvements he'd make in the spring. Why shouldn't she be part of the plans?

Now all that was out of the question. She went back into the main room and looked around. Her gaze fell on the small desk against the wall. She went over and pulled out a handful of papers. She'd seen them all before—who could live in another person's house for a month and not take a look at the few papers in it?

Stone hadn't left anything valuable in the house, but maybe there was something that would tell her where he'd gone. She threw the mail Sam had picked up down on the desktop. She'd already read the two letters—one from some store in Oregon City and the fateful letter from his niece. Of course, they weren't supposed to open them. Sam wasn't even supposed to get them from the post office, but Millie had envisioned the possibility of learning something useful if they did. And so it had seemed.

She'd prodded Sam into answering Anne Stone's letter—and a fat lot of good it had done them. She'd figured they could trick the girl into giving her "uncle" a loan at the least. But instead of taking easy pickings from the rich man's niece, they'd gotten a posse.

Ah, there it was. From the papers, she plucked a note from an outfitter in Scottsburg. *The supplies you requested will be ready when you arrive in late September.* So Scottsburg was the jumping-off place for David Stone's new property. She could go there and pick up his trail, with or without Sam.

She put the papers back in the desk's pigeonhole and hurried to the kitchen cupboard. A couple of empty flour sacks lay folded on the bottom shelf, and she grabbed one and began filling it with foodstuffs. No sense leaving good food here. After packing two sacks with supplies, she walked slowly about the room, looking at the furnishings with fresh eyes. What would help her along the way? Stone had left Sam well provisioned but had only left him a couple of dollars for emergency cash. That was long gone.

She picked up the small, decorative lantern from the desk. It had always appealed to her. If she didn't find it useful, she could sell it. She also pocketed a pen that looked like it was made of silver and a couple of sheets of paper, which she folded up neatly. One just never knew what one would need.

An afterthought sent her back to the kitchen shelves. She added a tinderbox and a few candle stubs to her stash, along with a tin cup, a plate, a fork, two knives, a spoon, and a small kettle.

Did she dare spend the night in the barn? She could leave her horse saddled in case a fast getaway became necessary. And she'd have the bundles ready to strap to the roan's saddle in the morning. She'd better pack some oats for the horses, too. In some ways, she hoped Sam would get loose and come back. In other ways, she

might do better without him. She reached for a second cup and stopped. She'd worry about Sam Hastings if and when he showed his face.

"You let him go?" Dan stared incredulously at the marshal. "I don't understand."

Bank sighed and polished the deputy marshal's star on his hunting shirt with his cuff. "I didn't have enough evidence."

"He was impersonating another man."

"Got no proof."

Dan eyed him critically. "Last night you said all that about the county clerk knowing the real David Stone."

"Well yes, there is that." Bank ambled to the small stove that heated the room he claimed as his official office and the attached cell. He picked a tin cup off a shelf and filled it with coffee. "I guess what I should have said was we've got no proof that the man I arrested wasn't also named David Stone."

Dan huffed out a breath. "So now he'll go back to Mr. Stone's house and squat there? Miss Anne has no recourse?"

"Well, no, I told him he can't do that. See, Mr. Skinner came by this morning. He knew right away that this wasn't Miss Stone's uncle—that is, the man who owns the property. Don't know if you realized it, but Eugene Skinner's a lawyer."

"I think he mentioned it the other day."

Bank scratched his chin through his beard. "Yeah, well, he's a lot of things, and that's one of 'em. I asked him to come take a look at the prisoner. He did, and he said it wasn't David Stone. But the prisoner insisted he *was* David Stone. He didn't have any proof, but he stuck to his story. Mr. Skinner said he wasn't the same David Stone who bought that piece of property last year and came in once a month or so for his mail. He said he happened to know *that* Mr. Stone had bought some land up Scottsburg way and was talking about prospecting up there."

"I don't suppose he could have told us that two days ago when

Miss Anne and I met him at the post office."

Bank shrugged. "He didn't know what was going on. Says he mentioned to his wife last night that two people was in looking for Mr. Stone—meaning you and Miss Anne Stone. But he wasn't sure if Stone was out to his farm or not."

Dan nodded. He guessed it made sense that Skinner had sent them to Stone's place without further explanation. He wouldn't want the postmaster broadcasting his private business to the world.

"Well, Miz Skinner told him that last week this other feller came in and took David Stone's mail." Bank started to take a sip from his cup then hesitated. "You want coffee?"

"No, thanks," Dan said.

"Right. Well, apparently the fella in question told her at the post office that he was Stone's farmhand and was watching the place for the boss while he went to look at his new property. But Mr. Skinner didn't know that when he saw you."

"That just beats all," Dan said. "Did she know the other man's name? I assume he's the one you had in the jail overnight."

"He didn't give it, and she didn't ask." Bank lifted his cup to his lips.

"So we're supposed to believe that David Stone hired another man by the same name to watch his place for him."

"I expect he was lying when he took the mail," Bank conceded.

"Yeah. He could be lying so bad that he's done in David Stone and taken over his property."

Bank frowned. "Murder?"

"Could be, don't you think?"

Bank stroked his chin. "Guess I'd better ride out there again and talk to some of the neighbors. Ask 'em when they last saw Mr. Stone. The real Mr. Stone, that is."

"Good idea. And while you're at it, ask if they know who this other man is and if they've seen Millie about the place."

"Yup. I'll do that. But I wouldn't put any notions of Stone being murdered into Miss Anne's pretty head."

"Don't worry, I won't suggest it." Dan crammed his hat onto his

head and beat it for the boardinghouse. He'd have to tell Anne that Bank had let the impostor go. She wasn't going to like that news.

Millie huddled in the alley between the barber shop and a freighter's stable. Her auburn hair was hidden under a drab poke bonnet, and she wrapped her shawl close. She risked a lot, coming into town this morning, but much depended on knowing what the uppity English-woman and her friends decided to do next.

Adams came out of the jail and hurried down the street. She reckoned Bank Raynor was still in there, and she surely didn't want him to see her. Probably Sam was in there, too, warming the bunk in a jail cell.

She waited until Adams turned a corner and set out after him. His long legs carried him quickly, and she had to lift her skirt and hustle, which garnered her curious stares from several pedestrians. He entered one of the more substantial houses near the river. Eugene City was just putting down its roots, and most of the residents lived in cabins or small houses thrown together out of logs or whatever lumber they could get their hands on. This one looked a little more respectable. She walked closer and spied a small sign swinging from the porch roof. ROOMS.

So, the so-called friends whom Miss Stone and Adams were staying with consisted of boarders. Unless they owned the boardinghouse.

"Millie?"

She whirled around. Wobbling down the street toward her on unsteady legs was Sam Hastings.

"What are you doing here?" She grabbed his arm and spun him around. He nearly fell over and clutched at her, leaning heavily on her shoulder. "I thought the marshal had you locked up."

"So he did, but Mr. Skinner came in this morning early and told him he had to let me go."

"And you headed straight for the nearest saloon." Millie shook her head and untangled his arm from about her shoulders. "If you can't walk straight, I don't want to be seen with you. Where were you headed, anyway?"

"Over to the livery. I got no horse, and the marshal said he wouldn't take me back to the farm. Said I have to stay away from there. 'Course, I have to get my stuff. And my horse. Got to get old Blue. I'm sure Mr. Stone would want me to have old Blue."

"Old Blue's not at the farm," Millie said.

"He's not?" Sam stopped in the middle of the dirt street and blinked at her. "Where'd he get to?"

She seized his wrist and pulled him out of the way of an approaching wagon. "I've got him and the mare outside of town. I packed up some stuff, but I didn't take your clothes because I figured they'd keep you in jail for a while."

"Well, they didn't, but I can't stay at the house. I don't reckon Mr. Stone would want me to now, anyways." He scowled at her. "I shouldn't have let you talk me into trying to trick his niece, Millie. That ruined everything. I had a nice, soft job there. Plenty to eat, a roof over my head."

"Oh, stop whining. There's still money in this. I can smell it."

Sam shook his head. "Don't see how."

"You wouldn't. Just come with me. You can take Blue out to the farm and get your clothes. I'm going to stick around town and see if I can find out what Miss Stone plans to do next."

"Why should you care?"

"Because her uncle has money. Buckets of it. Enough to set us up for life, unless I'm mistaken."

Sam considered that, puckering his brow and weaving on his feet with the effort of thinking. "Can't see how we'd ever get it now."

"You leave that to me."

"I can't believe Deputy Raynor let that thug go." Anne sat in the parlor of the boardinghouse with Dan, who had summoned her from her room on his return from a consultation with the deputy marshal at the jail.

The landlady came to the door with a laden tray.

"Here you go, miss. Tea just the way you like it. And I put some muffins and a few sugar cookies on. This gentleman has probably worked up an appetite already."

Dan grinned at her. "Thank you, Mrs. Brady. Your baking can't be beat."

"I agree," Anne said. "Eugene City may be a little rough around the edges, but your table is fit for royalty."

Mrs. Brady flushed to the roots of her wispy white hair. She set down the tray and waved a hand through the air, smiling. "Oh, go on now. You folks would flatter me to death."

Anne smiled as the older woman backed out of the room with a little bow. Of course the tea tray would be extra on her bill, but she couldn't bring herself to forgo the amenities. And Dan deserved it, after spending so much time sorting out her affairs with Bank Raynor. Two more months until she could draw more money from her trust; she'd already sent a letter by ship to the family solicitor, asking that he arrange for the bank at Oregon City to give her a payment early in January.

"Daniel, what do you think I should do?" She poured him a cup of the strong black tea and passed it to him.

"I assume you still want to find your uncle."

"Of course. That's my main purpose."

He nodded as he stirred sugar into his tea. "As I see it, he's away from home for an indeterminate period of time."

"Yes, but he should be coming back." She gazed at him bleakly across the tea table. She didn't want to voice the thought that Uncle David might be dead. No doubt Dan had thought of it, too, but she refused to give the idea credence. "Should I stay at his house, do you think?"

"Well, that depends. I'd think you have the right to if you want, and I can understand your desire to secure his property. But it's isolated. Mr. Raynor and Rob both seem to think a farm like that might be the target of thieves. Maybe even Indians who want to 'borrow' some beef."

Anne shivered. She certainly couldn't live out there alone. "I came all the way across the continent without having any run-ins with the natives. If you please, I'd rather not contemplate getting on their bad side now."

He chuckled. "I'm with you there. Well, you could stay here, I suppose, and ask Mr. Skinner to tell you when Mr. Stone next shows up to collect his mail."

That was out of the question, though she didn't say so. She couldn't afford to pay for her room and board until January. After that, it shouldn't be a problem, but in the meantime Mrs. Brady had to live, too. "I wonder what will happen to his cattle. The impostor said Uncle David hired him to tend things while he was away. Do you suppose he was telling the truth?"

"Your uncle wouldn't leave the place abandoned—not with livestock on it. Maybe that part was true. Anyway, Raynor said he'll go out there and see to the animals and talk to some of the neighbors. Maybe he can get a better idea of what's been going on."

"I'm glad to hear it. Maybe I should just stay put today and see what he finds out." Anne glanced uneasily toward the door. "Of course, I hate to keep Rob and Dulcie away from their home any longer than necessary. Or you either, Daniel."

"Don't worry about me. I'm here to help you see this through. And tomorrow's Sunday. We can attend church here in town and rest. Let's see what Bank turns up. Then if you want to stick around here for a while, you could tell the Whistlers it's all right for them to head on home. I'm sure Mrs. Brady would be considered an adequate chaperone for you if you stayed in Eugene."

"Well, I'll think about it. I do want you to know how much I appreciate your coming down here and giving up your time."

"Anne, it's my pleasure."

His deep voice and earnest gray eyes brought on a curious fluttering in her stomach. Anne sipped her tea, trying to analyze the sensation. She still didn't want to marry a man whose greatest ambition was to grow wheat. Not that farming was a dishonorable profession, but she was sure the life would bore her to tears. Still, if one

was honest with oneself, Dan Adams was a handsome man, and in the months she'd known him, she'd found him kind, thoughtful, and reverent. A lady could do worse.

By Sunday morning, Millie was ready to tear her hair out. Were these people going to just sit in Eugene forever? She'd spent two nights curled up in a bedroll in an unsuspecting farmer's barn outside town. The only decent boardinghouse was occupied by Anne Stone and her entourage. She and Sam could hardly show up there. And Deputy Raynor was watching the Stone place like a hawk. Sam had barely gotten away with his extra socks and gloves.

She and Sam had stayed outside most of Saturday, never remaining in one spot too long. But today was colder—a blunt reminder that November had arrived three days ago. She had a coat, but Sam's light wool jacket wouldn't be adequate for winter.

She picked wisps of hay from her hair and smoothed out her blankets. Why did she bother to worry about Sam, anyway?

He stirred and rolled over in the hay with a moan.

"Wake up," Millie said. "We need to get out of here. The farmer will be out to feed his stock soon."

Sam pushed himself up on one elbow and blinked at her in the dimness of the barn. "What are we going to do today?"

"We're going to find out what Miss Hoity-Toity Anne's plans are."

"How do we do that?"

A good question. Millie rose and gathered her bedroll and extra clothes. "I have ideas. Hurry up. We'll go someplace where we can cook breakfast first. The same spot we ate supper last night."

"All right, I'm coming."

She walked on the spongy hay over to the edge of the loft and climbed down the ladder, balancing her load. She almost wished Sam hadn't gotten out of jail and found her. He was just slowing her down. Why should she always have to wait for her stupid brother? Even after all these years, Millie cringed at the words that had leaped into her thoughts. Her stepmother had beaten her soundly for calling Sam that. She was forbidden to ever say the word *stupid*. Now, when she thought it, she felt the sting of the switch on her legs—twenty years later.

She opened the back door of the barn—the small door beside the manure heap—and slipped out. Just as she closed it behind her, she heard another sound—the grinding of the big front barn door as its wheels rolled along the track.

She caught her breath and listened, her ear to the crack she'd left between the door and the jamb. Was Sam still up in the hay mow or had he started down the ladder?

"Hey! What are you doing in here?" a man shouted.

"Me?" Sam asked. Millie could almost hear him gulp. "I–I'm not doing anything."

Stupid half brother.

CHAPTER 6

W e can't just go off and leave you here." Dulcie threw a pleading look at Rob over the dinner table. They'd just returned from the service at the rustic little church, and Anne had raised the question of the Whistlers going back to Corvallis without her.

Rob settled back in his chair with a sigh. "Now, sweetheart, Miss Anne is an adult. If she wants to stay and wait for her uncle, that's her right, and if she wants to head up into the hills looking for him, well, that's her right, too."

"But she's such a pretty young thing. She can't travel around mining country unchaperoned."

"I'll stay with her," Dan said.

"That's almost as bad," Dulcie replied. "I know you mean no harm, Daniel, but can't you see how it would look if Miss Anne traipsed about the wilderness with you?"

Anne decided it was time she spoke up. "Dulcie, dear, I know you mean well, but I'm sure Dan is capable of protecting me." She flashed a glance his way and saw him flush with pleasure and straighten his shoulders a fraction of an inch. She would have to be careful not to imply more than she meant where he was concerned. "And Mr. Skinner says there are towns all along the road to Scottsburg. We should be able to find respectable lodgings when we need them, at least that far."

"I wouldn't be too sure," Rob said. "Some of those towns are just a handful of cabins with a post office for miners and trappers."

"Nevertheless," Anne continued, "I'm sure Daniel and I can reach Scottsburg safely. And from there we should be able to reach Uncle David's mine within a day's travel, and I'll have my uncle to defend my honor."

Rob shook his head. "That sounds good, missy, but we both

know you've thought you were close to catching up with your uncle twice before and had to deal with disappointment. Supposing you get up in the Coast Range and he's nowhere to be found? Then what will you do?"

"We'll ride back to Scottsburg," Dan said firmly. "And if it looks as though we'll have to spend a night or more on the trail getting to the mine, we can perhaps hire a guide to take us. That's if I can't convince Miss Anne to stay in Scottsburg while I go and fetch Mr. Stone myself and bring him to her."

"No," Anne said, frowning, "I don't suppose you could persuade me of that."

Rob laughed. "You ought to have known better than to even think of it, Dan."

Dulcie leaned forward and shook an accusing finger under Anne's nose. "I know you're independent, but my question is this: When we get back to Corvallis, what will we tell Mrs. Bentley?"

"That's true." Rob rubbed the back of his neck, making a tortured face as he considered his wife's words. "Elise will be very unhappy. We told her we'd place you in your uncle's care or bring you back with us. No ifs, ands, or buts."

"Sounds like we'd better start practicing our 'buts,'" Dulcie said.

Anne chuckled. "Elise will understand. Won't she, Dan?"

He gritted his teeth. "Well. . .I don't know as she will. But I can't think of a better plan. Can any of you?"

"You'll take my horse," Rob said, and Anne took that as admission of defeat.

Dulcie nodded. "And my sidesaddle."

"Oh no, I couldn't," Anne said quickly. Part Rob from Bailey, his favorite mount? She wouldn't think of it.

"I don't see that you have much choice," Rob said. "Unless you have enough cash to buy a horse, and I'm not sure you could find a sidesaddle if you scoured Eugene City for one."

"But—"

"We'll be fine with the team and wagon," Dulcie said. "You'll have to go through your trunks today, though, and pack up what you

want for the journey. We'll take the rest back to our place and keep it for you until you come for it."

"That's very generous of you," Anne murmured. She couldn't think of anyone in England who would have shown her such kindness. "I promise I'll bring Bailey back to you safely."

"I'm sure you will." Rob cleared his throat and looked at his wife. "Well, sweetheart, do you want to set out tomorrow morning?"

"I suppose we should, though it's tempting to stay one more day," Dulcie said. "Anne needs time to sort through her luggage, and she might learn a little more about her uncle's doings."

"I'll repack this afternoon," Anne said.

Dan nodded. "I can bring the wagon over from the livery and load the trunks. And I'll make sure we have all the supplies we might need for the trip. Do you think we should take a pack horse?"

His question alarmed Anne. She didn't want Dan laying out money for her venture, and an extra horse was beyond her current means, especially if they planned to pay for rooms and meals along the way.

"We should do fine with Star and Bailey, especially if you think we'll find lodgings every night."

"Good," Dan said. "I don't expect we'll need a tent, but we might want to tote a couple of blankets just in case, and one kettle."

Dulcie laughed. "Anne, you'd better take a coffeepot and some coffee beans along for this young man. I've never seen such a coffee drinker."

"Well, Mrs. Brady makes it so well." Dan waved a hand in protest. "But you don't need to do that for me. I can go without coffee for a week if I have to. And we'll likely be able to find it wherever we stop."

Anne smiled and determined to slip a coffeepot and a small stash of ground coffee into her pack.

"Now, you'll want to head straight south to Cottage Grove first." Rob held out the map he'd asked the postmaster to sketch for him after church.

"Will we pass Uncle David's property?" Anne asked.

"Yes, you will."

She looked at Dan. "I'd like to stop in and see the neighbors Bank Raynor talked to, if you don't mind—the ones who said they'd look after the cattle until Uncle David returns."

"Certainly. We can go by David's house again, too, if you want."

"I don't see any reason to go there. Mr. Raynor said he looked around to make sure there were no valuables left in the house."

"If there were, that Millie probably pocketed them." Rob shook his head. "She was a sly one."

"Good thing I wasn't there," Dulcie said. "I'd have blacked her eyes."

Anne couldn't hold back a smile. "I'll miss you, Dulcie."

"Well, you'll see me again soon enough. I hope your uncle will bring you up to Corvallis, if only to get your trunks."

"He'll want to see Elise, I'm sure," Anne said.

"Good. I want to meet this famous English gentleman everyone's been talking about." Dulcie's eyes danced. "Imagine, meeting an earl out here in Oregon Territory."

Anne didn't deflate her spirits by explaining that her uncle wouldn't officially be the earl of Stoneford until he returned to England and claimed the title and the estate. She smiled at Dulcie. "I'm sure he'll be delighted to make your acquaintance. Yours and Rob's. After all, your husband saw me safely through many perils on the trail."

Dulcie reached for Rob's hand. "I almost wish I'd been along this summer. It might have been fun traveling with you and Elise Bentley."

Rob smiled at her indulgently. "No, darlin', you've told me a thousand times you don't want to make that trip ever again."

"It's true." Dulcie sighed. "When I first laid eyes on Oregon City, I said, 'Rob, please find a place where I can have a hot bath, and if I ever need to go East again, I'll go by ship, thank you very much.'"

Millie slipped behind a buckboard and ducked down. Dan Adams and his friend Whistler came out of the livery stable. She could hear

them talking as they walked past her hiding place.

"Are you sure you and Anne have everything you want for now?" the older man, Whistler, asked.

Adams had a brace of saddlebags thrown over one shoulder, and Mr. Whistler carried a shotgun.

"Pretty sure," Adams said. "We don't want to take too much up into those hills and regret having to haul it."

"Well, Anne won't have to worry about her trunks. We've got them strapped down tight in the wagon. We'll take them right back to our place in Corvallis, and she can pick them up when you come back."

They reached the street and headed off toward the boarding-house, and Millie could no longer make out their words.

Where was this wagon they were talking about, anyway? Adams and the tall trail master had driven into the livery ten minutes ago. Were they leaving the wagon right inside the barn overnight? They must be, with all their boxes and bundles in it—including the fine lady's kit and cargo. In the short time Millie had been observing Anne, she'd worn four different outfits, including two today alone. She'd set out for meeting this morning all got up in finery. Her hat matched her overskirt, and the lace on her bodice alone must have cost a month's wages.

Then this afternoon, while Millie had watched from behind a cedar tree on the edge of the yard, Miss Anne had gone in and out from the boardinghouse to the wagon and back with her bundles and frippery, wearing a brown dress of good quality wool, with black velvet-ribbon trim. Understated but elegant, just plain elegant. Four dresses were more than most Oregon women could lay claim to, and Millie could only imagine what lay in the steamer trunks Whistler and Adams had trucked to the livery in the back of the wagon.

She slid from behind the buckboard and flitted to the door of the barn. Cautiously she peeked around the edge of the door. The livery man was in there, feeding the horses fortunate enough to sleep inside. Soon he'd lock up for the night. Millie smiled to herself as she eyed the ropes wrapped around Miss Stone's trunks. Anything a man could tie, she could untie. It would just be a matter of coming back tonight when no one else was in the barn.

Hoisting her skirt, she hurried out to the street, watching out for familiar faces. She darted between two buildings and out behind them, toward the grove where she'd tied her chestnut mare.

In fifteen minutes, she'd reached the small sheltered meadow where she'd left Sam and Old Blue. Sam lay on the grass with his head on his saddle, while Blue grazed twenty yards away without so much as a hobble or a picket line to hold him.

"Why did you let the horse loose?" she cried.

Sam sat up and blinked as she jumped down in a swirl of skirts. "What? Old Blue will come to me."

To prove it, he rose, stretched, and ambled toward the roan.

Old Blue lifted his head, looked at Sam, and resumed grazing, but took a few short steps away from him, gradually swinging his hindquarters in Sam's direction.

"Oh terrific, now you won't be able to catch him," Millie said.

"Can, too!" Sam quickened his steps. Blue rewarded him by trotting a dozen steps away. He put his head down to the grass again but kept one ear cocked toward Sam.

"You are such a dolt!" Millie shook her head in despair as she opened her saddlebag. "You'll have to give him some oats or you'll never catch him. Lucky for you I scooped up a handful that had spilled outside the livery in town." She took out a knotted handkerchief, plump with her loot, and carried it to him. "We're fortunate that farmer didn't find our horses out behind the barn this morning."

"Wouldn't be my fault if he had." Sam gazed at her with an injured air. "You're the one who picked the spot to leave 'em."

Millie ignored that. "Get that horse and tie him up. I'll get out our lunch. We probably would have been safer if we'd stayed at Stone's place last night. Live and learn."

Sam scowled at her. "You blame me for everything, but it was your idea to move around and sleep in barns. You said the marshal would find us if we stayed at Stone's."

"And so he would have. He was out there again yesterday."

"How do you know that?"

"I learned a lot this afternoon. That's the other reason I wanted to stay someplace closer to town. We needed to stick close to Miss Anne until we knew what her plan was."

Sam watched her as she laid the makings of a campfire. "Do we know it now?"

"Yes, we do." Millie used the plural pronoun loosely. She wasn't about to disclose to her stolid half brother—whom she considered to be little more than half-witted—everything she knew. For one thing, if Sam had another brush with the law, he'd probably spill it. If not, he'd forget the critical bits of knowledge. No, it was best to tell Sam what he needed to know when he needed to know it. "Get that horse and then bring me some firewood."

"You gonna tell me our plan, Mill?"

"When you've brought an armful of sticks. Good, dry stuff, now. Don't bring me anything green. And don't call me Mill."

Why couldn't her mother have given her a pretty name—something flowing, like Victoria or Charlotte?

Sam carried the small bundle of oats toward the horse. Old Blue was curious enough to let himself be caught this time. When he was tied up, Sam trudged away toward the line of pine trees that lined the creek. Millie filled her one pot with water and considered her strategy. She definitely wouldn't tell him about the glorious dresses she was sure she'd find in Anne Stone's trunks. She'd think up an excuse to go back tonight. Maybe she could give Sam a simple errand to carry out while she went to the livery. If he noticed that she came back with an extra sack, she'd tell him she'd found some clothes and let it go at that. She'd choose carefully and leave Eugene with some assets for the days ahead.

But that was only a small part of Millie's plan. She needed her half brother to help her carry it out. Convincing Sam they should separate might be the most difficult part.

Dan looked up from fastening an extra strap on the pack he'd loaded behind Star's saddle. Bank Raynor was walking across the yard of the boardinghouse toward him.

"You folks heading out this morning?"

"Planning on it," Dan said. "You're out early."

Bank nodded. "I got a message last evening from Marshal Nesmith. Figured I'd best get it to Miss Stone before you headed out."

"What is it?" Dan tugged on the strap. Everything lay snug on Star's flanks. Way more gear than he liked to carry, though—he ought to have insisted on a pack horse.

"Seems there was a gent from New York who chased Miss Stone all the way out here. She mentioned him the other night—Peterson."

That grabbed Dan's attention. "Yes. Nesmith had him in custody when we left Oregon City. That was nearly two weeks ago."

"Well, he ain't there now."

"They've released him?"

"I'm not just sure what happened. All the marshal's note said was, 'Tell Miss Stone that Peterson is on the loose. She'll want to warn her uncle.' Now, mebbe you can make more of that than I can."

Dan puzzled over the message. "Not much, I'm afraid. I know who Peterson is, of course. I'm not sure we need to be concerned about him now that we're down here. But thank you."

Bank nodded. "Well then, that's all I came for. I hope you have a good trip, and that you find Mr. Stone in one piece."

"I appreciate it, sir."

"Right." Bank hesitated. "You watch out for Miss Stone, won't you, Adams? She's a pretty little thing. No bigger'n a minute, and I don't misdoubt she can take care of herself, but still—you don't want to put it to the test, do you?"

Dan nodded gravely. "I most surely will take care of her."

He smiled as he watched the old man walk away. Taking care of Anne would be his life's mission if he had anything to say about it. But he wasn't sure telling her that Peterson was out of jail would be the best way to do that.

Anne liked Uncle David's neighbors, the McIntyres, and wished

she'd stopped in and met them the first time she'd approached her uncle's farm. They might have saved her a lot of worry.

"I told David I didn't trust that feller he hired," Mr. McIntyre told her, shaking his head woefully. Anne and Dan had dismounted in the neighbors' dooryard to inquire about David's situation. "He's trusting to a fault, though. Said Sam would be all right, and what could he do wrong, anyhow? David left him with a score of cattle at pasture and five acres he'd planted to winter wheat. That was all the man had to watch out for. David couldn't see any harm in it."

"That's because he didn't know Sam's sister would show up," Mrs. McIntyre added.

"If she *is* his sister." Mr. McIntyre winked at Dan.

"He's not smart enough to lure a woman out here unless she was related to him," his wife said. "If your uncle weren't so softhearted, he never would have hired Sam Hastings to begin with. That man couldn't find a quill if he had a porcupine in his lap. Say, speaking of Millie, Sam came over here and borrowed my sidesaddle for her shortly after she arrived. They never brought it back."

"I wonder if it's still over in David's barn," Mr. McIntyre said.

"I wouldn't count on it," Dan told them. "Millie lit out on horseback the day we took the deputy marshal out there. I expect she's still got it."

"Well, I'll take a look around when I go over to check the livestock."

"But you *are* sure Uncle David went up to the mountains?" Anne asked.

"Oh yes," Mrs. McIntyre said. "He'd bought that property up there and said he wanted to go look it over and see if it was worth doing some mining on it."

Her husband ran a hand over his chin. "That's right. He'd been studying up on it, kind of as a hobby. I saw him the day he pulled out. Had all his gear on a pack mule. Said he thought he'd do a little panning in the creek that ran by his land, and if he found some color, he might even get a sluice box."

That news relieved Anne. She would stop wondering whether

Sam and Millie had done something awful to him.

"I wouldn't worry about him being gone several weeks," the man continued. "He was quite excited about it."

"Just like a boy," Mrs. McIntyre said. "But I expect he'll tire of it soon, now that it's getting colder. Can you folks stay to dinner?"

"No, thank you," Anne said. "I have news for my uncle that I really must get to him. We want to push on to Cottage Grove. Is there a hotel there?"

"Sure," said Mr. McIntyre. "Or you could spend less and get a better supper if you stopped with the Randall family. They're just past the feed store on the south edge of town. They take in travelers regular, and Mrs. Randall makes a fine chicken pie."

Anne looked up at Dan. "Sound good?"

"Sure does."

They set out once more at a quick trot. When they passed the lane to Uncle David's farm, Dan looked over at her with raised eyebrows.

"You sure you don't want to stop?"

"I'm sure." The cattle grazed peacefully inside the rail fence. She could see the barn's ridgepole in the distance. "The next time I see that place, I want Uncle David there, welcoming me to his home."

"All right, they're past Stone's place." From beneath the spreading branches of a pine tree, Millie peered at the retreating horses. "You wait half an hour. If they don't come back and no one else happens by, you can go fill out your supplies from the house. There's plenty of beans and cornmeal and raisins. Then follow along. We know they plan to spend tonight in Cottage Grove, so there's no hurry. When you get there, look around and find out where their horses are stabled. But whatever you do, don't let Adams or Miss Stone see you."

Sam scrunched up his face and wagged his whole body from side to side. "I don't see why you have to go on ahead."

"I told you. It's better if I get ahead of them. I'll see if I can get wind of David before they do. If I get to him first, I can soften him

up and maybe find out what he's really worth."

Sam shook his head. "That don't make sense to me. Why can't we stay together and just follow them to where he's at?"

Millie sighed in exasperation. "Because, you dunce, you're going to slow them down, remember? So I can get a good head start on them. The longer I have to get friendly with ol' Uncle David before Miss Anne shows up, the better."

"She'll just tell him how we tried to trick her."

"Not if things go my way. Now, you do as I say. Slow them down, throw them off the trail—anything you can think of. Give me time to find David Stone and learn whether his mining property is valuable. It could end up being worth more than his inheritance from his brother."

"Well, yeah." Sam's brow puckered. "I heard they're taking millions from the mines down Josephine way. I don't know why he didn't buy land down there."

"Because it's all bought up, no doubt. Now folks are sniffing around up this way, and he wants to get in on it early. You told me Stone is a smart man, right?"

"Oh, he's powerful smart."

"So he wouldn't get taken in by some swindler and buy worthless property. There's bound to be a little gold on it." Millie pushed the branches aside and walked back toward where they had tied the horses out of sight of the road.

"I don't see why he didn't just stay here and run his farm." Sam panted along behind her. "It's a nice farm."

"Sure, Sam. It's a wonderful farm."

Millie untied the mare's reins and led her out toward the road. By the time she was settled in the saddle, Sam was just coming out of the woods, tugging the roan along behind him.

"You're supposed to wait and make sure they don't come back," she said.

"Do I have to?"

Millie sighed. Sam was like a kid in some ways. "At least keep an eye out for the neighbors. If anyone comes along and asks what you're doing, tell them you came for your clothes."

"I got my clothes already."

"They don't know that."

"Oh yeah."

"And don't steal anything big. You know—that they could see."

Sam looked at her blankly as though the thought would never have entered his mind without her help.

"But get plenty of oats for Blue. Enough for several days."

"What about your horse?"

"We'll manage."

Millie turned the mare southward.

"Wait," Sam called. "How will I find you again?"

"If you ever catch up to David Stone, trust me, I won't be far away."

CHAPTER 7

Cottage Grove was a pretty little town on the edge of the Willamette River's Coast Fork. Anne imagined that every bedroom window had a lovely view of the mountains that folded in around it.

They found the Randalls' house without any trouble. The first man they asked pointed the way and declared, "You'll get some good eating there."

The sun was still higher than the hills to the west. It was a pity they couldn't keep riding for another hour or two. But they must bow to propriety on this journey if Anne hoped to face Elise and Dulcie again without shame.

"You'll have to bunk in with our boys tonight, Mr. Adams," Mrs. Randall said ruefully as she led them through the kitchen toward the stairway. "We've already got folks in the one guest room."

"That's fine," Dan said, but Anne felt bad for putting him in that situation.

"Miss Stone can take our daughter's room," Mrs. Randall added. "Mary Lou can sleep in with us tonight."

"We don't want to inconvenience you," Anne said.

"Let's not fuss about that," the hostess replied cheerfully.

Mr. Randall piped up from the corner by the stove, "If you was married, you could share the same accommodations, folks."

Dan went scarlet to his hairline.

"There's truth in that," Mrs. Randall said with a chuckle.

Her husband guffawed. "We got a preacher right down the street."

Dan looked helplessly at Anne. She decided the best thing to do was laugh with them.

"How nice for you. Daniel and I have been friends most of a year now, but we've no matrimonial plans."

"That's right," Dan said. "This trip is purely out of necessity."

"Too bad," said Mr. Randall. "Mighta made a nice honeymoon."

Millie had stayed well behind the pair until they took their horses off the trail to give them water. She hurried past, well out of sight, and then lit out for Cottage Grove. She made good time, galloping the mare most of the way. While the horse rested and grazed outside town, she went into the general store, bought a slice of cheese, and pocketed a pot of lip rouge and a tin of peaches.

She didn't let the horse rest long, wanting to be certain she'd cleared town well before Miss Stone and Adams showed up. Her next stop would be the little town of Anlauf, at a distance of about twelve miles. As she rode out of Cottage Grove, the road left the Coast Fork, skirted a pond, and followed Pass Creek, upstream and uphill, toward the divide. The road was passable for wagons, but still rugged, and she kept a steady, slow trot when possible. On the steeper grades, the mare walked.

She passed a few cabins, but the farther she went, the more desolate the landscape became. Reports Sam had brought in about the Calapooya Indians flitted through her mind. Had they really taken to the warpath again? She scanned the forest on both sides of the trail. The tall firs towered above her. She could see between their trunks for a ways into the cool shadows. Were angry warriors lurking there?

Something moved ahead of her, and the mare leaped to one side with a squeal. Millie's heart nearly jumped out of her chest. She kept her hands low, with tension on the reins.

Fifty yards ahead, two deer hopped across the road and disappeared into the trees.

She patted the horse's withers as the mare continued to prance and blow out air.

"Take it easy, girl. It was only a couple of deer. Settle down."

The mare crow-hopped one more time and minced forward with tiny, precise steps. As Millie's pulse slowed, she was able to

breathe normally again, but she didn't trust the horse with a loose rein for a good ten minutes. At last they settled into a road-eating trot. Millie thanked her lucky stars she hadn't wound up in the dirt with a broken neck.

She should have taken Old Blue, but Sam would have come after her. He claimed the horse was his since David Stone had left it for him to use. Millie was stuck with the thin nag she'd picked up in Champoeg without benefit of a bill of sale. Poorest horse she'd ever stolen.

Anne came down to breakfast in the Randalls' kitchen looking beautiful, as always. She wore her blue velvet habit and an adorable hat that looked as though it had come out of a shop window in New York. Dan supposed it was the only modest outfit she had for riding, but it seemed a bit overdone for the wilderness. She looked rested, and her eager smile when she met his gaze set his stomach fluttering. If only she weren't so lovely, he could bear it better.

"Good morning," she sang out.

"Sit you right down, Miss Stone," Mrs. Randall said. She indicated a place at the table next to Dan, where she had set out white china plates with green ivy painted around the rims.

Dan held Anne's chair for her and resumed his seat.

"How was your night?" Anne asked.

He wished she hadn't asked in the hostess's presence. He glanced toward Mrs. Randall's ample back and shot Anne a rueful smile. "Fine. Just fine."

Anne nodded in comprehension and shook out her napkin before spreading it in her lap. There would be plenty of time later to tell her how the three boys had offered him their bunks, but Dan had insisted on rolling out his blankets on the floor. It had seemed the polite thing to do at the time. But he'd reckoned without the oak planks beneath him or Petey's incessant snoring. Right now the prospect of eight hours or more in the saddle quelled all sense of adventure inspired in him by Anne's quest.

They finished their meal, and Dan rose to pay the hostess. Anne leaped up and followed him, opening her purse.

"Let me take care of it," Dan said softly.

"Oh no, I couldn't. In fact, I should be paying your way. This is my excursion, not yours, and you've given up much for my cause."

"Don't even think it." He smiled down at her. "It's a delight for me to be of service, Anne. I'm just glad you've allowed me to come along."

Her cheeks went a becoming shade of pink. "Thank you, Daniel. But you mustn't even think of paying my expenses. If you insist on paying your own way, at least let me keep my dignity and cover my own."

"Very well."

"My land, you folks are so polite it's painful," Mrs. Randall said.

Anne's flush deepened, and Dan regretted quibbling over money in front of the hostess.

"You've been most kind." Anne placed a few coins in the woman's hand and turned to the door.

Dan held out the money for his night's lodging.

"She's a proud one, isn't she?" Mrs. Randall asked, watching Anne step through the doorway.

Dan pulled back in surprise. "Oh no, she's nothing like that. She only wants to be clear that she's independent."

"Oh, she's a real lady, anyone can see that, and I don't doubt she can stand on her own two feet. But she's not averse to leading you about the territory, now is she?" Mrs. Randall chuckled. "How far are you folks traveling?"

Caution counseled Dan, and he replied, "We're heading over Scottsburg way."

"Ah. Getting the steamer there?"

"I'm not sure yet. Miss Stone has business in that area."

Mrs. Randall nodded. "It's not so bad to marry a woman who knows how to carry out her own business, you know." Her smile indicated that she was just such a woman and Mr. Randall was a fortunate man indeed to have found her.

Dan managed a smile. "I'm sure that's true. Thank you."

The children came in from their chores and began to set up for their own breakfast as he left the house. He found Anne in the barn working diligently at a tangle of leather straps, with a determined set to her jaw. Her eyebrows were drawn into a lovely pucker.

"What's the trouble?" Dan asked.

"Our bridles are all jumbled together, and these reins are tied in about a hundred knots."

"The boys must have done it when they came to do their barn chores this morning." Dan bent over the mess and frowned. "I can't believe their father would allow it, though, and it must have taken some time."

"It's a fine way to treat their paying guests," Anne said.

She carried the bridles to the brighter light at the open barn door.

"Would you like me to do it?" Dan asked.

"No thanks, I'm getting it. Why don't you go ahead and saddle up?"

He left her working on the knots and walked to where she'd placed her sidesaddle the afternoon before, on a wooden rack attached to the wall. He pulled it down and frowned in dismay as the cinch strap, girth, and stirrup tumbled to the floor.

"What on earth?" He sighed and stooped to retrieve the pieces.

"What is it?" Anne called.

"Seems the little urchins undid every buckle they could find and loosened the straps." The trick would cost them a good half hour in getting started. Dan had a mind to go find Mr. Randall and complain. But that would take another ten minutes.

He set the saddle back on the rack and began threading a leather strap through the slot at the top of the stirrup. No doubt entered his mind that his saddle was in a similar fix.

At last they had everything put back the way it should be.

"Ready to start," he asked Anne, "or are you exhausted?"

She chuckled. "I'm ready to get out of here—I'll tell you that."

They led the horses into the barnyard. Mr. Randall came around the corner of his house and stopped short.

"I thought you folks were gone already."

"We had a few things to take care of first," Anne said with her usual pleasant smile. "We're ready to start now, though."

"Well, have a good trip." Mr. Randall lifted his hat and watched in puzzlement as they mounted and trotted out of his barnyard.

"Do you think we'll be able to make Elkton today?" Anne asked.

"I hope so. We'll have to see how things look when we get a bit farther along." Dan had hoped they could make it to the next village in time for their midday meal and then press onward to Elkton. "I guess a lot depends on the terrain."

The information he'd gleaned in Eugene City told him that the distance from Cottage Grove to a small settlement at a river junction was about fifteen miles, and from there to Elkton, on the Umpqua River, was nearly as far again, but through less hospitable country. Several hamlets lay along the first portion of the journey, but beyond them they would see only a few cabins among the forested slopes. The road would take them over and between some rugged hills as they approached the Coast Range. Dan didn't want to risk being caught out in the wilderness after dark.

The trail swung westward as they left town, and they rode away from the river. The road bore deep wagon ruts in some places, and they let the horses pick their way between them, but for the most part the footing was easy.

"We'll follow Martin Creek for a while," Dan said, "and then pick up Pass Creek. The road pretty much follows the rivers through the mountains."

"It's a lovely day for riding," Anne said.

Dan had to agree. He settled back in the saddle and decided to forget about the mischievous Randall kids and enjoy this time with Anne. He reminded himself that these few days might be all he ever had with her. When it was over, she'd go back to England, and he didn't think she'd shed any tears over him.

Her friend Elise had changed her mind and decided to stay. How on earth had Eb Bentley won her over? Maybe he should have had a man-to-man talk with the gruff scout. Perhaps Eb could give

him a few tips on wooing English ladies.

After two hours on the road, they stopped to rest the horses.

"I think we'll reach Anlauf soon," Dan said.

Anne took a parcel from one of her bags and unwrapped four fluffy biscuits. "Mrs. Randall sent these along, and I have some raisins and cheese."

They sat down on the creek bank and watched the horses crop the grass.

After a few minutes of quiet, Anne smiled over at him. "This seems like when we were on the wagon train and stopped for nooning."

"Yes, only not so frenetic."

She laughed. "We had a few moments, didn't we? But Mr. Whistler claims our trip was singularly uneventful."

"I guess Rob ought to know." Dan took another bite of biscuit.

"I keep thinking about those people at Uncle David's farm," Anne said. "Sam Hastings and Millie."

Dan raised his eyebrows in question as he chewed.

"If he really was working for Uncle David, how did he expect to get away with impersonating him?" Anne shook her head. "I don't think Sam is very smart."

"Neither do I. We're well rid of him." Dan reached for his canteen.

"I wonder where he went after Deputy Raynor let him go."

Dan paused with the canteen partway to his lips. "Well, Raynor told him he couldn't stay at the farm." He shrugged. "It's not our worry now."

"I suppose you're right." Anne rose. "Do you think there's anything to see in Anlauf?"

"We'll cross the Territorial Road there. It goes on down to California."

Star jumped suddenly with a sharp squeal and kicked his heels at Bailey. Anne's horse responded with a snort and turned his hindquarters toward Star. The pinto gelding awkwardly hopped several steps.

Dan shot up off his log seat and called in a low voice, "Take it easy, Star. Calm down, fella."

The pinto stood shivering near the edge of the creek.

"What do you suppose startled him?" Anne asked.

"I don't know. Maybe a bee stung him." Dan looked all around but saw nothing that could account for the horse's actions. He walked over to Star and patted the trembling gelding's neck. "What's the trouble? Hmm?"

"It's a good thing we hobbled them," Anne said.

"Yes. Let's move on, if you're ready."

She nodded. "If you think Star is calm enough."

A faint rustle came from a thicket. Dan peered at the bushes but couldn't make out any solid shapes among the thick branches. An eerie feeling crept over him. Eugene Skinner had said the Indians in these parts weren't too happy since the white settlements had mushroomed. Could there be angry Calapooyas watching them?

Another rustle, fainter, drew his gaze to the tree line. His chest tightened as a dark-clad figure slipped between the close-growing cedars. Best not to tell Anne. He reached for Star's halter. "Let's go."

Millie trudged slowly into Elkton past noon of her second day on the trail, leading her horse by the reins. The worthless mare had thrown a shoe three miles back and limped so badly Millie knew she had to walk. It happened when they'd forded a creek. The horse had scrabbled in the rocky streambed and come out the other side minus a shoe. Millie blamed the horse for not being careful.

Stupid horse! She was glad she hadn't named her.

With any luck, she could pilfer a few coins and buy some lunch with it. But what was she going to do about the horse?

She turned and looked behind her. She'd gotten beyond Anlauf and stayed the previous night in a corn crib. She hadn't slept well and took to the road this morning feeling tired. The mare moved along well with a few stops for water and corn from the supply Millie had collected at her night's berth. She'd been pleased with her progress until their mishap while crossing one of the numerous creeks they encountered.

Ever since the mare lost that shoe, she'd feared Adams and Miss Stone would ride up behind her. But so far, she'd met only a few miners and a lone horseman coming from Elkton, and had overtaken a band of freighters heading there even slower than she was moving.

The freighters had called rude things to her and whistled. One had offered to let her ride one of his mules. Millie grimaced and shook her head as she remembered his boldness. Maybe she should have let her dignity slide and taken him up on it.

No, that wouldn't have ended well, she was sure. If she'd been alert, she wouldn't have let them see her at all. She had no doubt the freighters took particular notice of her and would be able to describe her minutely if anyone asked. She should have taken to the woods and worked her way past them without being seen.

"I really should have left you with Sam and made him give me Old Blue," she muttered.

The mare stretched her neck to the side and tried to grab a mouthful of dead grass. Millie jerked on the reins. "Oh, no you don't! Come on."

Elkton seemed a thriving community, compared to the hamlets she'd passed through earlier. Farms that held a prosperous air lay on the outskirts. The village itself boasted several large houses and businesses, a post office, and at least two houses with boards out front advertising ROOMS TO LET. A pocket of dwellings clustered near the point where Pass Creek flowed into Elk Creek. Beside a whitewashed, two-story house was a rail corral with a dozen or more mules and horses milling about inside. She decided that was as good a place as any to seek a new mount.

A three-sided shed sat at one side of the corral, but there was no barn. She couldn't see anyone about, so she led the mare over to the fence and tied her up. She was about to raise her skirt and duck through the fence rails when a door clumped shut. She looked under the mare's neck. A huge man had come out of the house and was approaching the corral. Worse, a short-haired, yellowish dog with a massive, square head trotted ahead of the man.

The dog barked fiercely. Her mare gave a squeal and jumped, crowding Millie.

"Help you?" the big man called. He clapped his hands together once, and the dog fell back, whining. "Sit," the giant said, and the dog plopped his hindquarters down in the dirt.

The man walked over and peered over the mare's back. "You want something, ma'am?" He towered like a rock formation, glaring down at her.

Millie swallowed hard and met his stony gaze. "Hello."

Slowly his sour face smoothed out to neutral then slid into a smile. "Well, well."

"I'm looking to trade my horse." It wasn't what Millie had planned, or the way she usually acquired a new mount, but sometimes a woman was forced to take extreme measures.

The man looked down at her mare. Millie retreated a step, so she could take him in without getting a sore neck. His bushy eyebrows tightened.

"This hoss right here?"

"Yes."

"She's lame."

Millie wanted to deny it, but that would be worse than useless. The mare stood with one foot—the shoeless one—tipped up and resting with just the tip of her ragged toe on the ground.

"She lost a shoe in the creek a few miles back."

The man grunted. "Bad place. People always cross there, but they should go upstream a ways. Well, I've got a ten-year-old bay gelding out there. He's healthy, but he's ornery. Or I've got a sixteen-year-old mare I could let go. She's sweet-natured, but she's on the thin side."

"Oh, I. . .well. . ." Millie hated being at a disadvantage. "Would you take my mare in trade?"

The man sighed. "I'll have to look her over." He took a step toward the mare's hindquarters, ran a hand down her flank, and stretched her hind leg out across his knee. After a moment he set the hoof down gently and straightened to his full height. Once

again, Millie was startled by his size and backed up a step.

"I'll need a horse that will take a sidesaddle." She wouldn't back down on that. She'd ridden the stolen mare astride all the way from Champoeg to Eugene City and vowed she'd never do that again.

He grunted and looked at the horse again.

Squinting against the rays of the sun, Millie studied the few horses among the mules in the corral. The bay horse didn't look bad at all. But where had all her confidence got to? She could usually talk her way out of any situation, but this time she wasn't so sure. Was it because he was so huge? Men didn't often intimidate her. She was smarter than most, so what was there to fear?

He moved around to the side where Millie stood and ran a beefy hand down the mare's off hind leg.

"You traveling alone, missy?"

Millie felt a rush of apprehension, another rarity for her. "No, I've got a couple of friends coming along, but they had to make a side trip on an errand. They'll be along before dark."

He eyed her sacks and bundles, tied to the saddle. "Her horn's pretty torn up. It'll take a while for her to grow it out again. I'm not sure I can shoe her for a month or two."

"Uh, I wondered—uh—how much you're asking. . . if I trade my horse, that is. . ."

"I'll have to get twenty-five dollars for the gelding, besides your nag. The mare I can let go for less, I suppose. Hate to, but. . ." He shook his massive head. Even standing beside Millie on level ground, he was a foot taller than she was. "Well, I'll take ten for my mare, along with your trade."

Millie huffed out a breath. She had less than a dollar in her pocket. "I'll have to think about it."

His eyes narrowed. "You ain't got the money?"

"No."

"Well, maybe when your friends get here. . ."

Millie considered her options. If she stuck around until after dark and stole one of his horses, he'd know who did it and set out after her. That was a hanging offense. Too risky. There might be a farm where the horses weren't too close to the house. She doubted that—there'd been too much talk about Indian trouble. Everyone would lock up their livestock at night and turn their dogs loose. She squared her shoulders.

"I don't suppose there's any place in this town where I could earn some money."

He smiled slowly and leaned toward her. "Well, now, that depends."

CHAPTER 8

Quickly Anne gathered the remains of their meal and tucked them away while Dan bridled both horses and put their hobbles in the saddlebags. They filled their canteens and mounted. All the while, Dan looked around, scanning the trees and the far bank of the stream. His anxiety made Anne want to gallop away from the spot as fast as Star and Bailey could run.

Instead they picked up a brisk trot and continued along the road. Dan's hand never strayed far from the butt of his rifle, where it traveled in the scabbard next to his right knee.

The road stayed within sight of Pass Creek most of the way. She enjoyed that at first, as the creek gave them a constant supply of water and provided some spectacular scenery as they wended their way through the hills. But now its babble covered other sounds she might have heard, and she wished they weren't forced to stay so close to it.

Dan stayed on edge, constantly watching, searching. He barely spoke to her until they began to pass a homestead here and there. She felt his relief as he relaxed in the saddle and smiled across at her.

"Almost to Anlauf."

A small village appeared between the high hills, and they approached the junction of their road with another that looked well traveled.

Dan slowed Star and waited for her to catch up. He pointed southward at the junction. "They say that road goes all the way to California."

Visions of gold miners and Spanish priests danced in Anne's mind.

"Of course, there're a lot of hostile Indians between here and there."

"Mr. Skinner said there's been fighting on the Rogue River," she said. "Is that near here?"

"It's a ways." Dan frowned, and she guessed that was because he had to give such a vague answer. Dan was a man of precision. No doubt he'd ask someone along the way exactly how far it was to where the hostilities raged and to the California border.

"Are we stopping here?" she asked.

Dan looked about, as though suddenly recalling the buildings around them. A grist mill rose by the edge of another large stream pouring into Pass Creek.

"Do you want to?"

"Not really. It's still quite a ways to Elkton, isn't it?"

"Yes. At least as far as we've already come today."

Anne stopped Bailey in front of what appeared to be a trading post. "Let's just stretch our legs for a minute and let the horses breathe."

Dan seemed agreeable. They didn't want to get caught on the isolated road to Elkton after dusk. Neither of them said as much, but the specters of Indians, wildcats, and ruffians hovered in Anne's mind. And there was always the question of propriety. She'd promised a number of people that she wouldn't be out alone with Dan at night. She wanted to be able to report to her friends later with a clear conscience. Not that Dan would try to take advantage of the situation. He was much too genteel for that.

Was that what made her categorize Dan as "unsuitable for husband material"? Was he just too much of a gentleman? The shocking idea brought heat to her cheeks. She slid to the ground without waiting for Dan to help her. As she walked about, pretending to take great interest in the tiny town, she wondered why she should blush over a dull man. She sneaked a glance back toward where he stood beside Star, working at one of the rawhide strings holding his pack to the saddle. True, Dan didn't have an adventuresome spirit. But he wasn't as bland as she'd found him a month ago.

They left Anlauf behind and rode steadily for two hours, stopped for an hour to let the horses rest, and moved on toward Elkton.

Where the road was overshadowed by huge pines, an eerie feeling swept over Anne.

"There's nothing like this in England. All the forests have been cut over and over for wood."

"I guess we've both seen a lot of new things since we joined the wagon train," Dan said.

Anne looked over her shoulder. As far back as she could see, something moved along the trail.

"Dan!" She reined Bailey in and swung around for a better look.

"What is it?" he asked.

"I'm not sure. I thought I saw a rider. But I don't see anyone now."

"Perhaps it was a deer crossing the trail."

"I don't think so. It looked like a grayish horse with a man on it, but it was way back there at the bend." She pointed.

Dan stared at the back trail for another moment, then turned Star. "Let's put a little speed on and get out of these woods."

Anne said no more but gladly urged Bailey into a canter. They rode side-by-side when the road permitted, and Dan let her take the lead when the ruts and washouts were bad.

They rounded a bend, and he pulled Star in, squinting at the trail ahead.

Anne rode up beside him. As far ahead as she could see, a line of pack animals plodded along the route.

"Freighters," Dan said.

"Can we pass them?"

"Should be able to." He glanced up at the bluff looming over them on the side away from the stream. "We might have to stay behind them for a while, but it won't be for long in any case. The town can't be far ahead."

As their horses trotted up behind the string of pack mules, the freighter who rode last in line swiveled in his saddle and looked back.

"Hello," he called.

"Good afternoon," Dan replied, riding ahead of Anne. "Where you headed?"

"Elkton, then Scottsburg," the freighter said.

"How far out are we from Elkton?" Dan asked.

"Less than two miles."

"That's good to hear." Dan looked back at Anne. "Not much farther."

The freighter stared past him, and when he focused on Anne his eyes bulged. "What do you know? This must be our lucky day—two winsome women in one afternoon." He laughed and met Dan's gaze but sobered when he realized Dan wasn't amused.

"Sorry, mister. No offense to your better half. It's just that we saw a rather robust redhead ride past us a couple of hours ago."

"Watch your tongue," Dan growled.

Anne pulled gently on Bailey's reins and fell back a little. Dan could get information from the rough freighters. She would keep in the background until he came and told her what he planned to do. Perhaps once they got beyond this hill, where the road squeezed between the creek and a steep incline, they could pass the mule train.

Sure enough, he soon turned Star and rode back to her.

"He says there's a place up ahead where we can get up off the road and pass them—where the hillside isn't so abrupt."

They rode at a walk for a few more minutes until the vista opened up ahead of them. The widening horizon promised open farmland.

"Come on," Dan said. "Let's get some speed up."

Anne urged Bailey to follow him, and they trotted off the path into the weeds and bushes. As they dodged between a few pines, she wasn't sure they were making much headway against the freighters. At last the ground evened out and they came to a farm with a hayfield bordering the road. They cantered along the edge, parallel to the long line of mules. More than thirty pack animals, all heavily loaded, made up the caravan. The drovers looked up one at a time, as she and Dan came into their peripheral vision. All of them stared at Anne, and she felt her face flush. Determined not to let them engage her in conversation, she gazed straight forward, at Dan's broad shoulders. He did make a magnificent figure on horseback. Why had

she never noticed that before? She could almost see him riding to hounds at Stoneford. He would enjoy the chase—but she doubted he'd take to the social life in the aristocratic circles of England.

At last they were past the freighters. Dan kept to the field a bit longer, and she was glad he didn't take her up onto the road immediately in front of their leaders. It was embarrassing enough to be seen with her hair coming loose and fluttering behind her. She did hope they found decent accommodations this evening. Something told her the muleteers would get rowdy when the sun went down.

As they neared Elkton, fatigue set in. Bailey's easy trot had become jarring, and Anne would have given much to stop the motion of the horse. When at last the town appeared, she gazed around in disbelief.

"Are we there? Truly?"

"Yes." Dan smiled gently at her. "I know you're exhausted, but really, Anne, you've been a wonderful traveler. You haven't complained once."

"And we'll make it to Scottsburg tomorrow?" Her voice had a plaintive note she regretted, but Dan's smile only deepened.

"Yes, dear lady. I'll ask about it, but I'm sure it's only half the distance we've come today, though we'll follow the Umpqua, and they say it takes more turns than a screwdriver."

She stared at him for a moment before her tired brain caught up. She laughed. "I don't mind a twisty river, so long as we get there. Oh Dan, just think! Scottsburg tomorrow, and perhaps I shall see Uncle David the next day."

Cautious Dan couldn't exult with her. He gave a judicious nod. "Perhaps. For now, I suppose we'd best find accommodations."

"Oh look! There's a place serving food." Anne pointed to a one-story building with a crudely lettered sign: MEALS.

"Did you want to eat?" Dan asked.

"Let's find rooms first. Perhaps it will be a nice boardinghouse with supper included. But I'll admit I'm hungry, and I'll wager you'd like a cup of coffee and some hot food."

"I wouldn't turn it down." Dan jerked his head toward a man

driving up the street in a farm wagon. "Why don't I ask this fellow if he knows where we can stay?"

Anne waited with the horses while Dan walked out to meet the farmer. The man halted his team in the street and talked earnestly for a couple of minutes, pointing here and there as he spoke. Dan took it all in, nodding at strategic points. He turned and jogged back to Anne while the farmer and his team clopped off eastward.

"He says there's at least three hotels or boardinghouses, all run out of private homes. The freighters will probably camp outside the village, so we don't need to worry about them crowding us out. One of the boardinghouses is right over there." He pointed across the street and down a bit, to a graceful wood-frame house of three full stories.

"That looks respectable," Anne said.

"Let's go and ask if they have two rooms." Dan untied the horses, and they decided to walk, leading their mounts the short distance.

The cushioned rocking chairs on the front porch tempted Anne, but she allowed Dan to guide her inside. In the foyer, an impressive, walnut-railed staircase wound upward. A table served as a desk, with a box divided into pigeonholes mounted on the wall behind it. The furniture looked solid and functional. Anne did not aspire to elegance on the frontier, just comfort, and the cozy fire burning in a stone fireplace assured her she would find it here.

A middle-aged woman came through a doorway and smiled at them. "Stopping over, folks?"

"Yes." Dan stepped forward as she moved behind the desk. "We're in need of two rooms, if you have them."

She frowned. "Well, I've got one nice front room you could have, but if you need another..." She peered past him at Anne. "Is it just the two of you, or do you have children?"

"It's just us." Dan's face colored beneath his stubble of a beard. The poor man! He was so shy, this must be quite a trial for him. Anne stifled a giggle.

"Well, we could put the lady in the front room," the landlady said, "but you, sir, would have to share with two of the miners."

"Oh well..." Dan glanced around at Anne. "What do you think?"

She walked over and stood beside him. "Might there be another place with more rooms?" she asked. "We thought we liked the look of your house, but Mr. Adams would prefer privacy, I'm sure." He hadn't squawked about sharing with the Randall boys in Cottage Grove last night, but Anne sensed that sharing a room with a couple of prospectors alarmed him. On the other hand, a gentleman like Uncle David would probably be classified as a miner in this situation, so perhaps bedding down in the same room with them wouldn't be too uncomfortable.

"Well, now, I've got a little room out back," the woman said. "It's not much—just a lumber room, we call it. It's off the woodshed, and we store trunks there. My Jack put a cot in there when he came home last summer, because his room was full of argonauts. If you want to see it, sir, maybe you'd consent to sleep out there. I could make the lady nice and cozy in the front room, and we wouldn't charge you much for the shed."

"That sounds agreeable," Dan said. "Thank you."

"Let's go take a look. If you're not put off by the boxes and trunks, we'll make a transaction here."

"And do you serve meals?" Anne asked as they followed the woman out to her spotless kitchen.

She lit a spill at her cookstove and used the roll of paper to light a kerosene lantern. "I put breakfast on the table at seven. Other meals, you have to go elsewhere. But there's a couple of places where you can get good, plain food." She led them out the back door and through an attached room with slatted walls, piled to the rafters with split firewood. "Here we go. I'm Jenny Austin, by the by. I only let this room now and again, but it's all made up fresh." She opened the door and walked in, holding the lantern high.

The windowless lumber room was as clean as the kitchen. Boxes, kegs, and a couple of trunks filled half the floor space. On the other side was a narrow bed bearing a quilt patterned with bright greens, reds, and whites. Nearby were a washstand and a crate set on end, with a calico curtain hiding the shelves of the improvised bedside table.

"It's not much, but such as it is, it could be worse."

"I'll take it," Dan said.

"Very well, then. If you want to bring in your things, I'll show the lady to her room." They followed her back through the kitchen. A tall, thin man wearing a vest and white shirt stood near the desk in the foyer.

"There's my husband," Mrs. Austin said. She introduced them and left the men to settle the registry and payment.

They were halfway up the stairs before Anne realized she should have given Dan some of her dwindling cash or else stepped up and paid Mr. Austin directly. She hesitated on the landing.

"Everything all right, dearie?" Mrs. Austin asked. "My Bill will bring your things up in a jiffy—or a couple of jiffies."

"I'm just tired, thank you."

"Well, you'll probably want the nearest eatery, then. Willis and Simpson's, near the bridge. The place doesn't look like much, but I'm told they've got a new cook and the pie's worth eating."

She led Anne into a charming room with rose trellis wallpaper and white muslin curtains. Mrs. Austin lit the lamp for her and spread back the covers. "There. If you want a fire, ask Bill when he brings your luggage. Or he can have one burning when you come back from supper. It's likely to rain tonight, and you don't want the damp to settle in your lungs."

"That's very kind of you," Anne said. "Would you please tell Mr. Adams I shall be down in ten minutes to go for supper?"

"I'll do that very thing." Mrs. Austin backed out of the room with a smile and shut the six-paneled door.

Anne almost felt as though she were back in St. Louis. The plump mattress under the crocheted bedspread called to her, but she brushed off her skirt and peered into the looking glass hanging over the maple dresser. The disarray of her hair alarmed her. If only Elise were here to dress it for her.

She took off her hat and removed the hairpins. It might take more than her promised ten minutes to repair this damage.

A tap at the door alerted her to Mr. Austin's punctuality. She

opened it to him and gratefully took her satchel from him.

Dan was waiting in a velvet-covered chair near the front desk when she descended the stairs a quarter of an hour later. He wore the same trousers he'd had on all day but had put on a fresh shirt and added a ribbon tie and somehow managed to shave in the brief time she'd allotted him.

"I'm sorry I've kept you waiting," she said.

"Not at all. Shall we go? A couple of other patrons came in from the restaurant and praised the new cook's venison roast."

"Indeed? I wonder what's brought such a masterful chef to this wilderness." Anne took his arm, and they walked out into the twilight. "Oh, the horses!" She glanced toward the hitching rail, where one sad-looking dun was tied.

"Mr. Austin assured me he would take good care of them."

"Good. Oh Dan, I need to settle with you about the payment for our rooms." She glanced up at him shyly from beneath the brim of her bonnet. This wasn't a subject a lady liked to broach.

"You mustn't think of that," he said. "We've discussed this before. Frankly, I was glad to have a chance to help out." He paused at the edge of the street and gazed down at her with gray eyes so compassionate that Anne almost blushed. "Anne, forgive me for asking, but perhaps it's time I did. Are you truly all right financially?"

"Oh Dan, please don't—"

Before she could say more, he held up a hand. "I'm sorry. I know how you dislike this type of discussion, but you've confided in me that the family fortune is slated for your uncle, not for you. I'm not a wealthy man, but I am able to see us through this expedition. If that would help you, just say the word."

Her face must now be a deep shade of scarlet that would draw unwanted attention. She looked down as she tried to regain her composure.

"Daniel, I appreciate your friendship and your generosity. What you say is true, but I should feel ill-bred and tawdry if I let a man— even a gentleman such as yourself—bear my expenses."

He grasped her hand where she'd tucked it through his arm and squeezed her fingers. "Dear Anne, I wouldn't want that. But neither would I want you embarrassed if your funds gave out on you. From here on, I'll keep paying my own share, and you just give me the sign if you need a bit of assistance, all right? We won't speak of it again."

She wanted to be cross with him, but she couldn't. Instead, her love of words betrayed her into a tiny smile. "And what's the sign, I wonder?"

Dan's worry creases smoothed out. "Why, just tell them your hired man will take care of the bill."

"Hired man? You should be a butler at least."

"I'm afraid the people here wouldn't know what to do with a butler. Maybe your guide?"

"How about my friend?" She returned the pressure on his fingers.

"I like that. Shall we?" He nodded toward the low building with the crudely painted sign board.

"Indeed. I'm famished." She stepped eagerly with him toward the ramshackle restaurant. She wouldn't consider what her British friends would think of this place, or even Elise, who had traveled across the plains with her. In truth, the place looked a bit homey in a crude way, a welcome refuge for travelers.

"Mr. Austin told me just before you came downstairs that those freighters we passed earlier brought an injured man in." Dan guided her out of the path of a wagon.

"Really? One of their men was hurt?"

"Not one of theirs. They said he'd passed them this afternoon, and then later they came upon him lying in the road. Apparently his horse had thrown him. The horse was off the road, grazing. But the fellow was out cold. They tossed cold water in his face and he woke up, but he appeared to be quite shaken, so they brought him in to town."

"Is there a doctor here?" Anne asked.

"Mr. Austin says there is—one the steamship owners brought in for their crews. I suppose he'll be all right."

A drop of water splashed on Anne's nose. "Oh dear, it's raining."

Dan seized her hand and pulled her the remaining few steps to the door of the restaurant.

Millie peered out the half-open kitchen door without losing a stroke in stirring her cake batter.

"You got that johnnycake ready?" Andrew Willis yelled. Her new boss seemed to have only one pitch to his voice, and it was aimed to carry over the roar of conversation in the dining room behind him.

"I just took it out of the oven."

"When will the next batch of stew be ready?"

"Not for another twenty minutes or so. The carrots are still crunchy." Millie leaned so she could see past him. If Anne Stone and Dan Adams showed up, she wanted some warning.

Andrew glowered at her, and Millie glared back. She could cook, but she couldn't work miracles.

"You should have started it an hour ago."

"How was I to know you'd have this many customers tonight?"

"They'll probably want some flapjacks and sausage then."

"You go ask them. Don't tell me what the clientele 'probably' wants."

He grimaced at her. "Oh, and one fellow wants jam for his biscuit. We got any jam?"

Millie stared at him. "How should I know?"

"You been cooking in here all day. You musta been through all the stuff." Willis stalked to one of the shelves, opened a small crock, and peered into it. "Ha!" He looked around, found a soup bowl and a spoon, plopped two scoops of preserves into the bowl, and strode back into the dining room, letting the door shut with a thunk.

Sweat streamed down Millie's face as she poured the cake batter into the one pan remotely the right size. She slid it into the oven, mopped her brow with the hem of her apron, and checked the fuel in the firebox. As much as she hated to increase the temperature of the room, she tossed in a couple more sticks of firewood. At the worktable, she cut several slabs of johnnycake and put them on plates.

She'd thrown open the back door ten minutes after she'd been hired, but the occasional breeze that wafted in was no competition for the heat radiated by the cookstove. For six hours she'd slaved to satisfy Willis's burgeoning flock of customers.

She strode out to the back stoop and flapped her apron in front of her face for a minute. The air had cooled since the sun dropped, and a welcome breeze came across the Umpqua. Millie let it caress her cheeks. She didn't mind working when that was the only option, but she hated to sweat. That made it harder to present herself as a lady.

The liveryman had frightened her for a moment, she admitted to herself. She'd feared his idea for her employment was something indecent, and Millie had her limits.

"Andrew needs a cook, over across the way," he'd said in a conspiratorial tone.

"A cook? For how many people?" Millie had stepped back to avoid his fetid breath.

"Oh, just everyone who passes through here." The man let out a big guffaw. "He ain't had a decent cook since Harry up and left for the gold fields."

"Harry?"

She wished she hadn't asked as she got a rambling tale of Andrew's business partner gone missing—otherwise known as Harry Simpson, formerly the best cook in Elkton. The liveryman walked over to the restaurant with her, making good on his promise to "put in a good word" for her. And when she'd earned ten dollars, he promised to trade his mare for hers.

Andrew Willis had hired her on the spot, and Millie had felt she had little choice, though the way he studied her figure made her flesh crawl. Every man in the rude café stared as well, and Millie had made one condition before she entered the cramped, untidy kitchen and donned Harry's abandoned apron.

"I'll not serve the customers, too. If you want me to cook, I can

do that. Mister, I can cook up a cyclone for you. But I won't carry it out to the men. Someone else will have to do that."

"Someone else" turned out to be Andrew himself. Millie wondered that he didn't have a wife or even some neighbor women who would like to work as waitresses, but perhaps the town was too rough and tumble for women. Whatever the reason, she soon found herself cooking ten dishes at once and trying to eke out Andrew's supplies to fill all the orders he brought her.

The door to the dining room banged again, and she slipped back inside.

"What are you *doing*?" Andrew yelled. "We've got hungry people out there."

"Just catching my breath. I'm like to die in here. Oh, there's your johnnycakes."

Andrew looked at the prepared plates and grunted. "I need two beefsteaks and some biscuits. And have you made gravy yet?"

"Beefsteaks?" Millie cried. "I haven't seen any beef except that one bone you gave me to put in the stew when the venison ran out."

"Hmpf. Guess I need to get out to the springhouse and bring in more meat."

"I guess you do. Bring some more chicken, too, if you've got it. I've made three batches of fried chicken, and it's all gone." She placed her hands on her hips. "If this is how it is every night, how did you and Harry keep yourselves in supplies?"

"It's been powerful busy today," Andrew admitted. "Guess people heard about you. Harry's been gone a week, and I've been dishing up pretty poor fare. Thought I'd lost all my customers. But when I put the word out this afternoon that I had a new cook and she was making a dozen apple pies, that's when they started lining up at the door."

"Well, there's not much pie left." Millie glanced over at the pie and a half on the sideboard. "You got any more apples?"

"Oh sure. I got a lot of those from the orchard over where the Hudson's Bay Company used to have its fort. I'll bring some in. You've got plenty of coffee, right?"

"Two pots full."

"Well, can you serve that up while I go out and get the stuff you need?"

"I told you, I'm not serving the clientele."

"Aw, come on, Charlotte." She'd told him her name was Charlotte when he'd hired her, as a precaution in case Miss Stone or Mr. Adams or even Sam came in and heard her name. Now she was glad she'd had the presence of mind to do that, since the new cook seemed to be the talk of the town.

"All right, I'll do one round of coffee and pie, and I'll tell folks who haven't had their main meal yet that we're working on it."

Willis grinned. "You're a capital girl, Charlotte. And I wouldn't say it in front of Harry, but you're a really good cook, too." He dove for the back door.

Millie looked at all her pots to make sure nothing would boil over in her absence and checked the progress of the cake. She grabbed two pot holders, took a steaming coffeepot in each hand, and pushed her way through the doorway to the dining room, shoving the door with her backside.

Freighters and miners erupted in cheering and whistling as she turned.

"Hey, you're better-lookin' than Harry!"

"Are you Charlotte? Bring some of that coffee over here!"

"No, darlin', pour mine first. I'm parched."

Millie stared at the room full of rowdy men and sucked in a deep breath. "All right, gentlemen. I've got ten pieces of apple pie left in the kitchen. If you want to get a slice, put fifty cents on the table, and I'll pick it up as I come around."

The men didn't disappoint her, but anted up as she made the rounds, filling their chipped mugs.

"Hey, sweetheart, how much do you charge for kisses?" one miner asked her.

"More than you've got in your pocket."

When she'd picked up five dollars, she called, "Sorry, fellows, the pie just sold out, but if you come back tomorrow, we'll likely have more."

A loud wail drowned her last few words.

Quickly she filled all the cups pushed toward her, dodging a few straying hands and tossing off retorts to their comments. Soon both pots were empty.

"Okay, folks, I need to go make more coffee and take the apple-sauce cake out of the oven. Those of you who didn't get pie, may I suggest cake or gingerbread? Andrew will be back any second to take your orders."

"Aw, Charlotte, whyn't you take 'em?"

"Because Andrew can't cook, and you all know that. So while I cook, he'll take orders."

As she pulled open the kitchen door, the street door opened and a cold draft swept through the room. She looked toward it and nearly dropped both coffeepots.

Coming through the doorway, clad in a stunning green-and-gold satin dress and a darling velvet cape and bonnet, smiling up at her handsome escort, was Anne Stone.

CHAPTER 9

Millie ducked through the kitchen door and set down the empty coffeepots. She tore off her apron and tossed it on the worktable. Her pocket was heavy with the pie coins. She hugged it close to her thigh as she ran to the corner where she'd left her coat and sack of clothes. Her saddle and other gear were at the livery with her lame mare, but she hadn't wanted to take a chance of losing the dress she'd extracted from Anne Stone's trunk, so she'd brought it along to Andrew's place.

She almost laughed at the thought of elegant Miss Stone sitting down to eat dinner amid the boisterous crowd of miners in the other room. If she weren't in such a hurry, she'd stick around to see whether she actually ate at Andrew's or went someplace else.

She pulled on her coat, hefted the sack, and dashed for the back door.

"Whoa, whoa, whoa!" Andrew was coming up the back steps. He shot out an arm to stop her from piling into him and dropped a plucked chicken and a basket of apples. The apples thudded down the steps and rolled hither and yon.

Millie tried to shove past him, but Andrew's fingers clenched her wrist. "Where are you going, missy?"

She stared into his suspicious face for an instant. "I've got to go out back. *You* know." She made a face that she hoped would imply her urgent need to visit the little building a lady would never mention.

"With all your stuff?" Andrew's eyes squinted into slits. "Not running out on the customers, are you? We've got a lot of dinners yet to serve tonight."

She sighed and pulled her wrist from his grasp. "Look, I need to leave. I'm sorry—it's an emergency. Just give me what you owe me, please." She was glad after all that she'd run into him. She'd have

slipped away without her pay, and she needed that.

"You ain't worked a whole day yet."

"Pretty near. I mean it, Mr. Willis. I need to get going *now*."

"Why? What's happened?" He looked past her into the kitchen.

"Nothing, but if I'm not in Scottsburg by morning, something awful will happen."

This didn't satisfy him any better than her earlier answers. He leaned against the doorjamb and studied her with an air of disapproval.

"You're lying. Why?"

"I'm not."

"You planning to ride to Scottsburg all by yourself? 'Cause the steamboat don't leave 'til morning. I know that for a fact."

She looked him over, wondering how big a fib he would swallow. So far she wasn't doing very well. And if he tried to collect money for the pies. . .

"All right, I'll tell you." She blinked several times and tried to conjure up tears. "I went into the dining room, like you said, and gave all the men their coffee. And some of them—" She sniffed. "Some of them said shameful things to me. Mr. Willis, I'm afraid of those men. Some of them have got no morals at all. Please let me go."

Andrew laughed. "You think you'll be safer on the road to Scottsburg than you were in my dining room? Girl, you're loony. What do you think would happen if one of them caught you a mile out of town, all by your lonesome? Besides, I won't let 'em bother you."

She achieved what she hoped was a pathetic quivering of her top lip. "I'm just so scared. And I'm nigh exhausted. I don't think I can cook anymore tonight."

"Well, you've got to. We have a business agreement. Come on, now. Fried chicken, more pies. . . I ain't paying you a cent until you do."

Millie let out a pent-up breath. "All right, but don't make me go out into the dining room again. I don't want them to see me."

"All right, Charlotte. Just you put your apron back on and get busy. I'll go deliver them pie slices and tell the ones still waiting to be patient. How do I know who gets the pie, now?" As he spoke, he picked up the things he'd dropped and placed them on the table.

"Oh, they'll know. Just ask who was promised a slice of pie." She dearly hoped they wouldn't tell him they'd paid her, but if they did, she guessed she'd have to hand over the five dollars.

Andrew loaded the tray and carried it into the dining room. The roar of voices and clinking of silverware on china burst through the doorway then quieted again as the door closed.

Millie looked longingly toward the back door. If she ran now, the liveryman wouldn't trade her a decent horse. She needed the pay Andrew had promised her. She couldn't think of anything more she could do to ensure that Anne Stone and Daniel Adams wouldn't learn who was cooking their dinner. Resolutely, she tied the apron around her again and picked up a limp, naked chicken.

The next morning, Millie crawled out of the hayloft in the barn behind a farmhouse before the sun rose and brushed all traces of her sleeping place from her hair and clothing. The rain had let up after midnight, and for a wonder she'd slept soundly. She hurried through the shadows to the horse trader's corral.

Her saddle was waiting for her in the flimsy shed, and she decided to go ahead and put it on the mare she was taking. If the owner came out before she was done, she'd pay him. If not, she supposed she'd have to go knock on his door and give him the money. She wished she dared to leave Elkton without paying for the horse, but that was too dangerous. He'd have the marshal on her for sure, and she couldn't stand for any delays now, nor too much scrutiny.

Just for a moment, she considered putting her saddle on the bay gelding, which looked to be in better shape than the mare, but she didn't have twenty-five dollars, and she'd never get away with it for less. The horse trader wasn't just big, he was shrewd. She threw one last wistful glance at the gelding. The horse she'd ridden into town got no notice. Millie was glad to be rid of it.

The liveryman arrived, rubbing the sleep from his eyes, as she tied her bundles to the saddle. She'd sneaked a small bag of oats from the farmer's cache last night and had slipped it into the sack with the dress she'd pilfered in Eugene City. At least her new mount would have a little nourishment later.

"Well, Miss Evans, you're about early." He frowned as he eyed the mare. "I guess this means we're doing business."

"Yes, sir, and I've got the money right here. Thank you kindly for recommending me to Mr. Willis."

His eyebrows shot up as she heaped his palm with coins and a few bills. "Well now. I heard there was big doings at Andrew's last night. I almost went over to see if I could get a piece of your pie."

"The pies sold out as fast as I could bake them."

"Do tell." The huge man slapped the mare gently on the withers. "She's a good horse. Treat her well, and she'll do the same for you."

"Thank you," Millie said. "Say, there hasn't been a fella around asking for me, has there?"

The man shook his head. "You did say you had friends coming in, but nobody's been here inquiring for a lovely young lady."

"Oh, thank you." Millie smiled up at him, knowing she'd get a lot further with him if she played along with his attempts at flirtation. "He's my half brother. Light hair, beard, not nearly so tall as you are." She blinked at him, disgusted with herself, but determined to leave a favorable memory, since she had to leave *some* impression.

"Nope, haven't seen him, but if he comes along, I'll be sure to tell him Miss Charlotte Evans was here."

"Thank you." She almost told him Charlotte wasn't her real name, but then what if Anne Stone made inquiries and learned she'd been here?

She swung up onto the mare's back.

"Her name's Vixen."

Millie almost shouted, "I don't ever name horses." Instead she gave him a farewell wave and set out on the westward road.

David Stone crawled out of his wilted tent and looked around at the sodden mountainside and the rushing creek. He hated rain. His bay gelding, Captain, named in a fit of nostalgia and yearning for his brother John, plodded toward him. He looked black when he was wet, and David regretted not having built a shelter for the horse.

Captain came over and rubbed his damp face against David's arm.

"Good morning." David rubbed between Captain's ears absently while he considered his course for the day. He'd have to make the trip down to Scottsburg for more supplies if he wanted to stay up here to prospect any longer. He and Captain both had survived on short rations for two days and would have a very skimpy breakfast.

Maybe he should just pack up his tools and go home. The rain swelled the stream and made it hard to work the sluice box—a difficult job for one man as it was. He should probably go home and see if that shiftless Sam Hastings had ruined his farm.

He walked back to the tent, with Captain tagging after him. Stooping, he pulled out his nearly empty sack of provisions.

"Here you go, boy." He'd saved the last, shriveled carrot for his horse. Inside the tent were his gold pan, spade, pick, and other tools. If he was going to break camp, he'd have to pack up everything. He hated to strike a wet tent. At least it wasn't raining this moment—but that didn't mean it wouldn't soon. He squinted up at the low clouds. "Well, Lord, shall we have a cup of tea, and I'll wait for You to speak?"

He always read a little scripture in the morning while his breakfast heated. Maybe God had a message for him today. Lately, he'd been feeling that his life was empty and hadn't a lot of point to it. He'd made money and lost it again, made friends and left them behind, fallen in love and climbed out again. He was forty-one years old, and this morning he felt ancient. He was so thin, he could count his ribs easily, and his left knee ached. The thought of riding all day with his foot confined to the stirrup made it hurt worse—but the prospect of standing in the icy creek wasn't much better.

How did he get to this place? Was he supposed be this age and not have loved ones around him? He'd bought the farm near Eugene as a place where he could settle down. So why couldn't he feel settled?

Captain nuzzled him for more carrots.

"Sorry, old boy. I haven't got any more. You'll have to make do with what you can browse on." He hated not having decent feed for the horse. He took out a small sack of rolled oats and set aside enough to make himself a small portion of oatmeal, then sprinkled the rest among the weeds. "There. See what you can make of that."

While his tea water and oatmeal heated, David opened his Bible and read a psalm. *"LORD, what is man, that thou takest knowledge of him! Or the son of man, that thou makest account of him! Man is like to vanity; his days are as a shadow that passeth away."* Wasn't that the truth?

His thoughts strayed, as they often had lately, to England. Stoneford. His real home. Was it time to go back? What would he live on, other than his friends' kindness? He'd have no income there. If he sold his mining claim and his farm, he'd have enough to take passage to England, but not enough to set himself up once he got there.

Maybe he should write to his eldest brother, Richard. Why hadn't he kept up the correspondence, anyway? Laziness, he supposed, and the difficulty of making sure he'd get a reply when he'd moved around so much. Now it had been so long since he'd written that he was embarrassed to barge into John's and Richard's lives again.

He recalled the days he'd dangled Richard and Elizabeth's infant on his knees. Little Anne was such a pretty mite. She probably had several brothers and sisters now. John must be married, too. David hoped so—hoped they were both happy and fulfilled.

The water boiled, and he jumped up to fix his tea. Sometimes it was hard to come by out here. A mercantile in Eugene stocked it for him, but the traders in Scottsburg had offered coffee instead. The stock David had carried with him was running out, like all his other provisions, and of course he had no milk to put in it.

He picked up his Bible and read the next verse aloud. " 'Bow thy heavens, O Lord, and come down; touch the mountains, and they shall smoke.' " He looked out over the hills, with the clouds rolling close to their summits. " 'Cast forth lightning, and scatter them; shoot out thine arrows, and destroy them.' "

Thunder cracked, and on the hillside across from the ravine where the stream flowed, lightning split a gnarled cedar tree.

Captain left off nosing about in the dead grass and snorted, whipping his tail back and forth. Raindrops splattered on David's head, and he slammed the Bible shut. He dashed to the tent and placed the book inside. Poor Captain. The horse would have to fend for himself in the storm.

David ran back to the fire and grabbed his pot of oatmeal and his cup of tea. Captain trotted off toward the lee of a rocky outcropping. David crawled into the tent and sat for a moment, listening to the rain pelt the canvas. A gust of wind shook it so hard he wondered how long before the whole thing would collapse on him.

"Well, Lord, if that's Your opinion, I'd say it's definitely time to go down the mountain."

Millie arrived in Scottsburg late in the morning. She'd shaken off Andrew's pleadings and refused to come back to cook breakfast. She'd made a good trade, as far as the horse was concerned. The new mare moved along briskly through the wooded hills. She'd met several horsemen and a couple of farmers driving wagons eastward and passed more freighters and some drovers taking a small herd of cattle west. The mare didn't balk at bridges, and she had a smooth canter—overall, Millie felt she'd spent her ten dollars well, and she still had the pie money in her pocket.

If she could have afforded the time, she had no doubt she could have struck an agreement with Andrew Willis by which they both profited. But she didn't want to work hard all day in a sweltering kitchen. She wanted to take things a little easier and be ready to go out dancing in the evening, instead of needing to soak her feet and tumble into bed.

No, she had no regrets about leaving Elkton. One thing troubled her, though: where was Sam?

She'd seen no sign of him. Because of Miss Stone's presence, she hadn't dared peek out into the dining room again to see if he came

into the restaurant last night. Before she went to the livery that morning to make her trade, she'd sneaked around to the stable behind the fancy boardinghouse. Sure enough, the horses Anne Stone and Dan Adams rode were in there. She was ahead of them now. She'd hoped to have a couple of days' lead on them, but she'd have to make do with a few hours.

But it would have been nice to see Sam for a minute. What was he up to, anyway? Not enough to hold her adversaries back, that much was obvious. Odd that he hadn't found her, though. Her lame horse should have told Sam she was in Elkton, and he could have located her if he'd hung around. She'd give him a piece of her mind next time they met.

A downpour broke as she reached the outskirts of town. She pushed the mare into a canter and rode the last quarter mile squinting against the fat raindrops that pelted her face. The brim on her hat served only to funnel the water into a nearly steady stream that poured down her back and soaked through her coat. By the time she saw a sign for a hotel, she was bedraggled and uncomfortable.

She threw the ends of Vixen's reins toward the hitching rail and ran up the steps. She shoved the door. It flew inward and crashed against the wall. The desk clerk and three other men in the lobby looked up.

"Sorry." Millie gave the clerk a weak smile and closed the door. Suddenly out of the wind and drumming rain, she wondered if she was going deaf. The four men still stared at her. Not the entrance she liked to make. She dredged up a smile and strode toward the desk.

"May I help you, ma'am?" the clerk asked.

She hesitated. She didn't want to blurt out a request for the rates in front of the other customers. You never knew when it would be advantageous to make a gentleman's acquaintance, and she didn't want them all to know first thing that she was nearly broke.

"Uh, yes, thank you." She raised her chin and hoped her disheveled auburn tresses held a hint of mystery, not complete squalor. "I wondered if you have a room free."

"Well, yes, we do, ma'am." The clerk turned the registry toward her. "That's a dollar a night."

"Oh." She kicked herself mentally for letting that give her pause. She had five dollars and seventy cents in her pocket, but she certainly didn't want the clerk to know that. With meals and care for the horse, that wouldn't last more than two or three days in this mining town. Her impulse to ask if they had a cheaper room might be a mistake, though. She picked up the pen. "I may wish to stay several nights."

"Of course. Our policy is, if you pay one night in advance, you can settle the rest when you leave."

"Perfect." With a flourish, she signed, "C. R. Evans." She didn't think Miss Stone and Mr. Adams knew her last name, and if they came in behind her, she doubted they'd recognize the name Evans. But sticking with the alias "Charlotte" that she'd used in Elkton seemed wise. One of the men who'd bought pie from her at Andrew Willis's establishment might ride over here.

"I have a horse outside," she murmured, in tones as like Anne Stone's as she could muster. "Do you have accommodations for my mare?"

"Yes, ma'am. I'll have somebody see to it. Fifty cents a night. Seventy-five if you want us to give him oats."

She nodded. "It's a brown mare with a sidesaddle—out front."

"Very good, ma'am."

"I shouldn't like the saddle to be ruined."

"We'll get her under cover right away, ma'am. Do you have bags?"

"Oh. . ." Millie couldn't think how she'd explain to the snooty clerk that she carried her clothes in a grain sack. "I shipped a valise that will probably come later when the freighter comes in, but there is a saddlebag and a sack containing a gift for my cousin. If your man could just bring those to my room. . .?"

He glanced down at the registry. "It'll be there before you get your bonnet off, Mrs. Evans." He smiled at her stupidly.

Was he making fun of her wet, drooping bonnet? It took Millie a moment to realize he was waiting for her dollar. Obviously he wouldn't put her horse under cover until she paid.

She took out the pouch her coins were in and held it below the level of the counter so that the clerk couldn't see how light it was. She placed the money beside the registry.

The clerk smiled and whipped the coins off the surface like greased lightning.

"Thank you, ma'am. It's room 202, up those stairs. Just throw the bolt when you're inside, and use this key when you go out." He placed a substantial steel key in her palm.

Millie paused, observing through lowered lashes that the other three men lingered and threw frequent glances her way. Maybe she could wangle a free dinner with one of them.

She cleared her throat and said to the clerk, "My cousin is to meet me here, but I've learned today that he'll be delayed. I may have to wait a few days for him to arrive."

"Very good, ma'am. If you need anything, just let us know."

"Do you serve meals?" she asked.

"Yes, we do. That door"—he pointed to her right, beyond the staircase—"is our dining room. They'll be serving dinner in about an hour, and supper from five to eight."

"Thank you." She lifted her skirt perhaps an inch more than was absolutely necessary and made her way leisurely up the stairs, well aware of the four pair of eyes watching her. Either she looked so outrageous they couldn't believe her, or she'd kept enough of her usual poise and comeliness to fool them all into thinking she was a lady. Time would tell.

A thought occurred to her, and she almost cast it aside, but its attractiveness made her pause with one foot on the next-to-top step. She would do it! But not until she'd had a chance to clean up.

A half hour later she again approached the front desk, this time without the audience of loiterers.

"Ah, Mrs. Evans." The clerk's eyes lit in appreciation. Apparently her ministrations to her hair and wardrobe were successful. "How may I help you?"

"My cousin mentioned that he hoped to meet a gentleman here. I thought perhaps you knew him—a Mr. Stone."

"Mr. David Stone? The Britisher?"

Millie smiled. "He's the one."

"He often stays here. In fact, I shouldn't be surprised if he came in today—or very soon. Would you like me to give him your name if I see him—or your cousin's name?"

"Oh that won't be necessary. I'll let my cousin handle it when he arrives. Thank you very much."

CHAPTER 10

Dan felt like an utter failure. He'd gotten Anne halfway to Scottsburg when the heavens let loose on them. They'd taken shelter in a thick stand of pines, but even so they'd been soaked to the skin within half an hour. The fierce wind tore at them and made his teeth chatter. Anne stood between the horses, leaning against Bailey's side and shivering uncontrollably.

People in Champoeg said this rain would keep up all winter. No snow to speak of this side of the Cascades, but lots and lots of rain.

He leaned close to her and laid his hand on her arm. "Anne, I don't think this is going to stop. I want to build a fire."

"Can't we just mount up and gallop for Scottsburg?"

"I'm afraid you'll be sick if you don't get warm soon."

"Maybe there's a house not far away, and they'd let us come in and get warm."

"Now that sounds like a good idea. Let me help you into the saddle."

Less than a mile farther down the road, they came upon a farm-house with a snug barn and fields spreading behind it. With a prayer of thanks, Dan led the way up the lane, dismounted, and knocked on the door.

It was opened by a sturdy girl of about twelve who looked him over suspiciously then called over her shoulder, "Mama! It's a half-drowned man, and there's a lady with him."

"What?" A thin woman of about forty hurried over, wiping her hands on her apron. She sized him up in a glance and looked out at Anne. "Oh sir, look at you! Bring your wife in. This isn't weather to be out in."

As Dan went back to get Anne, he heard the woman tell her daughter, "Go out and get Billy and Felix. Tell them to put these horses in the barn and brush them down well and feed them."

The girl threw on a hood and shawl and scurried out the door and around the house.

Dan raised his arms to Anne, and for once she let the reins drop and fell into his embrace. Her lips were blue. "Let me carry you."

"No, please." A look of alarm crossed her face. She gained her footing and leaned on his arm. "Thank you, Daniel. I shall be fine."

He hurried her inside, and the farm wife shut the door behind him. "Is she ill?"

"Just chilled through, but I fear she'll be ill because of it."

"Bring her right in here. She can lie down on my bed." The woman pushed aside a calico curtain in a doorway.

"Oh really," Anne said, "I'll be all right, now that we're out of the wet and the wind."

"Still, you'd like to change, wouldn't you?" the woman asked.

"You're right. That would be nice."

The woman smiled and eyed her cautiously. "English, aren't you?"

"Yes."

"I'm Lena Moss."

Anne held out her gloved hand. "Anne Stone. And this is my friend, Daniel Adams."

"Oh." Mrs. Moss looked from one to the other of them in confusion.

"We're not married," Dan said quickly. "I'm escorting Miss Stone to see her uncle in Scottsburg. This driving rain caught us."

Mrs. Moss's expression went from scandalized to soft with compassion. "Well then, let's see if we can make you comfortable. Do you have extra clothing along?"

"Yes," Anne said. "In my valise."

"I'll have the boys bring it in."

A few moments later, young Felix brought Anne's bag in, and Mrs. Moss led her into the next room. Dan took off his coat and hat, hung them near the door, and moved toward the stove. It warmed the kitchen end of the long room, ticking merrily away, and a coffeepot and a kettle of water on its surface sent off steam.

"Help yourself."

He turned to find Mrs. Moss behind him, bearing an armload of Anne's wet clothing.

"Cups are in the cupboard yonder." She nodded toward a large cupboard topped with rows of shelves.

Dan took down a china mug and poured himself coffee. Mrs. Moss brought a wooden rack from a corner and set about spreading Anne's skirt, petticoat, bodice, and stockings to dry.

"My husband went to Scottsburg this morning," she said. "He'll be back directly, unless he's decided to wait out the rain."

"It's a raw day." Dan could well imagine the farmer taking refuge in a haberdashery or a café.

The three youngsters tumbled in at the back door and bantered as they took off their wraps.

"Here, you!" Mrs. Moss shook a finger at them. "Stop that rowdiness, or you'll not have any cookies."

"Cookies?"

"Yes, Becky May Moss, but not for girls who charge in here behaving like hoydens."

Becky hung her shawl on a hook and faced her mother demurely. "Yes, ma'am. Shall I get a plate and offer them to our guests?"

"Now, that's better," Mrs. Moss said. She adjusted the position of the drying rack on the other side of the stove and walked toward the cupboard. "Give Mr. Adams some, by all means, and I expect Miss Stone would appreciate a few as well, once she's got her dry clothes on." She threw Dan a glance over her shoulder. "And you, Mr. Adams. When she comes out, please feel free to use our room. Your things are dripping wet, too, I've no doubt."

"I cannot thank you enough," Dan said. His wool trousers were beginning to steam and feel a bit too warm against his skin, so he moved his chair a little farther from the stove.

"I do hope the lady won't be ill," Mrs. Moss said. "She's just a bit of a thing, isn't she? Pretty."

"I brought the rest of the baggage up, Mama," Felix said. "It's in the woodshed."

"Well, bring it in here. Mr. Adams can't use it out there, now, can he?"

Felix opened the back door and lugged in Dan's valise and saddlebags. Billy shut the door behind him, giving Felix a playful tap as he passed with his hands full. Felix growled at him.

"That's enough," their mother said. "Put those things down and get your snack. And behave like civilized young gentlemen. Becky, you'll be setting the table for supper when you're done."

"Yes'm. Are they staying?" Becky cast an uncertain glance at Dan from the corner of her eye.

"Oh, we couldn't impose," Dan said quickly.

"Dear me, of course you could." Mrs. Moss brought a cast-iron frying pan to the stove. "The lady can't go on in this weather. You'll stay with us tonight." She eyed Dan archly, as though daring him to contradict her. "You, sir, will have to sleep upstairs with the boys. It's all right, though. They've got the chimney through their room, and you'll be warm. Miss Stone can take Becky's room."

Anne wouldn't like it one bit—being delayed another night from finding her uncle. "But we can't—"

"Don't fret, young man. 'Twon't be the first time Becky's stayed in with us."

The curtain in the bedroom doorway pushed to one side and Anne appeared in an attractive but serviceable gray dress with black braid. She'd combed her hair and pulled it neatly up into at twisted bun.

"Thank you so much, Mrs. Moss. I feel 100 percent better."

"You're most welcome, my dear. I was just discussing our arrangements for tonight with Mr. Adams."

Anne looked at him with arched eyebrows.

Dan stood and grabbed his valise. "Mrs. Moss can tell you. I'll step into the other room and get out of these damp things."

"Sit right down, dearie, and have a cup of tea with sugar. Since you're English, I'll warrant you like it with milk in it."

"Yes, thank you."

"And we've oatmeal cookies and. . ."

Dan pushed the curtain back and made good his escape.

David let Captain pick his way down to Scottsburg as fast as the poor horse wanted to go. He was not only laden down with David's weight and that of his mining gear, but everything was dripping wet. On a sunny day, David would have stopped to see Whitey Pogue, a crusty old miner with a claim lower down on the same creek as his own, but in this foul weather, he decided not to make the detour.

An hour before sunset, he arrived at the stable of the Miner's Hotel, the best hostelry in town. David unloaded his horse and rubbed him down while Captain dove into a ration of crimped oats. He'd much rather see to it himself than wait for one of the hotel employees to care for the horse. They might not give Captain the attention he deserved for his faithful service.

At last, weary to the bone, David trudged across the muddy barnyard and around to the front door of the hotel.

"Ah, Mr. Stone," the clerk called out. "I thought you might come in today."

"Yes, it's miserable up there in the hills." David couldn't help but notice the attractive woman with auburn hair who glanced up from her reading when he entered. She sat in a niche to one side of the room, on an upholstered settee where patrons sometimes met for conversation.

He took his key from the desk clerk. "Thank you, Ed."

"I'll get your satchel out of the storeroom and bring it right up. Will you be wanting a hot bath before dinner?"

David laughed, looking down at the mud-smeared clothing that clung to him. "It would be criminal not to, I fear. Bring on the hot water."

"And does your horse need care?"

"I put him up myself, thank you." David turned toward the stairs and was surprised that the woman he'd noted earlier had approached and stood near the newel post, watching him.

"Mr. Stone?" she asked.

"Yes."

"Mr. David Stone?"

"That's right."

She wasn't the prettiest woman he'd ever met, but she had an interesting face, and her hair shimmered in the lantern light, with red highlights in the brunette. Her dress was made of commonplace calico, covered by a silky shawl—an import if he wasn't mistaken.

"Do I know you?" he asked.

"Oh no, sir, but I heard the clerk speak your name. I'm visiting from Eugene City, and an acquaintance there mentioned you to me. She said you were over this way and it was possible I might meet you. I hope you don't think me too bold to approach you."

David chuckled. "Not if you don't think me too loathsome to approach in my present state."

She looked slowly from his face, which sported several days' growth of whiskers, down to his open coat and vest, his mud-spattered trousers, and his high leather boots.

"Oh no. Loathsome is not at all the word I would choose, sir."

To David's consternation, he felt the heat in his face. "Well, ma'am, you have the advantage of me. You know my name, but I haven't heard yours."

"Forgive me. I'm Charlotte Evans."

She held out a dainty, gloved hand, and he took it. The woman had a certain appeal—a forthright charm that many of the frontier women lacked. David studied her face for a moment. She'd used cosmetics, but with a light touch. Probably she was near thirty, but she had the assets to keep a man in doubt. And she seemed intelligent, something he liked in a woman but rarely had the opportunity to enjoy these days.

"Are you engaged for dinner?" he asked. "Perhaps we could discuss our mutual acquaintances in Eugene."

"Actually, I thought I was, but I'm not. My cousin was to meet me here today, but I've been informed he's delayed."

"Well then, Miss Evans, it would give me pleasure if you would dine with me. The hotel lays a creditable table."

"I should love to." She lowered her lashes and said softly, "Though it's Mrs. Evans. My late husband—" She broke off with a slight cough.

"I'm sorry. Forgive me."

"Don't distress yourself over it," she murmured. "James passed on five years ago, and I've begun a new phase of my life. In fact, that is why I'm here in Scottsburg. But perhaps that is better left to tell later. I'm sure you're anxious to get to your room."

"I'll be eager to hear about it. Shall we say in one hour?"

She bowed her head in assent.

David smiled as he hurried up the stairs. He hadn't expected a charming dinner companion tonight.

Millie spent the hour preparing for her dinner with Mr. Stone. Part one of her plan had worked to perfection. If only she had time to carry out the rest. She dressed her hair carefully, letting her curls tumble down from the bunch at the back of her head. She refreshed her powder and lip rouge with an expertise gained from years of experience.

Last, she wriggled into the gown she had obtained from the obliging Miss Stone. On her arrival at the hotel, she'd asked for two things—a hot bath and a flatiron to press her clothing with. She'd let go of a precious nickel to have the hired boy black her shoes. She'd have liked to have a prettier pair, but the hem of Miss Stone's gown was long enough to hide all but the gleaming tips of the only pair she had along on this journey.

She eyed herself in the mirror over her dresser, turning this way and that. She could think of no way to improve her appearance. She only hoped Stone's niece and Adams didn't show up at this hotel. They might—it seemed to be the nicest one in town, and the prices reflected that, as did David Stone's choice to stay here. The only thing she could imagine that would be worse than meeting Anne Stone in the dining room was to have Sam come bumbling in and claim her. Her masquerade with David would be over in a trice. She was glad her brother hadn't shown up yet—though she was a little concerned about him. Sam never learned how to take care of himself, and she despaired of ever teaching him.

Perhaps he was doing his job after all. So far as she knew, Adams and Miss Stone hadn't ridden into town yet.

The other vital ingredient for this evening was a plausible story. She went over the tale she'd concocted in her mind. David Stone must believe every word she said, and he must sympathize with her. She mustn't make her plight sound too pathetic, or he wouldn't want to get involved. No, she must present herself as a strong, charming woman in difficult circumstances. One who didn't need rescuing but was not above accepting the hand of friendship. One who valued a smart, competent, independent man. That shouldn't be too difficult to put across to Stone.

The fact that James Evans had left her a widow, though inconvenient at the time, was now an asset. She'd just have to be careful not to divulge too much about James, how he made his living, or the manner in which he had died.

She gave her hair a final pat and picked up the silky shawl. She'd never owned one so nice, and her gown was beyond anything she'd ever seen, let alone imagined. It was just the tiniest bit tight, but not so bad it made her look bulgy, and she didn't suppose the gentlemen who saw her in it would mind. The shawl would help hide her flaws, too. She didn't own a nice purse, so she tucked the pouch with its remaining coins into the pocket beneath her skirt. Gloves, courtesy of Miss Stone, and a fan she'd acquired without benefit of a receipt from a shop in Eugene completed her ensemble. She glided down the stairs well pleased with herself.

As she'd planned, David Stone was already in the lobby, waiting for her. He paced across to the front window and looked out at the rain-drenched street, his hands shoved into his pockets. She'd picked a handsome one. Tall, with only a hint of silver in his light hair. He'd reached maturity, but he was still in mighty fine shape. She appraised him as she would a horse and knew she'd pick this one out of a herd. The fact that he had means was crucial. His fine looks were a bonus.

He turned and started back toward her, letting his gaze swing over the lobby and up the stairs. With satisfaction, she noted the exact moment he saw her. His eyes lit, and his smile made her shiver with anticipation. She'd succeeded in part two of her plan.

She continued down, and he met her at the bottom of the steps.

"Mrs. Evans, you look lovely."

"Why, thank you."

He nodded in appreciation. "I haven't seen a woman so well-turned-out since I left St. Louis—or possibly even New York. I must say, it's refreshing."

"You flatter me, sir."

"Not without cause. Shall we?" He crooked his arm and offered it to her.

Millie slipped her hand inside his elbow. "Delighted, Mr. Stone. This is such a treat."

"Oh, you've sampled the hotel's cuisine?"

"No, I meant finding a dinner companion who can carry an intelligent conversation. You've no idea what a dearth of good company I've undergone since I left San Francisco a month ago."

"Oh? You came up from San Francisco? I've been thinking of traveling down there. You must tell me about it."

"Mr. Adams!"

"Yes, Felix?" Dan was still shaving when the boy burst into the loft room he'd shared with Felix and Billy the night before.

"It's your horse, sir."

Dan's stomach tightened. "What about him? What's wrong?"

"When we got out to the barn, he was loose and had his head in the oat bin."

"Oh no." Dan grabbed the towel and quickly wiped the lather from his face.

"We don't think he ate too awful much," Felix said. "And I know for certain sure he was tied when I left him last night. I put him away myself, and I *know* he was hitched. Besides that, we've never known a horse could unhook the top of the grain bin and open it."

Dan reached for his shirt. "Is he acting ill? Standing back on his heels? Nipping at his side or anything like that?"

"No, sir." Felix looked up at him oddly. "There's one funny thing, though."

Dan continued buttoning his shirt. "What's that?"

"Your bridle and Miss Stone's. They're all. . ."

Dan eyed him sharply. "What about them?"

"They're all tied together. Knots everywhere."

Dan froze with his hand on his cuff button. "Knots?"

"That's right." Felix gulped.

"You kids didn't do that, did you?"

"No, sir. We wouldn't."

"I didn't think so." What in the world was going on? Dan finished buttoning his cuffs and slid his vest on. "Take me out there and show me, please."

Felix dashed down the stairs, and Dan followed.

Half an hour later, he entered the Mosses' back door with Felix. Anne was already seated at the kitchen table with Becky, eating a hearty breakfast of eggs, sausage, flapjacks, and dried blackberries. A china teapot sat near her plate, with a pitcher of cream and a bowl of white sugar nearby.

"There you are," she said with a smile. "I thought you were still asleep." She picked up her knife and fork.

"No, I've been out to the barn with Felix." Dan pulled out a chair next to her and sat down. "Anne, I think we should leave as soon as possible. Will you be able to pack up your things as soon as you've eaten?"

She sat still with the knife poised over a flapjack, looking at him with troubled brown eyes. "Of course, Daniel. Is something wrong?"

He sighed. "You remember Cottage Grove? The way our gear was all knotted together?"

Anne smiled wryly. "How could I forget? But wait." She frowned and cocked her head to one side. "We thought the Randall children had done it."

"Well, I don't think that anymore."

She studied him for a moment. "I see."

"It's almost identical to the other job, and I'm pretty sure the Randall kids haven't followed us here."

"I should think not."

Dan shot a glance at Mrs. Moss. She was cracking more eggs at her worktable, but she made no pretense of not listening. "It gets a bit more sinister, I'm afraid."

"Oh?" Anne asked.

"Star was loose in the barn, and the grain bin was open."

"Oh no. Is he all right?"

"We think so, but I'll have to watch him closely today."

"But who—?" She glanced around. "Oh Daniel. I can hardly believe this is happening."

"Trouble with your horse?" Mrs. Moss asked.

"Yes. Your husband and the boys discovered it when they went out to do their chores," Dan said. "The odd thing is it's not the first time our tack has been tampered with like that."

Anne laid her knife down. "I'll go close up my luggage at once."

"No, finish your breakfast," Dan said.

"You eat, too, young man." Mrs. Moss shook her wooden spoon at him.

Dan smiled. "Thank you, ma'am, I will. But then we'd best get on to Scottsburg."

"I'll fill your plate right now. Becky, run out and see if you can find me a few more eggs, will you?"

Becky rose, carried her dishes to the sink, and took her hood off its peg. When she was out the back door and their hostess was bustling about to fix his plate, Dan lowered his voice and leaned toward Anne.

"There's something I didn't tell you, and I probably should have." He glanced up. Mrs. Moss was approaching with a mounded plate. "Oh, thank you. That looks delicious." He straightened and shook out the napkin at his place.

She set the plate in front of him. "You're welcome. I'll step out for another jug of milk, if you want a bit of privacy."

Dan smiled at her. "That's very kind of you."

Mrs. Moss slipped out into the woodshed, and he looked into Anne's troubled eyes.

"What is it?" she asked.

"Bank Raynor told me the morning we left that Peterson was on the loose. He'd gotten a message from Marshal Nesmith to that effect. I didn't see that it would help things to tell you, but. . .well, I should have, and I'm sorry. I also should have been more vigilant."

Anne stared at him. "You think Peterson would play childish tricks like this? That makes no sense whatever."

Dan leaned back in his chair. "I admit, I struggled with that. But who else, Anne? Think about it."

"I don't know who else, but Peterson wouldn't hang about and tie our reins in knots. Cold-blooded killers don't fool around and play pranks. He wanted to kill my uncle, Daniel. Don't you understand that? To him, Uncle David is a worth a lot of money—but only if he's proven dead."

CHAPTER 11

The ride to Scottsburg was mercifully short. Anne's habit was stiff from its soaking the day before. If only Elise were here—she would know how to clean it so that the velvet regained its soft pile. As it was, Anne didn't think she could stand to wear it in the saddle for a full day.

Mrs. Moss had given the name of a friend of hers. The widow kept a clean, respectable boardinghouse on a quiet side street of Scottsburg and charged less than the hotels. They found it without any trouble. Mrs. Zinberg welcomed them, smiling when Anne told her of her friend's recommendation.

"Oh, that's just like Lena. Isn't she the sweetest thing?"

"She took very good care of us," Anne said.

"She would. She's been extra kind since my William died. I'm moving up to Corvallis in the spring, to be with my daughter, but I'm getting by in the meantime."

"My dearest friend lives in Corvallis," Anne said. "I shall have to give you her name before we leave."

A gray drizzle threatened to become a steady rain, and Mrs. Zinberg hustled Anne inside. Dan carried in their bags.

"Why don't you get settled, and I'll take the horses to the livery stable," he told Anne.

Mrs. Zinberg said ruefully, "It's too bad for you to have to take them over there, but I haven't kept horses since William passed away. I'm afraid you'd find nothing for them to eat in the barn."

"It's all right, ma'am," Dan said. "I'm sure Miss Stone could use a rest."

"Shouldn't I go along to inquire about Uncle David?" Anne asked.

"It's raining again. I truly feel you're better off to stay where it's dry and warm."

"All right," Anne said uncertainly. "Just make sure they're talking about the right man, won't you?"

"I will. Tall, blond Englishman, right? Forty years old."

"Yes. I do hope you can find out where he is, or at least where his claim lies."

"Oh, this uncle of yours is prospecting?" Mrs. Zinberg asked.

"Yes, at least that's what we were told. He bought property near here and came to look it over. But he's been away from his farm more than a month, and we didn't know when he would return. I hope we haven't made a mistake in coming all this way."

"You go on, sir," Mrs. Zinberg said to Dan. "Ask at the post office. They should know if he's around here. I'll take care of Miss Stone for you, no fear."

Dan stood with his hat in his hand, waiting for Anne's approval. She sensed that it would hurt him somehow if she didn't let him do this for her.

"Yes, go," she said. "I'll be fine with Mrs. Zinberg."

Anne went upstairs to her snug room under the eaves and unpacked her satchel. Changing out of the itching blue habit into her gray dress lifted her spirits. Her hostess insisted on taking the heavy velvet riding dress and sponging it while she heated water for tea.

"You needn't," Anne said.

"But you'll want to wear it tomorrow if you're riding again."

Mrs. Zinberg was so matter-of-fact and Anne was so tired that she let her do it.

Anne sank into a well-cushioned rocker before the fireplace with a lap robe over her knees. As she watched the flames, she reviewed the journey she and Dan had made from Eugene to Scottsburg, but she could find no logical explanation for the pranks played on them. Peterson's intentions troubled her, but she couldn't see a way to find out his whereabouts.

When Mrs. Zinberg brought the tea tray, she smiled at the plump, graying lady.

"Thank you so much. This reminds me of home. We got a lot of

rainy days in England this time of year, and I would often sit near the fire and read."

"Oh, you're from England?" Mrs. Zinberg seemed unduly surprised by that. "I thought maybe you were from Boston or thereabouts."

Anne chuckled. "No, but I'd like to visit that city sometime."

"Tell me about England." Mrs. Zinberg passed her a blue-and-white china cup and saucer. She then poured out her own tea in a mismatched white cup and brown saucer. Anne suspected she had been honored with the only remaining matched pair.

"Of course it seems the dearest place on earth to me," she said. "Though Oregon is very nice—in fact, the climate seems quite the same. Of course, you have more hills—and bigger ones."

"Very large ones east of here," Mrs. Zinberg said.

"Yes. I saw some of those." Anne chuckled at the memories of her wagon trip. "Bigger trees, too. Much larger. And I've never seen such vast fields of corn. Wheat, that is." She shook her head. "In England, corn is grain of any type."

"Really? Then what is corn?"

Anne smiled. "That is maize."

"Ah." Mrs. Zinberg laced her tea with sugar and offered Anne the bowl.

"No, thank you. Was your husband a farmer?"

"No, he was a surveyor."

Within the next hour, Anne learned much of her hostess's story, her ills and her woes, as well as a few fond reminiscences of her husband and their two daughters, now grown and gone.

At last Mrs. Zinberg rose. "There, if I don't get moving, we shan't have any supper."

Anne looked about the room. "Do you have a clock? Dan seems to have been a long time in town."

"I expect he stepped into one of the taverns for news of your uncle and met some new friends, as they say." She smiled, but Anne shook her head emphatically.

"Daniel isn't like that. He never drinks a drop."

"Oh. Then I suppose he may have had some trouble getting word of your uncle and is asking more people." Mrs. Zinberg frowned and headed for the door to the kitchen shaking her head.

Her air of disbelief at the same time amused and troubled Anne. If Dan *were* a drinking man, she'd have no trouble imagining the reasons for his delay. But he was so sober and dependable it was hard to think he'd gone astray from his mission. Looking about for a distraction, Anne found a few books on a shelf. She took down one by Dickens and settled again in the rocker.

An hour later, Mrs. Zinberg laid the table and sat down with her knitting. She and Anne kept up a sporadic conversation about knitting, yarn, travel, and literature. At last a quick knock came on the door, and the lady of the house rose to open it.

Dan came in, dripping rain on the rag mat.

"I'm sorry," he said. "It's coming down quite hard now."

"Don't fret about the floor," Mrs. Zinberg said. "Hang your coat over there and come get warm."

Anne sank back in her chair with a sigh. Until that moment, she hadn't admitted to herself how worried she was. She made herself breathe calmly while Dan took off his coat, hat, and boots.

Mrs. Zinberg shooed him toward the fireplace.

"Warm your hands while I put supper on the table." She scurried toward the kitchen.

Dan scarcely waited until she was out of the room.

"I've some news of Mr. Stone, but I fear our journey is not over."

"Oh? I had hoped, but not expected, to find him here."

"As did I. But I learned where his claim is. It's several miles up in the hills, by way of what I'm told is a very rough trail."

"Can we do it in a day?"

"I'm not sure. Probably." He sat down in the chair opposite Anne on the hearth. "But to go the distance and get back to town safely before nightfall—well, that is debatable. In fact, several gentlemen debated it at length."

She smiled.

"Anne, the oddest thing happened."

"Oh?" She sat up straighter and tried to rid her mind of cobwebs.

"I saw a blue roan tied up in front of a saloon this afternoon."

"Is that odd?"

Dan seemed at a loss for words, but shook himself. "It seemed so to me. This roan was a dead match for the one we saw at your uncle's farm."

Anne sat forward in the chair and stared at him. "Do you think it was the same horse?"

"It couldn't be." Dan held his hands out toward the fire and gazed at the flames. "Could it?"

"There are lots of blue roans."

"Yes, and we didn't see that one up close. But it's thin like that one."

"Well over sixteen hands, I thought at the time," Anne said uneasily.

"More like seventeen. This one, I mean. I stood next to it and thought what a fine horse it could be if it were fattened up."

"Black mane," Anne said.

"Tail like a crow's wing."

They looked at each other.

"There was no brand on this one," Dan said. "I looked him over pretty closely, I'll tell you. Dark socks on his hind feet, and stockings on the forelegs. All four hooves are black."

"What about his face?" Anne asked. "Any markings there?"

"No, just speckled salt-and-pepper, like the rest of him."

She frowned. "I don't recall any markings on the other one."

"Neither do I. He's nine or ten years old, judging by his molars."

"And we've no idea how old the one at the farm was," Anne said.

"No, but I'll know this fellow, Hastings, if I meet him on the trail."

"There, folks." Mrs. Zinberg bustled in, wearing her apron. "Supper's all ready."

Dan rose and held out a hand to Anne. She let him assist her in getting out of the rocker.

"It can't be the same horse," she murmured.

"No, it can't."

"There was that time on the trail between Anlauf and Elkton when I thought I saw a gray horse behind us."

"I remember," Dan said.

They didn't speak of it during supper, but kept up a pleasant conversation with their hostess. Afterward, Anne drew Dan back into the parlor.

"We must go to Uncle David's land tomorrow, no matter what the weather."

"I understand your concern," Dan said, "but I don't want to take you out in inclement weather again. If it's raining in the morning, I think we should wait."

"I don't suppose you inquired about the owner of that curious roan you saw in town."

"I did." He grimaced. "I went inside and asked the barkeep. He said he didn't know whose it was for sure, but most of the men in there were regulars who were known to him. However, a couple of strangers had come in within the last hour, and he said perhaps it belonged to one of them. Then he looked about as though expecting to see them, but apparently they'd left. And when I went back outside, the horse was gone."

Anne tapped her chin. "Perhaps he'd already left the tavern when you were there and stepped into one of the shops."

"That's probably what happened. I missed him." Dan shrugged.

"We must leave early in the morning," Anne said. "If we find Uncle David, we can stay at his claim with him overnight. If not. . . well, we'll just have to turn around and make our way back down the trail."

Dan sighed. "I'm getting to where I feel I know you fairly well, Anne."

"Oh, do you?" She smiled at that.

"Yes, and that's why I went to the mercantile and stocked up on a few provisions for the trail. There'll be no boardinghouse up in the mountains. I got enough rations to last us a couple of days, and a packet of lucifers. I hope you won't think it too bold of me, but I

also purchased a cape for you. The shopkeeper told me the material sheds water well. Somehow they've woven some India rubber into it. Anyway, I thought you'd not be averse to another layer between you and the rain."

Anne hardly knew what to say in the face of his thoughtfulness. She couldn't offer to pay for the cape and other supplies—her funds were nearly exhausted and they might have a few more nights' lodging to pay for. Besides, it would hurt his feelings to suggest he'd acted improperly to buy her an article of apparel. She'd already wounded him enough by rejecting his suit. Why dash his fine spirits further by turning down a gift that could very well ward off illness?

"How kind of you. Of course I'll take it along. If we have another day such as we dealt with today, I shall find it my favorite piece of clothing, I'm sure."

"All right then. We'd best get a good night's rest. I'll load up our stuff at first light."

David smiled as the waiter set a slice of chocolate meringue pie in front of Charlotte and another at his place. Charlotte's expressive green eyes all but devoured the dessert.

"I'm sure I can't eat all of that," she said.

"It'll be fun to try," he assured her.

"Do you want this on your bill, sir?" the waiter asked.

"Oh yes, certainly," David said. He'd have to speak to the manager about the awkwardness of having the waiter mention the bill yet again when he was entertaining a guest. He supposed the man wanted to be sure he was paying for Mrs. Evans's dinner as well as his own—as if any man in his right mind would think he'd dine with a stunner like Charlotte and make her buy her own meal. Besides, he'd paid for her meal yesterday. He'd stayed in town an extra day, using the heavy rain as an excuse. How much of his behavior tonight was due to the lovely Mrs. Evans's presence?

She was prettier than he'd thought on first impression. Of course her cosmetics enhanced her natural looks, covering some freckles no doubt, and giving her eyes that smoky, adoring air. And her dress—it was as fine as any he'd ever seen in London. She'd certainly surprised him there. She was better gowned tonight than any other woman in the room—but of course, not that many women came to Scottsburg, and the farmers' wives usually dined at their own kitchen tables.

True, Charlotte had worn the same dress last night, but she'd explained that she'd come with only a small bag. The trunk she'd shipped seemed to have been delayed, and she contemplated shopping in the town's limited stores if it wasn't delivered soon. He might even stick around tomorrow and offer to escort her if the cousin didn't show up.

"Tell me more about your cousin," Dan said. "You mentioned that he's meeting you. What brings him here?"

"Oh, he's interested in mining. His work has something to do with geology. I'm not sure I understand it all." She chuckled and gazed at him from beneath her long, dark lashes. "What about you, Mr. Stone? You told me you have a claim nearby. How far away is it?"

"It's actually about two hours' ride downhill."

Charlotte laughed softly. "And uphill?"

"It can take me three or four hours. Have to baby the horse, you know, especially if he's loaded down."

"I imagine you're quite a horseman. How do our steeds compare to what's available in England?"

"It's been years since I was in England last, so I don't really know. There are some fine stables, of course."

"Now, did you live in the city or the countryside?"

"I usually stayed in the country. My father had a house in town—London, that is." David shrugged. He didn't like to talk about his family. People sometimes found that pretentious. "It belongs to my brother now. But I used to spend a lot of time there."

"London." Her eyes grew dreamy. "How I'd love to visit that city."

"Oh? I found it dull and full of smoke."

"Ah, men!" She smiled and took a bite of her pie.

To David's astonishment, the chocolate meringue had all but disappeared. Apparently Charlotte wasn't as stuffed as she'd claimed. His own piece was only half gone.

"Would you like more pie?" he asked.

"Oh well, uh. . ." She glanced at his plate. "No, I don't think so. Perhaps some coffee, or. . ."

He raised his eyebrows. Or what? Did she expect him to order wine? He wasn't sure they'd have it.

"I like a cup of tea after my meal," he said.

"So do I." She smiled and wriggled as though settling in for a long, cozy chat.

"You must tell me about your visit to San Francisco," he said.

She launched into a detailed and amusing description of the city, and David began to relax. She had obviously been there in person. Had he doubted her sincerity? He supposed it was just the old wariness from England—being skeptical of fellows who hung about wanting to be your best chum. That was one reason he'd never told anyone in America that he was the third son of an earl. Folks were never genuine with you once they knew that, and worse yet, people who wanted favors crept out of the woodwork.

But Charlotte seemed a nice enough woman. A bit forward perhaps, but who wasn't in these frontier towns? A widow with looks like hers wouldn't remain single long, and who could blame her for setting her sights on a likely prospect, a mature man with a bit of property—in short, himself? David was a bit taken aback by his own thoughts. Did she really only want to spend a pleasant evening with him, or did she aspire to something more permanent? And did he mind?

Years had passed since he'd let down his guard with a woman. But what was the harm? He'd lately pondered this very thing—finding a nice woman and settling down. Was Charlotte that woman?

He wondered vaguely if there was a place that offered dancing and immediately ruled it out. The hotel offered no entertainment. There just weren't enough decent women here to support a club or an assembly hall. Probably the only dancing in Scottsburg took place in the saloons. So what entertainment could a gentleman offer a charming lady?

The waiter brought their tea and slid a slip of paper onto Charlotte's saucer.

"Begging your pardon, ma'am, but I was asked to give you that."

David scowled at him. "What is that, Philip? I told you this all goes on my bill."

"It's nothing like that, sir. Someone inquired at the desk for Mrs. Evans."

"Oh." David turned and craned his neck to see if anyone was searching the room for Charlotte, but he couldn't see anyone in the doorway to the lobby. When he turned back to the table, Charlotte was perusing the note, holding it below the edge of the table. "Is it your cousin?" he asked.

"I—well, I'm not sure. Would you excuse me just a moment? I'll go and speak to the desk clerk about this."

"Allow me to escort you." David pushed his chair back.

"Oh no, thank you. I think I'd best tend to this myself."

She rose, and David stood. Unhappily, he stayed where he was as she walked toward the lobby. Every man in the dining room swiveled his head to watch her go.

"Can I get you anything, Mr. Stone?" the waiter asked.

"No. Thank you." He sat down with a thud and sipped his tea.

CHAPTER 12

W hat are you doing here?" Millie dragged Sam around a corner into the hallway that led to the kitchen and the rear entrance.

"You said to catch up to you. Well, here you are, and here I am."

"Where have you been?"

"On the trail."

Millie sighed. Sam was duller than a butter knife. "Do you have any money?"

He laughed. "No. Where would I get money?"

"I expected you to be creative. I personally spent an entire day cooking to earn enough money to replace my horse. I almost got caught at it by Miss Stone and her toady, Adams. I'd like to know why you didn't slow them down."

"I tried, Millie. But they're smart. And besides, I got hurt. I fell off my horse."

"Oh, you poor thing." She gave him a cursory inspection. "You look all right now."

"Can I stay here tonight?" Sam asked. "I'm tired of sleeping in barns and haystacks."

"Are you crazy? This place costs a dollar a night."

"Aren't *you* staying here?"

Millie put her hands on her hips. "I *told* you. I stopped and earned some money."

"I could sleep on the floor at the foot of your bed." Sam's hang-dog face made her want to scream.

"Oh, and how would that look?"

He shrugged and looked down at the floor.

Millie looked over his shoulder toward the lobby. The desk clerk was looking their way and frowning.

"Tell me quick—where are Miss Stone and Adams?"

"I lost 'em."

"*What?*"

"I told you, I got hurt, and it was raining, and I couldn't find out where they're staying here. Last night, I tied their tack in knots to slow them down, but I didn't want to follow them too closely and get seen. When I got to town I thought they might be here, but their horses aren't in the stable. I checked two other places, too."

Millie did some quick thinking. Apparently Sam didn't know David Stone was here or that she was having dinner with his erstwhile boss. She reached into her pocket and took out four bits. "Here. This is all I can give you. It only leaves me a few cents. Get yourself a room someplace if you can for that, and something to eat. And then you'd better find out where they are!"

"I saw Adams once."

Millie raised her eyebrows and leaned toward his face. "I thought you lost them," she whispered in a tone she hoped conveyed danger.

"So I did, but after I'd looked and looked all over town, I gave up and went into a saloon. Spent my last half dime for a beer."

"And?"

"In comes Adams, bold as brass."

Millie folded her arms and drummed her fingers on the sleeve of her fancy gown. "I'm waiting."

"He walks up to the bar and asks the barkeep if he knows David Stone."

"What did the bartender say?"

Sam shrugged. "I don't know. I scooted out the door while Adams wasn't looking. You told me I couldn't let him see me."

Millie sighed. "I don't suppose you followed him when he left the tavern?"

Sam hung his head. "He came out real quick, so I hid around the corner. Mill, he caught sight of my horse and went over to it and looked it all over and petted it."

"Oh, that's just great."

"Really?" Sam asked hopefully.

"No, not really! You are such an idiot."

"Well, I figured I'd best make myself scarce, so I hoofed it the whole length of the street and back. And when I got back to where Old Blue was standing, Adams was gone." Sam smiled as though she should pat him on the head now.

"So you lost him again."

"Well, yeah."

"Sam, listen to me. You are going to find Adams. And where you find him, you'll find Miss Stone. You are going to find out their plans. If they're going to try to meet up with Mr. Stone, you're going to stop them."

"What about you?" Sam asked.

"I'll be waiting here, on the off chance that Mr. Stone comes into town."

"What if Adams and Miss Stone go up to his mining claim?"

"Then you follow them. You've got to keep them from getting to Stone before he comes down here."

"Why'n't you just go with me? We could find him together."

"No," Millie said. If she could just keep Sam busy and Anne Stone out of the way for a few days, she might be able to reel in the rich uncle. "I think one of us should stay here. We don't want to miss him. You concentrate on slowing down Miss Stone and Adams. If that means you have to recruit some friends to help you, then do it."

"Friends? What friends?"

Millie clenched her fists. "Look, are you really this stupid? *Find* someone to help you."

"But. . . I've got no money to pay anyone, and I can't let Adams or David's niece see me."

"You'd *better* not let them see you. Now, excuse me. I have to get back to my dinner."

She flounced to the lobby in a swirl of skirts. Behind her, she heard Sam's plaintive, "Nice dress."

David was checking his pocket watch when she returned to the table. He jumped up when he saw her.

"I'm *so* sorry," Millie said. "I've kept you waiting much longer than I anticipated." She slid into her seat.

"Think nothing of it," David said. "I hope everything's all right."

She gave him a tight smile. "That was a friend of my cousin's. S—Stephen asked him to find me and tell me he should make it into Scottsburg tomorrow or the next day. I'm ashamed to say his 'friend' was a bit inebriated. He must have stopped at a saloon before he came here. It took some time to get the message out of him."

"I'm sorry."

The waiter appeared with a teapot in his hand. "Would you like more, madam? Sir?"

David looked inquiringly at Millie.

"Well. . .?" She returned his gaze.

"Philip informs me that there is a charming view of the moon on the river from the steamboat dock," David said with a glance toward the waiter. "I believe there'll just be a sliver of moon tonight, but we may not have a rainless evening again for some time. Perhaps you'd like to see it."

"I should like nothing so much as to see a cloudless sky, Mr. Stone." This was going better than she'd anticipated. Millie waited for David to come around and hold her chair as she rose.

"You might want a wrap," he said.

"Of course. It will only take me a minute." She glanced about apprehensively as they entered the lobby, but there was no sign of Sam.

"I'll wait for you right here," David said.

Millie hastened up the stairs. Part three, despite one snag, complete. Now for part four.

David was waiting, as promised, when she returned a moment later with her beautiful dress covered by her old woolen coat. She'd arranged the silk shawl over that, in an attempt to make it look less dowdy, and had freshened her lip rouge.

He offered his arm, and Millie mustered every ounce of charm she could find.

The brief walk to the dock gave their conversation time only to graze the top of Eugene society, for which Millie was grateful. Apparently David knew the Skinners and all the other pioneers

intimately, and her own ignorance would soon be manifest if she couldn't distract him from the topic.

A thin, dark-haired man leaned against one of the dock's pilings, smoking a cigarette, but aside from him, the pier was deserted.

"Lovely night," David said as they strolled along the dock. A much-scarred river steamer was tied up alongside, but the decks were empty.

"And not too cold," Millie said. She wondered if she could have gotten away with just the shawl—and a warm arm, of course, if she shivered.

"There's the moon." David stopped and gazed upward. Only the thinnest fingernail showed, but the stars glittered bright.

Millie gave the sight a proper moment of appreciation and looked back toward shore. "This is quite a pretty little town by starlight."

"Yes."

He was looking at her. She could tell, but she deliberately kept her gaze on the riverbank. The smoker tossed his cigarette in the water and ambled toward the center of town.

"You know, Charlotte, I was planning to return to Eugene tomorrow, but now I'm not so sure."

"Oh?" She looked up at him and blinked—only once, lest she overdo it and he think she was a flirt. "Is business keeping you?"

"Not really, but I'd like to be sure you're safe until your cousin arrives. And meet him if I can."

"Oh." She smiled. "That sounds like such a treat. I'm so glad we met, David."

He patted her hand and looked up at the moon again.

Was he shy? She hoped he wasn't the type who would take weeks to feel bold enough to steal a kiss. The whole fictional cousin business could get awkward if this dragged on too long. She couldn't get Sam to pose as her cousin, because David knew him. And last night he'd retired immediately after dinner, pleading fatigue. But really, she was quite pleased with the direction things were headed. She eased a little closer to him and dared to squeeze his arm the tiniest bit. David responded by pressing her hand against his arm ever so slightly.

Hadn't she heard somewhere that English men were cold fish? This one might take some work.

The town was just stirring when Anne and Dan made their way to the ferry and crossed the Umpqua. For once the sun shone, half-hearted and cool. Dan prayed it would last.

He entrusted the horses to the ferryman and stood with Anne by the rail. As the south shore approached, she looked back at the town.

"The sheer size of this land continues to astound me," she said.

"Yes, there's room for everyone," he said, but immediately he thought of the Indians lashing out against the encroaching whites not so far to the south.

"It's no wonder so many have come here from Europe," Anne said. "The prospect of owning land. . .for so many that's an impossibility in England."

Her troubled face led Dan to wonder if she felt guilty for being born into the noble class. In a similar fashion, he felt twinges of remorse when he considered how many Indians had been displaced for homesteads. Hector brushed that aside, insisting that things were the way they were, and the Adams boys could do nothing about it, so they might as well take advantage of the situation. But Anne was like him. They could not bear their cultural burdens lightly.

"Do you think Uncle David is safe?" she asked as the ferry drew close to its mooring.

"Of course. Why wouldn't he be?"

"Well. . .there's Peterson."

"The postmaster said your uncle came to fetch his mail about a week ago."

"That recently?" She turned toward him eagerly, her lips parted.

"Yes. I should have told you last night, but it slipped my mind. He said David's been in two or three times in the last month, and then went back to his claim." Perhaps they should have waited in

Scottsburg for him to return. If he'd tried harder, could he have persuaded Anne to wait at Mrs. Zinberg's house and let him make daily inquiries for her uncle? Dan strongly doubted that.

Star balked a little when it was time to step off the ferry. He wasn't usually afraid of bridges or rough spots in the road, but today he seemed a little skittish. Bailey, on the other hand, was as dependable as his master and stepped off as calmly as Rob would have.

Dan checked all the straps and buckles on Anne's saddle before giving her a hand up. She wore her velvet habit again, with the new cape snubbed behind the saddle's cantle with her blankets. He'd insisted they bring their bedrolls and camping gear in case they spent a night on Stone's claim with him, but they'd left some of their clothing at Mrs. Zinberg's, lightening their loads.

"How far is it?" Anne asked.

Dan pointed up the valley. "About eight or ten miles overall. We're to take this road for two miles, then turn off to the right and go up into the hills. The postmaster said it wouldn't be too rough, but I found another fellow who goes up there a lot—has a claim not too far from David's—and he said the last two or three miles make a rugged climb. He said to take our time so the horses aren't worn out when we hit the steepest part."

Anne set her jaw. "Then we'd best be going." She looked back toward the ferry slip. The boat had shoved off and was a third of the way back across the river. On the far shore, a horseman already waited for it.

They rode along for a half hour, saying little except for Anne's occasional exclamations over the lovely scenery and Dan's fretful observations on the clouds rolling in.

As they approached a stream, they halted their horses at the edge and stared at the scene before them. A log bridge decked with sturdy planks appeared to have fallen into the creek on the far end of the span.

"That's odd," Dan said. "The ferryman didn't say anything about a bridge being out."

"Yes." Anne pondered the logistics of it. "I'm no expert, but if it was washed out, wouldn't someone in Scottsburg have told us there was flooding?"

"Yes, and it wouldn't have gone down this quickly." Dan looked upstream and down. "I suppose we'll have to go along that path and see if there's a ford nearby."

They turned their horses onto the narrow path along the creek bank. Twenty minutes later, Dan found a spot where they could descend to the streambed and cross safely. The water was only a few inches deep, though it flowed swiftly. On the other side, they made their way back to their path and at last came to the far end of the bridge.

Dan dismounted and examined the supports. "It looks as though someone sawed right through the beams here."

Millie got up earlier than she wanted to. She had things to do if she intended to maintain the lifestyle she was growing accustomed to until she felt confident of asking David for a small loan without offending him.

The mercantile, perhaps. There were several small shops in town, but down near the steamer dock a large establishment catered to the miners and farmers. She'd go there first—that or a place where she could get breakfast for less than the hotel's exorbitant prices. She hurried down the street, wearing her calico dress and wool coat. She didn't want to look too prosperous this morning, or to stand out in any way, though most likely an auburn-haired woman men seemed to find handsome would not go unnoticed. With that in mind, she'd put her hair up and added a hat.

She found a bakery where several men were lined up to get rolls and pastry. She got in line. They all eyed her surreptitiously. This wouldn't do. She needed to go unwatched, if only for a few seconds. She left the line and gazed at the cakes and bread loaves in the case near the window, pretending to have trouble making her choice. When the line was down to one man, she stood behind him.

"There you go." The baker handed his customer a brown paper

parcel, and the man gave him a few coins.

Millie watched closely, but no change was handed back. Her disappointment hit a new low. The smell of the baked goods had her stomach rolling, and she'd hoped for a bun or two. She had only a few pennies left in her pocket.

"Help you, ma'am?" the baker asked.

"Oh, I—no, thank you. I changed my mind." She scurried out the door and stood panting on the sidewalk. It would be easier to pick a pocket, but she hated doing that.

"Morning."

She whirled toward the voice. A tall, thin man with a dark mustache nodded to her from where he leaned against the wall of the bakery.

She nodded and turned away.

"Didn't I see you with David Stone last night?"

Millie's heart lurched. She looked about, but no one else seemed to have heard. She eyed the man closely. The smoker from the dock? That must be it. She took one step closer.

"You know him?"

"Not personally."

"What is your interest in him?" she asked.

The man opened his jacket and reached into an inner pocket, coming out with a cigarette. "What's yours?"

Millie's heart paused and went on, faster. "None of your business. Good day." She turned away, but he leaped to her side and fell into step with her.

"On the contrary, I think we should have breakfast together and discuss it."

She eyed him askance. What was his game? Still, breakfast without having it added to the hotel bill. . .

"Are you buying?"

He smiled. "Of course."

CHAPTER 13

By noon Anne was certain. They were hopelessly lost in the rolling hills, and the temperature had dropped at least ten degrees since they left the ferry and detoured to avoid the damaged bridge. The clouds tightened overhead, obscuring the sun and threatening another bout of severe weather.

"Dan?" She urged Bailey forward and tried again, calling toward his rigid back, "Daniel!"

He turned in the saddle, a worried frown not hidden quickly enough.

"Perhaps we should go back and seek better directions."

Dan wheeled Star around and rode back to her. He stopped and eyed her sadly. "I'm afraid it's too late. Anne, I'm sorry, but I've no idea how to get back to Scottsburg."

They sat for a minute, looking around. The trail they'd been following had petered out, and Dan had tried to find his way back to it, but Anne didn't recognize anything she could see now. The wind snaked between the hillsides, and the bushes shuddered. A clap of thunder made the horses jump.

"I'm afraid we're in for it," Dan said.

"Should we go downhill until we find a stream?" she asked. "They'll all flow into the Umpqua eventually, won't they?"

"I...suppose so." He looked so contrite that she wanted to comfort him.

"It's as much my fault as yours," she said. "We probably went the wrong way back at that fork where I said to go right."

"Well, someone ought to mark these trails." Dan winced. "I'm sorry, that sounded rather petty, didn't it? I'm not usually a whiner."

"No, you're not."

The clouds let loose, and the rain dumped on them in huge

drops so thick they might have been poured from a giant vat.

"Quick! Get to the tree line," Dan shouted.

Star bounded away. Anne loosened her reins, and Bailey cantered after him.

When they reached the verge of the pines, Dan jumped down. He helped Anne alight and then walked between the trees, pulling Star behind him, shoving branches aside.

When they were well out of the open, he dropped Star's reins and came back to help Anne.

"Here, bring Bailey up near Star. I think they'll stay together. We'll get into the tightest thicket we can find and sit this out."

"Shouldn't we tie them up?" Anne asked.

"They ought to stay—they're both well trained. And if you tie them up and the thunder scares them, they'll likely break whatever you tie them with. We'd have to unbridle them and put the halters and lead ropes on to make them completely secure."

"All right." Anne could see that Dan was near his limit of patience, which was considerable. Still feeling guilty for losing the trail, no doubt. She let the reins fall.

Dan fussed with the knots on her saddle strings. "You'll want the cape now." He fumbled at the rawhide strings but couldn't untie them. "Bother." He shoved his hand in his pocket and came out with a folding knife.

"No, wait," Anne said. "Let me. I have fingernails." She didn't want to return Dulcie's saddle to her damaged. It took her a couple of minutes, but at last she got the knots loose. The rain continued to pelt them. Though the fir trees slowed it down, she would still be soaked again in a matter of minutes.

Dan grabbed the cape and shook it out, then wrapped it around her shoulders. "Come on!" He seized her hand and yanked her away from the horses.

"I thought I saw a big cedar over there." Anne pointed, and Dan veered the way she indicated. They crashed through buck brush and around firs. At last she spotted the down-slanting branches of an incense cedar, with dark, flat needles making a canopy near the ground.

"Under there," Dan said.

Anne looked back. "I can't see the horses."

Dan hesitated and craned his neck, looking. "Do you want me to bring them closer?"

A lightning bolt cracked and struck a tall fir tree not far away. The top splintered and crashed to earth. Immediately, thunder boomed so loud Anne's ears throbbed. She clapped her hands over them.

"No!"

"Then get under cover."

She hauled in a deep breath and dove under the lowest branches. The cape tangled about her, and she had to wriggle about to adjust it. She found she was almost able to sit up in the dim hideaway. Dan rolled in and fumbled about until he half-sat, half-lay on his back beside her. Neither of them spoke as the rain lashed the forest and the thunder rumbled, now distant, now frighteningly close. Anne drew up her knees and rested her head on them, closing her eyes.

After several minutes, the rain seemed to slacken.

"Anne, can you ever forgive me?" Dan asked.

"There is nothing to forgive. I forced you to bring me on this expedition." She raised her head and listened. "I do worry about the horses, though."

Dan sat up. "I'll go check on them."

"Please take this marvelous cape." She unfastened the button at her throat.

"Oh, I couldn't."

"You must. I shall come with you if you don't."

He chuckled and accepted it from her. "Don't know as I can put it on in this small space." He crawled outside, and Anne shielded her face as the swaying branches released a shower of droplets.

Dan was gone a good ten minutes, and the rain picked up again. She was thankful for what shelter she had, but her habit was damp through, and her feet were like ice. She began to fret about Dan and wondered how far he'd had to go to find their mounts.

After one especially loud *crash-boom* of thunder, the branch that

formed their doorway lifted and Dan crawled in, hauling the soaked cape behind him.

"They've worked their way down in a draw, but I think they'll be all right. The wind is probably milder down there."

"How far away are they?" Anne asked.

"Not that far. It just took me a few minutes to pick up their trail and follow them."

"Dan, you're shivering."

"Aren't you?"

"Here, let's not get grumpy."

"I'm sorry." He ran a hand over his face and sighed. "Anne, I've let you down."

"No, you haven't."

"Well, we differ in opinion on that. But I've got to get you back to Mrs. Zinberg's before dark. What would you say to striking out as soon as the lightning stops?"

Another flash punctuated his words, and they both waited for the thunder. It came just seconds later. Anne looked over at Dan. She could hear his teeth chattering.

She reached out for the edge of the cape. "Look, the outside of this is wet, but the inside feels pretty dry. What if we drape it over us, like a traveling robe? You need to warm up a little, Dan. I'm afraid you'll go hypothermic—is that the word?"

"I don't know, but I do feel as though I might freeze to death. I've got the lucifers in my pocket. If I thought we could build a fire. . . ."

"Well, come closer."

He didn't move.

"This is no time to be shy," Anne said.

Dan unbuttoned his jacket and slid over next to her. He folded back the side of his coat nearest her. She leaned closer and felt his warmth.

"Pull this cape up over your shoulder and put your arm around me."

"Anne—"

"Oh hush. It has nothing to do with—with anything other than survival." Her face flamed, but in the semidarkness, he wouldn't see that, and it actually felt good to have one part of her warm. She peeled off her soggy gloves and set them on the ground next to the tree trunk.

Hesitantly, Dan raised his arm and enfolded her.

"I fear my habit is so damp I won't be much help to you."

"No," Dan said in a strangled voice. "You're warm."

"Good." She very daringly slid her arm around his middle and laid her head against his chest. The pounding of his galloping heart rivaled the thrumming of the rain.

They sat in silence for a long time. Dan stopped shivering. Perhaps ten minutes later, his chin came down and rested gently on the top of her head.

Anne wondered if he was asleep. His pulse was still quite rapid, and she decided he wasn't. She'd told herself this was necessary, but now she wondered if he'd been right to object. Was she leading him on? She wished Elise was here to advise her. Dan was an honorable man, and she'd intended no harm. He was so warm and comfortable now, and his strong arm about her lulled her into thinking everything would be all right.

Some time later, Dan stirred and Anne jerked awake.

"What is it?" she asked.

"The rain has slacked. It's still very gray out, though. I wonder if the sun won't set early today. I'd best go for the horses."

"Let me come. I need to stretch my legs."

"All right, but you must put the cape on."

By the time they'd crawled out of their den, the front of Anne's habit was drenched again. She said nothing about her discomfort and donned the black cape.

"This way." Dan reached for her hand.

"Oh, I left my gloves in there."

"I'll get them." He dove into the hideaway again and thrashed about a bit, then appeared at the opening. "Here you go."

Anne tried to pull the sodden gloves on, but they resisted, so she shoved them into the pocket of her skirt.

They trudged through the woods in twilight until they came to a steep-sided ravine.

"Hold my hand," Dan said.

They slipped and slid down the incline.

"Where are they?" Anne looked all around, but saw no sign of the horses.

"They can't have gone far. I expect they went downhill." Dan pointed in the direction the ground sloped.

"Daniel?"

"Yes?"

"What will we do if we can't find them?"

"Please don't talk that way, Anne."

"All right."

Dan set out with a determined stride, and she followed, but she soon lagged behind him. She shoved through some underbrush, and a rope of vine maple snagged her shoe. She went down, floundering in the bushes. As she struggled to rise, she thought she heard a horse's snort, up the slope a bit to her left. She squinted into the darkness.

White patches. It had to be Star.

"Dan!"

"What is it?" He was fifty yards or more away.

"I think I've found them."

"Where are you?"

"Here." She tried to spot the white blotches again and began to labor up the side of the ravine.

A dark apparition darted from behind a tree between her and the place where she'd seen the horse.

Anne shrieked and fell back. "Daniel!"

The figure raised an arm over its head. "Horse mine!"

"I don't get it," Millie said. "What is it you want with David Stone?"

Peterson smiled and shook his head. "It's a business matter."

She sipped her tea. If she was going to spend a lot of time with an Englishman, she needed to learn to like tea. She'd eaten an enormous breakfast and managed to sneak a biscuit into her handbag while Peterson had left the table to get an ashtray. She didn't like him. At least not yet. She didn't trust his dark, calculating eyes and his thin, black mustache. But he held a certain fascination. Intelligent men always drew her. What exactly made him tick?

"Well, it's a business matter for me, too. I can't do anything to make David upset with me or to cause him to think poorly of me."

"Oh, I guarantee he won't think anything of the sort after I see him."

She eyed him suspiciously. Did Peterson know about this inheritance thing Anne Stone had mentioned? That must be it. He was going to tell David about the estate. She wasn't ready for that. Earning David's trust and admiration before he knew he was a rich man—well, a richer man—was crucial to Millie's plan. He had to believe she'd loved him before she knew about his finances.

"I don't know," she said. "What's in it for me?"

He drew on his cigarette and blew out the smoke. "Money, of course."

She frowned. He would offer that—the one thing she was desperate for just now. Unfortunately, to carry out her plan to set herself up for life, she needed cash enough to make a show of not caring about money.

"How much?"

"Twenty."

She let out a grim chuckle. "You're dreaming."

"Fifty then."

"Why don't you just walk up to him in the hotel lobby and tell him you want to speak to him?"

"It's important that we have privacy when I confer with him."

"Ah." She frowned and reached for her cup again. Seemed to her, Peterson could just tell David he needed to speak to him in private, but she didn't suggest that. For some reason he didn't want David to know he was here before the meeting took place. Sounded fishy. Still, she didn't want to talk her way out of this deal before she decided she didn't want it.

"How do I know that what you say to him won't be detrimental to me and my cause?"

He smiled. "And what exactly is your cause, Mrs. Evans?"

She gazed across the table at him. Frankness might be the best order of business—cut through all the chitchat.

"I want to marry him."

Peterson's mustache twitched. "I see." He picked up his coffee cup and took a sip.

Millie plunged ahead, hoping she hadn't ruined her plans as well as his. "Does that affect your business with him?"

Peterson's eyes narrowed to slits, and he set the cup down precisely in the middle of the saucer. "Not a bit."

"Tell me exactly what you want me to do."

"Take him away from the hotel—somewhere out in the open. The evening would be best."

"A little stargazing?" she asked.

"Perfect." He flicked his cigarette over the ashtray.

"And you'll just. . .materialize and tell him what you want to tell him?"

"Something like that."

"Why didn't you approach us last night? You saw us out walking."

"I had to be sure of my man. Now I am."

Millie leaned back and surveyed Peterson. He was too clever by half. She smiled. "The thing is I'm not sure that your business won't affect mine. Could you wait a day or two?"

"I hardly think so."

She sipped her tea again, thinking about it. Peterson was a man who played his cards close to the vest. He wasn't going to spill everything to her. But if she let on that she already knew his business, maybe she'd learn something.

"Is this about the business in England?"

His eyebrows rose.

"You know," she said in a cajoling tone. "The *family* business."

He gazed at her thoughtfully. "I've never been to England. What's going on over there?"

Millie clamped her jaws together. She was a fool. Now he'd suspect something. But if he wasn't here about that, what did he want?

This whole thing with David could explode in her face. If that happened, she'd need means to get away quickly.

"I'll need a hundred," she said. "In advance."

"Did you get a good look at him?" Dan held Anne by her arms and forced her to meet his gaze. "Was there only one?"

"Y–yes. He had garish black-and-red paint on his face, and—and feathers in his hair."

"What was he wearing?"

"A buckskin jacket and—oh, I don't know. Some sort of trousers."

"But there was only one Indian?"

Anne's teeth chattered as she nodded. "Oh Daniel, what will we do? He's stolen our horses."

Dan looked up the slope. He couldn't leave Anne here alone and run after the fellow. The Indian might have friends nearby. Dan had seen nothing but had heard faint hoofbeats retreating as he ran to Anne's side. He had to make a decision, and he only had one chance to make the right one.

"We walk the way we were going to go when we had the horses—downstream. Come on." He turned her away from where she'd encountered the savage and put his arm firmly about her waist.

"We c–can't just abandon Star and Bailey. Dan, I promised Rob I'd bring Bailey back in good shape."

He kept walking and pushed her along with him. "What do you suggest? We can't go and fight a savage for them."

"But—all our things are on the saddles."

Dan took two deep breaths before he answered. He tried to make his voice cheerful. "Not all. Only a few things, really. Most of our stuff is at Mrs. Zinberg's."

Anne planted both feet solidly, and he had to stop walking. "Those horses and the saddles are the most valuable things we have

right now. How can I repay Rob and Dulcie? Dan, my money is nearly gone until January. That's another six weeks. More than that." Tears flowed down her cheeks, joining the drops of mist that gathered there.

"Anne, dearest, you mustn't."

"Mustn't what?"

"Distress yourself. Rob and Dulcie will understand. The critical thing right now is finding shelter before dark. We can't stay out here all night."

Anne looked around, shivering. "N–no. We can't." She looked up at him, and for a moment he thought she'd regained control of herself. But her face crumpled, and she let out a sob. "Oh Daniel."

He folded her in his arms, and they stood in the darkening ravine. The rain spattered down gently on his hat and her cape and the trees. Would it turn into a violent downpour again? If he didn't find shelter for Anne soon, she might collapse.

She was a plucky girl. She'd sailed the Atlantic for her uncle and crossed the Rockies for him. She'd even faced down some unscrupulous men. But Lady Anne Stone seemed to have her limits. That came almost as a relief to Dan. Perhaps she wasn't impossibly above him, after all.

He held her a minute longer, thinking of their options, but he couldn't see a better plan than the one he'd stated. And every moment they waited, the darker it got. Could it possibly be that late in the afternoon?

"Anne, dearest, listen to me."

She gulped a few more shallow breaths then straightened slightly. "What is it, Daniel?"

"We can't go after that Indian and get the horses back. He's gone. I'm sorry about that, but we need to get started. We can't stay here, so we have to walk. Come. We'll follow the ravine."

"All right." She hiccupped. "I'm not sure how far I can walk, but I'll try."

She staggered along, and Dan held her up, willing her to keep going. The rain soaked them. Questions hammered him. Should he look for another sheltered spot? Should he stop and try to build a fire? How could he have been so stupid as to leave the horses unattended, with all their gear, including his rifle? The prospect of being out all night with temperatures in the hills plunging even lower—possibly below freezing—kept him moving.

Anne's steps dragged. Dan uttered the same phrases over and over. "We can do it. Don't give up. Come on. A little farther."

After perhaps an hour, they struggled down a rocky incline to the bank of a small stream. The ground was muddy in the bottom, so they had to stay up the slope a little ways, which made for awkward footing. Anne leaned into him, and Dan walked on the downhill side. They followed the rippling water, and around each bend he expected the view to open up and to spot a town, or at least a house or two. This brook had to dump into a larger waterway soon, didn't it?

The stream curved and wound through the woods, never seeming to widen. The shadows multiplied and darkened. Dan's mutterings began to sound nonsensical to him. Anne staggered and fell.

Dan stopped on a bed of orange pine needles and caught his breath. Anne sat crumpled with her dark cape and muddy blue skirt spread around her. He leaned over her.

"Come, Anne. We have to keep going."

"I can't."

"Yes, you can. Come on." He tugged on her arm, but she pulled away.

"Just leave me, Dan. You can go faster without me. I'll wait here for you to come back with help."

"No. I can't do that. What if the Indian came back?" He pulled at her hand, but it slipped out of his and fell to her side.

Anne looked up at him with a stricken expression. "He said, 'Horse is mine.' What if he only took one of them, Daniel?"

Daniel huffed out a breath. Maybe he should have gone up the hill and followed the thief. It was too late now, though. Anne wouldn't last going all the way back there, and he surely wouldn't desert her out here in the wilderness. He'd made a mess of things.

Her reputation was no longer a high priority, and when it came down to it, neither was finding her uncle. He needed to get her back to Scottsburg alive.

"Anne, I'm not leaving you."

CHAPTER 14

Anne stared up at Dan. Rain pelted her. It hit his hat and collected on the crown. When he leaned toward her, a stream of water ran off the brim and onto the ground between them.

What was it he'd said? She only wanted to rest. If they couldn't get out of this icy rain, she would pull her cape around her and roll up right here on the ground and not move until. . .sometime.

"Anne!" He prodded her shoulder.

She rolled away from him.

"Anne Stone! Shame on you! You're not a child. You know full well that I can't carry you, but I'll try if you don't get on your feet and walk."

"I can't."

Dan's face hardened. "Your father would be mortified if he could see you now. Didn't he teach you to have more grit than that?"

She opened her eyes just enough so she could see him beneath her lashes. Dan had never talked like that before. He was the perpetual gentleman. Night was falling, and his face showed up pale in the dim light. He was worried, not angry. Worried about her. She opened her mouth but nothing came out.

"All right, I'll carry you then." He stooped and clamped an arm around her back, pushing the cape in and groping for her waist. When his other hand touched her thigh through her skirts, she jumped away from him.

"What? Stop!"

"You won't walk, so I have to carry you."

"No, wait." She held out her hands in protest. "Give me a m—minute."

"You've had a minute. Come on, Anne. It's getting colder. You get on your feet, or I'll throw you over my shoulder. Which is it?"

She exhaled heavily and reached for his hand. Dan pulled her up.

"Good girl. Let's go."

He propelled her onward, along the bank of the stream. She trudged beside him, moving slowly. Her legs were stiff, and her feet were going numb, but she didn't dare stop. Something in his gray eyes and rock-firm voice had told her that he would make good on his threat. Dan would pack her home or die trying.

The stream wound downward, around a bluff. Dan was walking in water, lurching a little as he pulled her along. The rain pounded harder, and Anne kept her head down. She could barely see her feet in the darkness.

"I smell smoke."

She stopped and raised her chin. "What?" She turned her head and stared stupidly at Dan.

"Wood smoke. Someone's got a fire going. Come on." He squeezed her hand and dragged her forward.

Anne tried to hasten her steps, but her legs wouldn't obey her brain. They staggered onward until they rounded the bluff. Dan gave a whoop.

"Look! A cabin!"

Anne could smell the smoke now. She squinted where he pointed, and sure enough, a sliver of light came through the trees.

"Jump up."

"What?"

Dan positioned his arms. "Jump up and let me carry you across the creek. The cabin's on the other side."

"I can walk."

"I don't want you to get your feet any wetter. Come on. Let me."

He stooped, and she reluctantly put her arm around his neck. It felt heavy in the wet, freezing garments. Dan found strength somewhere to lift her and lurch across the stream. She feared he would drop her the way he had a week ago when they crossed the Long Tom, but he made it without stumbling. On the other side, he set her down on a rock and tottered up the bank. At last they stood at the door of a crude log cabin.

"Anybody home?" Dan called. He pounded two weary thuds on the door.

From within came a cautious voice.

"Who wants to know?"

David hurried up the steps to the post office and pushed open the door.

"Mr. Stone! Good afternoon." The postmaster whirled around to search the rack of pigeonholes behind him.

"Thank you," David said. "I guess you know what I want."

"Ha. If I could give people what they want every day, I'd be a very popular man." The postmaster turned and handed him an envelope. "That's it this time."

"Hmm." David took it. Nothing from Sam Hastings, but he'd asked Sam to send him a note every week to tell him how things were going at the farm. He'd been here a month, but he'd had no word from Sam.

"Someone was in here yesterday, asking for you."

"Oh?" David asked absently as he scanned the envelope. "If they come in again, tell them I'm staying at the Miner's Hotel."

"I'll do that."

He tucked the letter in his pocket and went outside. Must be an assay report on the ore samples he'd sent to San Francisco. He would wait and open it in his room. Now for some shaving soap, and then he'd stop in the stable to check on Captain. Or perhaps he'd go there first and take a look at the letter in the stable, away from prying eyes. Its contents might make a difference on his timetable. If the yield from his claim looked promising, he'd stay to put things in motion. If not, he might just sell out now and go back to Eugene. He had an idea he might invest in a stagecoach line between Eugene and Oregon City.

Of course, there was Charlotte Evans. He wouldn't mind seeing her again tonight. He hadn't figured her out yet. Her auburn hair

and green eyes had attracted him straightaway, and she'd come to dinner gowned like a duchess. She was hands-down the prettiest woman in Scottsburg, but she lacked a high-gloss polish.

For the frontier, her manners were passable, and he wouldn't ordinarily demand more than that. In fact, the woman he'd almost married in Missouri came from an unpretentious background. He'd never told her about his own pedigree. She'd loved him—or so he'd thought—and he had been ready to settle down. He wouldn't ask more of someone else, and yet. . .

Charlotte implied somehow that she was a tad above her neighbors. She wasn't snooty exactly, and he hadn't seen yet how she acted around other women. He *had* seen the way she held herself when she knew men were watching her.

Maybe seeing her in the company of other women was a good idea. He wished he had friends here in town—besides miners and dockhands—and someone was throwing a party. He could tell a lot about a woman from the way she carried herself at a social event.

He'd seen a couple checking in to the hotel last night when he'd gone downstairs to ask for some hot water. Perhaps he could "run into" the man in the lobby, and later in the dining room, he could introduce Charlotte. It seemed like a decent plan, and he became more aware of the people around him as he hurried down the street. He saw a few women, but most were hardened frontier wives. None that could hold a candle to Charlotte.

He frowned as he entered the dim stable. Whom did he think he was kidding? Would he dangle after Charlotte Evans if he met her in London? If he stood her beside Elizabeth Stone, his brother's wife, or even her lady's maid, Elise Finster, Charlotte wouldn't measure up. And if he were honest, she wasn't a woman he would consider taking home to Mother, if Mother were still on this earth. Charlotte had that worldly wise edge, like a woman who knew what was what but wanted him to believe she was innocent. When he was with her, that trait was easy to overlook. Should he be watching his back?

Dan had never been so glad to hear a crotchety old man's voice before.

"My name is Daniel Adams, and I've got a lady with me. Our horses were stolen, and we're lost. Can you help us, please?"

After a pause, the old-timer called, "Are you lyin'?"

Dan pulled back and stared at the crude door. "No, I'm not lying. Why would I do that? We're freezing to death out here!"

"Let me hear the lady."

Dan looked at Anne. She blinked up at him, her lips trembling. "What does he want?"

"Tell him your name. You can do it."

"I'm Anne Stone. Please, sir. We're like to die out here."

A thud came from within, and the door creaked open. Dan stood eye-to-eye with an elderly man whose flowing white beard resembled a frozen waterfall. His alert blue eyes peered at them from beneath white tufts of eyebrows.

"Well, lookee there. I've never had a lady grace my hearth before. Come in, missus. Do enter and be welcome." He stood back.

Dan grasped Anne's elbow firmly. "In you go." He gave her a little boost as she levered herself up the step and over the threshold. The old man slammed the door behind them and dropped the bar in place. The heat coming from a blazing fire shocked Dan.

He pulled off his gloves and turned to unfasten the hood of Anne's cape. He threw it back, revealing her porcelain face and the ridiculous blue velvet hat that had no business out here in the forest.

"Mm, mm," said the old man. "Ain't she just the purtiest? To what do I owe this honor?"

"It's like I said," Dan replied. "An Indian stole our horses, and—"

"Are you sure?" The old man's eyebrows sprang higher.

"Well, I didn't get a good look at him, but he scared Miss Stone half to death."

"Miss Stone?" The codger peered at Anne. "You kin to that

English feller up the mountain?"

"I suppose I am," Anne said. "Do you know David?"

"Know him? I've shared a beaver tail with him." He held out a hand to Anne. "Here, missy, come right over to the fire. You look cold enough to skate on."

Dan unbuttoned his coat with aching fingers. "Sir, we're much obliged. I think we'd have been in serious trouble if we'd had to stay out all night in this cold rain."

"Name's Pogue—Harlan Pogue, but folks call me Whitey." He stroked his luxuriant beard and winked at Anne. "They used to call me Blackie when I was younger. Can't figure that out."

Anne smiled and held her hands toward the fire. "Well, Mr. Pogue, Daniel is right. I believe we owe you our lives."

"Whitey, I told ya. Look at you. Shaking all over." The old man dragged a short bench over. "Sit yourself down."

While Dan removed his wraps and helped Anne get off her cape, coat, hat, and muffler, Whitey bustled about. He filled his coffeepot, threw more wood on the fire, and straightened the blankets on his bunk.

"There now, folks, in a few minutes we'll have some hot coffee for ya. Can't say as I've got any fancy eats, but there's some cornmeal porridge I can slice and fry with side meat."

"You don't have to feed us," Dan said.

"Oh? You got vittles?"

"Well, no. I'm afraid our supplies went with our horses."

"There you go. We'll have us some porridge and side meat after a bit." Whitey peered at Anne's face, frowning. "You feeling better, missy?"

"Yes, sir. Thank you." The color was returning to Anne's face.

"That's good." Whitey plopped down on the edge of his bunk. "I don't got any dry clothes I could offer you."

"We'll be fine," Dan said. His trousers were drying out, and his boots began to steam. He drew his feet back from the fire. He suspected Anne's heavy skirts and petticoats would take longer.

"This horse thief," Whitey said. "What exactly did he look like?"

Anne hesitated then gave him her sketchy description.

Whitey shook his head. "Don't sound right, and I know most of the red men in these hills."

"There's fighting south of here," Dan said. "Is it possible some of those Indians have moved up this way to get away from it?"

"I s'pose." Whitey shrugged. "I'm sure sorry that happened to you, missy. And you was out looking for your uncle, you say?"

"That's right. I haven't seen him since I was a baby." Anne gave him a shaky smile. "I've been trying to find him for nearly nine months now."

"Well, you're not awful far from his claim," Whitey said. "It's uphill and east of here. Tell you what. I could take you there tomorrow if it ain't raining so bad."

"Would you?" Dan asked before Anne could respond. "I'd be happy to pay you for your trouble."

Whitey waved a hand at him. "No need for that. I'd like to see Stone again myself. He tells capital stories." He leaned toward Anne. "So what brings you to find him now, missy, if you haven't bothered for most of your life?"

Anne smiled wearily. "My father passed away last year, and I've no close family left but Uncle David. My family had tried to write to him several times, but we hadn't heard from him for ten years. So I decided to look for him."

"And quite an adventure she's had," Dan added. "She made the wagon trip from Independence, and a swindler tried to bilk her, and now she's been robbed by an Indian and nearly frozen to death."

"Yup, that's quite a tale," Whitey said. "Well, we won't be too comfy tonight, all three of us in this little shack—more cozy than comfy, I guess you could say. But you'll be warm, and I'll put something in your bellies, and in the morning we'll see if we can find Mr. Stone."

"Can we get there on foot?" Anne asked.

"Oh, it's a rugged climb, but you don't look too spindly. I think you can do it."

Anne chuckled, and the sound lifted Dan's heart. She could

laugh, and less than an hour ago she was ready to give up and die. Later when she was helping Whitey wash their dishes in a chipped enamel basin, he brought in wood and water then sat listening to her banter with the old man. Whitey was obviously delighted.

Why had he ever set out from the farm in Champoeg? Dan wondered. He wanted to blame Hector, but he couldn't. His brother hadn't forced him to saddle Star and ride out. He wasn't sorry, yet . . .Dan couldn't imagine watching Anne sail away to England. He wanted to help her find her uncle and straighten out the whole mess about the inheritance, but losing Anne again might crush him.

She laughed, a musical sound that pierced him because he knew that he wouldn't hear it much longer. Dan squeezed his eyes shut. He should have stayed away and left her in Rob and Dulcie's care. Because once again, Anne was going to break his heart.

"It's chilly tonight," David said as he and Charlotte stepped out onto the front porch of the hotel. "Are you sure you want to walk?"

"I had my heart set on it." She looked up at him from beneath lashes that for some reason looked longer and more luxuriant than they were last night.

"I wouldn't want you to take a chill. And besides—there's no moon to see tonight."

She sighed heavily. "I suppose you're right. But the hotel offers so little entertainment."

"Perhaps we could scare up another pair and play cards." David steered her adroitly toward the door. "There was a couple just sitting down when we left the dining room. Perhaps they'd join us."

He could tell Charlotte wasn't completely mollified. What was going on? She seemed more insistent than a woman who just wanted to snuggle up to him would be. Although he hadn't done much snuggling lately, David was certain he hadn't forgotten how, and the woman involved was usually much more compliant than Charlotte.

They walked back through the lobby, and he looked around for likely companions for the evening. A thin man was reading a newspaper, and two other men sat in the nook to one side, smoking cigars and laughing. None of them struck him as what he was looking for.

"Perhaps they have a small parlor we could sit in," Charlotte suggested.

David almost offered the sitting room of his own two-room suite and changed his mind. He didn't really want to entertain a woman in his hotel suite, for one thing. Past experience had proven such action could be risky. For another, he happened to know that his was the only suite the hotel offered, and Charlotte might get her nose out of joint if she knew about it. The hotel usually opened it for David when he visited, and in times of great overcrowding—like the days when a new mine opened and the investors came to see it—they would put a bed in the sitting room and rent it as two separate rooms. He suspected it sat empty most of the time, waiting for the establishment's wealthier patrons to return.

Although Charlotte had seemed reluctant to go back to the dining room, she presented a charming attitude when David led her to one of the tables.

"Good evening, folks," he said.

The man and woman eating looked up in guarded surprise.

"Hello," said the man, standing. "Stone, isn't it?"

"Yes. We met this afternoon. This is Mrs. Evans." He looked at Charlotte. "Mr. and Mrs. Packer."

They all exchanged their how-do-you-dos.

"I hope you'll pardon us," David said, "but we had planned to go out this evening and the rain has discouraged us. We wondered if you by any chance would be interested in joining us for a quiet game of cards or just conversation."

The couple looked at each other. The woman's eyebrows rose, and he gathered she was passing the decision to her husband.

"Might be interesting," Mr. Packer said.

David smiled at the woman. "We wouldn't want to intrude on your plans."

"It sounds lovely," Mrs. Packer replied.

"Good. Why don't we wait for you in the lobby?"

"Perhaps the desk clerk could scare up a card table for us," Mrs. Packer said.

The gleam in her eyes made David wonder what he'd gotten himself into.

The next morning Whitey shared bacon, oatmeal, and coffee with Anne and Dan. When they'd eaten, Anne insisted on washing the dishes while the two men packed a small amount of gear.

Whitey tucked several small items and some jerky into a dirt-colored pack and added a long-barreled pistol. Then he strapped on a sheath that held a wicked-looking knife. Last of all, he hefted a shotgun and nodded at Dan.

"You got a pea shooter, Daniel?"

"No," Dan said. "My rifle was on my saddle, and I didn't bring a handgun."

"You orta have one," Whitey said. "Can you hit the broad side of a saloon?"

Dan smiled. "I reckon."

Whitey nodded and held out the shotgun. "Take this, then. I'll use my Colt if need be." He turned and looked at Anne, who was hanging up her rag of a dish towel. "Aw, I hate to take you out of here, missy, because I know the likes of you isn't apt to grace my cabin again. But"—he slapped his thigh—"I promised I'd take you up to David's claim, and so I will. Let's get crackin'."

They set out in the chill of dawn, but the sun soon made its way up over the hills to the east. Walking kept Anne warm, and within an hour, she paused to shed her cape. Dan rolled it up and carried it under his arm.

The path became steep, but Dan and Whitey made sure she found good footing. They came out in a clearing from which they could see all the way to the Umpqua.

"See the smoke yonder, from all the chimneys in town?" Whitey asked, shaking his head. "I don't wonder the natives are put out with us. Afore you know it, the forest will be all stripped off these hills."

"How far now?" Dan asked.

"We're more'n halfway." Whitey turned and picked up the path, which was little more than a deer trail.

They went downhill for a short ways and along a hillside.

Dan stopped and said, "I smell smoke."

Whitey swung around and stared at him. "You got a good nose, boy."

Dan smiled. "That's how we found you last night."

"It's true," Anne said. "Dan smelled your chimney before we saw the cabin." She sniffed the air. "I think I smell it, too. Is there a cabin up here?"

"Don't think so. Lot of claims," Whitey said, "though most fellas don't stay in the hills all winter. Most of them are packing up by now." He peered through the trees on the slope below them. "Well, let's move along quiet-like and see what we see."

He walked stealthily, lifting his booted feet high, and Anne almost laughed aloud. She looked at Dan, and he grinned. "When in Oregon, do as the locals do."

Anne followed Whitey, trying not to make a sound.

After a few minutes, Whitey stopped and looked back at Dan. "You still smell it?"

"I think so, but my nose may be getting used to it."

"There be a stream down in the draw." Whitey waved vaguely down the slope ahead of them. "I'm thinking someone's camped there."

Dan passed the cape to Anne and lowered his shotgun to the ready position. The two men crept closer, dodging from tree to tree. Anne held back a ways, but stayed within sight of them. Before long, Dan and Whitey stopped and took cover behind two trees. They peeked out and then conferred in whispers. What on earth were they looking at? She glanced over her shoulder, but saw nothing alarming there, and moved closer to the men. The babbling of a small stream reached her, but no other noise beyond the soft wind in the boughs above her.

Whitey was making signals to Dan, pointing and then making a circle with his finger. Dan nodded and slipped off through the woods to the left. Whitey tiptoed forward and a little to the right.

Anne crept closer and hid behind the tree where Dan had stood. She peeked cautiously between the branches of the bushy pine. Below her, on the bank of the stream, a man bent over a campfire. Grazing nearby were three horses. Anne could barely contain her excitement as she surveyed Bailey and Star. They looked fine, as did the rangy blue roan that cropped the dead grass near them.

She sucked in a breath and studied the man. His shabby buckskins looked familiar, but this was no Indian brave with feathers in his hair.

"Put your hands up," Whitey yelled from behind his tree.

The man jumped, dropping his tin cup into the fire, and whirled around.

"Easy now," Dan called from the other side of the clearing. "We've got you surrounded, mister. Put your hands nice and high, where we can see them."

Slowly the man complied. Whitey stepped out from behind the fir tree and walked toward him, holding his Colt pistol in both hands, trained on the man's chest.

"Just stand still now. You got any weapons?"

The man shook his head, then said something too low for Anne to hear. Whitey reached out and unbuttoned the man's jacket.

Dan came up from behind with the shotgun pointed at the man. "I got you covered, Whitey."

The old man pulled a knife from the prisoner's belt and patted his pockets, then stepped back.

Anne couldn't stand it any longer. She ran forward, gazing at the man's face.

"Dan, that's the man from Uncle David's farm."

"Thought so." Dan edged around to where he could see the prisoner's face, still aiming the shotgun at him. "All right, Hastings— and don't try to tell me your name is Stone. We know better. What are you up to?"

CHAPTER 15

W hat happened last night?" Peterson asked.

He and Millie had met at the café for breakfast again, though he hadn't asked her to. She'd gone there thinking he might show up. The food was good, and no one from the hotel was likely to see him here. Sure enough, as she tucked into flapjacks, eggs, and sausage, with a generous side dish of oatmeal, he slid into the chair opposite her.

"He wouldn't go out in the rain, hard as I tried to get him to go," Millie said.

"Hmpf. Didn't know he was such a namby-pamby."

"Well, a gentleman doesn't like a lady to get soaking wet and catch her death of cold." Millie picked up the pitcher and poured sorghum over her stack of pancakes.

Peterson picked at his eggs and biscuit. He left half of it and gestured to the waitress for more coffee. After she'd poured it and left the table, he leaned toward Millie.

"You'd better get him out there tonight. I'll be waiting."

Millie shrugged. "If it doesn't rain again."

"If it does or if for some other reason you don't hold up your end of the bargain, you'd best think about paying me back my hundred dollars."

"Can't," she said blithely.

"What, you spent it already in this miserable place?"

"Part of it."

His eyes narrowed. "Yes, I noticed you had some new fripperies last night. Well, you'd better keep our deal in mind. Because I don't like to be burned in a business deal."

He got up and tossed four bits on the table.

Millie watched him walk away. She liked him less the more she

saw of him, but she was in it now. She picked up the coins and put them in her purse before waving to the waitress.

"Yes, ma'am. Can I help you?"

"The gentleman had to leave, and I told him I'd settle up. How much was our breakfast?"

"That'll be thirty-five cents, please."

Millie opened her purse and fished around until she had the right change. "Thank you." She put the coins in the woman's hand and added a nickel. "Oh, that's for you." She smiled and hurried out to the street.

"You know this mangy critter?" Whitey asked.

Before Anne could speak, Dan answered. "We've met. He claimed he was Miss Stone's uncle, but she knew that wasn't true. Apparently he's followed us all the way from Eugene and stolen our horses."

"What do you need three horses for?" Whitey asked.

"Wait a minute," Anne said. "He can't be the man who took them. He's not an Indian." She stared at Hastings's sandy hair and scruffy beard.

"I'm thinking in the near dark with some war paint, he might pass," Dan said, squinting at Hastings. "Take a look below his right ear, Anne."

She moved around and stepped closer to Hastings. Dan raised the shotgun an inch as a warning to the prisoner.

She studied Hastings's profile and gulped. "It looks like red paint in his beard. But how—"

Hastings actually cracked a smile. "It warn't hard. I covered my face and beard with the stuff and scrunched my beard down into my coat collar. A little soot in my hair and a couple of feathers, and I fooled you, didn't I?"

Anne blinked at him. Was the man insane? She turned helplessly to Dan. "What do we do now?"

"We take our horses back," Dan said.

"But what do we do with him?"

"We'd best take him down to Scottsburg and turn him over to the law," Whitey said. "Stealing horses is a hanging offense, ain't it?"

"Wait just a second." Hastings still held up both hands, and he spread them in supplication. "I wasn't really *stealing* them."

"What are you talking about?" Dan asked. "You *did* steal them." Hastings's hangdog look raised Anne's ire. "You're insufferable."

"I was just trying to keep you away from David."

Anne stared at him. "Whatever for?"

Hastings's mouth worked, but nothing came out. He lowered his hands and stared at the ground.

"We almost died last night," Dan said. "Miss Stone was overcome by exhaustion and cold."

"Sorry," Hastings muttered.

Anne stepped closer. "Look at me, Mr. Hastings."

Slowly the man's gaze rose until he looked her in the eye. "I'm sorry, ma'am. Truly. I never intended to hurt you."

"Then why did you do it? Why don't you want me to find my uncle?"

"That should be obvious," Dan said. "He doesn't want us to tell Mr. Stone that his employee tried to defraud us and him. I wouldn't be surprised if when he gets back to his farm, your uncle finds that this man has squandered most of his resources."

"That ain't true!" Hastings looked so pained that Anne feared he would leap on Daniel—or burst into tears.

She exhaled deeply. "I hate to give up our quest even for a few more hours, but I think Whitey's right. We need to escort Mr. Hastings into town."

"I could take him," Whitey said. "I'll tie a noose around his neck and make him walk while I ride the horse."

Anne grimaced and looked at Dan. That sounded like an accidental suffocation waiting to happen, and she didn't like it one bit. If Whitey didn't strangle the man, Hastings might manage to escape. "What do you think, Daniel?"

"I hate to say it, but I think we should all go back to Scottsburg."

"We're not far from David's claim," Whitey said.

"He ain't there."

They all swiveled toward Hastings.

"What did you say?" Dan asked.

"I said David Stone ain't at his claim no more."

"Where is he?"

Hastings huffed out a big breath. "Down yonder in Scottsburg, I reckon. But I ain't supposed to tell you."

Anne frowned at him. "Are you saying my uncle is in Scottsburg now?"

"Uh...well..."

"I demand that you tell me." Anne clenched her fists. "What do you know, Mr. Hastings?"

"Well, I rode up to his claim first thing this morning, and he wasn't there. Just got back when you folks come by so neighborly." He eyed Whitey's pistol and Dan's shotgun. "I reckon he's down to Scottsburg. Or I s'pose he mighta gone back to Eugene, but I h'ain't seen him."

"We missed him," Anne said. The disappointment hit her hard. How many times could this happen?

"How can that be?" Dan asked. "I inquired at the post office."

"Easy to do out here." Whitey spat tobacco juice off to one side. "If David went down to Scottsburg yestiddy, he might be heading back up to the claim today. Too bad to be so close and not have a look. You might miss him again."

Dan nodded. "We should go up there. What do you say, Anne?"

Determined to eliminate the risk, Anne agreed. It took them less than a half hour to get to the claim. Anne stood beside the stream and gazed at the marks left by David's spade as he dug out dirt to sift for gold. His fire pit held cold ashes, and the flattened rectangle nearby showed them where his tent had stood. She could even see where his horse had cropped the grass.

"Told ya he warn't here," Sam Hastings said.

"Shut up." Whitey glared at him.

Sam shrugged. "I'm just sayin'."

"Well, don't say no more." Whitey looked at Anne. "What you want to do now, missy?"

She looked helplessly to Daniel. "Do you think it will do us any good to go back and ask around town for him?"

"I don't know what else we can do," Dan said.

"Maybe we should leave some sort of message here for him." The thought that she might miss him again depressed Anne horribly, and she was resolved not to lose a chance to make contact.

Dan rummaged in his saddlebags, but no one had any paper.

"Maybe we could write a message on this scrap of leather," he said.

Anne used a charred stick to write a few words on the leather. "Uncle David, looking for you. Anne Stone." She wrote the date and rolled up the improvised note. Dan tied it with a rawhide thong and tucked it firmly between two rocks on the fire ring, sticking out so that anyone building a fire there couldn't help but see it.

"There. If some skunk doesn't decide to chew on it, it should stay there." He stood and smiled down at Anne. "Ready to go back to town?"

"Yes." She hugged the black cape about her and took one last look over the valley. "I'm glad I saw this place, anyway." She turned to Bailey and sent up a silent prayer of thanks for the safe return of the horses.

"Mind if I ride along?" Whitey asked. "There's things I could use from the store."

"Wait a second," Hastings said. "Are you going to make me walk all the way to Scottsburg?"

"Why not?" Dan asked.

"We should get there before dark if you don't dawdle." Whitey grinned at Anne and put his foot in the blue roan's stirrup.

What was it about the river that Charlotte found so fascinating? David ambled along with her, not in a hurry. Did she only want to get him out of the hotel, away from onlookers? Personally, he'd

enjoyed their evening with the Packers last night. He'd thought Charlotte was having a good time, too, but she'd avoided committing to another session of cards tonight.

He didn't object to stargazing with a pretty woman. And his sporadic doubts about Charlotte were dim just now. She'd come down to dinner tonight in a new dress—plainer than the elegant one she'd worn on previous evenings, but perfectly suitable for the frontier hotel. She'd told him she'd found it in the mercantile. She seemed like a nice woman, and she was definitely intelligent. Perhaps he could learn to overlook her foibles. If she could put up with him, too, they might make a go of it. The fact that her cousin had yet to appear in town niggled at him, but that wasn't Charlotte's fault.

The road to the docks was the most traveled in Scottsburg, and the freighters kept it in good repair. This time of night, the riverfront was quiet except for a couple of saloons that fronted on the water. Shouts and raucous music wafted on the cool breeze. A man leaned against a piling on one of the smaller docks, smoking a cigarette. David had the feeling he'd seen the fellow before.

He led Charlotte away from that end of the road, heading instead for the steamer dock.

"I do love the night sky," she said, looking dreamily up at the velvety canopy.

"What do you like best about it?" David asked.

"It lets me think of things I never think about in daylight. Things I scarcely believe are possible at other times. But under the stars, I can think about anything. . .and forget things, too."

"What sort of things?"

Charlotte lifted her shoulders and shook her head slightly. "You know. All the sad things. Like being alone now and having to plan the future."

"You're going to live with your cousin and his wife, aren't you?"

"That's just a stopgap. Oh, they're nice enough, but I don't want to stay with them forever. You'll pardon me, won't you, if I say they're a bit provincial?"

"I'd pardon far worse things than that."

Her laugh rippled out over the water. "David, you make me feel so clever."

He smiled and paused when they came to the dock. "Would you like to walk out on the pier again?"

"I should like it above all else." She looked up at him coyly. "Well, not *all* else, but above most things."

The minx. She was the most outrageous flirt he'd known outside a saloon. And this talk of her lonely state and unsettled future—was that meant to draw on his chivalry and lure him in? He still liked her, but he wasn't sure he wanted to be caught, even though he longed for permanence.

"I'm sure you'll find a place you enjoy. And your cousin's household may surprise you. They may have connections you find very amicable."

"None so amicable as you, I'm sure." She squeezed his arm a little as they stepped onto the dock. "Oh David, I confess I shall miss you when I've left here."

Her burgundy lips assumed a pout that he found at the same time attractive and annoying. He'd never minded if a woman teased him a little, but tonight Charlotte seemed to go about it with almost grim purpose.

"Where did you say your cousin lives?" he asked as they strolled out onto the dock, the sound of their footsteps lost in the swirl of the river.

"Did I not tell you? It's in Salem. He assured me in his letter that he would meet me here, but now I wonder if I shouldn't have taken another ship and sailed farther north." She waved a hand in dismissal. "No matter. I shall stay here until he arrives now that we've set the place. And I'm fortunate to have such sympathetic company while I sit in this rather irksome town."

"You've made my stay more pleasant, as well."

"Have I, David? That gives me great satisfaction." She said the words almost seductively, peering up at him with a smile.

He felt suddenly uncomfortable. Charlotte's veneer had worn a little thin. He'd decided she was straightforward to the point of

bluntness. Now he didn't think so. She had plans that she hadn't stated, and he had serious thoughts about how much more time he wanted to spend with her. He shouldn't have walked out with her tonight—not that there was anything sinister in it, but she obviously hoped their relationship would not end soon. He turned toward shore.

"It's a bit chilly out here, don't you think?"

"Oh, let's not go back yet. I should be ever so warm if you'd just lend me your arm, David."

He heard her words subconsciously, but his mind had homed in on a figure on shore. A man walked up the road toward the end of the dock they were on. Was it the same fellow who'd been smoking down below? Perhaps they'd better wait until he passed before heading in.

"David, what is it? You haven't heard a word I've said."

"Oh, it's nothing." He glanced down at her and back toward the shadowy form on shore. The man had paused where the dock met land. He held something up. David's heart stopped for a moment as he realized the man held a pistol, then it went on beating at breakneck pace.

"Charlotte, my dear, I'm afraid we're about to be robbed."

"What? You can't mean it." She looked toward shore. "Oh no, David—"

A spark flickered near the man's hand, and something whizzed past David's ear, then a loud *pow* reached him.

"Get down!" He threw an arm about Charlotte and took a step back. They were trapped at the extreme end of the dock. David shoved her down onto the planking.

As he bent to shield her, something whacked into his arm and he heard another *pow*. Next thing he knew, he was falling off the edge of the dock, flailing as he plummeted into the icy water of the Umpqua.

CHAPTER 16

Millie screamed and stared at the man on the shore. She whirled and grabbed the post at the end of the dock and peered down into the swirling water.

"David! David!" Nothing answered her but the rush of the river. A desolation and fear she had never known swept over her, quickly replaced by fury. Its heat rose from deep in her belly and mounted to her neck and face. She clenched her fists and ran along the dock.

Peterson met her about halfway. Millie charged into him and pummeled him with her fists.

"What were you thinking? Why? Why did you do that?"

Peterson caught her wrists and held them firmly. "Easy now. Did you see him in the water? Where is he?"

"I don't know. You monster! Why did you shoot him?"

Peterson laughed. "What did you suppose I wanted from him?"

"I thought you wanted to talk to him. Do you mean to tell me that you had me bring him out here so you could *kill* him?"

"Could you please lower your voice?"

"No. I'll tell everyone who will listen."

"No you won't."

Millie stared into his dark eyes. "You promised he wouldn't think ill of me after you. . ." She caught her breath and ripped her hands free so she could hit him again. "I hate you. I hate you!"

"Talk is cheap, Charlotte."

He caught her hands again and squeezed them so hard it hurt. Millie stood still and stared up at him.

"Let me go," she said between clenched teeth.

"Why should I? You're in this with me, my dear. It's your choice. You can help me. . .or not."

She took a step back, but Peterson held tight to her hands. Tears

494

bathed her face, and it annoyed her that her hands weren't free to wipe them away.

"Just tell me why," she managed.

"If there was any other way, I assure you, I'd have found it. But Stone is only valuable to me if he's dead. It has to be this way. And we need the body."

Millie gasped. "What on earth do you mean?"

"The death certificate, woman! Come on. Help me find him and drag him out of the water. Then you can call the authorities and tell them whatever you like." He walked quickly along the edge of the dock, staring down into the water on the downstream side.

"I'll tell them, all right. I'll tell them you shot that man in cold blood."

"No, you tell them anything but that. Because if they come after me, I'll tell them how you took money to lure Stone out here. Do you understand?"

All the strength drained out of Millie, and she almost fell to her knees. In a flash she did understand. Her lungs squeezed, and a weight crushed her heart.

"Yes."

He nodded. "Then get ahold of yourself and help me. We can't let his body float off down the river."

They both walked to the extreme end of the dock and gazed downward.

"The water's not running that fast, is it?" Millie asked after an awful moment of silence.

Peterson peered out away from the dock and let his gaze track downstream. "I can't lose the body."

She said nothing but waited for him to speak again. He scanned the water continually. Millie began to think about trying to elude him. Could she outrun him to the end of the wharf? Doubtful. And if he caught her trying to escape, what would he do? He'd already killed a perfectly nice man and seemed to have no compunction about it. No one seemed to have heard the shot but her. At least, no one had come to investigate. He could kill her as easily.

And what would she tell the constable if she did get away from him? That she'd seen a man shoot another man, but there was no body and no evidence of the crime? If she named Peterson, he would deny everything and cast aspersions on her. . .or slip out of town before Millie finished telling her tale.

"Show me the exact spot he went in," Peterson said.

"Right here." She moved to the side of the wharf but turned half toward him, suddenly suspicious. What if he pushed her in? His only witness. But he seemed completely focused on finding David.

"I've got to get a boat." He stroked his mustache. "Can't have him floating all the way to the coast."

"I doubt you'll find him," Millie said. "The current probably pulled him under. He may never be found."

"I *have* to find him. I suppose the body could be caught under the dock."

She swallowed hard. "You can't just let him. . .disappear? He's been off at his mining claim. They might think he went back there. We could pack up his luggage and—"

"Stop babbling! I told you, I need a death certificate or all is lost." Peterson dashed along the dock, his shoes thudding on the planking.

Millie walked slowly toward shore. Peterson seemed to have forgotten her. He raced along the shore road toward the saloons. He'd said he needed a boat. No doubt he planned to poke about underneath the dock, in the eerie darkness. Well, he could do that alone. She turned in the opposite direction, though the road led past a looming warehouse and some shabby houses. She would take the long way around to the hotel.

David lay in the water on his stomach, hugging a piling about halfway along the length of the dock. The frigid water made his entire body hurt, but his arm was the worst. He touched it once and gritted his teeth. Clean through the muscle, he hoped. He concentrated on keeping his hold.

Above him, far away, he could hear their voices. First Charlotte's screams, then their feet thudding on the decking above him as he tried to maneuver his way beneath the dock and toward the riverbank. He felt his strength ebbing. As he shoved off from one piling and caught the next, it was hard not to be swept from under the dock and downstream. His head spun, and he clung to the piling. He must be losing blood, not to mention body heat.

He'd splashed into the water off the end of the dock, and somehow his momentum or the current had pulled him beneath it. He'd panicked at first, thinking Charlotte was alone and unprotected up there with a murderer. Then he'd heard her questions. "Why did you do it? Did you have me bring him out here so you could *kill* him?"

So. She was in some scheme and knew the gunman. But why? One thing he knew for certain—he wouldn't come out of hiding until they were gone.

As they walked along the dock and apparently searched the water for him, he grew weaker. Would they come down here and get into the water to search beneath the dock? He shifted his good arm lower, so that it was completely beneath the surface, just in case someone looking over the edge could glimpse the piling.

He heard the man's voice. It must carry some way—was there anyone else about to hear this thug?

"I've got to get a boat." And then, "I need a death certificate or all is lost." The heavier footsteps thudded toward shore.

It didn't make sense to David. He closed his eyes and tried not to lose his grip on the slimy post. Why would anyone need a death certificate? He opened his eyes. To prove he was dead, of course. But why? For whom? How could he be of value dead? There was his property, of course. But would someone kill him for an undeveloped farm and a not-too-promising mining claim? Did this man know something he didn't?

The voice sounded cultured but cold. Not like a backwoodsman or a hardened criminal. Who was he? David racked his brain for anyone who might hate him or even somebody who'd hold a grudge against him, but nothing came to him.

The lighter footsteps moved above him. Charlotte was still there. Should he let her know he was still alive? What would she do? She'd apparently betrayed him willingly, though perhaps in ignorance of the assassin's purpose. But David didn't have enough confidence in her to trust her again. He gritted his teeth and prayed in silence.

"I've got a place I can lock him up," the constable said. "Won't be the first horse thief we've kept in Fisher's icehouse until the judge said we could string him up."

Sam Hastings's face blanched.

"I'm not sure we want to go that far," Anne said quickly.

"Well, ma'am, did he or didn't he steal your horses?"

"He did," Dan said. Anne was obviously having second thoughts about turning the slow-witted thief over for justice. "Is it possible he could spend some time in jail for this, or even perform some labor in compensation?"

"You want him to work for you instead of hangin'?" The constable scratched his chin through his beard. "I dunno. Have to wait and see what the judge says, I reckon."

"We would plead for. . .for clemency. Wouldn't we, Daniel?" Anne turned her eloquent brown eyes on him, and Dan couldn't refuse her.

"Surely. We don't want this man executed."

"Thought you said he put you in mortal danger. Look, either you press charges, or you don't."

Anne plucked at Dan's sleeve and pulled him toward the door. "Excuse us, Constable. We need a moment to confer."

Dan followed her outside, where Whitey waited with the horses.

"We can't let them hang him, Daniel," she whispered.

"Well, Anne, it seems to be the standard penalty for his crime."

"What's that?" Whitey asked.

"They'll hang Mr. Hastings if we file a complaint against him for taking the horses."

Whitey spat tobacco juice between the roan's front feet. "Yup. That sounds about right."

"But. . ." Anne turned to Dan, her face contorted in dismay. "That makes us directly responsible for his death. We can't do that."

Dan hesitated. "What do you suggest?"

"Let's ask Constable Owens when the judge will make a ruling."

They went back inside and put the question to the constable.

"Well, now, I don't expect he'll be here for another fortnight. He only comes once a month."

Dan arched his eyebrows at Anne. Her tense facial muscles had relaxed.

"And you'll keep him locked up until the judge comes?" she asked.

"Yes, ma'am."

"Well then, Daniel, I see no reason why we can't get a good night's sleep and consider this again tomorrow, do you?"

"I. . .guess not."

"Might be a good idea," Constable Owens said. "Let me know when you decide. I'll hold him meantime, just so's we know where he is."

"You can't do that, can you?" Sam cried.

"I can, and I will."

Dan took Anne's elbow and guided her outside before anyone had third or fourth thoughts on the matter.

"It's too late to ask at the post office tonight," he said. "Let's go back to Mrs. Zinberg's and inquire first thing tomorrow."

"What about Whitey?" Anne looked over to where the old man stood beside the roan, scratching under its forelock.

"I suppose we should put him up for the night at a hotel," Dan said.

"It seems only fair—after all, he put us up last night, when we sorely needed it."

"All right. Shall we install him in town or take him with us to Mrs. Zinberg's on the chance she has an extra room?"

Anne smiled. "That depends. Are you willing to chance rooming with Whitey again if she doesn't?"

Dan laughed. "Could be worse, I guess."

Anne leaned toward him and whispered, "He's getting awfully fond of that horse."

"Yes. I suppose he'd like to have a mount of his own. But we can't just let him take it, even if its owner is a thieving rascal."

"I'll bet Hastings stole that horse from Uncle David."

"I hadn't thought of that," Dan said. "We can ask him tomorrow. But for now, let's go. It's getting cold again, and if we stay out much later, we'll frighten Mrs. Zinberg when we pound on her door."

He led Star over toward the roan and said, "Whitey, what do you say to accompanying us to our boardinghouse? We'll straighten all this out in the morning, and you can go home if you like, but we'd like you to have a good night's rest and a hearty breakfast first."

Whitey's eyes glittered. "That's right neighborly of you, son."

David's head cleared as he left the water and clawed his way up the bank. He'd said it was chilly before, but now he was soaking wet. The cold wind off the mountains could be lethal. Could he make it to the hotel?

Charlotte had finally left the dock, cursing as she went—not a section of her vocabulary she'd shown him before. What other talents were buried in the deeper layers of her personality?

He lurched onto the road and considered staggering the quarter mile to one of the waterfront saloons. Better not. That would attract attention. The assassin was looking for his body. The honorable David Stone would stay dead.

Down the road, a man came out of a saloon and strode up the boardwalk. David hobbled into the shadows. His arm hurt worse by the second, and he held on to it. He supposed he ought to be thankful it wasn't worse.

The cold air penetrated the layers of his wet clothing. If he didn't

get inside soon, he'd be in even worse trouble. When the pedestrian had passed, he left his hiding place. By alleys and back streets, he made his way toward the hotel. Each painful step was a trial. His mind raced while his body plodded, slower and slower.

A man wouldn't need legal proof of his death to jump his claim. In that situation, it would be better if his body were never found. The thug could just squat on the land and prospect. He could probably even get away with impersonating David if he stayed away from those who knew him in Scottsburg, or perhaps he could claim they were partners.

So what was this business arrangement Charlotte had gotten into? From the sound of things, she hadn't expected a murder attempt. The man had tricked her into luring him out where he could fire the fatal shot without an audience. But the gunman's plan included the filing of the proper paperwork. Whatever for?

Now, if this were England...

But the assassin wasn't British. Still, the thought wouldn't go away. David hugged himself, shivering violently. He hobbled through another alley and came out in the yard between the back of the hotel and its outbuildings. Should he get his horse and flee without telling anyone what happened? He'd freeze to death before he reached the next town.

He stopped and leaned against the wall of the hotel's woodshed, his left hand clamped over his wound. He should see a doctor. Or would that prove fatal? Someone wanted him dead.

His thoughts veered back to England. This might make sense there...but only if he were next in line to inherit an estate...say, Stoneford. A chill more bitter than that imposed by water and wind swept over him. This couldn't be connected to the earldom, could it? His teeth chattered, and he tried to clench them together, but he couldn't stop shaking. If he didn't get inside soon, the thug would get his wish. Sucking in a breath, he reeled toward the hotel's kitchen door.

Locked. David didn't think he had enough strength to get around to the front entrance. He fell against the door and raised his bloody hand to pound on the panel.

"Dear God," he ground out, "have mercy."

He lifted his left hand again and thudded his fist against the door. A rattle within startled him. He managed to draw back just before it opened, so that he didn't fall in.

"Help me," he said.

The rotund cook stared at him for a moment.

"Good heavens! Mr. Stone!"

David collapsed on the threshold.

CHAPTER 17

"Can you hear me, sir?"

David opened his eyes and blinked up at Ernie Bond, the hotel's cook. He reached out a shaking hand. "C–can you help me, Ernie?"

"What do you want me to do? You look half frozen."

"Help me get to my room."

"Yes, sir. Let me get Mr. Reed."

"No," David said. "Don't tell anyone."

Ernie swallowed hard and looked around the kitchen.

"I'm not sure we can do it without help, sir. We can go up the back stairs, but you've got the suite on the third floor, and that's a lot of steps."

"Then set me a chair by the s–stove. If I get warm, m–maybe I can walk."

Ernie bustled about and returned to give him a hand in rising.

"Easy, now. You all right?"

David groaned and pulled himself up, putting all his weight on Ernie's arm. They hobbled to a chair Ernie had positioned a yard from the big iron cookstove, and David sank into it.

"I've got a little coffee left. Let me get you some."

A moment later, Ernie held out the cup. David's fingers stung and prickled as the feeling began to return. "Can't—" He rubbed his hands together and grimaced.

"What happened to you, if you don't mind my asking?" Ernie said.

"Fell in the river."

"Bad place to be this time of year." His gaze fastened on David's sleeve. "You're bleeding, you know."

"Shot."

Ernie's eyes widened. "You need a doctor."

"Is there one?" At last David's hands stopped prickling and began to feel hot as the blood rushed through them. He reached for the cup.

"Oh yes. Doc Muller. Lives down the way. I could send the—No, I guess you don't want me to tell anyone. That's what you said before."

David nodded. "If I can get to my room, we'll see what's what." He clasped his hands around the thick china cup and sighed at the comfort of its warmth. Slowly he raised it to his lips and took a sip. The coffee was very warm but not hot.

"I can make a fresh pot," Ernie said. "I was about to close up the kitchen for the night. . . ."

"Don't bother," David said. "This is fine." He took a bigger gulp.

"Let's get that wet coat off you." Ernie took his cup away and worked at David's coat buttons. "You're lucky you survived."

David knew he was right, but his mind was too numb to form a prayer of thanks. The pain when Ernie tugged on his right sleeve jabbed him into sudden and complete alertness. He sucked in a breath and held it while the cook eased the coat off his other arm and dropped it on the floor.

Ernie moved away and returned with a heavy damask tablecloth. "I don't have a blanket. Put this around you."

"I'll get blood on it."

"You're shaking all over, Mr. Stone. Don't worry about the blood."

The weight of the dry cloth did feel good. Ernie gave him back his cup of lukewarm coffee, and he sipped it. As David thawed, other discomforts began to make themselves known. His feet ached, and his temple throbbed. He put his hand to it and winced. Had he hit his head on the dock when he fell? Maybe he'd stumbled going up the riverbank and didn't remember.

"We ought to do something about that arm," Ernie said.

David tried to look at the wound, but just moving his shoulder hurt more than it was worth.

"It doesn't seem to be bleeding much now, if that's any comfort." Ernie pulled the damask cloth over the injured arm.

"Probably the veins froze."

Ernie laughed. "When you think you can walk, I'll help you upstairs. Then I really should look at it or else get Doc Muller." Ernie looked toward the dining-room door. "Sometimes Mr. Reed comes out here in the evening. If you don't want him to see you, we need to do it soon."

"All right."

David handed him his coffee cup, and Ernie set it aside. He walked around to David's left side and stooped over.

"Put your good arm around my shoulders."

Even using his left side sent shafts of pain through David's body. He hung on to Ernie and pushed himself up. His head swam, and he stood still for a moment, gasping.

"All right?" Ernie asked.

"Yes."

"This way."

They staggered across the kitchen. David never should have sat down. Now his muscles had stiffened.

"My coat." They stopped and looked back. His sodden jacket lay in a heap behind his chair.

"I'll come back for it. We've got to get you out of sight."

Ernie half dragged him up to the first landing. David appreciated his not asking who had shot him or why—not that he could have answered the questions. Ernie seemed like a sharp-witted fellow. He understood the urgency.

A door opened down the hallway. David gritted his teeth.

"They won't see us unless they come down to this stairway," Ernie whispered. "But if anyone asks, I'll just say you came in drunk."

"Did I have a hat?" David asked.

"No."

"Must have lost it in the drink." Too bad. He liked that hat—and it would have helped shield his face. They swung around and started up the next flight of stairs.

When they reached the top, Ernie opened the door. David heard footsteps in the hall, coming toward the staircase. After a moment, they faded away.

"That was one of the geologists in 210," Ernie said. "He went down the main staircase."

"Did he see you?"

"I don't think so."

"Well, at least he didn't see me. That would make him stare."

"Yes. A fat man helping a scarecrow wrapped in a tablecloth to his room."

David laughed out loud. He couldn't stop chortling, until he shook all over.

"Hey, it wasn't that funny." Ernie eyed him askance from about six inches away. "Let's get you on down the hall."

"At least it wasn't someone I know," David said.

"Yes, like that pretty Mrs. Evans."

David's blood chilled. "If she asks about me don't tell her you saw me tonight, whatever you do."

"Does she have something to do with this?"

"Just play dumb."

"Got it."

At last they reached the door to David's suite. He patted his pockets, afraid he might have lost the key in the river, but he found it, with a sodden wallet, a few coins, and his pocketknife. He handed the key over, and Ernie opened the door while David leaned against the wall.

Inside his bedroom, he dropped the tablecloth and let Ernie help him strip off his wet clothing.

"That wound looks nasty. You'd best let me fetch the doctor."

David hesitated. "The fewer people who know about this the better."

"Yes, but you could die from infection while you're keeping your head down." Ernie took the clean handkerchief David supplied and tied it about the wound. Just his touch sent a fiery pain through David's body, and tightening the knot made him gasp.

"All right," he said, "but help me get warm first." The rooms were chilly, but while David pulled on long underwear and woolen trousers and a shirt, Ernie lit the fire on the hearth.

"You should go to bed and sleep."

David shook his head. "I can't stay here."

"Why ever not?"

"The person who did this might come looking for me here."

Ernie frowned. "Is there somewhere else you could go?"

"I'll have to think about it. I have a few acquaintances in town but none I'd call close friends."

"Well, I'll run for the doctor. Lock your door and wait." Ernie turned to go.

"I really don't want to sit here that long."

Ernie swung around. "I've got an idea. You could ask to switch rooms."

"Hmm, could we do that with no one else knowing?"

Ernie's slow smile gave him hope. "There's a small room under the attic stairs that is only rented out when everything else is full. I can get the key easily when Reed isn't looking."

David's mind raced. "But if all my things are gone, he'll think I skipped out without paying."

"Well, you can't stay here if someone's trying to kill you." Ernie frowned at him. "What do you suggest?"

David sank down on the edge of the bed, pressing on his wounded shoulder. If it didn't hurt so much, he could think.

"You're right. I need to get out of this room. But maybe we can leave my things here, at least overnight, and see if anyone comes around asking for me or tries to break into the room. What do they do if a hotel guest disappears without paying?"

"They'd pack up your things and hold on to them for a while, in case you came back, or in case a family member claimed them."

"Well, that's not going to happen."

"Won't anyone know you're missing?"

"I haven't kept in touch with my family for a long time." Not for the first time, David regretted not writing to his brothers more often.

"Tell you what," Ernie said. "If you think you'll be all right for ten minutes or so, I'll see if I can get Doc Muller. After he fixes you up, I'll help you get into the little room under the stairs. We'll take your wet things and just enough for you to get by on—so that it looks like you left all your stuff and disappeared."

"Yes. And I'll leave enough cash lying about to pay my bill."

"Oh, Mr. Reed will be very pleased if you do that," Ernie said.

David nodded. "Of course, there'll be something in it for you, too, Ernie."

"No need, Mr. Stone. I'm not doing this for pay."

"I know, and that tells me you're the sort of man I'd like to count among my friends."

Ernie ducked his head. "I'm honored, sir. Now I'd best get moving."

"My pistol," David said.

"Where is it?"

"In the bottom drawer." He nodded toward the dresser.

Ernie got it out and brought it over to him. "Is it loaded?"

"Yes. I want it handy while you're gone. I suppose I'll have to leave it behind when we move, though."

"Why?" Ernie asked. "No one can say you didn't have it on you when you disappeared."

"I like the way you think. All right, see if you can get the doctor. After that we'd better get me moved."

Ernie left, and David lay back on the pillow with the pistol lying on his chest and pointed toward the door. He wished the door was locked, but even if he made it over there now to lock it, he'd have to get up again when Ernie returned and unlock it. That might be too much for him. He'd have to depend on the gun if anyone else came before Ernie got back.

The temptation to close his eyes was too great. Slipping into semiconsciousness felt delicious. The pain in his arm still maintained a constant presence, but he was able to push it aside now that he lay prone and could relax.

His eyelids flew open. What was he doing? He couldn't go to sleep. An assassin wanted to kill him, and he'd flown back to the

first place the man would look for him. He forced himself to sit up. His head cleared a little, and he tried to stand but lurched and nearly knocked over the nightstand.

He got as far as the chair and clung to the back, panting and fighting a blackout. The fire was burning down, but he didn't think he had the energy to build it up again. He summoned another ounce of resolution and took two shaky steps to the dresser. Most of his valuables had been in his pockets tonight, but a few other things must go with him to the new room. He gathered a minimum of clothing, leaving enough to make it look as though he was still using the room. Most of the small gold nuggets he'd gleaned at his claim had already been cashed in, but he pocketed a small pouch he'd left covered by his extra shirts. The extra ammunition for his pistol would go with him. He'd better leave his rifle, much as he hated to. Charlotte or the killer might know he had one, and he certainly hadn't been carrying it the last time they saw him. His mining gear represented less of a loss. What about Captain?

He sank down in the armchair near the fire and pondered that. How could he keep his favorite horse without arousing suspicion? Captain was stabled out back in the hotel's barn.

His head throbbed now, and his arm screamed as though a hot iron seared it. Maybe Ernie or the doctor could help him figure that out.

When the door opened, he jerked awake. He'd slumped down, and the pistol had slid between his thigh and the chair's arm. As he fumbled for it, Ernie entered and spoke.

"Here we are. How are you doing?"

"All right, I guess." David gazed past him to the doctor.

"This is Doc Muller," Ernie said. "Mr. Stone."

The blond man looked to be ten years younger than David, well fed, and self-assured. He stepped forward with a black satchel in his hand and a rueful smile on his face. "Mr. Stone, I understand you met with an untoward happenstance."

"Nothing happenstance about it. The blackguard meant to kill me."

"Ah. Would you like to lie down while I examine the wound?"

David looked to Ernie. "Can we go down the hall first? I'm afraid they'll find me here."

"Of course."

Ernie scouted the hallway, then helped him up. Dr. Muller stood watch while they lurched along to a door tucked under the attic stairway. The cook seemed to have picked up a skeleton key on his outing, and they were soon inside. Ernie drew the drapes first thing. The cot wasn't made up, and he quickly spread a quilt on it.

"I don't want to bleed all over the bedding," David said. He looked around, but besides the bed, the room held only a washstand, a narrow dresser, and a stool.

"I'll go for some sheets," Ernie said. "Then I'll get your wet clothes while Doc sees to your arm."

"Oh, and I left a small bundle on top of the dresser. Bring that, too, please." David sank onto the stool. He was putting Ernie to a lot of trouble, but the cook remained cheerful.

"I may as well get that cloth off and take a look while we wait," Dr. Muller said.

"Better lay this down." David handed him the pistol, and the doctor set it on the edge of the washstand.

David nearly screamed when the doctor began to unknot the handkerchief Ernie had tied around his upper arm. He clenched his teeth and tried to think about England—Stoneford's fields would be damp and dreary this time of year, and the trees would have shed their foliage, but if he were there, he and Richard and John would be out hunting. Some different it would be from hunting in Oregon, though. The thought of donning a pink coat and setting off after a fox seemed almost ludicrous compared to the elk hunt he'd had last year. And no one hunting in the Oregon woods would wear something as bright as the scarlet material his pink coat was made from.

He managed to lie still while Dr. Muller lifted his arm and probed the wound.

"Seems to have gone in here and out here. That's good—we don't have to remove it. It did a job on your muscles, though."

"I'm thankful it's not worse," David said without unclenching his teeth.

"I'll clean it up and then bandage it well, but you've got to understand, a wound like this is prone to infection within."

"Do whatever you have to, Doc."

"You'll want it checked frequently. Of course it will be sore for several weeks. But if the skin around it becomes hot and swollen, and if it looks redder than normal, that means it's infected. You don't want to let it go if that happens."

"What can you do?"

The doctor sighed. "The best cure is to prevent it in the first place. So I will hurt you tonight to make sure it is thoroughly clean. This isn't a method many of my peers use, but I've found that patients do much better when I follow this procedure."

The door swung open, and Ernie came in carrying his things from the suite. "Here we go, Mr. Stone." He set the bundle on the dresser and dropped the wet clothes on the floor. "I'd better run down to the kitchen for your coat."

By the time he returned again, the doctor was cleaning up and putting his instruments away.

"I ran into Mr. Reed," Ernie said as he closed the door. "He asked why I was here so late."

"Is he suspicious?" David asked.

"I don't think so. I told him I wanted to start dough rising for breakfast. That means I'll have to come in extra early in the morning, but I don't mind."

"Is everything set in my old room?" David asked.

"Yes. I looked around in the sitting room as well as the bedchamber. Everything looks as though you stepped out for the evening and will return any moment. I made sure there's no blood or other telltale signs. And I soaked the tablecloth we used in cold water. It came out rather well."

"Thank you," David said. "Where's my soggy wallet now, Ernie?"

"Right here, sir."

"Good. Would you please give the doctor two dollars from it?

I've explained to him that I shall disappear as a hotel guest."

"That's right," Dr. Muller said. "I'll come and check on you to-morrow, but I shan't inquire for you at the front desk."

"If you come straight to the kitchen, I'll let you come up the back stairs," Ernie said. "No one will be the wiser unless one of the waiters is in the kitchen then."

"I'll make it a point not to come at mealtime." The doctor pock-eted the money Ernie gave him. "Thank you for paying promptly, sir. You're in the minority there. I assure you your location is safe with me."

Dr. Muller cracked the door open and went out, carrying his black bag. Ernie locked the door behind him, and David sighed.

"I can never repay you, but I'll make a down payment, Ernie. There's a little pouch in my bundle over there. That's for you."

"Oh Mr. Stone, I told you—"

David held up his good hand. "I know, but I want to give you this. It's a collection of small nuggets from my sluice box, and it should be worth about a hundred dollars. Don't say that's too much. It's not, and I have enough cash to get me home when I'm done here. But there's one other thing we need to take care of."

"What's that, sir?"

"I do want to pay the hotel bill. Perhaps we could leave enough money on the dresser in the suite to cover it? Then when Mr. Reed begins investigating my disappearance, he'll find it."

"Hmm. What if someone else goes in there first and 'finds' it?"

"The shooter, you mean?"

"Whoever. The cleaning woman, even. And once your absence is noticed, a lot of people will wonder what became of you. If Reed calls in the constable. . . Well, it wouldn't be the first time cash dis-appeared during an investigation, now would it?"

"What do you suggest?"

"You could put the money in an envelope with a note saying you plan to check out tomorrow and wanted to settle up in advance."

"Would that work? Reed would know it wasn't at the front desk when he left for the night."

"We'll leave it in the suite, then. Can you write a note if I bring you paper and pen?"

"Maybe." David yawned. He was tired out, but in addition the doctor had given him a powder to help him sleep. "Best be quick about it, or I'll be out cold." His brain was so numb he couldn't come up with a better plan.

Ernie hesitated. "Sir, don't you want me to stay here tonight? You need to rest."

"They won't find me here. You said no one uses this room most nights."

"That's true."

"Go on. What would your wife say if you didn't come home?"

"Wife? That's a good one."

"Still, I'll be all right. Leave me my pistol. I'll lock the door behind you."

"Let me take your wet things and get them dried and aired so you have a change in the morning. I might be able to do something about the bullet holes, too. . . ." Ernie held up the bloody shirt and shook his head as he surveyed the tattered sleeve.

"Don't bother," David said. "Just dispose of it discreetly."

"Well, sir, I could pick up anything you need at the haberdashery tomorrow. Too bad you have to leave so many nice things behind. . . ."

"Yes. I'll get on all right without them, but I wish there was a way to give some of it to you. Oh, that reminds me. Captain."

"Captain?"

"My horse. He's in the stable. I'd hate to lose him."

Ernie scratched his chin. "What if he sort of. . .checked out. . . before anyone knew you were missing?"

"Hmm. That might cause the assassin to believe I'm still alive."

"It might. Is it worth the risk?"

"What will happen if we leave him there?"

"Well, if we didn't leave the money to cover the bill the way we talked about, you could just leave the horse. Reed would probably sell him to pay your bill."

"My horse and gear are worth more than that, and besides, he's a good horse." David stifled another yawn.

"All right. I'll get the paper for you to write the note, and then I'll get the horse from the stable and take him and your wet clothes home with me. If nobody sees me, you're in good shape. I'll keep Captain until you're ready to travel again."

Ernie helped David get as far as the door, placed the pistol in his hand, and went out. David leaned against the jamb for a minute, listening to his new friend's retreating footsteps. He slid the bolt. He was just about to turn away when he heard soft footfalls in the hallway. He held his breath, wishing he'd doused the lamp. He heard a door open and close quietly, then more footsteps, so gentle he'd almost have said they were stealthy. Then all was quiet.

He stood there for a good five minutes—until his legs turned to lead. He couldn't stand any longer, even leaning against the woodwork. He staggered to the table and blew out the flame in the lamp, then lurched to the cot and lowered himself onto it with as little noise as possible.

CHAPTER 18

$\mathbf{M}$illie topped the second flight of stairs and stood for a moment on the landing to catch her breath. Which room was David's? He'd let fall last night that he was on the third floor. She didn't think many guests were staying up here. She tiptoed along the hall, studying the numbers painted on the door panels, mentally boxing her own ears for not discovering his room number.

At the opposite end of the building, across the landing and at the far end of the hall she was exploring, a door creaked. She stepped back against the wall and peered toward the sound. A man had just gone through a doorway down there, but where had he come from?

She hastened along the carpet runner, crossed the landing with a glance down toward the floor below, and glided on into the other wing. Two lamps turned low threw just enough light in the corridor to guide her.

At the extreme end of the hall, the door on the left seemed the most likely candidate for the one the man had escaped through. To her surprise, small, neat letters on it proclaimed a discreet STAFF ONLY. Millie turned the brass knob, and the door swung inward on an uncarpeted landing. She'd discovered the back stairs.

With a sigh, she closed the door again. The man she'd seen was no doubt a hotel employee. This wasn't helping her. She needed to find out where David had been staying. After a moment's thought, she went to the nearest numbered door—306—and knocked softly. No sound came from within. She tapped again, louder. Still no response. She tried the knob, but the door was locked.

She moved on along the hallway. On the third door she tried— a room close to the landing, a man's voice called from within, "Yes?"

Millie froze, every sense a-tingle.

A moment later, she heard a bolt drawn, and the door opened about six inches. A gray-haired man wearing dark trousers, an undershirt, and suspenders peered out at her.

"May I help you?"

Millie clapped a hand to her cheek. "Oh, I beg your pardon. I was supposed to meet my brother, and I thought he told me that his room was 303. I must have gotten the number wrong. Please forgive the intrusion." She fluttered her eyelashes and pursed her lips, on which she'd recently replenished her rouge.

"Oh well, certainly." The man hesitated. "Er, what does your brother look like?"

"He's a tall Englishman." She immediately realized her mistake and added hastily, "That is, he's spent a lot of time in England, and he's picked up the accent. That's what most people notice about him first."

"Hmm, I think he said good-day to me this morning—he seemed to be on his way out then."

"Oh, I've seen him since then, but thank you." Millie smiled and moved on toward the landing.

"You'd better ask at the front desk," the man called after her. His door closed.

She lingered on the landing. Was it better to disturb other guests and let them see her seeking a tall Englishman—and she needed to revise her story if she chose that option—or to inquire at the desk? She didn't want anyone connecting her to David's disappearance. Yet several other guests had seen them dining together this evening. Maybe it would be wise to ask about him. That would imply that she didn't know he wasn't in his room and healthy as a horse.

She hurried down the two flights of stairs.

A new clerk was on the desk—a younger, red-haired man who looked to be scarcely into his twenties. He stared brazenly at Millie as she descended the last few steps and strolled toward him.

"Well, hello," she said. "Haven't seen you before."

"I'm the night clerk. M—may I help you, ma'am?"

"Oh dear, I didn't realize how late it was. Mr. Stone had asked me to meet him for coffee when I returned from my evening out with friends, and I don't see him here in the lobby. He hasn't by any chance left a message for me, has he?"

"Uh... What's your room number, ma'am?"

"It's 202. Mrs. Evans."

He turned away and scanned the bank of pigeonholes behind him. "Nope. I don't see anything in your box."

She sighed and fluttered her lashes. "Perhaps he gave up on me. Let's see, he's way up on the third floor, isn't he?"

"Mr. Stone? I...uh...I think so." The clerk consulted the registry on the counter. "Oh, he has the suite. He's the English fellow."

"Yes." Millie's mind whirled. David had a suite? She hadn't even known the hotel possessed such accommodations. "Maybe he intended to have coffee served in his sitting room."

"Well, he hasn't asked for room service tonight, at least not since I've been here, but that's only the last hour or so."

"I'll go up and see if he's waiting for me. Uh, what did you say the number is?"

"He's in 304, but I can run up and check if you want, ma'am."

"Oh, that's all right. I shall have to go up to my room anyway, and if he's not in, I'll simply retire. Thank you very much...uh... what was your name?" She gave a smile she hoped dazzled the gangly young fellow, and he practically melted before her eyes.

"It's Ronald, ma'am."

"Oh please, Ronald. You may call me Mrs. Evans."

"Yes, ma'am."

She could feel his gaze on her as she sauntered to the stairs. She went along to her own room and gathered assorted hairpins, a nail file, and a pair of tweezers. One way or another, she was going to get into that suite.

Anne couldn't sleep. As much as she wanted justice, she wasn't sure that execution would be justice in Sam Hastings's case. The more she thought about it, the more certain she was that he hadn't acted alone.

"I ain't supposed to tell you," he'd said.

According to whom? she wondered. And hadn't he claimed he wasn't really stealing the horses but was only attempting to keep her from finding David? She'd assumed he meant because he didn't want her to reveal his attempt to impersonate her uncle. But would he follow her all this way for that? David would find out eventually. What good would it do Sam Hastings to keep her away from him for a while?

"If I don't find Uncle David, he'll never know I'm within ten thousand miles of here," she said aloud. Instead of trying to stop her from tattling on him, was Sam's goal to keep David from knowing about her?

She thought back over the two visits she and Dan had made to the farm when Sam pretended to be her uncle. She sat up in bed. The key to the puzzle was obvious—why hadn't she seen it before?

She threw back the bedclothes. In the interest of saving the horses, she'd packed light, which meant she hadn't brought her dressing gown. That meant she had to get completely dressed before she left her chamber. Without another woman to help lace her corsets, that took some engineering, but ten minutes later she surveyed herself in the mirror and decided her appearance lay within the bounds of propriety. She opened her door and tiptoed along the hall.

As she passed the room where Whitey had settled for the night, snores penetrated the pine door panels. Mrs. Zinberg's room was downstairs, for which Anne was thankful. She pulled up before the door to Dan's room and looked over her shoulder. Only a little light spilled through the casement at the end of the hall, and she was alone. Feeling slightly decadent, she tapped softly on the door.

"Daniel? Daniel, it's me. I need to tell you something."

She was about to knock louder when she heard him turn the knob. He stared out at her.

"Anne?"

His tousled hair gave him a boyish look that she found adorable

by starlight, and she smiled.

"What is it?" he asked.

Suddenly she realized anew how scandalous her behavior might seem.

"Oh! I thought of something. I'm sorry to wake you."

He smiled and opened the door wider, revealing that he was still dressed. "You didn't wake me. I couldn't sleep, and I was pacing the floor, thinking about what happened today."

"Me, too. Dan, don't you see? Sam Hastings wasn't in that bit of chicanery alone."

He stared at her for a long moment, then inhaled through his nose. "You're right. Of course. I should have seen it at once. The question is—"

Anne nodded. "Where's Millie?"

Whenever she got a new corset, the first thing Millie did was to sew a small pocket into it. Secure banking at its best. As she dressed in the morning, she patted the satin garment with satisfaction. She still had sixty dollars left from what Peterson had paid her—after a lavish shopping spree among Scottsburg's none-too-satisfactory retail establishments—and last night she'd added another ten.

She'd surprised herself when she shed a few tears for David into her pillow. It would have been grand to marry such a suave, handsome, wealthy man. Alas, that was not to be. From his room, she'd lifted his last gifts to her—a lovely little carved box containing a pair of onyx cuff links, a small Bible, and two five-dollar bills. She'd burned the envelope the money came in and the accompanying note: "I'll be checking out early. This should cover my bill. David Stone, #304."

Now wasn't that convenient of him to leave that before stepping out last evening? One would almost think he'd had a premonition that he might not return.

Poor David! She was still furious with Peterson and a little bit frightened, but she would never let him see that. In fact, she planned to be miles from Scottsburg before that shifty character was even out of bed. Too bad. She'd enjoyed this hotel. It was nicer than she'd expected in this rough river town, and so far she hadn't paid a cent. Two of her dinners went on David's bill, and thanks to him and Peterson, she had plenty to pay for her accommodations. She briefly considered skipping out without paying at all, but decided against that. She'd run up quite a bill, and it might be enough to make the manager set the constable on her. Of course, the constable would have his hands full with the disappearance of the hotel's most affluent guest. . . .

Her thoughts kept coming back to that. The shot in the moonlight, and David pitching over the edge of the dock into the river. Peterson's harsh words, and her aching emptiness. She was alone now, as she had been most of her life. It was up to her to distance herself from Peterson, who was obviously a very dangerous man.

A fleeting thought crossed her mind of Sam—where had he wound up? Was he still up in the hills, chasing Anne Stone and her stuffy bodyguard? She'd decided that's what Dan Adams was. Anne didn't give him enough encouragement to make him a lover or even a sweetheart. That girl had no passion. Millie could teach her a thing or two under different circumstances.

She sighed and settled her new hat on her upswept hair. Scottsburg needed a decent milliner, but this would suffice for now. When she got to San Francisco again, she'd buy a proper hat.

The hotel's breakfast was classier than what she'd gotten at the café with Peterson, though it cost nearly three times as much. Since she was paying this morning, she may as well stay here and enjoy it—and avoid the possibility of seeing Peterson again. That cook they had out back knew what he was doing. She'd take a leisurely breakfast, then pack her things in the new leather traveling bag she'd purchased, pay her bill like a decent lady, and collect her mount from the stable.

She opened the little carved box and gazed at the cuff links. Why had she taken them? She supposed she could sell them for a dollar or two in a pinch, but that wasn't the reason. David had worn

them their first evening together. When did she get sentimental? That attitude could get her in trouble. He'd planned to check out this morning. Did he intend to tell her last night, or would he have simply left without saying good-bye? She closed the box and tucked it into the drawer with her fine new underthings and extra gloves.

The leather-covered book was smaller than any Bible she'd seen before. Compact, for him to carry about when he traveled, she supposed. She hadn't thought too much about him being a godly man, but he had quoted something she was fairly certain came from the Bible as they walked toward the river last night—something about the heavens and God's glory. Mostly he seemed to favor Shakespeare and Edmund Burke for his quotations, but in any case, he was quite the scholar. The books in his farmhouse had told her that, and she'd expected him to be a little owlish, but he'd turned out to be far more dashing than she'd imagined.

Yes, he would have made a good husband. She'd never have had to worry about where the money for the tax bill would come from or struggle for the perfect word on any occasion. She could have tapped David for either at a moment's notice. She sighed and put the Bible in with the cuff link box.

When she opened her door, she took the precaution of looking down the hall first and waiting until the two men headed for the stairs had gone down. She didn't want to speak to any more people than necessary this morning. As she crossed the landing to the head of the stairs, she glanced up toward the third story. David's empty suite lay up there. Such a pity—she'd really liked him. But it was time to move on. She would have breakfast and then make one last purchase before leaving Scottsburg. With Peterson at large, she'd feel safer carrying a gun. A small lady's weapon, of course. She'd seen one in a shop yesterday and wished she'd bought it then.

She went down the stairs, avoided the desk clerk's gaze, and entered the dining room, knowing every eye was upon her. More than a dozen men were having their breakfast, and all seemed happy to have a pretty woman to look at while they did.

"Good morning, Mrs. Evans," the waiter said pleasantly.

"Won't you join me?" a smooth male voice asked.

Millie whipped around.

Peterson smiled. "I hoped I might see you again this morning. My table is right over here."

CHAPTER 19

I'm sorry I can't just let you have the horse," Dan told Whitey. "Until we see what happens to Hastings and perhaps determine whether the animal really belongs to him, I think we'd better keep it in Scottsburg."

"Makes no nevermind to me," Whitey said, but his mouth drooped behind the fluffy, white beard. "If you don't mind, I'll tag along when you go into town. Got no hurry to get back up to my cabin."

"We'd be delighted to have your company a bit longer," Anne assured him.

They enjoyed a hearty breakfast at Mrs. Zinberg's house.

"Not every woman knows how to fry an egg to perfection," Whitey said with a big smile for the widow.

"Oh Mr. Pogue, you flatter me."

"No harm in flattering one as deserves it."

Dan glanced over at Anne, who didn't try very hard to hide her smile. Was Mrs. Zinberg actually blushing? Maybe he ought to pay attention—the old man seemed to be a master of flirtation.

"I'll be going to worship service this morning," the widow said. "You folks are welcome to attend."

Startled, Dan realized he'd completely lost track of the days. He turned to Anne. "Would you like to attend church?"

"Very much."

He nodded. "I admit I was planning to check at the post office today, but that will be closed."

"Maybe we could inquire at some of the hotels before church," Anne said. "Mrs. Zinberg, what is the best hotel in Scottsburg?"

"Oh, that would be the Miner's Hotel."

"Hands-down," Whitey agreed.

"And there are several other boardinghouses," Mrs. Zinberg said, "but all the mining company investors and government officials stay at the Miner's Hotel."

"Let's check there first," Anne said. "And if you can tell us where some of those boardinghouses are, we'll try them if my uncle's not at the hotel."

"Mr. Adams, there's a small matter I'd like to speak to you about."

"Yes, ma'am?"

She looked a little embarrassed, and Dan wondered if she'd heard him and Anne talking in the middle of the night and jumped to conclusions.

"Well, perhaps I shouldn't mention it on the Lord's Day, but after hearing about your misadventures over the last two days, I did wonder if perhaps you wouldn't be in the market for a revolver."

Dan eyed her in surprise. "It wouldn't be a bad idea. I wished I had one when that thief made off with my horse and my rifle."

"Well, I have my husband's revolver, and heaven knows I would never use it. I don't even know how to load it. If you're interested in looking at it. . . ."

Dan glanced at Anne, who was calmly sipping her tea. She didn't seem to have a problem with him buying a handgun, or with him and their hostess doing business on Sunday. "Thank you, ma'am. I'd be happy to look at it."

The transaction was soon completed to both Dan's and Mrs. Zinberg's satisfaction. She allowed that she could use the extra bit of money more than she could a weapon.

Half an hour later, the travelers took their leave. Mrs. Zinberg all but simpered when Whitey bowed over her hand.

"If things don't work out for you in town, Mr. Pogue, you're welcome to return here for luncheon. I'll have plenty."

"Why, ma'am, that's a delightful invitation. I may avail myself of that."

Dan turned away to adjust his saddle's cinch strap. He never would have guessed the old miner had a deep vocabulary and courtly

manners up his worn flannel sleeve.

They rode together to Constable Owens's house.

"Good morning, folks. I expected you to come around."

Dan swung down from the saddle and gave Anne a hand.

"How's the prisoner?" he asked.

"Fine when I took him his breakfast. A little chilly, but my wife had sent over two blankets, and he had a coat. He's all right."

"We've decided to see if we can find Mr. Stone," Dan said. "He may be able to help us settle some questions. We'll come back here later and tell you what we learn."

"All righty. Say—have you checked the Miner's Hotel?"

"That's where we're headed," Dan said. He felt like the model of incompetence. He hadn't checked the Miner's Hotel their first day in town, but he should have. Had David Stone been two blocks away, and he'd missed him? But he'd asked the postmaster and been told David hadn't been in for a week. More likely he'd returned to Scottsburg right about the time Dan and Anne left to ride up to his claim.

He gave Anne a boost into Bailey's saddle and then mounted Star. They set out without any more words, but he could almost hear Anne's thoughts—how close had they come to running into her uncle on the street? Dan had led her on a wild goose chase that nearly ended in tragedy for nothing.

The hotel sprang into view—a large, three-storied house with rambling porches and lots of windows. It looked comfortable and more substantial than places miners and dockhands would stay.

In the lobby, a dignified man of about forty stood behind the desk, checking a guest out of the hotel. When the customer left, Dan stepped forward, with Anne and Whitey on his heels.

"Hello. We're here to see Mr. David Stone. This young lady is his niece, and we were told he may be staying here."

"Oh yes, Mr. Stone is a frequent guest," the clerk said. "I'll send someone up to see if he's in his room."

"Thank you," Dan said.

The clerk nodded as he came from behind the desk. "Would

you like to sit down while you wait? We're serving breakfast now. If you'd like, you can order coffee in the dining room."

Anne shook her head.

Dan said, "We're fine, thank you. We'll wait out here."

The clerk went through a doorway, and Dan guided Anne to a settee in the shadow of a folding screen. Whitey found a straight chair a short distance away and dragged it over. He plunked down in it opposite them.

"Well, it'll be good to see ol' David again," Whitey said.

Dan smiled at the old codger's designation of a forty-year-old as "ol' David," but Anne's face remained sober. She folded her gloved hands on her lap, but her gaze darted about the lobby. The clerk returned to his post a minute later, and he appeared to be busy with some papers.

"I do hope we find him in," Anne said. Anxiety lined her lovely brow.

Dan reached over and patted her hands. "I hope so, too. You've been through a lot, and this meeting is long overdue."

Five minutes later a boy arrived at the desk, red-faced and panting. He spoke in low tones to the clerk, who glanced their way, picked up something, and left the room with the boy.

Dan had a bad feeling about that, but he didn't say anything to Anne. Instead, he asked Whitey how the prices were on food-stuffs in the area. A grandfather clock in one corner ticked off the minutes, until he wondered if they would be late for church. At last the clerk reappeared, coming down the stairs this time, and walked across the lobby to where they sat.

"I'm sorry, but it seems Mr. Stone is not in his suite."

"Oh." Anne stared at him blankly.

"But he *is* still staying here?" Dan said.

"Oh yes. I'm sure he's only stepped out for a while."

Dan stood and stepped closer to the clerk. "Miss Stone has had an arduous journey to find her uncle. She is his nearest relation, and she's come to break news to him concerning a death in the family. If Mr. Stone has engaged a suite, would it be possible for you to allow

her to wait for him there?"

"Oh, I. . ." The clerk eyed him doubtfully then looked over his shoulder. Two men stood near the front desk looking annoyed. "I must go and help those guests check out. But I couldn't let you into the suite without permission from Mr. Reed."

"And who is Mr. Reed?" Dan followed the clerk as he set off across the lobby.

"He's the manager, sir. He should be here soon, and I'll let him know your request."

"Thank you." Dan walked back to where Anne and Whitey waited.

Millie doctored her coffee carefully and avoided meeting Peterson's gaze. Had she actually thought him attractive on their first meeting? He made her skin crawl.

"Now, as I see it, there are only two possibilities," he said in a low, businesslike tone. "Either his body washed downstream and has yet to be found, or he escaped alive, in which case it behooves the two of us to find him."

Millie contained her snort to a dignified *hmph*. If Peterson expected her to stay in Scottsburg, he was suffering delusions. The only thing it behooved her to do was to leave town as quickly as possible. And she could guess why Peterson wanted to find David— to finish off the job he'd botched the first time.

Was it possible that David was still alive? She sincerely hoped he was.

"If he came back to his room last night, he may be upstairs this minute," Peterson said. "Or he might have found a doctor. I'm sure I hit him. We need to inquire as to whether there's a physician in the area."

"Why don't you do that?" she asked in sugary tones. "But if we're going on with this charade, shouldn't I raise an alarm?"

"And have the authorities out looking for his corpse? Hmm, that might actually be to my advantage. I tried half the night to find him on my own, and I couldn't. There must be people hereabouts who know the vagaries of the river. But how will we explain to them that we think he's in it?"

"I don't know, but if David is still alive, I certainly don't want him coming back and finding me placidly eating breakfast with the likes of you." She drained her coffee cup and pushed back her chair.

"Wait," Peterson said. "I need to know what you're going to do—where you'll be."

"I'll leave you a note at the front desk."

"But I'm not staying here."

"You're not?" Millie asked.

"No. I only came in for breakfast and to see you."

"Where—" She stopped. What did it matter? She didn't intend to see him again. She shook her head. "I'll see if I can find out whether he came in last night." And what Peterson didn't know wouldn't hurt him. No way would she tell him she'd picked the lock on David's door last night. She turned and strode quickly toward the lobby. He couldn't jump up and pursue her without causing a scene—one Millie would make sure the hotel staff noticed.

Two steps into the lobby were enough to pull her up short. Five yards straight ahead, the hotel manager was in earnest conversation with Daniel Adams and Anne Stone.

"It's very irregular," Mr. Reed said. "We don't usually go into a guest's room uninvited or allow visitors to do so."

"But he's her uncle," Dan said.

"I'm sorry, but I have to ask: do you have proof of that?"

Dan looked at Anne. He wanted to get tough with the manager, but the request was reasonable. Anyone could waltz in claiming to be a relative of a guest and use it as license to ransack a room.

"I have a picture of him." Anne delved into her handbag and brought out the miniature. "It was painted when he was young—about twenty years old."

She opened the case and handed it to Reed.

"I also have a letter that he wrote to my father some time ago, when he lived in St. Louis."

Reed eyed the portrait and pressed his lips together. "Hmm. This does bear a resemblance to Mr. Stone."

Anne took the miniature back and gazed at it for a moment before closing the case. "You see, Mr. Reed, my father died less than a year ago. David is his younger brother, and he has no idea about my father's death. I went to St. Louis hoping to find him there, but I learned he'd moved to Oregon. Sir, I've been searching for him all this time. Please, if there's anything you can do to help me. . ."

Her vibrant brown eyes, along with her plaintive story and her charming appearance, would persuade any man, Dan thought. Sure enough, Reed seemed to waver. At last he shoved a hand into his pocket.

"All right. It's not real proof, but you look like a respectable woman. I don't mean to cast aspersions on you or to imply that I think you are not what you seem, but one has to be careful. Out here people frequently misrepresent themselves, and it's my duty to protect our guests."

"I understand perfectly," Anne said. "In fact, I appreciate your diligence. I assure you, I would not take unfair advantage of your kindness. I bear my uncle only goodwill, and this reunion means a great deal to me."

Reed pulled a large bunch of keys from his pocket. "All right, since the clerk has already checked Mr. Stone's rooms, I suppose we can go up." He shot Dan a glance.

Of course. That was why the clerk had hurried off after the boy had spoken to him. Probably dashed up the back stairs to scout out David's suite. That way, if the guest had passed out drunk, or if he'd died in the hotel room, the visitor wouldn't bear the shock of discovery.

Anne followed Mr. Reed up the stairs, and Dan followed as closely as her trailing skirt allowed. Whitey came last, gawking about at the carved woodwork, gilt-framed paintings, and hanging lanterns. At the first landing, as they walked around to mount the next flight, Reed looked back at Dan. "And this man is with you?"

Anne and Dan both glanced at Whitey.

"Oh yes, sir," Anne said. "He's a friend, both of mine and of Mr. Stone's. A mutual acquaintance who has been of great assistance to me."

Reed arched his eyebrows as though in doubt. "Very well."

They ascended to the third story, and he headed for one of the doorways leading off the corridor. A man carrying a covered tray came down the hall. He was already halfway along it, and he hesitated, then ducked his head as he passed them.

"Ernie," Mr. Reed said in surprise, "what are you doing up here in the middle of our breakfast hours? Shouldn't you be in the kitchen?"

The stocky man flushed slightly and looked down at the tray. "Oh yes, sir, I'm usually right there, but one of the guests was ill and asked for a tray."

"The waiter should have taken it."

"He was overwhelmed with folks in the dining room wanting this and that. It will only take me a moment."

Reed frowned. "We'll discuss this later. Deliver that and get back to your station."

"Yes, sir." Ernie glided down the hallway and exited through a door at the far end.

Mr. Reed knocked on the door to the suite, waited a moment, then put a key to the lock. He swung the door open and entered, looked about, then turned to Anne.

"Come right in, Miss Stone. I'm sure you'll be comfortable here. The clerk has already checked the bedchamber to make sure he hadn't simply overslept, but let me just make sure. . . ." He stepped through the connecting doorway. Dan heard a door open and close—probably the wardrobe.

"Well, he's certainly not here," Reed said with a frown as he reentered the sitting room. "His things look undisturbed. I'll check with our housekeeper, though."

"Why is that, sir?" Dan asked. "To see if the room has been cleaned already this morning?"

"Well. . .er. . ." Reed cleared his throat. "I noticed that the blankets are not on the bed."

They all stood in silence for a moment.

"What does that mean?" Anne said at last. "Did someone forget to make up the bed?"

Mr. Reed's forehead furrowed. "I'm not certain. I'm sure Mr. Stone *had* blankets. Perhaps he spilled something on them—coffee, or. . .or. . . Well, as I said, I will check with the housekeeper to see if she knows anything about it. If you folks would please make yourselves comfortable, I'll return when I find out anything. And if Mr. Stone comes in, we'll tell him that he has visitors."

"Thank you," Dan said.

By the time Reed was out the door, Anne had gone into the adjoining room. Dan went and stood in the doorway. She walked slowly over to the dresser.

"His razor is here, and a couple of papers." She turned away as though stifling the urge to open the drawers.

"Mr. Reed looked in the wardrobe," Dan said.

Anne strode to the walnut armoire and flung the doors open. Inside hung a wool jacket, a pair of plain twill pants, three shirts, and a droopy felt hat. She reached out and touched the sleeve of the coat.

"It looks as though he certainly planned to come back."

"He's probably down the street getting a newspaper," Dan said.

Whitey had come to the doorway, too, and he spoke up. "Like as not, he's over to the tavern right now and we missed him on the way."

Anne smiled faintly. "I dare say."

Dan said nothing. Anne couldn't know her uncle's habits and vices, and it might be true. The saloons out here might stay open on Sunday, too, as vile as that seemed. From what he'd gathered in the past weeks, Westerners didn't observe the Sabbath as strictly as most folks did back East—especially in mining towns.

Anne continued to scan the room and stepped to the washstand. "Daniel."

"What is it?"

"Could you come look at this please?"

He stepped over beside her. "What?"

"There are no towels. You know Mr. Reed commented on the bedding."

"Hmm. Maybe the housekeeper took away all the dirty linens but didn't bring the clean ones yet."

"Then why did she not take the sheets? That is very odd, taking the blankets but not the sheets."

Dan looked over at the bed. She was right about that.

"And Daniel. . ."

"Yes?"

"Please look closer at the rim of this washbowl."

Something in her tone put him on the alert. He stooped and peered at the edge of the large, white porcelain bowl. A small reddish smear on the rim set his pulse racing.

"Do you think. . .?"

Anne grasped his arm. "Yes, I do think. Look there." She pointed down at the floor and stepped back, holding her skirt against her legs.

Dan bent down and stared at the dark spot not much bigger than a half dime. Cautiously, he reached out and touched it with the tip of his pinky. He rose and walked to the window and examined his finger.

"I'm not sure, Anne. It appears to be dry, whatever it is."

She took out a handkerchief and picked up the water pitcher. "There's no water in here."

"Could be he washed and shaved before he went out this mornin'," Whitey said.

Anne ignored him. "There are a few drops in the bottom." She wiped the interior of the pitcher with her handkerchief, set down the pitcher, and knelt beside the stand. She dabbed at the spot and looked at her handkerchief. "I don't want to take it all."

She rose and walked over to Dan and held it up to the light. "There. I'll eat my two best hats if that's not blood."

CHAPTER 20

David startled awake when a key turned in the lock. He aimed the pistol at the door, but when the knob turned, it didn't open. A soft tap followed.

"It's me."

The bolt was still in place. David sat up and shook off the cobwebs.

"Hold on."

When he stood, his head reeled. He lunged for the door and stood leaning against it, panting, until the swirling blackness receded.

"Ernie?" he croaked.

"Yeah. Lemme in. Quick."

David fumbled with the bolt and opened the door. The cook squeezed in with his arms full of dishes and shut it.

"Man, you look awful."

"Thanks." David hobbled back to the bed and sat down.

"I can't stay. If the boss sees me up here again—"

"He saw you this morning?"

"Yeah. And get this—he was taking some people into your suite."

David's stomach dropped. "Really? Why?"

"Not sure. I heard someone was looking for you."

"Because I was shot at?"

"I dunno, but I saw a really pretty girl and two men. One was an old coot with a white beard, and the other guy was younger. Tall, decent looking. He'd shaved this morning, if that counts."

David rubbed his own stubbly chin. "Not sure if it does or not. Can you get my razor?"

"Not now. Those people are in there waiting for you."

"What on earth?"

Ernie shrugged. "I'll see if I can find out anything, but the boss will get mad if he sees me outside the kitchen again, and we start serving dinner soon. I brought you some more water and a sandwich and some cake. If there's any fried chicken left from dinner, I'll bring you some of that later."

"Thanks, Ernie. I forgot to ask you this morning about Captain."

"He's fine. He gets along great with my old nag. But listen, you've got to keep quiet, you hear me?"

"Absolutely."

"Good. 'Cause if Reed finds out someone's in here. . . Well, I wouldn't want to be around when he found out."

"The woman who was with Mr. Reed, it wasn't Mrs. Evans, was it?"

"Who?"

"The woman I had dinner with last night. She's a guest here—reddish hair, tall and regal looking."

"Hmm, no, I'd say not. I didn't want to look too close, on account of Mr. Reed being with them. She had dark hair and a fancy hat. Very handsome young woman. In her early twenties, I'd think. Fresh, young face."

"Well, that's not Mrs. Evans. She's a bit more mature. I wonder who it could be."

"Like I say, I'll see if I can find out more without stirring up suspicion. Maybe Elwood or Ronald on the front desk can tell me something. Now, I'd better vamoose. It's Sunday, and we serve a big dinner."

David managed to get to the door with him and throw the bolt as soon as Ernie left. He lay down again and stared up at the ceiling, wondering about the mysterious trio down the hall in his suite.

"You go on up to his room and knock on the door," Peterson said. "Make sure some other people see you going up there. Then you need to talk to the manager. Tell him Stone promised to meet you

at eight last night and he never showed up."

"Some of the hotel people saw us leave together around seven."

"All right, tell them that when you returned he had to go out on an errand but he promised to meet you again downstairs in an hour. He didn't show, and after a while you gave up and turned in. But then he didn't come down to breakfast this morning either. You're concerned, and he's not answering your knock."

"What good will that do?"

"Oh, come now, you can be persuasive. Insist that they open the door. Prove to the manager that Stone isn't there and most likely didn't come in last night."

Millie cast another glance toward the lobby. What would she do if Anne Stone and her friends came into the dining room? She supposed she could try to keep her face turned away and then sneak out after they were seated. Maybe she could hide her face with her fan.

"All right?" Peterson asked.

"I'm sorry, what did you say?"

"Insist that the hotel staff call the authorities in to look for Stone. Convince them that something awful has happened to him."

"And what if someone mentions you? A score of people have seen us together this morning."

"Tell them I'm an old friend who just got into town, and you wanted David to meet me. I'm staying at a boardinghouse down the street, if that helps. Go on, now. I'll inquire about a doctor."

"All right." Millie stood and grasped her purse and gloves. She dreaded going out to the lobby again, but there seemed no other choice. She walked slowly toward the doorway. A glance over her shoulder told her Peterson was paying the bill and would be right behind her. She peered out into the lobby.

She saw no sign of Anne and Adams. Her knees almost buckled, her relief was so strong. Now if she could just get her luggage and slip out without Peterson seeing her, he would think she'd gone up to David's suite. She might have ten or fifteen minutes before he came looking for her.

Too late. He'd turned around and was striding toward her.

Millie scooted toward the staircase. At the first landing, she paused, hoping Peterson had gone outside so she could end this charade and go straight to her room to pack.

He was leaning against the newel post, looking up at her. He touched a finger to his temple in a mock salute. Millie lifted her skirt a couple of inches and started up the next flight of stairs. That man was driving her insane. She had to get away from him—away from Scottsburg. If David was dead, Peterson could implicate her. And if the Englishman was alive, she doubted he'd want anything to do with Charlotte Evans now.

Three steps from the top, she pulled up short. People had come to the head of the stairs, intending to come down. She started to flatten her full skirt and then caught her breath.

"Aren't you. . .Millie?" Dan Adams asked, staring down at her.

Anne Stone's mouth opened, and her eyes went round. "Yes, she is, and unless I'm mistaken—Daniel, I believe that dress belongs to me."

Millie glanced down at her full skirt of fine polished cotton. Though she'd purchased two new dresses, she'd chosen to wear this one today. It remained the finest dress she'd ever owned, and she felt beautiful and confident when she wore it. Except when standing face-to-face with its rightful owner.

She whirled precariously on the stairs, held up her skirts, and barreled down to the landing. Without a glance to see if they followed, she ran around to the next stairway, dodged a drummer coming up with his sample case in hand, and ran down to the lobby.

She half expected to find Peterson waiting at the bottom, but he was nowhere to be seen. She flew past the astonished desk clerk and out the door. Gasping for breath, she ran along the porch of the hotel and down the steps at the side. Around the corner of the building, she dashed toward the stable. A plague on corsets!

She stumbled into the barn and looked around in the dim light. No stable hand was there to get her horse. With a sinking feeling in her stomach, she remembered telling the clerk yesterday that they could turn Vixen out into their pasture. She didn't have time for this.

She looked back at the hotel. No one had come after her yet.

She ran as fast as the constrictive undergarments would allow. In front of the establishment, several horses were tied to the hitching rail. One tall, speckled gelding with a coal black mane and tail caught her eye. He looked almost blue from a distance. She hurried over to him. Sure enough, that was Sam's saddle. Well, if her brother had come here looking for her, he'd get a surprise. She untied the roan's reins, sucked in as much air as her lungs could grab, and stretched her foot up to the stirrup.

She stood with one foot high off the ground, gasping and trying to summon strength to pull herself into the saddle. Behind her the front door of the hotel opened and banged against the wall. She didn't look back, but leaped upward and swung her right leg over the saddle without regard for modesty.

"Go, Blue!" She wheeled him and galloped off down the road.

CHAPTER 21

David leaned most of his weight on the sash of the tiny window in his room. He could see down to the street in front of the hotel. The sun was out, and he wished he could let some air into the stuffy little room. He shoved upward on the bottom sash with his left arm. The effort sent pain screeching through his shoulders and into his injured right arm. He ground his teeth and made one final push. The sash shot upward, and glorious air flowed in.

He hung on the narrow windowsill, gulping in the good mountain air. Now that he'd had time to rest, he had second thoughts about bringing in the authorities. He'd wanted to stay dead, so far as the shooter was concerned. But wouldn't he be safer with the U.S. Marshal on his side? A deputy marshal lived in Eugene. He doubted there was one this far from civilization, but there ought to be at least a constable in Scottsburg.

A wagon and team drove past the hotel, and he pulled back a little. No sense in letting the world see him hanging out the third-story window. Below and to his right, several horses were tied to the hotel's hitching rail. The one on the end was a tall, leggy roan that reminded him of the one he'd left at the ranch for Sam Hastings to use.

He heard the front door open, but the porch roof obscured his view, and he couldn't see who came out. Footsteps pounded on the porch and receded. Must have gone around to the side.

Two men came out of the hotel and ambled down the street toward the center of town. David stayed at the window, ignoring his headache and the searing pain in his arm. The breeze caressed his face. He'd deemed it prudent to leave his shaving equipment in the suite, but maybe Ernie could pick up another razor for him.

No. He was going to come out of hiding. As he straightened, a woman ran full tilt around the corner, from the stable area. She

paused for a moment then hurtled straight toward the hitching rail. A moment later, she'd untied the blue roan's reins and vaulted into the saddle in a whirlwind of skirts and petticoats. Spunky gal. She tore off down the street, clinging to the horse like a burdock, her auburn hair glinting in the sun.

He caught his breath.

Charlotte.

What was she doing? That couldn't possibly be her horse. A lady like Charlotte would have had a sidesaddle. In fact, he'd seen her horse in the pasture yesterday. It was a none-too-fine brown mare.

Below him an old man with white hair and a beard long enough to drag in his soup hobbled down the steps and yelled, "Hey! Come back here, you!"

David stared down the street where Charlotte's escape was now just an echo of hoofbeats. The old man turned and lunged back toward the front steps.

David staggered away from the window. He couldn't take any more of this lurking in a corner and not knowing what was happening. Charlotte stealing a horse? If she'd lure a man to his death, he supposed she wouldn't be beneath snatching a horse. And what about those people in his suite? Who were they? More assassins?

He grabbed his shirt and eased it on over his bandaged arm. The doctor had said he'd come back today, but David couldn't wait any longer. He was getting out of this box of a room and reclaiming his life.

"That is most definitely blood," Anne insisted. "We found it on the floor in my uncle's bedchamber, and there was a trace of it on the washbasin as well."

Mr. Reed, who had been summoned from somewhere deeper in the building, shrugged. "So he cut himself shaving this morning. I fail to see—"

"We both know he wasn't in his room this morning," Anne said.

"Yesterday then."

Anne stamped her foot. She was tired of gentility and courtesy. The desk clerk was worse than no help, and now that he'd found the manager, she was still being put off. "Why can't you be reasonable?" She turned to Dan. "Daniel, please get the constable. I've had enough of this nonsense. We're going to find out what's going on here, one way or another."

"Oh, I'm sure there's no need for the constable," Reed said quickly.

"What else would you recommend doing?" Dan asked. "It seems likely that Mr. Stone was injured. If he never came in last night. . . ."

"But Mr. Stone is an unpredictable man. He'll come here for a day or two and then go off to his mining claim. When he comes back, we open the suite for him again. Next thing you know, he'll be off to Eugene or who knows where."

Reed glanced toward the desk clerk, as if for confirmation. The young man, who leaned on the counter chewing a wad of spruce gum, nodded emphatically.

"But you saw him last night," Anne said.

"Well, yes," Reed replied. "He had supper in our dining room with Mrs. Evans."

"Mrs. Evans?" Anne asked. "Who is she?"

"Room 202."

"You mean she's a guest in this hotel?" Dan asked.

"That's right, sir. She's been here three or four days. Proper lady, I assure you."

"And she's acquainted with my uncle?" Anne frowned at him. This was the first she had heard of a woman connected to David.

"I wouldn't know if they were acquainted earlier, ma'am, but they've dined together the last several nights."

"I. . .see." Anne glanced at Dan, unsure how to proceed.

Dan cleared his throat. "She's not the same woman who ran out of here a moment ago, is she?"

"I couldn't say, sir," Reed said. "We've had some supplies delivered, and I was out in the kitchen."

"It was her," the desk clerk said laconically.

"I knew we should have stopped her," Anne said. "How could she have come by that dress? I'd hate to think she and Hastings robbed the Whistlers when they left Eugene."

"Oh really," Dan said. "Do you think they'd go so far? I mean . . .dresses look alike."

"That one was custom-made in Paris last winter, and I haven't seen the same material since we crossed the Atlantic. I'm saying it was my dress, Daniel. Not that it *looked* like my dress, or that I think it *may* be my dress. That was my dress—one I left in my trunk on Rob Whistler's wagon in Eugene. And now that Millie person has it."

Dan held up both hands. "All right, I'm convinced. I'll go for the constable."

Anne felt some mollification but also some shame at behaving so forcefully in public. Her intention was to learn the truth, not to humiliate Dan.

"I'll get him for you," Whitey said. He'd hung back during their conversation, but now he stepped forward. "It looks like it may be a while before you find ol' David, and I expect I ought to get back up to my cabin. But I can swing by the constable's and let him know you need him over here."

"Thank you," Dan said. "That would be very helpful."

"Yes, Whitey. Thank you very much." Anne held out her hand and squeezed the old man's fingers gently. "We so much appreciate your help and hospitality."

The old man nodded and ambled toward the door. Just as he reached the threshold, it occurred to Anne that they hadn't decided what to do about Sam Hastings's horse. They couldn't let Whitey ride off with it. Maybe he was shrewder than she'd realized—offering to fetch the constable and then head home while she and Dan were too distracted to think about the dubious ownership of the horse.

"Dan, do you think—"

Whitey's piercing yell cut her off.

"Hey! Come back here, you!" He shot back inside and scrambled toward them. "Somebody done stole my horse!"

As David reached for his jacket, a soft tapping came on the door. His heart accelerated. He stepped over to the door and waited, listening.

"It's me." Another tap.

He threw back the bolt and opened the door. Ernie ducked inside and closed it.

"Those people—they found blood on the floor in your room. I must have missed a spot when I cleaned up."

"Oh great." David grimaced. Now what?

"They're talking to the manager, insisting he call the constable in."

"Well, I was thinking I'd get out of this room anyway. The question is, should I sneak away or should I reveal everything and trust the constable to protect me? I'm not too confident right now, knowing the man who tried to kill me is still out there."

"I don't know." Ernie looked down at the pitcher of water in his hands, as if suddenly realizing what he carried. "Oh, I brought this as an excuse. And I have to get right down there. The dining room is open. But that woman keeps claiming you're her uncle, and—"

"What woman?"

"The one who was in your suite. She insists she's got to find you, and if Mr. Reed won't do something, she will." Ernie walked across the room and exchanged the pitcher of water for the half-empty one on the washstand.

"She said she's my niece?"

"That's what I said." Ernie turned and scowled at him.

"Did she give a name?"

"I don't know. I only heard a tiny bit myself, and the rest I got from a waiter. It's chaos down there right now, which is why I figured I could dash up the back stairs and warn you. They're making a to-do about the blood, and now some guy is claiming his horse was stolen."

"I think I may have witnessed that," David said.

"Really? So what do you want to do?"

"I think it's time I met this woman who claims to be my niece."

Ernie grimaced. "I'd love to see that, but if Reed sees me outside the kitchen..."

"Can you send someone to help me get downstairs?"

"How about I just help you back to your suite? Then when they come up to look at the blood spot. ..."

David clapped him on the shoulder. "You're a genius."

Ernie helped him into his jacket, and David pocketed his wallet and pistol. "All right. Let's go."

He hobbled down the hallway, leaning just a bit on Ernie. When they got to the suite, the door was ajar. Ernie peeked inside.

"Guess they left it open."

"All right," David said. "Go on down the back stairs. I'll be fine."

"You sure?"

He nodded. "No one's going to shoot me in front of Mr. Reed."

Ernie gritted his teeth. "I guess not. Let me know how it turns out, will you?"

"I sure will."

Ernie disappeared down the hall, and David walked slowly to the settee. He lowered himself to the cushions then took out his pistol and laid it on the seat beside him.

Before long he heard voices and footsteps approaching.

"I assure you, if he were injured seriously, Mr. Stone would have notified us," the manager said in his most pompous voice. "The fact that he is not in his rooms should tell you—"

Reed came through the doorway and stopped short, staring at David.

"Mr. Stone."

"Hello, Mr. Reed. What's all the fuss about?" David didn't feel like rising, but he could hardly remain seated when a woman entered the room just behind the hotel manager. He pushed upward with his legs and left arm, striving to control his facial expression and not give away his pain.

Reed approached with his hand extended. "Oh Mr. Stone,

you've no idea how happy I am to see you. How happy we *all* are."

"Uncle David?"

He looked at her then and stood still. She was the perfect image of her mother, Elizabeth. Her dark hair was pulled back in sweeping waves under a stylish hat, and her sweet, heart-shaped face took him back years, to Stoneford, leaving him no doubt that she was indeed his niece.

"Anne? How can this be?" He took a faltering step, and she met him in the center of the carpet and grasped his hands.

David ignored the pain and gazed down into her eager face. Could this be the dark-haired little sweetheart he'd bounced on his knee a score of years ago? The achy longing for England and Stoneford that he thought had faded to nostalgia reared up and called to him.

"Uncle David, I've looked so hard for you!" She burst into tears, and he did the only thing an uncle could do. He drew her into his arms, clenching his teeth against the fiery pain it caused him.

"Anne, my dear, I can't imagine how you ever found me. But—"

He looked beyond her and Mr. Reed, hoping to see his elder brother accompanying her. What he wouldn't give for a chat with Richard right now. His brother would know exactly what to do when one was pursued by an assassin and the woman one felt an attraction for turned out to be a blackguard.

Instead of his steady, practical brother, a grave young man hovered, watching Anne with obvious concern, but holding back to permit her a measure of privacy in the reunion. An older man, one with white hair and a long beard, stood in the door-way scowling, his face ruddy against the cottony beard. Whitey Pogue. What was the crusty old miner doing here with Anne?

"You must sit down and introduce me to your friend," David said. "Mr. Pogue and I are acquainted already." As an afterthought, he turned to the manager. "Mr. Reed, could we please have a tea tray and some refreshments sent up?"

"Of course, sir. I must say I'm delighted to find you looking so well. We were all worried when you didn't appear this morning. I hope you'll forgive me for opening your room to your niece."

"I'd expect you to do no less."

"Thank you. I'll go down to the kitchen and speak for a tray now."

Reed bustled from the room, dislodging Father Time from the doorway to do so.

Anne, meanwhile, had excavated a handkerchief from her reticule and was wiping her eyes.

"Sit down, dear," David said tenderly. "Tell me what has brought you here and how the family is doing."

"Oh Uncle David!" Her tears spurted out again, but she sat and arranged the skirts of her blue velvet riding habit. It looked as though the outfit had seen a great deal of the countryside lately, what with a film of dust over it and dried mud spatters along the hem. Even so, she looked more charming than any of the women he'd seen lately on the frontier—with the possible exception of Charlotte Evans, about whom he would reserve his opinion until he'd had more time to consider her precipitous flight on the stolen horse.

That thought brought him full circle to the white-bearded man, and David gazed at him. "I say, Whitey, was that your horse that was taken from the rail out front not ten minutes ago?"

Pogue's face went redder, and he blustered, "It most certainly was. That hussy jumped on him and took off without so much as a fare-thee-well. Took my saddle and all the stuff on it, too."

"And one of my dresses from Angelique in Paris, unless I'm mistaken," Anne said, "though I can't for the life of me understand how she got hold of it."

"How bizarre," David said.

Whitey turned his hat around in his hands, watching Anne for a cue. "I was about to go fetch the constable for Miss Anne anyhow, because she thought you'd been kilt or somethin'."

"Oh? I'm sorry I caused you such distress," David said. "As you can see, I'm alive and well. Mostly well, that is. Won't you gentlemen be seated, please?"

"How rude of me." Anne jumped up again. "Uncle David, it gives me great pleasure to introduce Daniel Adams. Dan has been a good friend and a pillar of strength to me since Independence, Missouri."

"Indeed." David eyed Adams openly. Anne was obviously indebted to the fellow. Was she in love with him? And did Richard know about him? This bore looking into.

Adams took a seat in an armchair and shuffled his long legs until he at last appeared to be comfortable. Whitey hesitated, sticking close to the door.

"That horse, Miss Anne. Shall I get the constable anyway, even though Mr. Stone ain't done in?"

"Oh, I. . ." Anne looked doubtfully toward Adams. "What do you think, Dan?"

"It wasn't our horse, Whitey," Dan said softly, as one would tell a child not to take the biggest biscuit. "Perhaps we should tell Constable Owens, but the man who owns the horse is the one he's got locked in the icehouse."

"Yes, that horse belongs to Mr. Hastings, like it or not," Anne said.

"Hastings?" David frowned at her. "Not Sam Hastings from my farm in Eugene?"

"The same, sir," Adams said. "He followed us here and tried to keep us from finding you."

David felt rather stupid as he stared at them. "But. . .whatever for?"

Anne looked uncertainly at Adams, then back to David. "We're not really sure, except that he tried to impersonate you when we arrived at your farm, and we think he was afraid you'd be angry when you found out."

"What?" David's jaw dropped, and he made himself close it. "I don't understand. Sam? Impersonating me?"

"It's quite a tale, sir," Adams said.

"Shall we send Whitey for the constable while you tell it?"

"That may be best," Anne said.

"I'll get right over there." Whitey turned to leave but whirled back for a moment. "Glad you ain't dead, David." He slipped out the doorway.

David put a hand to his forehead and laughed. "How did you link up with that old fellow? He's quite the character, you know."

"We gathered that," Anne said. "But he took us in when I was near freezing to death."

Adams shifted in his chair. "Yes. I truly believe Anne might not have survived the night in the mountains if we hadn't found Pogue's cabin. He was generous to a fault with his limited resources."

"That sounds like Whitey." David gazed down at his niece. "Now, suppose you begin at the beginning. What induced you to leave England?"

Anne's bittersweet smile told him her news would not all be pleasant. He reached for her hand.

"It's all right, my dear. Why don't you give me the worst of it right now? We'll fill in the gaps from there. Your parents—I hope they are well."

Her eyes shimmered as she raised her chin in resolution. "I'm afraid not. Mother's been gone three years now, and Father. . ." She drew in a ragged breath. "Father died about a year ago. I've been hoping to find you ever since."

"Oh, poor Anne. I'm so sorry to hear this." David felt the burning of tears in his eyes. How horrible for the girl to have lost both parents in quick succession. His own affection for Richard ran deep, and he'd been fond of Elizabeth as well, but he had all but cut the ties with his family these last twenty years. For Anne, however, the loss was incalculable.

"We sent letters." She swiped at a tear with her handkerchief. "Mr. Conrad, the solicitor, was quite diligent about it, but we couldn't learn where you'd gone when you left St. Louis. So I set out in March with Elise—do you remember Elise Finster?"

"Why, yes, I believe I do. She was employed at Stoneford, was she not? A pretty German girl."

"Yes indeed." Anne's smile broadened. "She'll be so pleased to hear you remember her. Anyway, she came with me. We found you'd gone to Independence."

"So you followed me there?"

"Yes. Again we were disappointed."

"My dear, dear girl. I'm so sorry I neglected to write and tell Richard where I'd gone. That was remiss of me. It was unconscionable."

"Well, we got a hint that you'd removed to Oregon, so we joined a wagon train."

He laughed involuntarily. "You and Elise?"

"Yes. It was arduous—and very educational."

"Quite." He chuckled again. "I can't quite take all this in. You and Miss Finster, driving an ox team?"

"We used mules. It was on the wagon train that we met Daniel and his brother."

David again surveyed Adams.

"Daniel and Hector were very helpful to us and became good friends," Anne said. "They took up farming near Champoeg."

Adams nodded gravely.

Anne continued, a little breathless, "And then Elise got married, and Daniel offered to accompany me to your farm."

"Elise married. . .who? Your brother?" David turned a questioning gaze on Adams.

"Oh no, sir, she married the wagon train scout, Eb Bentley," Adams said.

"Yes, and you'll like him, I'm sure," Anne said. "I do hope you'll be able to go to Eb's ranch in Corvallis with me and see Elise."

"Well, I. . .of course I'd like to see her. But today's events prompt me to think I should return to Eugene quickly and see what's going on at my property there. I've obviously stayed in the hills too long."

"Oh, the deputy marshal asked your neighbors to take care of your cattle," Anne said quickly. "That was after he arrested Sam Hastings for fraud. But he had to let him go. . . ." She shook her head. "I'm telling things all out of order. I'm sorry. But the thing that's most important, Uncle David, is the thing I most urgently need to tell you. The whole purpose for my journey, in fact."

"I. . .don't understand." What could be more important than telling him of Richard's death? And what urgent purpose would

retain its urgency for a year?

"It's. . ." She inhaled deeply and reached for his hand. "It's Uncle John, I'm afraid."

"John? What—"

It hit him suddenly, like an arrow out of nowhere. The thing he'd always considered so unlikely as to be impossible had happened.

"John is dead," he said.

The confirmation stared at him from her liquid brown eyes.

"Yes, dear uncle. In the Crimea, a year ago last summer. I'm afraid this means you are now earl of Stoneford."

CHAPTER 22

David rose and shoved his hands into the pockets of his trousers. He walked to the window overlooking the street and stood gazing out for a long moment.

Anne looked uneasily at Dan. The slight twitch of his lips was less than a smile, but still an offer of sympathy. They waited together, united in their knowledge. The pain and confusion that faced David now would bring some men to their knees.

The silence was broken by the desk clerk, who stood in the open doorway, bearing a laden tray. He puffed a bit, and his face gleamed red, with beads of sweat standing on his brow.

"Coffee and refreshments."

Dan jumped up and strode toward him. "Thank you. Let me take that."

The clerk passed the heavy tray to him with a sigh and closed his eyes for a second. "Thank you, sir. Oh, and I am to tell Mr. Stone that his horse is not in the stable."

David swiveled from the window, his eyebrows arched. "I beg your pardon."

"Your horse, sir. The stable man says it was missing this morning. He thought you'd gone out and taken him yourself, but apparently not. Did you? I mean, perhaps you left him somewhere."

David smiled. "Yes, that's exactly what happened. Thank you— you may pass the word that my horse is accounted for."

The clerk nodded but didn't move. David walked across the room and placed a coin in his hand.

"Thank you, sir." The clerk left then, and David closed the door.

"Anne, my dear, would you pour the— Oh, bother, he said coffee, not tea. Do you mind?"

"I can stand it." She leaned forward and arranged the four cups.

"I suppose Whitey will be back."

"And perhaps the constable with him," Dan said. "Shall I send for another cup?"

"Oh, let's wait and see what develops. He may have gone back to Mrs. Zinberg's for dinner. Uncle David? Milk and sugar?"

"I've gotten used to drinking it black since I'm so often in places where the accompaniments aren't available. Thank you." He took the cup and saucer she offered and sat down next to her.

"Daniel." Anne poured milk into his cup as she spoke then held it out to him.

Dan smiled. "Thank you."

Anne felt her face flush as she met his gaze. The simple fact that she knew how he liked his coffee and fixed it that way for him spoke volumes about their closeness. What must Uncle David think of them? She must make it clear very soon that she and Daniel had no romantic attachment.

"Care for a biscuit?" Dan didn't comment when she used the English word for cookies. When both men had chosen one from the plate, she set it down. Settling back on the settee with her cup, she eyed her uncle gravely.

"Now, what would you like to know first?"

"The peerage—the estate. If I decide not to claim it, what happens?"

"If you made a legal declaration to that effect, it would pass to Randolph."

"That fop?"

Anne cleared her throat, trying to keep a burst of laughter from escaping. "Uh, yes, that is what I'm told."

Uncle David shook his head. "I always thought you'd have brothers. And if not, why John. . ." His troubled blue eyes met her gaze. "I guess John has no heirs, or you wouldn't be here."

She smiled. "As much as I enjoy being in your company, I confess I should probably never have set out on this trip if the family had an heir safe at home. To my loss, I might add. Uncle, we live in a very small world at Stoneford."

"Yes. I found that out myself when I crossed the Atlantic. We make assumptions. . .however, to the point. Why should I go back?"

"But. . ." She'd never considered that he might not want to or that he would not consider it his duty to assume the earldom. "Do you love your life here so passionately?"

The bleak prospect of returning alone to England stretched before her. How could she go home without him? What life would she have there now? She couldn't imagine Merrileigh welcoming her at Stoneford, or that she would want to live under Randolph's protection. Even the cozy existence she'd imagined with Elise was no longer possible.

A sharp rap drew all their eyes to the door. Dan stood and walked to it.

"Who is it?"

"Constable Owens."

Dan opened the door and shook the man's hand. "Good to see you again, sir. Thank you for coming."

"Mr. Adams. I understand you and Miss Stone have another matter to discuss with me?"

"Yes, we do." Dan led him over to the settee.

David rose with some effort. Anne wondered at the grimace on his face. Was her uncle in pain? Perhaps that bloodstain was due to more than a shaving cut after all.

"This is Miss Stone's uncle, David Stone," Dan said.

"Oh sure, I've heard about you." Owens reached out to shake David's hand.

"No disrespect, sir," David said, "but I'm not shaking hands just now. I've got a bum shoulder."

"Oh. Sorry." Owens looked down at Anne. "Good day, Miss Stone."

"How do you do," she murmured.

The men sat down, and Owens said, "Now, what's this about a stolen horse? Whitey Pogue claimed some woman rode off with the roan he rode in on yesterday."

"Yes, that's true," David said. "I saw her jump on it from my window."

"But it didn't belong to Whitey," Dan added. "The man we brought to you—Hastings—had it."

"However," David said, "the horse actually belongs to me. I left it for Hastings to use when I left my farm in Eugene. Apparently he followed my niece over here in hopes of keeping her from finding me."

"Indeed?" Owens gazed at Anne with renewed interest.

"That appears to be true." Anne leaned toward Owens and spoke earnestly. "We told you yesterday how he'd stolen our horses in the hills and left us out there to wander in the cold and rain."

"Yes. You found Pogue's cabin and spent the night there."

Anne nodded. "Now it appears that Hastings wasn't acting alone. When we met him at Uncle David's farm, a woman was in residence with him."

"What?" David's eyebrows shot up. "I assure you, that was not the case when I left Eugene."

Anne reached over and patted his hand. "I'm sorry, Uncle. We haven't had time to tell you the full story yet. When we reached the farm, Sam Hastings pretended to be you, and this Millie woman served us dinner. I thought she was his wife at first, but now I have my doubts." She felt her cheeks color, but there was no varnishing the truth. "And when we arrived here this morning looking for you, here was this Millie coming up the stairs wearing one of my dresses that I had left in Eugene with friends. Somehow she's gotten hold of my luggage, I'm afraid."

"Yes," Dan added, "and she ran out of the hotel and jumped on Sam Hastings's horse and rode off."

David clapped a hand to his forehead. "Charlotte."

"Charlotte?" Anne asked.

"She told me her name was Charlotte Evans. I'm afraid I've been duped."

"Would you care to tell us about it, sir?" Owens asked.

"It's embarrassing to admit it, but I believe she set out to charm me. We dined together several evenings here at the hotel." His face hardened. "But there's more to it. It's not simply a couple of petty thieves hoping to lift my wallet or even take over my property.

Charlotte wanted to walk last night, and we went down to the river. We stood on the steamer dock for a minute or two, and I was shot at."

"Shot at? Oh Uncle David, that's horrible. Who would do that?"

"Not Sam Hastings," Dan said. "He was locked up in the icehouse."

Owens nodded. "I can testify to that."

David stood and with difficulty began to remove his jacket. "I almost sought you out last night, constable, but I decided to lie low and let the gunman think he'd succeeded."

Anne leaped up and helped him ease the sleeves of his jacket off. She gasped and stared at David's right arm. Beneath his shirt a bulk of extra fabric bulged, and a reddish brown stain had seeped into the white cloth of his shirt.

Dan jumped to his feet. "How bad is your wound, sir?"

"Not so bad I can't travel." David folded his jacket over the arm of the settee and resumed his seat. "One of the hotel staff brought a physician in last night to see to it, and I moved to another room so that I wouldn't be easily found if the assassin came here. That's why I wasn't here when you arrived this morning. My shoulder hurts, but I think I'll survive."

"The hotel staff?" Anne's eyes flashed in anger. "You mean they *knew* you were here all along and lied to us?"

"Only one," David said. "Don't blame Mr. Reed. We were very careful that he should not find out. You see, the man who tried to kill me is still out there, and I thought the fewer who knew my whereabouts the better."

"Probably true," Owens said, "but if I'd known, I could have gone looking for him. Do you know the man who shot you?"

David shook his head. "It was dark, and I saw him from a distance. But he was thin and agile. I think perhaps he was the same fellow I noticed loitering earlier. I wondered about him at the time—regular skeezicks of a fellow. I can't be sure he's the one who pulled the trigger, but if it was, he had dark hair and a mustache. Tall."

"A mustache?" Anne cried. She whipped around to look at Dan, and he nodded.

"That sounds like Peterson. Mr. Stone, I'm afraid there's more to this tale than you've heard yet." Her uncle eyed him levelly, and Dan felt suddenly that he was looking at a man of rare intelligence. David Stone might have chosen a simple life, but he was capable of running empires. Another small notion nagged him—should he address Stone as "my lord"? Dan shook off the thought. Here in America, people didn't bow to lords.

"All right, suppose we enjoy our coffee and you tell me about this Peterson." David chose a cookie from the serving plate.

"Mr. Owens, won't you join us?" Anne asked. We have an extra cup."

"Thank you, ma'am." Owens took a seat and accepted the coffee from her.

Dan sat down again. "I'll let Anne tell it, as she's privy to more details than I am."

"All right," she said. "Elise and I hired a man in Independence to drive our wagon for us. His name was Costigan. Later we found he'd pilfered your last letter to Father. I was carrying it with me on the wagon train. Costigan was also lazy. We fired him, and the wagon master ran him off the train. We puzzled over what his interest was in you. When we reached Oregon City, we found out. This other man, Peterson, had hired him to stop me from finding you. Peterson took a ship and arrived in Oregon about the time we did. He was asking about in Oregon City for you when we encountered him."

David sat in silence for a minute. He sipped his coffee and set the cup down. "Is this Peterson British?"

"No," Anne said, "but well you may ask. I have no proof, but I believe someone in England hired him to prevent you from claiming the peerage. Costigan was just a minion that Peterson hired. Peterson is the main one to be wary of—and even he is not the man behind the plot."

"So who is?" David asked.

Anne winced. "I don't know, but I have suspicions."

"My cousin Randolph?"

She let out a long sigh. "Who else would benefit from your death?"

David smiled grimly. "After I was shot last night, I heard the gunman say to Charlotte—that is, Millie, if what you've told me is correct—that he needed to find my body. I'd pitched into the river, you see."

"Oh Uncle David! How awful."

David squeezed her hand. "There, now. I'm sitting here with you, aren't I? The thing is, he told the woman he needed a death certificate and that I wasn't any good dead without it."

"So you're the fellow," Owens said with a mirthless laugh. "I got hauled out of bed about midnight by George Kidder. He's got a saloon down near the river. Said a fellow came in there yelling how a man had fallen into the river and they needed to find him and haul him out. George's place emptied out, and they had boats out, up and down the waterfront looking for this chap who'd gone in the drink. By the time I got there, folks were giving up and going back to their beer. I tried to locate the man who'd given the alarm at the start of it, and no one could point him out to me. I figured it was a mistake, or a cockeyed joke pulled by some inebriated lout. Either that or it was too late and the body would wash up downstream."

"How terrible," Anne said. "I'm glad you made it ashore, Uncle David."

"So am I, and that I eluded the man who started the whole thing." He shook his head. "I suppose it was that Peterson you mentioned. My question right now is whether or not Charlotte was in on it. She seemed shocked when he fired at me, but was she putting that on?"

"She's very good at dissembling," Anne said. "Daniel and I thought she might be the brains behind the impersonation after we'd met her and Sam Hastings. He didn't seem smart enough to think of it, much less carry it off."

David burst out laughing, and they all watched him, a bit uneasy. After a moment he sat back with a sigh. "Forgive me, but the

thought of Sam actually claiming to be me—it's preposterous."

"I doubt he could read half the books on the shelves in your farmhouse," Anne said. "By the way, was he supposed to be living in there?"

"Yes, I told him he could stay in the house and be comfortable. Didn't expect him to move a doxy in the minute my back was turned, though."

Anne's face flushed.

"I beg your pardon," David said.

"Well, sir," Dan ventured, "this whole thing has turned out to be quite serious. We thought Sam and Millie were amateur confidence artists hoping to get their hands on a bit of your money. You see, Anne had hinted at an inheritance from your brother Richard, and I suppose Millie picked up on that and thought she could lay hold of it—or some of it."

"That may be," Anne said. "And when she saw that it wasn't forthcoming in cash, she set out to find you and wriggle into your good graces."

"Is that what she was doing? Call me an idiot, but I was quite taken with her at first. She was pretty and had charming manners. Not timid, but a bit outspoken. And she dressed very well."

"In my clothes." Anne's lip curled. That point obviously rankled her as much as anything else.

"But when did this turn into a murder plot?" Dan asked. "They must have connected with Peterson somewhere."

"Yes," David said.

"He might have gone to them in Eugene and hired them the way he did Costigan," Anne said.

Owens stood. "We can speculate all day, folks, but it seems to me I'd best start looking for this Peterson chap. You don't think he stayed in this hotel?"

"He could have," David said.

"I'll ask. And if not, I'll start checking other hostelries."

"He didn't stay at Mrs. Zinberg's," Dan said as he got to his feet, "although Anne and I took Whitey there last night."

"And do I understand that you have Sam in custody now?" David leaned forward as if to rise, but Owens held out a hand to stop him.

"Don't get up, sir. Yes, I've got him locked in Fisher's icehouse until these two decide whether or not to press charges against him for horse stealing."

"I'd say not," Anne told him. "I mean, the horse is gone now, anyway. I'm sorry about that, Uncle David."

"It was a good horse, but if Charlotte's made off with it. . ." He shrugged. "I don't understand that. I thought she had a horse of her own stabled here."

"A quick getaway, I'd guess," Owens said. "And if she knew the horse and recognized it, she may have rationalized that it wasn't a crime to take it."

"Well, let's free Hastings, then," Dan said. "I'd hate for him to hang for this, even if he is a dimwitted scoundrel."

"Mr. Adams, would you mind going with me?" Owens asked. "Since you and Miss Stone brought Hastings in, I'd like you to sign a paper saying you've decided to drop the charge against him. That way I'm in the clear if anyone objects later to my letting him go."

"All right." Dan walked over to Anne. "You'll be all right for a short time with your uncle, won't you?"

"Of course."

David patted the pocket of his jacket. "I have a little Colt .44 insurance here, in case that fellow shows up again. And I feel bolder now that Constable Owens is on the lookout for him."

"I'll be back soon," Dan said. "Anne, I think it would be best if you lock the door while I'm gone." He didn't mean to alarm her, but with Peterson attempting to murder her uncle, he couldn't stress caution enough.

He walked over to the constable's house with him and waited impatiently while Owens got out the paperwork. He signed his name and put his hat on, declining Mrs. Owens's offer of coffee.

"I'll go right over and release Hastings," Owens said. "What do I tell him about that horse?"

Dan sighed. He wanted nothing more to do with Sam Hastings,

but he felt in some measure responsible. He had let Whitey ride the roan and hated to spoil the old man's pleasure in it, but he probably should have left the horse in Owens's care when they delivered Sam. The icehouse was at least half a mile away. He didn't want to leave Anne for very long with only her injured uncle to protect her.

"Tell him Millie took the horse."

"Millie."

Dan shook his head impatiently. "They said she was registered at the hotel as Charlotte Evans, but she was with Sam at David Stone's farm last week and called herself Millie. He knows her well, by the look of things. Just tell him. She had a brown horse in the hotel's pasture. Maybe he can use it until they meet up again." He had no doubt Sam and Millie *would* meet up again—if Millie saw a reunion as advantageous to herself.

"All right," Owens said, "but it's an odd way of doing things."

"This whole thing has been odd," Dan replied. He went outside and strode back to the hotel.

He passed quickly through the lobby, hoping to avoid Reed, the desk clerk, and anyone else who was curious about David Stone and the beautiful young woman who had come to see him. He took the stairs two at a time and reached the top of the second flight panting. At the door to the suite's sitting room, he paused and knocked.

"Anne, it's me."

A moment later the bolt was thrown and the door opened. Anne's eyes were bright and her cheeks scarlet.

"Dan, come in quickly. I saw him in the lobby."

"Who?

"That man. Peterson—he's here."

CHAPTER 23

Anne locked the door again and hurried across the carpet to the door of Uncle David's bedroom. Dan followed her, peppering her with questions.

"Are you sure? I didn't see him. Did he speak to you?"

"Yes, I'm sure, and no, he didn't speak. I went down to get some fresh water, and I saw him. He ducked into the dining room, but I am certain it was him. I couldn't mistake those calculating eyes anywhere, even if there are other men with mustaches like that."

Uncle David was leaning on the dresser, pulling clothing from the top drawer and tossing it into the valise Anne had set next to him on the floor.

"Adams, we've got to leave." He shoved the top drawer closed and tugged on the drawer pull for the second.

Anne stepped forward to help him open it. She suspected his wound was giving him more pain than he admitted to. "Here, Uncle David, let me do your packing. You sit down and rest."

"Should I go back and get Owens?" Dan asked.

"No time," David said. "We need to slip out of here before Peterson realizes it."

Anne threw Dan a glance trying to convey her concern. "Are our horses still tied out front?"

"Yes. They were when I came in. I could send word to the stable to have your uncle's horse ready."

David moaned.

"What is it?" Anne asked. "Are you ill?"

"No, I just remembered. I sent Captain home with a friend last night for safekeeping—or so I thought. I don't even know where Ernie lives, though."

"Ernie?"

His blue eyes took on a harassed air, and the fine lines at their corners deepened. "He's the cook, downstairs in the kitchen. He helped me last night—maybe saved my life. I thought I might stay in hiding longer, so I had him take Captain away. Didn't want the assassin who shot me to take him, or for Reed to sell him when I disappeared."

"I can go ask this Ernie where the horse is now," Dan said.

"Hold on," Anne said. "This Peterson is only one man. Why are we letting him scare us so badly?"

"Because he shot your uncle in cold blood and wants to finish the job?" Dan asked.

"We should be able to outsmart him. Besides, if we're going back to Eugene, we need to get the rest of our things from Mrs. Zinberg's house."

"True." Dan frowned. "If we rode back to Eugene on horseback, we'd be vulnerable to attack at any point along the way."

"But where else could we go?" Anne asked. "You and I don't need to go back to Eugene. We could go right to Corvallis. But Uncle David may want to get back to his farm." She turned uncertainly to her uncle. "You wouldn't be any safer at the farm than you are here."

"That's right," Dan said. "We need to deal with Peterson now. I'll bring Owens back. He went over to release Hastings. If we—"

"There'll be a steamship embarking in the morning for Portland and Oregon City," David said. "If we could get on it without Peterson's knowledge, we could get away without riding through the wilderness where he could ambush us. And much as I hate to admit it, I'm not sure I could stay in the saddle for two or three days."

"You're not really fit to travel." Anne laid her hand across his forehead. "You feel overly warm right now. I think we should fetch the doctor."

"He said he'd come by today," David said. "Of course, if he goes to that room where I was last night, he won't know where I've gone."

He took a step toward the connecting door and staggered. Dan jumped forward and grabbed his left arm. "Sir, you need to sit down.

It's all well and good to carry out heroics when you're healthy, but this is not the time. You need bed rest and a doctor to care for that wound."

"The man is ruthless," David said, but he let Dan lead him to the bed and sank down on the edge with a low moan. "Perhaps you're right, but. . .I can't bear to think of Peterson getting his way."

"He won't come and attack you in this room while Daniel and I are with you," Anne said.

"But he's waiting for me to leave the room. He's frustrated that he didn't get me last night. He might shoot me in a crowd now. He may be willing to take that risk if it's the only way he can get to me."

Anne watched Daniel. He seemed deep in thought. "What do you think, Dan?" she asked softly.

"Well, I think your uncle is right about Peterson's intentions and his resolve. But we should be able to stop him. And if Owens can't catch him, we can at least find a way to stay safe here until David is strong enough to travel."

"Perhaps the steamer is the best idea," Anne said, though she remembered with apprehension her seasickness on the voyage from England. "He wouldn't expect that."

"I don't want to lose Captain," David said.

"And I don't want to lose Bailey again." Anne placed her hands on her hips. "Dan, why don't you go down and speak to the cook and find out where Uncle David's horse is? And perhaps you could inquire discreetly about taking horses on the steamboat?"

"I'll see what I can find out, but I hate to leave you here with that scoundrel in the building."

"Just go down and see Ernie," David said, easing back onto the pillow. "Then we can decide what to do. And go down the back stairs."

"Where are they?" Dan asked.

"Go out the door and turn left. Past the main stairway, and all the way to the end of the hall, on the left again. They go right down into the kitchen. Ernie should be there."

Anne went over and lifted David's feet and slid them up on top

of the quilt. "You rest. I'll finish packing while Dan goes." She nodded at Dan and he slipped into the sitting room. She followed.

He'd paused by the hall door, waiting for her.

"Lock it behind me. I'll speak to you when I come back."

"All right," she said. "Don't let that monster see you."

Dan shrugged. "He may have seen me already. I didn't notice him when I came in, but I was avoiding looking directly at anyone. I didn't want Reed or one of his lackeys to stop me and ask questions."

"All right. Just hurry back."

He left, and she bolted the door and tiptoed back into the bedroom. David appeared to be sleeping, with his left arm across his eyes. She wished she had a blanket to put over him. No one had learned what happened to the missing bedclothes, but she suspected Ernie had carried them to her uncle's new room the night before.

Quickly she emptied the dresser and armoire, folding his clothing into the valise. He had a variety of clothes—well-worn work clothes and presentable dinner wear. The nicest coat and trousers weren't high-toned formal clothing, but nice enough for any restaurant in Scottsburg or St. Louis, for that matter.

Dan was gone a good ten minutes. When he returned, she was waiting near the door.

"I found Ernie," Dan said. "He's happy to hear that Mr. Stone is feeling better but was dismayed when I told him you'd seen Peterson lurking about. He doesn't know the man, but I told him it was the same person Mr. Stone believed shot him. Ernie took me to the door between the kitchen and the dining room and let me peek out at the diners."

"And?"

"He's there all right, eating his luncheon. Brazen of him, don't you think?"

"Decidedly." Anne drew him further into the sitting room but kept her voice low. "I think Uncle David is asleep. I've packed all his clothing, but I haven't gone over this room for personal items. Dan, what shall we do?"

"Oh, that's the other good thing. Ernie says he can bring

Captain—your uncle's horse—around to the inn's stable tonight. I was thinking that perhaps the three of us could get away to Mrs. Zinberg's and spend the night there. In fact, we might smuggle you out through the kitchen quite soon, and you could ride out to her house and tell her I'll come later and bring your uncle."

"What would you and Uncle David do in the meantime?"

"I'd stay here with him until the doctor sees his arm, and I'd also send an alert to Owens. Maybe he could pick up Peterson on some pretext or other and hold him until we get away."

"And ride for Eugene? I really don't think Uncle David could bear the strain or the jolting."

Dan gritted his teeth. "Well, this Ernie chap is very knowledgeable. He doesn't think we could take our horses on the steamer. But he says we could get a bigger boat in Reedsport and take the horses on board if we paid extra. He said boats leave there for the Columbia quite often."

Anne considered that. Uncle David would be sailing farther from his farm, but if she could get him to Eb and Elise's ranch, he could recover in peace. Elise would help her care for him, and she could return Bailey to Rob Whistler.

"I think I like that plan, though I confess I'm prone to sickness when at sea."

David awoke in a haze. Dr. Muller sat in a chair beside the bed, leaning over him, and was unbuttoning his shirt.

"Sorry to disturb you, Mr. Stone. I'm glad your niece is here to help you. But she tells me you intend to travel soon, and I'm not sure you're ready. Can I have a look at your arm, please?"

David tried to sit up. His whole body was sore, but his arm felt like molten lead and his head throbbed. He clenched his teeth and tried again, letting out a soft moan.

"Let me help." A young man stepped around the bed to the other side. It took David a moment to place him. Anne's friend. . . Adams, that was it. He wondered if Adams hoped to marry Anne

then slapped himself mentally. Of course he did! The young pup was besotted with her, though he managed to keep a rather cool exterior. But he'd followed her hundreds of miles for what? A bushel of trouble? No, he was in love with Anne, no question.

Between Muller and Adams, they got his shirt off without making him sit up, but the pain in his arm now eclipsed everything else.

Muller handed something to someone else. Anne.

"I want him to take a teaspoon of this dissolved in water. Can you fix it, please, Miss Stone?"

"Yes." She left the room, for which David was grateful.

The doctor deftly untied the strips of cloth holding the bandages in place. When he pulled them off, a different pain screeched up David's arm.

"Well, now, that looks as though an infection is starting." Muller shook his head. "I'll have to cleanse it again. I'm sorry, sir."

"I think we'd better forget about riding out of here tomorrow," Adams said.

"I should think so," the doctor replied. "Now, don't you worry, sir. I've got your niece fixing something that will help with the pain. I shan't poke around too much until you've got that in you."

Dan stood in the hallway talking to the hotel manager and Constable Owenss.

"I'll check all around town and see if I can find out where this so-called gentleman is staying," Owens said. "Meanwhile, Mr. Reed, if he's seen hanging about this hotel, you call for me, and I'll come run him in."

"Yes," Reed said. "We must protect our guests. Mr. Adams, I assure you, if I'd known someone meant to harm Mr. Stone, I'd have called in the constable at once. And to think the gunman was right here in our dining room this morning."

"Don't you fret," Owens said. "I'll raise a posse. We'll scour this town."

"Oh, and you'll see to the extra rooms for Miss Stone and me?" Dan said.

"Certainly, sir." Mr. Reed bowed slightly and turned away.

"Well now, gents." Up the stairs came Whitey Pogue. "You still here, Adams?"

"Whitey, I thought you went back to your cabin," Dan said.

The old man lifted his hands and shoulders in an elaborate shrug. "Got no horse now. It's too far to walk this afternoon. Reckon I'll wait until morning."

"Well, if you don't mind sharing, you can bunk in with me here tonight. I'm going to move our stuff from the boardinghouse so that Miss Stone can be nearer her uncle."

"Sounds dandy," Whitey said. "They got good, big rooms here—bigger'n my cabin, hey?"

"Yes," Dan said with a smile. "What did Sam Hastings say when you told him about Millie taking the roan?" Dan asked Owens.

The constable snapped his fingers. "Meant to tell you, but all this talk about an assassin drove it plum out of my head. He said that Millie person is his sister."

Dan stared at him. "His sister? They surely don't look alike."

"Well, half sister, he told me. He said he guessed it was all in the family, and if she took his horse, he could take hers. He set off for the hotel's stable, and that's the last I saw of him. Didn't see any reason to stop him."

Dan shook his head. "Wait until I tell Anne. We misjudged those two, at least on that score." He looked about the hallway and the stair landing. "I do hate to leave Anne here alone. Perhaps I should go get our luggage from Mrs. Zinberg while the doctor is still here."

"I could fetch it," Whitey said. "Reckon I could get everything using your horse, Dan'l?"

"You fellows work it out. I'm going to get some men together and start looking for Peterson." Constable Owenss strode toward the stairs.

Dan decided Whitey might be safer transporting the baggage than he would be, since Peterson knew him by sight. He gave the old

man plenty of money to cover their bill with Mrs. Zinberg and a note from Anne to the widow, detailing the packing of her belongings.

He returned to the bedroom in time to help the doctor clean up and settle the patient comfortably.

"He'll be out for some time," Muller said. "I gave him a hefty dose of laudanum. The fool thinks he can get up and take on thugs and ride off to Eugene. Well, he needs to stay put for at least two more days. I'll come by first thing in the morning and look at that arm again, but if the infection spreads, he may be here a long time."

Anne refused to leave her uncle's bedside, so Dan went downstairs and asked for a tray for her. He'd had no lunch—only a couple of cookies off the tea tray, but the dining room was deserted and the desk clerk told him he couldn't be served until five o'clock. When the clerk wasn't looking, he ducked through the dining room and peeked into the kitchen.

Ernie hovered over the huge black stove, stirring pots, and a boy of about sixteen sat on a stool peeling a mound of potatoes.

"Mr. Adams," Ernie said, looking up in surprise. "I hope Mr. Stone is all right."

"He's got a slight infection in his wound."

"Dear me. I hope it's not serious." Ernie shook his head.

"I'm not sure. The doctor seemed concerned, but I don't think he wanted to worry Miss Stone too much. And speaking of the lady, she's had no luncheon. Well, none of us has. They said at the desk that we're too late—"

"Nonsense. I can make you some sandwiches. How many people?"

"Two, I guess." It was probably safe to assume Mrs. Zinberg would feed Whitey something when he got to her house, and David would most likely sleep the afternoon away. "Just Miss Stone and me."

"Mudge, get some pie and a couple of apples," Ernie said to his helper. The boy laid down his paring knife and hurried to obey.

"We're taking rooms here until Mr. Stone is able to travel," Dan said.

"Probably best." Ernie swiftly sliced a loaf of bread and set about smearing it with mustard. "Anytime you want a tray, just let me know."

Dan sat down on a stool near the stove, glad to have found an ally in Ernie.

Millie loaded a tray with a coffeepot, two dishes of venison stew, and half-a-dozen slices of pie and shoved open the door to the dining room. She quickly delivered the stew and began making rounds about the dining room, refilling coffee mugs and selling pie to men who'd thought they would skip dessert.

Now that her prospects of marrying a rich English gent had fizzled and she no longer feared discovery by Anne Stone and Dan Adams, she'd figured Elkton might be a good place for her to pause. She was tired of running and scrambling and hiding. Andrew Willis was happy to have her back, and word of her return spread swiftly through the town. The dining room was packed for every meal, with freighters and miners forming a line outside while they waited for tables to free up.

With Millie in charge, Andrew had left on a three-day trip to Eugene to lay in more supplies. Millie's first actions had been to hire a waitress and a dishwasher. She met the waitress, Virginia, halfway around the dining room.

"You got any more fried chicken?" Virginia asked. "I've got four more customers who are hankerin' for it."

"I'll go dish it up." Millie handed her the coffeepot.

"Send Stubby out to collect dirty dishes, too," Virginia said. "I don't have time. The customers are still three deep outside waitin' to get in."

Millie hurried back to the kitchen. Where were all these men coming from? She supposed a lot of them were headed to the goldfields farther south.

"Stubby! Go pick up the empty dishes. Quick now." The grizzled man whom she'd hired for the job hated to carry the heavy trays of crockery, but Millie had warned him he'd have to during

their busy times. If he couldn't do the work, she'd hire someone younger. That had shut him up.

She put the money she'd collected for pie carefully into the two-gallon crock Andrew used for a cash box and shook her head. Andrew was such a trusting fellow. If she were of a mind to steal all his receipts for the day, it would be easy. But she'd promised herself she wouldn't do that.

She wasn't exactly sure what had happened to her between the Miner's Hotel in Scottsburg and here, but something was going on inside her. She'd decided first off to quit making her living by pilfering merchandise and cadging meals from men. Maybe it was the stolen dress that started her thinking she'd like to be honest. Anne Stone lived the way Millie wanted to live—but she'd never lifted a man's wallet and fled town in disgrace. Millie wanted what Anne had—dignity. Respect. Dare she think that someday she might attain self-respect?

Two nights ago when she'd checked into a boardinghouse at Andrew's insistence, she'd unpacked the small bag she'd gotten away with. David Stone's Bible and cuff links were in the bottom of it, along with her lip rouge and frilly garters. A wave of shame had swept over her—a rare occurrence in her lifetime. She had stolen a man's Bible, of all things. Was it for sentimental reasons?

She'd opened the cover and seen "David Stone, Esq." written in neat script. Esq. Esquire, she supposed, but what did that mean, anyway?

Out of curiosity, she'd sat down on her lumpy cot and flipped through the leather-bound little book. The tiny print made her bring the lamp closer, but she discovered several underlined places in the text. She browsed through the book, skimming the lines that he'd underscored. It made little sense to her—random thoughts that she supposed he'd found interesting. At last she'd laid it aside and gone to bed, exhausted from riding half the day and cooking the other half. Her last thought before drifting off to sleep had been that someday she ought to return the Bible. And the cuff links. And maybe even the ten dollars she'd stolen from his room. No, maybe not that. He would never miss it.

Now the thought came to her again as she arranged fried chicken and heaps of potatoes and squash on the heavy plates. She had stolen, and she ought to return the money—that and the pie money she'd taken from this restaurant a week or two ago. She owed Andrew five dollars. He'd never realized it and had gladly taken her back to work for him. He knew he was better off with her here in the kitchen, and she would make a pile of money for him. So why was her conscience bothering her about it?

Stubby dragged in, sagging under the weight of his laden tray. "Miss Virginia says hurry up wid the chicken dinners."

Millie arranged the plates carefully on a tray so that they wouldn't slide and lifted it to her shoulder. She shoved the door open and swished into the dining room with a big smile on her face. Men lingered for dessert when a pretty woman served them with a cordial manner. That was why she'd hired Virginia—a pretty farmer's daughter—over the more experienced older women who'd applied.

She caught Virginia's eye across the room, and the waitress pointed to the table of men waiting for their dinners. Millie wended through the close tables, her skirts brushing the men's chairs.

"Good stew, Charlotte," one of them called.

She smiled. "Thank you kindly."

"You can come cook for me anytime you get tired of this place," another said as she passed.

"Thanks—I'll keep it in mind."

She reached the corner of the room and lowered the tray to the edge of the table, balancing it there while she set off the plates one at a time.

"Mmm, that looks downright edible, sweetheart," one of the customers said.

"Enjoy it." She smiled at them all without making eye contact with any of them. "Save room for some of my walnut cake." She lowered the tray so that it was flat against her side and headed back toward the kitchen door.

"Millie?"

She whirled toward the familiar voice.

"Millie! Can't believe I found ya!" Sam shoved back his chair and stood, blocking her way. "I shoulda known nobody could make such good biscuits but you."

"Thank you. I'm working here now." She glanced at the other two men sharing his table and didn't like the look of them. Friends, or was Sam just sharing a table with strangers in a crowded restaurant? One had thick, dark hair and black eyes that raked over her. Had she seen him before? She looked away.

"Really?" Sam said. "You took a job? How long for?"

"I don't know yet. I might stay here. I like it, and my boss is real happy to have me cooking for him."

"Hey, Charlotte, how about some more gravy?" a man at a near-by table called.

Virginia sidled up to her. "I've got six more orders. You need to send this fella packing and get into the kitchen."

Millie bristled. "Don't tell me what to do, Virginia Shaw!" She looked back at Sam. "We close around nine o'clock. If you come back sober, I'll talk to you then."

Sam blinked at her guilelessly. "Sure, Millie. I can do that."

"Millie?" Virginia asked, peering at her vulturelike.

Millie whirled and headed for the kitchen, squeezing between the tables and laughing at the men's remarks.

Once in the kitchen, she stood for a moment breathing deeply. She hadn't counted on meeting up with Sam again, at least not this soon. She'd only been here a few days and hadn't really gotten herself established yet. As a good cook in high demand, she could earn a high wage here. She could be comfortable at the boardinghouse and put away a nest egg without having to do anything illegal. Andrew Willis would pay her well as long as she produced a lot of good food quickly.

Not only that, but when she'd taken Old Blue to the livery-man to see if he'd board her horse for her at a reasonable rate, he'd not only agreed at good terms, he'd done a little flirting with her.

Millie had the feeling the pick of the men of Elkton was hers, if she wanted it, to say nothing of all the miners and freighters passing through.

But Sam didn't fit into that plan. He'd come to her rescue a couple of months ago when she was down and out. Flat broke with no place to live, she was lower than the bottom of a mine shaft. She'd tracked him down at the farm where he worked and happened on a convenient circumstance. Sam's boss was away and had let him live in the farmhouse and tend to things while he was gone. Sam had invited Millie to come and cook for him temporarily. She'd moved in and taken over the household, bullying her brother into doing whatever she wanted and taking advantage of David Stone's supplies and the spending money he'd left Sam.

Now she felt a little guilty about that. Oh, it was far from the worst thing she'd ever done—and those things she felt even guiltier about. But she didn't want to connect with Sam again for any length of time. It would be too easy to fall back into his lazy attitude and her thieving ways. That was what she'd been—a thief. No denying it. And she wanted to change, to become something better. She could see now that she'd have to take up an entirely different lifestyle to do that. Elkton offered her a chance, and she was determined to make a go of it.

"Hey, you better check them pies," Stubby said.

As Millie shook herself out of her reverie and strode toward the stove, Virginia poked her head in at the door.

"Here's my orders—got nine now. Six for stew, three for fried chicken."

"Don't know if I've got that much stew."

"Better make more. They're still coming in the door."

Millie glanced at the clock on the shelf over the flour bin. "It's after eight o'clock. Just tell 'em they're too late and we're out."

Virginia screwed up her face like she'd been eating a sour pickle. "You got enough for these orders?"

Millie set a stack of soup plates on her worktable near the stove and started ladling stew into them. "Two, three, four. . . There's only enough for four."

"How much chicken?"

"Maybe six—your three and three more. After that we're down to pie and gingerbread."

Virginia trounced out the door without commenting on "Charlotte's" other name.

Somehow Millie made it through the next hour. When she was done cooking and dishing up food, she helped Virginia serve coffee and pie. They both carried heaps of dirty dishes to Stubby. At nine she put the CLOSED sign on the door, and at last the dining room began to empty. Sam and the dark-haired man sat at their table long after they'd finished eating, drinking cup after cup of coffee. Millie wished they would leave. She busied herself in the kitchen, tidying up and setting out what she'd need to start cooking lunch tomorrow.

She'd drawn the line when Andrew urged her to cook breakfast, too. Two meals a day was plenty, she'd told him. He'd work her to death if she'd let him. She'd worked from ten to ten the past two days, and she would soon be exhausted. As soon as Andrew returned, she'd have to sit down with him and thrash out some more favorable terms. And if he wanted to serve breakfast, he'd have to cook it himself or hire a morning cook.

Virginia hung up her apron, stretched, and said, "G'night. See you tomorrow."

"Is my brother still out there?" Millie asked.

"Who?"

"The fellow who wanted to speak to me."

"He's your brother? I didn't know. I tossed him out, along with the other stragglers. Sorry."

"Doesn't matter," Millie said. "You about done, Stubby?"

"Almost."

Millie picked up a dish towel and helped him dry the last rack of plates. At last he was ready to go, and she let him out the back door and locked it behind him. Then she took the money from the crock and put it in a cupboard with a lock. She got her coat, blew out the lanterns, went out the back door, and locked it behind her.

It was cold outside, and she pulled her coat closed. Walking around the corner of the building, she headed for the street and her boardinghouse. Two men detached themselves from the shadows at the front of the restaurant. Millie's heart pounded, but she stood still, realizing that Sam and his companion had waited for her.

"You done for the night?"

"Yeah, Sam. Where you staying?"

"We's camping down the creek."

She eyed the shadowy form behind him, sure it was the dark-haired man who'd been at his table. "Who's we?"

"Me and Lucky and a couple other fellas." He jerked his head toward the other man, and suddenly Millie remembered where she'd seen Lucky before. He'd been a chum of her husband, James's—one Millie hadn't cared to get to know too well.

"You wanted to talk," she said to Sam, ignoring Lucky. "You can't come to the place I'm staying this late."

"Can't we talk here? I was hoping I could wait for you inside, but that Virginia girl said we had to leave."

"What do you want to talk about?"

"I'm going with Lucky and the others. I want to know if you want to come with us."

Millie frowned. "Come with you where?"

"We're not sure yet, but Lucky thinks maybe over Fort Boise way."

"What do you want to go there for?" Millie's suspicions grew wings and began to fly.

"Looks like as good a place as any," Lucky growled.

"And nobody knows us there," Sam added.

"So?"

"Lucky thought your cooking was tops. He and the boys think it'd be terrific if you wanted to come see to us."

"What does that mean, 'see to you'? You want me to cook and clean house?"

"Well, we don't have a house," Sam said.

"Mighty good eats, ma'am," Lucky said. "Your brother says you have other talents, too."

"Other talents? What are you talking about?" She turned her

fiercest glare on Sam.

"You know," Sam said in soft, wheedling tones. "You're slicker'n anyone I ever saw at liftin' a wallet."

She stared at him, then at his shadowy companion. "No."

"Aw, come on, Millie. I told them about you, and they're counting on you. We'll need decent meals if we're going to make our living as road agents."

"Road—" She looked from Sam to Lucky and back. "No. Absolutely not. I'm done with crime, Sam. This is it right here for me. I'm staying here and working at the restaurant. I'm going to make an *honest* living. So forget it. And don't come around here bothering me again."

"Sounds like your sister needs a little persuasion." Lucky pushed past Sam and stood less than a foot in front of her, holding her stare. "Me and the boys'll take real good care of you, ma'am. That's a promise."

Millie ran her hand down her skirt until she could feel the comforting shape of the derringer she'd bought in Scottsburg. "No thank you, Mr. Lucky. That's final."

She was afraid he would insist, but Sam edged around him. "Come on, Millie. Please? We won't make you do anything you don't want to."

She strongly doubted that. "No, Sam."

"Then at least give Old Blue back. The constable in Scottsburg said you took him."

"Why should I?"

"Because Blue is my horse. And my stuff was tied to the saddle, too."

Millie almost protested, but the guilt that had plagued her for the last few days won out. If they got down to brass tacks, Old Blue belonged to David Stone. Did she want to start her new life with a stolen horse?

"What are you riding?"

"That horse you had—the plug of a brown mare."

Fair enough, Millie decided. She'd paid the asking price for the mare, and that was money she'd earned. Vixen wasn't as good a mount as Old Blue, but Millie didn't plan on fleeing the authorities again anytime soon.

"All right, I'll take Vixen back."

"What? You named your horse?"

"Oh, be quiet, Sam. Where is she?"

"Yonder." He jerked his head toward the hitching rail in front of the restaurant.

Millie sighed. "Wait here and I'll go get Blue for you."

"We might as well come with you," Lucky said, low and definite. Millie had a feeling not many people said no to Lucky.

She took a deep breath. "No. Stay right here. The lady I'm rooming with doesn't want to see any men hanging around. Sam, you wait here if you want to trade."

She walked out to the street and looked back. The two men were nearly invisible in the shadow of the building. At least they'd stayed put. She wouldn't trust that Lucky from here to the porch pillar. Above her, the sky was clear for once. The stars glittered like tiny lamps, lighting her way to the boardinghouse. Instead of going in, she walked around to the barn and went inside. Blue and the horse that belonged to the couple that owned the place whickered. Millie went to Blue's stall and patted his nose.

"I'm sorry, boy, but I've got to give you back to Sam. You were good for me." She put the saddle on him with Sam's bedroll still tied to it, bridled him, and led him out of the barn.

She had the assurance that this was right. She was giving the stolen horse back to Sam. From now on, settling Blue's ownership would be between him and David. Maybe if she started doing small good things, she could eventually become a good person. In fact, she would put a dollar out of her pay in Andrew's crock. If she did that every week for five weeks, she'd have paid back the pie money she took from him the first time she'd worked for him, and he would never notice. That would add to the "good" side of her behavior ledger. And she would read some more in the Bible tonight. What could be more virtuous than that?

She ignored the little guilt gnome that tugged at her sleeve to remind her that the Bible was stolen, too.

Back at the restaurant, Lucky and Sam emerged from the shadows. Sam untied Vixen and walked toward her. Before she could say anything, Lucky stepped up beside Sam.

"Your brother and I talked it over, ma'am, and we think you need to come with us."

CHAPTER 24

Millie's heart sank and hit bottom. "He's my half brother, and it doesn't matter what *you* think. I'm staying here."

Lucky's hand snaked to his hip, and he drew his revolver so fast she barely had time to shove her hand in her pocket.

"Mount up, Millie." His voice had a steel edge now. Sam hung back, looking worried but saying nothing.

Millie's pulse raced. "Give me Vixen," she said to Sam.

He moved forward and held out the ends of the mare's reins. She put Blue's leathers in his other hand, at the same time pulling out her derringer.

She whirled on Lucky, who stood only five feet away.

"I'm pretty good with this little peashooter, mister. If you still want your friends to call you 'Lucky' after tonight, you'd best mount up and ride out of here."

His eyes narrowed. Sam gasped, but Millie didn't spare him a glance, knowing Lucky could get the upper hand quickly if she let anything distract her. They stood for a moment glaring at each other over their guns' muzzles.

Lucky laughed softly. "She's a hard one, all right, Sam. Who'd have thought it to look at her? All right, Miss Millie, you win this round, but I won't forget it."

"Neither will I," she said.

Sam gulped and held out the mare's reins. "If you ever need a friend, Millie, come find me. And we'd still like to have you cook for us."

"Don't count on it." She took Vixen's bridle and turned the mare to shield her from Lucky's view as she led her away. After a few steps she heard their horses moving and looked back. Both men were mounting. She hustled Vixen along to the corner and got off the main road before they passed.

After two days of bed rest, David seemed stronger. Anne had hardly left the suite, sitting with her uncle's pistol in her lap whenever Dan went out. The cook, Ernie, came every day to see how David was doing, and Dr. Muller came at least once a day to examine his wound and monitor his progress. Whitey, seeing no benefit to wandering about town when he had no money to spend, had left them to hike back to his claim.

On the third day, David awoke grumpy.

"How long do you expect me to lie in bed?" he asked Anne. "Bring me some clothes. I want to get up and go down to breakfast with you."

Anne rose and went to his dresser, where she'd put the clothing she'd unpacked after they'd realized he couldn't travel. "I don't think you're quite ready for two flights of stairs, but perhaps we can have our breakfast at the table in the next room."

She laid out his smallclothes, trousers, and shirt.

"Where's my razor? I want to shave."

She smiled at that. "Get dressed first, Uncle David. Call to me when you're ready, and we'll see. Oh, and don't tumble off the bed trying to put your socks and shoes on. I can help you with that."

"I'm not an infant."

"Indeed." He sounded like an earl in that moment—one whose dignity had been questioned. She checked the water pitcher and went into the sitting room, closing the connecting door.

Dan's distinctive knock came at the hall door, and she let him in.

"Owens and his men haven't found a trace of Peterson. Once he left his boardinghouse, he simply disappeared."

"He probably rode out of town quietly that night." Anne glanced toward the bedroom door. "Uncle David is dressing. I must stay in case he needs help, but we'd like breakfast here. Have you eaten?"

"Not yet. I'll go down and speak for it."

"Thank you. We all need to eat a good meal. If the doctor approves, we may be able to leave today."

"Do you think so?" Dan asked.

"I don't think we'll be able to keep Uncle David down much longer. He wants to shave."

"He feels like a sitting target here," Dan said. "Do you really think Peterson would stick around?"

"You saw his persistence. He followed my uncle thousands of miles. I don't think he'll give up just because Owens is looking for him."

"I suppose you're right. Personally, I feel safer in here with walls around us and an officer of the law nearby. Well, I'll go down and ask for room service."

"Actually, I wouldn't mind a bit of exercise," she said. "If you don't mind staying here and playing valet if needed, I can order breakfast and then stop by my room to freshen up."

"All right. Just be careful, Anne."

She smiled. "I will. Did you want anything in particular this morning?"

"Eggs, maybe, and some flapjacks."

She went out and listened for the bolt to slide, then went down the stairs. At the second-floor landing, she peered over the railing and surveyed the lobby before continuing on her way. Peterson *must* be gone. At any rate, he wouldn't come back here where people would recognize him. But would he hire someone else to keep watch for him? The memory of Thomas G. Costigan on the wagon train brought an uneasy shiver. Anyone she met in the hotel might be in Peterson's pay, ready to pass the word to him when David left his quarters.

Anne had barely left when the bedroom door opened and David came out, walking slowly toward the table and chairs near the window. Dan rose and stepped toward him.

"Let me help you, sir."

"Thanks, but I need to practice using my legs. Can you help me get set up to shave, though?"

"Are you certain you want to do that?"

"Completely. But I'm not sure I can stay on my feet long enough to do it or have a steady hand if I'm swaying back and forth. Maybe you could put the basin of water and soap and razor on the table out here and prop up a small mirror so I can see what I'm doing."

"I'll get the one hanging over your washstand. Have a seat."

Dan waited until David had lowered himself with a sigh onto one of the chairs. Quickly he gathered the things he'd asked for from the bedroom, along with a couple of towels.

"Anne went down to order breakfast," he said as he reentered the sitting room. "By the time you're finished, it will probably be here."

Anne returned fifteen minutes later, wearing a fresh gown and with her hair cascading down the back of her neck in a most becoming style. Dan didn't know how she did it, staying up most of the night in her uncle's sitting room in case he needed her, but she managed to look so beautiful each day that she took his breath away. How he would go on without her when they finished this odyssey and she shooed him back to the farm, he couldn't imagine. He'd have to insist she sleep this afternoon. If David wanted to leave when his niece hadn't had a full night's sleep in days, he'd put his foot down.

An hour later, with breakfast done, the doctor came with an ebony cane for David to use to steady himself and took him into the bedchamber to check his wound. Anne and Daniel waited in the sitting room. Anne sat still on the settee with her hands folded in her lap while Dan paced from the window to the door and back, over and over. He wished he could remain as peaceful as she did. The confinement chafed on him, as did the uncertainty of their situation.

At last she broke the silence. "Dan, I know you want to get back to the farm and help your brother. Why don't you leave me in Uncle David's care? You've seen how much better he is."

Dan wheeled from the window and strode over to the settee. He sat down beside her and looked earnestly into her eyes.

"I can't do that. For all we know, that killer is still out there, just waiting for your uncle to leave these rooms. I wouldn't walk out and leave you in such a perilous situation." She lowered her eyelids, and he regretted speaking so frankly. "Besides, what makes you think I'd rather be puttering around the farm with Hector than here with you?"

Anne's eyes flew open wide for a moment then she looked away. "You didn't plan to be gone so long."

"No, but nothing could make me happier than staying by your side. I could wish the circumstances were less trying—that your uncle was well and that you could both travel on and resume your lives. But that would mean separation. Dearest Anne, please don't think ill of me for mentioning it. I've tried not to speak of this too often, because I know you don't share my sentiments."

"I won't say I do not care for you, Dan."

He was silent for a moment, unwilling to trust his voice. He sat back and cleared his throat. "That at least is a comfort. But I'm not sure you mean to give me hope."

"Hope is such a fragile thing. But I've discovered it fluttering inside me, even as I failed time after time to find my uncle." She started to move then hesitated. He eyed her cautiously, and at last she reached over and touched his hand. "Your presence has meant a great deal to me. In fact, your solid determination to finish the quest for the simple reason that it mattered to me has worked a slow, quiet course in my heart, until I find the prospect of parting company with you distressful." She looked away and whispered, "I believe we need hope. All the hope we can get. It's precious, don't you think?"

He turned his hand and clasped hers, not too firmly lest she pull it away. His heart thudded. "Precious indeed. Thank you."

The bedroom door swung open.

"Well, I can't say I approve," Dr. Muller said as he entered, "but Mr. Stone insists on traveling. His wound looks better—not so red and swollen. I believe we've got the infection licked. I'd rather see him rest a few more days, though."

Dan glanced at Anne. "Perhaps we could persuade him that Miss Stone needs rest herself before we move on."

"I'm fine," Anne said. "The fact that he's better gives me strength.

I'm willing to leave now if that is what he wants."

Dan nodded. "I can check on the steamers and see when the next one leaves."

David insisted on paying Dr. Muller generously, in case they did not meet again. Dan went down the stairs with the doctor and parted from him on the street. He strolled at a quick pace to the waterfront. No large boats were docked, so he ambled down to where two men were stacking crates on the end of the largest dock.

"No steamers today?"

"Should be coming in this afternoon," one of the men said.

"And going out again. . .?"

"Tomorrow morning."

"Thanks." Dan started to turn away then swung back to face them. "How big a boat is it? Will they take horses?"

"Doubt it. The deck area's pretty small, and they usually have it crammed with freight."

Dan walked slowly back to the hotel. He didn't want to leave Star behind, and he was sure David wouldn't want to part with Captain, either. As for Anne, she was committed to returning Bailey to Rob Whistler.

They reacted about the way he'd expected. After more discussion, he saw Anne to her room, where she promised to nap. David insisted he could fend for himself, so at about three o'clock, when the steamer's whistle sounded, Dan headed back to the landing.

He watched the passengers disembark and several men go aboard to make arrangements to have their cargo unloaded. When the dockhands started working, he made his way among them and up the gangplank.

The captain wasn't difficult to find. He stood just outside the pilot house, his blue eyes sharply watching the activity around him while he talked to two Scottsburg business owners.

Dan approached him and waited for a break in the conversation about freight.

"Help you, sir?" the captain asked.

"Yes, I wondered if you're heading out for Oregon City tomorrow."

"That's the plan, yes, sir."

"Would you take three passengers?"

The captain scratched his chin. "Could. Not much of a load going from here."

"And do you take horses?"

He frowned. "Look around you, man."

Dan gazed at the limited deck space on the small, squatty stern-wheeler.

"It can get pretty rough between here and the coast. You crowd three horses in here with passengers and cargo, and it can turn into a muddy ride. Then you get into open water, and you can't guarantee a thing. I have not slings to secure large animals with."

"So you wouldn't?"

The captain shook his head. "Don't care to risk it. Sorry."

Dan swallowed hard. "Not even from here to the coast? We might be able to get a bigger ship there."

"No doubt you could, but no, I won't take 'em on my boat."

Dan nodded. "I understand. Thank you."

Discouraged, he plodded back to the hotel. In his mind, he ticked off several options. They could sell the horses, which didn't seem agreeable to any of them. They might leave the horses in Scottsburg, to be retrieved later, but when? They could ride back to David's farm in Eugene, or to the coast, both of which promised to be dangerous.

He entered the lobby and headed for the stairs. As he passed the desk, the clerk said, "Hsst. Mr. Adams."

Dan paused and looked at him. "You wanted to speak to me?"

"Come closer, sir."

It was almost a whisper, and Dan was instantly alert. He walked over to the desk and said clearly, "Any messages for me?" He lowered his voice to a whisper. "What's up?"

"There's a man sitting yonder—don't look."

"I understand. What about him?"

"He asked for Miss Stone."

Dan tensed. "Is he a guest here?"

"No. I told him we couldn't give out information about our guests, like you said. He went out, but a little while later I went to get something, and when I came back he was sitting over there with the newspaper in front of his face. I ignored him. We've got no rule about people waiting for guests in the lobby, but. . .well, I thought you'd like to know."

"Thank you."

Dan walked deliberately over to the stairs and mounted them without looking toward the man indicated by the clerk. When he reached the first landing, he rounded the corner and paused long enough to look down and toward the sitting area. A young man with sandy hair and a heavy beard and mustache stared up at him over the top of an open newspaper. When he saw that Dan had noticed him, he averted his gaze to the paper.

Dan strode along the second-floor hallway to the far end. He looked over his shoulder then opened the door to the back stairs and ran lightly down them to the kitchen.

Ernie and his helper looked up in surprise.

"Mr. Adams," Ernie said. "I hope nothing's wrong upstairs?"

"No, our friend is gaining strength. But I wonder if I could ask a favor of you." He explained about the stranger watching the front entrance.

"I can go out through the dining room and see if he's still there, but if Mr. Reed sees me, he'll get upset." Ernie scowled. "He thinks I should stay in the kitchen all the time."

"I'll go," his helper said.

Ernie's face brightened. "Sure. We'll send Mudge."

His helper whipped off his apron and handed it to Ernie. "What do you want me to do?"

"You heard me describe the fellow in the lobby?" Dan asked.

"Yeah."

"Just see if he's still out there and tell me what he's doing."

Mudge walked out through the empty dining room. Dan and Ernie, peeking through a crack at the partially opened door to the dining room, had a limited view of the lobby beyond.

"Where'd he go?" Ernie asked after a half minute.

"Looked like he went over near the stairs," Dan said.

Half a minute later, Mudge breezed back in.

"Well?" Ernie asked.

"He wasn't sitting there, so I asked the desk clerk. He said the fella went up the main stairs after you did, Mr. Adams."

Dan looked at Ernie for a second then dashed up the back stairs. At the second-floor landing, he paused to calm himself and stealthily opened the door to the hallway. Halfway between him and the main stairway, a man leaned with his ear against the door of one of the guest rooms.

Dan strode down the carpeted hall.

The sandy-haired man whirled. His eyes popped wide and he backed away, but Dan was too quick. He grabbed him by the lapels and shoved him against the wall.

"What do you think you're doing?"

CHAPTER 25

David held his revolver trained on the scruffy man Adams had herded into his sitting room while Adams tied the fellow to a chair.

"What will we do with him?" Anne stood by wringing her hands.

Adams secured the knots he'd tied and stood looking at David. "He admitted he was hired to find you."

"Did Peterson hire him?" Anne asked.

"Someone did. He wouldn't say who."

David stepped toward their prisoner and aimed the gun point-blank at him. "I'm tired of this. Who's paying you? Give us a name."

"I don't know," the man sputtered. "He said he'd pay me a dollar a day to watch the hotel lobby and try to find out your room number and tell him if you ever left the room. He wanted to know if you planned to leave Scottsburg. It was more than I'd made panning for gold, and it sounded like easy work, so I took it."

"What did he look like?" Anne asked.

The man strained against the cords Adams had tied him with as though he wanted to move his arms when he talked. "I don't know. He was about forty, I'm guessing. Thin face. He had a mustache."

"A little pencil mustache?" Adams asked.

"Yeah. Skinny fella. Wore a suit like a dandy."

"We'd best turn this man over to Owens," David said.

"What? I didn't do anything!"

"You're in the employ of a killer," Adams said.

The prisoner's face blanched. "I swear I didn't know. I thought he just wanted to get in with Mr. Stone. I had no idea he wanted to harm anyone." He looked up at David. "No offense, mister, but he said you wouldn't give him the time of day and he had a business deal he wanted to talk over with you. He wanted me to tell him where you'd be, so he could find you outside the hotel. Said they wouldn't let him wait around the hotel anymore."

"More like, the constable is watching to see if he comes here," David said.

"So what do we do now?" Anne asked again. "I could go for Mr. Owens."

"We need to leave this town," Adams said. "If we stay here, Peterson's going to find a way to get to your uncle. But we can't—" He broke off and glanced at the prisoner. "Let's not discuss it in front of him."

"All right, I'll guard him," David said. "Get Owens, and we'll be rid of this baggage."

Adams hurried out, and Anne went over and locked the hall door behind him. The prisoner's eyes followed her every move.

"Why don't you go lie down?" David said.

"I don't think I care to be alone right now."

David could see the sense of that. With the certainty that Peterson was still about, lying in wait for them, sending Anne to her own room down the hall might not be the most brilliant plan. "At least sit in my chamber," he said.

Anne threw an uneasy glance at the prisoner and nodded. "All right. I shall think about our options."

All was quiet until Dan came in twenty minutes later with Owens in tow. Anne came and stood in the connecting doorway.

"Well now," the constable said, looking over the prisoner. "Billy Harden. You went bust on your claim, I heard. What are you up to now?"

"Nothing," the prisoner said. "I swear." The version he gave the constable squared with what he'd told them before.

Owens leaned toward him with glinting eyes. "Where's this man at now, Billy?"

"I don't know."

"But you had a way to report to him. Where were you going to meet him?"

The prisoner was silent for a moment. "Will you let me go if I tell you?"

"No."

"But, Mr. Owens, I didn't do nothing."

"Maybe it was all in ignorance—that wouldn't surprise me a bit," Owens said, "but now you know that man meant to harm Mr. Stone. So tell me what you know."

"What do I get if I tell you?"

"You don't get strung up, that's what you get."

Billy stared at Owens. "You can't hang nobody without a judge says so."

"Oh, can't I?"

Anne looked horrified, and David threw her a surreptitious wink. Owens wouldn't have the stomach to lynch a prisoner, but they couldn't have Anne ruining his strategy by protesting too heartily. His niece had been through a lot, but it seemed she was still tenderhearted enough to spare a criminal.

"He gave me two bits and said to go to the Big Tree Saloon tonight, down by the river, and he'd find me."

"Hmm." Owens frowned at him. "You giving it to me straight?"

"Sure am."

Owens gestured to David and Adams to join him, and the three stepped out into the hall.

"I'll try to get him over to the icehouse without a lot of people seeing me, but it'll be hard to take him out of this building unnoticed, especially if someone's watching."

"There's stairs for the staff that go down into the kitchen," Adams said. "You could take him that way and out the back."

"Good. I'll lock him up and see if I can get wind of this Peterson." Owens shook his head. "Persistent, isn't he? I was sure he'd left town. He must have a big payday riding on killing you, Mr. Stone."

"I hate to think it, but it seems you're right," David said.

Owens untied the prisoner, and Adams showed him the back stairway. When he returned, David told Adams and Anne, "We need to sit down right now and decide what we're going to do.

Personally, I don't want to depend on Owens to catch that thug Peterson."

"I agree," Adams said. "What I didn't have a chance to tell you is that the steamer is too small to take horses on the deck. The captain wasn't open to it, and I could see why. But Anne and I don't want to give up our horses, and I know you don't either, sir."

"We could head out for your place in Eugene," Anne said doubtfully.

"Too risky," David said. "He could bushwhack us anywhere along the way."

"How about this," Adams said. "I could go back to talk to the captain again and make it look like I was buying tickets on the steamer. If I asked him nice, he might put it about that we were taking his boat tomorrow. He's going down the river and up the coast to the Columbia, then to Oregon City."

"And what would we really do?" Anne asked, her eyes bright.

"Start out tonight when it's full dark and ride to the coast. If Peterson figures out we left on horseback, he'd probably expect us to ride east. But we go west instead, and follow the river road to the coast."

"What's the point, other than to confuse him?" David asked.

"We could get a bigger ship at Reedsport or Gardiner, board it with the horses, and sail to Oregon City. A steamer would get us there in less than two days."

"Then you'd be nearly home, and Uncle David and I could ride down to Corvallis to Eb and Elise's ranch," Anne said. "I like that plan. Can you stand to be away from your farm a little longer, Uncle David?"

"That doesn't matter much. It's staying alive I care about."

Anne's face sobered. "Maybe we ought to stay right here until Owens catches Peterson."

"We've done that and he hasn't even laid eyes on the fellow," David said. "How long do you think we should we hide in this hotel? It's been days already."

"Your uncle's right," Adams said. "Peterson is staying out of

sight. Unless he makes some big blunder, we're at his mercy. He could wait forever, though I don't think he would. I wish I knew where he's hiding."

"Must be boarding somewhere," David muttered. "But I don't want to stay here any longer. Let's get out of Scottsburg."

"All right," Adams said. "I'll go have a word with the steamboat's captain."

Ernie sent the dishwasher up with a tray of sandwiches and coffee at one o'clock. "Did anyone see you in the hall?" Dan asked when Mudge set it on the table in the sitting room.

"I don't think so."

Dan put fifty cents in his hand. "I'd like you to go out to the stable with me after we've eaten. Can you have our horses ready at ten o'clock tonight if I show you our animals and gear?"

"Yes, sir."

Dan nodded. "Try not to let anyone see you going into the stable, either. If anyone who works here asks, tell them you're serving a guest, but don't give out our names."

"Yes, sir. I'll keep mum. No worry there."

"Good," Dan said. "When do you finish in the kitchen? I'll come down and go with you."

"I could slip out for a few minutes around half past eight, sir."

Mudge left the room, and Dan locked the door behind him.

Anne had set the sandwiches and cups out on the table near the window. She looked over at Dan. "We're putting an awful lot of faith in that young man."

"Yes, we are." Dan could only pray that their trust was not misplaced.

They gathered at the table and ate their meal. Ernie had included a plate of raisin tarts and a dish of sautéed apples. Afterward, Anne sat quietly on the sofa, mending one of David's socks, while the men settled the details of their escape.

"I expect Peterson knows what rooms we're in by now," David said.

"Just the same, it doesn't hurt to exercise caution." Dan sat and studied him, thinking. David's height and bearing made him difficult to mistake for anyone else, and once he started talking there was no question. "When we leave, you should go out separately from us. Maybe through the kitchen door. We could meet you a short distance away with the horses."

David frowned but nodded. "All right. Less chance of him getting on to our plan that way. You and Anne get the horses, and I'll meet you down at the junction."

"I think that would be best," Dan said. "Even if Peterson sees Anne and me leaving, he won't see you. But stay out of sight."

"I've learned to sneak through the shadows." David's wry smile lacked any mirth.

Dan glanced at Anne. "Is this plan acceptable to you?"

She nodded, but her face had paled. Dan wished he could reassure her that all would go well and they would soon be away from this place and safe. Together and safe.

They waited in the hotel suite with the drapes drawn through the afternoon. At first all was quiet, but David became restless again. He paced for a while, then sat down on a chair facing Dan.

"Adams, I've decided what I want to do."

"Tonight, sir?"

"No. In the future."

Anne gazed at him in dismay.

Before she could speak, Dan said, "And what is that, sir?"

"I want to start a stagecoach line from Eugene to Corvallis. Heaven knows we need one."

Dan nodded, considering the idea. "If one was in place, Anne and I could have gotten to your farm much quicker. I think it's an excellent idea."

"They're bringing the mail up from San Francisco overland," David said. "Why stop at Eugene? The roads need some improvement, and we'd need better ferries and a couple of stout bridges, but whoever had the mail contract could get money from Washington for those things."

Having seen the hazards of the route firsthand, Dan began to warm to the idea. "You could offer daily service between the two cities. Or at least three coaches a week each way."

"Excellent. We'd need a station halfway, where they could change horses, or possibly two swing stations. But one driver could easily make the full run."

"I wouldn't mind being a station agent," Dan said.

David blinked at him. "Wouldn't you? I thought you were set to grow wheat."

"My brother's more keen on it than I am." He tried to imagine what the station in Corvallis would be like—hustling whenever a coach came in, changing out the teams of horses, loading the mail and freight. The passengers would go in to eat dinner.

That stopped him cold. Who would cook dinner for the guests? Before he could check the thought, he imagined a small, dark-haired woman in an apron standing over an iron cookstove. She looked uncannily like Anne. He glanced over at her. Anne had stopped her darning and was watching him.

He smiled. Anne hadn't known the first thing about cooking, or even how to light a fire, a few months ago. But she had a quick mind, and he figured she could learn to cook for a crowd if she put her mind to it.

"What's funny?" David asked.

"Nothing, sir. Not funny exactly. I was just thinking how our perspective changes over time. I never thought about freighting or driving a stagecoach before, but I think I'd like to be involved in such a venture, especially on the organizational end. Buying horses and making sure things run smoothly down the line."

"You could do it," Anne said. She turned to her uncle, her face earnest. "Daniel has a good mind for seeing problems and finding the solution."

"Hmm. Well, I'm about done with placer mining, and I may decide to sell my farm, too. Or I could use it for the home station on the southern end of the line, though a place in town would probably be better. I wonder if there's a good spot available in Eugene. I'll have to talk to Skinner about it."

"But—" Anne frowned. "Won't you be going back to England, Uncle David?"

He sighed and burrowed down in his chair. "Haven't decided yet."

That surprised Dan. Stone could finance a stagecoach line here and go back to his position of wealth and power in England. He'd thought that much was a foregone conclusion. From what Anne had said, the estate must be large, with a sizable fortune entailed. Who would turn down such an opportunity?

The other side of the coin was the danger such a position brought. Why would a man take on the responsibility if it meant others constantly tried to kill him?

"I'll admit I'm ignorant in such matters," he said, "but it seems to me that accepting this earldom would be dangerous to you, Mr. Stone."

David turned languid eyes upon him. "I doubt it would be more dangerous than what I'm enduring now."

"That's so," Anne said, taking another stitch. "Once you're established as the earl and settle down to run the estate and—"

"And marry suitably, thus providing a direct heir or two," David said drily. "Yes, becoming entrenched in British society is probably the best way to insure my life if I decide to claim the peerage. But I can't help feeling I'd be much freer and happier if I simply said no."

Anne lowered her sewing and stared at him. "You couldn't. You wouldn't."

"I could, and I might. All it would take is a letter. And I might." He laughed at Anne's horrified expression. "Don't you see, my dear? If I stood before a judge and signed a letter saying I give up any claim to my brother's estate, no one would want to kill me. Cousin Randolph would inherit, and Peterson would leave me alone."

"How would Peterson know to do that?" Dan asked.

"I haven't figured that out yet. I suppose we could have a copy of the letter hand delivered to him, if we knew where to find him."

They sat in silence for a full minute.

"Please don't do it," Anne said at last. "I do value your life, Uncle

David, and your liberty to do whatever you wish with your life. If you want to stay here and open a stagecoach line with Daniel, why, that would be wonderful. Yet I'd hate to see you make a hasty decision. Please think of all the people in England who depend upon Stoneford. And think of your cousin running the estate. I can't say I like that picture."

"Nor do I," David said. "He was always a selfish twit."

"I fear he hasn't changed much—and his wife! Always one to live beyond her income. Randolph and Merrileigh would run through the fortune in short order if their present spending is any indication. Then where would the tenants be?"

"And this is the man who's hired Peterson to kill you," Dan said. "This spineless, spendthrift cousin."

"So it seems," David said. "I can't think of anyone else with a motive. And it's like Randolph to hire someone else to do the work for him. It's true I don't like to hand the estate over to him. It's not an easy choice."

"Then don't make it hastily," Anne said.

"How is this cousin paying Peterson?" Dan asked.

"Yes. He hasn't much spare money." Anne eyed the sock in her hand as though she detested it. "He must be giving Peterson a lot."

"Probably promised to pay out of the estate when he gets it, other than expenses," David said.

Dan shook his head at the waste, let alone the depravity of it. Imagine what an honest man could do with the money this cousin was spending to kill David. It boggled the mind.

Anne picked up her needle once more. "Well, I think you should take your time deciding what to do. And regardless of your decision, we should send a letter to the solicitor, telling him I've found you and that you are alive."

"So far," David said.

Anne frowned at that. "Please don't speak so. If we let Mr. Conrad know you are safe, I expect he will tell Cousin Randolph. Then perhaps Randolph will leave you alone."

"I doubt it," David replied. "For one thing, he has no speedy way to call off his hound."

"And if we found a way to prove your cousin's involvement," Dan said, "would he be disqualified from inheriting the estate? If so, who would be next in line?"

"A good question," David said.

"Randolph's son, I should think." Anne continued stitching, but she didn't seem at ease.

"He's got children, then?" David asked.

"Yes. Two of them—a boy and a girl."

"Well, he's far ahead of me in that, though he must be six or seven years younger."

"Spoiled and ill-mannered, the lot," Anne said.

David sighed. "I should have married sooner. Then you wouldn't have all this trouble I've caused you."

Anne clipped her threads and laid the scissors aside. "I rather hoped you had. Elise and I speculated on the wagon train whether we might find you settled and the father of several little Stones."

"There was a girl in Independence," David said with a faraway look in his eyes. "I thought she might be the one. But by the time I got around to asking if I could court her, she was looking at someone else." He shook his head. "I didn't do so well at farming there, either. I'd done better as a shopkeeper. I sold out after a few years and got enough to stock three wagons full of merchandise to bring to Oregon."

"So that's why you left Independence." Anne's sympathetic gaze would have cheered most men, but David still looked sad.

"The only thing is, it's mighty hard to get a wagon heavily loaded over those mountains."

"Tell me about it," Anne said. "I sold a trunk of ball gowns in Independence."

"Really? That was indeed a sacrifice, my dear."

Dan smiled. "Wait until you hear about the fellow who told us you were buried out behind his house."

"What?" David arched his eyebrows.

"Oh yes, Herr Schwartz nearly had us convinced you'd died on the trail."

"Schwartz? I remember him."

"Well, Anne and Miss Finster saw through him," Dan said. "But your niece has undergone a great deal for you."

Anne reached over and patted Stone's arm. "I don't want you to feel you have to return to England, Uncle David, but at least inform the solicitor that you're alive. If you don't claim the estate and title within a few years, the crown might dispose of the property and appropriate the money."

"I suppose you're right." David's reluctance was obvious.

Dan stood. "I was thinking I'd make a quick trip to the mercantile for some extra ammunition. I could take a letter if you want to post one. It might be a good idea to have one on the way before we leave here."

"I agree," Anne said. "And I'll send one to Elise as well. I know we hope to see her in a few days, but if anything should delay us, at least she'll know our plans."

"Does she know you've found me?" David asked.

"Yes. I wrote while you were resting and recovering."

He nodded. "All right, I'll fetch some paper and write to Conrad. Heavens, he was old when I was a lad. He must be positively doddering now."

David rose and walked unsteadily to the desk, using the cane Dr. Muller had provided.

"May I help you, sir?" Dan asked.

David looked down at his arm, still swathed in a sling. "I believe I can write a few lines, but perhaps you'd best open the ink for me."

He sat at the desk for several minutes, scratching away with a pen. Anne borrowed a sheet of paper from him and composed a note to Elise. At last both missives were ready to post, and Dan put on his coat and prepared to leave for the post office.

"If you'd like anything from the store. . ."

Anne tilted her head to one side, sending highlights from the lantern glinting over her dark hair. "Rations for the ship, I suppose. Something we can carry and eat easily, without needing a fire. I've no idea if we'll be able to buy things like that when we reach the coast."

"Or have the time to do so before we sail." David reached in his pocket and took out a silver dollar, which he handed to Dan. "Get some jerky and ship's biscuit, if they have it."

Anne made a dour face. "I suppose that's practical."

"It's only for a short time, and only if we need it," David assured her.

"All right," Dan said, "and shall I inquire for your mail, sir?"

"Yes. Let me write a note to the postmaster, or chances are he won't give it to you."

Finally Dan set out, hoping the post office was still open. The sun had gone down, and the temperature had dipped. At least the sky was clear tonight.

The postmaster was coming out from behind his counter when Dan entered.

"Well, now, you just caught me," he said. "Adams, wasn't it?"

"Yes, and I have a note from Mr. Stone, asking you to give me his mail. He and his niece also entrusted two letters to me for mailing."

The postmaster scrutinized David's note and compared the writing to that on the letter addressed to Andrew Conrad, Esq., in Middlesex, England. He turned and dropped it into a box and placed Anne's letter in a mailbag. He scanned the rack of pigeon-holes on the wall behind him.

"There's nothing here for Mr. Stone today. Anything else I can do for you, sir?"

"No, thank you. But we'll all be leaving Scottsburg tomorrow by the steamer, if anyone should ask."

"Ah, then I should forward any incoming mail for Mr. Stone to his home in Eugene?"

"That's correct."

Dan drew on his gloves and went out into the dusk. A flicker of movement at the corner of the building drew his eye. Had someone just ducked back into the shadows? The back of his neck prickled. He'd never been fanciful, and he didn't for an instant think he'd imagined it.

He turned and strode quickly toward the general store, where

several lanterns burned brightly inside. If Peterson or his hirelings lurked about, Dan wouldn't give them a chance to work mischief tonight.

CHAPTER 26

Anne had a nap after Dan returned from the post office. He came and knocked on her door as promised when their supper was delivered from the kitchen. She freshened up quickly and was only half surprised to find Dan coming up the stairs when she opened the door to the hallway.

"Your uncle sent me down to settle the bill for all of us," he said.

"Oh." She tried to read his face. "That was kind of him."

"Extremely. He had me tell Mr. Reed we'll all leave in time to make the steamer in the morning."

Dan seemed uncomfortable with that statement. He'd probably worked hard to word it so that he wasn't lying about their departure time. She started to close her door.

"Want to bring your last bundles over to Mr. Stone's room?"

"All right." She went back in and placed her hairbrush and gloves in her bag and looked around to be sure she hadn't left anything. Dan leaned against the doorjamb, waiting. He smiled when she turned toward him.

"All set?"

"Yes." They went out, and she locked the door. "What should I do with the key?"

He held out his palm. "I'll slide it under the door on our way out. But not until then, in case you want to go back in for something."

"Daniel, you've been so good to me and Uncle David. I'm sorry for the discomfort we've caused you."

"Think nothing of it. If I can just deliver you safely to Eb Bentley's house, I'll be satisfied."

His tone brought a wave of regret, and she touched his sleeve. "Satisfied, but not happy?"

He started to speak but shook his head slightly. "Come. Let's eat, and I'll take the last of the bags down. Mudge will be coming before long for instructions. I'll show him exactly where our stuff is in the stable, and we'll pack all of your uncle's gear and our extra baggage on the pack saddle."

"I'm so glad you were able to find a mule for his things," Anne said as they walked down the hall toward David's room.

Dan grimaced. "I traded his sluice box and other mining gear toward the price of the pack mule. I just hope I didn't attract too much attention doing it."

"Peterson, you mean?"

"Yes. Something tells me that man doesn't miss much. If he sees we've bought an extra mule, he'll figure out that we're not sailing from here on that little steamer."

"I hope not. And we'll be much more comfortable without having all our bundles hanging about us on the horses."

They reached Uncle David's room, and Dan looked back toward the stairway then knocked on the door. A moment later it opened.

"Everything's ready," David said. "Past ready—getting cold."

"I'm sorry," Anne said. "I should have moved a little faster."

"Forgive me." David bowed his head in contrition. "I'm afraid I left some of my manners at Stoneford."

They sat down to eat. Ernie had sent his best, in Anne's opinion. The cook had shown himself a true friend to her uncle. The roast beef, baked potatoes, corn, and squash went down well. She'd asked for tea, and it was there in a silver teapot. Dan drank it with them, though she knew he preferred coffee.

He smiled when she handed it to him, already laced with milk and a little sugar. For a moment she wished they were in England, in the parlor at Stoneford—but the image of Dan calling there at tea time didn't fit. How many times last summer had she put a tin cup of coffee in his hand at the end of a long day on the trail? That was Dan, not high tea and evening dress for dinner.

Or was it? She'd seen Uncle David in both worlds now, and he seemed as much at home here, in the raw West, as he had been in

England. Perhaps Dan could straddle both comfortably, too. Did she want that? The idea startled her. She'd spent many hours mulling the possibility of staying in America. Always she knew she didn't fit in his farming future. But Dan in England? He might blend in very well. But he'd probably disdain the wealthy people she'd always associated with and befriend the tradesmen and village folk. Her old friends wouldn't abide it and would cut her cold. What was the use of thinking about it?

They talked quietly through the evening, and it seemed to Anne that the two men had their stagecoach line planned, almost down to the last horseshoe nail. She tried not to take it too seriously, yet her fears strengthened as she listened. David might actually do it—and never leave Oregon.

Mudge came on time, and he and Dan went to the stable for half an hour. Shortly after Dan returned, Ernie came to get the tray.

"I thought you'd have gone home by now," David said.

"I should've. We had a lot of folks in for dinner tonight, but I wanted to say good-bye, sir. It's been a pleasure serving you and your friends." Ernie nodded at Anne and Dan.

"You've been very helpful," Anne said, "and tonight's dinner was wonderful."

Dan murmured his thanks, and David stood and shook the cook's hand.

Ernie picked up the laden tray and rested one edge on his shoulder. David walked with him to the door.

Ernie paused and looked back at Dan. "Mudge says he'll do everything just the way you said, sir."

Dan nodded. "Thanks. We appreciate it."

David let Ernie out and secured the door then checked his pocket watch. "Well, another hour."

"Yes." Dan fell silent. Everything had been said. If they could only get away clean. . .but speaking of it would make Anne anxious, so he said nothing.

"About that stagecoach line," David said, ambling to his chair.

"Yes, sir." Dan sat a little straighter.

Anne caught her breath. Here it was again. Her uncle was obsessed with the idea.

"Whether I go to England or not, I think it would be a good investment. Now, I figure I've got to stay here over the winter anyway. Don't want to sail this time of year, and the overland route is impassable now."

"Well, yes," Anne conceded. "I thought I'd stay with Elise, or—" She looked hesitantly at David.

"You can stay at the farm in Eugene with me, if you like. Or I could winter in Corvallis. Let's see what the wind brings when we get up there, shall we?"

"Of course," she said.

He turned back to Daniel. "But we could get a lot of things in place this winter. I want to talk to someone in Oregon City about this. I'm pretty sure the mail coach only goes as far as Corvallis right now, but if we had a plan ready for taking it the length of Oregon, why, I think we'd have a good chance of getting a contract."

They talked on for the next hour. Dan had an idea how much livestock would cost, and David, having run several stores, could figure fairly close on harness, grain, building supplies, and other commodities that a stage line would need.

"It's certainly doable," David said. "And I think I can sell my mining claim. That would give us some working capital."

Anne noted he'd said "us," linking himself to Daniel. Uncle David seemed serious about the venture, but what role would Dan play? Would he be a hired station agent, or would her uncle make him a partner? Dan wouldn't have nearly as much money to invest. But he looked utterly content, discussing the business as if it were a fact.

He gazed over at Anne, and her heart fluttered. Ever since that night in the hills, when he'd lectured and bullied her, she'd sensed a change in her feelings toward Dan. They hadn't talked about it, but he'd saved her life—no question about it. And he'd called her "dearest Anne" in the tenderest, most endearing way. She would never forget it.

Yet since then, they'd ignored what had passed between them. They'd rarely been alone, it was true—first with Whitey's presence and then Uncle David's, but still... She could not deny that she was closer to loving Dan than ever before. His friendship went deeper now. He'd seen her at her worst.

Did he still dream of marrying her? Why would he, when she'd told him no so many times? She wondered what she would say if he gathered his courage and asked her again. But maybe he was past wanting her now. Had she annihilated his love up there in the hills?

He'd kept his politeness since then, and he'd always been quiet. On the wagon train, she'd caught him staring at her several times with a moon-calfed, lovesick gaze. She hadn't seen that in a long time. Did that mean he was over his infatuation with her? Or had it solidified into something else? Part of her hoped it had, and part of her was repelled by the thought. It would only be harder to return to England if his love was the deep, true, forever kind. Last summer, she'd taken his admiration for a boyish crush and thought he'd be over it by winter. But if he knew the real thing, did she really want it to pass?

He smiled and looked away—back to her uncle. Anne took a shaky breath.

"It must be time for Anne and me to go out," he said.

David extracted his pocket watch and opened it. "Ten o'clock. Go then. I'll see you in ten minutes at the junction."

They all stood. Anne stepped toward David, suddenly loathe to part from him.

"Uncle David—"

"It's going to be fine," he said. "And I'll be careful."

She smiled. Even though they'd been apart so long, he knew her thoughts.

"You're very like your grandmother," he said.

Anne barely remembered her grandmother, the countess before her mother. "I like that," she said. "Please tell me more about her next time we're at leisure."

"I shall." He stooped and kissed her cheek.

Anne went to the table near the door and retrieved the bonnet that matched her riding habit. She put it on while Dan and David shook hands and Dan put his coat on. He came over and held her cape for her.

"Good-bye, Uncle David," she said.

"Godspeed."

David waited until they had gone down the back stairs. They would sneak out and make their way to the stable, trying to avoid being seen by any other patrons or the hotel staff. Three minutes found the limit of his patience. He put on his wool jacket. Anne had mended the tear where the bullet had pierced it, and he could barely tell where the rift had been. Bless her heart, he hoped she didn't get killed for coming to find him.

He clapped his hat on, turned out the lamp, and grabbed the last bag—his small crocodile leather kit of personal items. He still wondered what had become of his Bible and his onyx cuff links. Probably the chambermaid had taken a fancy to the cuff links, but a Bible seemed an odd choice for a thief.

In the hall, he locked the door and slid his key beneath it. The Miner's Hotel had been mostly good to him. If he ever came to Scottsburg again, he'd probably stay here. He flitted quickly down the carpeted corridor to the back stairway door. As he opened it, a door farther down the hall opened. No time for indecision. He ducked into the stairway and pulled the door closed behind him, taking care to do so quietly.

The stairway was pitch-dark. He ought to have brought a lantern or a candle. Had Anne and Adams gone down here without a light? He found the railing and clung to it. His heart pounded as he felt his way, step by step, down the narrow staircase. It curved near the bottom and apparently had a few triangular treads. He nearly plunged downward before he realized it, but he caught himself on the railing and managed to reposition his feet in time.

After the turn, he could see a sliver of light shining through the crack at the bottom of a door. Why hadn't Ernie or Adams or someone warned him about this treacherous avenue of escape?

At last he felt the door panels and fumbled for a knob. Instead he found a thumb latch. It lifted, and light bathed him. He squinted and took a moment to orient himself. It was a pale light really, coming from the next room—the dining room, he supposed. He was in a large kitchen and could make out the bulk of a cookstove, tables, and cupboards.

He edged toward what he assumed was the back wall and slammed into the corner of a table. He sucked in a breath and gritted his teeth. Why on earth hadn't he come down when Anne and Adams did, or asked Ernie to show him the way out?

At last he found the back door. Adams had left it unlocked. A fine mist was falling outside. Next summer it would be bone-dry and hotter than a griddle, but for the next few months, this chilly rain would stay with them. He shivered and turned up his collar.

He was tempted to walk around the hotel and look toward the stable to see if they were in there. But he'd promised to go straight to the rendezvous, so he ambled out to the edge of the street and stood for a moment, looking all about. Far down the road, near the smithy, a couple of people were walking, but they were headed the other way. David turned to his right and kept to the shadows of the buildings as he worked his way to the meeting place.

A narrow alley ran between a boardinghouse and a feed store. He slid into it and leaned against the wall of the feed store. He could see the junction, and there didn't seem to be a better spot to wait where he couldn't be seen from a distance. He folded his arms and slumped against the log wall. He could hear the river in the distance, soft but insistent. An occasional voice called out indistinguishable words, and a couple of dogs traded noncommittal barks. An owl flew overhead, so low he heard its wings flap, and he shivered. This was the sort of place where that thug would gladly kill him. Was he a straight-out idiot to come out here alone?

He looked up at the sky. Still cloudy, and black as the inside of a hat.

"Lord," he said softly, "I sincerely hope we know what we're doing. Seems to me we maybe ought to have prayed about this plan before we settled on it. Something doesn't feel right."

Anne waited while Daniel opened the door to the stable. It creaked so loudly she was sure everyone in the hotel could hear it.

"Let me light a lantern," Dan whispered. "They have one hanging just inside the door here."

He stepped inside, and Anne paused, holding the door open to give him a little light, though that was meager. The moon was either hidden by clouds or not yet risen. She hadn't kept track of it since they'd gotten to Scottsburg. Dan probably had—didn't farmers always know the phase of the moon and when it would rise, the way sailors and fishermen knew the tides?

He rummaged about, and soft pats and rustles came to her. A horse nickered. At last Dan scratched a lucifer, and the flame spurted. He lit the lantern and adjusted it. Anne squinted and looked away from the glare. After a few seconds she could see the inside of the barn, and she moved inside and shut the door behind her.

"You get Bailey and Captain," Dan said. "I'll get Star and the mule."

Anne could see all four animals, tied in straight stalls on the right. Their hindquarters and flowing tails showed, all in a row. The last one's tail didn't flow, however. It was scruffy and short. The mule, no doubt.

She walked into the stall with Bailey first. The chestnut gelding greeted her with a soft neigh. Her sidesaddle was in place. She patted his neck and shoulder.

"Hello, boy," she murmured, raising the saddle skirt so she could check the girth. She tightened it then fumbled for the fastener on the short chain that held him. "Are you ready for a midnight ride?" She got the snap off his halter and let the chain fall. Putting one hand on Bailey's nose, she backed him slowly from the stall.

"Is there a place to hitch him?"

Dan, in the next stall with his bright pinto, looked around and pointed. "There's a ring in that beam."

On the other side of the center aisle, iron rings were mounted in the thick, square, upright posts that supported the roof. Anne led Bailey to the nearest one. She had no lead rope on him. Mudge had put his bridle on over the halter so that he could leave the horse bridled but hitched up in the stall. She looped Bailey's reins through the ring and went across the aisle to get Captain.

As she entered the stall, the horse shifted and snorted.

"Easy," Anne said. Dan was taking Star out of the stall next to Captain's. "What's the matter, boy?" The bay gelding moved over as far as he could away from her.

Something else moved, near the horse's head, and Anne jumped back with a gasp. She was not alone in the stall with Captain.

"What—?"

A firm hand closed about her wrist and jerked her forward, toward Captain's head. The horse squealed and strained against his chain, trying to get away from them.

"Daniel," she screamed.

A man hauled her close to him and clamped a hand over her mouth.

"Hush," he hissed in her ear. Her heart hammered. The man pulled her closer, an unyielding arm about her waist, until her body pressed against his. Horrified, she struggled. The hand that had silenced her released her, but he reclaimed her wrist and twisted it.

"Let me go," she gasped.

Another voice stilled her struggles.

"Put your hands up, Mr. Adams." She jerked her head around. Dan had dropped Star's reins and was halfway between his pinto and her position. He stood stock-still now, staring at her with a tortured expression on his face as he slowly raised his hands above his shoulders.

Two paces behind him stood a young man with a revolver pointed at Dan's back.

Anne's heart plummeted. "Mudge."

"Quickly," the man behind Anne called. "Tie him up, and make it tight."

It had to be Peterson, Dan decided, though the man was hidden in the shadows. Captain snorted and pulled against his halter chain. The man shoved Anne out past the horse, and Dan saw him clearly at last. Peterson held Anne before him with his right arm, and in his left hand, held to the side of Anne's slender neck, was a long-barreled pistol. Her lovely face was a stark white, and her dark eyes loomed huge and pleading.

Peterson turned sideways and aimed squarely at him. "Snap it up."

"Let her go," Dan said.

Peterson laughed.

"Please." Dan held the man's malevolent glare. "I'll do whatever you say. Just keep Miss Stone out of this."

"That's rich," Mudge said as he patted Dan's coat. He found his revolver right away and removed it. "Gimme your wrists. Put 'em behind you." As soon as Dan complied, Mudge began wrapping them with some type of cord or light rope.

"She has nothing to do with this," Dan said, never looking away from Peterson's stare.

"She has more to do with it than you do." His lips curled and the mustache twitched as he spoke. "Somehow I don't think her uncle would run as quickly to rescue you as he would his darling little niece."

Dan thought for a moment his heart had just plain stopped, but it kicked and raced on, faster now. Peterson would use Anne as bait—he should have foreseen that. And where did that leave him? Most likely shot and dumped in the river.

"Where is Stone?" Peterson asked.

Dan eyed him in silence.

Peterson tightened his hold on Anne and ran the muzzle of the pistol up to her ear. "Tell me where he is."

Dan tried to swallow the boulder in his throat. *He won't kill Anne*, he told himself. *He needs her to get David in here.* But he didn't dare trust that instinct completely.

"We left him in his room," Anne said.

Dan wanted to applaud her. He gave Peterson a grim nod. "He won't come down until we give him the signal."

"And what's the signal, dear friends?"

Anne stared at Dan, panic in her dark eyes. Silently she pled with him, and Dan read the message as clearly as if she had it painted on her forehead. *Don't betray my uncle. If one of us has to die, let it be me, not the earl of Stoneford.*

"We're to take the horses out front," Dan said, amazed at how steady his voice sounded.

"Watching from his window, I suppose," Peterson said. "When he sees the horses out by the hitching rail, he'll come down."

Dan said nothing. It was as good an assumption as any—and it would get them out of the stable at least. David should be well away from the hotel by now, but maybe if they got outside, they could attract the attention of Mr. Reed or the desk clerk—even one of the other guests.

"No, that's not right," Mudge said.

Dan could have kicked himself. Mudge had heard the whole plan. Or had he? If he knew they were meeting David at the junction, why hadn't he told Peterson?

"They were talking about meeting someplace."

Peterson scowled. "Tie his feet, too."

"Sit down, Mr. Adams," Mudge said.

Dan sat on the dirt floor, and Mudge found a short piece of rope. He looped it around Dan's ankles, but the rope went over his boot tops, so it didn't feel too tight. His hands, however, had been bound in an uncomfortable position, and he was beginning to lose feeling in the fingers of his left hand.

"Are you fond of that young man?" Peterson asked in a dangerous voice, so low Dan barely heard the words.

Anne choked out a yes.

"I assumed as much. I'm sure you'd hate to see him suffer."

"What do you want?" she asked.

"Only a chance to talk to your uncle in private."

Anne grimaced but said nothing.

"Now, Mudge is going to take a couple of these horses out in front of the hotel," Peterson continued. "When your uncle comes down and sees him, Mudge will tell him there's a little holdup and some of the gear needed to be repacked. And Mr. Stone will come out here where I can talk to him. And you—you just be ready to greet him as though everything is going forward, you understand?"

"N–no," Anne said.

Peterson sighed. "And I thought you were an intelligent young woman."

"Anne, don't listen to him," Dan said.

Peterson turned his head and glared at him. "Gag him."

"Yes, sir." Mudge looked around stupidly and patted his pockets. A moment later he knelt and stretched a sweaty-smelling bandanna across Dan's mouth.

"Open."

"You want to kill me? I won't be able to breathe."

"Not sure it matters," Mudge said.

Aghast at his apathy, Dan said, "How could you—"

Mudge slid the cloth between his teeth and pulled it tighter.

Dan gave up and tried to keep from retching while his captor secured the knot. When Mudge had finished, he shoved Dan down on his side.

"Drag him into that last stall," Peterson called.

As Mudge took hold of his boots and jerked him over the dirt floor, Dan caught sight of his revolver, lying against the divider between two empty stalls.

He could only be thankful that the last stall on this side was used as a tool room. A feed bin and a couple of barrels stood on the straw-strewn floor. Saddles, harness, and small tools hung on nails, and a shovel, a pitchfork, and a dung fork leaned against the outside wall. He couldn't see Anne or Peterson from the position Mudge left him in. The pungent earth and musty straw smells mingled with the scent of the filthy rag in his mouth and heady whiffs of manure and leather.

"Take those two," he heard Peterson say, and a moment later, hooves clumped on the dirt floor. The big front door was rolled open, and a wave of colder air swept through the stable. Horses shuffled, and the door moved again on its metal rollers; then the barn fell still.

What was Peterson doing now? Did he still hold Ann against him, with the pistol touching her head? Dan was consumed with anger and the need to see them, to know Anne was all right. Another question ate at him. Had Mudge picked up his gun, or did it still lie there in the straw a few feet away?

They waited without talking for what seemed eternity.

The drizzle let up, but that was small comfort to David. What was taking them so long? He'd expected them to be along by now. He pulled out his watch, but there wasn't enough light to read it. He shoved it back in his pocket and patted the Colt revolver in his coat pocket.

"Come on, Anne. Where are you?"

He ought to have gone with them. This slinking in the shadows didn't suit him. Even as he considered jogging down the street to the hotel, he remembered the night he was shot. Sometimes clinging to the shadows was best.

His new resolve to wait patiently lasted all of two minutes. Something was wrong. It had to be! He tiptoed out of the alley and huddled behind the steps to the feed store, peering down the street. He couldn't tell exactly where the hotel lay, but he suspected the highest roofline he could make out belonged to it. Maybe it was time to take a risk.

Hauling in a deep breath, he rose and scrambled around the steps, trying to run stealthily. He was getting a bit old for this sort of thing. Hurrying past two more closed businesses, he flattened

himself against a jutting front porch. Only one more building between him and the Miner's Hotel. Lamps gleamed in several of its first- and second-story windows. The third floor, where he'd stayed, was dark.

Leisurely hoofbeats clopped on packed earth. Were they leaving the stable yard at last? David squinted into the darkness and made out two horses. They passed through a square of lamplight cast from a window casement. The first horse had a rider; the second bore an empty saddle. David waited. The rider didn't look quite right for Dan. And where had Anne gotten to?

The rider stopped near the hitching rail and gazed upward, toward the hotel's top-floor windows. What was he looking at? David followed the fellow's line of sight upward, but the rooms on the third story were still dark.

It hit him suddenly, as though a steer had kicked him. The man was watching his window. Dan wouldn't do that. Dan knew he was waiting at the junction—or should be. David's hand crept toward his revolver, though why he wasn't sure.

Who was that man? It couldn't be Peterson. This one slouched in the saddle. Peterson might be a rogue, but sloppy he was not. Impeccably dressed, well groomed, and superior in posture, from all David had learned about him. Quite the gentleman, until one got to know him better.

The rider slid to the ground and walked quietly up the hotel's front steps. Something about him made David tense. It was Mudge, the kitchen lad. Why was he out front with two horses? Something had gone awry.

David drew his revolver and slipped from his hiding place to the edge of the hotel's porch. All was quiet. He bent low and slunk over to the horses. Captain whickered softly.

"Hello, old man." David ran a hand along the bay gelding's flank. "What's going on, eh?"

Hitched to the saddle by a long lead rope was Anne's horse, but Anne was nowhere to be found. And what about Adams and his paint horse? David eyed the closed door to the hotel lobby. Had they gone back inside? One thing seemed likely—Adams's horse and the pack mule were still in the stable out back. David tiptoed to the corner of the building and peeked around it. Light from a lantern shone through a narrow opening at the stable door.

"Sit there." Peterson gestured with his pistol toward a keg near the door of the stable.

Anne walked toward it slowly. The big, rolling door was nearly shut. She couldn't possibly open it and get out before he would catch her—assuming he would scruple to shoot at her. Not knowing what else she could do, she went to the keg, sat down, and arranged the skirts of her riding habit.

"Do I need to tie you up?" Peterson asked.

She frowned up at him. "What do you mean?"

"I mean, will you try to escape if I don't?"

"Of course."

He sighed and looked about for rope. She almost laughed at the ease with which she'd distracted him. Unfortunately, his search took him between her and the door.

"This will do. Hold out your hands." He came closer, carrying a short length of manila rope.

She raised her hands in front of her. He didn't force her to put them behind her, so she didn't protest. He pulled the rope tight enough that she winced and tied the knot a couple of inches above her wrists. She wouldn't be able to reach the short ends. Now she'd be helpless if Uncle David needed her.

Peterson planned to kill him—she had no doubt about that. And what would become of her and Dan afterward? Surely he wouldn't just turn them loose to testify against him. Maybe he didn't want to kill them all here in the barn. It would be easier to dispose of them if he took them all away from the hotel.

Would he really kill three people to ensure that David never claimed the peerage?

She shivered.

Peterson stood near the crack in the door, not two feet from her, peering out toward the hotel. She gazed along the length of the stable. Star was still tied in the center alley, where Mudge had tied him up before he left, and the pack mule remained in his stall. The butt of Dan's rifle stuck up out of the scabbard. If she could reach it. . .but would that do any good? She seemed to recall that the gun wouldn't fire until a cap was applied to the action or some such thing. She should have paid more attention when her father hosted shooting parties.

She'd heard nothing from Dan since Mudge had dragged him out of sight. Was he all right? Maybe Mudge had bludgeoned him before he left.

She swiveled her head and eyed Peterson again. He was still looking out the doorway. She measured the distance to the horse with her eye. How long would it take her to run the five or six yards?

"Don't even think about it," Peterson said drily.

She swallowed hard. The beast couldn't really read her mind, but he'd like her to think that. He probably thought she was considering braining him with something. But what? Nothing small and solid enough was within reach.

Again she gazed longingly at Star. The pinto snuffled and strained against his lead rope. He couldn't quite reach the straw on the floor.

Between the horse's feet, Anne glimpsed the sheen of lantern light on metal.

David kept to the back wall of the hotel as much as he could, tiptoeing around a pile of firewood and a two-wheeled cart. The stable loomed ten yards away, and the soft lantern light still spilled out the crack at the front door. Someone was in there, probably Adams and Anne, but he had to be sure. He crouched over and ran to a haystack near the barn. For a full minute, he stood still, waiting for his breathing to slow and listening. All he heard from within was a horse's occasional stamp.

The clouds overhead parted, letting the moon peek through for a few seconds. He took a good look around the yard, then hustled toward the rear of the stable. He'd just spotted a back door when the clouds drifted over the moon again. If only it wasn't locked.

The thumb latch clicked, and David froze. Even a sound that small might carry to his enemy. He tried pushing, with no success, and pulled instead. The door moved reluctantly toward him. An odd sound caught his attention—a pulley? He realized the door had a weight attached, so that when a person let go, the weight would fall and the door would close itself. No curious horses would accidentally get out the back door.

He held it open about three inches and peered inside. The glow from the lantern at the front of the stable barely reached back here. Was he looking into a back room or tool shed? Another few seconds of scrutiny told him he was looking into an end stall used as a feed room. David listened but again heard nothing out of the ordinary— which in itself was odd. Shouldn't Anne and Adams be talking as they prepared to leave? Shouldn't he hear them moving the gear or leading out the mule and Adams's horse?

He moved the door outward a couple more inches. It creaked softly, and the rope on the pulley moved. He held his breath. Nothing else seemed to change.

Slowly, he eased the door open a bit more, until the gap was wide enough for him to squeeze through. With agonizing slowness, he let it come back to the frame with the thumb latch depressed. He kept the fingers of his other hand against the jamb at the risk of smashing them, to be sure there was no sudden *thunk* when the door moved into place. He let go of the thumb latch and exhaled.

For a long moment he stood in silence, letting his eyes adjust and trying to determine what was around him and how best to proceed. The glow came from ahead and to his left, where it seemed a wall stuck out, shielding him from view of anyone in the stable. He stepped forward gingerly, feeling for obstacles on the floor with his feet. When he reached the edge of the divider wall, he eased forward and took a quick look, then dodged back.

Midway down the barn aisle, Dan Adams's horse was tethered,

saddled, and ready to go. So why hadn't Dan left yet? David had received a hazy impression of a man standing by the door at the front of the barn, with his back turned to the stable. He pulled in a breath and held it, then looked around the wall again.

The man's build was too slight for Adams, and he wore a neat, town-gent's suit. Peterson. The scoundrel moved his head, and David swiftly drew back behind the board wall. Where was Anne? Had the blackguard hurt her?

A soft noise reached him from immediately on the other side of the flimsy wall. There must be a horse in the stall behind it.

David bent his knees and searched for a crack through which he could spy on Peterson, but the only one he found didn't give him a view of the far reaches of the building. He was mulling whether or not to risk peeking around the edge again when he heard the man say, "Stand up." Cautiously he peered around the divider.

Peterson moved to the right of the big door and returned a moment later, holding Anne by one arm. Her hands were bound in front of her. Peterson spoke to her, but David couldn't make out the words.

Behind him he heard a soft grunt—or more like a muffled groan. He turned and squinted into the inkiness of the stall. A barrel, the long handle of a tool, a dark bundle on the floor. He went over and felt the dark lump cautiously. A boot. A leg. A man.

"Adams?" he whispered.

Another soft grunt. David patted along the figure gently until he reached the man's head. A gag was tied in his mouth. He helped the poor fellow sit up and fumbled in the darkness until the cloth fell away.

"He's got Anne," Adams croaked out in a whisper.

"I saw," David replied. "What should we do?"

"Untie me. Do you have your gun?"

"Yes."

"Give it to me," Adams said. "If you go out there, he'll kill you."

"Oh, and he'll welcome you like a long-lost chum."

Adams sighed. "What, then?"

David fingered the knots in the twine that held Adams and gave up. He pulled out his pocketknife. "Hold still." A moment later he'd sliced through the twine. Adams's hands fell to the floor with a quiet thump. They both stopped breathing.

After a moment's silence, David whispered near his ear, "We need to hurry. I saw Mudge going into the hotel." He pressed the pocketknife into Adams's hand.

"He was going in?" Adams began to saw at the cord around his ankles. "We told him you would meet us out front if we took the horses out there."

"Mudge must have got tired of waiting for me."

"All right, I'll go out the way you came in and see if I can keep Mudge away. You wait here and see if you can get the drop on Peterson."

David couldn't think of a better plan. "Has he hurt Anne?"

"No, she's the bait."

Adams crept on all fours to the board wall and peeked around it. He rose to a crouch and ducked toward the back door. David wished he'd warned him about the weight and the noisy door, but it was too late. He winced and waited, pointing his revolver toward the opening of the stall.

Adams had apparently paid attention when he heard David enter; he opened the door slowly and almost silently. When he'd disappeared through it and let it come gently back into place, David let out his breath.

The paint horse shifted around so that he stood sideways across the aisle, and David couldn't see Peterson well—only his feet and a bit of Anne's dark skirt showed under the horse's belly. Hoping the horse would also hide him from their view, David crept forward and across the center alley to the divider near the pack mule's stall. He flattened himself against the low wall. When he stole another look, Peterson still held Anne. Maybe he'd attribute any sounds behind him to the animals.

David checked his revolver. He wouldn't dare use it unless he had a point-blank shot. Otherwise, he might hit Anne. But he was

sure Peterson wouldn't hesitate to fire on him.

He peered around the divider again. Peterson was rolling the door back. When it was open about eighteen inches, he stopped.

"Where is he?" he called.

David shrank back behind the wall again, certain the "he" Peterson inquired about was himself. If the assassin knew he crouched a few yards behind him, he'd sing a different tune. But now his accomplice must have returned. Mudge. They never should have trusted that boy. Ernie had proven himself, but the kid only saw the money he was promised.

And where was Dan Adams?

Anne flinched when she heard quick footsteps on the driveway. Peterson's breath tickled her neck as he stared out into the darkness, and she shuddered.

He shoved her aside suddenly and rolled the door open wider. Mudge must be back; he wouldn't give Uncle David such an open reception.

"Where is he?" Peterson called.

"Beats me," came Mudge's reply from outside.

Anne glanced down at her bound wrists. Was this the time for her to attempt a move?

Peterson leaned toward the doorway and let his hand, and the pistol, dangle at his side as he listened to Mudge.

"I went up to his room," Mudge began, and Anne took quick stock of Star's position.

The pinto was broadside in the aisle now, his head drooping as though he dozed. She pulled in a deep breath and ran.

"Hey!" Peterson cried.

She didn't look back, but grabbed as much of her heavy skirt as she could, hiked it up, and flung herself under the startled horse's belly. Star grunted and shuffled his feet. Anne ducked her head and rolled on the dirt floor in a swirl of skirts, right underneath the pinto and out beyond him. Star whinnied and pranced, pulling the lead rope taut. Anne crawled on her knees and elbows and at last grasped the prize.

She turned awkwardly and rose to her knees with Dan's revolver clutched in both hands. Movement to her left caught her eye, and she flicked a glance toward the mule's stall. Her throat tightened when she saw her uncle crouching behind the wall that separated it from the adjoining empty stall.

Dan could see them both talking in the shaft of light from the barn doorway. Mudge was giving a cursory account of his search for David Stone. When Peterson jerked around and yelled, he knew the game was over.

Dan used the only weapon he had—a stick of firewood he'd snatched up on his stealthy trip around the barn. He ran from the corner of the stable to the partly open door and swung at Mudge's droopy hat. The young man took a step into the opening as Dan delivered the blow, so it landed with less force than he'd intended and glanced off. At first he thought it had done no good, but Mudge paused for a moment then dropped like a stone in the doorway.

Dan looked over him. Star gave a shrill whinny. The lantern hung near the door, and its light showed Star, his white markings prominent, still tied in the middle of the barn, but backing and pulling against the rope. Between him and the horse, Peterson stood with his back to Dan, his pistol raised and pointing toward Star. Dan's throat went dry as he scanned the stall openings and brought his gaze rapidly back to Peterson. The killer took a step away from him, heedless of Dan's presence.

Stooping over Mudge's body, Dan grabbed the young man's belt and rolled him over. As he'd hoped, a pistol was stuck in the front of the belt. Dan grabbed the butt and worked the gun out of Mudge's clothing, praying Peterson wouldn't look back.

"All right, Miss Stone," Peterson said in a voice like granite. "You're too old to play hide-and-seek. I see your dress plainly. Now come on out."

Dan swallowed hard. He was after Anne, not her uncle. Perhaps

he still had no inkling that David was in the stable.

Peterson walked forward, leading with his pistol, until he was next to Star. He patted the trembling horse's flank behind the saddle and pushed Star's hindquarters aside.

"Come now, Miss—"

Peterson broke off as David rose from behind a stall divider to his right. He swung toward the Englishman. Dan aimed instinctively and pulled the trigger, getting only a faint *click*.

He wasted only a fraction of a second absorbing the fact that Mudge's pistol either wasn't loaded or had misfired. In that moment, Peterson swung his gun to point directly at David.

"Well, Stone, so you came to me after all." The two men stood for an instant with their weapons poised.

Dan pulled the trigger again. It clicked, and he threw it to the floor.

Peterson caught his movement or the sound and looked toward him at last. The hesitation was enough of a distraction. Dan dove toward him, hoping he could take Peterson down before he gathered his wits and fired.

But instead of aiming at Dan, Peterson whipped back toward David and pulled the trigger. Dan slammed into him as another gun discharged, and they both fell to the floor. Star squealed and sidestepped.

Peterson wasn't moving. Slowly, Dan pushed himself up to his knees. Peterson lay on his back, staring at the ceiling. He sucked in a breath, his face contorting. Blood soaked his shirt and coat, the stain growing as Dan watched. He leaned down and grabbed the shirt fabric and yanked, ripping the buttons out. The massive wound was too great. Dan clamped his teeth together.

Peterson's eyes sought his. "It's bad."

Dan nodded.

"I would have got him."

"Yes."

Peterson gritted his teeth and moaned.

David straightened and came from the shadows to stand beside

Dan and gaze down at his enemy.

"We'll tell Stone's cousin you failed," Dan said grimly, looking down at the dying man.

"Cousin?" Confusion clouded Peterson's gaze.

"Randolph Stone."

"I. . .don't know. . ."

"The person who hired you. Randolph Stone." Dan couldn't keep the anger out of his voice, and he hated that. This man still had power over him, even now.

"No." Peterson pulled in another breath. "That's not. . ." He went limp, staring sightlessly. Dan stared down at him for a moment, his mind whirling. He rose and looked over at Anne. She huddled on the floor close to Star, holding his revolver, her face set in shock.

"Anne, you all right?" David called. He nodded to Dan. "See to her." He knelt beside Peterson and put his hand to the man's throat.

Dan hurried to Anne and knelt beside her. "Anne, dearest, are you all right?"

She looked up at him with stricken eyes. Very carefully she held out the revolver. Dan started to take it by the barrel, but drew back when he felt its heat. Carefully he took it from her by the butt and placed it on the floor.

With tears swimming in her eyes, she held out her arms to him. Dan cut the rope on her wrists and pulled her close. For as long as she would let him, he would stay there with her, with his arms around her. She didn't cry, but her breath came in quick jerks. Dan rubbed her back slowly.

"It's all right, darling." He kissed her temple and folded her against his chest.

After what seemed like a year, and at the same time the flicker of an eye, David came over and stood in front of them, his feet planted a foot apart, hands on his hips.

"Is she all right?"

Dan nodded, though he was sure that on some levels Anne was far from fine.

"Good. I've tied up Mudge."

"Peterson?" Dan asked, but he knew.

David shook his head. "We'll need to get the constable. I suppose it's safe for me to show myself outside now."

"I'll go," Dan said.

"No. Stay here with her."

"You don't know where Owens lives."

"Tell me," David said.

Anne gave a little sob, and Dan patted her shoulders while he described the house to David. "It's not far. I think it's the third one past the smithy, and set back from the road. Clapboards, but no paint."

"I'll be back in a few minutes. If Mudge wakes up, let him rant. But do not untie him. You hear me?"

"I hear you," Dan said.

"Do you want to reload before I leave?" David touched the revolver with his boot toe.

Reluctantly, Dan stirred. He'd be foolish to sit here with Anne, a dead man, and a trussed-up thug without loading his gun.

"I'll do it," David said, stooping to pick it up. "You got what I need in your saddlebags?"

"Yes."

David walked to Star's side. He was surprisingly efficient and brought Dan's revolver back a couple of minutes later. He rested his hand on Anne's head for a moment. "I'll be back, my dear."

"Thank you," she choked out.

Dan looked up at him. "Take Star. I know it's not far, but it'll be quicker if you ride."

"All right. David stepped over Peterson's legs and untied Star. He led him to the door and carefully maneuvered him around Mudge's prone form. He shoved the big door farther open and led out the pinto. A moment later the door closed, all the way this time.

Dan sighed and settled more comfortably on the floor. Anne nestled into his embrace.

"Daniel?"

"Yes?"

"I killed him, didn't I?"

Dan swallowed hard. "I'm not sure. It happened so fast."

"Uncle David didn't reload. He never got a shot off. And I saw Peterson fall—the hole in the back of his coat. I did that."

Dan tightened his hold on her. "I'm sorry. We don't have to tell the constable."

"No, it's all right. We should tell him the truth."

The ache in Dan's throat was impossible to swallow away. "I love you," he whispered. She was silent for a moment, and he regretted his words. She already had more than enough to distress her. "I'm sorry. I shouldn't have said that. Forgive me."

"No."

He drew back a little and eyed her cautiously. "You won't forgive me?"

"No, Daniel. Say it as often as you want. I'll never tell you not to again."

He looked into her sad, dark eyes, still not certain he read her mood correctly.

A faint smile curved her lips upward. "I love you, too. I've been so foolish, but I expect I'll mend my ways from now on."

Dan bent toward her, still swathed in disbelief, and kissed her gently. Anne slid her arms up around his neck.

"When Uncle David comes back, will you take me to Mrs. Zinberg's? I don't want to stay in the hotel tonight."

"Of course."

Bewildered but thankful, Dan kissed her again.

CHAPTER 27

Two weeks later, Anne helped Elise Bentley set the table in her ranch kitchen for seven. Dan had ridden down to Corvallis from his brother's place, and Rob and Dulcie had driven over from their neighboring ranch to join Anne, Eb, Elise, and David for supper.

"I suppose it's unrealistic to think we could keep your uncle here any longer," Elise said as she laid out the plain, white ironstone plates.

Anne walked along behind her, placing the silverware at each place. "He said that as soon as he and Daniel settle the details for the stage line, he's going back to Eugene to look for a suitable building. He's serious about it, and he wants to get started before someone else does."

Elise smiled but shook her head. "It's wonderful having him around again, but I keep wondering if he's even thinking of going back to England."

"Not for a while, I'd say." Anne went to the cupboard for cups and saucers. "Of course, he can't until spring, but I don't know if he even wants to go then. He's having too much fun here."

"I should hate to see him go," Elise said, "and yet. . ."

"Yes. I feel the same way. I'm delighted to be with him again, after all these years, but I can't help thinking how much he's needed in England."

Elise smiled. "Now that his arm is getting better, there's no holding him down on this stagecoach business. If he took half the energy he's putting into that and put it into Stoneford, why, the estate would flourish and the tenants would prosper."

"Yes," Anne said. "I can't help feeling he's sorely needed there. But of course, he seems to have become quite attached to the freedom he has here. I believe he sees this stagecoach line as a challenge.

He's determined to see it succeed."

"I wonder. . . ." Elise eyed her thoughtfully.

"What?" When she didn't reply immediately, Anne's anxiety mushroomed. "What are you hinting at?"

Elise smiled. "Maybe it's Dan that he wants to see succeed."

"I don't understand." The truth was, Anne did understand. She dipped milk into a pitcher and avoided Elise's gaze.

"I'm just saying, maybe he sees Dan as a good prospect for a nephew-in-law and wants to help him escape his brother's farm for your sake."

Anne tried to formulate a retort, but she couldn't. Instead, her cheeks began to burn. She put down the ladle and carried the pitcher to the table. Without turning around, she said, "I do love him."

"Do I dare hope you're staying and will be a somewhat close neighbor?"

Anne shrugged. "I hope that as well. But Dan hasn't—"

"Don't tell me he hasn't renewed his suit. Whenever he's around you, he can't take his eyes off you."

She smiled at that. "I'm afraid I'm as bad now. But he hasn't spoken again. Perhaps I put him off too many times. I thought before we left Scottsburg that we'd reached an understanding."

"Perhaps you have. Dan is a practical man. He probably wants to be sure of what he's offering you this time before he makes the offer."

That prospect heartened Anne. She strained to catch sounds from outside.

"I hear a wagon driving up. That must be Rob and Dulcie. Is everything ready?"

Elise opened the oven door, and a cloud of roast beef–scented air wafted through the room.

"Yes, I believe so." Elise closed the oven and took off her apron. Together they went out to greet the Whistlers.

Dulcie hugged Anne and Elise and hovered over Rob while he unloaded the dishes she'd brought—two pies and a pot of beans, though Elise had assured her she didn't need to cook a thing.

Anne went to the team's heads. Bailey was in harness with Dulcie's mare. Anne stroked the gelding's nose.

"Hello, friend."

Rob smiled as he passed her, carrying the bean pot. "He seems none the worse for his sea voyage."

They all sat down to dinner. Eb carved the roast beef, and Elise served up the beans while the other dishes were passed around the table. For the first few minutes, the talk centered on the food and life at the Bentleys' and Whistlers' farms.

"How are things at your brother's place?" Rob asked Dan.

"Going well, sir. Hector accomplished a lot while I was gone. He expects his fiancée to come by ship next year."

"Sailing around the horn? She must be a brave woman," David said.

"I'm afraid the things Hector told her about our journey here dissuaded her from traveling overland," Dan said.

"Our trip last summer wasn't half bad." Eb held his cup out toward Elise, and she rose and took it from him. She returned a moment later with a coffeepot and poured his cup full.

Eb took it and set it down. "Somebody asked me t'other day if we were going to take another wagon train next year." He looked across the table at Rob.

"Not me! I promised Dulcie I was done with wagon trains."

"That's right," Dulcie said. "I'm surprised you'd even consider it, Eb, with your new bride and all."

Eb smiled. "Oh, I'm not going anywhere."

Elise said nothing but smiled as she made her way 'round the table dispensing coffee.

"And what about you, Mr. Stone?" Rob asked. "What are your plans?"

"I'll be going back to Eugene City soon and settle up there," he said.

"Going to England?" Dulcie asked.

"Weeell..." David looked over at Anne. "I've about made up my mind to stay another year. Daniel and I have a scheme we want to try—stage coaching from here to Eugene. We ought to be able to tell in a year's time whether we can make a go of that."

"Mr. Stone's found a place in town where they want to have the stagecoach station," Eb said. "Personally, I think it's a good idea."

"Daniel will man the station here, and I'll set up in Eugene," David said. "I intend to talk to Mr. Skinner when I get back there and see what's required for a mail contract."

"Well, now. You're giving up wheat farming?" Rob said to Dan.

"Yes, sir. My brother can do most of it, and I'll go up and help him when I can, for planting and harvest. But Hector's agreeable."

"So, Anne, if I stay in Oregon another year and go back in the spring of '57, will you make the journey with me?" David watched her closely, and again she felt her cheeks warm.

"Well, I. . . I'm not certain, Uncle David."

He smiled. "A lot can happen in a year or eighteen months."

"Yes."

Dan cleared his throat. "I believe Miss Stone may have other plans, sir."

David's eyebrows rose. "Oh? You believe, or you know?"

"Yes, tell us, Dan'l," Eb said.

Rob grinned at him. "You'd better make certain."

Dan looked from one to the other, seemingly uncomfortable. Anne decided anything she could say would only worsen the situation, so she busied herself with cutting her meat.

"There now, leave the boy alone," Elise said. "Eb, could you please pass the biscuits?"

"Mr. Stone," Dulcie said, "I've been wondering what would happen if you go back to England. Would you feel safe with your cousin still about?"

"That's a good question," David said, frowning. "You see, before Peterson died—that is, the man who wanted to kill me—he said that my cousin wasn't the one paying him."

"It sure seemed like that was what he meant." Dan shot Anne a quick glance and then looked away. He was just as glad to have the subject changed, she was sure, even if it was to a gruesome topic.

"But who else could want you out of the way, Uncle David?" she asked.

"I've thought about it a lot, and I've come up dry. Perhaps we'll hear back from Mr. Conrad in a few months, and he can tell us if there's any evidence that my cousin was behind it all. Meanwhile, I intend to go on living."

"Sounds like a good plan," Rob said. "Now, tell me, sir, will you be buying horses for the stagecoaches, or mules?"

The talk went back to the business for quite some time. When the meal had ended, the ladies cleaned up the dishes. When Elise went out to hang her dishcloth on the clothesline, she came back with a message for Anne.

"Dan says when you're done, he'd like to have a word with you. He's out on the side porch."

"Oh. I was going to sweep the floor," Anne said.

"I'll do it. Fetch your cape and go on. Don't keep that young man waiting."

Anne smiled at her. "I always did obey you, Elise."

"Yes, you were an exemplary child."

A minute later, Anne was out the kitchen door. Dan jumped up from his perch on the porch railing.

"Anne! I was hoping I'd get a word with you."

"Take several, if you've a mind to."

He smiled, and the worry lines eased out of his face. "I hope I didn't embarrass you too deeply at dinner."

"Everything you said was true."

He stepped a little closer, and her heart beat faster.

"Anne, I do hope you'll stay. I didn't mean to presume upon your thoughts about the matter, but a few things you said on the ship. . ."

She looked up into his gray eyes, usually so calm. Today they seemed a bit anxious. "I meant to encourage you. Am I horrid for being so bold?"

He smiled and reached for her hand. "I almost said, 'Do you mean it?' but I know you wouldn't say so if you didn't. Anne, are you truly thinking you might make your permanent home here?"

She chuckled, conscious of her own ingrained sense of propriety and his even stronger reticence. "That depends on so much, Dan."

"Oh?"

"Dare I say it depends on you?"

He caught his breath. "Anne, my dearest, if you would marry me, I'd do everything in my power to keep you happy. I wouldn't stick you off on the farm, away from your friends. You could be here in Corvallis, near Elise and Dulcie. And I wouldn't work you to death at the stage stop."

"I'm not afraid of hard work, Daniel."

"I know you're not. But I wouldn't like to see you worn down by it. I spoke to your uncle about it. He said we should hire a cook and a couple of tenders for the animals. He thinks we can do that and still make a profit."

"We shall see about that—about hiring a cook, I mean. Having extra help would be nice, though."

"Oh Anne, does—" He dropped to one knee and held her hand in both of his. "Will you, Anne? Will you marry me?"

She touched his cheek. "Yes, Daniel. I think we shall have splendid adventures together."

He sprang to his feet and pulled her into his arms. "Oh Anne, if it gets too tame, we'll take a ride up into the mountains."

"Lovely—so long as we don't encounter any cutthroats or grizzly bears."

He frowned for a moment. "I can't guarantee that. You and your uncle seem to attract swindlers and assassins. I've never seen a grizzly bear, though."

She eyed him askance. "Oh Daniel! Kiss me, or I'll retract my answer."

Without another word he complied, and quite handily.

On the last Friday in March, Dan's brother, Hector, rode down from Champoeg and stayed with him at the small house he'd bought in Corvallis. After breakfast on Saturday, they dressed in their best.

Dan put on the suit he wore to church each week, a new shirt and tie, and the silk top hat Hector had persuaded him to buy.

They walked over to the little church where Eb and Elise Bentley had been married in the fall. The minister greeted them. They sat down in the back pew, talking quietly. Dan's stomach was a bit on the roily side. He got up and walked to the door and looked out. Two riders had just entered the churchyard.

"Here's Eb and Elise."

Hector came out and greeted the Bentleys with him.

"How's the farm?" Eb asked Hector, whom he hadn't seen since they'd disbanded the wagon train in late October.

The two were soon engrossed in talk of crops and livestock.

"Where's Anne?" Dan asked Elise.

"Her uncle's bringing her in the wagon. But they were waiting for Rob and Dulcie."

Dan nodded and took a deep breath.

Elise smiled and touched his sleeve. "You look fine today, Daniel. How do you feel?"

"Not half bad." He grimaced. "Well, maybe half."

Elise laughed. "Anne is very excited, but she won't let on."

"No, I don't expect she will." It gave him a perverse pleasure to know that his coolheaded bride was nervous, too.

"How are things going?" Eb asked. "Anne says the stage line opens next week."

Dan grinned. "That's right. We're all set, and we've had people buying tickets already. Mr. Stone's got the station in Eugene set up, and we've got two stops along the way where we'll change teams."

"I admit I wondered this winter if it would all come together for you," Elise said. "I'm glad it has."

"Thanks." Dan didn't mention his main motivation—he'd promised Anne to have their house bought and furnished and the stagecoach station operational before the wedding. She hadn't insisted on it, but Dan didn't want her to jump into marriage and the chaos of setting up the business, too. He was confident that with her uncle's guidance for the next year at least, the line would succeed.

"David's been a really hard worker. When something didn't want to happen, he grabbed both ends and made it work."

Eb laughed. "What about those swindlers? Any word on them?"

"No. The marshal thinks Millie and Sam have left the territory."

"Good riddance," Elise said. "Anne got a letter from England day before yesterday, you know."

Dan stared at her. "No, she didn't tell me."

"The solicitor says Mr. Stone's cousin denies having anything to do with Peterson or the attempts on David's life. He said there's no evidence that Randolph Stone was involved."

"Huh." Dan frowned at Eb. "What do you think about that?"

"I think the cousin's lying. What other explanation can there be?"

Elise shrugged. "At least no one's tried to harm David since he left Scottsburg in November. I hope that's the end of the matter."

A team of horses pulling a wagon clopped into the yard.

"There's Rob and Dulcie," Elise said, waving to them. "David and Anne won't be far behind. Daniel, you'd best get inside now. Can't have you seeing Anne before the ceremony."

Dan grimaced at her. "That's silly."

"Come on." Hector laid a hand on his shoulder. "If the bride wants to follow some harmless tradition, what do you care?"

"That's right. It'll be worth it," Eb said with a wink at Elise.

Dan went back into the church with Hector. The minister met them halfway down the aisle.

"Most of the guests are here," Hector told him. "We're apprised that the bride is on her way."

"Oh good, good," the minister said. "Perhaps you gentlemen would like to come to the front of the church. I'm sorry we don't have an organ, but Miss Stone had me engage Harold Scully to play his fiddle. He just came in the back door."

A gray-haired man wearing a passable black suit and carrying a violin stepped forward and nodded to them. "Gents. It's a pleasure."

Dan and Hector shook his hand.

"Harold plays at all the dances," the minister said.

Dan eyed him with some trepidation, but Scully laughed. "It's

all right, sir. I can play slow tunes, too, and hymns."

A flurry at the door drew their attention. Eb, Elise, Rob, and Dulcie entered, along with several other women Dan recognized from church services and one man looking rather ill at ease. They all sat down on the benches, and the minister walked over to greet them.

He returned a moment later. "Mr. Adams, I'm told the bride and her uncle are ready. How about you?"

Dan swallowed hard and looked at Hector, who chuckled and slapped him on the shoulder.

"He's ready, Parson."

Dan nodded. "Yes, sir."

The minister nodded to Scully, who began to play a soft, sweet melody. The door opened once more, and Dan straightened his shoulders and looked toward it. David Stone held the door while Anne squeezed her voluminous skirt through the doorway. She smiled at her uncle through the filmy veil that hung from her bonnet.

Dan's stomach lurched. She wore a dress fit for Queen Victoria herself—white, with ruffles and flounces and bits of lace. And Anne's face shone. She held his gaze as she walked slowly the length of the aisle, holding David's arm. Dan hardly glanced at the tall Englishman, but he had an impression of an immaculate, finely tailored suit of formal clothes worn by a handsome man of substance.

They reached him, and David stood between him and Anne for a few minutes while the minister welcomed the guests and offered prayer.

"Who gives this woman in holy matrimony?" the minister asked.

David Stone took a deep breath. In his cultured tones, he said, "In the absence of her beloved parents, I do."

He moved aside and placed Anne's hand in Dan's.

Dan gazed down into her trusting brown eyes.

"Daniel," the minister said, "do you take this woman to be your lawfully wedded wife, to love and to cherish, to have and to hold from this day forward?"

"Yes, sir."

Behind him, Eb and Rob chuckled.

Dan said quickly, "I do, sir. I most assuredly do."

Discussion Questions

1. Anne has devoted nearly a year to looking for her uncle. At what point should she decide it's time to give up?

2. Dan knows from the beginning that Anne does not want to marry him, yet he joins her on her quest. Give two good reasons for him to do this—and two for him to put it to rest and go home.

3. Millie's morals slither all over the place. Was she justified in selling Andrew's pies and keeping the money? Name two other unethical things she did in the story. If you knew she was wearing a stolen dress, what would you do?

4. Why didn't David write to his family? Based on this, do you think Anne's expectations of her uncle were overblown?

5. What did you expect transportation, commerce, and communications to be like in 1855 Oregon? How did the characters cope with the primitive methods they had to use?

6. Do you think Millie is redeemable? How about Sam? Peterson?

7. If you were Anne, and Sam stole your horse, would you turn him over to the constable, knowing he might be hung for the offense?

8. How is Anne's quest as much a search for herself as it is for her uncle?

9. Anne suffers a great deal of anxiety over the fate of Bailey, the horse she borrowed from Rob Whistler. How does this compare with Sam's feelings about the blue roan?

10. How was Millie affected by her theft of David's things from his hotel room?

11. Anne has gone through nearly all of her annual allowance, but she hates the thought of borrowing from anyone. Unlike Millie, she can't just steal a few dollars. What would you recommend she do in her situation?

12. Anne is surprised that her uncle isn't eager to rush back to England. What is keeping him in America? In Oregon?

13. Why didn't Millie want to stay with Sam at the end of the story? What do you predict for Millie's future?

A LADY IN THE MAKING

CHAPTER 1

1857 The Dalles, Oregon Territory

You lied to me, Sam." Millie Evans peeked out the window from behind the half yard of muslin that served as a curtain. Outside the shanty they rented behind the feed store, a tall man with thick, dark hair and a week's growth of beard stood smoking a cigarette.

Millie turned back toward Sam and glared at him. "You said you were looking for a job, but you went and found that despicable man and brought him back here."

"I was looking for a job," Sam sputtered. "But I couldn't find one, and then Lucky turned up."

"Oh, sure he did. Like a bad penny. I suppose you just happened to be in the saloon when he dropped out of the sky."

Sam cringed, and she shook her head in disgust. "I came to The Dalles because you told me we could make an honest living together. Big laugh that turned out to be. And now you've brought *him* here. I told you before, I will *not* go live with a pack of outlaws."

She stalked to the wall and pulled her apron, extra dress, and shawl down from where they hung on nails and threw them on her bed. She stooped and felt underneath the end of the bed frame for the handle of her worn valise. Listening to her half-brother was the biggest mistake she'd ever made.

"Aw, come on, Millie. I just want to make things better."

"Better?" She pulled out the traveling bag and plunked it on the bed. "How is going into crime better?"

"You can have better things. You know. Clothes and—and jewelry, maybe. Lip rouge, stuff like that. It'd be better than scraping by like we are now."

"Is that what you thought when you went with Lucky last year?"

"Well, no."

"Exactly. But then two months ago, you wrote to me and said you were leaving the gang and you were ready to settle down in a nice little house somewhere with me."

Sam hung his head, and his face colored. "I'm sorry, Millie." Neither of them had to speak of the money he'd earmarked to buy that little house. He'd lost it all gambling by the time Millie had traveled up here from Elkton. A woman who'd lived thirty years and more ought to know better than to trust a gambling man, even if he was kin.

"We got by," she said. "Between my baking and laundry, we've been eating."

"But I don't want you to have to work so hard, Mil. I know I haven't helped much." That was an understatement. Sam's contributions to their funds had consisted of money he'd pilfered or won at cards. She suspected he only got the latter by cheating.

"If you want to go back to the gang, go ahead, Sam. I'm not going with you, and that's final."

"But—"

"No." Millie folded her best dress. She'd stolen it from a proper lady's luggage more than a year ago, and it was getting threadbare now, but she still loved it. She placed it in the valise and added the apron, her extra stockings, and her few cosmetics. Last of all she put in a brown, leather-bound book and a small wooden box. She walked to the shelf near the stove. "I'll leave you ten dollars. I'll need the rest."

"Where are you going?" Sam's plaintive expression almost made her relent. Though he was past thirty, his boyish face and memories of their knockabout childhood together kept her from despising him. But she'd had enough.

"I haven't decided yet." She opened the coffee tin she kept money in, peeled off the amount she was leaving him, and shoved the rest into her pocket. She'd been saving every penny she could, and had hoped that soon they could move to a real house, even though they'd have to rent one and not own it as they'd planned.

Good thing she'd saved most of what she had left when she got here, and hidden it where Sam wouldn't likely look.

"I'll send Lucky away," Sam said.

"For good?" Millie went to the window and pushed back the edge of the curtain with one finger. Lucky still stood there. He tossed his cigarette butt to the ground and crushed it with the heel of his scuffed boot.

"Well, I don't—see, I—Lucky needs me, Mil."

She dropped the curtain and placed her hands on her hips. "He needs you? Oh, that's rich." She'd known the man slightly when her husband was alive. Lucky was bad news then, and she had no doubt he'd grown worse over time.

"No, he does. See, one of his men died, and another's hurt."

"Ha. Killed during a robbery, no doubt."

Sam ignored that. "He really needs me, and he says I'm a good man and he wants me to come back. And if you'd come and help us out—"

"What, nursing wounded thieves and cooking for them? No, thank you." She went to the dish cupboard and scanned the contents. She couldn't take all of their meager belongings. She chose her best paring and chopping knives and an enameled tin cup. She tucked them into her valise and closed it.

She put on her shawl and best bonnet.

"Good-bye, Sam. I'm sorry it turned out this way. Be careful."

"No, wait!"

He followed her out the door.

Millie didn't so much as glance Lucky's way. She strode across the yard between their hovel and the feed store, aiming for the back door of the store. Better to go where other people would see her.

Sam trotted up behind her. "Millie, please."

"Go back, Sam."

He grabbed her elbow and spun her around. "What's happened to you? You're different than you used to be. Did you get soft, Mil?"

"I wouldn't call it that. But I *have* been thinking about right and wrong."

Sam lifted his battered felt hat, scratched his head, and settled the hat again. "We didn't used to think about that much. Just about what we'd eat next."

"Well, those days are over. For me, anyway. Now I know there are things we shouldn't do—things I *won't* do ever again. And stealing is one of them."

"You can just cook if you want to. We wouldn't make you steal. It's too bad though—you were good at it."

"That's enough." She glanced quickly about to be sure no one else was near enough to hear. At the feed store's back door, she left him and entered the shadowy building. Not for the first time, she felt somewhat relieved at leaving her half-brother behind. She cared about him, yet Sam didn't seem to want to change. He didn't like to work, and he seemed to prefer living on the shady side of the law. Well, she'd walked away from that once, and she liked the glimpses she'd had of a better life.

Sacks of feed and fertilizer were stacked to the ceiling in the dimly lit feed store. She wound her way toward the front, where light shone in through two dusty windows.

The store owner nodded at her. "Miz Evans."

Millie paused. "My brother and I will be giving up the rooms out back. I believe our rent is paid through the end of the month."

"What? Oh. Well, I'm sorry to see you go."

She said no more but hurried out and turned toward the stagecoach station. There should have been a stage leaving town that afternoon. She didn't really care what direction it was pointed, though she didn't want to go back to Elkton. The traffic to the gold mines had slowed to a trickle along that route. Trade was so slim her boss at the old restaurant had closed up shop and retired. There wouldn't be a job for her there.

When she reached the stage office, the coach was nowhere to be seen. She went inside and walked to the ticket counter.

"Where to, ma'am?" the clerk asked.

"Where can I go for less than eighty dollars?"

The clerk laughed and quickly sobered. "Well, let's see now." He consulted a book on the counter before him. "Boise, Salt Lake. . .you might connect from there for someplace farther east, but there's no direct line, ma'am. If you want to go west, you could get to Portland, Vancouver, Oregon City, Eugene—"

"There's a stage going out soon, isn't there?"

"Yes ma'am. They're around back, switching the team. They'll leave in"—he pulled out his pocket watch as he spoke and opened it—"ten minutes."

"East or west?"

"Eastbound."

The door opened, and Sam came in, panting. "Come on, Millie." He walked over to the counter and tugged at the handle of her satchel.

"I am not going with you." She glared at her brother. At least he hadn't brought Lucky inside, but the outlaw was probably lounging outside by the hitching rail.

"So, are you going to buy a ticket?" the man behind the counter asked.

Millie glanced at him. "Please excuse me a moment." She grabbed her brother's sleeve and pulled him aside. "I'm serious about this, Sam."

"But you said you'd stay with me."

"That was when you said it would be just the two of us—like in the old days, when we were at Mr. Stone's farm in Eugene."

A man wearing a woolen suit came in and walked to the counter. Millie edged Sam farther away from them.

"Mr. Stone is gone now, Millie," Sam said. "And I tried to get a job. You know that."

She tossed her head. "You didn't try very hard." Lowering her voice, she added, "And running with a gang of road agents is *not* a job."

His face fell. "Aw, come on. You didn't used to mind lifting things here and there. You had a real knack for it. You didn't do so bad convincing fellas to give you money either."

She pulled back and glared at him. "What are you implying?"

"Nothin'. I'm just saying, you worked for that Andrew fella, and you got chummy with Mr. Stone—"

"David Stone never gave me a cent." She clenched her teeth and pushed back the memory of picking up ten dollars off the gentleman's dresser. "Andrew Willis, on the other hand, was my employer. I cooked in his restaurant, and he paid me a fair wage."

"A pretty good wage, if you ask me."

"I *didn't* ask you. But good cooks are at a premium out here." Although that hadn't helped much in this town. She baked bread for a restaurant and a boardinghouse and sold a few pies to the officers at Fort Dalles, but she knew she could do better in a bigger town.

"Well, if you come cook for us, we'll pay you. Lucky says so."

"With what? Your loot?" She glanced toward the ticket window. The man now purchasing a ticket was watching them with apparent interest. She set down her valise, seized Sam's sleeve, and hauled him outside and down into the dusty street. Lucky stood several yards away, near their horses. She turned her back to him. "Sam Hastings, you listen to me. I don't want to live on the wrong side of the law." She didn't say *again*, but she didn't have to.

"Might be in your best interest to come along with us, Miz Evans," Lucky drawled.

Millie whirled and found him not two feet behind her. He moved quietly for a rugged man. He stood with his thumbs tucked into his gun belt, watching her with a self-satisfied smirk, as though he knew her type and how phony she was. Well, she wouldn't give him the satisfaction of having her cook so much as a cup of coffee for him.

"I'm not interested."

"Sam and I have an extra horse for you to ride. He's tied up yonder with our nags." Lucky pointed down the street with his bearded chin.

Millie looked and saw the horses tied up in front of a saloon. So he'd come expecting to take her along. He and Sam must have planned it all out this afternoon while they shared a bottle of whiskey.

"Just come on along with us nice like, and take a look at our place. You can maybe fix supper tonight."

"And if you don't want to stay, I'll bring you back to town in the morning," Sam said.

"After breakfast," Lucky added.

"Yeah. After breakfast." Sam grinned at her.

"No thank you." Millie gathered handfuls of her skirt and prepared to mount the steps to the stagecoach station and buy her ticket. The agent had said she could afford one to Salt Lake and go east from there. That's what she'd do. Her cousin Polly lived at Fort Laramie. She had married a preacher. Maybe Polly and her respectable husband could help her find honest employment. And she'd put as much ground as she could between herself and Sam's outlaw cronies.

Strong fingers clamped around her upper arm. "I said it's in your best interest to go with us." Lucky's cold tone sent a jolt of fear through Millie.

She turned around swiftly, swinging her other arm as she whirled. She struck him hard on his fuzzy cheek and lunged away from him, stumbling over the bottom step.

"You little—"

"Hey!" A stern-faced man strode up the street from the direction opposite the saloon. "What's going on here?"

Millie righted herself, wincing at the pang in her ankle where it had connected with the step. "It's all right. I was just going in to buy my ticket, and I fell."

Lucky's eyes narrowed. Sam stood a couple of steps behind him, staring, his lower lip trembling.

"Are you sure you're all right, ma'am?" the newcomer asked.

"Yes, thank you." She gave him a delicate smile. He wore work clothes, and he was youthful and big enough to give Lucky pause. A farmer, most likely. "I bumped my ankle when I stumbled. Would you mind, sir, if I took your arm while I get up these steps?"

"My pleasure, ma'am." The young man crooked his elbow, and she placed her hand in the bend, leaning on him just a little as they maneuvered the steps. She didn't look back.

As soon as they were inside and the door closed, she turned to him and whispered, "I cannot thank you enough. You must be careful when you leave here, lest those thugs lurk about to harm you."

His eyebrows shot up, and he pulled off his hat. "Indeed. Then they *were* ill-treating you. I thought so at first, but you were so cool, I'd changed my mind."

"That big fellow is one to watch," she said.

The customer who had come in to buy a ticket earlier turned away from the counter, tucking his wallet away. He touched his hat brim as he passed them and went out.

"Well, now," the clerk said. "Made up your mind, have you?"

"Yes." Millie stepped up to his station. "I'd like a ticket to Salt Lake, please, unless you can get me through to Fort Laramie."

"Can't do that, ma'am, but I hear the Mormons are setting up for a mail route from Independence to Salt Lake. Most likely they'll take you through in one of their wagons." He named the price to Salt Lake City. Millie winced but took out her purse.

"They lowered the prices this week," the clerk said, as if hoping to console her. "Trying to break the competition."

She gulped, thinking of the few dollars left in her purse after she'd paid out the price of the ticket. If not for the reduction in fares, she couldn't have bought passage to Salt Lake, and she wasn't sure she could afford to get to Cousin Polly's home. She hated the thought of getting stranded along the way.

"Ma'am," said the young man who had rescued her, "it would be my pleasure to buy you dinner at the boardinghouse down the street. And to bring you back here to make sure you board safely."

Millie smiled at him. "Thank you so much, but there's not time, I'm afraid."

"That's right," the clerk said. "Stage is comin' around now." He nodded toward the window. Millie turned and saw the coach, with the driver and shotgun messenger perched high on the box, pulling up outside.

"Then I must board right away." She hoped the young man would stay close. With him, the driver, and the shotgun rider handy, she ought to be able to get into the stagecoach without interference from Sam and Lucky.

The young man flushed and looked down with a sad smile playing at his lips. "Then it's my loss. I do wish you a good trip."

"Thank you." Millie judged him to be six or eight years her junior—perhaps four and twenty. Just the age when young men tend to think older women are intriguing. Especially attractive older women, and Millie would never be so self-deprecating as to think she didn't fit the bill.

The clerk cleared his throat. "Your ticket, ma'am."

"Oh yes. Thank you so much." Millie put the bit of pasteboard into her purse. "May I leave my valise here?"

"You may. I'll see that it's loaded."

She retrieved it from the corner, where she'd left it to converse with Sam fifteen minutes earlier, and passed it to the clerk.

"Best get aboard," he said. "The driver won't wait."

The young man smiled down at her and again offered his arm. "Let me see you off, ma'am." He didn't ask her name, and Millie didn't give it. She'd be just as glad not to have her name associated with the two rather scruffy men watching from a few yards away. The clerk followed her out and passed her valise up to the shotgun rider on top of the coach. Her gallant young escort stepped up and opened the door for her. She threw a sidelong glance toward her brother. Sam and Lucky stood near their horses, watching them, but didn't approach.

David Stone leaned back against the leather seat and closed his eyes. Not for the first time, he wished he'd ridden horseback instead of taking the stagecoach. But he couldn't take a horse with him on the ship to England, so it was no doubt better to have left it behind. The fact that he owned a small stagecoach line in western Oregon didn't make this journey any less tedious.

The Stone line that he'd run for the last year had two coaches more comfortable than this one. David rode them himself at least once a month, when he went to see his niece, Anne, and her husband, Dan. Daniel Adams was his partner in the business, and he'd proven himself an apt driver and a good businessman. If only David could ride his own line all the way East.

The one bad thing about the Stone line was its length, or lack of it. The route only ran from Eugene to Corvallis, though he and Dan had discussed pushing it through to Oregon City and Portland in the near future. But it hadn't happened yet, so he had to sample other stage lines on his journey. He anticipated several weeks of this tiring travel. Why hadn't he just boarded a ship in Newport? While the thought of rounding the Horn didn't scare him, his niece, Anne, had pleaded with him not to risk it.

"They need you in one piece in England," were her exact words. Well, the way they'd rattled over the road toward The Dalles, he might not get out of Oregon intact.

The stage had dropped into a rut as they approached the town, throwing him against the side wall. The wound he'd received eighteen months ago still ached sometimes when he was tired or racketed around the way he was now, and the jolting sent a deep pain through him. As they waited for the new team to be hitched properly, he rubbed his right shoulder. He quit when the man opposite took notice.

The stop near Fort Dalles would be brief. At least they'd gotten a passable dinner earlier, at the home station. The tenders at the swing station changed the teams swiftly, and the driver soon guided the coach around to the front of the building. David sighed as the door opened to admit another passenger.

"Watch your step, ma'am," said a young man outside.

David turned his head to peer at the new arrival. Sure enough, a woman placed a dainty foot on the coach step. The rancher sitting beside David scooted across to the seat on the opposite side, where a tool salesman was sitting. Great. Now David would have to share a seat with the woman, and he'd have to put up with a big hat, skirts, and no doubt a parasol and a bundle or two.

She paused in the doorway, took stock of the situation, and eased onto the seat next to him. David nodded without making eye contact. Oh well—the other men would have to watch their language and refrain from smoking, but that wouldn't bother him any.

"Good day," she said pleasantly.

He stared at her. The broad brim of her hat shaded her face, but the voice...

The two men opposite murmured a greeting. She settled back in her seat and turned to look at him. The smile on her lips froze.

She blinked at him and narrowed her gaze. "Why—Mr. Stone?"

David gulped and stared into the beguiling green eyes of Charlotte Evans—the woman who had tried a mere eighteen months past to cheat him out of his fortune.

CHAPTER 2

Millie sat rigid on the seat for the first hour, trying not to let any part of her person or her clothing touch the elegant Englishman beside her. With two other passengers in the small enclosure of the stagecoach, they could hardly discuss their last meeting or their mutual acquaintances. David Stone seemed just as indisposed to converse as she was. He'd developed a deep interest, it seemed, in the scenery they flew past as the stagecoach rolled eastward along the Columbia River.

She couldn't maintain that posture forever, especially in a vehicle that lurched and swayed in a manner that made her stomach roil. Her gloved hands, clenched in her lap, at last relaxed, and she allowed her aching back to curve a bit against the seat back. She longed to remove her large hat, but there was no place to lay it, and her valise had disappeared into the boot at the back of the coach. She cursed her own vanity. Why hadn't she worn her plain calico bonnet and not this fancy hat? She'd bought it last year, with money ill-gotten when she betrayed the man beside her. Just thinking about it made her ill.

They must be halfway to the next stop. As soon as they arrived, she would speak to Mr. Stone in private. She must make him understand that she had changed.

The two men across from her watched her, the one dressed as a farmer surreptitiously, and the businesslike one with open admiration. Millie concentrated on keeping her expression neutral. A lady mustn't betray her inner thoughts any more than she should reveal her inner layers of clothing. She avoided looking at either of them, and in consequence her gaze collided once with David Stone's.

That flicker of a moment—coupled with the brief appraisal she'd made on entering the coach—told her that he was as handsome as ever. The tall, blond man was about forty, very fit and good-looking. She knew from experience how charming he could be. But now his blue eyes held a clear dislike bordering on contempt. She looked away and shivered.

If only she'd changed her ways before they met—what might have happened then? But at that time, she'd been godless and without scruples. The way things had gone, she doubted she could ever regain his respect and admiration. But she might be able to partially right the wrong she had done him.

By the time they'd crossed the John Day River at McDonald's Ferry and reached the station on the other side, she feared her spine was jostled beyond repair and she might not be able to climb down from the coach.

"Twenty-minute stop to change the teams," the station agent announced as he opened the door. "The necessary is out back."

The men hung back, waiting for her to disembark, so Millie pushed herself forward off the seat. Her lower back muscles screamed as she emerged through the doorway and groped for the step. The agent offered his hand to assist her, and Millie clutched it.

"Thank you," she gasped as she reached terra firma and inhaled as deeply as her corset would allow.

She made the requisite trip "out back" and returned to the yard, grateful that the men had waited there until she was finished. The driver was applying grease to the wheel bearings while the tenders swapped the team for four fresh horses. The shotgun rider stood by, chatting with the station agent.

Millie approached them with a smile, and they immediately broke off their conversation. The shotgun rider whipped off his hat, and both men returned her smile. Once again, Millie had proven to herself that if a woman acted self-assured and at ease, other people would respond in like manner. At least, decent men did.

"Help you, ma'am?" the station agent asked.

"Yes, thank you. I wondered if there's a way for me to send a message ahead to Fort Laramie and have it get there before I do."

"Not much goes faster'n this stage, ma'am," the agent said.

The shotgun messenger frowned. "Well now, Billy, that ain't the strictest truth. You know, if she was to hit it just right, she might get a military messenger to carry a letter for her."

"I s'pose that's true." His companion nodded. "Sometimes the army will send dispatches and such, and they travel pretty fast. Could be someone will pass you heading out from Fort Dalles or one of the other posts along the way. Might beat the mail coach. Not by much though."

"Oh. Is this a mail coach?" Millie asked.

"No ma'am. This line doesn't have the contract for that." The station agent's face was so sour she feared she'd touched on a sore spot. His competitor must have reeled in the lucrative contract.

Her hopes to inform Polly of her impending arrival dashed, Millie broached her next question.

"Would it be possible for me to retrieve something from my valise?" she asked the shotgun rider.

"Surely, ma'am."

He had her bag down in an instant, and Millie quickly removed the small items she wanted. She thanked the man and stepped away.

She hoped for a word with Mr. Stone before she boarded, and so she waited a few yards away from the coach, watching the men complete their work.

She'd written to Polly last fall, when the restaurant in Elkton closed, about the possibility of visiting her. But once she'd decided to stop at The Dalles with Sam, she'd sent a note saying she guessed she would postpone the trip. She hadn't wanted to cut off the option, but she'd really hoped things would work out with Sam this time. What had she been thinking?

To her relief, David Stone soon appeared around the corner of the building, and she stepped briskly toward him.

He glanced about as though hoping to spot an avenue of escape, then stopped and waited for her to reach him.

"Mrs. Evans."

"Mr. Stone. I wondered if I could have a private word with you, sir."

"I see no need for it."

"Oh, but I do. Great need."

"I've nothing to say to you, Charlotte." He blinked and looked away.

She realized he'd slipped, not intending to use her given name. She'd be flattered that he remembered it, except that was the assumed name she'd used when she tried to lure him into a hasty marriage. His cheeks colored, and she looked down at her hands.

"It's Millie actually."

"Indeed." He strode past her and opened the door to the coach.

His accent still thrilled her, though she understood he'd been in America more than twenty years. Whether he'd been farming or mining since she last saw him, she didn't know, but the clothes he wore gave him an aura of success. A well-cut suit of good cloth, pearl buttons on the figured satin vest, and a hint of subdued luxury—a plain gold watch chain peeking out near his belt. If he was still farming, it was for the entertainment of it.

She walked over to him, afraid for a moment that he'd climb into the coach and shut the door in her face. But he stood there with a resigned air, holding it for her. She might have known he would retain his manners, even though he obviously despised her.

Once in the stage, she hesitated then turned to address him. "Would you like to sit on this side, or do you prefer your former seat?"

"It doesn't matter."

She moved over to the farther side of the seat and settled her skirts about her. For an instant, she wished she'd worn her finest gown. Then she recalled that David's niece had told him Millie had stolen it from her, so that would never do. Her cheeks heated at the memory. He had every right to think ill of her. But she might not get another chance to speak to him in private, so she turned to him as he sat down next to her.

"Forgive me, but I must have a word with you."

"I really see no advantage to that, Mrs. Evans."

He'd left the door open, and at that moment the farmer and the man in the suit climbed in, followed by another man, this one wearing a plaid flannel shirt and worn whipcord trousers. The three eyed her and David, and lined up across from them on the opposite seat. Between them, a bench seat would accommodate more passengers, but no one wanted to sit on that without a backrest unless it was absolutely unavoidable. So now she had one man beside her avoiding her gaze and three across the way ogling her. Millie resigned herself to endure the next twenty-five miles with nothing resolved between her and the man she might, under other circumstances, have truly loved.

David crossed his arms and leaned his head back as the stage began to roll toward the mountain crossing. Charlotte Evans, of all people. Or Millie, as she now claimed. It figured that she'd deceived him in that, too. Could there be another person on earth he would less like to have met up with? And to be forced to sit beside her for—how long?

Why, oh why hadn't he simply declined to get back in the coach? He might have had to wait a couple of days to catch another stage, but a quiet interlude in the Oregon wilderness would be preferable to several hours locked in a box with Charlotte.

"Good day, ma'am," the newcomer on the seat opposite David said, staring at Charlotte.

"Good day," she replied.

"Going to Boise?" he asked.

"And beyond."

He nodded.

"I'm going to Boise myself," said the farmer. "I hope you have a pleasant journey."

"The same to you, sir."

Charlotte knew how to speak prettily without encouraging a fellow; David had to hand her that. She was so good at the role, he'd thought her a true lady.

"I'm going to Boise as well," said the man in the suit. "Henry McCloskey's the name."

"How do you do," Charlotte said.

"What's your line?" the man next to him asked.

"I represent the hardware trade."

"Aha, a drummer," said the farmer.

"A sales representative, sir."

The man chuckled. "Well, I've got a hunnerd and twenty acres in the Owhyee Valley—I run sheep mostly. Name's Stoddard."

The three men chatted among themselves, occasionally throwing a question Charlotte's way. After a half hour, the newest man, who had declared himself a miner, eyed David keenly.

"And you, sir? What do you do?"

"I'm half owner in a stagecoach line," David replied.

McCloskey's eyebrows shot up. "Not this one?"

"No, thank heaven."

The three men chuckled. David couldn't resist a sidelong glance at Charlotte. Her lips curved in a genteel smile.

"Not from these parts," the miner said.

"No, sir, though I've been in Oregon six years."

"He's a Britisher," Stoddard said with an emphatic nod that crumpled his beard.

David said nothing, which he supposed some might consider rude, but he didn't want to talk about himself. Already he'd given out more information than he wanted Charlotte to know. The fact that he'd made a success of the stage line since he'd last seen her might be enough to set her scheming. What would happen if she knew he was on his way to England to claim a large estate?

At last they reached another way station and stopped to change teams. They all got out to stretch their legs, and Charlotte let the other passengers drift by and then grabbed David's sleeve.

"Please, Mr. Stone. I really must speak to you. Forgive me for being such a pest."

He gazed pointedly at her fingers, clutching his broadcloth sleeve. Charlotte pulled her hand away as if it had burned her.

"I'm sorry. But you must believe me when I say that I've changed since last we met. I do hope you'll find it in your heart to forgive me for the wrongs I committed then."

David observed her through slits of eyes. He didn't believe a word she said. If her urgent news was that she no longer took part in swindling innocent people, or that she wouldn't conspire to have him murdered this time, she could save her breath. He'd had a few hours to think about it, and he suspected she'd been keeping track of him.

"Tell me," he said, "did you take the same stagecoach as I did by design?"

"Oh no, sir," she cried. "That was purely coincidence, I assure you, though if I may be so bold, I'd call it a providential one. I've repented of my wrongdoing. I'm grateful that God allowed me a chance to tell you so."

David scowled. Now she was bringing the Almighty into it. If she thought that would convince him, she was wrong. It only made him more suspicious.

"So where *are* you traveling to?" he asked at last. "You said beyond Boise."

"That's correct. I'm heading to Fort Laramie. I hope to live with my cousin, who is married to a minister there."

He nodded, thinking about the length of that journey. They'd be confined in the coach together for several days. He shuddered.

Charlotte—or rather, Millie—had turned her attention to her rather bulky handbag. Perhaps this would be a good time to disengage himself.

"Excuse me," he said.

"No, wait!" Her bewitching green eyes held dismay, almost panic. "I have something of yours. I need to give it to you."

"Something of mine?" He frowned but waited. She drew out a small, leather-covered book and handed it to him. "Your Bible, sir. Please forgive me for taking it."

David took the familiar book and held it tenderly, stroking the soft leather. He'd wondered how it had disappeared from his hotel room in Scottsburg a year and a half ago. He should have known. But even given Charlotte's character, he never suspected she'd steal a Bible. Money, yes, but God's Word? Hardly.

"And this." She held out a small wooden box, and David frowned. "What's that?"

"Why, your cuff links, sir." She glanced off to the side, as though to be sure no one else could overhear. "I'm truly sorry."

David tucked the Bible under his arm and took the little carved box. He lifted the cover and stared down at the onyx cuff links his grandfather, the fifth Earl of Stoneford, had given him on his twelfth birthday. He'd known they were missing, but he'd suspected one of the hotel staff had pilfered them from his room while he was recovering from a wound. He'd never had an inkling that Charlotte had been in his room, much less ransacked it.

"Thank you." He tucked the box in his coat pocket, and his fingers wrapped around it for a moment. How close he'd come to losing his heart to her—but all she'd made off with was his cuff links. He'd been blinded by her charms. The knowledge left him feeling witless and old.

She looked up at him with a pained expression. "I took ten dollars, too, from your dresser. You'd left it there with a note to the hotel owner, saying it would cover your room."

"Indeed?" He stared at her, unable to think of anything more trenchant.

She nodded. "I burned the note. And I spent the money, I'm afraid. I promise I'll pay it back though, as soon as I'm able. If you'll give me an address—"

"Forget it," David said. He was touched that she'd returned his keepsakes—the onyx cuff links were actually worth more than the money she'd stolen. But there was no way he'd tell her how to reach him in the future. He never wanted to see her again.

Her stricken face reminded him of how much he'd cared for her. Charlotte could be so charming. . .pity she'd gone so wretchedly wrong.

"I read some in your Bible. The truth is, that's partly what brought me to change my ways. And so I thank you for that."

David hated the way her guileless manner played on his

sympathies. She was a fake and a fraud. He knew that. But she was very good at it. "Look, I have a new Bible now. Keep this one if you like."

She gasped, and her face lit with surprise and joy. "Oh, thank you, sir. If you're sure—I'd love to keep it, above all things." She took it from him with trembling hands that appeared almost reverent.

"Yes, well, let's say no more about this. The past is the past." He touched his hat brim and turned away. If he made a beeline for the outhouse, she could hardly chase after him and press further conversation on him. But he wondered—was even a tenth of what she'd said the truth?

CHAPTER 3

Millie was not completely surprised that David Stone shunned her. After all, she had stolen from him and tried to lure him into marrying her so she could live in style. Without meaning to, she'd endangered his life.

If only he'd give her the chance to show him that she had transformed into a new Millie Evans.

She almost laughed aloud at the thought. He hadn't even known her real name. She'd introduced herself to him as Charlotte Evans in Scottsburg, because it sounded more elegant than Millie, and he'd still thought the name belonged to her.

The stagecoach jostled and swayed. She was very careful not to move too close to David. More than anything right now, she wanted to avoid giving him any new reason for displeasure.

She was pleased to see that he'd recovered from his mishap. He looked as handsome as ever—tall, fair-haired, with compelling blue eyes—and if anything, more prosperous. The stagecoach line was news to her. So he'd given up farming and prospecting and invested in a real business. She was certain it would thrive under his guidance.

Where was he going? He hadn't chimed in when the others had discussed their destinations. Maybe he was thinking of expanding his stage line and had come to check out some of the roads. Perhaps he contemplated adding this very line to his own. Hadn't the ticket agent in The Dalles said prices were lowered to break the competition? Wouldn't that be ironic, if he was riding this coach to see if he wanted to annex the entire line? She'd ascertained long ago that he was shrewder with financial matters than he was with women. If only certain people hadn't interfered, she'd have reeled him in and had a fine husband.

She turned her face toward the window and silently scolded herself. She must stop thinking that way. God certainly didn't want her to go on viewing David Stone as a potential husband, rich or otherwise. If she wanted to please the Lord—and she did now—she had to get those thoughts right out of her head. But it was hard to do when he was sitting right smack beside her.

The stage kept rolling, day and night. They stopped only to change teams. At swing stations, they had twenty minutes to tend nature's needs and perhaps grab a quick bite of something. Home stations served full meals, and they had a half hour at those. Of course, they had to pay for every bite they ate, and Millie's funds dwindled quickly.

On the second day, they climbed out at a home station and the men hurried inside.

"Taking dinner, Mrs. Evans?" McCloskey, the drummer, asked.

"Oh no, thank you." She'd bought one full meal the day before and had decided she'd have to limit herself to one per day and perhaps a biscuit and a cup of tea in the mornings. If she could hold off and buy her full meal in the evening, she'd feel as though she'd accomplished something and deserved her supper.

"You hardly ate any breakfast," McCloskey protested. He hadn't shaved for at least two days, and a grayish stubble speckled his chin. "Come on, lass. I'll treat you."

Millie was tempted to accept, but David lingered near the door to the station, conversing in low tones with the shotgun rider. Was he listening to see what she would say? Even if he wasn't, he'd see her eating with McCloskey.

Besides, Millie would feel beholden to the drummer for the rest of their journey. Was that what he wanted? Would he expect something in return? Most men did expect a profit on their investment.

"No thank you," she said. "I'm really not very hungry. I'll have something this evening."

McCloskey frowned. "Coach make you queasy, does it? I don't think this one's as well sprung as some. Sure you won't join me?"

"Quite sure." She gave him a cool smile.

"All right then." He lumbered inside.

Her stomach growled, and Millie hurried around the corner of the building, out of sight and sound of David and the shotgun rider.

As they journeyed over the Blue Mountains, David asked himself many times why he was doing this. The air dropped below freezing at night in the upper altitudes, and he wasn't about to cuddle up to any of the other passengers. They huddled under the buffalo robes the driver distributed. Millie Evans kept to her corner, thank heaven. The male passengers took turns on the backless bench seat in the middle. McCloskey, Stoddard, and the miner—whom he'd learned was named Tuttle—stayed with them. Other men came and went, from one stop to another.

By the time they wound down out of the mountains and approached the Grande Ronde River, they had eight men and Millie, all bound at least as far as Boise. They sat three to a seat, unless one or two ventured up to the roof, where some claimed they could sleep.

All of the others tried to engage Millie in conversation. She answered them politely but did not encourage them. David ignored her.

He felt an occasional twinge of guilt that he hadn't offered her a modicum of protection by continuing to sit next to her, but he couldn't bear to be any closer to the woman. As soon as it became necessary to admit a third person to their seat, he retreated into the other corner. After that, they had to put up with whomever chance—or Providence—placed between them. For one stage, a matter of a couple of hours, it was a slightly inebriated farmer who reeked of manure and cheap ale. Poor Millie-Charlotte spent most of that time with her handkerchief close to her nose. Everyone concerned breathed easier when he got out at the next station and did not return.

They headed down a rather steep portion of the trail, pushing David back into his seat corner and making the men opposite brace themselves. Those on the middle seat clung to the leather straps that hung from the ceiling. David took his watch out for a quick look, though he didn't like to show it often among strangers. They'd make Brown's Town by sunset, he hoped.

A sudden jarring sent the drummer completely out of his seat and crashing into a rotund traveler sitting in the middle. The coach listed to one side—David's—and the driver erupted in coaxing "Ho's" and "Whoa now's" designed to convince the team to stop.

As soon as the coach halted, the driver hopped down and could be heard breaking the no-cussing rule as he examined the vehicle. A moment later, the door swung open.

"Sorry, folks," the shotgun rider said almost cheerfully. "Got to have you all step out. We seem to have busted a wheel."

Millie accepted his hand and climbed out first.

"Do you have a spare?" Stoddard asked.

"Nope, but we're only three miles from Brown's. I'll take one of the horses and ride in to tell the station agent. He'll send out a wagon with an extra wheel and a man to help change it."

"How long will that take?" McCloskey asked as he squeezed out the door.

The shotgun messenger frowned for a moment, sending his droopy mustache askew. "Couple of hours, maybe."

"But we'll go on tonight?" McCloskey apparently was in a hurry to get to Boise with his sample cases.

"I expect so, if we get it fixed in time. They don't run the ferry after dark here."

The driver, meanwhile, was unhitching one of the leaders for him. He clipped on shorter reins that they carried for emergencies, and the shotgun rider trotted off toward the river.

David strolled around and eyed the broken wheel with misgiving. Unless he was mistaken, when they'd hit that rock, they'd also cracked the axle.

"I say, if it's only three miles, I might set out and walk for a bit."

The driver pulled a twist of tobacco from his shirt pocket. "Well now, I make it to be about that far. You armed, mister?"

"Yes, actually. Am I apt to need a weapon?"

The driver shrugged and leaned on the unharmed wheel. "This road's been hit before. Been awhile, but I figure that means it's about time I got held up again. Bein' stranded out here ain't good."

David surmised that he'd have as good a chance of keeping his wallet if he walked. The broken-down coach might draw in road agents the way a carcass drew vultures.

"I guess I'll chance it then." It would put him out of range of Millie's piteous gaze, if nothing else. He certainly didn't want to give her the opportunity to seek him out again.

"If we get goin' before you're to Brown's, I'll pick you up." The driver took a big chaw of tobacco. Apparently the halt gave him license to break the spitting rule as well as the cussing one.

David patted his pockets. Wallet and pistol were in place, along with the box from Millie and a few coins. If he was ambushed, he'd lose the cuff links again. But he didn't like the odds any better if he stuck them in his luggage and left them with the disabled coach, so he set off with them in his coat pocket. He deliberately didn't look back. If Millie watched him walk away, he didn't care, and he didn't want to make eye contact and give her hope that he'd stop and talk to her—or worse yet, let her walk with him.

It wasn't Millie, but the sheep farmer, Stoddard, who tagged after him.

"Hey! Mr. Stone!"

David kept walking but looked over his shoulder, only as far as Stoddard's jogging figure, not back to where the others clustered.

"Walking in to Brown's Town?"

"That was my plan," David said. "Thought I'd stretch my legs."

"Mind if I join you?"

He seemed a stout enough fellow, not overly talkative, and he wore a Colt revolver strapped about his waist.

"Fine by me," David said.

They walked along companionably for ten minutes before Stoddard said, "Is that Mrs. Evans an acquaintance of yours?"

David grunted, wondering what he really wanted to know. "I met her once before."

"She a widder woman? I didn't see no weddin' ring."

"I believe so," David said.

They walked in silence for another ten minutes before Stoddard said, "I don't reckon she'd take to a sheep farmer."

David smiled grimly. "I cannot speak for her, but from what little I know, I don't think you can afford her taste."

"Ah."

They'd walked about two miles when a wagon passed them bearing their shotgun rider and another man, with the replacement wheel. The men waved and drove on. David and Stoddard finished their journey in silence and without sign of highwaymen. In less than an hour, they sat together in Mr. Brown's dining room, making up the first supper sitting of the stagecoach passengers and thus getting the best portions of the fried chicken and having the leisure to enjoy it. The driver who would take them onward also ate when they did, grumbling between bites about the delay.

The stagecoach didn't arrive until nearly two hours later, as the sun slid behind the mountains. The passengers went inside to eat hastily, while the coach and horses were ferried across the river. David noted that this time Millie headed inside. She must be purchasing the meal this evening.

"Hey," Stoddard called to him, "we can ride over with the coach if we want. We'll get there afore the rest and can get good seats."

David boarded the ferry with Stoddard. It was hard to feel smug about it though, when they couldn't travel on without the people they'd left behind. He felt a bit sorry for them all—they hadn't gotten the exercise that he and Stoddard had. At least he felt more prepared to get back in the stagecoach and on the road again.

On the other side, David was the first on the coach, and he claimed his comfortable corner again. Stoddard took the one across from him. The other passengers came across the river as twilight descended. Millie, unfortunately, was one of the last to board and lost her usual spot. She settled demurely on the middle seat with two rough-looking fellows. The one nearest her appeared to keep inching closer to her, until Millie looked in a fair way to tumble to the floor.

"I beg your pardon, sir," she said when the coach had been underway for ten minutes. "Could you possibly give me a little more room?"

"Hmpf. Bit of a thang like you?" the man said. He scooted over, but not very far. The first time they rounded a corner, he slid back toward her.

It was dark now, with only a sliver of light shining in from the lanterns on the front of the stage, and David couldn't see much of what else was going on, but suddenly Millie leaped up and whacked the man with her handbag. Since it held David's Bible, he imagined it packed a wallop.

"How dare you?" Millie said in tones that would have frozen the river if they'd still been on the ferry.

David couldn't sit by any longer. "Here, ma'am. Take my seat."

Though he couldn't read her expression, he sensed her hesitation. "Why. . .thank you, sir!"

With some awkward shifting as the stage rolled on, they managed to exchange places without landing in anyone else's lap. David held his ground against the encroaching fellow to his left—though he suspected the offender was less eager to claim more territory when an alluring woman was not involved. But David found it necessary to cling to one of the hanging straps, and his right arm was soon aching dreadfully. This was the shoulder in which he'd been wounded, and after five minutes, he turned around on the seat and faced the other way so that he could reach the strap with his left hand. The next two hours were torture.

Charlotte, he thought. *No, Millie. If she hadn't boarded this stage, I'd be sitting in comparative comfort.* He was glad his back was to her now. He didn't want to see her, even in the scanty light they had.

Even so, in his mind he saw her lovely dark red hair, piled high as it had been in Scottsburg when they'd dined together. Her skin was as white and smooth as ever, her eyes as vibrantly green. He gritted his teeth and tried to think instead of Stoneford. Once there, he'd be thousands of miles from the woman he disliked more than anyone else on earth.

CHAPTER 4

At midmorning of the following day, they reached the verge of the Snake River. At long last, Millie was putting Oregon behind her. What a pity that part of her past traveled with her. She tried to avoid looking at David, since he so obviously shrank from contact with her.

"All out," the station agent called as they pulled up in his barnyard. As she descended from the coach, he droned, "Dinner inside, two bits. The ferry will take you across in thirty minutes. All luggage will be ferried with you."

"Are the horses going across as well?" she asked, looking about for a fresh team and seeing none.

"Nay, madam. This coach and team will stay on this side and head back for Fort Dalles tomorrow. You'll board a new stage once you're over the water."

Millie gulped and looked toward the river. She didn't like water, and the Snake looked rather treacherous. She remembered that fateful night in Scottsburg when David had plunged into the Umpqua. That river had been much calmer. This one, high with snow melt from the mountains, twisted and writhed its way through the wilderness.

Three of the passengers had left them, and Stoddard and McCloskey would part company with them across the river. Perhaps they'd be less uncomfortable now. Millie had pitied David after he took her spot on the center bench, but she'd been more grateful than she could express. She'd tried to express her gratitude at the next stop, but David had brushed her aside. Embarrassed? What gentleman would be ashamed of his gallantry? More likely he was still angry with her.

A married couple joined them at the station on the western bank of the river. Though Millie was glad to have another feminine presence—the men had grown weary of not swearing or smoking, and the miner had taken to chewing tobacco and spitting frequently out the window, though the rules forbade it. She hoped that with Mrs. Caudle's arrival, this would stop.

They were all ferried across with their bags. The water swirled and tugged at their low, flat craft, but strong cables and ropes held it from being swept downstream. Millie clung to one of the railings and stared at the pile of luggage, which was secured to the deck with ropes. Mrs. Caudle looked a bit green-faced, and Millie imagined she presented an equally distressed picture.

At last they landed, with only one of the passengers being ill, and that one of the men. The new coach was waiting for them on the eastern shore and carried the eight of them to the station yard a short distance away, where the luggage was put down for those who had finished their journey.

"Good-bye, Mrs. Evans," McCloskey said before disembarking.

"Farewell, sir. I wish you Godspeed."

The salesman tipped his hat and left them to claim his valise and sample cases.

"We'll have to make up some time," the new driver said.

"Aye, see if you can make up half an hour on this stage," the station agent told him. "But whatever you do, don't have another wreck."

"Don't you worry," the driver told him. "I know this road like I know the back end of my wheel horses. We're all rarin' to go."

Mr. Caudle paused before entering the stage. "What about Indians, sir? Have they bothered the traffic along the trail this year?"

"Not yet, and please God they won't," the driver replied.

"I admit I'm a little nervous, since that massacre—"

"That was nigh three years ago, sir." The driver seemed a bit disgruntled at having the safety of his bit of trail cast in doubt.

"But they shut down Fort Boise—"

"True, but there be troopers back and forth. They man the

cantonment near Fort Hall every summer, and they've set up for the season, to make sure wagon trains get through safely. Now, let's get aboard and head out, shall we?"

Geography wasn't Millie's long suit, but she knew they were still many miles from the vicinity of the old Fort Hall. She hadn't given much thought to the Indian troubles in Idaho when she'd bought her ticket. She was in Idaho now, and she'd have to trust God and the cavalry to see her through.

They set out again with only six aboard, and the miner made no secret of his plans to leave them at the next stop. Millie sighed and leaned back against the leather-covered headrest. She'd hardly slept a wink last night. Perhaps she could catch a nap now. Though she could barely imagine sleeping with the intriguing David Stone so close, her exhaustion would surely come to her aid in that matter.

Her hope of slumber soon drifted out the open window. Although the party had become smaller, the atmosphere in the coach had not improved. Mrs. Caudle sat between Millie and her husband, and the most notable thing about her was her heavily applied scent. Millie barely had time to recognize it before her nostrils were overcome and it became a stench.

Mrs. Caudle plunged into conversation at once, introducing herself and insisting the others give their names and home towns.

Millie pasted on a smile. "I am Mrs. Evans, and I'm lately of The Dalles, but I'm traveling to Fort Laramie to visit my cousin."

"Oh, how lovely for you, my dear," Mrs. Caudle said, laying a moist hand on Millie's wrist. Her cloying perfume caused Millie to swallow hard and avoid inhaling deeply. "And has Mr. Evans remained at home?"

Millie hesitated and shot a quick glance at David, but he was staring out the window.

"Mr. Evans met his demise several years ago," Millie murmured.

"Ah, what a shame."

Not really, Millie thought. If he hadn't gotten himself killed when he did, he probably would have beaten her to death. Of course, she would never say such a thing to anyone. Sam knew she'd been unhappy, and he'd seen her once or twice with bruises on her face, but even her half-brother had no idea the extent of her suffering under James Evans's hands.

"So he is at home after all," Mrs. Caudle said sweetly. "At home with the Lord."

Millie couldn't respond to that. She took out her handkerchief and put it to her nose, not to cover her sorrow, but to filter the overbold perfume of her seatmate.

David said merely, "David Stone, of Eugene." His words were few enough that his accent was not obtrusive, and no one commented on it. The others gave a bit of their background.

When the turn came to Mr. Caudle, he gave his name—Robert Caudle—and said, "I'll let Agnes tell it."

Mrs. Caudle chuckled. "Ah, my husband is too modest."

Millie got the feeling this was the moment she'd waited for, and sure enough the lady continued with relish.

"Mr. Caudle is headed to Washington to help lobby for statehood. He'll be attached to our new senator's office. Isn't that delightful?"

Millie and a couple of others murmured their assent.

No one seemed desperate to hear more of Mr. Caudle's official duties or how he came by this position, but his wife held forth anyway.

David sat across from Millie, in the same corner he'd started out in at The Dalles. After a few minutes, his eyes closed, but she couldn't tell whether or not he was sleeping. He was too genteel to snore or let his head loll to the side.

Millie leaned toward the window, hoping to catch more of the breeze. After a while, she rested her arm on the window ledge, her handkerchief clasped lightly in her fingers.

"Don't you think that's true?" Mrs. Caudle leaned closer and elbowed her sharply.

Millie jumped, a bit startled at the woman's audacity. Her handkerchief flew from her fingers.

"Oh!" She tried to look out and behind the coach, but the bit of white muslin was gone on the perpetual breeze.

"What is it?" Mrs. Caudle asked, louder than necessary.

"It's nothing," Millie said. "Just my handkerchief."

"What? You lost your handkerchief? Robert, quickly! Pound on the ceiling and tell the driver to stop."

"Oh no," Millie said quickly. "Please don't. There's no need."

"But madam, if you lost a piece of your property," Mr. Caudle said, leaning forward to peer at her with all the ostentation of his position, "of course we can ask the driver to stop."

"Yes indeed," his wife added. "Those men work for us, after all."

By this time the three men opposite were all paying attention, though none of them spoke. David hadn't moved, other than to open his eyes in narrow slits. As soon as Millie glanced his way, he closed them again.

"Please don't," she said, leaning past Mrs. Caudle to appeal to her husband, and thus getting a strong whiff of the by-now nauseating perfume. "I should be excessively embarrassed if you asked them to do that. It was nothing but a scrap of muslin, and we're running late already. I shouldn't like to cause another delay. Indeed, that handkerchief is not worth the trouble."

"Hmpf." Mr. Caudle sat back and folded his arms. "Very well then."

Millie exhaled and closed her eyes for a moment, relieved to have averted the halt. The other men would no doubt have resented her for the rest of the journey if she'd demanded the driver and shotgun rider stop and look for her handkerchief or wait while she did so. She already knew how the driver would feel—he was bound to make up lost time and would see her as a troublemaker. And Mr. Stone? David appeared to have drifted back into slumber, but she wondered if he wasn't very busy thinking behind those closed eyelids. Thinking bad thoughts about her.

David tried to ignore the conversation on the other side of the coach. The Caudles, while attempting to be pleasant, were anything but.

He had to give Millie credit—she maintained a gracious demeanor but did not prompt the loquacious Mrs. Caudle to ramble. Alas, the woman needed no encouragement from others; she achieved it under her own steam. If only Millie were a little less polite and would tell her to be quiet.

The handkerchief episode surprised him mildly. Millie was determined not to delay them all. Her attitude reminded him of the Charlotte he'd liked so well in Scottsburg—before she started hounding him to take her out walking every evening and led him into chaos. She seemed a modest, somewhat self-effacing, and, yes, charming lady. Of course, he knew too well now that she was not what she seemed.

Because of Charlotte, David had become much more cautious where women were concerned. He'd left England a bit spoiled for romance by a crush on his older brother Richard's wife. Elizabeth Stone would never, ever so much as hint at impropriety, but David adored her. His niece, Anne, didn't know—she was only an infant then, and David would never admit to anyone how much he'd admired Anne's mother. But his wanderlust, combined with the pain of knowing he would never be able to openly love Elizabeth, had driven him from Stoneford and England. That and the fact that he'd had no responsibilities to live up to. Richard inherited the earldom, and there was John between them in age. David was certain he'd never inherit the title, and so he was free to follow adventure wherever it led him.

That turned out to be America. He'd recovered from his heartache after a while and had become enamored of a young woman in Independence, but that had gone nowhere. He'd moved to Oregon, undergoing a few flirtations over the years, but had never come close to thinking he'd found the right woman.

Charlotte had interested him far more than the wide-eyed girls on the wagon trail or the jaded women in the western towns. Quite striking, she was, with that rich red hair and those startling green eyes—rare coloring, and she wore it well.

He realized with a start that he was staring at her. He closed his eyes again. Best not to look at the woman. She was lovely on the outside, but her heart would drag a man to destruction.

A sudden bang outside the coach brought him upright.

"What was that?" Mrs. Caudle screeched, clutching her husband's arm.

Before Mr. Caudle could answer, two more pops and a blast from directly over David's head confirmed what he already knew. Those were gunshots, and they were under attack.

CHAPTER 5

G et down," David called to the ladies, reaching inside his coat for his pistol. The two other men on his side of the stage also produced weapons, but Mr. Caudle, it seemed, was not so well prepared.

Millie gazed at him, her green eyes huge in her white face.

"I advise you ladies to sit on the floor. You too, Mr. Caudle, if you've no pistol." David moved to the middle seat and maneuvered to see out the window and forward, but only trees met his view.

Another shot fired from above him. He hoped the shotgun rider's aim was true.

The coach continued to roll, and the driver's whip cracked several times.

"Up, there, boys! Go!" The driver's yells seemed ineffective because a moment later the coach stopped so suddenly that David was thrown forward onto his previous seat. Mr. Caudle catapulted to the floor, where his wife and Millie had taken hasty refuge.

David could imagine only two things that would stop the coach so suddenly without any noise of breakage—one of the horses must have fallen in harness, or the outlaws had felled a tree across the road and they'd plowed into it. An unearthly shriek came from one of the team, and he pitied the poor animals.

"Hands in the air!"

"All right, all right," the driver said grumpily.

"Throw down the box."

A moment later a thud evidenced the driver's compliance.

"You got mail sacks?" the gruff voice demanded.

"Nope, nary a one."

"Awright, git down. Both of you."

In an odd way, this conversation bolstered David. It meant both the driver and his shotgun messenger were still alive.

A shadow fell over the passengers, and the door flew open.

"Don't shoot, fellas," the driver cried.

The masked robber held him around the neck, a pistol aimed at his temple. "Come on out, folks."

David hesitated and eased his pistol into his coat pocket.

"Throw yer guns out." The outlaw was bigger than the driver and easily kept him under control. "Come on, gents. I know some of you have revolvers. Let's see 'em."

The other two passengers, who were nearer the door, tossed their guns out the window. David wondered if he was foolish not to follow their lead.

"Only two?" The robber asked.

A second outlaw scooped up the revolvers and tossed them forward of the coach, then came to the doorway.

"Well now, what have we here? Ladies!"

Mrs. Caudle raised her head and held out a beseeching hand. "Oh please! Don't hurt us. I'll give you my pearl necklace."

"That's right nice of you, ma'am."

David eyed the second robber carefully. That voice seemed somehow familiar. He wore a cloth tied over his face, but his straw-colored hair showed beneath a battered felt hat. His blocky build and dull gray eyes were all David needed to identify his former farmhand, Sam Hastings.

"Everybody out," the man said, standing back. "And no funny business. Ladies first."

Millie rose shakily, looking decidedly ill.

Mrs. Caudle almost tumbled out, talking the whole while. "You mustn't hurt anyone. I'm sure we'll all cooperate. Just take what you want and be on your way."

"Hush, you!" The robber prodded her with the barrel of his rifle, and she squealed and jumped aside.

Millie held up her skirt, exposing a shapely ankle, and followed Mrs. Caudle outside.

The outlaw gave a little gasp as she poked her head out the door.

"Mil—er, watch your step, ma'am."

David held back and climbed down last. He pulled his hat low over his eyes, but there was no way he wouldn't be recognized. Of course, the man he feared would know him had never been the brightest penny in the cashbox.

The passengers lined up, with David at the end nearest the stagecoach. One man trained his gun on them while the stockier robber collected the valuables. He began with the Caudles, relieving the lady of her necklace, her earbobs, and a handful of coins from her purse. Mr. Caudle contributed a watch, his wallet, and two cigars. David resigned himself to giving up his watch—he'd bought it during his storekeeping days at wholesale, so he wasn't overly attached to it—and rejoiced that he wasn't wearing the onyx cuff links. If they didn't search him, perhaps he'd keep those and a reserve of bills tucked into a tiny pocket Anne had sewn inside his boot top.

He had no intention of opening fire. It wasn't worth the risk with two women present and several unarmed men. Besides, now that he was out of the stage, he realized there were at least five outlaws, maybe six. As he'd feared, one of the team's horses was down—a big, brown wheeler. The other five stood uneasily in harness, shifting and snuffling. If the robbers left with their loot, the driver and shotgun rider would have to cut the traces and reconfigure the rest of the team.

Two of the outlaws had climbed to the roof of the coach and were going through the luggage. A fifth gang member was packing the contents of the treasure box into a sack for easier transport.

A shot—too loud and too close—spun David around. Mr. Caudle apparently wasn't unarmed after all. He'd brought out a small pistol and let the man with the rifle have it.

The one holding the bag of the passengers' belongings stood uncertainly for a moment. That was Sam for you, always a half-second behind. The thought flashed through David's mind as he whipped his own revolver from his pocket.

By the time he had the gun out, Sam had moved, and quickly.

He fired in Mr. Caudle's direction and jumped behind the stagecoach. Mrs. Caudle screamed as her husband went down.

David whirled and let off a shot at the robber drawing a bead on him from the top of the stage. The man jumped back and dropped his revolver over the edge of the roof. David didn't think he'd hit him, unless in the hand, but he swooped on the brigand's revolver and backed toward the woods with a gun in each hand.

"Run! All of you take cover," he said without looking around at the others.

The passengers scattered, and he heard branches breaking and brush rustling as they obeyed—all but Mrs. Caudle, who sank to her knees beside her husband's inert body, still screaming. The stage driver snatched up her husband's pistol and joined David in keeping up a stream of fire toward the robbers while the other passengers retreated, and the shotgun rider managed to grab the rifle dropped by the outlaw Mr. Caudle had shot. The three of them backed into the woods, keeping up their fire.

"How much ammo you got?" the driver yelled to David from his refuge behind a big fir tree.

David patted his vest pocket. "Six more rounds and whatever's left in this gun I picked up." He fumbled to reload his own.

"I think this is empty," the shotgun rider said hefting the muzzle-loading rifle he'd picked up. He'd fired its single shot during their retreat. "Wish I coulda got one of them revolvers they took. Jay?"

The driver peered at them from behind his tree and waved Mr. Caudle's revolver. "I fired two shots. Don't know how many are in this thing."

The road agents seemed to be conferring. David hoped they weren't cooking up a plan.

"Here. I think there's a couple of rounds left in there." He passed the outlaw's gun he'd confiscated to the shotgun rider. The three of them might have a dozen rounds. If used well, that might be enough.

He turned and squinted into the dim woods behind them. Millie was peeking from between a couple of smaller trees, her wide-brimmed hat easy to see. David waved them back, hoping she'd read his signal to get farther into the forest.

A sudden thought chilled him. Had she signaled the robbers by letting her handkerchief fly out the window? Maybe she had a gun in that bag with his Bible.

Millie knew she ought to forge farther into the woods, but she couldn't tear herself away. Did David know that was her brother out there?

Mrs. Caudle's screams tapered off into wrenching sobs. All else was quiet, except for the snorting of the horses and occasional shrieks from the felled wheeler. Millie glanced at the other two male passengers, who huddled behind trees. She edged out from her cover and flitted up to where she could hear David and the other men talking.

"Think they'll leave now?" the shotgun rider asked David.

"I don't know. If Caudle hadn't brought that pistol out, they'd no doubt have left us alone."

The driver dashed between the trees to where they stood. "I have another gun in the driver's boot. I wonder if they're still up there by the coach. Maybe we could get it."

"Is there anything I could do?" Millie asked.

The three men turned their rather disdainful gazes on her.

"You'd best get back with the others, ma'am," the driver said.

"Hey," a man shouted from up near the stagecoach, "You done shot Lucky."

The shotgun rider let out a grim chuckle and said softly, "Not so lucky today, was he?"

"You can't git away with that," the robber yelled.

"Sounds like they want more trouble," the driver said.

"We don't have the ammunition to hold them off for long," David said calmly.

Millie gulped. "Listen, they probably wouldn't shoot me. I could go out there and try to calm Mrs. Caudle down. Maybe I could pick up one of the passengers' pistols. Or cause a diversion so that one of you could get them."

"Too dangerous," the driver said.

"I wouldn't hide behind no woman's skirts, anyhow," the shotgun rider muttered.

David turned his head and trained his eyes on her—glacial blue in shadow of the trees. "They wouldn't shoot you because one of them's your brother. Isn't that so, Mrs. Evans?"

"What?" The driver stared at Millie.

Her throat tightened. She wanted to deny it, but she couldn't.

"Yes. It was Sam who held the bag."

David nodded. "As I thought. Did you signal them to attack?"

"What? No!"

David looked at the other two men. "She lost a handkerchief out the window just minutes before the road agents stopped the stage."

The driver and the shotgun rider stared at her, and their gazes weren't kindly.

"I didn't know," she cried, but their faces held patent disbelief. "You must believe me. I left The Dalles to get away from my brother. I refused to—" She shook her head. What did it matter? Now that David had spoken against her, they would never believe her.

David seethed inside as Millie shuddered and wilted. Did she expect him to protect her in this nefarious game? Sam Hastings had impersonated him once and tried to claim David's belongings. Did he know about the estate in England? Maybe he and Millie had come up with this plan to finally get rid of David and go claim his wealth and position.

"Millie!" Sam stayed hidden, but his voice came loud and clear. "Come on, Millie. You come with us."

Millie raised her chin. "No! Go away!"

"Come on, Mil!"

"I told you, no!"

David edged over to another tree, wondering where the other robbers were. Why should they hang around now, other than to attempt to get Millie to join them? Was she really a confederate of theirs?

He caught his breath. Through the trees, he'd spotted a saddled horse. At least one of the road agents had left his mount unattended.

He was about to move toward it when Millie cried, "David! Look out!"

Rather than turn toward her, he swung toward the flicker of movement he'd caught from the corner of his eye and fired two rapid shots. The outlaw went crashing through the brush toward the horses.

Behind him, more gunfire erupted. David hoped the unarmed folks were keeping low, but he didn't have time to look. He stumbled toward the road, conscious of the three meager shots he had left. When he came to the tree line, he looked up the road, forward of the stagecoach, where the harnessed horses plunged, neighed, and kicked at each other in their frenzy to escape. Sam was helping an outlaw mount his horse. So, Caudle hadn't killed Lucky after all. The big man lay low over his horse's neck and headed away from the altercation. Three more horsemen appeared out of the woods to the side. David raised his revolver but doubted he could make the shot from this distance. Still, he couldn't bring himself to fire at Sam when Millie stood nearby.

The driver ran up beside David and let off a shot, then his revolver clicked as Sam Hastings swayed, clutched his chest, and fell to the dusty road.

The driver swore. "At least I got one of'em."

The other outlaws were out of range now, galloping away eastward, leaving Sam behind, lying in the dirt as a cloud of dust swirled in the air and the stagecoach team thrashed and screamed.

Before David could catch his breath, Millie dashed past him, holding up bunches of her skirt and gasping for breath. She ran to the outlaw lying in the road and knelt beside him.

"Sam! You big old oaf! Why did you do this, Sam?"

David tucked his pistol inside his coat and walked heavily toward her. He patted his pockets for his handkerchief and found it crumpled beneath the cuff link box.

Millie had torn off the cloth that had masked her brother's face. Sam's eyes were shut tight, and his mouth twisted as he pressed both hands to his chest. Blood oozed between his fingers, and his labored breathing set David's teeth on edge. He knelt in the dirt across from Millie. She tossed him a glance. David could see that the wound was beyond what little help a handkerchief could offer, and he tucked it back in his pocket to keep it clean. Millie would need one later.

An odd feeling seized David, as though he was watching this tableau from outside the frame. Millie had saved his life back there when she'd warned him. Offering a clean handkerchief seemed poor recompense.

"Sam, I'm so sorry," she choked. "Hold on now. We'll take you to a doctor."

Sam coughed, and blood splatted from the corner of his mouth. "I'm past doctorin', Millie. You get Old Blue, huh? Take care of him."

"Old Blue?" Millie looked around in distraction.

"Is he there?" Sam asked.

"Yes, I see him." The roan had run a little way after the band of outlaws but had stopped and was nervously snatching mouthfuls of grass at the edge of the road, keeping an eye on the activity near the coach.

Sam pulled in a shuddering breath. "He's a. . .good hoss."

"Yes." Millie sounded as though she were the one strangling.

The driver went to his team, but after he and the shotgun rider had somewhat calmed them, he came over and stood gazing down at Sam. "Is that the one? Her brother?"

"Yes." David stood and brushed off his knees. "I'm afraid there's nothing we can do."

The driver inhaled deeply through his nose. "Caudle's dead, but the fella he shot got away. Hal and I will see about getting the team set to go. We need to get these passengers to the swing station. It's about five miles. As soon as I pass the stage to another driver, I'll come back with some men and all the horses we can harness to once, and we'll drag ol' Star off the road." He nodded to the downed coach horse.

David nodded. "If it will help you, that blue roan the outlaw was riding can pull in harness."

"You sure?" The driver eyed him with speculation.

"Yes." David didn't bother to explain that Old Blue had belonged to him, once upon a more-trusting time.

Millie burst into tears and flung herself on Sam's body. David guessed her brother had breathed his last. He stood in confusion. He ought to offer his comfort or at least some show of sympathy, but how could he? Her brother was an outlaw and had brought him nothing but trouble. So far as he could see, she was in on the robbery plot. The best thing he could do would be to distance himself from her.

"Best let her have a few minutes," he said to the driver. "Let's see about the harness."

The three of them—David, the driver, and the shotgun messenger, Hal, managed to get the straps off the dead horse without cutting any of them. It was an awful job, and they had to call upon the other two men to help roll the dead animal partway over, but at last they freed all the leather. David's clothes were bloody when they finished. Old Blue sidled and snorted a bit when buckled in next to the remaining wheel horse, but he didn't protest too violently, which encouraged David. Maybe they'd get to the next stage stop without further incident.

Two horsemen rode up from the direction of the river as the passengers were preparing to enter the coach again. After a brief explanation of what had happened, the two farmers on horseback decided to finish their journey with the stagecoach for safety. The shotgun rider tossed Blue's saddle and bridle into the boot, and they set off with Sam's body on the roof and Mr. Caudle inside with the sober passengers.

Millie and Mrs. Caudle sat together in the front, and David joined the two other male passengers on the rear seat, with Mr. Caudle lying on the bench in the middle. The two women wept incessantly—Mrs. Caudle with a loud keening and Millie in stoic silence. The tears streamed down her cheeks, and she swiped at them periodically with David's handkerchief.

The next forty minutes dragged on and on. No chatter relieved the tension. The only interruption to Mrs. Caudle's crying was when they started up a steep incline and her husband's body slid off the seat, landing on the boots of the three gentlemen at the rear. She let out a scream, but David held out a hand toward her.

"Please, madam, control yourself. I believe your husband will rest easier on the floor until we reach the station. It's not far."

Millie put an arm around Mrs. Caudle and drew her back against the leather cushion. "There now, my dear. The Lord is welcoming him into glory. You must think of that and calm yourself."

"But what of his trip to Washington?" Mrs. Caudle wailed. "Oh dear, I haven't any black. I wonder, can I get dress goods in Boise?" She began her keening again, and Millie sat beside her with tear tracks glistening on her cheeks, patting the older woman's hand and murmuring her sympathy.

Thoughts of glory would give Millie no comfort. David eyed her with new respect. Heaven's gates would not open for Sam Hastings, he had no doubt about that. Millie must know it, too, and yet she offered sympathy without bitterness to Mrs. Caudle.

CHAPTER 6

They arrived at the swing station, and all tumbled out. The bodies were removed from the stage, and Mrs. Caudle sat down with the station agent to make arrangements for transporting her husband's remains back to Oregon. Millie could see no alternative to having Sam buried there at the station. A small graveyard on the hill above the road was the resting place of two previously departed travelers, and the tenders, who took care of the teams, offered to dig a grave.

She had no money to pay them nor to hire a room for the night at the stage station. The few coins she'd had left were in the outlaws' sack. Sam must have passed it to one of the others, as it wasn't found at the scene of the robbery after they fled. That fact also left Mrs. Caudle destitute. The two male passengers grumbled about their losses as well, though each had planned for such an event and concealed some money about their persons. Sam had never reached David and the shotgun rider with his sack, and so the driver and the two women were the only ones who lost all their valuables.

The agent, a Mr. Kimball, remarkable for his fiery-red hair and beard, refused to make the driver wait. To Millie's surprise, David let the stage go on without him. She'd figured he'd want to get as far from her as he could. Instead, he got a cup of coffee from Kimball's wife and took it outside. Millie and Mrs. Caudle sat down in the dining room.

"We don't normally serve meals," Mrs. Kimball told them, "but sometimes it's a plain necessity."

She served the ladies tea and biscuits.

"I can't eat a bite," Mrs. Caudle said, so Millie felt justified in eating all four biscuits. No telling when she would get another meal.

683

Mrs. Caudle had arranged for one of the men to build a coffin for her husband.

Mr. Kimball brought her some money, saying, "I've changed your ticket for you, madam, so that you can head back to Oregon on tomorrow's westbound."

"And they'll carry Mr. Caudle, too?" the widow asked in a quavery tone.

"Aye, they should be able to put the box on the roof." Mr. Kimball refunded most of her money for her husband's ticket, since he would travel for less as freight, and so the lady had enough money to see her home. He'd kept back enough to pay for the materials for the coffin and to pay the man who built it fair wages.

Two hours after they arrived, he came back into the house and approached the table where they still sat. "The grave is ready, Mrs. Evans."

Millie rose, feeling stiff and empty. Sam wouldn't even have a rough coffin, as Mr. Caudle would. But Sam had grown up poor, and she didn't think he'd mind.

David Stone and Mrs. Caudle joined her. Mr. Kimball drove the ladies in his wagon to the burial plot among the weeds, and David walked along behind, with the two tenders. The four men lifted the body out of the wagon bed and lowered it into the ground, wrapped in a blanket Kimball had given for the purpose—saying he would add it to Mrs. Evans's bill.

She didn't know how she'd pay for that, and she supposed she'd be charged for the night's lodging as well, but she wasn't about to reveal her penury to the host now.

Her tears welled up as the men settled the body in the hole. Poor Sam. He'd had no idea how to go about living, and so he'd done it badly. Some people learned from their mistakes, but Sam wasn't that kind. The fact that Millie hadn't been able to help him—had in fact, up until the last few months, encouraged him to live in crime—saddened her.

God had grabbed hold of her and changed her. Even if she looked the same on the outside, she was different in her heart. She ought to have done a better job explaining that to Sam.

The tenders climbed out of the grave and stood back, leaving the passengers and the station agent near the edge. Mr. Kimball opened his Bible, and Millie sobbed.

David should have left with the stagecoach, but he felt so guilty, he couldn't go on and leave Millie to bury her brother alone. He told himself repeatedly he had no reason to feel remorse. Sam had brought this on himself. And David owed him no loyalty. Still, he stayed.

As they stood by the grave, Kimball read a psalm from his battered Bible. The sun set behind the mountains, and David's mind roamed.

Kimball startled him by saying, at the end of the psalm, "Mr. Stone, would you say a few words?"

David nearly choked but managed to turn the reflex into a cough while he did some quick thinking. He couldn't say what a fine man Sam was or that he was in a better place.

"I was sorry to see Sam Hastings come to this end," he said. "He chose his path, and this is where it led him. May we all learn from this and seek to do what's right. Shall we all recite the Lord's Prayer together?"

That ensured everyone closed their eyes and didn't stare at him. They repeated the words together, with even Millie joining in, her voice faltering toward the end as she wept. David passed her another clean handkerchief—the last until he managed to have some laundry done. She accepted it meekly and pressed it to her eyes.

The two hired men stayed behind to fill in the grave, and David walked back to the station house. He let the wagon outdistance him. When he came to the barn, Kimball was unharnessing his horses, and the ladies were nowhere to be seen.

The blue roan nickered from a nearby corral, and David walked over to stroke Old Blue's nose. They would have to pay for overnight accommodations, and he doubted Millie's purse could stand the strain. He walked into the barn.

"Mr. Kimball."

"Yes?" The host hung a set of harness on a peg and turned toward him.

"That roan horse that belonged to Mrs. Evans's brother—perhaps you might consider buying it from her."

Kimball's eyes narrowed. "Don't need another saddle horse."

"No? He's a good mount, and if nothing else, you could resell him."

Kimball scratched his chin through his red beard. "Maybe so."

David took that for what it was worth and strolled to the house. They spent a bleak evening there. Mrs. Kimball prepared a room for Mrs. Caudle and Millie, but David had to bunk in with the tenders in a small room partitioned off in the barn. One of them stayed up late, constructing a casket by lamplight for Mr. Caudle's remains, and his sawing and pounding kept David awake.

The next morning a westbound stage went through and took Mrs. Caudle and the corpse of her husband. Everyone around the station seemed to breathe easier after that. A couple of troopers came by, bound for the Green River, and Millie prevailed on them to take a letter for her.

Another eastbound stage would not pass through until the next day. David borrowed fishing gear from their host, paid twenty-five cents to Mrs. Kimball to pack him a lunch, and set out for a leisurely ramble along a stream. Anything to avoid seeing Millie's tear-reddened eyes all day.

He found a place to sit in the shade and half-heartedly cast his line. If he'd claimed Old Blue, he might have ridden him on eastward. David began to wish he'd forsaken the stagecoach line and gone on alone, despite the risks of facing Indians and robbers. But it was too late for that, and if Mr. Kimball bought the horse, Millie would have enough to allow her to eat between here and Fort Laramie. He leaned back and settled his hat lower, prepared to catch a nap.

He was almost put out when he started getting nibbles, but after he pulled in his first fish—a foot-long trout—he began to feel a little more enthusiastic. As the sun began to lower, he ambled back to the station with four good-sized fish. Mrs. Kimball accepted them with thanks and told him he wouldn't have to pay for his supper or breakfast, since he'd earned his keep. She also informed him that a small wagon train of freighters had passed through heading west, the first of the season.

After supper, Kimball approached David as he lounged in a rocking chair on the porch.

"The lady said that one of the outlaws stole the roan from you, and I should bargain with you for it, sir."

David eyed the fellow in surprise. Millie obviously needed money, yet she'd passed up an easy deal? "No, he didn't steal it. The horse belonged to her brother. Give her the money."

Kimball hesitated. "All right, then. He's not much of a coach horse though. I suppose I could sell him as a saddle horse."

Remembering the dead horse at the scene of the robbery, David arched his eyebrows. "Did our driver yesterday speak to you about removing the dead horse from the road?"

"Yes sir. My men went out this morning with a team and cleared it before the westbound got there."

David nodded. "Good. And don't forget, Mrs. Evans has a saddle and bridle to sell you with that roan."

Kimball left him, and David rocked and watched the stars grow brighter.

"Mr. Stone?"

"Yes?" He turned at the soft, feminine voice.

Millie left the doorway and came over close to him.

"The station agent has offered me thirty-five dollars for the horse and saddle. I know he's worth more than that, but I haven't time to stop and find another buyer."

"Do as you wish," David said.

"But Old Blue is yours, sir."

David stood, shaking his head. "No, I gave him to your brother. And I told Kimball to deal with you."

"I thought you might like to keep him or try yourself to drive a better bargain. Sometimes a man can do better than a woman at this type of business transaction."

687

David felt his face flush. He wanted only to end this embarrassing conversation. "Char—Mrs. Evans, your brother had that horse for nearly two years. I gave him Old Blue to use while he was in my employ, and once we'd parted ways—well, I never expected to see the horse again. Please consider it your brother's gift to you, as he wished."

"I can't do that. Please!" Tears streaked her cheeks.

David sighed. He'd run out of handkerchiefs, an untenable situation for a gentleman. "If there had been time before Sam died, I'd have told him to consider the horse his, to do with as he pleased. Since there was no such opportunity—I felt the time was better left for you to say your good-byes—I didn't make it a formal gift to him. But I'm telling you now: That is how I looked upon it. I never thought to reclaim the horse."

"You're very good, sir, considering how Sam and I treated you."

"That is neither here nor there. If you wish, you may tell Mr. Kimball I said that horse and his saddle are worth at least fifty dollars, and he ought to give you that much. He has to resell it, and of course he wants to profit by the transaction. But I think fifty would be fair in this case."

"Thank you. I'll tell him." She smiled ruefully. "I considered keeping him and riding on by myself, but they say it isn't safe in these parts."

"So I've heard. Despite the fact that stagecoaches seem to draw outlaws, I believe you're safer with the stage than you would be alone in this wilderness."

"Yes, my conclusion as well." She drew in a breath, and for a moment David saw again the beauty he'd squired in Scottsburg. "I'll bring you the money—"

David held up his hand to silence her. "Let us say no more about this."

Millie ducked her head and turned away.

David knew he couldn't sit opposite—or worse yet, beside—her tragic figure for days or even weeks as they journeyed east across the Oregon Trail. Before retiring to the barn for the night, he sought out Mr. Kimball. He'd have to wait another two days for the next stage, but in David's mind, it would be worth it. He had no deadline, and he would be much more at ease if he didn't have to board the same stagecoach as Millie.

The next day, an hour before noon, the stage approached from the Snake River. The tenders had the fresh team ready, and Millie came out of the house dressed as she had been the whole trip, in a plain but serviceable dress. She'd replaced the wide-brimmed hat with a cloth bonnet.

Mr. Kimball walked to the coach and opened the door. The four passengers inside got out to stretch their legs. Mr. Kimball handed Millie inside. She peered out the window. David could tell the moment she spotted him on the porch. Her brow furrowed. She was wondering, no doubt, if he was going to board. He turned and went into the house. Mrs. Kimball was pouring coffee for one of the eastbound passengers, and David got a cup from her.

Ten minutes later, the stagecoach left with a blast of a horn and a drumming of hooves.

Mr. Kimball came inside a moment later and walked to where David sat. "Mrs. Evans asked me to give you this."

David unfolded the paper. Two five-dollar bills fell out on the table. She must have written the note earlier and planned to give it to him in the stagecoach, where he couldn't escape. He shouldn't feel guilty that he'd forsaken her company. The woman was relentless. Still, he felt a pang as he read her words:

Mr. Stone—

> *I don't presume to call you David now, though you once asked me to. Thank you for your assistance at this difficult time. This money replaces what I took from you in Scottsburg. I beg you to believe me, that I am not the same woman you knew then, and I am very sorry. I had no part in the holdup, and I had no inkling Sam and his cohorts were planning it. God has forgiven my sins, and I hope someday you will, too.*
>
> *Mildred Evans*

CHAPTER 7

Millie huddled in her corner of the seat, avoiding conversation. The stage headed across the Idaho Territory and would dip south when they neared the old Fort Hall. They would follow the wagon train route most of the way, though it was too early in the season to meet many emigrant trains. Freighters were another story. Many mule trains were heading west with supplies for merchants in the Oregon Territory.

Millie's spirits sank to an all-time low as she contemplated Sam's death and David's final insult—he'd refused to travel on with her. She had no doubt that his reason for not boarding the coach was her presence. He would rather stall in the wilderness an extra two days than share the same space with her. When she'd first realized they were fellow travelers, her heart had leaped. She'd had her chance to apologize and return his property. If only he would believe in her once more—but perhaps that was too much to expect.

Tears sprang into her eyes, and she reached for her handkerchief. Her hand came out with David's crumpled one. She'd intended to wash it at the Kimballs' and return it, but she'd forgotten. If she ever got his address again, maybe she could send him a dozen nice handkerchiefs.

Immediately she knew that would be foolish. David couldn't bear to be with her. He certainly wouldn't want to receive another reminder of her wickedness. He might even think she was mocking him—after all, he'd gotten that ridiculous notion that she'd signaled Sam and Lucky by dropping her handkerchief out the window. If she didn't care so much for his good will, she would find that amusing.

The driver yelled, and his whip cracked. Millie gasped and clutched the handkerchief to her breast. Not another holdup. If Lucky's men had found their way over here and gotten ahead of them again, she'd give them a piece of her mind.

The recollection that Lucky had been shot—Mr. Caudle had fired his pistol point blank into the man's abdomen—set her head whirling as the stage leaped forward and the team's hooves pounded on the trail. Sam's death was probably due to his kindheartedness in helping Lucky get on a horse and escape. She seriously doubted that the outlaw was in any condition today to ambush stagecoaches.

Nothing halted their progress now, and the horses ran on for what seemed an age. The passengers held on to whatever they could grab to brace themselves. No one spoke, but all had strained faces. The driver continued to urge the horses on, but no percussions of gunfire came, and no shouts to halt and deliver their money.

At last they pulled into a farmyard and stopped between a large barn and a snug log house. A moment later, the door opened, and the shotgun rider said cheerfully, "All snug and sound, folks."

Millie accepted his hand and stepped down into the chilly twilight air of a mountain valley.

"What happened?" demanded the passenger who disembarked behind her.

"Saw a few Injuns," the man replied. "There's been some trouble through here lately, and we didn't want to take any chances. Hard on the horses, but here we are."

A man came from the house and shouted, "You boys are early."

The driver went over to talk to him. Millie assumed he was the station agent. She made her way around the house in search of the "necessary." When she came back, the driver met her near the steps.

"Not going on tonight, ma'am. You might as well get some supper and see if they've got a bed for you."

Merrileigh Stone sat in the tiny chamber she optimistically referred as the morning room, working on her needlepoint. This house, set in an unfashionable quarter of London, wasn't large enough or grand enough to hold too many rooms for the master and mistress to lounge about in, but one needed a place to carry out the humdrum business of life without worry about mussing the rooms visitors might see.

Smaller and less formal than the drawing room, this parlor took the abuse of the family and saved the more elegant furnishings of the other room for company. Merrileigh preferred to conduct most of her daily business here. Another advantage of the morning room—it allowed her a view of the hall if she positioned her chair just so and left the door open. Through the aperture, she could see anyone going in or out of her husband's study across the passageway.

This morning the objects of her attention were her husband, Randolph Stone, and a young man of slight build and plain mien, his only remarkable feature a shock of wavy blond hair that many a maiden would envy.

He was dressed nearly as well as Randolph. His suit might not be of as nice material, or as flawlessly tailored, but it was fashioned of sturdy fabric and quite stylish. The young man would pass as suitably dressed in nearly any group of London men, though he obviously didn't belong to the class known as "gentlemen." A professional man with a good position.

After a scant twenty minutes closeted with the young man in his study, Randolph saw the visitor out and then came to the morning room. As happened too often these days, Randolph was unable to keep a scowl from his face. Sometimes Merrileigh didn't think he even tried, though she found it most unattractive.

She looked up from her needlepoint. "What is it, my dear?"

"Nothing of consequence."

"Wasn't that Mr. Conrad's man?"

"Yes. Iverson. I don't like him."

"That is neither here nor there. What did he say?" Merrileigh set her needlework aside, rose, and gave the bell pull a tug.

Randolph sighed and slouched into a chair. "My cousin David is returning to England."

Merrileigh clenched her teeth. They'd feared this turn of events for some time. "Rather brazen of him, after all this time."

"I couldn't say," Randolph drawled. He stifled a yawn, as though bored to death with the topic, but his wife knew better.

"Why shouldn't you say?" She rounded on him and glowered at

his lazy form. "If you only cared a bit more, Randolph, we might be living at Stoneford this very minute."

"I don't see how. So long as David's alive, we shall never have that estate." He squinted at her with a bitter air. "You must let go of the bone, Merry. There was a short time when we thought we might have a chance, but I know now I shall never be Earl of Stoneford."

"And why shouldn't you? For years we thought the man was dead. If that were true, you'd have stepped in when Richard died. You were ready to do that. You were *here*. And where was your cousin?"

"Off shooting buffalo and chasing Indians, I expect. Something like that."

"Yes, and I say—"

Merrileigh broke off as the maid entered, bearing a tea tray. She resumed her seat and waited until the maid had unloaded the tray and left them. The mistress lifted the teapot—a charming porcelain pot decorated with violets, but she wished she could replace it with a Doulton tea set. Perhaps one day. She poured two cups full and doctored one to Randolph's taste.

"Here you are." She held out the cup, and he came to get it from her, then resumed his seat.

Merrileigh reached for the second teacup. "As I was about to say, David has done nothing—absolutely nothing—to entitle him to claim his father's title and fortune."

"Other than be born the earl's son," Randolph said drily.

Merrileigh ignored that. "You, on the other hand, have remained close at hand, ready to serve at an instant's notice."

Randolph gave her a wry smile. "Unfortunately, that instant never came, and I was never called to do my duty."

Her lip curled, and she took up the sugar scissors. She needed *something* to sweeten her day.

"I had resigned myself to never knowing one way or the other whether David was alive," Randolph mused. "The sting was fading."

"Yes, and you were set to live out your days a tragic figure." She stirred the sugar into her tea. "Mr. Stone, you know my feelings on the subject."

He frowned at her. "Really, my dear, your suggestion that we take some action—well, it was out of the question. You knew we had no money to search for David, and to what end? To confirm that I would never be earl?"

"Or to confirm his death, in which case you would be. To me, that is worth risking a lot."

"But we didn't have a lot. You knew the limits of my income when we married."

Indeed, she had, but her parents had encouraged the match anyway.

"And when Anne so gallantly decided to brave the frontier, the savages, the bison, and all the rest of it. . ." He shrugged and sipped his tea.

"Yes, you were content to let the late earl's daughter do the work."

"Why not?" Randolph sat straighter and eyed the tea table critically. "I say, do we have any biscuits?"

"Only these shortbread wafers."

"I detest those bland things."

"Then find a way to increase the household budget."

He scowled at her, and Merrileigh scowled back. Both knew they were fortunate to have a cook, a parlor maid, a house maid, and a footman. Merrileigh had hoped that by now they would have increased their income and Randolph would have loosened the purse strings a bit. Unfortunately, that hadn't happened. The few timid investments he'd tried had lost value.

"Perhaps if Albert's school wasn't so costly. . ."

Randolph let out what sounded like a snarl. "You know we can't afford a live-in tutor. We've been all around that several times. There's not room in the house for one, anyway, let alone enough money for his salary."

Merrileigh said quickly, "Yes, I know, my dear. I was merely wishing."

Albert would, in a few short years, be ready for university if they decided to send him. Merrileigh didn't think they'd be able to afford that either, but Randolph was adamant that the boy needed to be prepared to earn a living. She wouldn't bring it up now—she was in no mood for another argument. But personally, she thought the money would be better spent to buy him a commission in the Royal Navy. Once he became a ship's officer, the Queen would pay for his upkeep. And now that the war in the Crimea was over, even an army commission might not be too bad.

Randolph shrugged. "Maybe by autumn we'll be invited to a house party at Stoneford. It will be good to see the old house opened again. I wonder how the shooting will be."

Merrileigh's hand trembled as she raised her cup to her lips. How could he be so accepting and unambitious? Randolph seemed to have given up all hopes of having prospects. So long as friends invited him to house parties in the country now and then and received him at their card parties and balls in town, he didn't care. But she cared.

One of Merrileigh's greatest humiliations was the inability to reciprocate the invitations they received. How long would their friends keep hosting them when she and Randolph had no country house to invite them to visit? Even a simple dinner party was difficult in the cramped, unfashionable townhouse.

If she'd only known when she married him how little prestige she would have, she might have refused Randolph's suit. Of course, she'd been on the upper edge of what was called "the marriageable age" at the time, and her father had bade her consider that Randolph Stone might be her last chance. She was not homely—some considered her fairly pretty, she knew. But without a fortune, she was low on the list for suitors. Randolph's proposal had perhaps saved her from disgrace and ridicule. As Mrs. Stone, she could secure her place in society.

But she'd soon found that Randolph, though received in polite society, had little of the popularity David and his brothers had enjoyed. It seemed the Stone name carried little cachet without money. Time to have another talk with her brother.

CHAPTER 8

Millie's journey to Fort Laramie took weeks longer than she'd expected. Stalled in Idaho while the cavalry dealt with the Shoshone and Bannock, she eventually met a small band of civilians heading eastward. With a small military escort, they traveled to the Loring Cantonment, from where a lieutenant was about to embark for Fort Laramie with an escort for emigrant trains.

"We'll need to travel fast," Lieutenant Fenley told the men of the party. "We have to get through the Shoshone territory quick, and the Sioux aren't happy either. We've had word of them gathering and letting off steam."

"There'll be a lot of wagon trains coming through," said John Collins, whose family had had enough of the West.

"It will be our job to see that they make it safely through to Oregon," Fenley replied. "Our company will join the first westbound emigrant train we meet and escort them through Indian country. Then we'll go back for the next one."

"You won't go all the way to Fort Laramie, then?" asked another of the drivers, a freighter heading for Missouri to purchase supplies for merchants on the Columbia.

"Only if we don't meet a wagon train coming through," Fenley said. "It's early yet, but you never know."

Millie negotiated a place for her valise in Collins's wagon, and they set out the next day. Millie helped Collins's wife cook, much to the lady's relief. The couple had three young children, and it was all Mrs. Collins could do to keep them away from the fire, let alone cook over it.

Millie's skill was soon rumored throughout the company, and since most of those traveling were men—only one other woman besides Millie and Mrs. Collins had joined them—she was soon able to make an arrangement with several gentlemen. They provided the supplies, and Millie cooked for them whenever the wagons stopped. The Collins family gave her their protection and a place to sleep at night near their wagon. Her other clients paid cash.

Rather than going to Salt Lake, as Millie had originally expected to do, they headed more directly to Fort Laramie and took the Sublette Road, bypassing Fort Bridger as well. Millie had turned down two marriage proposals by the time they reached the Platte River. She didn't want to marry a soldier she barely knew, who'd be off most of the year guarding settlers and dodging Indian arrows.

They found that stagecoaches were traveling regularly along the Platte, with mail for the Mormon settlements. Millie had enough money to procure passage on one of their eastbound coaches. At last she left the Collins family and the military escort behind and ventured on in the stagecoach, which would travel day and night until they arrived at Fort Laramie.

This was hard, Millie thought. She hadn't planned to spend the whole of the spring traveling and then begin a new life. But she needed this. Needed to forget the past—her life with Sam, and before that her short and stormy marriage to James Evans. And she needed to let go of her memories of David Stone and the hopes he'd inspired in her. She'd almost succeeded in quelling her unfulfilled dreams until she met him again on the stagecoach.

She'd have to focus on the future. Find a new place for herself. Because David was out of the picture and out of her life.

David surveyed the small enclave at Schwartzburg, thankful to have gotten this far. He remembered the place from his westward journey. It was run by a shrewd German at the time, but Anne and her friend Elise had told how the men on their wagon train had exposed Schwartz's criminal activity and handed him over to the cavalry. They'd left a young man in charge of the station. Anne and the wagon master had asked him to check on the fellow and send them a note telling them how things were going at Schwartzburg.

Pretty well, from what David could see. The corrals were full of healthy-looking livestock. An emigrant train was camped a mile west of the trading post, and a dozen or more travelers had ridden or walked back to deal with the trader.

Inside the post, a tall, handsome young man stood behind the counter.

"Help you, sir?" he called as David walked in.

David ambled over to the counter. "Are you Georg Heinz?"

"Ja."

David smiled and held out his hand. "Greetings from Mr. Rob Whistler, the wagon master who set you up here."

The young man frowned for a moment. His eyes narrowed as though he was putting together what David had said, and then a smile broke over his face. "Ja. Herr Whistler."

Another man, older and a bit stooped, with gray-sprinkled hair, lumbered over carrying a burlap sack. He set it on the counter and looked up at David.

"Georg's English is getting better, sir, but if there's anything you need help with. . ."

"You're working here with him?" David asked.

"That's right. My name's John Kelly." The storekeeper shook David's hand. "Georg took me on a couple of years back. My wife and I thought we'd stay a few months while we got over the grippe and got our strength back, but we like it here, and Georg asked us to stay on."

David nodded. "I'm glad it worked out for all of you."

"You're an Englisher?" Kelly asked.

"That's right."

Georg's eyes widened. "You are the one?"

"What one?" David asked.

"The one Herr Schwartz said was buried out back?"

David laughed. "I've heard that story from my niece. I'm him all right. But as you can see, I'm still alive."

"That is good, sir."

"Yes," David said. "Very good. Can I write a note and send it on the next westbound? Mr. Whistler and my niece wish to know how you're faring, young man."

"I do well," Georg said.

Kelly nodded. "He's a good lad. A good businessman, too, and an honest one. He's put by a good nest egg and hopes to get himself a wife one day."

David just had time to write his letter and post it before the stage driver blew a blast on his horn. Although the stage was uncomfortable and crowded, it rolled steadily eastward, carrying David closer to England with each revolution of the wheels. He had even met a few interesting people during the last two weeks. One, a man with an interest in a New York rail line, had visions of taking the railroads west. Another fellow traveler was a government man who'd been sent to Utah to try to negotiate with Brigham Young over the accommodation of federal troops there. He gave the opinion that there would be a war with Young's followers before the year was out, which set all the passengers on edge and sparked a debate that lasted nearly three hundred miles.

But the best thing about the stagecoach, in David's opinion, was simple: It was now free of Millie Evans.

Merrileigh hated to part with even four pence to go out visiting, but the cost of an occasional hackney to bear her across town was far less than keeping a horse and carriage—even if she and Randolph had had ample room at their modest establishment, which they didn't.

She must have a serious conversation with her brother, Peregrin Walmore. Rather than wait for him to come around to the house, she decided to descend on him. Peregrin hadn't the means to maintain his own house in London, but he shared a rented house with two other young men. His annual income was enough for a minor gentleman to live frugally, but Peregrin shared Merrileigh's tastes, and therefore could not live frugally.

An amiable fellow of one and thirty, he supplemented his

income by gambling and trading horses. Unfortunately, sometimes his trades and his card games went sour, leaving him frequently out of pocket. If his modest fortune had not been tightly tied up, she had no doubt he'd have blown through it long ago. As it was, he lived large each time he received his allowance and cadged off his friends for the rest of the quarter.

Though Peregrin's interest in the Stone family's fortune was peripheral at best, Merrileigh hoped she could convince him to become her ally. This investment might be more lucrative for him in the long run than the faro table at Tattersall's.

Peregrin knew how much his sister had hoped the death of Richard Stone, the seventh Earl of Stoneford, would bring the title to Randolph. None of that would have been possible if Richard had fathered a son. Or for that matter, if either of his brothers, John and David, had had sons. The three brothers had flagrantly shirked their duty, so far as Merrileigh was concerned. Richard had one girl, Anne, but neither of the other brothers had married or produced an heir, to her knowledge.

Their cousin Randolph, however, had outdone them all, producing Albert as well as a daughter, Francine. Merrileigh considered she'd done her duty well—though a second boy wouldn't have been unwelcome. Still, her husband had a sturdy heir. If only Albert were old enough to help her now.

But Peregrin would have to do. Even though the young man was perhaps not the paragon of virtue and fine character that one could wish for, her brother was certainly capable when he was sober.

She descended from the hackney before his house. Much to her chagrin, Peregrin and his two comrades lived on a better street than she did. She bade the driver to wait, realizing it might cost her an extra twopence. But that was preferable to chasing down another hack later.

Sweeping up to the front door, she lifted the knocker and gave it three peremptory raps. A moment later, a footman opened the door—a gawky boy whose pale hair stuck up in odd lumps and pinnacles.

"Is Mr. Walmore in?"

"Yes marm. This way, please."

The boy held the door while she entered, then awkwardly sidled past her to lead her to the drawing room. Merrileigh hated this room—the dark paneling and high, narrow windows reminded her of a solicitor's office. The three young men sharing this house really should hire someone to overhaul the decorations. She didn't suppose they had the funds between them though, and if they did, they probably wouldn't care to spend them on household niceties. Single gentlemen weren't prone to do a lot of entertaining in their homes.

She settled in on the worn horsehair sofa and rehearsed how she would tell her tale to Peregrin. He was already aware of her husband's situation, which should make it quite simple to understand.

Since Richard and his next brother, John, had died, only David stood between Randolph and the earldom—and the grand estate at Stoneford. How Merrileigh had hoped that David had also met an early end. It seemed so likely. He'd left England twenty years before Richard's death, and after the first ten years of his absence, the family hadn't heard a word from him. So why couldn't he have conveniently died in the American wilderness—leaving behind proof of his demise of course?

Alas, that cheeky girl Anne—Richard's only daughter—had traipsed across the ocean and found her uncle David alive and well, presumably panning gold and guzzling whiskey in the Oregon Territory. If Merrileigh had had anything to say about it, the unworthy churl would have died then and there. But Merrileigh didn't get everything she wished for. Not without hard work, anyway.

Peregrin arrived five minutes later, disheveled and wearing his dressing gown. Merrileigh frowned but refrained from expressing her displeasure. At least he was home and willing to speak to his sister before noon.

"Good morning." She turned her cheek for the expected kiss.

"Ho, Merry. What brings you out so early?"

"My husband's cousin David."

"Oh? What's the word now?" Peregrin lowered his voice and

glanced toward the door. "Hold fast." He walked over and closed it, then returned to settle in beside her on the sofa.

"Randolph received word from the solicitor's office that David is on his way home."

"Oh. That rots."

"Well, Randolph can only think of delightful fall weekends at Stoneford with his cousin, but I tend to share your opinion."

"If David comes home, it pretty well means your Albert will never have a chance at the title." Peregrin stood and walked to the fireplace. He leaned with his elbow on the mantel, his brow furrowed. "What's to do? I suppose you can't break the entailment, now that David has turned up."

"We couldn't anyway. Believe me, I made sure Randolph pursued an inquiry in that direction. No, the only way he can come into the earldom and install our family at Stoneford permanently is in the tragic event that David dies."

"Mmm. No kiddies, what?"

"No. That's one good thing. Mr. Conrad showed Randolph a letter he received from Anne last year, shortly after she'd located David. She stated straight out that he hadn't married, and so had no male heirs." She let that sink in. Her brother generally saw the lay of the land if you let him look it over at his own pace.

"So." Peregrin's face brightened. "If old David doesn't get him a bride, Randolph is still in line."

"Exactly." She smiled at him, feeling they were halfway to understanding each other.

A discreet knock came on the door panel. Peregrin strode over and opened it. "Hope you don't mind—I asked for coffee."

Merrileigh's mouth curled. She couldn't stand the stuff. She declined a cup and waited patiently while the footman served Peregrin. Once the servant was out of the room, she cleared her throat, ready to approach the topic again.

"Now Perry, I didn't tell you this before, and perhaps I should have, but the fewer people who know, the less likely it will get back to those we don't wish to know it."

"Oh? What's that?" He took a sip from his cup.

"Two years ago, when Anne Stone first took it into her head to go to America and find David, I felt it was in our best interest—Randolph's and mine, and of course Albert's—to try to find out quickly whether or not David was still alive."

Peregrin's sandy eyebrows arched. "Oh? Well yes, I can see that it might be an advantage to know, but surely Anne—"

"To know before Anne knew," Merrileigh said deliberately.

He set his cup down on the saucer. "Go on."

"Randolph wouldn't hear of spending any money on it—he couldn't see the need. He was content to sit back and let Anne spend her funds to do the job."

"But you weren't."

"No. It was my opinion that our interests would be better served if we were one step ahead of Anne. If we *knew*."

Peregrin's eyes opened wide, and he pulled his head back. "Why, Merrileigh, you shock me."

CHAPTER 9

David stepped down from the cramped stagecoach and looked around. Fort Laramie had sprawled since he'd passed through nearly seven years ago. It looked almost a proper town now, and the walls of the old stockade—Fort John—were left in disrepair. The main buildings of the present, garrisoned Fort Laramie weren't fenced in. The large barracks dominated the other structures, and the Indian encampments seemed smaller than he recalled. The place had looked overrun with tipi villages last time he was here. One of the passengers had said something about the army making the Indian bands move several miles away to protect the grazing for their animals and those of the emigrant trains. Probably a good decision.

"One hour," the station agent bellowed. "Dinner available next door. They've got fried chicken today."

David arched his back to stretch out the kinks and turned toward the station house. It was a bit past noon and quite warm for early June. An hour's reprieve sounded good. He'd ridden the last fifteen miles squeezed in between mail sacks in a covered farm wagon the Mormon fellows called a stagecoach. At least they were getting through.

"Mr. Stone!"

A dreadful feeling hit him, like a pebble plinking off his head. He'd told himself he'd be safe from Millie Evans if he only ate supper and got back on the stage, without strolling down the street or even glancing about the fort's parade ground.

Slowly, he turned toward the voice. Sure enough, Millie was hurrying across the street toward him, her feet raising a small cloud of dust that accompanied her wherever she walked. She wore a dainty hat, and beneath it her hair glinted red in the sun. He was surprised that she had on the same faded traveling dress she'd worn two weeks ago. Had she completely lost her wardrobe and her sense of fashion?

"Thank heaven! I was afraid you'd take the Salt Lake line and I'd miss you entirely." Her smile seemed a bit strained.

"Oh?" David did not see any point in telling her how he'd had to piece together tickets on one local line after another to get this far. She had no doubt done the same thing. The overland mail contract to California had gone to John Butterfield, but he was setting up a southern line. The man was probably wise to go through Texas and New Mexico Territory, as the stages wouldn't have to deal with winter weather, but it certainly didn't make travel any easier in the North.

"If I'd had any idea what the route was like. . ." Millie shook her head. "That doesn't matter though, does it? We've both come this far. I've been meeting every stage for the last week, hoping I'd find you."

"Indeed?" David normally spoke more than one word at a time—in fact, his family and friends would say he was an adept conversationalist—but Millie's effusive welcome tied his tongue. Apparently his efforts to disconnect from her had failed. He cleared his throat. "Might I ask why you were so eager to see me again?"

She put a hand to her brow. "Of course. How uncivil of me. But you see, I'm near desperate. Might we find a place to sit down, and I will tell you my predicament?"

"Well. . ." David couldn't truthfully think of a reason to refuse. "I suppose so, but I need to be ready to board the stage again soon."

She nodded. "I hope to find a way to travel on it myself."

"Oh? I, er, understood you were planning to make this place your new home."

"I was, but—" Millie glanced toward the stage driver, who was throwing luggage down willy-nilly in the dusty street. "Oh sir, your bags. You'll want to watch them here."

"What? I say!" He strode to the edge of the street. "Sir, I plan to go on with you."

"You'll have to wait," the driver said. "The colonel has several sacks we need to add to the load. Unless you want to ride on the roof, but we're tying some freight on there."

The station agent came to David's side.

"I'm sorry, sir. I only just got the word. Most likely the tavern next door can put you up for the night."

Dazed, David looked from his discarded valise to the station house and back. "All right, yes. Thank you." He glanced at Millie, who hadn't budged an inch. "Uh. . .Mrs. Evans, perhaps you will be my guest for dinner?"

She smiled, not the winsome smile meant to charm a man, but a beatific expression of gratitude. David got the uneasy feeling he had restored her faith in mankind, and he didn't like meaning that to Millie.

He found himself sitting opposite her ten minutes later in what looked to be a perfectly respectable dining room.

"It transforms into a wicked saloon after sundown," Millie confided, "but during the day it's not so bad."

He couldn't help wondering if she'd seen the inside of the place after dark. They both fell to their dinner, and he noted that Millie ate as much as he did. Had she gone hungry these last few weeks? He couldn't help a pang of remorse.

When David had finished the main course, he stirred the coffee placed before him. It seemed the proprietor had no tea. "Now, Mrs. Evans, could you please tell me what this is about? And let's be direct, shall we?"

"Yes, indeed." She brought a fan from her handbag and fluttered it before her face, sending a little backhand of a breeze David's way, for which he was thankful. The heat had nearly driven him to strip off his coat, which he would rather not do in public.

"It's my cousin, Polly."

David lifted his cup. "She being the relation who lives here?"

"Did live, sir. She's gone on."

David paused with the cup nearly to his lips. "Gone on to. . . ?"

"To glory, sir. She and her husband both. Her husband was the fort's chaplain this last year and a half, but now they are without one—until the army sends another, that is. Polly and her Jeremiah are buried in the graveyard."

"I'm sorry." David set his cup down. It seemed somehow disrespectful to slurp his coffee when speaking of the deceased. "What will you do now?"

"That's just the thing. I don't know. I've had to spend the money you so graciously let me keep from the sale of Old Blue just to get this far and survive here. Lodgings and food. I earned a bit on the way, cooking for the people I traveled with. But that's run out, and now I've not got enough to go on. I fear I'm stuck here."

David winced. At least she was telling him straight out instead of hovering around and pilfering from him. But how did he even know she was telling the truth? Maybe she knew she couldn't charm him again, so she had switched to a different tactic. But how did one convey such a delicate thought? He didn't wish to insult her if she was truly destitute. Coming on the heels of her bereavement for her brother, even David felt the cruelty of the situation.

"So you've spoken to some of your cousin's acquaintances?" he asked.

"Yes, several. They've been quite kind, especially the colonel's wife. The colonel even gave me five dollars, but he said that he couldn't do anything officially."

"And your cousin's belongings?" David picked up his coffee cup then, to give him something to do besides look across the table at Millie. She did look rather fetching in that hat, though the dress was as drab as dishwater.

"Oh, they're to go to Polly and Jeremiah's daughter. She's married and has five children, but her husband is coming, or so I'm told, to settle the estate and auction their things."

"Ah. Perhaps if you waited for him. . ."

"No, I can't ask them to take me in."

"What will you do then?"

She let out a big sigh and clasped her hands on the table. "I have a plan."

David raised his cup slightly in a sham salute. "Always a good idea."

She smiled then, and his stomach flipped. She really was lovely, even now when she was poor as a church mouse.

"Yes, I always thought so." Millie sipped her coffee.

"And your plan is. . . ?"

"Well, if you hadn't come along, I'd have continued as I have the last several days, walking about town and seeking work. But employment seems hard to come by here." She raised her fan before her face and waved it, hiding her expression as she added, "Oh, there are jobs, of a sort, but I don't want that sort."

"Ah yes."

Millie wouldn't engage herself as a barmaid or worse, of that he was sure. Better to latch on to a well-heeled gentleman passing through. Like himself.

She surprised him by saying, "I'm known as quite a good cook, and I'm willing to do housework or laundry if I must, but they have plenty of laundresses for the fort, and the officers hire enlisted men very cheaply to do for them. I had no luck at all seeking a domestic position. At least, not without other requirements, which I refuse to meet."

Her face flushed, and she fanned herself again.

"Yes, well, a military post is no place for a decent single woman."

"Thank you, sir."

So. He'd designated her a decent woman. Now he would probably have to help her out of this scrape or forever bear the guilt of depriving her of the chance to live an upright life.

"I have friends near Philadelphia. I grew up outside the city. I feel sure I could find an old acquaintance who could give me a reference for work."

He cleared his throat. "Perhaps I could have a word with the colonel."

"Thank you, but I doubt it would do any good."

"Well, since we'll be here until tomorrow, I might walk over to his office." A sudden thought struck him. "And where are you lodging?"

She looked away. "They've let me use a little room in the officers' building, but I fear I've displaced a young lieutenant, and they will

all be glad when I've left."

At least she hadn't needed to resort to a tavern. "Have the officers' wives been courteous to you?"

"To some extent. There are only three ladies at the fort now. I am told they expect more this summer, but it's clear I can't receive their charity much longer."

With a sigh, David set his coffee cup down. "Well, since I have the afternoon free, I suppose I'll stroll over to the fort." She wanted him to promise more than that, he could see it in those tragic green eyes. But he couldn't. Not yet. First he wanted to verify her story. He wouldn't wish any woman to be forced into her situation, but he wasn't about to be duped again.

He pushed back his chair. "Perhaps we shall meet again later."

She opened her mouth and closed it.

David paid for the food and walked out into the bright sunlight. The wind over the prairie made the air bearable. He'd left his luggage in the tavern owner's keeping, and now he took his time getting over to the fort. A sliver of conscience chided him—he ought to have escorted Millie to some safer place, but where would that be?

It took only minutes and a confident attitude to admit him to an audience with the colonel. He explained his circumstances and quickly told the officer he'd taken a room at the tavern and planned to take the next day's stage eastward. He didn't want the man to think he was here to ask a favor for himself.

"I ran into Mrs. Evans at the stage stop," he said, watching the colonel's face. "She's an old acquaintance of mine."

"Oh yes. Charming lady. Such a pity." The colonel shook his head.

"Yes," David said. "She told me of her cousin's passing."

"And her husband as well. He was an excellent chaplain, but he insisted on doing a lot of mission work among the Indians. I fear it killed him."

"Oh?" David frowned. "I thought illness took them."

"So it did. Diphtheria, if our surgeon is correct. There was a small outbreak among the Brule Sioux. Mr. Morton wouldn't stay out of their camp. He did great kindness to the Indians of course, but his job was to see to our men's spiritual needs. Because he tended to the savages, he's no longer with us."

"Ah. But Mr. and Mrs. Morton were Mrs. Evans's relatives?"

"So I understand. My wife was very friendly with Polly Morton. She informed me that on her deathbed Polly was fretting. She'd just received a letter saying her cousin was coming for a visit, and she wanted everything neat and clean. My wife assured her we'd get a striker— that is, an enlisted man—to redd up the house for her. Unfortunately, I ended up hiring a couple of men to pack up their belongings instead."

David left the colonel's office vaguely ill at ease. Millie's story seemed to be true, and the cousin had indeed expected her arrival. That was comforting. The part that bothered him was his perceived responsibility. What did Millie expect him to do?

He supposed he could pay her way back to civilization. He hated to have her further indebted to him. But he couldn't drive off and leave her here. No gentleman would do such a thing—even to a woman of questionable character.

"And how did your venture turn out?" Peregrin took a sip of his coffee and waited for his sister to continue.

She grimaced. "I sank all I had into it. All I could lay hands on without arousing Randolph's suspicion, that is. If he ever learned that I'd gone ahead without his knowledge. . ." She shook her head. Perhaps it was best not to give her brother the details. Peregrin would probably not scruple to hire thugs to get in the way of someone he didn't like, but she couldn't bring herself to admit she'd done just that. "Anyway, nothing came of it, and I used up all my year's income as well as a bit I'd tucked away, and loans from several friends."

"I seem to remember you touching me for some cash about that time."

"Yes, well. . .I'm afraid I wasn't forthcoming in my reason for needing it."

"You told me you'd lost heavily at cards, and you didn't want Randolph to know."

Merrileigh waved her hand in dismissal. "I paid you back eventually, and all the rest, but I went without the least luxuries for months on end."

"I know what that's like," Peregrin said. "Seems like I'm never flush more than a week after I get my quarter's allowance."

"That's because you keep gambling when your luck runs black. You just don't know when to hold off on betting."

Her brother smiled impishly at her and ran a hand through his hair, which disarranged his golden locks even more, putting her in remembrance of the footman who'd let her in. Did none of these young men care about their appearance anymore?

"Still, if I hadn't given you a round sum back then, I could have covered most everything in '55, and I surely would have come even last year. Here I am still out five hundred pounds."

"Good heavens." Merrileigh winced, knowing she had little chance of convincing her brother to risk more of his income. Her own annual pittance, which her grandmother had left her, was spent during the first three months of the year to pay off her dressmaker for last year's expenditures and for food and wine served at two dinner parties which she absolutely *had* to host to avoid letting herself and Randolph look like cheap hangers-on. Oh, and two new dresses and a few trifles her husband would doubtless refer to as "fripperies." But they were necessary, every one. A lady couldn't appear at an assembly wearing last year's gown, or take a promenade in Hyde Park sporting an outdated chapeau. It simply wasn't done.

"Does that crestfallen demeanor tell me that you'd hoped I could stand you another sum so that you could try to—oh, I don't know. What is it you think you can do about all this, Merry? Do you hope to hinder David from coming home and laying claim to the title?"

"Well. . .would that be so unreasonable?"

Peregrin laughed. "Not to my way of thinking. Why, if I had one half-wild cousin blocking me from a huge fortune, I'd—well, never mind what I'd do. But I think it's safe to say you must be careful to whom you present this idea."

"I'm well aware of that." She scowled. "It was such a blow when

I learned my first attempt had failed."

He straightened and eyed her with new realization. "Don't tell me you hired someone to go over there and—"

She smiled sheepishly. "Perhaps you also recall me asking if you had any contacts in America. Specifically in New York."

"Why, yes. I thought it odd at the time. I suppose I thought maybe you would pass a name on to Anne if she wanted to hire a private detective."

"Not Anne. Me. I sent word ahead—by a ship that sailed just days before Anne's." Merrileigh laughed. "She didn't tell us her plans. We wouldn't have known if Conrad hadn't told my husband. He was awfully embarrassed about it—said he shouldn't have let it slip. But I seized the opportunity and set someone up to watch her and see if he could find David before Anne did."

Peregrin shook his head. "I'm speechless. You ought to have told me, Merry. I could at least have helped you set things up."

"You're right, I should have. I'm sure now that he bilked me out of far more than his services were worth. But toward the end—ah, toward the end, I was so excited. It was all I could do not to tell Randolph. I'd had word from the fellow I hired. He was close, he said. It was to be over within a matter of days. And then the next thing I know. . ." She sighed. "It was all for naught, and we heard from Anne that David was safe."

"That's bad luck."

"Yes. I haven't had the heart or the means to try again, but now it's becoming urgent. In David's latest letter, he told the solicitors he planned to leave Oregon this spring—a month ago, in fact, as soon as the mountain roads were open."

"What, he's going it overland?"

"Apparently. He could be nearly to New York by now."

"Surely not."

"That is my hope, that it will take him much longer than it took the ship that brought us the news. But when Conrad's man came around to see Randolph the other day, he said we could look for David by fall."

"And you still don't feel you can bring Randolph around to where he'll commiserate and try to do something?"

Merrileigh shook her head. "I brought it up once, way back before Anne left, and he was scandalized at the thought. I daren't suggest that we might have the power to change things."

"Haven't we, though?" Peregrin met her gaze with anxious blue eyes.

Merrileigh smiled. She had not misjudged her brother. His wit might be even keener than she'd thought. "I should have put it all before you the first time."

"Yes. Perhaps we could have worked together to a happy outcome. But you have to understand, Merry. I haven't any money I could lend you now—none."

"What about your friends?"

"Heavens, no. I can't ask them for anything right now."

She sighed. "I wonder if I could borrow enough to send someone to New York."

"Have you any jewelry—"

Merrileigh gritted her teeth and shook her head. "I'm afraid not. Nothing that would bring enough." Again, it was probably best not to tell everything she knew.

"Well, maybe you could go around to the solicitor and see if they've heard any more from David."

"That might help," she said. "Though I think we need to have someone on the spot. I mean, if we wait until he sets foot in England, the danger would be much increased."

"Yes. It would be better to send someone over there—someone you trust. You know David's sailing from New York?"

"I believe so. Perhaps Mr. Conrad's office can say for sure." Merrileigh rose. "Thank you, Perry. Talking to you has been a great comfort, even if you can't help me in other ways. I needn't remind you to keep this to yourself."

"Of course. I hope you find someone to help you—and the means to underwrite the venture. And be assured I'll support you in any way I can."

She had no doubt of that—after all, this venture was in Peregrin's best interest, too. If his sister rose in fortunes, he would go up a notch in society's stock. Of course, he'd probably come around more often for help with his debts, but Merrileigh wouldn't let that bother her if he helped her and Randolph get discreetly into the position of largesse.

He saw her to the door. She had forgotten all about the hackney until she saw it sitting there in the street.

"Oh dear, I didn't expect to be so long. . . ."

"Now, that I can cover." Peregrin hurried away for a minute and returned with a few coins in his hand. "There you go, Merry. I wish I could invest in your adventure, but this will have to do."

CHAPTER 10

Millie sat as long as she felt comfortable in the dining room, lingering over a second cup of coffee and a slice of cake that the owner said came with the meal. When men began to come in and line up at the bar for drinks, she felt their eyes on her and decided it was time to leave.

She thought about asking for the piece of cake David didn't eat but gave up on it when a trooper came to her table and said, "Share a drink with me, ma'am?"

"No, thank you." She scurried out into the sunshine and walked toward the parade ground.

What would she do if David wouldn't help her? She'd never felt so powerless. She didn't even have a horse. If she stole one from the military enclave, no doubt she'd be tracked down and hanged.

Why hadn't Polly and Jeremiah settled in a nice, quiet town? Most places she could find work. She'd offered her cooking skills at the tavern, but the owner wasn't interested in a cook. He wanted saloon girls, and Millie was determined not to sink to that level.

She could go back to her old ways of stealing, but where would that land her? The only alternative she could think of was to marry one of the cavalrymen—which would take time and would likely lead to a miserable existence. Or she could wait for a wagon train to come through and see if she could attach herself to it. She didn't want to go westward again though, and nobody was apt to take her along when she couldn't pay for her own supplies.

Tears flooded her eyes, and she wiped them impatiently with her sleeve. *God, I've begged You to help me find a way to support myself. You're supposed to be with me. Why do I feel so alone?*

She smiled wryly. At least now she'd have a chance to return

David's handkerchief. She'd washed it several times after soaking it with her tears—tears for Sam, for Polly and Jeremiah, and for remorse over the past. If she were honest, she had also shed tears for David and what might have been.

He came around the corner of the men's barracks thirty yards away. Should she approach him? She stood still, gazing at him. He cut such a dashing figure, even after weeks of rough travel. His carriage did that, she supposed, even more than the well-cut clothing. But now she was more interested in his mindset.

Lord, You say in the Bible You'll help Your children. I need that help now.

How could she bear it if David rejected her pleas and left the fort without giving his aid?

He looked up and saw her. His steps faltered for an instant, then he came on. Millie inhaled and raised her chin. She had always prided herself in being able to command a serene expression in any circumstances, but now she didn't know how to compose her face. The grieving sister? The gracious fellow traveler? The desperate pilgrim?

Without thinking about it, she mirrored David's countenance—brows lowered, lips slightly parted, eyes somber.

Dear Lord, she prayed, *please soften his heart so he can help me this once.*

He walked across the open parade ground and stopped a yard from her. Millie waited for him to speak.

"I am sorry about your cousin."

"Thank you." She clenched her teeth, determined not to cry. Even if he refused to help her, she would not let him see her weep again.

"And you feel that if you got to Philadelphia you could find proper employment?"

"I'm sure of it. There are many opportunities there, and I do have skills." She couldn't stop herself from taking a step toward him. "Mr. Stone, if you help me, I promise to repay—"

"Please." He held up a hand, and his expression told her she'd crossed the line with him. David had enjoyed her company when he could think of her as a genteel lady. When she sank to the level of an impoverished widow begging for aid, his whole attitude toward her had changed. "I shall not expect any repayment. Just. . .get to where you can establish yourself in a respectable manner." He took some money from his pocket. "Here is ten dollars. I shall purchase your tickets, but I would appreciate it if you use this to buy your own meals and necessities. If you need more, tell me."

"Oh, sir." The tears spilled over, to Millie's dismay, but these were tears of relief. Even though he didn't want to be seen paying for her meals—he probably would rather she didn't acknowledge him at all when other travelers were about—she would be grateful to him for the rest of her life. God had used him to answer her pleas, and the Almighty, at least, would not be embarrassed when she expressed her gratitude.

Her cheeks flushed as she accepted the money. "Thank you. I shall endeavor not to embarrass you on this journey." That seemed paramount to sustaining their relationship for the next thousand miles.

He nodded. "I shall arrange the tickets. Be at the stage stop in the morning."

The hack pulled up in Chancery Lane, one of London's stodgiest business streets. Merrileigh gathered her skirts in preparation to climb out. It wouldn't do to trip over her wide crinoline and fall on her face. The footman opened the door and held out a hand to steady her. She stepped down without mishap and eyed the discreet sign beside the modest, half-timbered building: JONATHAN CONRAD, ESQ.

Conrad's firm had been the Stone family's solicitors forever, so far as Merrileigh knew. Probably since the first earl. She had never had occasion to visit them personally before today.

She hesitated. It was risky. She mustn't spill any of her intent. But still, if she hoped for any sort of a chance for Randolph to become the new earl, she needed information. Already her mind raced ahead to what she would do with that knowledge. She would need an emissary. Perhaps she could ask Peregrin to find a man she could trust among his acquaintances. But could she have confidence in one of his friends? Letting too many people in on the plan was dangerous. No more blunders! She squared her shoulders and walked to the door.

In the office, a clerk took her calling card and bade her sit in the antechamber while Mr. Iverson finished with another client. A moment later, a door to an inner room opened, and a gray-haired gentleman with luxuriant whiskers emerged. He turned and spoke to the man behind him.

"Pastiche. That's the one you want to back on Saturday."

Iverson, the junior partner, appeared in the doorway, and over the older man's shoulder, Merrileigh glimpsed his regretful smile.

"I'm not a gambling man, sir, but I wish you well."

"Ha! You'll wish you were. Pastiche. He's the horse to be beat, I'm telling you. You won't get a better bit of advice than that."

Iverson continued to smile as the gentleman limped toward the outer door, but shook his head. The clerk, meanwhile, had risen and handed Mr. Iverson Merrileigh's card and then hurried to open the door for the departing client.

Iverson stood for a moment, fingering the cream-colored card. It ought to impart to him Merrileigh's station in life, imprinted as it was with a nosegay of geraniums and white violets, signifying gentility and modesty. After a moment, he looked up and smiled uncertainly.

"Mrs. Randolph Stone. How do you do, ma'am?"

Merrileigh rose and gave him a slight curtsey. "I do fine, sir."

"I'm afraid Mr. Conrad is not in the office today. He only comes in two days a week now. Perhaps you would like to come back on Monday."

"On the contrary," she said, looking him up and down, "it is you I wish to see, Mr. Iverson."

"Ah. Then come through, please." He stepped aside to let her pass and said to the clerk, "Tea in my chamber."

The inner office had only one window, rendering it quite dark. Iverson's desk was positioned before it, no doubt so that he had the advantage of the light while he went about his tedious duties. Shelves on two sides of the room held leather-bound books— legal tomes, she assumed—and pasteboard file boxes. No doubt the Stones' lives and her chances of living in luxury, as opposed to threadbare gentility, lay in one of those files, gathering dust.

Iverson sat down behind the desk, eyeing her warily. "Well then, Mrs. Stone, what may I help you with?"

Merrileigh leaned forward with what she hoped was an engaging smile. "I was wondering. . .is there any new word from Mr. David Stone? The family is quite anxious to welcome him home."

"No, nothing since what I shared with your husband a few days past."

Merrileigh smiled regretfully. "Pity. I hope to host a dinner party for him shortly after his arrival. You will give us word if you hear anything, won't you?"

"Surely. I shall communicate anything of that sort to Mr. Stone. Your husband, that is."

She nodded. "I suppose I'm too eager to move forward with my plans. You know, it helps the hostess to think ahead when it comes to staging a social event."

"Of course."

Still, she wasn't sure he wouldn't mention this call to Randolph on their next meeting, and that could cause some friction. Merrileigh settled back in her chair and cleared her throat. "Mr. Iverson, I'd like to be sure you understand that I am not here on behalf of my husband. In fact, Mr. Stone has no idea that I've come to see you."

He gazed at her blankly. "All right."

"Don't misunderstand me. We're all delighted that my husband's cousin is coming home."

"Yes," Iverson said. "It will be good to have an earl in residence at Stoneford once again."

"Yes." Merrileigh decided to advance a bit further and see if she could determine where the man's loyalty lay. "My husband and his cousin have always got along very well. When they were lads, that is. As you know, they've not seen each other for more than twenty years."

"Yes, so Mr. Stone told me. Mr. Randolph Stone, that is." Iverson nodded happily.

"To be sure. But you must understand, that though they are quite amiable toward each other, they are, in a sense, adversaries."

"Adversaries?" Iverson sobered. "I'm not sure I understand you, ma'am."

"Why, David Stone, and only David Stone, stands between my husband and the earldom. You must see that."

The young man picked up some papers from the desktop and tapped the edges on the desk, straightening them. "I suppose, in a sense. . ."

A quiet knock in the door drew his attention, and Merrileigh felt his relief that the conversation had been interrupted.

"Come in," Iverson called.

The clerk brought in a tray with a teapot, two cups and saucers, a pitcher of hot milk, and a cone of sugar.

"Ah, here we are," Iverson said with a smile. "May I pour for you, Mrs. Stone?"

"Yes, please."

When they were settled with their tea and the clerk had backed out of the room and closed the door, Iverson said carefully, "Now, Mrs. Stone, I must tell you that if your husband has a notion of—"

"I told you, my husband doesn't know I am here."

"You did say that, but even so, I must say that if he hopes to break the entailment—"

Merrileigh laughed, and Iverson stared at her, his face flushing.

"Sir, as to my husband and his notions, well, truthfully, he hasn't any. It is I who make the inquiry. Not for my husband—he is content to let his cousin resume his place at Stoneford. Not for myself—for I know my place, and I am satisfied with my position in life." It was a lie, but she hoped the color it brought to her cheeks would be interpreted as modesty. "I am asking on behalf of my children, sir.

For it is they who will suffer."

"Suffer?"

"If David Stone were to die this instant, my husband would become Earl of Stoneford."

"Well, yes," Iverson said cautiously. "That is, if Mr. David Stone has no direct heirs."

"But he hasn't. Mr. Conrad told my husband last winter, when your office first heard from David, that he was living in the Oregon Territory, unmarried. Without issue, as the law says—no children. And that means that if my husband did ever inherit the title, our eldest, Albert, would follow him."

"Well. . .he would certainly be the next in line if that were the case." Iverson frowned at her. "But madam, as I was going to tell you before, if you have any idea of the title bypassing Mr. David Stone and coming to your husband—or your son—without going through proper channels, well, that would be quite impossible. However, if you did want to pursue such a notion, it would be best for you to seek out an attorney not connected to the Stone family. You see, whatever happens, we here at Conrad and Iverson are committed to serving the earl. And right now the heir apparent to the title is David Stone."

"Oh please." Merrileigh touched a hand to her lips. "I hadn't a whisper of an idea that we would try to break the entailment. No, that belongs to David, if he is able to claim it."

"Then I fail to see the purpose of this conversation."

Merrileigh studied him thoughtfully. The junior solicitor did not seem at all inclined to favor the idea of Randolph or Albert being in a position to inherit the earldom. She must tread carefully.

She shrugged and gave him a smile. "I expect you'll think me silly, Mr. Iverson, but I thought perhaps it would be in the family's interest to send someone across to—to ensure David Stone's safety. We all know he was attacked in Oregon."

"Yes." Iverson rubbed his jawbone absently. "Odd thing that. We never did find out what was behind it."

"I suppose it was a random incident," Merrileigh said quickly.

"Some Yankee thug out to rob him. But really, I think it might be wise to send a...a sort of bodyguard to meet him in New York and accompany him here."

Iverson shook his head. "I regret to say, ma'am, that the trustees are not allowed to spend money on such an agenda. But I understand that Mr. Stone is not destitute, that he has made a small fortune under his own auspices in America. If he feels he needs guarding, he is perfectly capable of hiring some trustworthy men to look out for him."

She sighed. "I suppose you are right and there's no need for me to worry. Forgive me for wasting your time, sir." It was clear that the solicitor would not prevail upon the trustees for an expenditure of that nature, and therefore any possibility of Merrileigh persuading the emissary to do a little extra work on her behalf was out of the question. She rose and gathered her reticule and fan.

Iverson jumped up. "Not at all, ma'am. I'm sure Mr. Stone would appreciate your concern."

"Hmm. It will be a relief to us all when he's home and officially instated."

"Then we agree." Iverson smiled and guided her to the door.

Merrileigh bid him good day and went out to her hackney. She wished she hadn't come. It was worse than a wasted half hour—she'd put a hint in Iverson's mind that she opposed David's claiming his title. And Iverson had neither confirmed nor denied her mention of New York as David's port of embarkation. She'd have done better to keep quiet. And now she had to pay for the time the cabby had waited for her—Peregrin wasn't here to play the gallant for his sister this time. She felt very sour indeed when she descended from the carriage in front of her house and handed over several coins to the driver. Where would she find a man to carry out the task she wanted done for the pittance she would be able to offer?

CHAPTER 11

David purchased two tickets the next morning, relieved that he was able to book passage through to Independence. Millie was prompt, meeting him outside the stage stop. She carried the same battered valise she'd left The Dalles with. David made sure no one was watching them when he handed over her ticket. He then strolled over to watch the tenders hitch up the team, thus avoiding conversation with her.

"We'll be meeting a wagon train on the first stage," the driver told him. "A couple of troopers from their escort rode in last night. Said they're camped six miles east of here."

"Will that delay us?" David asked.

"Naw, we'll go around 'em."

Two men joined them in the coach—bearded men dressed as farmers. They seemed to know each other but said little. David let Millie and the others board first and wound up sitting beside her. He kept to his corner, and she stayed in hers.

They met the wagon train head-on a few miles out. The wagons were strung out in four or five columns to lessen the dust, but even so, it choked the coach passengers. They kept the windows shut, but it drifted in through cracks and settled on their clothing. David's eyes began to water. Millie, he noted, was still using the linen handkerchief he'd given her in Idaho Territory. No matter—he still had half a dozen, and had found a laundry on one of his delays. By this time he knew well enough to carry two at all times.

Hers looked clean when she took it out. That meant she'd washed it at least once, maybe several times. Millie somehow kept a clean, neat appearance under the abominable travel conditions. He did wonder about her scanty wardrobe. Perhaps she'd never had many clothes, only given the illusion of bounty as part of her confidence game.

He wished he could chat with the wagon master or his scouts and pick up some news, but probably what he'd heard at the fort was as fresh as any these travelers would have.

Nebraska seemed endless. David reminded himself countless times that crossing it had taken much longer when he'd done it with three freight wagons. Ten or fifteen miles a day was all they'd done on that trip, at the pace of oxen. The stagecoach was doing ten times that, easily.

Whenever possible, he avoided sitting next to Millie or directly across from her. Still, she looked and smelled better than a lot of people they wound up sharing their cramped space with. Looking at her was preferable to gazing at some grizzled old prospector or a glittery card sharp.

David kept his mind from dwelling on Millie by thinking about England. If all went well, he'd be at Stoneford in a couple of months. He looked forward to spending autumn at the country estate. He hoped the letter he had sent via ship before leaving Oregon had reached the family's solicitor by now.

Of course, he'd communicated to the solicitor earlier. David's niece, Anne, had insisted he do so shortly after she'd found him in Oregon and broken the news of her father's death to him. Even if David never claimed the estate and the title that went with it, she had prevailed on him to let Conrad know he was alive and eligible to do so. That would put many minds to rest in England, she had said.

Now David wondered if that had been the wisest course. After all, an assassin had tried to kill him eighteen months ago. His right shoulder still ached every time it rained, and probably would for the rest of his life. Who had paid Peterson? They'd never found out.

If only the experimental telegraph cable under the Atlantic was completed. He could get a message to Conrad in minutes, if that succeeded. At least when he reached St. Louis, he'd be able to send a telegram to New York and have it forwarded to England on the next steamship.

At a way station came a welcome break from his reverie. The passengers all got out to use the necessary, then boarded again. The other two men lingered, and for a few minutes, David and Millie were the only two in the coach. The silence between them stretched into awkwardness. A real gentleman would make polite conversation. Most women would have spoken unbidden. David suspected Millie didn't dare utter a word for fear of offending him.

At last he could stand it no longer. "You seem to bear the rigors of the journey well, ma'am."

"Thank you. I cannot complain—but if I did, it would do no good."

He smiled. "Indeed. I give thanks often that we're moving forward. I ask no more."

She nodded, then said hesitantly, "Might I inquire after your niece's health, Mr. Stone?"

"Anne? She's fine. Married and happily settled."

"Oh? I'm pleased to hear that. Has she gone back to England then?"

"No, she married an American. Daniel Adams. He was with her in Scottsburg."

Millie's cheeks pinked up, the highest color he'd seen in them since the day of Sam's interment. He realized that Millie had met Anne and Daniel at the time when Sam had impersonated him. Perhaps she was thinking now of the gown she had stolen from Anne's trunk. But David could never mention that. Only a churl would overtly remind her of her past. And she said she'd changed. Had she really? None of the other passengers had complained of missing wallets or trinkets. Perhaps she really had given up stealing.

Her choice not to attach herself to one of the cavalry officers at Fort Laramie still stymied him. Wasn't that one of her old tricks? Playing up to a man with means? Perhaps none of the unmarried men at the fort had enough income to suit her. And of course she'd rather get back East, where the standard of living was higher. The Millie—or rather, the Charlotte—he knew wanted a much higher standard than a career army man or a farmer in some soddy could give her.

He found it ironic that Anne had married a farmer-turned-stagecoach-agent, and her lovely personal maid, Elise Finster, had settled for a rancher who'd been the scout on their wagon train. And here was Millie, born into poverty, yet apparently too good to marry an American pioneer. With her looks and domestic skills, she could have had her pick of men in Eugene. But it seemed she needed a man of a higher class. Well, if David had anything to say about it, she would never know that he was born to the aristocracy. So far as he knew, she'd never learned about the earldom waiting for him across the Atlantic. If she found out about that, he feared she would try again to sink her claws in.

"Now was that the gentleman who. . ."

The door to the coach opened, and Millie let her sentence trail off unfinished. David was just as glad. Too close an examination of their mutual acquaintances could only lead to further embarrassment.

The two hayseeds got in, followed by a man dressed in somewhat dandyish clothing—though if David thought about it, they probably considered him a bit overdressed himself. This man he judged to be in business of some sort, and it wasn't long before he found out.

The dandy sat directly across from David, and he introduced himself to all and sundry with a booming voice that bounced painfully off the ceiling. "Kendall's the name. I'm with the Northern Pacific Railroad."

"Oh, scouting out some new routes?" one of the other men asked.

"Something like that."

Kendall proceeded to fill them in on his travels and complain about the necessity of depending on stagecoaches.

"It won't be many years before you can travel from one ocean to the other by rail," he declared. "And you can rest assured that journey will be more comfortable than this one."

He moved on to describing the short lines being built in California. "We'll be pushing up to Oregon soon and then who knows where."

David stopped listening. It would be awhile before they took rail service to Eugene, where his stage company was based. By then,

Dan and Anne ought to have a nice nest egg. Dan could go back to farming if he wanted. Or if he preferred, he could take Anne to England. David would find a place for him at Stoneford. Maybe he should hold the position of land steward open until he knew what Dan wanted to do.

"And you, sir," Kendall said heartily, fixing his gaze on David. "Where are you bound?"

"Oh, I'm just a traveler headed home." Immediately David wished he'd worded his reply differently. The three men plied him with inquiries about where "home" was and what he'd been up to.

David smiled as blandly as he could. Americans just didn't seem to understand the concept of ennui, however, and he felt he had to answer.

"Yes, I'm from England. Haven't been there in many years."

"And you're going there now?" Kendall asked. "Tell me, how are the railroads there?"

David laughed. "I'm afraid there were none when I left, sir. I was but a youth, and things have changed greatly."

"Ah. I expect you'll find everything modernized. Will you be going to London?"

"Perhaps. But I plan to go directly to my family home, in the country."

He glanced over at Millie. Her green eyes watched him, and he thought he detected a great deal of speculation and scheming.

Merrileigh hurried to the hall when she heard her brother's voice. As the footman took his hat, she beckoned to him and then retreated into the morning room. If Randolph had the chance, he would spirit Peregrin off for an hour to talk about horses and tailors and who knew what.

"Good day, Merry." The tall young man stooped and kissed her cheek. He was smiling, which made her curious.

"Good morning, darling. I've rung for fresh tea. Do sit down."

Peregrin took a chair nearby. "So. Anything new on the matter we discussed a few days ago?"

"Well yes, I have a great many thoughts on the subject." Merrileigh picked up her fan and fluttered it languidly. "It appears that Mr. Iverson and associates are firmly attached to David."

"As they should be," Peregrin said.

"Yes. Alas, they've served all of the Stones since Randolph's grandfather's day or earlier, so they are our solicitors as well. But that becomes a conflict of interest in this matter, I'm afraid."

"So, you're going to consult a different solicitor?" Peregrin frowned at her. "That will take money."

"I daresay. But there's something you need to know." She leaned toward him and studied his face. Her brother might not be as shrewd as she would like, but he had common sense and a bit of pluck. She hoped he would fall in with her newly formed plans to bring home the title. "Perry, I'm determined that my son shall one day own Stoneford and the title that goes with it. And I'm ready to move toward that end."

Peregrin frowned. "You indicated that this is not the first time you've made an attempt to—shall we say—swing the pendulum of fate in your direction."

"It's not. I hired a man who came highly recommended to me. An American known for his efficiency and discretion."

"And yet he failed."

"Yes." Merrileigh sighed. If only Peterson had succeeded in carrying out her plan. But the scanty information she'd been able to gather since that disaster told her only that her distant employee— whom she had never met—had reached his demise in Oregon. She wasn't certain, but it seemed likely that David Stone had killed Peterson in some sort of altercation. David had certainly been badly injured and taken some time to recover.

She would never reveal any of that sordid business to anyone— not even her brother. And the person who'd recommended the emissary—a sharp old friend of her father's who had spent time in America—was gone now. Took a tumble off his hunter last spring and broke his neck. She didn't know anyone else to turn to if she wanted to hire another emissary willing to carry out her scheme.

No, if she was going to do anything, it had to be on her own, and with only one other person—someone she could trust implicitly. She'd decided Peregrin was that person. Perry, if he thought he stood to gain by it, would do a great deal for her.

She leaned toward him and lowered her voice. "I have a new plan, and I'm ready to put it in motion."

Peregrin's eyes flickered. "Indeed? I take it Randolph doesn't know?"

Merrileigh smiled ruefully and shook her head. "No idea at all."

CHAPTER 12

Missouri

Millie had nearly reached her limits of overland travel—but she had also nearly reached the end of the stage line. At Independence, they could take a local railroad line to St. Louis, cross the river on a steamer, and from there it would be smooth going to Philadelphia by train. She could hardly wait to leave the crowded, smelly stagecoaches behind.

The station agents had packed in as many passengers as possible for the last six or eight stages, and wedged mail sacks between them. Sleep was nearly impossible, though Millie's eyelids drooped constantly. She made some attempt at each stop to freshen her appearance and always tried to be one of the first back inside the coach, so that she could claim a corner. Even so, discomfort reached new levels.

Nine people squeezed inside, and three or four rode the roof. Extra bags were tied on top with them. Millie didn't know how the six-horse teams could pull the weight.

David largely ignored her these days, though he did ask her once—quietly, at a nighttime way stop—if she needed more money for food. He seemed to have an endless supply of cash. Fortunately for both of them, Lucky's gang hadn't made it down the line to David when they were collecting donations.

Beside Millie sat a man who had obviously never ridden a stagecoach before. Not only were his clothes too clean and nice for the rough traveling conditions, he had also made no effort to hide his prosperity—something discreet gentlemen like David Stone did not flaunt in public, knowing it would make him the target of pickpockets and outlaws.

The newcomer wore a snowy-white shirt with a winged collar bearing points so crisp and sharp that Millie smiled and endeavored not to look at them. The collar was of the "patricide" fashion, so called because of a story in which a young man went home after a long absence and embraced his father. His collar points were so sharp that they cut his father's throat. It was all Millie could do to hold back a chortle.

The man's black frock coat was perfectly respectable, but again a bit overdone for travel, with a velvet collar. His outfit was completed with a woolen vest and black trousers. His watch chain draped conspicuously across his middle, from pocket to button hole, and his pristine cuffs were held in place with monogrammed gold studs. He balanced a top hat on his lap. The odor of the pomade that kept his hair in formation was not unpleasant at the outset, but as time passed, Millie found it annoying in the closed space.

Several of the men seemed inclined to converse. One, a Mr. Nelson, had journeyed a couple of stops westward to investigate the possibility of opening a dry goods store.

"My stores in Independence and St. Joseph have been quite successful," he said with a satisfied smile. "I envision expanding westward as the rail lines grow."

"Sounds like a good idea," said a man wearing rough trousers and an unmatched sack jacket.

"And you sell ready-made clothing?" the dandy asked.

"Yes sir, but we have a tailor employed at each store, to make alterations as needed. In Independence, we have enough business to keep a seamstress employed full time as well. She does dressmaking in addition to the alterations, and we have a large yard-goods section."

"It sounds like a store I should like to patronize," said the woman who sat with her husband opposite Millie.

The merchant turned and smiled at her. "Oh yes, ma'am. If you are in Independence any length of time, you must visit Nelson's Dry Goods and Sundries."

The woman fluttered her eyelashes at her husband. "Well, Mr. Brackett, perhaps we shall have opportunity to do that."

"Perhaps."

Her husband seemed to feel no need to elaborate, but Mrs. Brackett beamed on the merchant. "We are visiting his family for a few weeks."

"By all means, then," Mr. Nelson said, "I do hope you will stop by." He glanced at Millie. "And you, ma'am. I'm sure you'd find our merchandise to your liking."

"Thank you," Millie said. "I am going on to St. Louis, so I doubt I'll have time."

"Oh, I am going to St. Louis as well," said the dandy.

Millie gave him a polite nod.

He fingered the knot of his Windsor tie. "Perhaps we shall ride the train together."

She mimicked Mr. Brackett and said only, "Perhaps." She hoped her tone and brevity would send the dandy a message that he could clearly read—that she didn't wish to divulge her personal plans to him or the rest of the company.

"My name is George Andrews," the dandy said.

Millie nodded. Several of the other passengers were watching her, and she knew she would be insufferably rude not to divulge her name.

"Mrs. Evans."

"Pleased to make your acquaintance," Andrews said with just a hint of triumph in his tone.

"Evans," said Mrs. Brackett. "Are you related to the Cleveland Evanses?"

Millie puzzled over that. "I don't think so, ma'am. I've never been to Cleveland, and so far as I know, Mr. Evans had not either."

"Was that thunder?" one of the men on the middle seat asked.

Millie perked up and listened. They were less than a day from Independence, and she didn't want anything to slow them down now.

Sure enough, an ominous rumbling sounded above the rattling of the wheels and drumming of hoofbeats.

"I do hope we shan't run into a bad storm," Andrews said, leaning toward Millie to look out her window—or perhaps that was a pretext to lean closer. She pulled back and tried to flatten herself against the seat cushions. His well-oiled hair came within two inches of her nose.

"Really, sir," she gasped.

"Oh. Pardon." He resumed his former position, and Millie grabbed a deep breath.

A flash of lightning illuminated the inside of the coach. Mrs. Brackett was clinging to her husband's arm. The seven men's faces glared stark white for an instant. All seemed to be frowning, except David. Millie caught only the merest glimpse of his expression, but he looked rather amused.

A moment later, rain pummeled the stage, and someone on top gave a shout. Scuffling and thumping on the roof brought Millie a mental image of the hapless "outside" passengers pulling their coats over their heads and burrowing down amidst the luggage to make less-tempting targets for the lightning.

"Has a stage ever been struck by a thunderbolt?" She wished she hadn't spoken aloud, as Mrs. Brackett began to simper and fuss to her husband, and several of the male passengers began telling horrific tales of stagecoach disasters, whether involving lightning or not.

Since leaving Oregon, Millie had driven through several storms, some of them severe, but this one seemed more determined than the others. Wind rocked the coach, and the horses began to snort and whinny, pulling unevenly with jerks and sudden starts.

One of the men swore—in the darkness, Millie couldn't tell who the offender was, except that it wasn't David or the dandy. The horses settled into a pounding gallop, and the coach hurtled along. The driver's even-toned calls to the team were interspersed with thumps on the roof and muffled shouts from the men riding there. How on earth did they stay on? Millie had heard a man saying he'd tied himself to the roof the night before, so he could sleep without fear of falling off. Perhaps they were all anchored to the top of the stage like hog-tied calves waiting for a branding iron. She shuddered and clung to the edge of her seat, bracing with her feet so she wouldn't slide into Mr. Andrews.

After two or three minutes, the horses slowed somewhat, and she unclenched her fists. The coach settled into a steady, swaying pace as the thunder abated.

The next flash of lightning showed seven faces much relieved—and David Stone, apparently asleep, with his hat tilted downward so that the brim hid his eyes.

"And so, you see, it's time to hire someone else to go across the Atlantic," Mereleigh said in a matter-of-fact tone as she poured out the tea. "I had thought at first that perhaps Conrad's associates would send a man and we might persuade their fellow to take our part."

"Pay him off, you mean," Peregrin said.

Merrileigh glanced toward the doorway. "Please, dear, you never know when one of the servants will appear, or when Randolph will pop in."

"Of course. Forgive me."

She nodded and passed him his cup. "They do have an agent who conducts business on the continent for them, but they're not inclined to send anyone to America. In fact, Iverson seemed to consider me a bit of a mother hen to think David couldn't get himself home without assistance."

"So, what do you intend to do? Hire someone in America again?"

"I don't think there is time, even if we knew whom to contact."

"Whom did you contact before?"

"Someone Colonel Waterston had met. I simply told him I needed a person who could do any sort of job and not be too scrupulous about it."

Peregrin blinked at her in surprise. "Didn't the old boy want an explanation?"

"Oh, I made one up. Something about Father having invested in the States and been bilked. I said I wanted someone who could put things right for me. The colonel never batted an eye."

"Really?"

"Yes, but of course he is dead now, and I don't want to leave any sort of a trail leading back to me—correspondence or bank drafts, any of that."

Peregrin nodded. "So, what will you do?"

"I thought I'd send someone from England."

"Is there time?"

"I think so. There's a steamship leaving Liverpool on Monday for New York."

"So quickly?" Her brother sipped his tea, frowning. "Have you the funds to pay someone and buy his passage? And how will you hire him? Cast about Soho for a footpad or some such person? Really, Merry, it's too dark. And too dangerous for a lady to get involved in."

"That is why I need your help."

"My help?" Peregrin laughed. "You want me to hire an"—he looked cautiously toward the doorway and whispered—"an assassin?"

"Heavens, no. I just want you to help me get the money. Then we'll worry about finding someone who can. . .who can keep David from returning to Stoneford. That's all."

Peregrin was silent for a long moment. Did he not understand? Or maybe he understood every word and was too appalled to speak.

If her brother decided to call a halt to her scheming, Merrileigh would be at his mercy. Any time she stepped astray, he might tell her husband and his cousin what she had attempted to do—and what she had already done. Her heart lay like a stone in her breast while she waited for a clue to Peregrin's thinking.

"I know you haven't much money of your own, Merry."

"No, and I daren't ask for any from Randolph. He'd demand to know why I needed such a sum."

Peregrin swallowed hard. "How much are we talking about?"

She tried to give a casual shrug, but it turned out more of a nervous jerk. "The last attempt cost me several thousand."

"Really?" Peregrin's eyes flared, and his mouth crinkled into a jagged line. "And here I've just cleared my debts and thought perhaps I could be of assistance."

"You've cleared your debts?" Merrileigh pounced on it with glee.

"Oh Perry, I've always had faith in you."

He sat back, grinning. "I had a very good night on Saturday last. I kept winning and winning. It seemed like a dream. And the last round, I thought, 'Am I an imbecile? What if I lose it all now?' But I won again! And I pushed back my chair and left the game."

"I'm so proud of you!" She eyed him severely. "Now don't you go thinking how much you might have won if you hadn't quit."

He shook his head. "No. Instead I was thinking of you, Merry, and how much it would mean to you that I'd paid off my own gambling chits and caught up on my bills, instead of dunning you or old Randolph to tide me over."

"Oh, it does, truly."

Peregrin smiled. "There's not much left over, but—"

"How much is 'not much'?"

"Forty quid, but it's got to last until my next allowance—"

Merrileigh leaped up and paced to the window. Could they pull this off? It would cost her dearly—and more so if Randolph got wind of it. But the possible reward was so alluring. Lady Stoneford. A countess. Mistress of the estate. No more wrangling over expenses. She could have an allowance ten times what she got now, without causing Randolph a twinge of apprehension.

She clenched her teeth. When she'd learned that her first attempt at stopping David had failed—after months of careful planning and thousands of pounds sunk into the endeavor—she'd felt she would never recover. But Randolph never learned how much she'd lost, nor where she'd spent the money.

She'd borrowed from friends and taken an advance on her small yearly income. Though it had pierced her deeply, she'd sold a diamond necklace she'd inherited from her aunt and replaced it with paste. If Randolph had any idea! But he wasn't all that observant, and she didn't wear the necklace very often. When he'd insisted she wear it this spring to a gala event, she took out the replacement, which looked generally similar to the original, and he hadn't noticed the difference.

"If only we had a way to increase what little we have," she murmured.

"Yes. Believe me, Merry, if I had a bundle, I'd loan it to you. You've helped me so many times." Peregrin set down his teacup and stood. "Well, I suppose I'll toddle across the hall and say good day to Randolph before I go."

"Oh, must you leave so soon?" Merrileigh fluttered her fan. "I hoped you could stay to dinner."

"Afraid not." He grinned at her. "My mates have been so good about springing me a loan when I needed it that I thought I should treat them tonight."

She frowned. "But darling, you'll go through your forty pounds quickly if you start that sort of thing."

He shrugged. "Can't be helped. I've touched both the fellows more than once, and it's my turn to show a little generosity. And after we eat, there's a pastiche at the Golden Door this evening—"

"Pastiche!" Merrileigh nearly shrieked the word.

Peregrin halted and eyed her cautiously. "Yes, that's what I said. We're going to the theater. Hedgely's cried off to take Miss Linden to an assembly, but—"

"It's a horse." Merrileigh hastened to his side. "Do you know of a horse called Pastiche?"

"What? A horse? Hmm, well yes, now that you mention it. Old Cardigan's got one."

"Lord Cardigan? Good heavens!"

"No, not him. His uncle. Or are they cousins? Doesn't matter. It's Edmund I'm speaking of."

"Of course." Merrileigh nodded. "I saw him at Conrad's two days past—the day I spoke to Mr. Iverson."

"Oh?" Peregrin shrugged. "Bit of a stiff shirt, if you ask me."

"But he owns racehorses."

"Yes, he's part owner in an Irish stud, I'm told. Brought over a couple of three-year-olds for the season. That Pastiche you mentioned is one of them."

Merrileigh touched her closed fan to her lips and smiled. "Yes. How fortuitous."

"How do you mean?"

"I think this is the opportunity we need."

"Opportunity for what?" he asked.

"Why, to increase our funds."

"*Our* funds?"

"Cardigan seemed certain his horse will win on Saturday."

"Well. . .doesn't every owner think his horse will win?"

"I suppose so," she said doubtfully. "No, darling, I think this is a sign."

Her brother grimaced. "I'm not so sure, Merry. You know I can't get down to nothing again so soon. It would be horribly bad form."

She turned to him eagerly, excitement building in her chest. "But you'll win. I know you will."

He smiled indulgently. "I'll give it a try."

"And if we win, you'll go?"

"Go where?" Peregrin's eyes clouded. "You mean me go to America? Good heavens, Merry! I'm not sure I could. . .well, do anything permanent. I never knew David Stone before he went away, but his brother was a good chap."

"You can't think about that." Merrileigh seized his wrist. "Think of the good that will come to us if he never returns. If he met with an accident, I'd be in a position to favor you."

"With what? Invitations? I mean, a good time is nice, but really, Merry—"

"I'd pay you two thousand after Randolph came into his title. I might not be able to get it right away, but I promise you, over time, I'll give it to you."

Peregrin's eyes narrowed, and he inhaled slowly. "I will consider it. And now I must pay my respects to Randolph." He winked at her. "Or should I say, the future earl?"

CHAPTER 13

W ouldn't you know it?" the dandy asked. "It's the last river we have to ferry, and it's flooded."

"That shouldn't matter," said one of the men who'd been riding on the roof of the stagecoach in the rain. "What's a little more water?"

"The current is unpredictable," the station agent said. "We dasn't take the horses over until things look calmer."

David sighed. Farther east, they would leave the horses behind and get a fresh team on the other side. They were still far enough into the frontier that the horses had to ford or ferry with them.

But another day wouldn't really matter to him. Besides, it would be good to sleep in a bed for a change, instead of propped up on the stage seat. Now that they were closer to civilization, they had a full quota of passengers on every leg of the journey, which meant they had no room to stretch out to sleep as they rode.

He made a trip out back to wash. When he came inside, the odors of stew and cinnamon struck him and set his mouth watering. Millie was off to one side with the station agent, speaking to him earnestly. At least a dozen people sat around two tables in the dining room, and he realized another coach had also halted here. The station agent's wife was plying them with chicken stew, cornbread, and pie.

David decided he'd better speak for a bed quickly, given the number of passengers needing accommodations. He stepped up behind Millie, hoping to be next in line.

She cast him a glance over her shoulder and immediately her anxious wrinkles smoothed out. "Oh Mr. Stone. I'm told there is only one room left, and—"

"Your wife says two dollars is too much, but I could put six men in there for fifty cents apiece," Mr. McLeary, the station agent, said, as though daring David to refute his logic.

"Well, first of all, we aren't married."

"Oh. Sorry. My mistake. Well, I certainly can't give a whole room over to one woman."

David looked around the room. He spotted only one other woman among the passengers, sitting at the far end of the room, deep in conversation with the man seated next to her.

"And what is that woman doing?"

"Why, she and her husband hired a room before your stage even got here. Their two sons are with them, so they took a full room for the family."

David frowned. "I don't suppose that lady would go in with Mrs. Evans and let another man take her place?"

"I highly doubt it," McLeary said primly.

"Well, what are the other gents doing?" David tried to remain calm and sent Millie a glance he hoped she would take as reassurance.

"I told the last three they'd have to sleep in the barn. I'm only charging a dime out there."

"Then I suppose that's where I'll be tonight. But you certainly can't send Mrs. Evans out there." David took his wallet from his inside pocket and took out two one-dollar bills. "Here. Mrs. Evans shall have the room you spoke of. And don't you think for one instant of putting anyone else in there with her."

Millie grasped his sleeve, but not before the station agent had seized the money.

"Oh, you mustn't. It's too much."

"I know it's too much, but it's the way it is." David fished in his pocket for a dime and handed it to McLeary. "That's for me." He pulled Millie aside. "Do you have enough left for supper?"

"Yes." She looked down at the floor, her face coloring. "Thank you."

"Good. Have a pleasant evening." He walked away in search of his own meal, knowing McLeary and his family would speculate mightily over this friendship. He wished he'd been more alert and taken care of the lodgings first thing.

He wasn't surprised when Millie approached him later. Outside, the rain continued to fall and the wind howled. The passengers who had rooms retired early. The men who'd been relegated to sleep in the barn sat around the dining room stove, telling yarns and drinking coffee or whiskey, as their preferences fell. David kept quiet but listened with half an ear.

About eight o'clock, Millie came down the stairs and asked the agent's wife if she might get a cup of tea. While she waited, she looked David's way. He made himself turn his gaze away quickly, but most of the other men were ogling her. Millie was wearing the lovely gown she'd worn in Scottsburg. He wondered why she had put it on in this rustic place. Was she out to snare a man this evening?

"My, don't we look fine?" Andrews murmured.

David shifted in his chair and took a swallow of coffee.

A moment later, Millie was at his elbow.

"Excuse me, Mr. Stone. If you don't wish to speak to me, I understand, but I thought perhaps we could have a word."

As David rose, Andrews winked at him, but David ignored him.

He followed Millie to the far end of the room, near the kitchen door, carrying his coffee mug with him. He pulled out a chair for her at the end of one of the tables and sat down kitty-corner from her.

"You're looking very elegant this evening," he said.

"Thank you. I didn't like to wear this dress, but my traveling clothes needed washing so badly, I felt I should take advantage of the stop. This is the only thing I had available that wasn't in dire need of laundering."

"Aha." What she said made perfect sense—his own stock of shirts was getting quite soiled, but he'd had no opportunity to have them laundered lately, and he was sure he smelled no worse than the other men they traveled with. At least Millie had a washbowl in her room where she could rinse out a few items.

"I hope you won't think I put it on to taunt you." Her lovely green eyes studied him anxiously.

"Because you were wearing that frock the last time I saw you? In Scottsburg, I mean?"

"Yes. That and. . .well, your niece must have told you it was her dress."

"I seem to recall her saying as much. But she didn't know how you could have come by it."

Millie's cheeks went scarlet, and she looked down at her hands. "I took it from her luggage in Eugene. Her friends were taking her trunks to their house to keep for her, and I—I took it from their wagon."

David nodded. Rob and Dulcie Whistler, who had escorted Anne to Eugene in her search for him, had surmised as much.

"I regret the action deeply," Millie said, "but I haven't the means of making restitution just now."

David wished she hadn't brought it up. Or had he been the one to steer the conversation? No matter—they were both thoroughly embarrassed now. But that was progress, wasn't it? He doubted Millie had known how to be ashamed when she'd first worn the dress. Here she was, talking of restitution.

He cleared his throat. "I'm sure Anne doesn't expect anything of the sort."

"No, but it was wicked of me. I see that now. Perhaps you could give me her address, and later on I could send her the cost of the gown."

"No need." Hearing from the thief who stole her belongings was probably the last thing Anne wanted now. And Millie would no doubt be staggered to learn the cost of that gown. Anne had probably had it sewn by a skilled modiste in London or Paris.

"But I would feel better, sir."

"Perhaps she would feel worse."

"Oh." Millie eyed him pensively. "I hadn't thought of it that way. You're saying it is kinder not to remind her?"

David shrugged. "Let the past go, Mrs. Evans. That is my advice."

"I've sought to do that, but it's been difficult."

"Yes, I can see that." He took a sip of his cooling coffee.

The mistress of the house bustled in from the kitchen with a tray and set it down beside Millie.

"There you go. Sorry it took so long, ma'am."

"It's quite all right," Millie said. "Thank you."

"Ten cents, please," said Mrs. McLeary.

"Oh." Millie's eyes went wide, and a panicky look drew her mouth in a pucker.

David reached automatically for another coin. "I'd like more coffee as well, please."

"Certainly, sir." Mrs. McLeary accepted his money with alacrity and headed into the kitchen again.

"I'm sorry," Millie said. "I didn't think she would charge me for a cup of tea, after I'd paid full price for supper."

"Ah, but that was more than an hour ago." David smiled. "These folks have us over a barrel, as the saying goes, and they seem eager to take advantage of that."

"Well, thank you for your courtesy and generosity." Millie looked anxiously toward the window. "This storm! What if it doesn't let up?"

"Then we may be here awhile."

She winced, and David could almost read her thoughts.

"Don't fret, Mrs. Evans. I have enough to see us both through."

Tears stood in her eyes when she turned to face him. "But I shall owe you such an awful lot."

"There now, don't weep on me. I'm running out of handkerchiefs."

Her startled look made him chuckle. The hostess returned with the coffeepot and topped off his mug. David lifted it and winked at Millie. "To good weather."

Her smile was only a bit watery as she lifted her teacup. "And a swift journey." He noted that her hand trembled as she took a sip.

Merrileigh Stone could scarcely wait to see her brother again. She'd persuaded Randolph to take her to a large, noisy party thrown by a woman her husband detested. Mrs. Simwell held a rout once each season and invited far too many people. Her father had made his vast fortune in coal, and many of the aristocrats snubbed the couple. But Chester Simwell was a likable man, the younger son of the younger son of a knight. Barely in the upper class. Yet he was so much fun that the men of the ton embraced Chester and tolerated his wife when they couldn't get around it.

Randolph took a few turns about the dance floor but tended to slink off into a corner with a few of his cronies to chat with a glass of punch in his hand. Merrileigh danced a couple of times, but mostly she worked her way around the room, conversing with dowagers and watching the door for her brother. Peregrin had promised her by way of a note that he would see her at the Simwells' tonight.

Midnight was nearing before he arrived. As soon as he'd greeted the hostess, Merrileigh pounced. She knew his habits. If she didn't corner him quickly, Peregrin would slide off into the card room, and she wouldn't see him again before dawn. She seriously doubted Randolph would last that long.

"Perry! Come here." She plucked at the sleeve of his rather flamboyant blue velvet tail coat and practically dragged him into the adjoining room. It held a pianoforte and a few chairs, and Mrs. Simwell referred to it as the music room.

"What's got you in a dither, Merry?" her brother asked. "Don't tell me. It's about David Stone."

"Shh. Yes." Merrileigh closed the door and unclipped her reticule from her sash. "I've got thirty pounds more for you."

"Really?" His eyes lit. "How did you get it?"

"I told Randolph I needed a new corset and shoes for tonight. Of course, my old corset doesn't show—it will last for some time yet—and he was good enough not to pay any mind to my shoes this evening. He never noticed they are the same pair I bought last fall with new buckles." She hiked her skirt a few inches and smiled down at her kid slippers.

"A most accommodating man, your husband," Peregrin said with a saucy grin.

"I think so sometimes. I'll tell you, I was very surprised he came across for me. I think he's happy because Albert is doing so well at school."

"Ah. So we have your son to thank for this piece of good fortune as well."

"Indeed." Merrileigh took out the cash Randolph had given her the day before and handed it over. "I was afraid he would say no or tell me to have the bill sent to him. So I told him I wanted to be sure I didn't start incurring debts for him, and he seemed to think me a considerate and frugal housewife."

Peregrin guffawed and then looked quickly over his shoulder toward the closed door. "Sorry. Now, I take it you want me to put this with my bit for tonight?"

"Only if you feel lucky."

"All right. I'll see how things are going."

"Perry, if you're losing, you'll walk away from the table, won't you?"

"Yes, darling. Don't worry. And whatever I win, I'll put it all on Pastiche tomorrow?"

"Yes. Everything. If we win tomorrow, we'll have enough to send a man to New York and intercept David."

"But if we lose? Merry, can you stand that?"

"I. . .don't know. Just don't tell me how much you have tonight unless you've kept even or worse. If you come out ahead. . ."

"Oh, I see. You won't miss it if you don't know how much it is?"

"Something like that. And you mustn't breathe a word to Randolph. He's not above betting now and then himself, but he'd kick up an awful fuss if he knew what I am up to."

"No fear." Peregrin leaned down and kissed her cheek just as Merrileigh's friend, Lady Eleanor Fitzhugh, opened the door of the music room.

"Oh, excuse me—dear me, Merrileigh! It's you and your *brother*. I thought I'd interrupted a tryst."

Merrileigh laughed. "Nothing so exciting, my dear. Just catching up on things with Perry. We don't see enough of each other these days."

"That's right," Peregrin said, edging toward the door. "I'll drop by and see the kiddies one day this week, Merry. Oh, and do tell Randolph I want to see his new shotgun." He nodded with a dazzling smile toward Eleanor and ducked out.

Eleanor frowned. "Dash it, I wanted to make him promise to

dance with my Cornelia. She thinks he's ever so handsome."

Merrileigh grinned. "Well, he is." For the moment, she was inordinately pleased with her brother, and with herself. "I suppose Randolph is looking for me. He'll want to go home as soon as supper is over."

"I thought this party was a little better than the usual Simwell standard, didn't you?" Lady Eleanor asked as they glided toward the door.

"Oh, I don't know. . . ." Merrileigh realized she'd been too focused on her scheme with Peregrin to pay much attention to the decorations, the music, or the other guests' evening wear.

"Did you see the flowers in the little drawing room?" Eleanor took her arm and led her back toward the crowd.

CHAPTER 14

David lay wrapped in a blanket in the hayloft in the barn. Below him, the extra horses from the stage line's stalled coach teams snorted and stamped. Four other men had staked out spots in the mounds of loose hay and burrowed in for the night. The rain drummed on the roof for the first hour, but then it let up.

Maybe they'd be able to cross the river in the morning. David sent up a quick prayer to that effect. The delay in Idaho, where they'd buried Sam Hastings, had been less depressing than this place. And less expensive.

Thinking of money made him think of Millie. He wished she'd leave him alone. Yet he anticipated seeing her again in the morning. Would she wear the drab traveling dress, or would she enter the stagecoach in Anne's gown? The men in their party had thronged her as soon as she and David had ended their conversation. The dandy—Andrews—was bolder than the others. He'd tried to draw her into conversation and had even offered to buy her a drink. Millie had brushed him off with the rest by giving a cheerful *goodnight* and escaping to her room. That had made David feel perversely contented.

Now he pondered the things she'd said to him over tea. Since they'd left The Dalles, she'd told him several times that she was truly sorry for what she had done in Scottsburg. To all appearances, her penitence was real. Why couldn't he accept that? He supposed it was his male pride that still stung.

She'd said tonight that she prayed for him—that all would go well for him. That bothered him perhaps more than his attraction to her green eyes and appealing face. How could he think she and God were on speaking terms? That seemed a little farfetched to him, knowing she'd lived for some time by stealing and deceit. Shouldn't he be the one praying for her?

He'd watched her on the stagecoach, and honestly, he hadn't seen any behavior on her part that he could criticize—other than asking him for money. He hated it when acquaintances approached him for loans. In the old days, he would have given her a set-down.

The only thing was, now he knew the cruelty of the West. There was a sort of unwritten code of chivalry out here. Not all the men he met were gentlemen, but very few would leave a woman stranded in the wilderness when they had the means to help.

David rolled over in the hay, comforting himself with that knowledge. He hadn't helped her because she was Millie. He'd have done the same for anyone.

But she *was* Millie. And this Millie held up well under strain and hardship. She exhibited great patience and discretion. And her green eyes danced through his mind whenever he tried to sleep.

He just wished he could know for sure that she was telling the truth and that she had really repented. She'd mentioned reading his Bible. Was that true, or had she said it to gain his sympathy? He pressed his lips together in a firm line. A bewitching smile wouldn't fool him again. Still—if he knew she'd truly settled things with the Almighty, would he feel differently about her? He told himself he would not, but he couldn't be certain he believed that.

One of the other men coughed and rustled about in the hay. David wondered what these rustics would say if he told them they were sharing their hay mow with an earl. He smiled in the darkness. They wouldn't believe him, not a man of them.

Millie rose early. The stage station was packed to the rafters with stranded travelers waiting to cross the river. The agent and his wife had their hands full, and this might be the one time during her journey when she stood a chance of earning some money. Her brown traveling dress was still damp around the hem, but she put it on anyway.

She tiptoed down the stairs and through the dining room. Two men had spread their bedrolls on the floor near the stove, and she didn't want to awaken them. She pushed open the kitchen door. Sure enough, Mrs. McLeary was coaxing the coals in her cookstove into life. Her eyes were rimmed below with dark circles, and her shoulders had a weary stoop to them. Millie eased into the room and shut the door softly.

"Good morning."

Mrs. McLeary jumped and dropped her poker with a clatter loud enough to wake everyone in the house.

"I'm sorry." Millie hurried forward to pick it up for her.

"What do you want?" Mrs. McLeary eyed her suspiciously. "Breakfast won't be served for another hour."

"I thought perhaps I could help you this morning." Millie smiled. "You have so many guests, surely you could use a bit of help setting the table or serving coffee—anything that will ease your load, ma'am."

"Well. . ." The hostess's eyes narrowed. "Can you make biscuits?"

"Oh yes. How many do you want?"

"Ten dozen."

Millie smiled. "Give me an apron, and point me to the lard and flour, ma'am. The first batch will be ready by the time you have the oven hot."

Mrs. McLeary opened a cupboard and tossed an apron to her. "Good, because I'll be hard-pressed to fill those men up. My hens only gave eight eggs this morning. Maybe I should charge extra for the eggs."

Appalled, Millie tried to stay calm as she tied the apron strings. "You seem to have plenty of side meat. Perhaps you could scramble the eggs and give them each a small portion. Or if you have plenty of potatoes, I know a recipe for an egg and potato dish that goes well in the morning. Oh, a bit of cheese helps it."

"Yes, I've got spuds and some cheese," Mrs. McLeary said grudgingly. "I guess that would be all right."

"Marvelous. And have you any dried apples?"

When the men started filtering to the dining tables an hour later, the women were ready with mounds of biscuits, a large crockery bowl of applesauce, fried bacon, and a large pan of what Mrs. McLeary told them was "my special breakfast ramekin." It gave off such a tempting odor that all of the diners accepted a portion.

Mrs. McLeary scurried into the kitchen with an armful of empty dishes. "Is the new coffee ready? My, they like your egg-potato dish, Mrs. Evans."

Millie, who was elbow deep in a pan of dishwater, smiled. "Oh, I'm glad. And yes, I think that pot of coffee should be just about drinkable by now."

"Would you care to serve it?" Mrs. McLeary asked doubtfully.

Millie took that as praise—the hostess was willing to let her appear in the dining room and perhaps acknowledge her part in the success of the meal, rather than keeping her hidden in the kitchen. But Millie felt she'd gain more by working hard and letting someone else take the glory.

"No, you go ahead, ma'am. I'm making fine progress on these dishes."

Mrs. McLeary cast a glance over the sideboard, where Millie had set the clean cooking pans to drip dry.

"I must say, you're a regular plow horse when it comes to kitchen work."

"I'll accept that as a compliment."

The hostess picked up the coffeepot. "It was intended for one, to be sure. I don't suppose you'd consider stopping here for a while? As a cook?"

"No, but thank you. I hope to press onward as soon as the river permits it." Millie couldn't imagine the station agent paying her much, and when the flood season was past, they might not want her at all. Best to move on. She hummed as she plunged a stack of dirty plates into the water.

"Oh, and be sure you eat, too," Mrs. McLeary said. "Heaven knows you've earned it."

"Thank you, I shall."

That was two bits she'd saved David, Millie reflected as the hostess left the room.

The dining room door flew open, and Mr. McLeary lumbered in. His gaze settled on Millie. "Ah, Mrs. Evans. How nice of you to help my wife this morning."

"You're welcome, sir." Millie kept scrubbing away at the cheese baked on to a tin pan.

"I knew someone other than my wife made those biscuits—she hasn't the touch for them."

Millie smiled.

"And that potato ramekin, as she calls it, was mighty tasty."

"I'm glad you enjoyed it, sir."

Mr. McLeary nodded. "If you're interested in finding work, ma'am, I'll pay you a dollar a day, and you can have Sundays and Thursdays off. We don't generally get any stagecoach passengers for meals on those days."

A dollar a day was a decent wage for most jobs, especially for those a woman might find, but it was much less than Millie had earned when cooking in a restaurant that catered to miners. Beside, this stage stop was fairly isolated. There wouldn't be any social life to speak of. Where would the cook sleep? In one of the rooms they now rented out for guests? Or would they stick her in a tiny cupboard with a cot? Though she wasn't afraid of hard work, a life of drudgery and fending off men's advances didn't appeal to Millie. Philadelphia, with her connections there, was her best chance at finding a new and pleasant life.

"I do thank you for the offer, sir, but I must go on with the stage."

"Hmm." McLeary frowned. "Well, the river's still too high for you to go today. Too dangerous."

"Oh?" She looked up at him as she squeezed out her dishrag. "Do you think we shall be able to cross tomorrow?"

"Perhaps. And if you want to keep helping my wife today, I'll pay you that dollar, and you can have your meals besides."

"Thank you. I'll accept, if you don't charge for my room tonight either."

He opened his mouth as if to protest then grimaced. "You drive a hard bargain, Mrs. Evans, but my wife gets quite harried when we're filled up with guests. It's a deal."

David reached for a third biscuit. For once, a stage stop provided ample food for the travelers. Perhaps it was because they were stranded and the owners wanted to keep them from complaining overmuch. This breakfast seemed vastly better than last night's supper. Though not ill-tasting, the stew had been a bit watery and bland. That and the cornbread had been served in stingy portions. But these biscuits—David had never tasted better.

The driver who'd brought them to McLeary's the day before reached past David for the butter.

"They must have a new cook. I've never knowed Miz McLeary to make such fine biscuits before. Even the coffee's good."

"Oh?" David looked down the table, where their hostess was refilling some of the other men's cups.

The one woman dining with them said loudly, "This potato and egg dish is delicious. Would you share your receipt?"

Mrs. McLeary hesitated, then laughed. "You've caught me out, ma'am. 'Tis not mine at all. The other lady what's staying here made it from scratch, and not having a receipt book or anything."

Other lady? David glanced quickly about for Millie, but she was nowhere to be seen. He'd assumed the noise of the overly full house had kept her wakeful last night and she had slept late. Had she really risen early to cook for them?

When Mrs. McLeary came down the table with the coffeepot, he held out his mug. As she poured, he said softly, "Pardon me, ma'am, but did I understand you to say that Mrs. Evans cooked this meal?"

"She gave me a bit of assistance this morning." Mrs. McLeary didn't seem happy with the accolades the others were giving the food. "That's not to say she did it all, by any means, but I was telling Mrs. Willard that Mrs. Evans did volunteer her way of making the egg dish. We were short on eggs this morning, you see, being as we have so many guests."

David nodded. "And where is Mrs. Evans now?"

"Oh, she's about," Mrs. McLeary said vaguely.

David said no more but finished his breakfast. Afterward, he went outside and strolled toward the river. The water roiled among the trees, which rose from it like pilings. It lapped at the doors of a barnlike structure, and two men stood next to the building, mournfully watching the swollen river.

David ambled toward them and called, "Are you the ferryman?"

Both men turned toward him, and the older one nodded. "I am, sir."

"What's the forecast? Shall we get across soon?"

The gray-haired man shook his head. "She's crested, but you see the ferry." He pointed, and David saw the flat boat then, tied to a tree several yards out from shore.

"The dock's clear under water," the ferryman said. "Wish I'd put a longer rope on the ferry. We may lose it yet."

"If you're lucky, you might get over tomorrow," the other man said. "Or the next day."

David thanked them and walked back to the house. On impulse, he walked around to the back. The kitchen door on the back porch stood open, and he looked inside.

Millie was wrist deep in a large pan of dishwater. The plates and cups flew through her hands, into the suds. Scrub, turn, swish, and she dropped one in the big kettle beside her, which David assumed was clean water. Scrub, turn, swish, plunk. After repeating the motions half a dozen times, she shook the drops from her hands and picked up a pair of tongs, then proceeded to pluck the clean dishes from the rinse and place them to drip dry in a rack.

Mrs. McLeary came back from the dining room with a tray of dirty coffee cups and silverware. She set it on the sideboard near the dishpan, and Millie went back to her routine of scrub, turn, swish, plunk.

David almost stepped into the kitchen, but he thought better of it and backed away, slipping down the steps and around the corner of the house in silence.

He went to the barn and rummaged through his luggage. His leather-bound Bible met his fingers, and he pulled it out. Near the barn door, he found a keg of horseshoes. Placing a short board across the top, he made a stool. For the next half hour, he read undisturbed and closed his eyes to reflect and pray.

Lord, I don't know what to ask for. My instinct is to plead with You to get me away from this place, but You know better than I do. Bring us along in our journey in Your own time.

At the sound of men approaching, he opened his eyes. Two of the tenders came into the barn.

"Mr. Stone." One of them nodded to him as they passed and went on to care for the idle teams.

David rose with the vague feeling that there was something important he should have prayed about, but whatever it was had slipped his mind now. He climbed the mow ladder and put his Bible back in his valise. Too bad he hadn't brought another book along. He hadn't seen any reading material in the station house, but perhaps the McLearys had some books in their private quarters.

He ambled across the yard. The ground there was still muddy, though the grass around the house had dried in the sunshine.

The station agent was inside, sorting mail from the sacks the stages had brought in. It occurred to David that the longer they remained stranded, the more people would collect at the stage stop. The hay mow might be as full as the house by tonight.

"Mr. McLeary," he called, walking over to the agent's sorting table. "I wondered if you had any books about the place."

"Well now, we used to have an old volume of Edmund Burke's essays that a lawyer left here, but it disappeared last spring. I suspect the division agent swiped it, but he won't admit it. And there was a copy of *King Lear* kicking about. I'll ask the wife."

"Oh, don't bother, sir," David said. The shotgun messengers for the two stalled eastbound stages had a card game going in one corner, and a couple of passengers off the second coach were seated with mugs before them. David headed toward them, but Millie came out of the kitchen carrying a pitcher of water, and he found himself smiling at her.

"Mrs. Evans, I am told you had a hand in preparing our sumptuous breakfast this morning."

"Well, yes."

"That was a proper meal, if you'll allow me to say it. Very tasty."

"Thank you." Her long lashes swept upward, revealing her captivating green eyes, but she quickly veiled them again. "I trust you had a restful night, sir."

"Perhaps not as restful as some, but more so than others," David said, thinking of the stamping horses beneath the hay mow and the rustling noises and snoring that wakened him repeatedly in the darkness.

She nodded and gave him the ghost of a smile. "I expect that's right. And if you'll excuse me, I shall rest myself. The house seems to be quieter now than during the night."

He inclined his head in a bow and watched her go up the stairs. Millie really was a charming woman. Quite personable, and that auburn hair. . . Though she must be at least thirty, she'd kept her youthful grace and winsomeness, not to mention her figure, which of course, a gentleman never would comment on. If she'd been born to different circumstances, she could have fit easily into his social circle in England. David couldn't think of another woman besides his niece or Elise Bentley that he'd rather make small talk with at a party.

He turned away with a sigh. What was he thinking of—social circles indeed! This was America, where such things didn't matter. Perhaps he could get a cup of coffee and join the other men. Their conversations started up again, and David became aware that they'd stopped talking while Millie was in the room. It seemed every man's eye was drawn to her, and they'd all postponed their business until she'd left.

CHAPTER 15

A commotion in the hall disturbed Merrileigh. She and her husband were just having tea with the children, and then she would dress for a card party at the Fitzhughs' home. She did hope this interruption wouldn't force them to change their plans.

The maid entered with a perturbed look on her face.

"What is it, Mary?" Merrileigh asked. "Did someone come in? I heard voices."

"It's Mr. Walmore, mum. He insists on seeing you."

Randolph frowned. "Tell him to come on in."

The maid looked doubtfully toward Merrileigh.

"I'll go and see what he wants," Merrileigh said quickly. Pastiche's race must have been over two hours ago, and she dearly wanted to hear the outcome, but not in front of her husband.

"Father, do you think I'll be able to go shooting with you in the fall?" asked Albert.

That's it, Merrileigh thought. *Distract your father for a few minutes. That's all I need.* She smiled as she crossed the hall to the morning room. What good children she had!

"Perry, what's to do?"

He turned toward her, and she caught her breath. His hair stood on end, as though he'd run his hands through it many times. His cravat was undone and hanging loose about his neck, and his complexion was pale as ice.

"What's happened?" She strode to him and took his hands. "You lost, didn't you?"

He frowned and shook his head rapidly. "No. No, I won. You were right about Pastiche."

"Then—what's the matter?"

"Merry, you'll hate me so!"

"Just tell me."

"Hedge and I went round to the club after the race, and Lord Brampton was there. He wanted to get up a game of faro."

"Faro?" Things fell rapidly into place in Merrileigh's mind. "You didn't. Tell me you didn't lose the whole bundle."

"No, but. . ." His breath came in shallow gulps. "Merry, he accused me of cheating."

"What?" She stared at him. "Are you mad?"

"No, but he was. Stark, raving insane. He claimed there was no way I could be so lucky."

"Lucky? You mean you won again?"

"Bless you, dear." He reached a trembling hand into his coat pocket and pulled out a fistful of notes. "Five thousand pounds I came away with."

Merrileigh's jaw dropped. "You. . .you won that much?"

He nodded. "Last night after the game at Tattersall's, I had six hundred. After the race, I had two thousand and a half. And Brampton and the others—Merry, I clipped their wings but proper, I'll tell you."

She laughed. "But that's wonderful!"

Peregrin sobered and shook his head. "No. No, it's not. He accused me of cheating, and. . ." He stared at her, his face stricken. "I must bolt, Merry."

"Bolt? What are you talking about?"

"The old curmudgeon wanted satisfaction."

"You mean he wants to duel you?"

"Worse. He pulled a pistol then and there."

"But. . .what happened?" Obviously her brother was still in one piece. Merrileigh wanted to shake him and make him blurt out the story faster.

"Hedgely put a gun in my hand."

"What? You're joking! He's your friend."

"Yes. Said he would stand as my second."

"But. . .there are rules."

"Yes, and laws, too. We broke every one of 'em. Brampton refused to wait until dawn. He was going to blow my head off."

Merrileigh drew in as deep a breath as her corset would allow. "What did you do?"

"Blew his, of course." Peregrin hung his head. "What on earth am I to do? Hedge told me to run out the back. The club had to call the coppers in, you see."

"Naturally." Meredith swallowed hard. "You'll have to leave England."

"That's what I said. They'll have me in irons if I don't. Merry, they might hang me. I mean—he was a lord."

"But you kept your winnings."

"Yes. Hedge and Rutherford scooped the bills off the table and stuffed my pockets and told me to run for it. Said they'd handle the police, and no one would dispute the money was mine. But I don't dare to go home for my things."

"Let me think." Merrileigh pressed her hands to her temples. "We can't stop the scandal now. We must tell Randolph." She raised her hands. "Oh, not everything, just the part about the club and Brampton. That ship that's leaving Liverpool—you can make it if you have a good horse."

"You still want me to go to New York?" Peregrin stared at his sister with a silly twist to his lips and his eyebrows nearly meeting his hairline.

"More than ever now. Only we won't tell where you've gone. Not even Randolph will know." Merrileigh said. "Your winnings will keep you for a long while, especially if you're careful and don't gamble." She nodded slowly. "You stay here. I'll bring Randolph in so you can tell him. I'll suggest we send our footman around to get your clothes. Just don't tell Randolph that you have a destination in mind. Say that you'll run for it and hop on the first ship you find that's ready to sail. He won't know that I am aware of where you're going."

"And I hoof it to New York and try to find David?"

"Yes. If we can fix it so that Randolph comes into the title, he might be able to fix it for you later, so that you can come back. Do you understand?"

Peregrin nodded. "Merry, I'm scared."

"Don't be." She gave him a quick hug. "Buck up, little brother. And my previous offer stands. Two thousand."

"Half my winnings are yours." His brow furrowed, and the rest of his face tightened.

"Take the two thousand out of that. You have plenty to live on in America for a long time."

The door opened, and Randolph came in.

"Hullo, Perry. You look awful."

The fact that her brother didn't laugh showed Merrileigh how shaken he was.

"I'm afraid I've pulled a stunner, Randolph. Don't hate me. I was only defending myself."

"What?" Randolph stared at him, then swiveled his head to look at Merrileigh. "What's going on?"

"Sit down, my dear," Merrileigh said. "Peregrin has a tale to tell, and then he must flee. Meanwhile, I propose we send Thomas to pack a bag for Perry and bring it here."

Randolph eyed his brother-in-law severely. "What? You've got in so deeply you're ruined?"

"Worse than that, I'm afraid."

"Sit, dear." Merrileigh practically pushed her husband into a chair.

Peregrin walked shakily to a chair opposite Randolph and sat down. "I've shot a man. A lord."

"What on earth?"

Merrileigh gave a quick account, which Randolph punctuated with questions. At last he took out his handkerchief and wiped his brow.

"I suppose you're right. There's nothing for it but to skip until things blow over." He looked up and scowled at the miscreant. "Perry, how could you?"

"It wasn't his fault," Merrileigh said.

"Couldn't you at least have shot him in the arm?" Randolph asked.

Peregrin lowered his head into his hands. "He was going to kill me. That's all I knew. It was him or me. And now I can't show my face in London."

"More like the whole empire." Randolph stood with a sigh. "I shall ask Thomas to go round to your lodgings and pack your things. But you can't stay here long. Most likely the police will come here when they don't find you at home or at your club."

"Thank you," Peregrin choked out. When Randolph had left the room, he looked bleakly at his sister. "I'm not sure I'll be able to carry it out."

"What? New York?"

"You know."

She gritted her teeth. "This is for more than just money and position now, Perry. If you ever want to come back to this country again, you need someone in a high place to watch out for you and smooth the way."

He nodded, raking a hand through his wild hair. "Yes. I see that. But I had no idea at first that you wanted *me* to carry it out. Perhaps I could hire someone there."

"Discretion is of the utmost."

"There was so much blood."

Merrileigh swallowed. "Well, the first thing is to get you off English soil. You've never been to New York, dearest. You'll find it exciting. And there's absolutely no one else we can trust in this matter."

Peregrin frowned. "I say, it's hard when I've just lined my pockets. I was looking forward to living large for a short time at least."

"Well then, go and live large in New York. But do not let David Stone set foot on the deck of a ship. You can cut all the capers you want, so long as you see that through. And keep me informed. When Randolph thinks it's safe, we'll tell you, and you can come home."

"But my friends! Hedge wanted me to go to Ascot with him,

and Rutherford is getting up a house party in a couple of weeks."

"Hedgely has done enough for you, don't you think?" Merrileigh couldn't keep the bitterness from creeping into her voice. "Besides, they have horses in America."

Peregrin fingered his cravat, which usually hung in a beautiful waterfall. "Lord Raglan's nephew is in New York, I believe. Might be one to show me about, with no questions asked."

Merrileigh reached for the fan she'd left on a side table and opened it to cloak her expression. "Yes, that's right. Make all the friends you can. It may help you later. Didn't Lady DeGraves marry an American plantation owner?"

"He's in the Carolinas, dear. Not close to New York at all."

She shrugged. "Just put on a good face. And never talk about this to anyone. Ever. If it comes up, tell the truth—it was self-defense. If the man were a commoner, you'd be in the clear. Most people will understand that."

He nodded. "What if David has already boarded a steamer?"

"I think it's too early, but if you miss him, we'll have to deal with the consequences."

"And what if I miss the steamer in Liverpool?"

Merrileigh pursed her lips. She had researched the available berths well during the past few days. "There's another leaving from Dover on Tuesday next, but you must do all you can to make the one in Liverpool. And Perry, these steamers are so efficient. You'll be there in two weeks, and you'll miss some of the hot, muggy weather while you are at sea."

Peregrin smiled wryly. "How delightful. Can't argue with a good sea breeze, can you? Hmm. Always thought that if I got too deeply in debt, I could skip to America or Australia."

"You'll be fine," Merrileigh whispered eagerly. "When you return in a year or two, your name will be clear. Your friends will want to hear every detail. You'll be in demand for parties. People might whisper behind your back a bit, but the young ladies will find you mysterious and dangerous." She fluttered her fan.

"You make it sound like a good thing."

"Men who weather a good scandal are the most fascinating, you know. They're said to make good husbands, too."

"If you say so." Peregrin's face scrunched up in puzzlement. "America's huge, you know. How could I be certain whether or not he'd left port already?"

"I'll ask Randolph to contact the solicitor—not Conrad. The young one, Iverson. I'll send you a letter as soon as we learn anything."

"Where?"

"Hmm. I believe there's a hotel called the Metropolitan. Lord and Lady Wingford stayed there. I'll write to you there unless I hear first from you, with a more complete address."

He nodded his consent. "I suppose I shall have to travel without a valet."

"You goose!" Merrileigh spanked his hand with her fan. "It's not as if you have a private valet now. You three fellows share one footman, and you know it."

Her brother squared his shoulders and pursed his lips. "Hogg's not a footman. He's our houseman, thank you very much. And I was thinking of hiring my own valet. If I didn't have to spend all my winnings on a voyage, that is."

Merrileigh eyed him narrowly. "Hogg? You could at least call him something more dignified."

"That is his name."

She scowled, wondering what sort of name that was. She called all her parlor maids Mary, no matter what their real names were. "Well, if you do hire a valet, make sure you get one with a dignified name. If you're careful, you can hire one."

Randolph entered. "I've dispatched Thomas. Merrileigh, if we're going to the Fitzhughs' tonight, you'll have to get dressed."

"Oh. Yes." She looked uncertainly at Peregrin. "I hate to leave you, but if we don't show up, Eleanor will be very cross at me."

"I suppose the story's already all over town," Peregrin said.

Randolph frowned. "Then we must go out and stand up for you. Do you have funds?"

Peregrin nodded. "Yes, thank you."

Randolph looked distinctly relieved. "If what you've told us is true, then it *was* self-defense. Get us an address as soon as you can, and we'll let you know if the coast is clear. But if Brampton's people want to prosecute, I suppose you'll have to stay away."

"Do you think it will go worse for him if he flees?" Merrileigh asked.

"I don't know. But if he stays, they might hang him quickly to satisfy the screaming aristocrats."

Perry's complexion took on a greenish tinge. "I'll go. And thanks." He extended his hand.

Randolph shook it. "I'm sorry this happened, Perry. Rent a horse, now. Don't mess about with a coach or anything like that. Too easy to trace. And if you have a choice, the farther away you land, the better. Canada, the Indies. . ."

"Right. I'll just stop here until your man returns with my bag."

Merrileigh stepped up to him and kissed his cheek. "This will all turn out, Perry." Would he have the nerve to carry out her request? She turned away, aware that she might never see her brother again.

CHAPTER 16

Millie laid aside her Bible—David's Bible—when someone rapped on her door.

"Who is it?" she called.

"It's McLeary. Can I talk to you?"

Millie frowned and rose from the bed, where she'd lain down and napped for an hour before reaching for the book that now meant so much to her. She supposed it was time to go back to the kitchen and help Mrs. McLeary.

She brushed her skirt smooth and quickly patted the impression of her body from the quilt. A glance in the looking glass showed that her hair was passable, and she opened the door six inches.

"May I help you, sir?"

"I'm hoping so, Mrs. Evans. See, the missus don't feel so chipper. She wondered if you was up to fixin' the midday meal by yerself. She started beans and put bread to rise, but now she's feelin' all-overish."

"Oh, she must lie down," Millie said. "I shall come down directly, sir. Just leave all to me. Oh—" She paused with her hand on the edge of the door. "How many are we for dinner?"

McLeary ran his meaty fingers into his beard. "Hmm. Seems to me about twenty. No, if you count the drivers and shotgun riders, I suppose nearer twenty-six."

"Has another coach come in, then?"

"Yes ma'am. The ferrymen want to put the nosebag on here this noon as well."

She grimaced. "I'll plan on thirty then. How does the river look?"

"I think she's startin' to ebb. But no one will cross today."

"What about dishes? Do you have enough?"

"I'm thinkin' two sittings."

Millie nodded soberly. "And could you get someone to wash them, please? I'll have my hands full."

"Mm. I'll put one of the tenders to work. They got nothin' to do today, since the stages ain't runnin'."

He left her, and Millie quickly washed her face and hands, ran a comb through her hair, and took an apron from her satchel. Mrs. McLeary's aprons could wrap around her twice, and she'd rather wear her own.

She retrieved the Bible and laid it reverently on the upended crate beside the bed. "Lord, give me strength, and thank You for this opportunity," she said aloud.

David ignored the temptation to join his fellow travelers in raising a glass of beer. A couple of them couldn't seem to quit after one or two, or even three, though it was still an hour shy of noon. He stuck to his coffee.

Listening to their stories passed the time. One of the shotgun riders tried to coax him into a card game that now had five participants, but David waved him off with a smile.

"I'm not much of a gambler, sir. But enjoy yourselves."

"Well now, I recollect back in '41, when I first saw the Rockies," one of the passengers said. His full beard and worn buckskin jacket led David to believe the man, who was about his age, had a history with the mountains. He seemed about to draw the longbow, as the old-timers said when one set out to tell a story, and he had an appealing manner of speech. David took a deep swallow of coffee and settled back to hear the tale.

Despite the overcrowded inn, the travelers spent a quiet day. The sun shone gloriously throughout the afternoon, lending a touch of unreality to the scene. With such favorable weather, they ought to be moving toward their destinations, yet here they were, becalmed at McLeary's way station, listening to a rough man regale them with an account of his early trapping adventures.

The meals constituted the highlights of the day. The dishes at dinner, though plain fare, hit the gustatory spot. David thought the beans were especially well seasoned, and the cornbread melted in his mouth—not the dry, crumbling version they'd eaten their first evening here. Pudding and cookies followed, fit for a king, or at least the ruler of a small duchy.

Millie was again absent from their table, and David wondered if she was behind the toothsome menu. Mr. McLeary served their main course, but when it was time to refill the coffee cups and pass the desserts, Millie emerged with the host. She wore a colorful, pieced pinafore apron over her plain traveling dress. From across the room, she might have passed for a twenty-five-year-old farmer's wife. A very pretty farmer's wife.

David tried not to follow her with his eyes. When she came near, he smiled and thanked her but said no more. The other men all got a word in, teasing and trying to flirt with her.

"Capital food, Mrs. Evans," called Andrews, the dandy from their stagecoach.

She cast a charming smile his way. "Thank you, sir." She moved on to the next diner, and Andrews stared after her with a silly, vacant look on his face.

"This your cookin'?" one of the drivers asked her.

"Some," she said briskly. "Mrs. McLeary had things started."

"Why'n't you take a stroll with me after dinner?" the driver said. "I'll show you round the barn and all the corrals."

Millie laughed and moved away with her tray. "I think not, but thank you, sir."

Supper turned off even better. David had heard in the interval that Mrs. McLeary kept to her bed all day. He couldn't wait to see what Millie produced for them, and he was not disappointed.

Yet another stagecoach arrived from the west, and Mr. McLeary apparently felt it was time to sacrifice a few chickens. What Millie did to those birds he would never know, but the fried chicken surpassed anything David had ever had the privilege to taste. Mashed potatoes would have been the perfect complement, but it was too early in the season for those, and it seemed the McLearys' supply from last fall was exhausted. When he tasted Millie's rice dish, he forgot about

potatoes. This was even better.

Where had that minx learned to cook like this? Was she born knowing about herbs and sauces and how to cut lard into pastry dough? He doubted it, but she certainly had a gift. Even the greens went down well. The only part of the meal he would criticize if asked—which, of course, he wasn't—would be the bread. It was disappointing after the feather-light biscuits they'd had at breakfast.

Of course, David thought as he sipped his perfect coffee. Mrs. McLeary had started the bread before she succumbed to her illness. The jelly and pickles of course, were hers. The rest was Millie's. The smooth, flavorful gravy, the tart lemon pie with toasty-browned meringue topping and flaky piecrust.

With so many guests crowding the tables in shifts, he couldn't hope for a second slice, so he left the dining room satisfied yet slightly wistful.

He considered going around to the back kitchen door and offering his compliments to the cook but thought better of it. After all, he wouldn't want Millie to think he was going soft on her again—though many a man would marry a woman on the spot if he knew she cooked like an angel.

No, he wouldn't think about that. He'd escaped her clutches once. Nothing could induce him to get close to her again. Beneath that appealing exterior lay a hardened, unscrupulous soul, whether she admitted it or not.

The odd thing was, other than her appeal to him at Fort Laramie, he hadn't seen her grasping for anything on this journey or chumming up to a man, though she'd had plenty of opportunities. She was as pretty as ever—nay, beautiful, if you replaced the apron and threadbare dress with a proper wardrobe and loaned her a hairdresser for an hour. Millie Evans would stand out in any company.

But for some reason, she no longer sought to stand out. Rather, she tried to avoid notice. Very strange.

The next morning, Mr. McLeary announced at breakfast that they would cross the river on the ferry as soon as they had eaten. Millie hurried to put out the food and an extra pot of coffee, then dashed up to her room to gather her things. The passengers from her coach would be in the first group crossing.

As they walked toward the river carrying their luggage, she could see the brown expanse before them. It still overflowed its banks and spread wider than it should, but the ferryman seemed confident they could cross safely.

The swirling water frightened Millie. She'd crossed many a stream in her day, but not at flood stage. Still, the ferry appeared to be sturdy. The ferryman said it would take two trips to get them all across. She considered holding back and seeing how the first group did, but all of the others from her coach were taking the initial trip. It she waited for the next, she would delay them. Or perhaps they would go on without her. Tales ran rampant of drivers leaving without passengers who were late.

Their coach and team had to cross with them, though the other stages would stay on the west side of the river. What if the horses panicked in midstream? She wished the stage line could just have another coach and team waiting for them on the other side.

The animals were loaded first and securely hitched to iron rings in the ferry's deck. Since the dock had been damaged in the flooding, the ferry was brought close to shore, and a sturdy plank ramp was constructed for animals and people to use in boarding.

Once the coach and team were secure, Millie and her fellow passengers, along with the travelers from the second coach, were permitted to board.

The family that had shared the inn with them went first, and the wife seemed surefooted when she embarked, though she did hold fast to her husband's arm as they ventured onto the ramp.

Millie had no one to help her. She gathered handfuls of her skirt and set foot on the end of the gangplank. The boards quivered just a bit. The ferry was tied fore and aft to pilings, so the boat would not move during this process, but still it swayed a little. Millie gulped and stepped forward.

"May I assist you?"

It was Andrews who had spoken. Millie had avoided him as much as possible during their stay at the McLearys', and when he'd attempted to engage her in conversation, she'd made sure others were included. Treat them all alike, she'd told herself. That was the key. Don't let any one man think you're singling him out for special treatment.

Only one man in the party stood a chance of snaring her heart—indeed, it was half caught already. But David Stone remained aloof so far as Millie was concerned. He had praised her cooking, but not overmuch, and for the last two days he had greeted her pleasantly if they happened to meet in a doorway. Other than that, he'd barely spoken to her during their delay at the stage stop.

Since adolescence, Millie had instinctively allowed men to help her. She had come to expect it, and it was one of her tools in working toward success. Most men would offer to help a woman, especially if she was neat and ladylike in her appearance. If she was pretty to boot, she could choose whose arm she wished to hold. In this case, Andrews was first in line. Glancing about, she saw at least three other men fall back with disappointed frowns. Perhaps if she had paid them more attention at breakfast this morning, they would have been bolder in offering their protection and aid.

At once she felt a pang of remorse. Since she'd turned to the Lord, she'd begun to learn that God looked upon men—and women—differently than mortals did. And using another human being for one's own gain and comfort was not acceptable in God's view. Millie strove to attain humility and selflessness in her new life, but those lessons went down very hard. She was still trying to fathom their meaning and what good could come from self-effacement.

Now she felt she should accept the gentleman's offer, but with reservation. She gave Andrews what she hoped was a modest and thankful smile, but one that did not promise anything beyond her gratitude.

He responded with a generous grin and patted her gloved hand reassuringly. "We shall be fine, you'll see. Why, in thirty minutes we'll be over and ready to move on."

"I do hope you're correct, sir," Millie murmured.

Andrews's expression deepened into caring concern. "My dear Mrs. Evans, I've longed to converse with you. Perhaps we shall have the opportunity now, and I shall be allowed to distract you from the disagreeable manner of our voyage."

"Indeed." Millie supposed she could stand a half hour's conversation with him in exchange for having a robust young man standing solidly beside her during the crossing. As they stepped off the gangplank onto the ferry, he steadied her and then drew her toward the center, where the ferryman was tying down the luggage to keep the weight low in the craft. Once the coach was on solid ground again, the baggage would be reloaded in the boot and on the roof.

"Does the water frighten you?" Andrews asked.

She opened her mouth to lie and stopped short. Even in polite conversation, she was sure the Almighty would expect the truth. Still, she didn't want this man's overbearing sympathy. "A bit," she managed. "But not overmuch."

"Then let us stand in the center, near the stage. If you wish, you can hold on to the door handle for support."

"Thank you."

Two other gentlemen soon joined them. They held back a bit, seeming bashful in her presence, yet drawn to her. One in particular—a shopkeeper from St. Joseph, she'd learned—seemed especially determined to further his acquaintance with her.

David, on the other hand, flicked a glance her way as he boarded and turned at once toward the bow, where he stood with a couple of other men, partially concealed from Millie's view by the lead horses' heads.

The ferryman closed the gate on the landward side of the craft, and they started across. The current pulled at the boat, and Millie leaned a little, trying to remain steady.

Something struck the side of the ferry, and the craft lurched. The horses whinnied and shifted, and Andrews shot out his other arm to steady Millie. Behind her, the shopkeeper also reached to keep her from stumbling. Caught between them, Millie began to feel like a piece of cheese between the two halves of a biscuit.

Her cheeks heated as she pushed slowly away from them. "Thank you, gentlemen, but if you'll excuse me, I'll stand by the rail."

The ferry still swayed, and she staggered between the other passengers to grasp the peeled log that formed the railing around the sides. The muddy water was only inches below her feet, and the movement of the craft prompted her to cling to the log. Her stomach heaved, and she raised her gaze quickly to the shore. The distance to the far shore was not great now. Trees swayed in the breeze, and a cluster of people awaited their arrival. No dock stood in place, just a landing where the ferryman would run one end of the craft aground. They wouldn't need to use a gangplank, and Millie was grateful.

"I hope you're well, ma'am."

She gasped and looked up into David's blue eyes.

"Quite."

He gave her a half smile, nodded, and edged away.

So. He wasn't totally ignoring her. Millie took some consolation from that. She squared her shoulders and resolved to keep her wits and maintain her balance.

Millie held her own, David had to give her that. She didn't let any of the men take liberties, and she didn't look to them for favors. She could take care of herself, and she seemed to want to do that, so he let her.

Something about the entire situation went against the grain with him. He'd been reared to be a gentleman and to make the way easier for ladies whenever it was within his power. But he kept telling himself he'd done more than his share for Millie already. Besides, he wasn't 100 percent convinced yet that she was a lady.

The ferry bumped the landing hard, and everyone struggled to keep their feet. The horses scrambled for purchase on the deck. Millie flew to her knees on the rough planking.

David stepped quickly to her side. "Are you all right?"

"Oh, I. . ."

He held out a hand. "May I help you?" At least three other gentlemen eyed them with disappointment and turned away.

Millie grasped his hand and rose slowly. "Thank you."

"Are you certain you're not injured?" He wanted to ask if she'd hurt her knees, but that would be most improper. One never insinuated that a lady had limbs beneath her skirt.

"I shall be fine, thank you."

He nodded. "Let me see you ashore."

"Oh—my bag." She glanced toward the pile of luggage.

"I'll see to it."

He turned and located the ferryman's helper and gave him four bits. "Please take my bags and Mrs. Evans's to shore, would you?"

"Glad to, sir." The man pocketed the coins and grabbed the bags David indicated. The passengers disembarked first and gathered to one side of the landing to watch the ferrymen unload their coach and team.

Millie gazed at the tenders while they hitched up the horses, and David gazed at Millie. He didn't sidle up to her like three or four other fellows tried to. He imagined that if he stepped back, she'd have plenty of gallants to hand her into the coach.

Two passengers left them immediately for destinations in the town, and another went off in the second coach, which was bound for a local train depot. David had weighed the options and decided to ride the stage to the railroad station in Independence, where he and Millie could catch a train to St. Louis. Once they were across the Mississippi, he intended to buy her a ticket to Philadelphia and be quit of her. He saw no reason whatsoever to stay in her proximity once he was sure she had the means to reach her friends.

He turned to make sure their bags were loaded and allowed Andrews to offer Millie his assistance in boarding. To David's surprise, when he entered, he landed next to her and was a little confused as to how it had come about. Had she somehow shuffled and arranged it? Andrews was sitting on her other side.

For some reason, the other men felt they were now well enough acquainted with Mrs. Evans to chatter away at her all the way into town. David said little, though Andrews made repeated attempts to lure him into the conversation.

"Won't you tell us a bit about England?" the dandy asked after a while. "I misdoubt any of us has been there."

David shrugged. "Parts of it look like western Oregon Territory."

"Have you ever been to London?" another man asked.

"Yes, I have. It's quite a place."

"Have you seen the Queen?" The dandy leaned toward him.

"No. When I left England, she was not the Queen. Her uncle William was on the throne then."

"Ah, William IV," Andrews said sagely. "I don't expect you ran in his circles."

"Uh. . .no."

The other passengers laughed, and one of the men on the middle seat winked at David. "Not one of them lords, eh, Stone?"

David smiled but considered it wise to remain silent. The alternatives were to lie or to spill his lineage, so he let them think the other man had made a clever jest. Millie, however, eyed him in silence from beneath her long lashes.

They rode along for some time in amiable conversation, and he thought they must be drawing close to Independence. The horses topped a long hill and started down the other side. The stage lurched forward suddenly, and the driver yelled, "Whoa, you! Slow down, boys."

They plunged downhill at an imprudent pace, and the men on the middle and rear seats braced themselves. Loose articles hurtled to the floor, and Millie grabbed David's arm. The coach continued on, bumping and jolting, and the driver's yells turned to curses.

A sharp drop on one side signified that the wheels had gone off the edge of the road. They slipped across the seats and slammed against the folks on the far side of the stage.

"We shall overset," Millie cried. Her green eyes filled with terror, and she clung tightly to his arm.

"Cover your head!"

It was all David had time to say before the coach tumbled on its side and the horses screamed. In the midst of a fierce clattering and cracking, Millie flew into David's lap, and they both rolled with the stage. He yanked her to his chest and held her close for a second, but the coach crashed into something and jolted her away from him.

CHAPTER 17

Millie moaned and stirred. Someone was yelling, and a horse shrieked piteously. The whole side of her face smarted, and she put her hand to it. It hurt to open her eyes, but she tried to get her bearings. She lay atop a tangle of bodies—all male but hers. She cringed away and winced at the pain in her wrist.

"Anyone alive in there?"

It was the shotgun rider's voice. His head appeared above Millie, poking in through the window, which was now part of the ceiling.

"Y–yes," she managed to say and reached a hand toward him.

"Easy, ma'am. We'll get you out."

She wondered how he and the driver had escaped injury, but they both seemed to be in one piece. Probably they jumped off the box when they saw that the stage was going over.

The driver appeared on the far side of the damaged vehicle, and she realized then that the bottom of the coach was ripped half away. The driver squeezed in between a broken floorboard and the end of one of the seats.

"Come on out this way, ma'am. Looks like you're the topmost one and the easiest to get out."

It took both of them to pull her through the opening, and her skirt snagged on a splintered board. Before she could tell the men to stop pulling, a rent a foot long ventilated her brown bombazine skirt.

She stood shakily and looked around. The screaming horse lay on his side. The other three were unhitched from the wreckage, but still in their harness, standing off a ways and huffing out deep breaths.

"Is he going to be all right?" Millie asked, indicating the injured animal.

"Not sure." The shotgun messenger grunted. "We'll check him over once we get all the passengers out."

"Of course." Millie stepped away from the shattered coach.

"Whyn't you see to Stone?" the driver said as he dove toward the hole in the floorboards once more.

"Stone?" Millie whipped her head around, looking for David.

"He's yonder," the shotgun rider said glumly, pointing up the hillside down which they'd evidently plummeted.

A figure in dark clothing lay halfway up, sprawled near a large rock. Millie gasped. He must have been thrown out through the gaping hole in the floor as they rolled.

She hiked up her skirt and staggered up the slope. At least her limbs worked. How many of her fellow travelers were severely wounded?

She reached David's side and fell, panting, to her knees.

"Mr. Stone!"

He lay face down, and she grasped his shoulder to turn him toward her but stopped. One of his pant legs was saturated with blood, and his leg's crooked attitude made her heart sink. If nothing else, his leg was broken. She'd heard people could bleed to death if the large blood vessel in the leg was severed.

She didn't want to cause him more harm, but she couldn't let him lie there bleeding. She wondered if she could find the source and put pressure on it. That was the way to stop it, wasn't it? She touched his leg gingerly, but he didn't react. Her cotton glove came away red with his blood.

The terrible thought seized her that he might be already dead. She tore off her gloves and scooted around to his other side. She peered down at his pale face. Reaching out hesitantly, she put her fingertips to his neck. She couldn't feel his pulse, but at that moment he took in a shuddering breath.

Her relief was so great that she felt lightheaded. Surely they should loosen his necktie and collar. What else could she do to make him comfortable without causing more hurt? At the bottom of the hill, the driver and shotgun rider pulled a man from the debris. They laid him on the grass and turned back to get another. Millie counted three passengers down there—one sitting up and rubbing his arm, and the other two prone and still. It would be a while before anyone came to help her.

Frantically, she tugged at David's coat. If she could get her hands in his pockets, she would surely find something useful. David Stone never went anywhere without a clean handkerchief.

David awoke to a loud noise. At first he thought he was in the middle of a gun battle again. He opened his eyes to blue sky, green grass, and pain.

A handsome woman with auburn hair glinting in the sun leaned over him.

"Charlotte." It came out a whisper, but she heard, and she smiled.

"It's Millie, but yes."

He tried to sit up and fell back at once with a groan. The stabbing pain in his leg ran all through him and left him breathless, with a tight, sick feeling below his breastbone.

"Am I shot?"

"No, but you're hurt bad. Relax, Mr. Stone. I've got a farmer bringing some blankets to carry you on. We'll get you to Independence and a doctor."

He tried to sort that out while taking a few careful breaths and looking up at the high branches of a tree that waved gently overhead. A cool breeze lifted a few strands of his hair.

"Was there a shot? I thought I heard. . ."

She grimaced. "That was Gip. He had to put down one of the horses."

"Gip?" David blinked up at her, feeling as though they'd shared a long history, but he couldn't remember the half of it.

"He's our shotgun rider. The driver couldn't do it, so Gip did. It's very sad, but better a horse than a man."

"Yes, indeed." David gritted his teeth. "If I may ask, what happened?"

"The stage went off the edge of the road and tumbled down this hill. Gip said the horses bolted, and the driver couldn't stop them. The stage is now a heap of kindling. I think you fell out when the floorboards ripped open."

David couldn't think of a response. This tale was so bizarre, no one would believe it. It might make for good drawing room talk, though—if he survived.

The pain swept over him again, and he gasped.

Millie touched his brow gently. "Try to relax, Mr. Stone. We'll get you to a doctor as quickly as we can. Your leg is bleeding a lot, but I've tied a cloth around it, and I don't think you'll die of it."

She sounded dubious, and he didn't ask for particulars.

"Does anything else hurt?" she asked.

"My head aches. And my side." He patted his ribcage and winced.

"Hmm. Your breathing is all right though."

"Seems so." He squinted up at her. When she moved her head, the rays of sunlight made vagrant wisps of her hair gleam like firebrands.

"Ah, here's the farmer."

Millie stood, and David tried to see the man she had mentioned, but that involved moving more than his head, and it wasn't worth the stabbing pain.

"This 'un?" a man said.

"Yes, take him first."

"Looks like there's a lot of people hurt down yonder."

"You take this man *now*," Millie said firmly. "I'll help you, if you and your son can't do it."

"Maybe one of them other fellas—"

"They are busy with the other passengers. You said you can't get your wagon any closer."

"No'm."

"Then let us get Mr. Stone into it, and you can take us as quickly as you can to a doctor and send others back to help the stage-coach men."

"Awright."

They shuffled about him, and he lay panting and trying to assess his wounds. His leg. How bad was it really? Were his ribs broken? How would they ever get him to the wagon? He was at Millie's mercy.

"Hey!"

At the shout, David rolled his head slightly and gazed down the slope. The driver was climbing the hill toward them.

"You!" he yelled. "Help us get those men up to the road."

Millie stepped around to where her skirts blocked David's view of the driver. "Mr. Stone is likely to bleed to death if we don't take him straight to a doctor. We'll send help back to you."

"I got four men down there in about as bad condition," the driver said testily.

"But Mr. Stone is up here, and we can have him in the wagon in five minutes. If we wait while you cart those men up here, he may die."

David let the air out of his lungs in a *whoosh*. Was he really that bad off, or was she just being bossy, exaggerating his injuries to get her way? He did feel lightheaded, and he had barely stirred.

"How far is it?" the driver shouted.

The farmer was closer than David had realized, on his other side. "Nary a mile and a half."

After a pause the driver said, "All right, but you hurry back here. We'll get those others up if we can. We need help right away though. If a doctor can come out here, it would be good."

"Let's go," Millie said grimly. "Sir, you and your son lift him. Be careful. I'll move his leg over onto the blanket while you get the rest of him."

The farmer hesitated, and Millie cried, "Now!"

She was barking orders like an enraged fishwife, which David found oddly comforting and reassuring—it confirmed his assumption that she wasn't a real lady at all, though she could don a cloak of gentility when it served her purposes. Right now, he didn't need a lady. He needed a tough, determined advocate. It seemed

Millie fit the bill.

The farmer snarled and grabbed him roughly under his shoulders. His strapping son bent on David's other side. David braced himself for their rough touch, but when his leg jostled, he tensed and then surrendered to the swirling blackness.

Peregrin Walmore leaned out the window of the hack, gazing at the buildings that lined the street. He was here, on the infamous thoroughfare known as Broadway, in New York City. Though nothing here was more than two hundred years old, he couldn't help being impressed. While not London, the city had a busyness, a vitality about it that warmed his blood.

The cabbie stopped before a row of fashionable shops whose windows displayed clothing, home furnishings, and exotic foods. The door opened, and Peregrin blinked at the driver.

"Are we there?"

"We are, sir."

Peregrin hopped out on the sidewalk, and then he saw the sign, high on the side of the four-story brownstone edifice: METROPOLITAN. This was the hotel, all right.

"Where do I go in?"

The cabbie nodded toward a door topped by an awning. "Yonder, sir. Your hotel takes up an entire city block. The bottom is all shops and such."

"Very impressive." Peregrin stroked his new mustache as he deciphered the man's words. The accent was going to be a challenge; he could see that.

"Well said, sir. I'll give your luggage to the boy."

"Oh, yes." Peregrin swiveled and saw a young man in a smart uniform approaching. He took out his purse and paid the driver, adding an extra coin.

"I say, how would I go about finding out whether an acquaintance has sailed for England yet?"

The cabbie frowned. "Hmm. Not sure. P'raps you could ask at

the desk. Some of these desk clerks can work wonders."

Peregrin approached the door gingerly. A man in a long livery coat smiled at him.

"Good day, sir. Welcome to the Metropolitan."

"Er, thank you," Peregrin said. "Do I just..."

The uniformed man opened the glass-paneled door for him. "Right up the stairs to the lobby, sir."

"Thank you." The carpeted stairs muffled his footsteps. The curved mahogany railing was a wonder, smooth as glass. On the walls along the stairway were paintings of harbor scenes and the city skyline. Peregrin emerged into a chamber as large as a ballroom and as elegantly furnished. The settees, chairs, and side tables appeared to be European-made. Paintings hung in ornate gilt frames, and a magnificent chandelier illuminated the cavernous room.

In a daze, he glided toward the counter that must be the check-in desk. He'd never imagined Americans could build such a lovely hostelry. It was as good as anything in London—more ostentatious than most. He could understand why traveling aristocrats made this their temporary home.

"May I help you, sir?"

"Oh yes, thank you. I should like apartments, please. A bed-sitter if you've one available."

"Certainly, sir." The clerk went on to list several options.

Peregrin ventured uncertainly, "And what is the price of the three-room suite, as opposed to the bed-sitter?"

The clerk smiled as though the British accent amused him. At any rate, Peregrin was a bit put off by the prices. He wasn't bad at mathematics—he fancied that was what made him a moderately successful gambler—and he was fairly certain he'd done the mental conversion correctly. He hadn't expected to pay so much for a room. If he paid full price, his funds would run low within a few months, and he might be on this side of the ocean for years.

Perhaps he could stay here for a few days while he got his bearings, and then move to a less-expensive establishment. That was it. He felt better just working that out.

"Thank you. I'll take the bed-sitting room, please."

"And how long will you be with us, sir?"

"Oh, well, what's today?" He flushed at having shown his ignorance, but after all, he'd just stepped off a steamship.

"It's Tuesday, sir. June second."

"I expect I'll stay until Friday, then."

The bellboy arrived with his luggage, and the desk clerk gave the boy Peregrin's room number. Before turning away, Peregrin put forth his question on how to locate someone in as vast a city as New York.

"Did he stay at this hotel, sir?" the clerk asked.

"I'm not sure. A lot of our friends do, but I expect there are a great many hotels in New York."

"Hundreds. Do you know the name of his ship?"

Peregrin winced. "No, afraid not. Only that he planned to come overland from Oregon this spring and sail from New York."

"Oh, if he's coming that far, I doubt he's reached the city yet," the clerk said. "If you like, I can check our registry for the last month and our upcoming reservations and send word up to your room."

"Thank you." Peregrin slipped him a quarter-dollar and hoped it was enough.

"Oh, and you might inquire with the steamship companies," the clerk added. "I can't do that myself—haven't time—but you might hire someone to do it for you."

Peregrin mulled that over as he followed the bellboy up another flight of stairs and down a hallway that seemed longer than the carriage drive to Stoneford—the place his sister hoped one day to rule over as mistress. Lady Stoneford. He hoped he wouldn't disappoint her. He hated to let Merry down, and she had ways of making one uncomfortable if that happened. Though he loved her, they were very much alike in that way. He had no doubt she'd manage to punish him somehow if he failed, even from across the Atlantic.

CHAPTER 18

"Gently, gently," Millie called, her distress jacking her voice higher than its normal alto timbre. They'd torn over the road to town, with her urging the driver to make all speed possible, though it jostled her uncomfortably in the wagon bed. She was glad David wasn't conscious during that mad ride.

She looked away as the men lifted David's inert form from the back of the wagon onto a wheeled cot. But she had to look back to make sure they were handling his leg carefully, so as not to cause any further injury. If she had anything to say about it, David would get the best care available.

The fellow helping the farmer and his son looked to be in his late twenties. He moved swiftly but seemed to know what he was doing.

"Are you the doctor?" she asked.

"Yes ma'am. Are you the wife?"

"No. I'm a fellow passenger, but I was previously acquainted with this gentleman. Please give him your best care."

The doctor straightened and glanced at her. "From what your driver tells me, I should hurry out to the scene of the stage accident."

Millie glanced uneasily at the farmer and back to the physician. "I understand. But if you can just take a quick look at Mr. Stone's leg and make sure the bleeding's stopped. His pulse is faint—you must have seen that yourself when you examined him a moment ago. You wouldn't want him to bleed to death while you drive to the crash."

"I've got to be going," the farmer said.

"Help me get him inside," the doctor told him. "I'll send my wife to get someone to go with me, but I can't move this fellow to my examining table alone."

As she followed them into the house, Millie spotted a modest signboard hanging on the wall beside the front door: MARTIN LEE, M.D. A pretty young woman stood in a doorway, watching anxiously as they wheeled the cot past her.

"Jane, hop over to Billy Croft's and see if he can help me. There's been a stagecoach accident on the river road, and this man is the first of several casualties. And if his boy can go round to Dr. Nelson's, I'd appreciate it. We need all the medical help we can get."

Millie noted how quickly the woman moved to obey, without questioning her husband about the situation. Apparently Mrs. Lee was used to taking her husband's orders.

Millie didn't wait for an invitation but trailed the men into a room set up for patient care. The farmer helped transfer David to the table and then left, but within five minutes the man called Billy appeared.

"Want I should ride out there, Doc?" he asked from the doorway.

Dr. Lee glanced at Millie. "Mrs. Evans, was it?"

"Yes sir."

"What do you think? Should we send many men to the accident?"

"I think they'll need help. There were nine of us in the coach when it overset. I saw the driver and shotgun rider moving about afterward—they pulled me from the wreckage. But most of the others are injured, I fear."

"They're off the road then?" Dr. Lee asked.

"Yes. Down a steep hill—it will take some labor to bring them up."

"I'll get my wagon and a couple other fellows if I can," Billy said.

Dr. Lee opened a cupboard and stuffed a bag with rolled bandages and some short sticks. "Take these. If Mr. Stone can wait, I'll ride out in a few minutes."

Billy left, and the doctor turned back to David. "You done any nursing?" he asked Millie as he unbuttoned David's waistcoat.

"Some," Millie said.

"Wash your hands yonder." The doctor nodded toward a wash-basin on a stand in the corner and took a pair of scissors from a drawer. He began cutting David's pant leg open without another word.

Millie looked down at her hands. Blood and dirt caked her fingers. She poured water into the basin and used the bar of soap in a dish next to it. After pouring water over each hand, rinsing thoroughly, she dried them on a towel that hung at the side of the stand.

"All right, what can I do for you?" she asked.

"Go to the kitchen and see if my wife has a kettle of hot water on the stove. She usually keeps one going for me."

It took Millie only seconds to find the kitchen and lift the steaming kettle from the stove. She carried it back to the treatment room. Dr. Lee had David's lower leg exposed and was swabbing at it with cloth. He nodded toward the chest of drawers that held his instruments.

"Take one of those pans on top and pour hot water into it. Get a clean cloth from the second drawer and soak it for me."

Millie obeyed and watched him clean the blood from David's leg, revealing a jagged gash with blood still oozing from it and a stark bit of white bone poking out.

"This is pretty mean looking. There's wood in the wound—at least one long sliver, maybe more. I'll have to take it out. I won't put the cast on his leg until the swelling's down, but I need to close this wound."

"It's broken," Millie said, feeling rather stupid.

"Yes, and badly so." Dr. Lee glanced up at her. "Can you hold his leg for me? Rotate it like this?" He showed her how she would need to hold it so that he could work on the wound with both hands.

Millie stepped closer and reached out to help. A wave of embarrassment washed over her. She was touching a man's. . . limb. . .with her bare hands. She glanced at Dr. Lee, but he was intent on preparing his instruments. He picked up a needle and some sort of thread or fine cord.

"I'm not bad at threading needles," she said.

He kept on with his task. "I'm not bad at it either." He poked the end of the thread through the eye of the needle. "But thank you."

He didn't seem to notice her flushed face but bent over his work.

785

Hurried steps came through the house, and Millie looked toward the doorway.

"Hold still," Dr. Lee said sternly.

She turned back to the job, but she'd gotten a glimpse of Mrs. Lee, entering briskly.

"Can I help?"

The doctor didn't look his wife's way but asked, "Do I need to go out to the stagecoach?"

"Dr. Nelson is going now. Billy and two other men saddled up to ride with him and assist."

Dr. Lee grunted. "Well, we'll probably have more patients coming in soon. I might do better to stay here and be ready when they arrive. Prepare the bed in the isolation room for this man."

Mrs. Lee whirled and left the room.

"Steady now," said the doctor. "I think I've got the bleeding stopped, but I need to set that leg." A moment later he clipped his thread and straightened. "All right, you can let go."

Millie released her hold on David's leg and arched her aching back.

"I don't think he'll wake when I shift his leg, but I want you to hold on to him anyway, just in case. I had a man sock me in the kidney once when I thought he was out cold."

Millie looked down at her hands, found a finger that wasn't too bloody, and brushed back a lock of her hair. "Just tell me what to do, Doctor."

When he roused, David was lying on a bed, or at least something more comfortable than the ground. The pain in his leg was unbearable. He ground his teeth together and sucked in a breath. The movement caused a sharp pain in his side, and his head felt as big as a bushel basket, but all of that was dwarfed by the agony of his leg.

He peered through slits between his eyelids. A lantern cast harsh light over the room. When he moved his head, a rustling sound warned him that he wasn't alone. Millie appeared at the bedside. Her hair was disheveled, escaping from the knot on the back of her head, and dark circles rimmed her eyes, but if possible, that only made her prettier.

"Mr. Stone."

He blinked, but she still looked a bit hazy. "Where are we?"

"In a doctor's house on the outskirts of Independence."

"We crossed a river. Not the Missouri."

"One of its tributaries."

He started to nod but winced and kept his head still. "I was injured."

"It was after the river crossing. The horses were skittish, and they ran away." She pushed back a lock of auburn hair, and he watched, fascinated, as it fell forward again.

"I remember." He wanted her to talk some more. Her voice was gentle, musical, familiar. "What's the damage?"

"Your left leg is badly broken. Dr. Lee fears you have at least one broken rib as well, and you may be concussed. But you still came out better than the stagecoach."

"Oh?"

She nodded. "It's matchwood. Two of the passengers died."

That knowledge landed on him like a rock on his chest. "Not Andrews?" For some reason, he hoped the dandy had survived. Maybe it was because the fellow was likable—and they both admired Millie in their own way.

"No, he's stove up some, but he'll be all right. I didn't see the worst of it. Once Gip and the driver hauled me out, I went up where you were."

David vaguely recalled her telling him about Gip on the hillside.

"The gentleman from Illinois was one of the deceased. I'm not sure of the other. I think he was one of those in the center when we crashed." She pulled a chair close to the bedside and sat down.

"Well. At least you came through all right."

Her face went sober. "Yes. I'm very thankful."

"How long have I been here?"

"Since yesterday afternoon."

He stared at her until his headache made him close his eyes for relief. "Yesterday? We've been here a night already?"

"Yes."

"Where did you stay?"

"After I'd done what I could to help Dr. Lee, his wife took me to an inn about a mile away. I spoke for a room for you, for when you can be moved."

Just the thought of being moved again clamped David's teeth shut tightly.

"Dr. Lee wanted to keep you here a few days," Millie said matter-of-factly. "But a couple of men were worse off than you, so he said to find a place where I can tend to you, and he'll call on you daily until you're better."

"Where you. . ." David broke off, startled. Did the doctor think Millie was his wife? It seemed he'd be plagued with that assumption until they parted company. And when *would* they part company, anyway? "You mustn't delay your journey for my sake."

She smiled indulgently. "And who would care for you? I don't mind. Really." Her face flushed, and he thought she was quite beautiful.

He closed his eyes to shut out the sight of her. He didn't *want* her hovering over him and blushing like a schoolgirl. And he certainly couldn't let her take on his personal care. Surely he could hire an experienced manservant. . . .

Nonsense, he told himself. A valet in the rambunctious young town of Independence? Only a deluded man would think that.

The truth hit him squarely between the eyes. Millie couldn't go on without him, short of lifting the price of a ticket from his wallet. She was stuck here until he gave her the means to leave. He looked beyond her, seeking a bedside table or a dresser.

"What is it?" she asked.

"I just. . .wondered where my things are." He shifted enough to look down at his own body, covered by a sheet and light blanket. Unless he was mistaken, he wore nothing but his underclothing.

Now it was his turn to blush.

"Your trousers were beyond repair," Millie said bluntly. "The rest of your things are over there." She pointed over his prone form, toward the other side of the room, but David hadn't the energy to roll over. Even if he had the strength, whatever entrapped his injured leg would probably prevent that.

She bent closer and smoothed the edge of the blanket. "Don't worry, Mr. Stone. All of your belongings are safe. When you're ready to get up again, I can go to a haberdashery and find some suitable trousers to replace the ones you had on in the crash. Or perhaps you have others in your luggage. Gip brought it here last night, but no one has opened it."

David could think of nothing to say but "Thank you."

After all, she was not the only one in need. Yes, she was dependent on him now. But even more desperately, he needed Millie.

CHAPTER 19

Millie's eyelids drifted down, and she jerked suddenly awake. She shifted in her chair and straightened her shoulders. She supposed it was foolish to sit here at David's bedside all night. She ought to go across the hall to her own hotel room and sleep for a few hours.

But she couldn't stand the thought of him awakening alone in the strange room and trying to move about. Dr. Lee had not yet put the cast on his leg, and David might do further damage if he thrashed around.

No, she would stay here until morning, and then perhaps she could pay Billy, the young man who carried bags and did other chores and errands for the hotel owners, to sit with him while she got a nap. Uncomfortable as she was, she would rather stay in case David needed her.

Dr. Lee had dosed him heavily with laudanum before they moved him here. David had protested at first, but the doctor assured him that he wouldn't give him too much of the drug, and that he would regret it if he refused. The trip was apt to be excruciating if he wasn't medicated in advance.

Millie had heard stories about people who were given too much of the concoction. It could stop your heart, some said. She didn't blame David for being wary. Not only was there a danger of overdose, but he was also the type of man who liked his wits about him. Knowing he hadn't been in control of his faculties for hours at a time was probably a great frustration to him in his lucid moments.

At last he had given in, but he'd looked almost fearful. Millie was sure the pain and the uncertainty about his recovery had much to do with that. He looked like a frightened little boy as he lay waiting for the doctor to mix his tonic. Out of empathy so sharp that it hurt, Millie had reached for his hand and held it until Dr. Lee had the dose ready, and then she'd helped prop David up so that he could drink it without spilling.

She'd sat beside him afterward, while Dr. Lee repeatedly checked his pulse and respiration rate. David didn't seem to mind when she reached out and patted his hand. When he slipped gently into slumber, the doctor summoned another man to help him get David into the wagon.

That was nearly twenty hours ago. Millie didn't have a clock, but she consulted David's watch occasionally, to reassure herself that the night was not really endless.

David hadn't stirred for the first eight hours after they put him to bed in the hotel room. It was only as night came on that he began to move slightly now and then, and sometimes he let out a sound that might have been a garbled word or a moan. Millie felt his brow frequently, but he didn't seem to have any fever. She used it as an excuse to brush the blond hair back from his forehead. He really was a striking man.

While the light lasted, she read off and on from her Bible. To save lamp oil—which guests must pay to replenish—she used a candle once true darkness had fallen. Candles cost less and gave enough light for her to get about the room, but the single taper's illumination was too dim for her to read by without sitting very close to it and squinting. She'd put the volume aside hours ago and sat quietly, thinking about David and Sam, and even James, whom she rarely contemplated anymore.

She was growing very fond of David—again, she realized. She liked him even more than she had when she first knew him. He was smart and discreet, though his personality was not the warmest. He seemed to reserve the easy camaraderie she knew he was capable of for those he knew well and trusted.

Even the fact that he now eschewed her fueled Millie's admiration for the handsome Englishman. After all, a true gentleman should avoid women like her—or such as she had once been. She didn't take it as snobbery. Rather, she thought he might be quite devout, though he didn't broadcast it. She'd had his Bible for some time now and had seen how well-worn it had become. She'd found dozens of passages underlined within the book, and her heart sang when she read them, because they often spoke to her own spirit, and she felt she shared something with him.

Dawn had turned the room gray when she startled awake again. A sharp pain hitched between her shoulder blades. She'd slumped in the chair, and she'd probably have a crick all day from it.

She arched her back and stretched her arms and legs. She glanced toward the pillow and froze. David's eyes were open.

She jumped from the chair and bent over him. "You're awake. Can I get you some water?"

He nodded, and she poured some from the pitcher on the washstand into a tumbler.

"It's time for your medicine, too. Past time. I should have given it to you an hour ago, but I'm afraid I fell asleep."

He blinked and said in a low, raspy voice, "Where are we?"

"At a hotel. Remember, Dr. Lee got some men to help move you?" David shook his head.

"Well, we're settled in here, and you must tell me if there's anything I can do to make you more comfortable. I need to mix your laudanum, but take a sip of water first. You'll feel better."

She helped him raise his head enough to take a small swallow from the glass.

"There. Now just lie still—"

"I need to get up."

"Oh dear." She'd feared this. "You can't. You see, your leg is badly fractured. I'll have to help you."

He stared up at her. She'd never seen a man look so terrified.

"Or perhaps I can rout the boy out, though I hate to wake him."

"Boy?"

"The one who carries the bags in for people."

"Get him."

Millie decided it was best to do as he wished. She set down the medicine bottle and scooted for the back stairs. If Billy wasn't about yet, perhaps Mr. Simmons, the hotel's owner, was. She'd try the kitchen first. Surely the cook would be there and could advise her.

Fifteen minutes later, David wished he hadn't sent Millie away so fast. The boy might be able to help him tend to his personal needs, but he wouldn't trust the lad to mix the opium tincture, and he hadn't allowed Millie time to fix it. Consequently, the screaming pain in his leg got worse and worse.

He hated to take the laudanum. When he didn't, he could think without it clouding his mind. But the pain! He supposed he'd have to give in to the opiate for a while longer.

At last he was settled in the bed again, though he wouldn't say he was comfortable, and the boy stood back.

"Anything else I can do for you, sir?"

David said between clenched teeth, "Send Mrs. Evans in."

"Right."

A moment later Millie was at his side.

"I'm so sorry," she began, but David raised his hand to cut her off. "Laudanum."

"Of course."

She went to the washstand and began to measure and stir.

"Here you go, sir."

David shuddered as he swallowed it. The vile stuff would put him into darkness for several hours, but by now it was obvious he needed the dose.

"There!" Millie smiled down at him and took the tumbler away.

"I'll need to send a letter right away," he managed.

"Of course. I'll get paper and take it down for you."

He nodded, saving his breath. She left the room, and he let his head sink into the pillow. He wasn't sure he could stay awake until she got back. At least he had someone looking out for him, and for that he was thankful. Before he could form a coherent prayer of thanks, she was back.

"I have a scrap here. If you'd like to tell me what you want in the letter, I'll take it down. Later I'll get some good paper and an envelope and write it over nice."

He blinked up at her, trying to make sense of her rapid speech.

"Mr. Stone?" she asked doubtfully, a stub of a pencil poised over her bit of paper.

"Yes. To my solicitor, Jonathan Conrad. His address is in my valise. Tell him I will be delayed. And whatever the doctor said about recovery time." David couldn't recall anything Dr. Lee had told him, but a month was batting about in the recesses of his mind. He would lose a full month. At least. "Millie?" He looked up at her suddenly, a fearful thought seizing him.

"Yes?" She leaned close.

"I will get better, won't I?"

"Of course!"

He exhaled. "My leg?"

"Once the swelling is down, Dr. Lee will put a plaster cast on it. Later today, I expect, or perhaps tomorrow. Now, I shall write this out for you and have it ready for you to look over whenever you feel up to it."

"Thank you."

"Would you like anything to eat?" she asked.

"No, I. . ." He closed his eyes and let go of the worries and the pain, drifting into misty dreams.

"New York? What is your brother doing in New York?" Randolph Stone waved a sheet of paper over his head as he entered the morning room.

Merrileigh flicked her fan open and fluttered it before her face. "Goodness, Husband! What is all this to-do?"

"Here's a letter come from Peregrin, and he's in New York, at one of the finest hotels. I thought he'd cut and run to Australia, or at least to Canada. How can he afford to gad about in the best circles in New York? He says he met up with Freddie Wallace's cousin and went with him to a card game. What on earth is that lad thinking?"

Merrileigh stood and plucked the letter from his hand. "Come now, dear. What's the harm in his enjoying a little company with a fellow Britisher? And Perry left here with enough money to keep him in style for a bit."

"But he's likely to be in exile for years. And a card game is what put him in this fix to begin with." Randolph sighed and strode to the bell pull. "Your brother never did have any common sense. When he's flush, he lives high, and when he's broke, he cadges on us. Well, I don't intend to be sending him an allowance to keep him at the Metropolitan, I'll tell you that."

Merrileigh skimmed the letter quickly. "Relax, Mr. Stone. He says right here he walked out of the game ten dollars to the good. So long as he's winning, you won't have to support him."

"Oh wonderful. My brother-in-law is now supporting himself as a professional gambler. That is so much better." Randolph rolled his eyes and yanked the bell pull.

A moment later Thomas appeared in the doorway.

"Yes sir?"

"Sherry," Randolph said.

"Yes sir." Thomas went to the sideboard and poured his master a glass of wine.

Merrileigh turned the sheet over and caught her breath. Apparently Randolph hadn't read this far, to where Peregrin mentioned that he'd put out some feelers but hadn't caught word of David yet. The foolish boy! He hadn't bargained on Randolph opening the mail before she did. Usually she had first look at the post, but not today. At least he'd worded it so that she could make a plausible explanation if need be.

"Oh, Conrad's man was here earlier," Randolph said.

"Was he?" Merrileigh jerked her head toward him. She'd gone out for two hours after lunch to make a few courtesy calls and leave her card at a few of her acquaintances' homes. Nothing ever happened when she was on the premises, but set foot outside, and the fireworks began.

"Yes. They'd had a letter from David."

"Indeed?" Merrileigh tucked Peregrin's letter into her sleeve. She would peruse it again later in private. "What did he say? Is he coming soon?"

"Apparently not. He's stalled in the middle of the country."

"St. Louis?"

"No, but somewhere out there." Randolph frowned and sipped his sherry. "Said he'd had an accident and would be delayed several weeks." Randolph grinned at her, obviously delighted with himself. "Independence, that's it. The name of the town, I mean."

Merrileigh shelved that bit of information for later contemplation as well. "Did he say when he expects to arrive?"

"Iverson thought it would be at least a month."

"Oh."

Randolph chuckled. "Maybe he'll run into your brother. Wouldn't that be a corker?"

"Yes," Merrileigh said thoughtfully. "Wouldn't it just?"

CHAPTER 20

I'll need to send another letter." David's voice held authority that Millie hadn't heard in more than two weeks. She turned from where she'd been arranging his clean linen in the dresser and stepped over to the bedside, glad he was feeling better. His will to do something showed her that the pain no longer overpowered him. "Of course. I'll get you some paper and ink."

She went downstairs and stopped at the desk in the front hall, where Mr. Simmons was bent over a ledger.

"I'm in need of stationery, sir. I don't suppose—"

"Oh yes, Mrs. Evans. I took your suggestion and laid in a supply."

Millie smiled. "That was good of you, sir. I'm sure other guests will be pleased, too. I'd like two sheets, please, and an envelope."

The first time she'd written a letter for David, she'd had to go out to find a mercantile for the supplies. She'd purchased a small bottle of ink and a pen at the time. She was grateful she wouldn't have to do that again.

She got the stationery she needed from the landlord and thanked him, then went back up to David's room. He was still awake, scowling at the ceiling.

"There, I think we're ready," she said cheerfully. "I only got one envelope."

"That's enough—unless you need to send a letter as well."

"No, I've no need, but thank you." She hesitated.

He raised his head suddenly, fixing her with an inquisitive stare. "Did you pay for it yourself?"

"This time, yes. But earlier, I. . .there were some coins in the pocket of the trousers you wore at the time of the accident. Dr. Lee cut the trousers off you, and. . .well, I salvaged the contents of your pockets for you." Her cheeks flushed, and she couldn't look him in the eye.

"Did you pay the doctor?"

"Yes, and the man who carted us here. I'm sorry, Mr. Stone, but I had to take the money for them from your wallet. I didn't ask you then. You were indisposed." Unconscious, actually, but she didn't like to remind him of his weakness too vividly.

"Bring it here." He stirred and gasped, sinking back onto the pillow, his face ashen.

Millie grabbed the wallet from the dresser and hurried to his side. "Are you all right?"

"No."

"What can I do?"

He said nothing but stared upward with clenched teeth.

She wanted to give him another dose of the painkiller, but Dr. Lee had told her yesterday to lengthen the intervals between doses, lest David become addicted to the stuff. "It will be time for more laudanum in an hour."

"Yes." It was barely a whisper, and she thought that an hour must seem very long to a man in pain.

She put his wallet in his hand, and he held it up where he could see it. He inspected the contents.

"What do I owe you for the stationery—and anything else you've paid for yourself?"

"Nothing." Need she remind him that every cent she had came from him to begin with?

He withdrew a dollar and handed it to her. "You must have used up most of what I gave you before."

"Well. . .yes. Thank you." She pocketed the dollar. "Would you like to dictate your letter now?"

"Yes. Do you mind? It pains me to sit up, and I don't think I'm ready to undertake it myself."

"I'd be happy to."

He dictated slowly, so that she could write nicely as he talked. The message was destined for his niece. Millie's color heightened as she wrote the name, but neither she nor David said anything about Millie's past connection to Anne.

"My dear niece," David said. "I regret to inform you that I have been delayed in my travels. The stagecoach on which I was bound for Independence met with an accident, and it seems my leg is broken. I've been sequestered two weeks in a hotel on the outskirts of town. The doctor assures me I shall have full use of the limb again within a month or so. Meanwhile, I submit to the kind ministrations of others. You probably will not recognize this hand, for the letter is penned by one who has been of assistance to me.

"Do not worry, dear Anne. Your uncle may be nearly twice your age, but I assure you that I will mend. Please tell Daniel I am confident leaving all in his hands so far as the line is concerned. I trust the arrangements we made earlier are working smoothly. I expect that I shall be gone from here by the time you read this, as the overland mail is so slow. I am now at the Frontier Hotel in Independence, but if you have urgent news, a missive might catch me at Astor House in New York before I sail. With great affection, your uncle."

Millie wrote it as neatly as she could and blew on it to dry the ink before handing it over to him to sign.

"I expect she'll be relieved to hear from you," she said.

"Yes, though this news may unsettle her. I almost hate to tell her. There's nothing she can do, and I don't like to worry her. Still, if I don't tell her and she learns of my mishap later, she'll be upset that I didn't say anything."

"She can pray for your speedy recovery, sir."

"Yes, there is that." He gritted his teeth. "I shall have to sit up a bit if I'm to sign that."

"Are you sure you want to?" Millie asked.

"Yes. I want her to see by my signature that I'm well enough to write it."

She put an extra pillow behind his shoulders, and he let out a groan as he shifted.

"I'm sorry," Millie said.

"No matter. Hand me the pen, please."

His face had gone white, but he managed to write his name with a confident flourish. Then he thrust the pen into her hand and sank back with his eyes closed, his mouth in a tight line.

Millie set aside the letter and pen. "I think we can give you the laudanum now, Mr. Stone."

"Good. I think I'm ready for it, thank you."

Sweat trickled from his temple down his cheek as she held him up to drink the dose, and Millie fetched his towel to wipe it away.

"I'm sorry you feel so bad."

"Ah well, the doctor assures me I'm healing. I daresay it's not as bad now as it was at first, but we forget, don't we?"

"Yes, mercifully, we do. Would you like to rest now?"

"I would. Oh, Anne's address. . ."

"She's Mrs. Adams, is she not? Of Corvallis?"

"Yes. Mrs. Daniel Adams. . ."

"That's all I need then."

She removed the extra pillow and arranged the bedclothes neatly. David was already asleep when she turned away.

She folded the letter and put it into the envelope. *Mrs. Daniel Adams, Corvallis, Oregon,* she wrote across the front. She decided to take it directly to the post office, rather than relying on Mr. Simmons to get it there swiftly.

The owner of the Frontier Hotel was greeting a new customer when she passed through the lobby, but when she returned, he was in the dining room, drinking coffee.

Millie hesitated, but she wondered if David had enough money left to get them both to the East Coast. She'd counted his money the first time she opened the wallet, and she'd felt seven shades of guilty ever since. There was plenty for the journey, for both of them. But David hadn't planned on stopping six weeks or more in Independence, and he probably had not yet paid his passage to England.

She couldn't leave him now. If she did go her own way, he would save money by not having to pay for her food and lodging. But he was completely helpless. For at least three or four more weeks, he would need someone to do everything for him. The hotel owner wouldn't do it. The bellboy could do only so much. The doctor had no nurse to spare. Millie couldn't see any way around it. She couldn't let David spend all his money to keep her near him, but she couldn't leave him alone either.

She would have to get a job.

As she approached Mr. Simmons's table in the corner of the otherwise-deserted dining room, she worked up her courage.

"Sir," she ventured, not quite looking into his eyes, "I'm known to be a good cook, dressmaker, and housekeeper. Would you happen to know of any employment openings a lady could fill?"

Peregrin was delighted to have a letter delivered to his room. Mail from England—imagine that! His sister's flowery hand greeted him. Of course—who else would write to him here? He held the envelope to his nose for a moment. Did it smell faintly of English roses, or was that his imagination?

He'd been in New York near a month, and so far he'd accomplished little but deplete his funds. He'd lost a few hundred pounds at the last couple of poker games he'd indulged in— and heaven knew his lodgings cost enough. He'd hoped they'd let him run up a tab indefinitely, but the management insisted, politely but coldly, that he pay on a weekly basis.

If he didn't start winning again soon, he'd have to move to a cheaper establishment. He'd hate to do that and give up all the amenities here, but realistically, he had to plan on an extended stay in America. And that meant frugality. Unless of course, he wanted to seek employment, but he shuddered at the thought. What was he good for, anyway? Not manual labor. He supposed he might get on as a bartender or some such occupation. He certainly knew how to pour a drink.

He carried Merry's letter to the desk and slit it open with his ivory-handled letter opener. He'd bought that at a shop on Fifth

Avenue, along with a silver pen and some paper and ink. Probably should have saved the money, but one needed basic supplies if one was going to carry on correspondence.

Dearest Brother,
How delightful to receive a missive in your own hand.

Really. Who else's hand did she think he'd write in?

I'm so pleased that you've found a comfortable, if temporary, place to stay, and that you've run into some acquaintances.
You'll be pleased to know that Randolph caught wind of his cousin's situation today. It seems David has been delayed for several weeks in the town of Independence. I am not sure how far that is from New York—perhaps you could investigate. It might behoove you to go there.

Peregrin scowled at the words. Independence! Wasn't that the place where folks gathered to form emigrant trains before going into the vast wilderness that comprised the West? He read on.

I don't know what's keeping him there—I believe Randolph said something about a mishap. Anyway, if he sent the message two or three weeks ago, he's likely still there. Perhaps Nigel Wallace can enlighten you—or someone at the post office or railway station.
At any rate, after going over your missive again, I was pleased with the information you'd gathered on steamships, but I must warn you. Randolph opened your letter while I was out. He did it in all innocence. I'm thankful he didn't read as far as the second page, however. When I returned home, he was sputtering about the fact that you'd gone to New York instead of Canada or New South Wales. Be very careful, dear brother, what you say in your future letters.
Perhaps we should work out a code, so that if Randolph

*reads another letter, he won't realize that you are interested
in his cousin. Perhaps we could use another name. Instead of
David Stone, you could say "Donald Steppington" or some
such thing. Just make up a name with the same initials, and
I will understand. And don't mention Independence. You
might say Freedom instead. You see, it's all very simple. Your
friend Donald has left Freedom and hopes to return home
soon. Something like that. Or you might say—if it were
warranted—that poor Donald met with an untimely demise.
Oh dear, you can work it out, I'm sure. We simply need to
practice discretion.*

    *With that in mind, I urge you to destroy this letter after
you've absorbed its contents. We wouldn't want your friend
Donald to stumble upon it, now would we?*

Your affectionate sister,
Merry

Peregrin stood for a long moment, staring at the signature. He'd
hoped, as he settled into his new life, that Merry had given up the
ridiculous scheme. It appeared not. She wanted him to go through
with it. It was up to him to stop David Stone from boarding a ship
for England—ever.

He sighed heavily. It was too bad. He might have made a good
life for himself here if he had a run of luck. And Nigel Wallace had
promised to introduce him to some people in the higher set of New
York society. Now it appeared he'd have to move on to some frontier
backwater.

Well, he might as well enjoy himself tonight. There was a game
on at Nigel's lodgings. He could spend the afternoon learning all
he could about Independence and how to get there and then pass
the evening singeing the other fellows' tail feathers. Maybe he'd
leave the Metropolitan with more swag than he'd brought.

CHAPTER 21

David sat up on the edge of the bed, determined to get dressed without help. It was high time he was up and about. Dr. Lee had left him a pair of crutches, saying that, as it had been nearly four weeks since the accident, he could begin hobbling about the room. He mustn't attempt the stairs yet, but even a foray down the corridor would be a relief. David had never in his life grown so sick of a room.

Millie had been a tremendous help, he had to admit. She'd done everything from seeing that his clothes were laundered to reading aloud when he was bored—which was often. And who knew what she'd done during the times when he'd been unconscious or in a drugged sleep?

But he wasn't about to let her help him put his trousers on. Now that he was fully aware of what was going on, he deserved to have his dignity preserved. If need be, he'd summon the innkeeper or the bellboy. They'd been pressed into service several times to help David bathe. But this time he resolved that he didn't really need either of them. With a bit of patience and determination, he could do it himself.

The pants were of coarse whipcord, not something he would have chosen himself, especially in this stifling July heat. But Millie had of necessity purchased what the storekeeper had shown her for a man his size. His only other pair was of fine quality and matched his tailcoat. Millie didn't think the cast would fit through the trouser leg, so she'd gone shopping for him and found these.

She'd offered several times to help him try them on, but he'd put her off repeatedly. The fact that she'd been married didn't matter one whit. Even the thought was unseemly.

But today he'd been granted permission to stump about with the crutches, and he couldn't wait another moment. He'd asked early on for a wheeled sick-chair, but Dr. Lee hadn't been able to come up with one, and anyway, the formidable stairs would have curtailed its usefulness. For the last week or so, he'd gotten as far as the armchair a few feet away, but getting to it had been a trial. He looked on the crutches with great optimism—but he'd need the trousers on before he could appear outside the confines of his room.

He made an attempt to work the garment over his cast and nearly fell off the bed in the effort. His dismal conclusion daunted him—this pant leg would not fit over the cast either, though it was cut much looser than his formalwear. He would certainly have to replenish his wardrobe when he reached New York. He couldn't arrive in England so poorly outfitted.

Disgusted, he reached for the dressing gown Millie had left looped over the bedpost at the foot of the bed. He donned it whenever he had to leave his bed of necessity, but so far that had only been for brief and painful moments. He would suffer agony gladly, rather than have Millie or some stranger tend his basic needs with a bedpan.

But today he wanted freedom. And he would not give up.

He knotted the belt of the dressing gown, seized the crutches, and fitted them under his armpits. The doctor had assured him they were the right length for a tall man. David tested his weight on them and hopped experimentally to the window, keeping the foot of his injured leg a hair's breadth off the floor.

At last he stood before the casement. Millie had kept the window clean—he'd seen her wash it at least twice since they'd been here. He looked out on the street three stories below. The thoroughfare was rutted and muddy, and across the way were a saloon, a laundry, and a disreputable-looking ironmonger's. That accounted for a lot of the noise that annoyed him during the day. But it was a different scene than he could glimpse from his bed or even from the chair, and he drank it in. By leaning on the crutches, he was able to shove the sash up a few inches, but the air outside seemed no cooler than what he had in his room. He shut the window so dust and bugs wouldn't come in.

His thoughts flew beyond Independence, all the way to England.

His letter to Jonathan Conrad must have reached its destination long ago. He'd asked to have that one sent to St. Louis, and then across the Mississippi, and on by express train to New York, where it would be put on a steamship. Steamers made the voyage in less than two weeks. He might get a return message any day.

He turned and swung his way toward the dresser. Hadn't the doctor said he might try a little weight on his foot now? He rested the bottom of the cast on the floor and stepped gingerly on it. His leg ached, but the pain was not unbearable. He kept the greater part of his weight on the crutches, but used his damaged leg for gentle support.

Immense satisfaction filled him when he reached the oak dresser. He balanced with the crutches and picked up his wallet. He still seemed to have most of the money he'd had before the accident. Of course, more bills were secured in his boot top, but that was money to be used only when the unforeseen occurred.

At that thought, he grimaced. If this wasn't unforeseen, what was? He might well need to delve into the hidden trove to pay for his ship's berth to England.

He stumped to the wall where his coat, vest, and a shirt hung from pegs and checked his pockets. His documents and letters from Conrad were also intact, and he let out a sigh of relief. Apparently Millie had kept her paws off his belongings. Hard to believe, but he couldn't think of anything that was missing. Even the little box with the onyx cuff links was in the side pocket, but he'd fully expected to find that. After all, it would be a bit blatant for her to steal them again.

As he thought it over, it seemed odd that he had so much cash left. He hobbled to the chair and sank into it, suddenly weary. His leg ached, stretched out before him, and he clenched his teeth. The angle of the rigid cast caused him quite a bit of pain. He shifted in the chair, wondering if he could get up again unassisted, but that seemed unlikely. He hoped someone would come along before it became too unbearable.

At a tap on the door, he called, "Come in," almost joyfully.

Millie entered, her eyes sweeping over him in surprise.

"Well now, look at you! Are you all right?"

"It hurts a bit to have my foot resting on the floor like this, but I really hate to get back in bed."

"A pillow under your heel, perhaps?" Millie laid a book on the bedside table and picked up one of the two pillows he'd been using. She fluffed up the feathers inside and knelt. "There, now, I'll just lift your foot and slide it under."

He grimaced as she moved his leg, but as soon as the feather pillow was under his foot, the pain lessened.

"Ah, that's what I needed. Thank you." He refused to think about how much of his person she was viewing.

"Would you like the other one as well?" she asked.

"No, I think not."

She rose and brushed her skirt with her hands. "This might be a good time for me to change your bed linen, if you're comfortable there for ten minutes."

"As you wish." It felt odd, sitting there and watching her work like a chambermaid. David wondered if he ought to look into hiring someone to come in and clean. Or would the hotel pay someone to do that?

"Millie. . ." He'd taken to calling her that—when, he couldn't say. Somewhere between seeing her bully the men on the hillside and the tenth time he watched her straighten his bedclothes.

"Yes?" She turned with her arms full of cotton sheets. Her face made a rosy contrast to their whiteness, and her fiery hair caught a ray of sun from the window, topping off the image like the flame of a burning candle.

"You oughtn't to do all this for me."

"Nonsense. We've had this conversation before. You did much for me, and I'm happy to return the favor." She stepped toward the door, but when he spoke again, she stopped.

"Millie, how are you paying for our rooms? Have you told the innkeeper I'll pay him, and he trusted us, or what?"

She turned, her green eyes wide. "Oh, he expects you to pay for your own room, sir. I gave him five dollars the first week we were here, out of your wallet. I expect he'll tot up your bill any time you want it."

"And yours? Did you give him something down on your own as well?"

"Only for the first week. I've been able to keep my account current since then."

"You have? But how?"

"I. . .I've been cleaning other people's rooms and doing laundry for the hotel while you slept." Her cheeks had gone pinker, and her eyes flashed a bit, as though she dared him to tell her she was behaving in a vulgar manner.

"I see."

She nodded and went out the door with his sheets.

David struggled with the conflicting thoughts teeming in his mind. A lady wouldn't do such a thing. But would a real lady let a gentleman—even if he were a friend—pay for her lodgings? And was he her friend, when it came to that? Another part of him raised a defiant chin and asked whether it mattered if she was a "real" lady or not. Millie, it seemed, could cook like a fine chef, work like a deckhand, and take charge of a situation like a gunnery sergeant. In the face of such evidence, what did gentle birth and impeccable manners matter? Yet something buried deep in his psyche raised a stubborn hand and cried, "She would not be received at Almack's."

Millie returned a few minutes later with an armful of clean, folded sheets.

"There, this will just take a minute." She laid the stack on the dresser and shook out the bottom sheet, sending it in a glorious, white pouf, like the filling sail of a schooner, half the width of the room.

She hummed as she spread the sheet and tucked it in all around. David watched her quick, deft hands.

"It's a magnificent day outside." She smiled at him across the featherbed. "Not too hot. Perhaps I can open the window."

"That would be nice." He didn't mention dust or bugs. Odd how much more beauty she saw in the day than he had, and he was the one who'd been confined.

She crossed to the casement and pushed the sash up, securing it in place with a wooden block. This time a breeze fluttered through, setting a stray tendril of her hair dancing.

"There!" Millie stepped back from the window. "I read in the scripture that 'This is the day which the Lord hath made.' It struck me that every day is His day. Some of them we like more than others, but still, the Almighty gives us what He deems best. And today He gave us a stunner." She went back to the dresser, snatched a pillowcase from the pile, and worried the extra pillow into it.

A stunner, David thought. *Yes, and there's one right here in my room.*

Appalled at the thought, he looked toward the window, where the breeze flirted with the muslin curtain. How little he had thought about God this past month, and how much about David Stone and his comfort or lack of it. Perhaps he could take a lesson from this common woman who seemed to have undergone a massive change of heart.

Unless this was all a show, for his benefit. Was she still trying to lure him in? He didn't feel as though she was. For several weeks she'd been friendly, helpful, and almost unfailingly cheerful. She had assured him countless times that he was healing and would soon have his strength back. But she had never once cast sheep eyes at him. Was it possible that she was no longer interested in him as a man?

Millie spread the top sheet and laid the quilt over the whole.

"That's it, but for the pillow under your foot," she said. "When you're tired of sitting, I'll help you back to bed and put a new slip on that one."

"Millie, do you suppose there's a minister nearby who might visit me?"

Her eyebrows shot up, and he thought how delicate and well-shaped they were.

"Why yes. I've met one, as a matter of fact."

"You have?"

She nodded. "I've been going to a church a couple of blocks away.

The pastor and his wife have treated me very kindly. In fact, they've been praying for you, sir. I hope you don't mind. I didn't give a lot of details, just told them an acquaintance of mine was badly injured."

David blinked at her. She hadn't mentioned going to church nor making new friends. But then, he hadn't known she was working in the hotel either. Millie, it seemed, was a woman of discretion, and also a woman of mystery.

"Would you like me to invite him here?" she asked.

"Yes, thank you. I do wish I could get downstairs."

Millie shook her head. "Two flights. It would never do at this stage. You must be patient."

David sighed. Not for the first time, he wished she'd been able to secure rooms on the ground floor. "I suppose you're right. Could you help me back into bed now? My leg is beginning to ache."

"Of course." Millie paused to look at his pocket watch, which had made its home on the bedside table since they moved in. "Look at that! It's an hour past the time when you can have more laudanum. I do believe you're getting better, sir, but I'll fix you a dose after you're in bed if you want it."

"I think not. Is that a new book?"

She glanced at the volume she'd brought earlier. "Oh yes, it is. A Mrs. Fleming, in 201, had it. She finished it this morning, and she offered to lend it to me. She says it's prodigious exciting. Alexandre Dumas."

He smiled. "Would you—oh, I don't suppose you have time."

"To read to you?"

He ought to just read to himself. He was turning into rather a lazy fellow. But the truth was, he liked the way she read aloud. She brought the characters right into the room.

"I think I could stay half an hour," she said.

"Thank you," he said meekly.

Millie knocked on the door of David's room. She'd left him twenty minutes ago, clean shaven, washed, and brushed. On her way out of the hotel, she'd sent the bellboy up to help him put on the trousers she'd modified by slitting one leg to allow the cast to go through. She hoped the venture had been successful.

"Come in," came his voice, and she pushed open the door.

Her gaze flew to his armchair, positioned beside the window. David sat in it, fully clothed. The trouser leg was pinned together so that one hardly noticed the cast—well, not much. And he wore his exquisitely made shirt, tie, and jacket.

She smiled at him. "Mr. Stone. Glad to see you looking so well. I've brought the Reverend Mr. Harden."

The pastor stepped past her and extended his hand to David. "I'm pleased to meet you, sir."

"Mutual," David said, stretching to shake hands. The two were about the same age. Mr. Harden was several inches shorter than David, and his complexion and hair darker. David's features relaxed as he looked him over. "Won't you sit down, sir?"

Mr. Harden sat opposite him, and Millie was suddenly loath to quit the room. But she knew she ought to, so she cleared her throat and gave a little curtsey.

"I'll leave you gentlemen alone. May I bring a tea tray up?"

"That would be nice," David said. "Thank you."

She bowed her head slightly. *Why am I acting so servile with him? Just because he's rich doesn't mean he has to treat everyone like servants.*

If the truth were told, he had not treated her like a domestic. Instead, he'd been generous to her and grateful for her ministrations— as a friend would be, not a master. And he'd never asked her to scrape and curtsey.

"Thank you, Mrs. Evans," Mr. Harden said.

Millie managed a little smile and swept out of the room. She closed the door behind her and stood for a moment in the hallway to catch her breath.

What would David say to him? Would he tell the minister how she'd tried to cheat him once and had nearly gotten him killed?

She bit her lip. Why should she fear that? David was a gentleman. Besides, she had already told Mr. and Mrs. Harden much of the tale herself. But how differently would the situation appear from David's viewpoint? And had she colored her account to show herself in a more favorable light than she deserved?

There was no sense fretting over it. Today was washday at the hotel, and she'd be busy all afternoon.

Dear Lord, it's up to You. If You want Mr. Stone to sully my reputation—well, I suppose I deserve it. Teach me not to be so proud. I've really no reason to think highly of myself. No reason at all.

Resolved to complete her day's work well, she gathered her skirt and flew down the stairs.

CHAPTER 22

David spent the most enjoyable hour he'd had since he left Oregon. Millie brought a tea tray fifteen minutes after the minister's arrival and retreated again with a cheerful wave, though she looked a bit tired. Now that he thought about it, Millie often had an air of fatigue. The innkeeper was probably demanding too much of her. He turned his attention back to his visitor, making a mental note to ask her about it later.

Joseph Harden was a most amiable man. He didn't swing every topic round to theology, but once they got into it, he turned out to have a most practical view of Christianity. He also knew the minister who had held the pulpit at the church David had attended many years ago, when he lived in Independence, but informed him that a different man now preached in that church.

David liked Harden and soon found himself revealing his situation in a general way—no specifics.

"Of course I never expected to inherit from my brother Richard. I thought he'd have a dozen progeny, and if anything should happen to prevent that, why then, our brother John would step up."

"So very tragic that you are the last brother," Mr. Harden said.

"Yes. Of course, I would gladly have given Richard's daughter a home, but an odd thing happened when she came to Oregon to find me."

"Oh? What was that?"

"She fell in love with a plain but honest man." David smiled, remembering how Anne would flush whenever Dan Adams came around. "He's a capital fellow, and he's making her a good husband."

"At least that part of the tale ends happily."

"Yes." David frowned as he recalled other moments in Oregon.

"What is your overall impression of Mrs. Evans?"

"Oh, she is most amiable, Mr. Stone, and she has a tender heart."

David considered that.

"You seem troubled by this assessment, sir," said Mr. Harden.

"Oh no, not at all," David said. "This past month, I've found her to be as you say." However, he kept thinking about the minister's words.

"Come now," Harden said. "You have known her longer than I have, haven't you?"

"Yes, I first met her more than eighteen months ago, out in western Oregon. But she was...considerably different then."

Mr. Harden's features sobered. "Yes. She has told my wife and me some about her past. I must say, we admire her. With God's help, she has made some commendable changes in her life, both inward and outward."

David eyed him in surprise. "She is now penniless and dependent upon the kindness of a slight acquaintance. How is that a better outward situation than when I first met her? She was staying then in a hotel a bit better than this one and dining well each day. She owned a horse, at least, and seemed to have no shortage of money."

"Ah, it is not up to me to divulge the things she told us, Mr. Stone. I assumed you knew her fairly well and what her life has been like since her husband died."

"I know she was not completely honest, if that is what you mean."

Mr. Harden smiled ruefully. "Shall we let it rest there, then? Let the cloak of charity cover her past transgressions. Millie Evans is now a sister in Christ. For all I can tell, she is sincere in her new faith, and she has given up her old habits. While she may not be affluent now, she has nothing to hide, and I assure you, your wallet is safe in her presence."

David froze for a moment. It sounded as though Millie had confessed her sins rather particularly to the pastor. If she were still in the fraud business, would she have done that? Or was this all part of an even larger, more sweeping scheme? He'd begun to trust her, but was that wise? One thing was certain—until he was 100 percent confident of her honesty, Millie must not learn about Stoneford.

He'd been extremely careful since their unexpected reunion not to let a word of his expectations pass his lips—to Millie, or to anyone else he met on the journey. He believed she remained ignorant of the title and fortune awaiting him in England. He intended that it should stay that way. Therefore, he would not now discuss the matter further, not even with a man of the cloth. He'd told Joseph Harden he must settle his brother's estate, but no more, and so it would remain.

"Mr. Harden, I do hope you won't take me amiss when I ask you not to reveal anything I've told you about my purpose in returning to England."

"Rest assured, it shall not leave my lips, sir. And how does the doctor say you are progressing?"

"Quite well, though from where I sit, it seems to be rather a slow process. He's letting me put a little weight on my leg now. I hope within a couple more weeks to cast aside the crutches and resume my journey."

"And Mrs. Evans will travel with you?"

David blinked at him. "We haven't discussed it recently. I had told her before our accident that I would give her enough for her ticket to Philadelphia, where she has friends. Now that I'm getting about a little, perhaps I should ask if she'd like to go on now. She need not wait for me."

"Indeed?"

"I'm sure I can tend my own needs now," David said uncertainly, glancing about the room. At the moment it was clean, but only because Millie had kept it so. Without her, when would his bed be changed again, or his shirts washed, or the floor swept? He supposed there were other hotel employees who did such tasks for other guests, but thanks to Millie, he hadn't had occasion to meet them.

When the minister took his leave, he smiled and extended his hand to David. "May I call upon you again, sir?"

"I should like that excessively. I'm afraid I suffer great boredom within these walls."

"Then I promise to return before too long."

"Thank you. I shall look forward to it." David smiled until his visitor was out the door, and then let out a low moan. His leg ached horribly, and he wanted only to get back to bed. But who would help him?

He struggled to rise but fell back into the chair with a painful thud.

A moment later there was a tap on the door.

"Come in!"

Millie peeked round the edge of the door. "I saw Mr. Harden leaving. Would you like some assistance?"

David gritted his teeth. "Yes, if it's not too much trouble."

She hurried into the room, her lovely face lined with worry. "Are you all right, sir?" She stooped and let him drape an arm over her shoulders. "There now, one—two—three."

David pushed himself upward. He couldn't help but notice how gentle she was, and yet she had the strength of a woman who knew hard work. He realized he was looking at her lovely hair and thinking how soft it must be. He looked away.

"Steady now." She stood still for a moment, letting him collect himself. "Ready?"

"Yes."

"It's only three steps."

He wanted to tell her he could make it just fine if she'd hand him the crutches, but the truth was he felt weak as a newborn colt. He let her support him as he hobbled the short distance. He tried not to lean too heavily on her, but he liked the way her shoulders were at just the right height for her to fit beneath his arm. They reached the bed, and he sat on the edge quite precipitously. She lifted his injured leg gently, swinging it onto the mattress.

"I should have laid back the covers," she said.

"Leave it," David gasped.

"Yes, I shall. Let me take off your shoe, and then I'll get you a blanket and some laudanum. Next time, perhaps you shouldn't sit up so long."

"I'll be fine." He spoke rather crossly, though he didn't intend to. It was her femininity that flummoxed him, he thought, and the fact that he liked her more and more without wanting to.

Millie only smiled. "Of course you will."

Peregrin lingered in New York three more days after he received his sister's letter. He hated to leave his nest at the Metropolitan, but on Friday night it became clear that he must waste no more time. That was the night Nigel Wallace's friend, Lionel Baxter, took him for every cent he had on him and a thousand dollars more in IOUs.

Appalled at his losses, as each hand played out, Peregrin insisted on going one more. Finally Nigel would hear no more and insisted it was time they cleared out. Peregrin was nine-tenths drunk, and Nigel dropped him off at the hotel and bribed the doorman to see him safely up to his room. It was a good thing Nigel was feeling generous, or Peregrin might have spent the night huddled on the sidewalk.

He awoke Saturday morning with a splitting headache. He put on his dressing gown and rang for breakfast. When the bellboy delivered it, Peregrin remembered he had no more cash. He would have to get to the bank Monday morning. He told the bellboy he'd tip him double when he got the ready, but the young man was not pleased.

He would surely spend a dull weekend, since he was short of funds. Why had he put so much in the bank, anyway? That was a mistake. He swallowed down the herb tea that was brewed to help dispel hangovers.

When his headache receded, Peregrin admitted to himself that he'd banked the larger part of his funds—two thousand dollars—as a safeguard against the very thing he'd done last night. And now he owed half of that to Lionel Baxter. He'd better pay Lionel off and hop a train to Independence. If he put off Merrileigh's business much longer, he might end up flat broke and unable to carry it out.

On the other hand, if he stayed in New York, Merry might send him some money.

He decided against asking, as it would probably take close to a month to receive her reply. She'd said nothing about sending more money in her letter, and he'd better not count on it. He'd left London with enough to keep any man in good shape for a year—he'd have been the first to say so. He'd gone through two-thirds of it in a couple of months. It was up to him to use the rest wisely.

He frowned at himself in the large, gilt-framed mirror. How could he have lost so much in one game? If he went back to Baxter's tonight...

No, that would never do. Baxter had said he wouldn't play with him again unless he put the money on the table. No more IOUs.

Wearily, Peregrin began to lather his shaving soap. He sorely missed his houseman, even though he'd had to share Hogg with his housemates in London.

Somewhere between the first nick on his chin and knocking the water pitcher over as he grabbed for a towel, it occurred to Peregrin that he could get his money from the bank on Monday and leave for Independence without paying a visit to Lionel Baxter. The fellows would have no idea where he'd gone to. He hadn't told even Nigel Wallace that he planned to go there, for fear of exposing his scheme with Merrileigh.

He liked the idea. He could disappear. With his two thousand dollars intact. He doubted Baxter would pursue him all the way across the Mississippi, even if he did get wind of his flight. Would he? A man might chase him across England for less, but England was such a small country, compared to this one.

Peregrin was just unbuttoning his shirt—he'd done it up wrong and came out with a button too many—when someone knocked on his door.

He stepped closer. "Who is it?"

"A friend of Lionel Baxter's."

Cautiously, Peregrin unlocked the door and opened it a crack.

A man the size of a plow horse shoved it open, throwing Peregrin back. The giant entered, with a companion close behind.

"I say," Peregrin stammered.

The giant tapped his palm with a stick about a foot and a half long. "Mr. Baxter says good morning. And don't forget to visit the bank first thing on Monday."

"Er. . .right." Peregrin looked from the man to his smaller but more sinister chum. The second man had a jagged scar running from one cheekbone to his chin. He stared ominously at Peregrin.

"Give him my best, won't you?" Peregrin tried to affect a carefree smile.

It slipped a little when the big man said, "Don't fail him, or you'll wish you'd never set foot in New York."

CHAPTER 23

When Dr. Lee paid his next call on David, Millie waited in the lobby until he came down the stairs, and then she followed him outside.

"How is Mr. Stone doing?" she asked.

"Ah, Mrs. Evans. I hoped I would see you. The patient was in a restless mood today. Apparently he overdid a bit yesterday."

"I'm afraid so. I shouldn't have let him sit up so long with his visitor. I didn't realize he was in pain the entire time."

The doctor nodded. "Give him the regular doses of laudanum today. Tomorrow he might slack off again, if he feels better. Now, you mustn't let him do too much too soon. And whatever he tells you, I think it would be unwise for him to travel for several more weeks."

Millie swallowed hard. "That long?"

"Yes. Perhaps another month. He's not healing as fast as a child would. But he is healing. That itching he complains of is part of it. But I won't remove the plaster for at least two weeks more. And even then, it will take him a little while to regain strength in those muscles."

"I see."

Dr. Lee nodded and untied his horse from the hitching rail. "Mr. Stone seemed to think you might be traveling on soon without him."

"I have no such intentions," Millie said.

"Good. I fear he'd injure himself again if you—or someone else capable—were not here to keep him from doing so."

"I shall stay as long as he'll put up with me," Millie said. "I hope that will be until he's ready to travel again."

820

"Excellent." Dr. Lee laughed. "I take it you have some history with him. He told me today that every time he's around you, he winds up injured."

Millie stared at him. "I should hope he didn't imply that I had anything to do with causing the stagecoach accident."

"Oh no, he said it in jest. I saw the scar on his shoulder and asked him about it. He said he'd suffered a gunshot wound not long after he'd met you. He didn't say the two events were connected—in fact, I got the feeling he made it sound that way just to get a laugh from me."

"Oh, I see. Actually, I hadn't seen him after he received that wound until we met again on a stagecoach this spring."

"Ah. Then it's as I thought—I shouldn't take seriously his allegation that you are a dangerous woman." The doctor winked at her and climbed into his buggy.

Millie stood for a long moment staring after him, her hands on her hips. Of all the disgraceful nerve.

David had found it hard to concentrate since the minister discussed Millie with him and told him that he believed her faith was genuine.

"Trust her, and let God handle the rest," Mr. Harden had said.

It appeared that Millie was now trustworthy, so far as money and trinkets were concerned. But what of his heart? That was a different matter, and David had no intention of entrusting it to her again. Not that he had been so foolish on their first acquaintance— but if the truth were told, it was a near thing.

Instead of the languid lady he'd met in Scottsburg, Oregon, or the shameless fraud, she was now a capable nursemaid and housekeeper. When he remembered her conduct after the stagecoach accident, David felt she should be made a brevet general for her valor in combat.

But that did not mean he wanted to form a permanent attach-ment with her. In fact, he intended to send her off soon. Very soon. If only Dr. Lee weren't so pessimistic. Surely he'd be able to fend for himself within a couple of weeks. He had made a joke of Millie's ministrations when the doctor asked about their relationship. The physician only wanted reassurance that David had a competent attendant, he was sure, but the topic was a delicate one. Sooner or later, he had to face it head-on.

The morning after Dr. Lee's visit, after much thought, David summoned the innkeeper, Mr. Simmons.

"How may I help you, Mr. Stone?" Simmons asked, approaching his bed with a smile that promised to meet any need—for a price.

"I should like to know how much I owe you, sir."

Simmons told him the total. "Will you be leaving us soon, sir?"

"No, not for at least two weeks, perhaps longer, but I'd like to keep my account short. Oh, and Mrs. Evans said she's been paying for her own board and lodging?"

"That's right, sir."

"Well, she's been a great help to me, and I'd like to give you enough to bring my bill and hers up to date and pay for the next fortnight in advance. Is that amenable?"

"Very much so."

David paid the man from his wallet, and a few minutes later Simmons left well content with his long-term guests.

Millie, however, seemed far from pleased when she brought up his supper that evening.

"Mr. Stone!"

"Ah, Millie." He'd loafed about all day and was tiring of his bed again. He nodded at the tray she carried. "Is that my supper?"

"It is."

"I should like to sit in the chair to eat it, if you don't mind."

She frowned but set the tray on top of the dresser. "I suppose you can, but when I say it's time to retire, you must obey."

He laughed. "And now you're my governess, it seems."

"Not I. Those are Doctor Lee's orders. You must be cautious."

She brought his robe and crutches, and after a bit of exertion and fussing about his dressing gown, he made it into the chair.

"Now, what is this about you paying my bill?" she asked.

"It's nothing. Bring the tray, please."

"Not until I hear a satisfactory answer. I am able to pay for my own expenses now, and you know it."

"How do I know it?" David asked.

"Because I told you so."

"But you might have need of your earnings when you travel on to Philadelphia."

"Then I shall have to earn some more."

David sighed. "Don't be difficult, Millie. Come now, I'm hungry. What's on the menu tonight?"

"A nice beefsteak, potatoes, squash, and some rather dry cornbread." She made no move to retrieve the tray.

"All right, going to be stubborn, are you?"

"Difficult times call for extreme measures."

David threw his hands up in exasperation. "Difficult times? You think a disagreement with me is a dire situation?"

"Indeed, sir." She regarded him with steady green eyes. "Through all our acquaintance, I think we've managed to be civil to one another."

"That's neither here nor there. You're wearing yourself out, and I won't have it."

"Oho."

"What?" he asked.

"Telling me what you will and won't have, so far as my behavior is concerned."

He clenched his teeth, seeing that he must take a new tack. "Millie."

"Yes sir?"

"It's only that I don't want you working day and night to earn your keep. You've been tending to me, and I'm happy to recompense you for your time and labor. You don't need to take on these other exhausting jobs."

"But you are feeling better now, sir. You've said so yourself. And so you will be needing less care, am I right?"

"Well, I hope that is true. I don't need dosing so often, and I think I shall soon be dressing myself without assistance."

"So I shall be getting more rest," Millie said. "I don't mind earning an honest living."

"I didn't say you should, madam." Really, she was impossible. He'd tried to smooth her way, and she was taking offense.

"Mr. Stone, I think we both agree that I should maintain my independence if I am able. You must admit that it was never your intention to support me."

He felt the blood rush to his face. "Well, no. Hardly."

"I rest my case, sir. And I shall be paying my own way from here on. I hope to earn enough by the time you've recovered to buy my own ticket to Philadelphia." She picked up the tray and brought it to him.

"I suppose everything is cold by now." He picked up the napkin and spread it over his front.

"Oh, and you're going to get crotchety again?" She placed her hands on her hips and glared at him. "Mr. Stone—"

"Now, Millie, I don't know what's gotten into you, but you've 'Mr. Stoned' me too many times. You told me recently to call you by your given name, and I believe I once asked you to use mine. So why can't we be on equal footing?"

She lowered her gaze, and her cheeks went pink. "That was a long time ago, sir."

"Yes, I suppose it was. But you don't mind my calling you Millie."

"I thought it would be easier for you. More natural."

He thought about that, and he didn't like the implications.

"Oh. So you think I'm used to ordering servants about, is that it? You suppose I look on you as I would a scullery maid or an undercook?"

"Well. . ." She turned away and spread up the covers on his bed.

"I do not see you in that way, and if you insist on calling me 'Mr. Stone,' then I shall go back to 'Mrs. Evans.'"

"Whatever you wish. Now eat your supper, or it really will be cold."

"I don't suppose. . ." He glanced toward the dresser.

"What, you want me to read? We've finished *The Black Tulip*. I hoped to find a volume of Dickens at the ordinary, but the only one they had was *David Copperfield*, and you told me you've read that."

"Well, perhaps you could read me a chapter or two from the Psalms."

She froze for a moment, then nodded. "I shall be happy to."

She fetched his new Bible from the dresser—the one he'd bought in Oregon after she made off with the other—and drew a chair close.

"Any special chapter?"

"I've always been fond of the thirty-seventh."

She turned to it and read it with great spirit, as though giving a dramatic recitation. When she lowered the book, she sighed. "I don't think I've ever read that before. It's lovely."

"Millie."

"Yes?"

"Why did you take my Bible?"

For a long moment, she was silent.

"I don't really know. I thought you were dead when I took it, and I was feeling horribly guilty. I saw it lying there in the hotel room, and I was curious about you. When I opened it, I saw that you'd marked some of the verses, and I thought perhaps I could learn more about you if I read what you'd thought was important. I never knew anyone who wrote in a Bible before—well, except births and deaths. But I thought you'd been a very special man, and I'd gotten you killed. And I—well, I just took it."

He felt as though he'd missed something important—something crucial to Millie's story. He also knew that when he returned to England, he would never look at servants in quite the same way.

Peregrin waited until eleven o'clock Monday morning before going to the bank. For one thing, he'd slept late. For another, he didn't want to run into Lionel Baxter's "friends."

He kept a sharp eye out as he left the Metropolitan and hurried down the street. He wished he could afford a cab, but thanks to the two ruffians, he hadn't a cent until he made his withdrawal from the bank.

Instead of just getting out Baxter's thousand, or that much plus a bit more for his ordinary expenses, Peregrin closed his account.

"Leaving us, are you, sir?" the teller asked.

"Yes, I'm—" Peregrin caught himself and avoided blurting out his destination. One never knew who was listening. "I'm headed for Boston."

"Boston? Ah, well have a good journey." The teller counted out his money and smiled at him.

"Thank you." Peregrin put half the bills in his wallet and split the rest between a couple of pockets. If he were held up—as he'd learned New Yorkers were apt to be—he didn't want to lose all of his cash.

He hurried back to his hotel room and began to pack. What he wouldn't give to have Hogg there to do it for him! He supposed he could ring for the bellboy, but then he'd have to tip him.

He threw his clothes and toilet articles, along with his stationery, into his valise. He decided to leave the bottle of ink, though he hadn't used a quarter of it. Such a mess it would make if it leaked on his limited wardrobe.

On second thought, he ought to send a note to Merrileigh. With a sigh, he unpacked his silver pen and stationery case. After a moment's thought he scrawled,

> *Yr letter rec'd. I am going to Freedom to visit my friend, Donald*

Peregrin scratched his head, trying to recall the name Merrileigh had invented. It started with *S*. That was all he could remember. After a couple of minutes he gave up and wrote "Smith."

> *. . .Donald Smith. I am told the Sanders is a good hostelry there. You may direct any correspondence to me there.*

He considered what he'd written and wondered what sort of chaos that would cause. Would Randolph or somebody else send him mail at the nonexistent town of Freedom? Or maybe there was a town by that name. Oh well, Merrileigh would have to figure it out.

Now to get to the train station undetected. He briefly considered leaving without paying the hotel bill, but that seemed counter-productive. Lionel Baxter wouldn't alert the police to his transgressions at the card table, but the hotel manager would call them in a second if he realized a guest had left without paying up. No way around it.

He carried his bags down and stopped at the front desk.

"Checking out."

The desk clerk looked at him in surprise and said, rather loudly, "What? Leaving us, Mr. Walmore?"

Peregrin looked over his shoulder then leaned toward the man. "I'd like to keep it quiet. You see, my—my friend is always after me to borrow money, and I'd prefer he didn't know where I've gone—or even that I've gone, if you take my meaning—at least for a while." He slipped a dollar bill across the counter.

"Oh yes, I see, sir. Just a moment, and I'll total your account. You just paid on Friday, so it won't be much. Would you like the doorman to call a hansom for you while you wait?"

"Er, yes, that would be fine. And could I leave this letter here for the post?"

At last he was able to get away. He paid his bill, paid for the letter to England, tipped the doorman, paid the driver when they got to the station, and gave him an extra dime for a tip. Peregrin went inside, bought a ticket, and tipped a porter for carrying his valise to the platform. All the while he felt his life's blood was trickling away with the coins. The large amounts he'd lost at the gaming table weren't the half of it. It was this daily drain on his funds that had brought him to this pass.

He boarded one of the passenger cars and huddled in a seat near the back of the carriage, watching the doors with apprehension until they closed. At last the train set off westward, and he was reasonably sure the thugs hadn't followed him.

CHAPTER 24

I don't see why you can't go down to the dining room for dinner tonight." Dr. Lee eyed David's leg in its plaster cast critically. "Take it easy, and have a stout fellow to lean on, and if you need it, get two to help get you back up again."

"I'll be fine," David said.

"I know you think that, but it's been six weeks since you took a flight of stairs, let alone two. It will be a big exertion, and you may need to rest awhile before you come back up to your room."

"Don't you worry about me."

The doctor shook his head. "I won't waste time worrying, but I shall have a word with Mrs. Evans before I leave. One thing about her—I know that if she's on duty, you'll mind."

David's jaw dropped, but he quickly closed his mouth. He did have a point. Millie bossed him around like she did everyone else, now that he was getting better. "Time to practice walking in the hall," she would say, with no room for protest, and "Don't toss your laundry on the floor, sir," and "Surely you can do that for yourself now."

"Remember," the doctor said, closing his bag, "you have a compound fracture that is still healing. I know it seems like it's been a long while, but it would be easy to overdo now. Go slowly, and build up your activity gradually. Keep using the crutches for a few days at least, until you feel steady. I'll bring you a cane next time I come."

"So, when can I travel?"

Dr. Lee hesitated. "Not for a while yet. I'd like to take the cast off next week, and I would like to see you at least one more time after that. We'll see if you get your strength up. Then we'll talk about travel."

When the doctor had left, David got up and walked slowly to the window, stepping gingerly on his left foot. His leg ached a little, but that would pass in time—Dr. Lee had said so.

About fifteen minutes later, Millie arrived with his clean laundry.

"I'm going downstairs for supper tonight," David said eagerly. "The doctor said I may."

She smiled indulgently. "I saw him, and he told me. That's wonderful." She opened a drawer and tucked a few clean garments into the dresser. "I asked Billy to come up at five o'clock and help you downstairs."

"Who is Billy?"

She frowned at him. "He's the young man who carries luggage for people. He's been in this room at least a hundred times since we've been here. Don't you know his name?"

"He told me it was Wilfred."

"So it is, but his friends call him Billy."

That struck David as odd—foremost because Millie was implying that she was Billy's friend. It also seemed to him that a boy named Wilfred ought to be called Willie or Fred.

"So he'll still answer to Wilfred?"

"I should think so, especially if you give him a half dime for his trouble."

"Ah." David peered at Millie, but her green eyes were inscrutable. Did she think he was treating Wilfred in that "servant" way? Perhaps he was, but he didn't think it would be proper to treat the young man like a chum. "I suppose I should put on a clean shirt and a tie if I'm going into the dining room."

"Trust me, the dining room here is very informal. However, I'd be happy to lay those things out for you if you wish." Millie stepped toward the armoire.

"Thank—" David stopped short. He ought to be doing things for himself now. After all, he was able. And Millie wouldn't be with him forever. "I can do it," he said.

"All right. And are you content with those trousers?" She looked his pants up and down.

David squelched his natural embarrassment. He was too old to blush when a woman looked him over. "Well, I guess I'll have to be, since they're the only pair I own that fits, at least until I'm rid of this cast."

"Yes, that's true." She walked over and stooped, then twitched the material at the level of his knee. "Stand up and let me adjust that. I think I can do it a little better, so the pins don't show." She held up his crutches while he positioned himself.

"Hmm." Millie tugged and fussed with the fabric. "I suppose I could baste you into them."

"Is that necessary?"

"No, I don't think so." Finally she stood. "There. You'll pass. Now, is there anything else I can do for you, or shall I see you in the dining room?"

"Meet me there," he said. "It will be like old times."

An odd look crossed her face, and he wished his comment hadn't slipped out. The less they thought about Scottsburg, the better.

Peregrin arrived in Independence at dusk on a Sunday. He'd waited out two days of rain in St. Louis, at a dismal hotel with bland food and sluggish room service. The train he'd ridden from there to Independence had nearly deafened him, and he had several small holes in his suit, where cinders had fallen. But he was here at last.

He had several ideas on how he would find David Stone. The town was not very large, and there couldn't be many hotels a gentleman would patronize. More to the point, how would he stop David from going on to England?

He'd half expected to find the town buttoned down for the Sabbath, especially at this hour of the day. To his surprise, he found that the West was apparently as rowdy as it was rumored to be. Taverns and saloons esteemed all days alike and kept their doors open. Some of them, in fact, had no proper doors, but only hinged panels that reached neither the threshold nor the lintel. Men were entering and emerging from these watering holes in steady streams.

Peregrin decided to stop at one first thing and get rid of the smell of the locomotive.

The hotel he'd heard about, to which he was duly directed by two somewhat inebriated loafers and a bartender, turned out to be not a tenth as good as the one he'd left in New York, and Peregrin mourned his losses, especially when he learned that this one charged nearly as much as the Metropolitan had.

"I say," he sputtered to the desk clerk, who hadn't a proper desk at all, but a wobbly table in the entry hall. "How can you charge so much for such a small, shabby room?"

"Think of all the trouble we must take to bring in supplies, mister." The clerk looked him testily in the eye. "Everything in this place was floated up the river. It takes a lot of muscle to freight in amenities."

"Hmpf." Peregrin looked him up and down. "Well, I'd like a bath in my room, and when I'm done, I'll have you send up my supper by room service; there's a good chap."

The clerk stared at him for a moment. A smile spread slowly over his face.

"Ain'tchu somethin'? We don't do no room service, mister, and the closest place you can get a hot bath is down the street. The laundry on the corner will give you one if you treat 'em nice and show your silver." He looked down at Peregrin's baggage, which he'd dropped on the floor while signing the register. "Oh, and you'll have to haul your own truck upstairs tonight. Jojo's sick."

Peregrin shook his head and stooped to pick up his bags. There had to be a better hotel in this town. There just had to be. He couldn't imagine Anne Stone staying in this monstrosity, but he was sure he'd heard she'd gone overland to Oregon, and chances were pretty good she had passed through this place.

The room was tiny and none too clean. He put his bags next to the bed, freshened up, and went out again in search of supper. Apparently this hotel served only breakfast to its patrons. On the street, he met a pair of rudely dressed men. If the filthy state of their clothing was any indication, they came straight from a farm into town without cleaning up first.

"Say, gents, is there a good place to put on the feed bag near here?" he asked, smiling brightly.

They stared at him.

"What did you say?" one asked.

"Is there an eatery close by?"

"Oh. Surely." The rustic turned and pointed. "Up yonder to the corner and turn left. Casey's."

"Thank you," Peregrin said.

The other man elbowed his companion. "Of course, if it's drink you be wantin'. . . ."

"Oh? And where might a man find a glass or two and a card game?" Peregrin asked. He'd learned in New York that Americans played more poker than anything else, so he didn't ask for a game of whist or faro.

"You oughta come with us if you've a mind to sit in on a game," the first man said.

"Can I get something to eat there?" Peregrin asked, torn between his empty stomach's needs and his love of gambling.

"Sure—well, maybe. Or you can go eat at Casey's and come on down to the Bear Paw afterwards."

It was a difficult decision, but Peregrin decided to get a meal under his belt first thing. He knew his head would stay clearer for the game if he put something solid down first. His two new friends told him how to get to the Bear Paw, slapped him on the back, and sent him on his way.

Millie asked Mrs. Simmons, who held sway over the dining room, to hold a small table in reserve. She went back to her room and freshened up and then waited near the bottom of the stairs as Billy went up to help David.

Getting him down the two flights of stairs took its toll, as Dr. Lee had predicted. David had apparently insisted on leaving his crutches behind. Millie frowned, but perhaps that was wise—they might be too cumbersome on the stairs. The satisfaction on David's face when he reached the bottom testified that he felt it was worth the trouble.

"Mr. Stone, you're looking very chipper." She stepped forward and took his arm. "Thank you so much, Billy." David didn't reach for a coin—he seemed preoccupied with maintaining his balance—so she took a half dime from her pocket and passed it to Billy.

"Thanks, Miz Evans," he said, pulling at his forelock.

"Oh," David said, blinking at her. "I should have—"

"Forget it. Let's get you to a chair. I asked Mrs. Simmons to let us have one of the smaller tables, over to the side, so we won't be right in the middle of the traffic."

In the doorway, David paused, looking around a bit anxiously at the roomful of townspeople, farmers, and adventurers. "Is it always this busy?"

"Supper is very popular here. You know Mrs. Simmons is an excellent cook—you've been eating her meals for some time now."

"Yes." David walked slowly with her along one side of the crowded room to their table.

If Mrs. Simmons weren't such an accomplished cook, Millie reflected, she might have had a chance of getting a job in the kitchen here instead of doing laundry and cleaning. She would have much preferred cooking—but Mrs. Simmons also had a sharp tongue and was very jealous of her territory. Keeping out of the kitchen was no doubt less stressful than the job of cook's helper, even if the work Millie did now was harder physically.

Once they were seated, a homely girl whom she had learned was the Simmonses' niece came to stand beside the table.

"What can I get you folks?" she asked.

David stared up into her abundantly freckled face for a moment, then looked across at Millie.

"You like the fried chicken," Millie said. "Today they also have corn chowder, beef stew, and pork cutlets."

"Ah." David looked less lost. "I'll try the chowder, and then I'll have some chicken. What about you?"

"I'll have the beef stew, please, and biscuits."

"Put Mrs. Evans's meal on my bill, won't you?" David said cordially.

"No, don't do that." Millie frowned at him and leaned across the table. "Mr. Simmons allows me my meals as part of my wages."

"I see." David raised his eyebrows and smiled at the waitress. "Cancel that last request."

"Yes sir. Would you like coffee?"

"Gallons of it."

When the girl had gone to give their order, Millie smiled at him. "Does it feel good to be out in company again?"

"Very good. In fact, I feel so well that I think I'll be able to fend for myself soon."

She nodded and spread the calico napkin in her lap. "Now that you're getting about more, perhaps we could ask Mr. Simmons if he can give you a room on the first floor—or at least the second."

"That would make things easier," David said, "though I do hate the bother of moving."

She smiled at that but said nothing. David resisted any sort of change in his routine when it was first proposed. She'd found it surprising in such an energetic man, but she'd decided it was his way of trying to retain some control in his helpless condition.

"Dr. Lee says I'm not quite ready to resume my journey," David continued, "but I see no reason for you to remain here."

"I. . .beg your pardon." She hadn't supposed he wished her gone just yet, though Dr. Lee had said David mentioned the possibility. She looked across the table into his blue eyes. "I'm not displeased to stay a bit longer."

"Surely you'd rather get on to Philadelphia and get settled. I know you've been anxious to get to your friends and find a permanent situation."

His smile made her heart flutter. How could he be so charming while pushing her away?

Her cheeks grew warm, and she looked down at the tablecloth. "Do you wish me to leave?"

"I wish you to be happy and secure, Millie. You've been very kind and generous with your time and attention, but I can manage now, if you want to go."

The freckled girl, Sarah, came with her tray and put a plate of biscuits on the table between them. Carefully, she eased a bowl of stew off and set it before Millie, then presented David with his corn chowder.

"Butter, jam, and salt is yonder," she said, nodding toward a sideboard where the guests were expected to help themselves. "Anything else?"

"Just the coffee," David said with a smile. Indeed, he seemed to have regained his pleasant demeanor and left the crotchety complaining up in the third-story room.

"Oops. I'll bring it straightaway." The girl whirled about, her skirts billowing.

Millie couldn't help smiling. This *was* like Scottsburg, in some ways, though she no longer tried to beguile him into buying her meals. But she'd enjoyed his company immensely then—as she did now, when he wasn't talking of getting rid of her.

"Now, Millie—"

She stifled her laugh with her napkin. He'd sworn not to call her that anymore unless she used his first name.

He eyed her suspiciously. "What?"

She shook her head and waved one hand. If she told him what amused her, he'd make sure he stuck to his hasty proclamation, and she didn't want him to go back to formalities with her. But if she called him "David," would he think she was trying to coax him into friendship as she had once before? She didn't want to summon back his distrust.

He frowned but went on, "I was only going to say that you should go on as soon as you can. It's August already, and you'll want to get to Phila—"

"Would you please stop talking about that?" she asked, more sharply than was necessary. She lowered her gaze. So much for convincing him she was no longer a woman of the rough frontier.

"I beg your pardon."

David was staring at her. She could feel it. After several seconds, she looked up at him.

"You aren't eating."

"I'm wondering if I've made you cross," he said.

"No, I—" She sighed. "Mr. Stone, if it's all the same to you, I'd rather stay."

"Stay? In Independence? Do you mean. . .you want to settle here, instead of going on to Philadelphia? I realize you've made some friends here. The Hardens—"

Millie shook her head vigorously. "That's not what I mean. I'd like to stay with you until you're certain that you're well. If you don't mind, that is. Mr. Stone, I have no desire to surfeit you with my company. If you truly wish for me to leave. . ."

Now he was smiling, almost gleefully. Millie's cheeks flushed. Was she making a complete fool of herself?

"As a friend," she said hastily. "I feel a certain responsibility to you now, since you were so kind to me, and I wish to stay as long as I can be of help to you."

David said nothing for a long moment. Finally he nodded. "All right. I don't mind, but there are two things we must address."

What on earth? She shot him a keen gaze, but his eyes still held a hint of amusement, and she looked down at her plate. She really was hungry, and the beef stew smelled delicious. She reached for her spoon.

"What two things?"

"First of all, *Mrs. Evans*—"

She winced involuntarily.

David, on the other hand, grinned. "I knew it. You hate for me to call you that."

She shrugged and said carelessly, "It's my name."

"Yes, but I'd rather call you Millie."

She said nothing, knowing what was coming next.

"Or Charlotte, or whatever you desire," David said softly, almost caressingly.

Her cheeks now felt as if they were on fire. "Please. You know that 'Charlotte' was a ruse. In short, I lied to you back then. I don't lie anymore. My real name is Mildred."

"A lovely name. May I use it instead of Millie?"

She nearly strangled to get out, "As you wish."

"Ah. Thank you. And I also wish you would call me David."

"For old times' sake?" she asked cynically.

"No. Not at all. I should like to mark this as the beginning of a new phase in our acquaintance."

"What is the second matter?" she asked uneasily, not willing to commit to anything yet, even something so small as how to address him.

"The second matter—"

"Here you are, Mr. Stone."

Sarah arrived with the coffeepot so precipitously that she bumped into the table, and Millie feared she would slop hot coffee all over David. She opened her mouth to issue a sharp rebuke but clamped it shut. The new Mildred would hold her peace and let the gentleman deal with it.

"Oh, I'm so sorry." A few drops of coffee had sloshed on the table.

"Think nothing of it," David said. He set his cup closer to Sarah so that she could fill it more easily.

"Is there anything else I can bring you?"

"No, thank you."

When she was gone again, David inhaled deeply and looked over at Millie.

"Now, where were we?"

"Your dinner is getting cold." Millie took a bite of her stew.

"So it is. But I'd like to put this traveling matter to rest."

"Oh? Then perhaps we shouldn't discuss it any further."

David frowned and shook his head. "No, I want to settle it. I still need help, Mildred. I admit that. If you leave, I'll probably have to hire someone for the next couple of weeks. If you truly wish to stay, I'd be happy to have you continue as my—shall we say, my aide?"

Millie took a sip of water but had trouble swallowing around the lump in her throat. She blotted her lips and finally met his gaze. "Yes, David. I accept."

He smiled. "Good." Then he frowned. He looked as though he would speak again, but instead he began to eat his chowder.

CHAPTER 25

"Y ou win again, Cy," crowed the fellow called Jim. He grinned around at the others, showing his brownish teeth. "We'uns are goin' to lose our shirts if this keeps up."

Peregrin lifted his glass and took a swig of his beer. Most of the players at the table were locals, but a couple were men just passing through town. Cy, Jim, and the shaggy man known as Beater, which Peregrin optimistically assumed was his surname—though it seemed many a man jettisoned his real name when he crossed the Mississippi—gathered at the Bear Paw nearly every night to play poker. They must win a good portion of the time, or they wouldn't be able to sustain the regular game.

They probably viewed Peregrin as one of the well-feathered strangers, ready to be plucked. Well, he'd have to teach them a thing or two. They had no idea what sort of card player they were up against.

Last night, they'd jollied him along and played the game almost carelessly. Peregrin had listened to their stories of the frontier and stood them all a couple of drinks. But tonight they were joined by two strangers, and the three locals seemed more serious, more intent, and more ruthless. Peregrin had come out three dollars to the good last night, and they'd parted with a general feeling of camaraderie. But tonight—tonight he got the feeling the boys were out for blood.

Beater proved it when he raised the ante by a hundred dollars, not the customary dollar or two. Surprised the man could lay claim to that much, Peregrin eyed his hand dubiously. Did he want to lose that much, along with the easterner whom Beater seemed eager to trounce? His beer hadn't yet clouded his judgment too much. He didn't stand a chance of winning this round.

He looked over at Cy. Peregrin had learned last night that the scruffy farmer had sixty acres outside of town. Cy and his two buddies had seemed to like the Englishman, and they'd treated him like a long-lost chum. Did they still feel that way? Or had he been bumped into the same class with the other newcomers tonight?

Cy winked at him. Peregrin felt suddenly wiser—and smarter than the travelers who'd dared to take on these fellows.

"I'm out." Peregrin folded his cards. Let Beater take this one. He'd jump back in on the next hand.

Cy nodded. "How about you fetch us another drink, Perry?"

"Glad to." Peregrin rose and walked to the bar just a little less steadily than usual.

Merrileigh would be proud of him for keeping his head.

"Listen to this," David said eagerly. He stood leaning on his crutches while Millie adjusted his clothing, and in his hand was a letter from his niece.

"Hold still, please. I'm trying to fasten these hooks." Millie tried not to let the impatience she felt show in her attitude. She'd spent three hours yesterday shopping for the right trousers and a piece of material that would match—or near enough that no one would notice. It had taken her half of today to alter the pants to her satisfaction.

"Are you sure this will look all right in church?" David asked.

"Yes, I'm sure." Millie had slit the inside seam on the left pant leg and inserted a gusset of the extra black cloth. Then she'd sewn a row of tiny hooks and eyes beneath the flap of material. If her painstaking work didn't pay off, she would be sorely disappointed.

"Well, you must hear Anne's news. I'm delighted that she and Daniel have added a little Adams to the family."

"What?" Millie blinked up at him. "I had no idea."

"No, well... Anyway, they have."

"That's wonderful." Of course he, being a gentleman, would never have mentioned that Anne was in a delicate condition. Still, it felt odd, having been so close to David these past four months and not having known anything about it.

"They've named him Richard, after Anne's father."

"Oh, how nice." Millie could barely see the dark little hooks against the black fabric, but at last she managed to fasten the last one. "There!" She sat back on her heels. "I think no one will have an inkling that you're wearing a cast."

"Won't my left. . .limb. . .look fatter than my right?"

"Well of course, but who will notice? If you wear your nice frock coat, and with the crutches—"

"I shan't use the crutches."

She looked up into his stubborn gaze. "I see."

"I shall be fine with the cane." David flicked a glance toward the stick lying on the bed.

"Well, your one leg is a bit out of proportion, but the black cloth helps hide that. I really think this is the best we can do."

"Hmpf."

What was he thinking? When he got that faraway look in his eyes, she couldn't follow him.

"Do you have a better idea?" She almost hoped he didn't, as it would negate all her labor.

"If I were in London, I'd wear a caped greatcoat."

"Ah. Well, we're not, and I don't think I could find one of those in Independence, especially not in August. You'd look more peculiar wearing a heavy woolen coat in this heat than you do with an odd leg."

He winced, and she supposed he felt she was being indelicate. Of course she wouldn't chatter on about a gentleman's legs in public. She wouldn't so much as glance at them. But he didn't know how discreet she could be.

She stood and reached for the cane. "Take a turn down the hallway, and see what you think."

He did so, holding himself almost straight. She could tell he attempted to limp as little as possible. When he came back into the room, she tilted the mirror on top of the dresser.

"Look in here. Tell me if you don't see a fine gentleman."

David looked grudgingly. "I suppose it will have to do."

"Yes. If you wish to go to church this week, it will."

"And there's no way Dr. Lee would consent to remove the cast tomorrow?"

"No way on this green earth."

He sighed. "All right then. And you've spoken for a buggy?"

"I have. A driver will bring it here Sunday morning in plenty of time. I shall return it after our outing."

She could tell he wasn't entirely satisfied with that arrangement, but she wasn't about to change it now. She gathered up her sewing things and put them in the small bag where she stored them.

"Now, if you'll excuse me, I need to put in a few hours working for the Simmonses this afternoon. I shall see you at supper."

David's expression fell even more. "Of course. And thank you."

She wished she hadn't mentioned her work, but she'd taken the equivalent of nearly a full day off, unpaid, to see him decently clothed for church. Mrs. Simmons had a long list of chores she'd wanted completed this morning. Millie would do well to finish it by evening. If only David had been content to wear the pinned trousers to church! But no. She could understand his feeling on that. She didn't think he was an especially vain man, but who could feel confident with pins and a streak of plaster showing? It would be worse than a lady allowing her petticoats to show.

After four days of gambling and wending home to his cramped hotel room half drunk in the early morning, Peregrin came to a decision. It came about when he woke past noon with a violent headache and five hundred dollars less than he'd had the day before.

He examined himself distrustfully in the mirror. His eyes were bloodshot, his hair matted, his face covered in an unbecoming stubble—and his hands shook so badly he didn't dare shave.

Turning away in disgust, he cursed the shabby hotel. In New York he'd have rung for a houseman and asked for a drink and a moderate breakfast. He could even get someone to shave him there.

Here, he was on his own.

Sinking down on the edge of the narrow bed, he considered what to do. First, he decided, he would dress and go downstairs to partake of breakfast. A look at his watch disabused him of that notion. It was closer to dinnertime, and he couldn't get a midday meal here. He would seek out a restaurant and then look for a better hotel. His pitcher held water, and he poured some in a cup. A swig of the lukewarm liquid took away some of the stale dryness in his mouth. With trembling hands, he dressed and added another task to his mental list: find that laundry where he could get a bath. Both his clothes and his person badly needed cleansing.

Finally he brushed his hair almost flat and made a fair attempt at shaving. It took him awhile to staunch the bleeding from the three nicks he made, but at last he felt he was ready to venture into the daylight world of Independence.

Once more he faced his reflection.

"Buck up, old boy."

He scowled at himself. He couldn't keep on like this. Freedom from responsibility was nice to a point, and he enjoyed not having anyone looking over his shoulder and scolding him when he behaved badly. But he knew he must change his ways, or he'd wind up penniless. His luck had turned sour since he'd come to America, and he had enough sense left to know that this wasn't the time to push it.

He needed to stop both drinking to excess and losing money. Immediately. If he went on the way he was, he'd be penniless within a week.

And he needed to do two positive things, also at once: find better lodgings and start looking for David Stone.

Millie considered it a triumph when she got David to church on Sunday. Not that he resisted—in fact, he was eager to go. The Hardens had invited them to take dinner at the parsonage after the service.

Getting David dressed and groomed for church was her first

challenge in the morning. She got ready early, putting on her brown traveling dress and her best hat. She sent Billy to set out David's shaving things and help him into his clean smallclothes and a shirt she'd starched and ironed to perfection, along with the modified trousers. When she came upon the scene, David was tying his necktie, and Billy was hovering with the cane. Apparently Billy had managed all the hooks, as she couldn't discern from two yards distant where the gusset met the seam.

David looked so handsome, she caught her breath and studied his reflection in the looking glass. His face seemed to have dropped ten years. She realized that she had grown accustomed to the lines and pallor the pain had brought to his face since the accident. Now he seemed more like the dashing gentleman she'd first met in Oregon. Not young, but certainly not old. A man in his prime.

She noted that he was also looking at her in the mirror. His hands had stilled with the ribbon half tied, and his blue eyes searched her face for—what?

Smiling, she stepped forward. "Don't you look fine? Billy, thank you for helping Mr. Stone this morning."

"Yes'm." Billy ducked his head in acknowledgment and sneaked a glance at David.

"Give him two bits, will you, Mildred?"

She went to the bedside table, where David's latest reading material and a few coins lay near the lamp. Twenty-five cents was an awfully large tip for the boy, but she didn't argue. David was in a sunny mood this morning, and who was she to dispute his largesse?

"Thank you," Billy muttered. He turned to observe David, who had finished with his necktie and now reached for his frock coat. "Help you, sir?"

Billy held the coat and handed David his cane as he turned.

"Thank you, Wilfred," David said. "Will you be able to help me down the stairs now?"

"Surely can, sir."

"Good. Let me just get my wallet."

"Shall I bring your Bible?" Millie asked.

"Thank you."

She picked it up from the dresser and placed her own smaller brown one on top. These and her handbag she carried down in the wake of the two men. David really was doing better these days, though he still had to pause on each step and make sure he was balanced before venturing to the next.

The buggy was waiting, with the driver's saddle horse tied behind it. When David was seated and Millie had taken the reins, the driver tipped his hat and rode off on the horse.

"Let me drive," David said.

Millie eyed him askance. "Do you think you're ready?"

"Of course I'm ready. It's my leg that was injured this time."

She flinched at the "this time," a flagrant reminder that she'd as good as caused his earlier shoulder wound. Well, it wasn't her fault that the stage had overturned.

"I'm in the driver's seat," she pointed out.

"So what? I'm sure the horse won't mind, so long as I adjust the reins."

She wanted to dig her heels in, but it struck her suddenly that the mood for the day lay in her lap. Did she want a peevish, out-of-sorts man with an acerbic tongue to accompany her today, or a charming gentleman who'd had his first opportunity in months to drive? She suspected that men of David's social caliber looked upon their right to drive the same way some women regarded their right to pour tea.

She said no more but handed over the reins and whip.

They reached the church in good time, as David didn't allow the horse to slack. She helped him to the ground and then unhitched the horse, led him into the shed beside the church, and covered him with a blanket the owner had provided. During this interval, David stood waiting and frowning. Did he think he was in danger of being perceived as a lesser man because the woman accompanying him tended the horse? Such notions bordered on the ridiculous, but Millie could see this wasn't the time to say so.

"Didn't you used to live in Independence?" she asked as she

removed the horse's bridle.

"Yes. Five years. I kept a mercantile."

"Do you want to visit any of your old acquaintances, now that you're feeling better?"

"Don't think so."

Millie was not too surprised at this—more than a decade had passed since David's move to Oregon. A lot of the people he'd known in Independence had probably moved on, too. Apparently he hadn't formed close friendships here in the past, which made for fewer complications now—though the distraction of a larger social circle might have been welcome during the healing phase.

When she was ready, she took their Bibles and her purse from the buggy. David offered his left arm and carried the cane in his right hand. He halted only a little as they walked to the church door.

When they reached the heavy portal, he pulled on the handle and staggered a bit, catching himself with his cane. Millie grabbed the edge of the door and put her strength into the pull. Together they got it open, and David leaned against it.

He caught his breath and nodded. "After you, madam."

He was treating her like a lady. Not that he'd ever disdained her, but when they'd embarked on the stagecoach journey, he'd held himself aloof and made it plain that he wanted nothing to do with her. Now he was going as far as his health would allow to be courteous—beyond that, to pay small but welcome attention to her.

Millie smiled at him. "Thank you."

The church pews were about half-filled, and Mr. Harden was just taking his place on the platform at the front.

"I see a place there." Millie pointed as discreetly as she could to a half-empty bench near the back.

David nodded, waited until she laced her hand once more through the crook of his arm, and then led her toward it.

"She's a hard worker," David said, watching Millie from a distance. He and Pastor Harden sat in the parsonage garden, talking and drinking coffee in the shade while Millie and Mrs. Harden strolled about looking at the hostess's flowerbeds. Apparently Mrs. Harden loved to garden and used her blooms in decorating the sanctuary.

"Does that surprise you?" Joseph Harden asked.

"Some. When I first met Millie, I saw her more as a lady of leisure. A woman of means."

"But you've told me that was a false impression."

"Yes." It still troubled David. "She's always working now. She says that I don't need her, so she can spend all day cleaning and doing laundry for other people."

"She wants to support herself. To prove she's not helpless—or dependent on you."

David nodded. "I suppose you're right. One thing she was then and is still—she's independent. I think she hated having to rely on me. But I didn't mind helping her." After a moment, his conscience prompted him to add, "Well, maybe at first. I was afraid she saw me as easy pickings—again."

"But you don't think that now?" Harden said.

"No. I've watched her long enough to know this new attitude of hers is genuine. A lazy person wouldn't keep up the drudgery so long. And most thieves are lazy."

"Mildred has told my wife and me quite a bit about her early life." The minister eyed him thoughtfully. "It's not my place to reveal any of that to you, but I believe we know her well enough to assure you that she has truly changed her ways. She wants to please God now, and she's contrite about some of the things she did in the past—including the plot she became involved in that nearly killed you."

"She's told me she didn't know that fellow wanted me dead."

"And we believe her." Mr. Harden sipped his coffee.

"Did she tell you how she got her Bible?"

The minister smiled. "Yes, she did. And she said she had some cockeyed notion at first that if she read from it, she'd atone somehow for what she'd done. But the message touched her heart, Mr. Stone. I firmly believe Millie is a true sister in Christ now."

David watched the two women and mulled that over. Would

this have mattered to him ten years ago? It did now, but for most of his life, faith had not been the prime criterion he considered in a woman. Instead, if he were looking for a wife, he would look at her family's pedigree, her appearance, her manners, and her fortune or lack of one.

Millie had no family to be proud of. The only one of her relatives David had met died while committing a robbery. She was pretty, in an earthy way, with her glossy auburn hair and green eyes. Her complexion was quite good, and when she was able, she dressed well. But today she wore a simple brown dress that had neither style nor allure. He studied her posture and her manner as she conversed with Mrs. Harden, and he found nothing to criticize. Of course she didn't have two dimes to rub together. But was fortune really that important?

"You have long thoughts, Mr. Stone."

"Yes." He turned his attention back to Mr. Harden. "Did she really think she could redeem herself with good deeds?"

"She had some idea along those lines, I believe. That if she did more and more good, and if she turned aside when tempted to do evil, this might save her, and eventually she could become a good Christian through her own efforts."

"I trust you and your wife were able to set her on the right path."

"She'd discovered her error by the time she came to us. She realized what she'd believed didn't fit with what Christ said. That she had to trust Him in order to be relieved of her transgressions."

David inhaled carefully. He'd had many long hours in his bed at the hotel to consider this very thing. "I'm afraid I was a rather proud and vain young man and did not improve much with age."

"Oh?" Mr. Harden smiled. "Is that still your outlook, sir?"

David shook his head. "Twice in the past two years, God has laid me low. The first time, I made a slow recovery, but I renewed my fellowship with the Almighty."

"Praise be."

"Yes. This time, the Lord is showing me other lessons."

CHAPTER 26

Peregrin entered the doctor's office and looked around. Two men and a woman holding a baby sat in the waiting room. He took a seat. About ten minutes later, a pretty, round young woman came from deeper in the house.

"You can go in, Mrs. Jackson."

The baby's mother rose and shuffled through the doorway. The woman who'd directed her looked at Peregrin.

"May I help you, sir?"

"Yes, I hope so." Peregrin stood and walked over to her.

For several days, he'd inquired for David Stone at various hotels, but without success. He was beginning to think he'd missed his quarry after all. David must have gone on eastward. Peregrin feared he'd have to give up.

His search had brought one good result—he'd found a couple of hotels that offered better rooms than his own and promptly changed his lodgings. He'd taken his time settling in and getting used to his new environment. And he'd found a higher class of poker game in one of the other hotel guests' sitting room. But he hadn't allowed himself to get in too deep again. Right now he had nearly as much cash as he'd arrived with, and he intended not to lose it all.

He was determined to catch wind of David. That took precedence over everything else. A newcomer at the poker game last night had mentioned that he'd taken an English gentleman from a stagecoach wreck a couple of months previously. Peregrin had perked up at that news. It was the first clue he'd gotten, and on inquiry, the man had told him that he'd delivered the gentleman to a local doctor's house. Peregrin had gotten the address, and this morning he'd found the office and was feeling hopeful.

"I'm looking for a British man," he said with a smile that he hoped was winsome.

"Oh, an acquaintance of yours, sir?" Her face lit up, and she smiled back. His accent seemed to have that effect on American women.

"Yes ma'am. And I heard that Dr. Lee treated such a man several weeks ago. I'm trying to find him. Uh. . ." He glanced about. The other two men were listening, but he couldn't see any way out of letting them hear. "His name's Stone."

"Oh yes," the woman said. "The doctor tells me Mr. Stone is on the mend. He'll probably leave town soon. He's very fortunate to have made a good recovery."

Peregrin nodded, smiling. "I'm so glad to hear it. Could you tell me where he's lodging, please?"

"Well, I don't see any harm in that. Are you a relation of his, sir?"

"No. Well, yes, in a spotty sort of way. My sister is married to his cousin, don't you see?"

She laughed. "Yes, I do see. Well, you might try the Frontier Hotel." She gave him directions and assured him it wasn't far.

Peregrin thanked her heartily and departed, avoiding the other men's direct gazes. People would remember him, but there was no help for it. He'd have to leave town as soon as he'd finished his business, that was all. Even better, he could wait until David left Independence. Perhaps he could follow him and make sure David's next mishap took place a good distance from here. Then people wouldn't connect it to his inquiries. Maybe he could even travel with David.

Peregrin liked that idea. Why shouldn't he march right up to Stone and introduce himself? They did have a social connection, and he could use that to gain the man's confidence. Of course, he'd have to make up a story explaining his presence in the middle of North America, but that shouldn't be too difficult.

If they traveled eastward together, Peregrin could watch for an opportunity to complete Merrileigh's commission unobtrusively. Maybe David would fall off a moving train in some isolated part of the wilderness. And who would know if he hit his head as he fell—or before?

"Does this mean he can travel?" Millie stood in the doorway of David's hotel room, after having been summoned by Dr. Lee.

"Yes," the doctor said, "I think he's ready. You'll take the train to St. Louis, not a boat?"

"We thought we would," David said.

Millie said hesitantly, "There's been talk of disease spreading on the steamboats."

"Yes, and I thought it would be simpler to take the railroad. Of course, we'll have to cross the Mississippi by steamer, but that shouldn't be so bad. Mrs. Evans will make sure I'm comfortable, won't you?" David smiled at her across the room.

"Of course." Millie entered and stood at the foot of the bed. It was so good to see David looking happy and eager to get on with life.

"I am going to remove the cast now," Dr. Lee said. "Mrs. Evans, would you be able to get me a large basin or box to put the plaster in? I don't want to make too big a mess. You might want to bring a broom as well."

"I'd be delighted." Millie dashed down the back stairs to the kitchen and found a large enameled wash pan. In it she placed a dustpan and a couple of rags.

Mrs. Simmons was chopping onions at her work table, and she eyed Millie testily. "What are you up to?"

"The doctor's taking the cast off Mr. Stone's leg."

"Ah. I suppose that means the two of you will be leaving us soon."

Millie wanted to say, "I hope so," but that would be rude, so she said only, "Perhaps." She grabbed a broom and scooted back into the stairway with her unwieldy load.

Was she really eager to leave Independence? David, she knew, could hardly wait to depart from this hotel. When they left here, they would also separate, if not immediately, then surely after they crossed the Mississippi. She'd come to dread the day.

Lately he'd grown more solicitous of her, taking pains not to cause her extra work. She'd praised him for taking on his own care and becoming self-sufficient once more. But the truth was, she missed spending time with him. More than two weeks had passed since the last time she'd read aloud to him. David had gone up and down the stairs slowly, but unassisted, the past two days. Without the cast, he'd be chafing to resume his travels.

When she got back to his room, Dr. Lee had already begun to cut through the plaster and had removed several large chunks, which he had placed on a newspaper.

"Ah, there you are. Thank you, Mrs. Evans." He dropped the next section into the wash pan.

Millie dumped the debris he'd already created into the pan and concentrated on not looking at David's limb while the doctor exposed it. She felt her cheeks flush anyway and decided sweeping the floor would give her a good reason to look elsewhere.

"It would be wise to take a few extra days here to exercise a little more," Dr. Lee said to David. "In moderation of course. Walk down the street tomorrow morning and get a glimpse of the town. Perhaps buy your train tickets for a few days hence."

"I suppose we could do that," David said, a little of his old stubbornness creeping into his tone. "I should rather leave tomorrow."

"I know," Dr. Lee replied, "but you want to make sure your leg will support you before you set out. Your muscles have grown quite weak from lack of use during the last two months. Take Mrs. Evans or someone else with you when you walk. And take the cane along, too. You might suddenly get a cramp or lose your balance—you just never know. Give it a few days, and then, if you're feeling well, go ahead and make your journey."

All of this made perfect sense to Millie, and she hoped David would see the wisdom of it and take the doctor's advice. She would hate to see him have a setback, even though his recovery meant they would soon be parting.

"It's getting late," she said. "Probably it will be suppertime when

Dr. Lee finishes. But in the morning, we could take a stroll, as he suggested, and see how you do. I really think going to the dining room and perhaps a walk around the hotel grounds would be plenty for this evening. Don't you?"

David frowned but raised one hand in defeat. "You may be right. Let's see how it goes."

She nodded, and something in her heart contracted. Her job now was to make sure David was capable of leaving her behind.

Peregrin entered the Frontier Hotel. He decided that he wouldn't get far if he tried to conceal his purpose. He would use the direct approach, as he had at the doctor's office. He reached for his wallet and walked to the desk.

"Are you wanting a room, mister?" the innkeeper asked.

"Well no, actually I'm here to visit one of your guests. Mr. Stone."

The man smiled, and Peregrin decided he might not need to bribe him after all.

"Mr. Stone? Sure, we've got 'im."

Peregrin was almost surprised that he'd at last found the man he'd sought so long. He let out a quick laugh. "Honestly? He's here?"

"Tall English gent with a broken leg?"

"Yes, I suppose so. I'd heard he was injured. Didn't know his leg was fractured."

"Oh yes. Been staying here nigh on two months now."

Peregrin smiled. "My good man, I see that you serve meals here. Tell me, do you also take a bathtub to a guest's room when he wants one?"

"Nope, but we've got a bath shed out back. You can get your hot bath out there when you've a mind to. You're English, too, ain'tcha?"

"Well yes." Peregrin frowned, wondering if he should admit it, but he supposed it wasn't any use to try to hide the fact. But should he risk taking a room here? The scents of chocolate cake and frying chicken, wafting from the kitchen, swayed him. "Would you have a room free?"

"Yup. You want ter be next to Mr. Stone?"

"Oh no," Peregrin said quickly. "In fact, a different floor is fine."

"Awright. Got a room on the second-floor landing." He passed Peregrin a key. "Sign here. You'll want to catch Mr. Stone today or tomorrow though."

"Oh?" Peregrin eyed him keenly. "Why is that?"

"The sawbones came 'round and took the plaster off his leg this afternoon. Mr. Stone says he'll likely leave in a day or two. Mrs. Evans is trying to talk him into staying out the week, but I doubt he'll be here that long."

"Mrs. Evans?" Peregrin asked.

"The woman what came here with him. Millie, her name is. Millie Evans."

"Indeed." Peregrin would have a juicy morsel to tell Merrileigh in his next letter. David Stone had a woman traveling with him. Very interesting.

Simmons shook his head. "We sure will miss her when she's gone."

"Why is that, sir?"

"H'ain't nobody cleans as well or gets the sheets as white as Mrs. Evans. I'll have to send the linen out to be laundered again. Well, nothing good stays, does it?"

"If you say so."

Simmons shrugged. "Anyway, Mr. Stone's in 302. You talk just like 'im. It beats all."

Peregrin pondered Mr. Simmons's words as he climbed the stairs to the second-floor landing. He'd best send a note to Merrileigh right away. He hoped he could wire the message to New York, but even if he could, it would still take ten days or so for it to reach England from there by ship. Perhaps he'd send a short message for now, and save the news about David's female companion until he knew more. But he needed to tell Merry he'd found David—alive, but injured, and, most importantly, unmarried.

CHAPTER 27

Millie insisted that David sit and rest while she packed his valise, though he would much rather have handed things to her or even done the packing himself. She'd taken away all his shirts and linen but what he was wearing that morning to launder them, and now she had a big stack of clean clothing to fold and stow in his two traveling bags.

"I put a new button on this shirt," she said, folding the one that was now his second best. "And I mended the tear in the sleeve of the plaid one."

"That old thing." He'd worn the plaid shirt while puttering about his farm in Oregon and had brought it along mostly in case he needed to do something that would get him dirty. "I suppose I shall have to buy an entire new wardrobe when I get to England, or decent folks won't receive me."

She paused and frowned at him. "Is that so? And here I was thinking how splendid it is that you have so many shirts and such a fine frock suit, not to mention the tailcoat and trousers, besides your everyday."

"Oh." He'd never thought of it quite that way. Even when he'd divested himself of most of his worldly goods, he was still much better off than many of the people around him.

"Do you want to keep these?" She held up the two pairs of trousers she had modified to fit over the cast.

"I hardly think so."

Millie shrugged. "I shall take them to Mrs. Lee then. They might keep them for another patient, I suppose—or someone could put them back to rights for a person without a plaster cast. The black pair is quite good quality, and I hate to see it wasted."

"Do whatever you wish," David said.

Millie folded them carefully. "Perhaps Rev. Harden could use the black pair if his wife gives them some attention and removes the gusset."

"Fine."

"I'll leave out the things you'll need tomorrow," Millie said.

"I still don't see why we can't board the train tomorrow morning." David winced at the sound of his own voice. "Sorry. That's childish of me, isn't it?"

"Getting a bit anxious now?" She smiled at him. "One more day. Dr. Lee insists."

"Yes, yes." He huffed out a breath. Part of him wanted to bound down the two flights of stairs and stride off to the railroad station this minute. He'd been stalled far too long on this trip. The sooner he got to England the better.

But another voice within him cautioned that all too soon he'd be pining for America—the rough beauty of the West and the gentler exuberance of the East Coast. And beyond all of that, he would miss a certain lady.

Yes, she was a lady. He'd settled that in his heart. Millie had some unpolished facets, but she had more substance than most Englishwomen could imagine. Oh, he knew the British were supposed to be staunch to the bone, but nowadays he felt a lot of the upper class in England were too soft by far.

Millie could outride, out-cook, out-scrub, and out-sew most of the women he'd known in his homeland, and on top of all that, she could shoot and drive and do business as well as most men. She might not play the harpsichord or speak Italian, but what did those things matter?

She shook out one of his under-vests, and David looked away, embarrassed that she was handling his personal things. She did it matter-of-factly, almost the way a servant would. But he'd long ago determined he wouldn't treat her like a servant or think of her as one. Whether a woman became a duchess or a maid was in most cases an accident of birth. Look at Elise Finster, his niece's lady's maid. She'd begun life as a lowly servant girl. Now she was the wife of a well-respected, independent rancher in Oregon.

Why couldn't Millie cross the line in the other direction? An American woman of questionable birth and rearing, to be sure. But she had the stuff that would let her hold her head high in the finest of company.

"There. That's the lot. I'll put your bags in the armoire. Anything else I can do for you now?"

"No, I don't think so. Thank you."

"Well, then, I'll be off. Mrs. Simmons wants me to wash dishes tonight, which will probably last until bedtime."

"You shouldn't have to do such mean work."

She laughed. "Why not? Somebody has to do it. And they're paying me."

"Not nearly enough, I'll wager."

He looked at her again. Her thick auburn hair was pulled up on the back of her head, and she wore a plain calico dress, one she'd bought a few weeks ago to wear while cleaning, in order to save her traveling costume and her one "good" dress. An urge came over him to see her again in a well-cut gown of fine material, this time with jewels at her throat and her ears, and an ivory-cased fan at her waist, with her beautiful hair cascading about her shoulders. It could happen, if he weren't so set in his ways.

It was not the first time David had contemplated the matter. He pictured Millie—no, Mildred—on his arm at a ball. Suitably gowned and coiffed, she could stand next to any Englishwoman and compare favorably. And if she had the fortune to allow her to stop working so hard, her roughened hands would soften. Yes, Millie with the advantages of, say, his niece, Anne, could hold her own in any social circle. Because she knew how to charm people. She listened and learned. She studied and mimicked. She could be more polite than the Queen herself.

And she would do everything necessary to avoid embarrassing a man who treated her well. He knew this somehow without being told—without being shown beyond what he had seen of her already.

With a little training, he was sure she could pass for a countess. Could even *be* a countess. Almost, David felt a man could marry her and take her into the highest of English society and not be shamed.

But more importantly, in Millie's company, a man would never be bored.

Peregrin lingered on the third-story landing, watching the door of room 302. He also kept a sharp eye out to make sure nobody else came along and found him loitering. He was still undecided on how to go about Merrileigh's commission. Should he introduce himself to David or remain in the shadows? The woman accompanying David was an unknown quantity. Perhaps he should learn more about her before he made himself known. She might be an obstacle.

A door at the end of the hallway opened, and a woman emerged. Peregrin had previously scouted this doorway and found that it gave on a dim, narrow stairway that he assumed led down to the kitchen. The woman now walking toward him wore a dress his peers would call dowdy, topped by a large apron. One of the hotel staff, no doubt, though she was quite pretty. Fiery highlights shone in her dark hair as she passed beneath a wall lamp, and she carried herself well. In better clothes, she might dazzle him.

All of this Peregrin learned in a quick glance as he moved toward the head of the main stairs. He started down and darted another look over his shoulder. She paid him no attention but was opening a door across the hall from Stone's. Peregrin descended a couple more steps, paused, and turned to go back up, as if he'd forgotten something.

When he reached the landing again, the woman had disappeared. Softly, he walked past her door. It was numbered 303. Could this be the woman that Mr. Simmons had described—David's companion of the laundry talents?

This bore looking into. It seemed odd that David would allow a woman traveling with him to do laundry for the hotel. Had the next earl lost all his money? Peregrin could hardly believe she was working to pay for their lodgings. What gentleman would ask his lady friend to support them? Such an attractive woman must have some options other than drudgery. Surely she would have little trouble finding herself a husband.

It was a regular bumblebroth. Peregrin decided to take supper elsewhere—not in the hotel's dining room—and give it some more thought.

David was in pain. Millie could tell as soon as she saw his face. The fact that he hadn't dressed, but sat in the armchair wearing his dressing gown, confirmed her impression.

"Your leg hurts." She crossed to his bedside table and picked up the laudanum bottle. "Let me fix you a dose."

"No," David said sharply.

She turned and frowned at him. He'd been so polite the last few days!

"I'm sorry," he said. "I only mean that I don't want to take the stuff. It makes me groggy, and I can't think clearly."

"But if you are in pain. . ."

"Pain is not the worst thing in the world."

"Ah." She stood with the bottle in her hand, waiting for a cue from him as to what to do. He had overtaxed himself yesterday, but she wouldn't say that. He could figure it out for himself, and if she stated the fact, it would only irritate him.

"I believe we were going to the train station to buy our tickets," he said.

"Yes, but it's too far for you to walk, especially if your leg is bothering you."

"I daresay you're right. Can we get a carriage? Or even a farm wagon?"

Millie considered that. "It would be much simpler if I go. I can walk it in half an hour, while you rest."

"I hate resting. It's all I ever do."

"But if you do too much now, you'll have a setback. Then where will you be come time to travel?"

He looked away and rested his chin on his hand. "I suppose you're right—but I don't like it."

She laughed. David never liked it when someone else was right. "Just tell me what you want, and I'll get it. I suppose you want a through ticket to New York if they have such a thing."

"No doubt we'll have to go to St. Louis first. Get across the Mississippi, and then deal with the ticket question again."

"You're probably right. Shall I get two train tickets to the ferry, then, and we'll cross together?"

"Why not?"

"Would you like me to help you back into bed before I go? I could ask Billy to bring you a breakfast tray."

"I think I'll sit here, but I would like the tray, thank you." David's blue eyes seemed melancholy today.

"Perhaps some willow bark tea would ease the pain, though it's not nearly so strong as laudanum. I'm sure Mrs. Simmons keeps some in the pantry."

"All right." He looked up at her suddenly. "Mildred, there's something else."

Something about his tone softened her heart, and she stepped closer. "What is it?"

"I think I'd like to travel with you as far as Philadelphia. I can surely get a ship from there for England."

This unexpected news set her pulse off in a jagged path. "I expect you could, but why?"

He shrugged and looked out the window. "I should worry about you if you went off alone."

She wanted to laugh. She'd been fending for herself for years, and she didn't need an escort. But the simple fact that someone cared about her welfare touched her heart. And this wasn't just anyone. It was David.

She closed the distance between them and bent to touch his hand. "Thank you. You don't need to, but that—that means a good deal to me. I'll see about the tickets."

"All right. Take the money from my wallet." He turned his hand and clutched her fingers for a moment, then let them slide from his grasp. "I shall see you later, then."

"Yes, I'll be back before dinnertime."

She'd gone to his room prepared to take breakfast with him and then set out for the train station, so after she got the money for the tickets, she went right down to the dining room. This morning she would eat alone, as she had for many weeks.

Last night she'd given Mr. Simmons her notice, so she'd have to pay for the rest of the meals she ate here, but that was all right. She needed the next couple of days to tie up the loose ends for their travel. She'd saved enough to purchase her own fare to Philadelphia, with several dollars besides. With care, she could keep herself until she found work in the city.

In the dining room, she ordered David's tray, but only coffee and biscuits for herself—the cheapest thing she could get and still fill her stomach. She was eating a bit later than her normal hour, and only a few guests were still in the room. In the far corner sat a gentleman she didn't remember seeing before. A new guest, no doubt. He looked to be about her own age, and handsome in an ornate sort of way. She decided it was his well-cut coat and the necktie at breakfast that gave her this impression—that and the way he'd combed his hair. She doubted most men in Independence had more than a nodding acquaintance with a looking glass. This one had obviously spent some time gazing into one. He seemed more intent on his newspaper than his meal, however.

As she ate, she mulled over what David had said. Her heart was tearing in two. On the one hand, she was glad he wanted to stay with her a little longer. But he showed no regrets about their imminent parting. In fact, from what he'd said this morning, it appeared he wanted to see her safely to her destination, and then be rid of her once and for all. These last few days, he'd seemed to truly enjoy her company, but that was coming to an end. It still seemed to Millie that he couldn't wait to be rid of her, although his conscience bade him to make sure she was safe.

A steady ache formed in her chest, and she feared she might begin to weep. That would never do! Just because she'd developed feelings for a man was no reason to fall to pieces. She wouldn't call David an uncaring man. Indeed, lately he'd shown himself quite compassionate. But he didn't love her, and in spite of her efforts to resist the longing, that was what she truly desired.

What would he say if she bought her ticket for a different day than his and refused to travel with him? That seemed a bit crass, in light of his past kindnesses. Furthermore, she knew she could never bring herself to do it.

Millie finished her coffee and resolved to make the most of her limited time with David. Inside, she might be mourning as they rode the rails eastward, but she would show him her charming, lighthearted demeanor. Once she'd fancied marrying him—for his fortune, nothing else. Now she couldn't care less about that. She loved him with all her heart. But she would never let him know.

Peregrin watched the auburn-haired woman over the top of his newspaper. This was the mysterious Mrs. Evans who was traveling with Randolph Stone's cousin. She was pretty enough, even in the stark morning light of the dining room. She wasn't wearing an apron today, but a practical, coarse calico dress. She wore a hat as well, and that looked to be of better quality than the dress. So. . .she was going out.

Peregrin had hoped David would come down to breakfast so he could get a look at him. But it seemed he was keeping to his room this morning. Just how ill was he?

Should he wait for this Mrs. Evans to leave and then run up to David's room? Peregrin decided against that. He wasn't ready to carry out Merrileigh's ultimate wishes yet—not here, in the hotel. And it might be best if David remained unaware of his presence a little longer.

Mrs. Evans rose, and Peregrin made a quick decision. He cast aside his newspaper, laid a few coins on the table, and followed her out. She was already striding rapidly up the street. He'd have to dash to keep up, and Peregrin wasn't the sort of man who liked to hurry. But if he hired a hack, he'd have to instruct the driver to hover behind her—a distasteful position. Besides, there didn't seem to be any hackneys lingering about the hotel this morning.

Shank's mare it was. He set out briskly, telling himself she wouldn't go far. What woman would set out on foot to walk more than a few blocks?

The streets were crowded with wagons, saddle horses, and pedestrians. The emigrant trains going west this year had all left, his poker-playing friends had told him. For the next couple of months, people headed the other way would come through. The town was growing ever larger, and thousands more would pass through next spring, headed west.

Peregrin couldn't see what the attraction was. More land like this to break with a plow and till? He supposed that for the lower classes, the prospect of a few acres was alluring. Personally, he'd rather have stayed in the more settled and civilized East.

Mrs. Evans turned out to be a difficult person to follow. She moved quickly through the morning crowds, apparently focused on her destination. Peregrin dashed after her, trying to keep an eye on her bonnet.

About twenty minutes later, he pulled up, wheezing and clutching his chest, before the railroad station. She must have gone in here. He hadn't actually seen her enter, but she'd headed up this street with a purposeful stride, and the station was the largest building in the vicinity. He stood on the corner, catching his breath and waiting. Surely she'd come out again. Unless she took a train. But no—she hadn't carried any luggage.

He congratulated himself on this keen deduction. He was really getting rather good at this cloak-and-dagger business. Mrs. Evans must have come to buy tickets. That meant she and David planned to leave Independence soon, perhaps today or tomorrow. He'd come just in time.

He pulled in several steadying breaths. His pulse began to

slack off. At that moment, the woman in question emerged from the station. She didn't dawdle but headed immediately back the way she had come. As she reached the corner where Peregrin stood observing her, she glanced at him.

"Good morning," he said cheerfully, lifting his hat.

She nodded and started to pass, then stopped dead in her tracks. She whirled around. "Didn't I see you at the Frontier Hotel this morning?"

CHAPTER 28

David lay on his bed, rubbing his thigh and wishing the pain away. He ought to have listened to Millie and taken the laudanum this morning. At this rate, he wouldn't be fit to take dinner with her, let alone travel tomorrow.

He glanced about the room. Where were those crutches? Millie must have put them away in the wardrobe, since he hadn't used them for a day or two. Oh well, he could reach the cane. Perhaps if he hobbled out into the hallway, he could summon Wilfred to come and give him some laudanum.

What was he thinking? That boy couldn't mix the dose. Millie always did it. He supposed he could mix it himself. He seemed to recall that half a teaspoon made the usual dose, in a glass of water. Maybe he'd use only half that. He truly didn't want to lose consciousness for hours, just to stop feeling as though his leg were being crushed under a boulder—or a stagecoach. The willow bark tea probably helped some—everyone swore by its curative powers—but a strong cup of it hadn't seemed to take more than the sharpest edge off his pain.

Perhaps he could lessen the discomfort if he put his mind to something else. Or someone else?

Millie.

There, he might as well face the facts and stop trying to trick himself. He wanted Millie for his bride. How sharply would his friends in England cut him if he arrived with Mildred as his legal wife? Of even more concern, how badly would they treat Millie? Could she stand up to disdain and scorn? He wasn't sure he could abide with that. If people were going to treat her abominably—or just ignore her, which in London was even worse—he might lose his

865

good nature. But so much in English society depended on having the good will of the upper crust.

"What am I thinking?" he said aloud. "Millie can pull it off. Why, with two weeks in New York, I can outfit her like the countess she'll be and teach her how to address the nobility." She could probably dance already, and he had no doubt she could handle the staff at Stoneford. She had a commanding manner when she needed it and could give orders that other people sprang to obey.

And she was lovely. Not a sugary-sweet debutante, but a handsome young widow who knew her way around the lamppost. She picked up on nuances quickly. Yes, he could give her sufficient training in the time it would take to cross the Atlantic. Millie would be accepted—and loved—as his treasured bride. As Lady Stoneford.

"Oh. . .well. . .uh. . .yes, I believe you might have." Peregrin whipped off his hat and bowed at the waist. "I did take my breakfast there. Came out for a constitutional afterward."

"Indeed?" Millie surveyed the man in the smartly tailored suit with some misgiving. It seemed very odd that a man had set out for a stroll and gone in the same direction as she had and kept pace with her as well. "It's not been thirty minutes since I left the hotel."

The man didn't quite meet her eyes. "Oh yes. I like a brisk walk after breakfast, don't you know."

"You're English, aren't you?" He was about thirty years old and had a pleasant face, but what had really caught her attention was his accent. In those few words, she knew he was not only British but also of gentle birth. And how did she know this, she asked herself. Because he talked like David of course.

"Why yes. I've only been in this half of the world a few weeks. Liking it, rather, though it's a bit rustic."

"I suppose so," she said, though to Millie, Independence was as big as any town she'd seen in the last twenty years. Philadelphia would probably shock her when she saw it again. "Excuse me, I must be going." She turned away.

"Might I not accompany you back to the hotel?" He hopped along to catch up and fell into stride with her.

She shot him a sideways glance. He was a bit forward and overeager, but really, he behaved no worse than scores of other men she'd encountered. And the poor fellow probably knew no one in the area. He looked like a gentleman. Could she assume he would behave like one? And his presence would keep other men from accosting her. Really, what was the harm?

"I suppose you might," she said demurely.

"Oh, thank you, madam. I shall be honored."

He didn't offer his arm, and Millie was glad. That would be spooning it on a bit thick.

"I do hope your visit to the depot doesn't foreshadow a journey in the near future," he said.

"Why yes. I shall be traveling soon."

"What? Not leaving us? But I've only just made your acquaintance." He touched her sleeve and stopped walking, peering down at her in consternation.

"Really, sir," Millie said, a bit more severely, "you haven't made my acquaintance at all."

For a moment he gazed at her in assessment, and Millie fancied his eyes took on a bit of a gleam, as though he was accepting a challenge. He bowed slightly.

"You're absolutely right. Since we have no one to perform the ceremonies, allow me to introduce myself. The name is Peregrin Walmore."

She wanted to repeat the strange name, just to hear the cadence on her tongue, but she managed to get by with only a slight twitch of the lip as she thought about it.

"That's a very odd name, sir. I've never heard one like it."

"Oh, it was quite the fashion in England some years back, which I suppose is why my mother chose it."

"I see."

"And your name, if I may be so bold?"

She hesitated but could see no reason not to divulge it. All of the hotel staff knew her and would probably not scruple to give another guest her name.

"Mrs. Evans."

"Ah."

Millie began walking again, and Walmore hurried to keep up.

"May I inquire how Mr. Evans is doing? Is he traveling with you?"

"No, Mr. Evans has left this mortal life."

"My condolences." His smile belied his words. "So you might say your husband has journeyed on before you."

Millie said nothing. She strongly doubted James had passed through the pearly gates, and she certainly didn't want to follow him in his otherworldly travels.

"Might I invite you to take dinner with me this noon?" Walmore asked.

He did have a charming smile, and that delightful accent that was so like David's. It occurred to Millie that having another English gentleman approach her in the frontier town amounted to a coincidence so large as to be unwieldy.

"May I inquire what you do for a living, sir?"

"What I do?" Mr. Walmore blinked down at her. "Well, I've a couple of thousand a year, if you must know, but that's a bit brash, isn't it?"

"I don't understand you." Millie stopped walking again. "I didn't ask your income, sir. I asked your profession."

"Ah, I see. As a matter of fact, I am of the class that has a living but does not need to *make* one."

"Oh. A gentleman, as they say."

"Well yes."

She nodded and walked on. She decided to ask David if he knew anything about the Walmore family. "And where in England do you reside, if I may ask?"

"You may. My father's house is in Reading, and I myself am lately of London. And where are you from?"

"I was born in Pennsylvania, but my mother married a man with a restless foot." A wandering eye, too, but that was none of his business. "We eventually moved to San Francisco, and later to Oregon Territory. I have recently come from there."

"I see. A westerner."

"Yes." She doubted he knew where the places she'd mentioned were located, or had any idea of the vast distance she'd covered in the last few months. She opened her mouth to ask if he knew the Stone family in England, but something held her back. Perhaps it was the memory of Peterson in Scottsburg—the man who had persuaded her to deliver an innocent man into his hands. It might be wiser to ask David first whether he knew a family in England named Walmore.

This man would have been only a boy when David left his homeland, but he spoke as though his father still lived. She walked onward, mulling this over.

"So, will you dine with me?"

She glanced at him and shook her head. "I'm afraid not."

"Oh, you wound me." He put on a smile that was winsome indeed. Under other circumstances, Millie would have gladly accepted this handsome young man's invitation. "Dare I hope I might prevail upon you to join me at supper?"

"I. . .I don't think so, Mr. Walmore. I am assisting a person who has been ill, you see, and I may be needed. I'm often required to help at mealtimes."

"Ah." He eyed her thoughtfully.

"Watch out." Millie thrust out a hand to stop him. Walmore was so engrossed in the conversation, he'd almost stepped off the walk at a corner, into the path of a mule team.

"Oh. Quite." He pulled back and waited with her until the big freight wagon had passed. "Allow me." He seized her hand, tucked it through his arm, and hurried her across the street.

"Thank you." Millie removed her hand from his elbow as soon as they were safely on the boardwalk beyond the intersection.

"So. . .no supper either?" he asked genially.

"I do thank you for your offer, sir, but I shall be otherwise occupied." They were within sight of the hotel, and she gave him an impersonal smile. "Excuse me, won't you? I'll go around to the back and speak to Mrs. Simmons about my friend's meal."

She bustled away before he could say anything about her friend or dinner or any other topic. She'd skip through the kitchen and up the back stairs. There was no point in forming a new acquaintance, since she and David would leave tomorrow. The young man was probably all right—but she'd grown wary. And she wasn't looking about to replace James.

Peregrin stood on the sidewalk in front of the hotel, gazing after Mrs. Evans. From behind, she looked like an ordinary woman dressed in attire suitable for the working class. Only the carriage of her shoulders and her more elegant hat, with a faint glint of reddish hair peeping from under it at the nape of her neck, bespoke her quality. Their short acquaintance had convinced him that she was a woman of substance. Not wealth, perhaps, but she had an innate savoir faire he hadn't expected. Perhaps that was what attracted David to her.

Now that he thought about it, most women in her situation would have remarked on the other Englishman she knew. Mrs. Evans was cautious, which was not to say secretive, but she was protecting David. Or perhaps it was more a matter of safeguarding her own reputation. That was probably it—she didn't want other people to know she was traveling with a man. He should have guessed it at once.

With no inkling of how to proceed, Peregrin decided a trip to the Bear Paw wouldn't be amiss. A pint of beer might help him sort through his options. If only he could get some good British ale in this desolate place!

He entered the saloon a few minutes later and looked around. Seeing none of his new friends, he strolled to the bar and ordered a beer. As he waited, he was startled by a heavy hand laid on his shoulder.

He whirled and found himself staring at the chest of a huge man. Craning his neck back, he looked upward into the face of the giant who had accosted him at the Metropolitan Hotel in New York.

"Well now, Walmore, we meet again. Ain't that sumthin'?"

CHAPTER 29

Millie tapped on David's door and received a hearty "Come in." She opened it and peeked inside. Pastor Harden was sitting with David near the window.

"Oh, I'm sorry to interrupt," she said. "I just wanted to tell you that I have our train tickets in hand."

"Well done," David said.

Mr. Harden stood. "We'll be sorry to see you go, Mrs. Evans, but I'm glad you'll be able to get on with what you want to do."

"Thank you." Millie wasn't exactly sure what it was she wanted to do—that seemed to have changed since she arrived in Independence. But now was not the time to discuss it. "Our journey has been enriched by meeting you and Mrs. Harden."

"Indeed it has," David said. "I say, Mildred, would you be able to ask the kitchen to send up coffee for Mr. Harden and me?"

Millie smiled. "I'll fetch it myself, as soon as I drop my things in my room."

"I hate to see you go to the trouble," Mr. Harden said.

"I don't mind."

"Join us, if you'd like," David said, smiling at her across the room.

While the prospect was tempting, Millie felt he would be better off to have a last private conversation with the minister. "I have my packing to do, but I'm happy to bring a tray for you."

She hurried across to her own chamber and left her shawl, hat, and purse on the bed. After smoothing down her hair, she went out again, locked her door, and went along to the back stairs. While she could have gone down the front stairs, this way was more direct, and she'd have no chance of running into that other Englishman on this route.

She puzzled over him again. What was he doing out here? He'd admitted he had no business interests, and he'd mentioned no friends or acquaintances or a further destination. Perhaps she should have accepted his dinner invitation so that she could learn more about him. It really did seem odd that a young, well-to-do Englishman should come to Independence, Missouri. If he wanted to go to the gold fields, wouldn't a man of means sail to Panama and take the railroad across the isthmus?

Perhaps it would be a good idea to speak to him again and pump him for more information. If David wanted to go down for dinner, they might meet him in the dining room. Or maybe that was what Walmore hoped would happen. She shivered. David had better stay in his room until she learned more about the young man.

As she stepped into the busy kitchen, Mrs. Simmons fixed her with a disapproving frown.

"Millie? Thought you weren't going to work today."

"I'm not, but Mr. Stone is entertaining the reverend and would like coffee for him and his guest. I thought I'd save you some trouble and fix it myself."

"Fine, but you can be sure it will go on his bill."

"I wouldn't expect anything else, ma'am." Millie went about preparing the tray, avoiding Mrs. Simmons's sour gaze. She knew David would prefer tea but had no doubt requested coffee for the minister's sake. She fixed a pot of tea and a mug of coffee and added a small pitcher of cream and some loaf sugar to the tray.

"I see you have a few muffins left from breakfast. May I add a couple?" she asked the innkeeper's wife.

"Just leave my Charles one of the apple ones."

"Certainly." Millie added two spoons and napkins to the tray and lifted it. The burden would be tricky to carry up the winding back stairs, but she could do it.

A few minutes later, she emerged in the third-floor hallway, puffing a little. She rested the tray on the windowsill at the end of the hall for a minute and caught her breath. She didn't want to bother David, but perhaps it would be best to put in a casual inquiry now.

She hefted the tray again and went along to his room. At her knock, Mr. Harden opened the door.

"Ah, let me take that for you," he said.

"Thanks, but I'm fine." She passed him, walked to the small table beside David's chair, and lowered the tray, setting the edge on the surface.

David reached over to help her set the dishes off the tray.

"Oh, you fixed me a pot of tea. That was very kind of you, Mildred."

She smiled. "I thought you might prefer it. And Mrs. Simmons had some muffins left from this morning."

"Very nice."

She straightened and set the tray over on his dresser. "I'll leave you gentlemen, but I wanted to ask you a question first, Mr. Stone." She still used his surname in front of other people. She wouldn't want anyone to assume their relationship had become more personal than was seemly.

"Oh? What is it?" David asked as he poured tea into his cup.

"I met a man this morning. He's a new guest here. And it seemed a bit odd to me—he was at breakfast when I ate, and then he followed me to the train station."

"What?" David set the teapot down with a clunk. "A man is following you?"

She felt her cheeks warm. "Well, he said he was only out for a walk, but I was moving quite quickly. He asked me to have dinner with him at noon. I turned him down, but—well, I thought—in light of—" She threw a glance Mr. Harden's way in apology. She didn't think he knew everything about her past with David, though she'd given him an abbreviated account. "Well, the thing is, he's English, like you."

"That does seem odd," David said thoughtfully. "Did he mention me?"

"No, which I found even odder. Wouldn't that be the first thing Mr. Simmons would tell another Englishman when he checked in here—that one of his countrymen was staying in the hotel?"

"Perhaps." David sipped his tea absently, then seemed to recall what he was doing and set it down to add cream. "I don't suppose he gave his name?"

"Yes, he did. It's Walmore."

"Walmore. . ."

"Do you know anyone by that name?" Mr. Harden asked.

"I don't think so," David said. "No, wait. It almost seems that Anne told me something. . . . Ah yes, that's it. She said my cousin married a Walmore. Mary, I think. Something like that."

"Your cousin?" Millie stared at him.

"Might bear looking into," David said pensively. "Yes, I believe she said my cousin Randolph's wife was a Walmore. There was a family. . . ." He shook his head. "Not in the top tier of society, but respectable, I'm sure."

Millie watched him, fascinated. It was as though he'd become a different man, in a different time and place. The type of man who would know in an instant whether or not someone belonged to the highest circles of English society.

He smiled at her. "Perhaps I should make this gentleman's acquaintance."

"Or perhaps you should not," Millie said.

"You're not thinking—" He paused, eyeing her with speculation. "You are, aren't you?"

Mr. Harden watched them with obvious interest but said nothing.

"Well, one can't be too careful," Millie said.

"Yes, especially if one is prone to accidents." David nodded, and she was sure he'd reached a decision. "If you're game, Mildred, you shall go down to dinner without me in an hour. And if this gentleman is about, perhaps you could further your acquaintance with him."

"What?" Peregrin stared up at the big man, whose leathery face was set in a gruesome sneer. "I—oh—please—"

During his stammering the giant and another fellow pushed him down the boardwalk and into a secluded alley between a haberdashery and a carriage house.

"Please," Peregrin said. "Whatever do you want? This is highly irregular."

"Is it, now?" the giant asked. "Hear that, Teddy? We're irregulars."

"Right," his partner said.

The bigger man grabbed the front of Peregrin's shirt and twisted it with his fist. "You know what we want, Walmore."

"Er. . .do I?" Peregrin blinked and turned his face, owl-like, from one to the other, terrified that they would beat him and unable to think of a reason why they shouldn't.

The giant shoved him against the wall. "You do. The same thing we wanted in New York. Baxter's money."

"Oh." Peregrin gulped. "I thought you looked familiar, but since we've not been introduced—"

"Idiot," said Teddy.

The giant hit Peregrin, landing a wallop just south of his left eye. He gasped and sagged back against the rough boards behind him.

"I'm Wilkes," the giant said. "Sorry, but I ain't got no calling card. So fork over the blunt."

"The. . .uh. . .I'm sorry, but I don't believe I have what you're looking for. That's why I left New York."

"That warn't smart," Teddy said.

Wilkes continued to hold Peregrin by his shirtfront. "You told Baxter you'd get it for him. Now, you give it over, or we'll have to make you regret it."

"I already regret it," Peregrin said, "but I can't pay the thousand I owe him."

"It's twelve hunnerd now," Teddy growled.

"That's right," Wilkes said. "Baxter had to send us out here after you, and that's expensive. You need to pay up, or it'll be even more." He clamped one massive hand around Peregrin's throat and pushed his head back against the wall.

"I can't, I tell you," Peregrin gasped.

"Why not?"

"Lost it."

"That's bad."

"Ask 'im how much he's got," Teddy said, elbowing the giant.

"Yeah," Wilkes said. "How much you got, Walmore?"

Peregrin was finding it hard to breathe with the man's huge hand compressing his throat. "Let me go," he squeaked.

Wilkes released his hold, and Peregrin sucked in a big breath, doubling over and grasping his thighs.

"Don't get sick on me," Wilkes growled. "How much you got on you?"

"On me? About thirty dollars."

"What?" Wilkes grabbed his arm, jerked him upward, and punched him in the stomach. "You better say you got more in the bank, pal."

When the swirling kaleidoscope faded, Peregrin held his abdomen and tried to think fast. If they knew he had eight hundred in cash, they'd take it all, and he'd have nothing left to work with. "I've only got five hundred," he gasped.

"Awright, let's go get it," Wilkes said.

CHAPTER 30

Begging your pardon," Mr. Harden said. "I don't want to intrude, but it seems you are suspicious of this Walmore fellow. If I'm able to be of assistance, I'd be happy to serve you."

Millie eyed him thoughtfully. "What could you do, Pastor?"

"I thought perhaps, since David is going to keep to his room, I could go down to dinner with you."

"He might not want to talk to me if I've another gentleman with me." Millie looked to David. "What do you think?"

"That's true," David said. "Perhaps I should just go and seek him out. Find out if he means to meet me or not."

"You must safeguard your health," Millie said, "if only for the journey."

Mr. Harden's eyebrows shot up. "You don't think this man would harm Mr. Stone, do you? Is this a matter for the constabulary?"

"Oh, I doubt it," David said. "It's just a case of once bit, twice shy where I'm concerned."

"But still, it might be good to have another person at hand who knows the lay of the land," Millie said.

"How about this?" The pastor seemed eager to take part in the drama, and Millie listened with growing approval. "I could go home and get my Isabelle to come and eat dinner with me here at the hotel."

"It might be helpful," Millie said. "If Mr. Walmore became obnoxious, I could appeal to the Hardens as an excuse to leave his company."

"Isabelle would love a chance to eat out," Mr. Harden said, smiling at David.

"All right, but only if you do it at my expense," David said.

"Oh no, you mustn't." The minister flushed.

"Yes, I must. This is purely for my welfare, and I insist on seeing to it. Mildred, would you bring my wallet, please?"

Millie fetched it with alacrity and handed it to David, who took out a dollar bill and held it out to Mr. Harden.

"Please, sir. I will consider it money well spent. Not only will I be sure Mildred has a friend nearby, but also you and your wife, who have been so kind to us both, will have—I hope—a pleasant meal."

"If you insist," Mr. Harden said, tucking the money into his waistcoat pocket. "But I must hurry home and inform Isabelle, so that she knows before she has dinner on the table for me."

"If it's any inconvenience, do not bother to come back," Millie said. She didn't think Isabelle, who was of a sunny temperament, would object, but some women would want to be told in advance of such a venture.

"No fear," Mr. Harden said. "We shall be in the dining room by a quarter till noon."

"Excellent," Millie told him. "I shall go down a little after that. I was hoping to avoid Mr. Walmore for the rest of the day, but now I hope very much that he turns up for dinner."

Peregrin staggered up the stairs to his room with Wilkes and Teddy right behind him. The only way to get rid of these two was to pay them something. He'd have to be careful and not let them know that he was holding out on them, or they might kill him.

He unlocked his door with shaky hands. The two thugs followed him in, and Teddy shut the door.

"Where is it?" Wilkes asked.

"I'll get it."

"No, tell me. I'll get it."

Peregrin swallowed. His Adam's apple hurt, where the giant had squeezed it. He had some cash hidden in the dresser drawer, as well as some in his luggage, besides the bit they'd already taken from his wallet. He hoped he could satisfy them with one stash and keep them from tossing the room looking for more.

A LADY IN THE MAKING

"It's in my valise. There's a purse under my clothes."

Teddy pawed through the bag, not seeming to notice how few clothes were in it. Most of them were now in the dresser, but Peregrin studiously avoided looking in the direction of that article of furniture.

"This is only four-fifty," Teddy whined.

"You said you had five hunnert." Wilkes came toward him menacingly.

"I thought I did. You got some out of my wallet."

"Thirty-two dollars and change."

"Well, that's it then." Peregrin tried to smile, but he felt sick to his stomach, and his throat and face hurt.

"You better get the rest," Wilkes said, towering over him.

"How am I supposed to do that? You're not leaving me any capital to work with. I can't even go out and join a poker game tonight."

"You got friends?"

"Not here."

"There must be somebody you know."

"Uh, well. . ." Peregrin thought of David Stone, but he couldn't drag him into this. That would alert David to his presence and put the wind up so far as Peregrin's integrity went. And he couldn't borrow seven hundred dollars from a man and then do him in, could he? Of course, if the one he borrowed from was dead, he'd be less apt to ask for a repayment of the loan.

Peregrin shook his head. It was all so confusing and gruesome. Bad enough to plan an accident for an upstanding gentleman, but to use him to repay a gambling debt. . . That was beyond dishonor. Peregrin knew that he could never again respect himself if he followed through with this.

No, he wouldn't breathe a word about David if he could possibly get by without. If he could just make these fellows go away, maybe he could escape them and flee. He had no idea where he would go, and they'd taken the bulk of his remaining funds. But he couldn't stay here.

"I'll see what I can do." Peregrin attempted to brush his shirt

879

into smoothness, but it was grimy and creased now. "Why don't you gentlemen come back tomorrow, and we'll see if I've been successful, what?"

Wilkes looked at his chum questioningly. "What say, Teddy? Shall we give him a few hours to come across?"

"No more'n that. I'm sick of this place. I wanna get back to New York."

"All right." Wilkes fixed Peregrin with a malevolent scowl. "You've got until three o'clock. We'll be watching the hotel. Meet us out front with the dough."

"Dough?" Peregrin frowned. "I say—"

"The money, you numbskull," Wilkes said.

"Oh. Right. But what if I can't get it by then?"

"Then we'll take it out of your hide."

Teddy smirked. "That's right, chum. Baxter told us if we couldn't squeeze the twelve hunnerd out of ya, to do whatever we wanted. So think hard about getting every cent."

"And don't even think about running," Wilkes said, giving his shoulder a little shove. "We'll be watching you."

"Right." In spite of his roiling stomach and throbbing face, Peregrin straightened his coat and tie. He walked to the door and held it open.

As the two men passed him, Wilkes turned back and pointed a finger so close Peregrin could have bitten it. "Three o'clock. Don't be late."

Millie went down to the dining room, wearing her best dress. She didn't like to draw attention to herself, but past experience had shown her that this outfit would impress an English gentleman. Of course, the gown was somewhat the worse for wear now, but she'd kept it mended and fairly stainless. Before donning it, she'd carefully pressed all the wrinkles out of the wide skirt.

Every eye was upon her as she entered the dining room. Simmons's niece turned her way and gaped at her. Millie hid her smile. The waitress probably wondered if she'd spent all her earnings on clothing.

Millie didn't see Mr. Walmore, but the pastor and his wife were seated at one of the center tables and already had soup and biscuits before them. Millie smiled at them but didn't stop to speak. She didn't want Walmore to see her with them if he should walk in behind her.

A man who'd been staying at the hotel for several days jumped up and stood in her path.

"Good day, ma'am. Care to join me?"

"Oh, no thank you," Millie said, and she brushed past him.

She was afraid some of the other guests would come and sit with her—people usually shared tables when the dining room was busy. She took a seat at the end of one of the long tables, with two seats between her and the nearest diner. She avoided looking around at people, so as to discourage them from engaging her in conversation.

When Sarah came to her side, Millie gave her order for soup and corn pone. She laid a hand on the girl's arm and leaned toward her.

"Do you know Mr. Walmore? He's a guest here."

"That new fellow?" she asked. "Funny accent?"

"He's the one," Millie said. "Has he been in for dinner yet?"

"Don't think so. I'd have seen him."

Millie nodded. "Thank you. Oh, and I'd like a pot of tea, please."

The freckle-faced girl arched her eyebrows. "A whole pot?"

"Yes, please." Millie smiled at her. She could see that Sarah was trying to work this out in her mind. Millie usually had a cup of coffee with her meal. Few people asked for tea, and even fewer for an entire pot. But then, Millie had never appeared wearing such a fine dress either.

"Is Mr. Stone coming down to join you?"

"I don't think so."

"Oh." The waitress turned away, frowning.

Millie smiled to herself and then glanced about surreptitiously. Mrs. Harden caught her eye and gave a slight nod, then looked back at her husband. The door from the front entrance opened, and in came Mr. Walmore. He kept his head down and shuffled between the tables, hardly looking at other people, but taking tiny glances ahead as he searched for an empty seat. When he noticed Millie he started to smile, then winced.

Millie caught her breath. A red and purple bruise spread over Walmore's left cheekbone, and the flesh around his eye was swollen and discolored. She'd seen quite a few black eyes in her day—mostly on Sam—but this one was a prizewinner.

She pushed back her chair and half stood.

"Mr. Walmore! Won't you join me?"

"Oh, uh…Mrs.…uh…Evans, isn't it? Are you certain you—"

"Yes. Please, sit down, sir. Are you all right?" She hoped her concern for his injury was enough to atone for her earlier refusal to dine with him.

His rueful smile was somewhat of a grimace. "I shan't say it's not painful."

"Dear me, what happened?"

"Oh, I…I misjudged which way a horse was going to move."

"I see." Millie shook her head. "I don't suppose you want to see a doctor?"

"No, it will be all right in a couple of days."

She doubted the bruises would fade in a fortnight, but the swelling would probably be gone in less time. The waitress was approaching with a brown teapot on a tray.

"Well please, go ahead and order your dinner," Millie said. "And feel free to share my pot of tea. I'm sure I won't be able to drink it all."

"Most kind of you," Mr. Walmore murmured.

Sarah set down the teapot and turned to him with a smile. "Help you, sir?" Her smile skewed. "Oh my! That's a beaut."

Mr. Walmore chuckled. "I expect it looks worse than it feels. I'd like some roast beef, if you have it."

"Not until suppertime, sir. This noon we have soup and lamb chops and chicken and dumplings."

"The chicken, then. Thank you."

"Oh, and we'd like an extra cup for Mr. Walmore," Millie said.

The waitress flicked her a glance. "There's cups and things yonder, with the butter and jam."

"Right," Mr. Walmore said, rising. "I'll get it."

He didn't seem to worry about the fact that Millie had reversed her position by welcoming him at her table. Perhaps he thought she was just being flirtatious earlier when she turned him down. Millie wondered how to bring him around to talking about David without mentioning the gentleman's name. She decided to pry a little into Walmore's history first.

When he returned with his cup and saucer, she smiled across the table at him. "I'm afraid they don't bring milk for the tea unless you ask them, and I forgot."

"Well, when the girl comes back, we'll put in a request, hey?" If his face wasn't so colorful and puffy, he would no doubt look very charming.

"So, Mr. Walmore, what brings you to Independence?" Millie asked.

"Oh, business. You know. How about yourself?"

This seemed to contradict what he had told her earlier, when he'd implied that he was a gentleman of means who needed no business. It certainly bore further investigation. "I'm just traveling through. Returning from the West. Uh. . .what sort of business?"

He hesitated. "Just looking over some property for a friend. Are you traveling alone? I believe you told me you've been helping an invalid?"

"Not an invalid precisely. One of my fellow travelers was injured in a stagecoach accident, and I stayed here to help."

"Oh, I see. That was most compassionate of you."

"I don't know. . . . It seemed the proper thing to do."

The waitress brought Mr. Walmore's plate of chicken and dumplings. While she set his dish down, Millie dipped a piece of corn pone in her soup and ate it. She wondered if that was considered proper etiquette and shot a glance at her dinner companion, but he wasn't looking at her. Even so, Millie picked up her spoon and determined to eat as aristocratically as she could.

"I wonder if we could get a little milk?" Walmore asked the waitress.

"Milk?" Sarah shrugged. "I suppose so." She flounced away, clearly baffled that a grown man would wish to drink milk with his dinner.

As they ate, Millie continued to ply him with questions. Before long she had him telling her about London. None of his stories had to do with industry or business, but rather he told her about parties he'd attended, and his club—which, it seemed, was like a private restaurant for gentlemen—and his friends' horses and equipages and their impromptu races down Jermyn Street.

"Your friends must be men of means," she said, picking up her cup. Over the rim, she glanced toward the Hardens. The waitress was serving them pie.

"Oh yes, they're good chaps."

"I'm surprised you wanted to leave them and come out here."

"Oh." Walmore sobered and speared a dumpling with his fork. "Well, business. You know."

Millie decided she wasn't going to get anything pertinent from him, and at last she declined dessert and gathered her things. "I must go upstairs and pack. I expect to travel tomorrow. It was pleasant eating with you, Mr. Walmore."

"Oh, indeed. Thank you for allowing me to join you."

He stood and bowed. Millie gave him a smile and walked away.

Peregrin ate two pieces of pie and emptied the teapot. He supposed he'd have to go down to the saloon to get a real drink to top off his meal—but would the two thugs let him?

Sitting through dinner with Mrs. Evans had been an ordeal. What was she scheming at? She'd flat out rejected his invitation this morning, and then she practically forced him to sit with her. If he hadn't feared that Wilkes and Teddy would thwart him, he would have gone elsewhere for his dinner just to avoid meeting her again. And then she turned all charming.

No matter. Now he needed to formulate a plan. Her chatter had kept him from thinking things through. If he wasn't going to try to borrow from David, what *was* he going to do? He needed money, and quickly.

He couldn't up and kill the man here, or he'd be found out. On the other hand, if he did, he might be able to lift some funds from David's person or luggage. And he needed cash if he was going to flee from Baxter's thugs.

Carefully he weighed the options. He really disliked the idea of harming Randolph's cousin, on a purely physical level. However, if he didn't somehow stop David, Randolph and Merry would never own Stoneford. And he might need their goodwill in the future, not to mention a loan now and then. So he *had* to do something to keep David from returning to England. . .permanently.

But if he hung about Independence too long in order to do that, Wilkes and Teddy would hound him, in which case his own life would be worth less than David's. That giant, Wilkes, could crush him like a gnat.

Peregrin touched his cheek gingerly and winced at the pain. He did not want to deal with Wilkes again, but if he lingered until three o'clock, he would have no alternative. The scant three hundred dollars he had left would take him back East. Perhaps that was best. He couldn't return to New York, where Baxter was, but some other city, perhaps.

On consideration, it appeared that he had two possible courses of action. He could either flee from his adversaries immediately or stay to carry out Merrileigh's business. His fear of Wilkes loomed larger and more immediate than his desire to please Merry—tempered as it was with his distaste for completing her charge. He drained his teacup and mustered his courage.

Millie passed the Hardens' table and gave a little nod. They appeared to be finished as well. She went into the lobby, if one could call the dim entrance hall that, and waited near the stairs. A moment later, the couple emerged from the dining room.

"Do you have time to come up to Mr. Stone's room?" Millie asked.

"Should we?" Mr. Harden glanced at his wife and back to Millie. "Did you learn something?"

"No, not really. He never mentioned David or the Stone family. He seems a rather vacuous, lazy fellow who likes to go about with his chums and watch horseraces."

"Ah," said Isabelle Harden. "Perhaps you'll have to be more direct."

"Yes," Mr. Harden said. "You might have to ask him flat out if he knows Mr. Stone."

"I guess it comes down to that if we want to know what he's about," Millie said.

"Speaking of his rather nebulous activities," Mrs. Harden said, "did he explain to you why his face is so disfigured?"

"And was it that way the first time you met him?" the reverend asked. "You didn't mention it."

"No, he looked fine this morning. He said something about running into a horse."

Isabelle frowned and shook her head, as though she'd never heard anything sillier.

Millie looked back toward the dining room. "Do you think I should—"

The door opened, and Mr. Walmore, glorious in his multi-hued bruises, emerged.

"Mr. Walmore," Millie called without benefit of further deliberation, "come and meet my friends."

He looked at her, startled, and approached, uneasily eyeing the couple with her. "Hullo."

Millie put on her brightest smile. "I was just telling Mr. and Mrs. Harden about you." She smiled at the couple. "This is Mr. Walmore, a guest here."

"How do you do," said Isabelle.

Mr. Harden shook Walmore's hand. "Pleased to meet you, sir."

"Likewise," Walmore said.

"When Mrs. Evans told us about you, we of course thought of our other acquaintance here at the hotel," Mr. Harden said. "Pray tell us, are you acquainted with Mr. David Stone?"

"I—" Walmore blinked at him, then shot a glance at Millie. "Uh, Stone, you say? Here in this hotel? I don't believe—"

"He's from England," Millie said quickly. "We thought perhaps you knew him."

"Oh. Well, there are lots of people in England."

"True."

He hesitated. "There was a family. . .hmm. . .country estate. . . well, I wouldn't say I'm chummy with them, but if that's the family you mean. . ."

"It may well be," Millie said. "I'm sure Mr. Stone would be happy to make your acquaintance."

"Oh well!" Unless she was mistaken, Walmore's face flushed, but it wasn't easy to tell because of his injuries. "Er. . .not sure I know the chap personally. Perhaps. . ."

"May we look for you in the dining room this evening?" Millie asked. "Say, six o'clock? You could meet him then."

He chuckled, but it sounded a bit nervous. "You Americans eat so awfully early, what?"

"I suppose we do," Millie said. "Would seven be better?"

"Oh no, six is fine. And now, if you'll excuse me. . ."

"Of course," Millie said.

The Hardens bade him farewell, and Walmore strode to the front door. He opened it and stood for a moment, looking out. To Millie's surprise, he backed away from the door and turned about. He kept his head down and didn't meet her gaze as he walked quickly to the main staircase.

"Well!" Isabelle said when he'd disappeared above.

"Well indeed," her husband mused. "Didn't want to come out and say he knew the Stones, did he?"

"No, he certainly didn't," Millie said. "What shall I do?"

"I suppose you should tell Mr. Stone and let him decide whether he thinks it would be a risk to come down to supper.

"Yes. I can't think of anything else."

"Well, we really ought to go home," Isabelle said. "I left the girls alone, and they're good girls, but I don't like to be gone too long."

"Yes, and I must work on my sermon this afternoon," her husband said. "Please thank Mr. Stone. I'm sorry you didn't learn something useful."

Millie shook his hand and gave Isabelle a brief hug. "Thank you both for your kindness."

"You're welcome, dear," Isabelle said. "Have a safe journey. Joseph and I shall be praying for you."

Millie hurried up the stairs. She had a feeling David wouldn't be pleased, but there wasn't much she could do about that.

CHAPTER 31

Peregrin hurried to his room and hastily threw all his things into his bags. He could leave word for Millie Evans that he'd been called away suddenly. He had to leave quickly. If he stayed around for a couple more hours, Wilkes and Teddy would pay him another visit and thrash him—or worse. They were lurking directly across the street, in plain view. When he'd looked out, Wilkes had leered at him, while Teddy calmly whittled away at a stick with a lethal-looking knife. Peregrin shuddered and pocketed the stash of money from the dresser drawer.

Fleeing now would mean he wouldn't meet David Stone tonight. But if he came face to face with Stone, he doubted he'd have the nerve to go ahead with Merrileigh's request. No, it would be better to leave before the thugs' deadline expired.

He flirted with the idea of going up to David's room now and introducing himself. But what then? He'd already convinced himself that he couldn't kill the man in his hotel room and get away with it. He doubted he could steal from him either, without being caught. And one could hardly barge into a fellow's chamber and say, "Hello, I'm a social connection of your family's. Would you give me a loan?"

On top of all that, Merrileigh would be furious if he borrowed from David for his own purposes. And she'd still expect him to turn around and kill the poor man. Why had he ever told her he'd do it? Peregrin clutched his head with both hands. Was he insane?

Best to make a run for it. If all else failed, he would appeal to Stone, but it seemed horribly bad form to cadge from a fellow you planned to kill later.

He couldn't walk out the front door, or they'd see him immediately. Besides, his luggage was too heavy to carry all the way

889

to the train station, and it would make him conspicuous. After some thought, Peregrin went downstairs and found the boy, Wilfred, and paid him to go and hire a rig at the nearest livery stable.

"And tell the driver to be sure and come to the back door," he said sternly.

It was almost too easy. He gave Wilfred enough money to cover his hotel bill and a tip. With the rest of the three hundred dollars he'd salvaged divided among his pockets and a five-dollar bill in his shoe, he urged the driver to head out the lane behind the inn and take a back street for the first few blocks.

He hoped a train would be ready to leave when he arrived, so that he could board it at once, with no waiting about on the platform. He didn't particularly care where the first train was headed.

Over and over he played out his conversations with Millie Evans. How close were she and David? If he *had* gone up to Stone's room, would she have been there? Maybe he should have stayed and tried to set up David's "accident" at once. Or if he could have hidden from the thugs long enough, maybe he could have gotten into Stone's room while he was at dinner. Other scenarios appeared, now that he was out of striking distance. Could he have killed him and taken all his money, so that it looked like a stranger had robbed him?

The driver pulled up before the depot and climbed down to set his bags out. Peregrin paid him, though it hurt to part with more of his funds. Now to buy a ticket and board a train. He wouldn't feel safe until the wheels were rolling over the rails.

He didn't even make it to the ticket window. Wilkes stepped out from the shadows at the depot entrance and yanked him aside.

"Going someplace, Walmore?"

"Uh. . ." Peregrin swiveled his head and took in Wilkes's sneer and Teddy's grim face. "Just seeing off a friend."

"Oh, and taking his luggage in for him, were you?" Teddy asked brightly.

Peregrin's stomach dropped. He should have taken a steamboat instead of the train. But they probably would have followed him there as well. He let go of the bags, and they thudded to the ground.

"Come on." Wilkes steered Peregrin toward the street. "Get his baggage, Ted."

"Listen, this isn't what you think," Peregrin said.

"And what do we think?" Teddy asked as he bent to pick up Peregrin's fine-grained leather valises.

He had no answer, and Wilkes pulled him along roughly until they came to a gap between a saloon and a wheelwright's shop. The giant shoved Peregrin into the alley and pulled him up behind the saloon.

"All right, give up everything you've got, right now. Then we'll talk about the balance."

"But I. . .I haven't anything," Peregrin said.

"Oh, and how were you going to buy a ticket, then?"

"Besides," Teddy said drily from behind him, "we saw you pay off the liveryman. You've got *somethin'* in your pocket, man."

"I should have gone down with you." David tapped the floor hard with his cane. He shouldn't let Millie run this fox to earth for him.

"If all goes well, you'll see him tonight. Then maybe we'll get to the bottom of it." Millie shook her head ruefully as she gathered the dishes from David's dinner and stacked them on the tray. "I'm sorry I didn't find out more for you."

"Well, it's clear he had no intention of making himself known to me."

Millie clamped her teeth together and puzzled over Walmore's behavior. "You don't suppose he could be telling the truth, do you, and he barely remembers your family?"

"I don't see how. I mean, if his sister is married to Randolph, every member of the Stone family in England was probably at the wedding."

"Maybe he's just slow-witted."

David shook his head. "I don't know. But I can't see how he can have helped knowing who I am." He laughed and gave a little shrug. "There. Perhaps I think too much of myself. I suppose it's possible no one in England remembers me."

"Oh, I doubt that," Millie said.

Yes, David reflected. The Earl of Stoneford was known throughout British society. Not that Richard had carried himself with pomp or self-importance. He'd been a regular fellow, whom everyone liked. But he was conspicuous in his position. If Walmore hadn't lived under a rock near the Scottish border, he *had* to know who the Stones were. Especially if he was related to Randolph's wife.

"Well, I'm through being helpless. I'm going to meet this fellow, one way or another."

"Fine," Millie said. "We'll go down at six and watch for him."

"No. I want you to ask Simmons for his room number. I intend to pay a call on Mr. Walmore. At once."

Wilkes held Peregrin pinned against the saloon wall, and Teddy moved in. He drew back his fist.

"Wait! Don't hit me. Please."

"Why not?" Teddy asked. "I been wantin' to pound you all day."

"There is something I could do."

Wilkes let go of him with one hand and waved Teddy back. "Spill it."

"There's a fellow at the hotel. I don't know him really, but I believe we have some mutual acquaintances. I don't know if he has any money or not, but perhaps I could ask him to help me."

Wilkes scowled. "We're not talking about borrowing a buck here."

"I know," Peregrin said hastily. "This fellow—well, he seems pretty well set up. He may not be able to give me anything, but it might be worth a try."

Wilkes looked at his pal. "What do you think, Teddy?"

Teddy scratched his head. "How well do you know this gent?"

"Uh, well. . ." Peregrin gulped. "He's connected to my family."

"What do you mean, connected?" Wilkes asked. "Like he's hitched to their mule team?"

"No." The more Peregrin thought about it, the better this idea seemed. He forgot all his previous objections. Surely if David knew it was a matter of life or death, he would come through. "He's actually...well, my sister's married to his cousin, but he doesn't really know me."

The two thugs frowned at each other.

"You're both staying in the same hotel, and he's married to your sister, and he doesn't know you?" Teddy asked.

"That's not what I said. His *cousin* is married to my sister."

"Oh." Teddy looked doubtfully to Wilkes.

The giant shrugged. "Has he got the ready?"

"I don't know. Maybe. His family's swimming in it. But he hasn't seen me since I've been here."

"Do tell." Wilkes relaxed his grasp on Peregrin's shirt. "So you're going to renew your acquaintance with this sort-of kin of yours and see how much you can get from him. You got that?"

"Yes."

"First, give us every red cent you have on you or in your things," Teddy said. "No holding back."

"Yeah." Wilkes grinned. "And Teddy, you can hit him once if you want, for holding out on us this morning. But just once."

"Is that really necess—" Peregrin gasped as Teddy's fist rammed his stomach. He doubled over, fighting dizziness and nausea.

After a few seconds, his spinning world began to slow down. Wilkes took hold of his coat collar and pulled him erect.

"All right, now. Give it up. All of it."

Peregrin fumbled for his wallet. Before he could open it, Teddy plucked it from his hands. He riffled through it and handed it back to Peregrin empty.

"Now the rest," he growled.

"The rest?"

Wilkes hit him hard, a little higher than Teddy's blow, and Peregrin saw colorful flashes of light. He couldn't haul in a breath. He sank to the ground and felt himself sinking into darkness. When he could register that he was still alive, Wilkes was rifling his pockets. Maybe if he feigned continued unconsciousness, they'd take his cash and leave him alone.

"Well, that's another two hunnert," Wilkes muttered.

"Here's another wad." Teddy pulled more money from Peregrin's trouser pocket.

"Come on, Walmore, on your feet." The giant lifted him bodily, and Peregrin couldn't see any sense in flopping back down in the dirt.

He opened his eyes slowly and hung on Wilkes's meaty arm. "Wha—"

"You're going back to the hotel," Teddy said.

Wilkes nodded, grinning. "That's right. You find this friend of yours and put the squeeze on him. We'll be waiting outside—and watching both doors. You hear me?" He shook Peregrin as though trying to make his instructions settle quicker.

"Yes!" The shaking stopped. Peregrin stood still for a long moment as he caught his breath and rubbed his abdomen.

"What's the matter?" Teddy asked sweetly. "You look like you got a bellyache."

Peregrin grimaced and set out for the hotel without looking at them. He could hear their footsteps behind him as he staggered from the alley. Once he got out on the street, passersby stared at him, but he kept his head down and trudged for the Frontier Hotel.

David rapped smartly on the door of 201. He waited, but no sound came from within. He looked at Millie, who stood beside him.

"Try again, just in case," she said.

He lifted his cane and used the handle to knock—a loud, authoritative sound.

After a few seconds, he turned away. "All right, he's not in."

"I guess we'll have to wait until supper and see if he shows up," Millie said. "Come, let's get you back upstairs."

David huffed out a breath. "I'll be glad when we put this place behind us."

"And that will be at first light," Millie said cheerfully. "Come. Just one more night here and we're off."

Peregrin entered the hotel at half past four. He ought to go right up to 302 and accost Stone, but he didn't like the idea. Better to keep his supper engagement and approach the matter like a gentleman. Perhaps he could get some money out of David without telling him everything.

A mirror graced the wall in the entry, above a horsehair-covered settee. Peregrin caught a glimpse of his battered face in it as he passed through the lobby. What would Stone think of his appearance? Had that gentleman ever been attacked in the street? Mrs. Evans had shown sympathy, but Stone might just peg him for a fool.

He stopped at the desk and got his key back. Mr. Simmons welcomed him back and assured him his room was as he'd left it. Resigned, Peregrin dragged himself up the stairs. He ached all over, and his stomach and breastbone were tender and sore. His cheek still smarted some, too, and his head throbbed unbearably. He might as well have thrown himself in front of a battering ram as to face those two thugs.

His hand shook as he unlocked the door. He would lie down and try to rest for an hour. What else could he do?

If he lingered in his room, would Wilkes and Teddy storm the establishment and come after him, as they had before? He hoped not. If they did, he would tell them David was out and he hoped to see him at supper. That ought to work, or it would with any reasonable man.

Of course, Wilkes and Teddy were not always reasonable.

Peregrin wished he had a bottle of whiskey, but there was no way he could get past the bloodhounds to buy one, and Mr. Simmons had already informed him that he didn't serve liquor. Besides, if he spent part of his last five dollars on drink, he would be truly destitute.

Always before, he'd had his friends to fall back on until his next allowance came through, or else he could go join a friendly card game with the hope of winning a few pounds. In a tight pinch, there was Merrileigh and her husband, slightly better off than middle class. His sister could be counted on for short-term small loans, so long as he didn't ask too often.

But now he was left to his own devices, and it felt horrid.

CHAPTER 32

Millie and David entered the dining room at quarter to six. A strong odor of cooking grease wafted out from the kitchen. Millie surveyed the patrons.

"He's not here. Let us find a table with an extra seat and watch for him."

They claimed one that would allow them to observe the door and ordered tea.

"We expect Mr. Walmore to join us," Millie told Sarah. When the waitress had left them, she appraised David. He was a bit pale, but that was understandable. He looked fit, and his tailored clothing and impeccable grooming set him off as what he was—a fine English gentleman. She had no doubt that within a few weeks he would regain his strength and agility.

"What are you smirking at?" David asked.

"Was I smirking? I suppose, if you want the truth, I was thinking how different you look from the first time I saw you."

He frowned for a moment. "Oh yes, in the lobby of the hotel in Scottsburg. I believe I'd just come in from my mining claim and was sadly in need of a bath."

She laughed, glad they could mention it without either of them prickling. "You were a handsome man then. It was obvious to all that you didn't avoid hard work."

"As opposed to my appearance now?"

She shrugged. "Those who know you realize you are a complex man, Mr. Stone. But yes, those who've never made your acquaintance might, on first glance, assume you are a man of leisure."

"And those who met you for the first time tonight would find you a fascinating woman—one whose acquaintance they longed to cultivate."

She felt her cheeks flush. "Thank you, sir." He'd never spoken to her in such a manner, not even in Scottsburg. His words confused her. She would like to think he'd changed his opinion of her, but still he intended to leave her in Philadelphia and sail out of her life. That much they both understood. The rest was still murky, and a change of subject might be in order.

"How is your leg?"

"Better. In fact, I felt hardly a twinge as we came down the stairs."

Sarah brought their tea and set out the pot and three cups. "Do you want to order now?"

Millie looked to David, quirking her eyebrows.

"We might as well," he said.

"All right, it's roast beef or fried fish tonight."

They told Sarah their wishes from the limited menu. A few minutes later, Millie glimpsed Walmore, peering in at the doorway.

"He's here," she whispered to David.

When Walmore's gaze landed on her, she smiled and beckoned discreetly. His face was still hideously discolored, and he moved slowly. As he approached their table, David rose.

"Mr. Walmore, may I present Mr. Stone?" Millie said.

"Good evening, sir." Walmore extended his hand tentatively, and David shook it.

"Have a seat." David resumed his place, and Walmore sat down opposite him, with Millie between them. "That's quite a badge you're wearing on your face, sir. May I ask how you got it?"

Walmore put his fingertips up to his swollen cheek. "I hate to admit it, but I ran afoul of some rather obnoxious thugs."

Millie arched her eyebrows. "That's not quite what you told me this morning, sir."

"Well, no." He gave her a deprecating smile. "One doesn't like to admit to a lady that he's been bested at fisticuffs and robbed."

"Robbed?" Millie said.

"Really, sir! Have you spoken to the constabulary?" David asked.

"No. No, I haven't."

"Why ever not?" Millie asked.

"It's not a happy tale." Walmore looked at David. "I hoped perhaps I could have a private word with you later, Mr. Stone."

David's eyes narrowed, but he said affably, "Of course." He looked up as Sarah approached the table. "Oh, here's the waitress. Why don't you order your dinner, Mr. Walmore, and we'll talk of more pleasant things for now."

When he had ordered, the newcomer fixed his tea and smiled at Millie. "So, you are both leaving Independence tomorrow—is that correct?"

"Yes," she said.

"I'm thinking I may leave, too," Walmore said. "I've not had the best of fortune here."

"Are you going back to England?" David asked.

"Not just yet, but I shall head back to the East Coast."

"Ah." David waited until the waitress placed his and Millie's plates before them and took Walmore's order before changing the subject. Millie just sipped her tea, unfolded her napkin, and smiled.

"Now, tell me, sir," David said, "is your family not connected with mine by marriage? It seems to me that my niece said my cousin Randolph married a Walmore."

"That's correct. My sister. Merrileigh, her name is. They have a townhouse in London."

"Yes, and Randolph's father had a small country house as well. . . ."

"I believe that's gone out of the family since you left England," Walmore said. He took a quick gulp of his tea.

"I see. Well, it's quite a coincidence us meeting up on the frontier like this." David smiled at him, but his tone clearly asked for information.

"I came out here to see a bit of the West," Walmore said. "Oh, and a friend asked me to look over some land. But since I'm now nearly penniless, I think I'd best head back to civilization and see if I can't recoup my losses."

"Perhaps your bank could send you some money here," David suggested.

Walmore frowned. "Unfortunately, I closed my bank account in New York when I left there. I'm afraid I'll have to rely on the charity of friends until I can get a bank draft from England." His eyes flickered, and Millie wondered if he really thought he could do that. Maybe he was just saying it so they wouldn't think he was a complete derelict. But from her experience, she felt it was more likely he was sizing David up as a potential "friend."

"I wish you the best," David said and turned back to his meal.

They continued eating, and the two men discussed a few mutual acquaintances. Mr. Walmore described some recent happenings in London and occasionally shot a remark or a question Millie's way, but he seemed intent on winning David over.

Sarah had just delivered three slices of apple pie and a fresh pot of tea when Walmore smiled ingratiatingly at David and said, "I suppose your first order of business on British soil will be to claim your late brother's title."

Millie caught her breath. She didn't mean to stare at David, but she couldn't help it. Why hadn't she known about this? It made sense, starting with the day Anne arrived at the farm in Oregon, telling her and Sam that David had inherited something from his brother. Did no one in America know that he was a true aristocrat? He must have kept it a secret. All the way from Oregon to Independence, he'd certainly been reticent about his background. He had mentioned a country home once or twice, and lately he'd let fall a few tidbits that led Millie to believe his family traveled high in London society. But she'd never dreamed he held a title. Or would, it appeared, when he returned to England.

David was looking at her. She reached for her teacup as a way to camouflage her dismay. How could she have allowed herself to hope he was warming toward her? A lord would never marry someone like her. And he'd done all in his power to make sure she knew nothing of his true situation.

"Mr. Walmore," David said evenly, "I'd appreciate it if you didn't speak of this matter. It's not settled yet, and I don't wish people to hear rumors and speculate."

"Of course not, sir. Forgive my thoughtlessness. But I wish you the best."

David nodded and took a bite of his pie.

Millie could scarcely keep her cup steady enough to take a sip. Would David be willing to talk to her about this later? Or would he deposit her in Philadelphia without explanation and go off to live in his castle?

"Won't you come up to my room, Mr. Walmore?" David said when they all had finished their dessert. "I believe we can talk privately there."

"That's most kind of you," Walmore murmured.

David rose, but his stiffness slowed him, and Walmore jumped to pull out Millie's chair before he could.

Her features were impassive, but her cheeks bore spots of high color that David didn't think were caused by rouge. He'd have to tell her everything now. She probably deserved to know. He almost wished he'd told her earlier, but he couldn't change that. She would be discreet about it—he was sure of that now. Keeping Walmore quiet might be more difficult.

When they reached the stairs, Walmore said, "Lean on me, if you will, sir. I see that your injury is not completely healed."

"I'm fine," David said, slightly annoyed. "I shall come along a little slowly, but I'll get there." Using his cane and the railing, he mounted the first few steps as vigorously as he could. The pain in his bones was still there, but much less than it had been previously, and he was able to put up a good front for the first flight. Walmore himself seemed to limp a bit, and David wondered how badly he'd been beaten.

They reached the landing, and Millie gazed at him anxiously.

"One minute," David said, leaning heavily on the railing. He tried not to pant, but to breathe slowly and normally.

"I say, my room is right here," Walmore said. "You could come in there for our chat if you wish. I could help you up to your own room afterward."

David hesitated. Millie looked alarmed. Was she worried about leaving him alone with Walmore? He supposed he would feel a little less vulnerable if they met in his own room. He had a sitting area there, and Millie would be just across the hall. He could leave his door open to reassure her. After the attacks on him last year, he supposed it made sense, though this fellow seemed rather a vacuous young whip, one of the useless, idle society lads he disdained. He'd refused to become like Walmore—that was part of coming to America in the first place. He'd never wanted it said that he was the lazy third son of an earl who never got his hands dirty.

"I think perhaps I'll be more comfortable in my own chamber," he said. "My leg still pains me some, and Mrs. Evans can help me get settled before she leaves us." Millie gave a tiny nod. David wished he could speak to her without Walmore overhearing. He smiled and set his cane on the first step of the next flight. "Shall we?"

A few minutes later, they had reached the sanctuary of his room. With a sigh, he sank into the chair by the window. Millie set the straight chair in place for Walmore.

"Shall I get your medicine, Mr. Stone?" she asked.

"Oh, no thank you," David said. "I think I'm all right for now."

They both knew she'd dosed him shortly before their trip to the dining room. Millie must be giving him an opening to keep her there a little longer.

"It's warm in here, however," David said. "I'd appreciate it if you'd crack this window open and leave the door ajar when you leave."

"Certainly." Millie opened the window a few inches, as he'd requested. It did let in a soothing breeze, and it also gave credence to his ruse about leaving the door open.

"Well, gentlemen, if there's nothing else. . ." She gazed expectantly at David.

"I shall call out if I need you."

She nodded and left the room. David had no doubt she would also leave her door open and be ready to return at an instant. This, he hoped, would serve as notice to Walmore that any funny business would come home to rest squarely on him.

And now, he thought, how long before he asks for money?

Peregrin sat facing David Stone, completely at a loss for words.

"Tell me what happened when you were robbed," Stone said. "Did it take place here in the hotel?"

"No, out on the street. A couple of fellows accosted me. One was a huge brute. I tried to put up a fight, but that was a mistake."

"It usually is," Stone replied. "So, I suppose your pockets are to let now."

Peregrin winced. "I'm afraid so, sir. They took everything I owned but five dollars, which I had hidden away. If not for that—well, let us just say that by the time I settle my bill here, I shall be strapped. I doubt I can get passage back to New York."

Stone sighed and eyed him thoughtfully—disapprovingly, Peregrin felt. "I don't like to see a countryman in need. But neither do I like to give out large sums of money, especially to people I don't know."

"Perfectly understandable," Peregrin said quickly. "In fact, I feel the same way, sir, and it pains me greatly to ask you to come to my aid."

"Well, I shan't leave you here in dire straits. After all, you are connected somewhat to the family." Stone reached inside his coat—for his wallet, Peregrin hoped. Of course, his plan to ask David to cover his entire debt to Baxter and his flunkies could hardly come to fruition now. He'd look awfully shabby if he touched David for more than the minimum to get him to New York.

Instead of a wallet, however, Stone brought out a pair of railway tickets and squinted at them.

"Let's see, our train goes at 7:20 in the morning. Can you meet us at the station by seven? Or ride with us if you like. I'll purchase your ticket then, and you can go with us as far as Philadelphia. I'm going to escort Mrs. Evans to her friends there, before I go on to New York."

"That's very good of you."

Inside, Peregrin fumed. He wasn't going to hand over a cent.

Not one penny. How was that supposed to help him with Wilkes and Teddy? Should he tell Stone everything and throw himself on his mercy?

"Well then," Stone said cordially, "we shall see you in the morning."

Peregrin caught his breath. He hadn't expected to be dismissed quite so summarily. But if he showed displeasure, Stone might back out on his offer to buy his train ticket. Peregrin rose.

"Yes, indeed. Thank you very much." At the doorway, he dared to turn back. "I don't suppose. . ." He appraised David's impassive face. What plausible excuse could he give to elicit a few more dollars? "Well, I don't like to mention it, but I had hoped to see a medical man before I leave here. I'm afraid those thugs cracked a rib or something." He rubbed his abdomen, which truthfully was very sore.

"I doubt any doctor would come out tonight unless it was an emergency. But go around to Doctor Lee this evening if you want. Tell him to add it to my bill." David rattled off the address.

Peregrin blinked. Best to just accept that graciously, he supposed.

"Thank you, sir." Recognizing defeat, he bowed himself out of the room. The door across the hall stood a bit ajar, but he could see no sign of Mrs. Evans in his brief glance. He strolled to the landing and down to his room below. Now what? He certainly couldn't go out to consult the doctor, much as he would like to. His head ached terribly, and his ribcage pained every time he moved. But he'd hurt a lot worse if he tried to leave the hotel again without paying Wilkes and Teddy.

For the next hour, Peregrin paced his room. What could he do? Maybe if he sneaked up to David's room in the night, he could take his wallet and. . . No, as much as Merrileigh would like to see the job done, he wasn't going to raise a hand against David Stone in this hotel. He would be the first suspect. But if he met Stone and Mrs. Evans in the morning and got on the train with them. . .

He fetched up by his window and peered out around the edge of the curtain. Teddy stood across the street whittling, as seemed to be his hobby. No doubt Wilkes was nearby. Or perhaps they spelled each other so they could eat dinner in turns and not lose sight of him.

As he watched, Wilkes joined Teddy. Peregrin drew back a little. The two talked for a minute. Teddy shook his head and whittled. Wilkes crossed his arms and leaned against the building, watching the hotel.

Millie hustled to get their bags out to the landing in the morning. She'd suggested that David shave the evening before, to save time. Yawning, Billy answered her summons and carried their bags down. The driver she'd engaged was on time, but there was no sign of Walmore. She tipped Billy and ran upstairs to see that David got down in one piece.

They met on the second-floor landing. David was moving fairly confidently, using the cane more as an accessory than a crutch.

"Where's Walmore?" he asked first thing.

"Haven't seen him," Millie replied.

David nodded to the door marked 201. "That's his room. I'll see if I can raise him."

"All right. I'm going down and make sure the bags are all loaded. If Mrs. Simmons is up, I'll see if she has hot water. Maybe you can get a cup of tea."

"No time." David strode to Walmore's door and rapped on it with his cane.

Millie bustled on down the stairs. Let David handle this. The young paragon of British indolence was probably sound asleep. Would David wait for him? She strongly doubted that. David was a good traveler and never missed a departure unless he meant to. Rather wise of him not to give Walmore any money, nor purchase the man's ticket until they reached the station. He was a shrewd businessman, and she liked that in him.

The driver lounged on the seat of his wagon but straightened when she came out of the hotel, wrapping her shawl snugly about her shoulders.

"All ready now?" he asked.

"Almost. Mr. Stone is checking on the third member of our party."

"Got plenty of time, have you?" the man asked.

"I should think so." The sun was barely over the horizon, and that meant they had about an hour before train time. Even so, Millie looked anxiously back toward the door. As of yet, there was no sign of David or Walmore. Across the street, a large man rose from behind a rain barrel, stretching. Had he slept there? Maybe he fell into a drunken stupor in the shadow of the building last night. Millie looked hastily away. Had she seen that big fellow before?

"You can climb up if you want to, ma'am."

She glanced at the driver, then the wagon seat, and decided to wait until David was present. Besides, what kind of gentleman told a woman to climb up without getting down to offer his assistance?

At last the door of the hotel opened. Billy ambled out carrying two leather bags.

"Where is Mr. Stone?" Millie asked when he reached the wagon.

"He's dressing the other gent."

Millie sighed. "All right. After you put those in the wagon, could you give me a hand up, Billy?"

He smiled at her. "Sure can, Miz Evans."

He'd been so helpful over the past two months, and so good-natured, that on impulse Millie dug out an extra half dime for him.

At last David came out, followed by a rumpled and scruffy-looking Walmore. The young man hadn't shaved, and he wore his hat pulled low over his face, shadowing his black eye.

"Jump in," David said, indicating the wagon bed. He climbed up beside Millie. When Walmore had dragged himself up over the wheel and thumped into the back with the luggage, the driver cracked his whip smartly, and they moved off up the street toward the train station.

Millie looked back and saw the large man by the rain barrel staring after them.

Peregrin shuddered and hunkered down in the wagon bed. Wilkes was on watch across the street, and he'd seen him. He could only hope that the two thugs would not confront them. If he stuck close to Stone and Mrs. Evans, perhaps he could get away with this, but those two were persistent.

The early morning streets were all but empty, and the horse trotted right along. Next thing Peregrin knew, they were pulling the baggage out of the wagon, and David paid off the driver. Peregrin grabbed his own luggage and flung a glance over his shoulder. So far, so good. Wilkes would have had to hoof it mighty fast to get here by now, and Peregrin was banking on the giant's having to go round up his friend first. With any luck, they'd lost the pair. Of course they'd seen all the bags loaded, but they just might head for the steamboat docks first.

Inside the station, he waited impatiently for the others. Of course, being a gentleman, Stone was pampering Mrs. Evans. Peregrin supposed he oughtn't to have dashed inside so quickly, but he wanted to get off the street and out of sight. A minute later, they entered with the remaining luggage. Stone was limping but couldn't use his cane because both his hands were full of baggage.

"I say, let me help you," Peregrin dropped one of his own valises and stepped forward. "Forgive me, I should have thought."

"I hoped the driver would carry our things in," David said, "but he wanted to go. I'll see about a porter once we've purchased your ticket."

Peregrin broke out in a sweat while he waited. He couldn't stop staring at the main entrance to the depot. Mrs. Evans stood serenely beside the pile of luggage while Stone completed the transaction at the ticket window. Finally Peregrin had the ticket in his hand.

"I can't tell you how much I appreciate this." He glanced once more toward the door, hoping he would never need to explain the exact depth of his gratitude.

"Don't mention it." Stone waved a porter over and showed him his ticket.

"You want to go right out there, sir," said the porter. "Your train is just pulling in. I'll take your luggage to the baggage car."

"Thank you." Stone put some money in the man's hand and

took Mrs. Evans's arm. "Come, Mildred." He threw a glance over his shoulder.

Peregrin pasted on a smile and hastened after them, leaving his bags with theirs. The train chuffed in, and they all stopped on the platform and clapped their hands to their ears. Once it had stopped, they had to wait for disembarking passengers to climb down. Peregrin thought he might die of apoplexy if they didn't get aboard soon.

At last they were seated in the passenger car. He deliberately avoided a window seat, not wanting a chance of Wilkes and Teddy spotting him from outside. The wait for the wheels to start rolling seemed interminable, but Stone and Mrs. Evans chatted amiably.

Peregrin noted Stone's attentions to the lady—nothing excessive, yet when he inquired whether she was warm enough and had sufficient room for her sundries, Stone sounded as solicitous as a new husband might on his honeymoon. All his addresses lacked were *my dear*s and *darling Mildred*s. Peregrin didn't doubt for half a second that David Stone was a smitten man. Perhaps he could use that to his advantage. He only hoped that dear Mildred didn't get in his way when the time came to execute the rest of his plan.

CHAPTER 33

The ride to St. Louis took most of the day, but David found the journey almost pleasant with Millie at his side. It would have been even more enjoyable if Peregrin Walmore had not sat opposite him.

The young man appeared to be ill—apart from his black eye. His nerves apparently jangled badly, so that he jumped every time someone came down the aisle from behind him. He perspired copiously, though the railway car was not overly warm.

At one stop, they got up to stretch their legs, and David managed to take him aside for a moment.

"Are you all right, Walmore?"

"What? Me? Oh, I'm fine, sir."

"I thought perhaps you were ill. You did say the men who robbed you roughed you up a bit."

"I'll be fine, I assure you. I just. . .travel doesn't agree with me."

"I see." David wanted to ask why on earth he'd come all the way across the ocean and halfway across the continent. But he would leave impertinence to the young.

Millie had found an urchin selling sandwiches and apple fritters on the platform, and David willingly handed her enough money to purchase a lunch for the three of them. Walmore seemed very grateful and stammered out an offer to pay for his own, but David didn't want to see him hand over his last few coins. He wasn't heartless. Assuming, of course, that Walmore was telling the truth about his funds.

Millie exhibited more courtesy and charm toward their new companion than David felt, and he was proud of her. Aside from her accent, no one would think she was any less a lady than Anne.

He wasn't the only man observing her. Walmore seemed quite taken with her, and David intercepted the gazes of several other male passengers who also found Millie pleasing to look at.

And why not? Her face and form would attract any man, and she had an alluring combination of good health, an active spirit, and a pleasant demeanor. She was also a thinking woman, and a spiritual one. In short, she had every quality one would expect in a lady. So why should she not be designated such?

By the time they reached St. Louis, David's mind was made up. There was no one else he would rather have beside him when he took his title—or when he returned to his childhood home. Mildred Evans was the perfect candidate to become the next Lady Stoneford.

Peregrin feared that, for Mrs. Evans's sake, Stone would insist they spend a night in St. Louis. They reached the city late in the day, and the lady did admit to mild fatigue, but she insisted they should push on if possible.

This greatly relieved Peregrin. He wanted to keep moving until they were far away from Independence. And he doubted he'd ride all the way to New York. That would be foolhardy in his current situation. He'd have to find another coastal city where he could set himself up comfortably and yet not run into Baxter's minions. Perhaps he could cash in part of his ticket before they reached New York and fade into another municipality.

The ferry embarked just before sunset, and they were able to get a light supper on board. Once they reached the other side, a hack took them from the ferry dock to the railway station. To Peregrin's dismay, they had a two-hour wait. Their train would travel through the night, and Stone tried to engage a compartment, where they could sit in privacy, but none were available on this train. They would have to sit in a car with rows of seats, among the other travelers.

They escorted Mrs. Evans to the door of a ladies' waiting room in the depot, where she could rest in safety. Stone was of a mind to wander about the station and perhaps buy a newspaper. Peregrin would have preferred to stay out of sight, but there was no gentlemen's waiting room. He reasoned that he'd eluded his pursuers and had nothing to fear. Still, he couldn't help looking about for Wilkes, who would stand out in any crowd.

After a short while, Stone invited him to walk a couple of blocks to stretch his legs and buy something for them to eat on the train. Peregrin decided it was better than lolling about the depot, where he could be easily spotted. They found a general store still open, and Stone purchased a basket and filled it with crackers, dried fruit, peppermints, cheese, and jerky. After they returned to the station, they kicked about for another hour until their train was ready, and at last they were able to retrieve Mrs. Evans and board.

Rather than discuss his own activities or draw suspicion by inquiring about Stone's affairs in England, Peregrin asked him about his life in the West. Mrs. Evans seemed interested, too, though Peregrin had been under the impression that the two had known each other in Oregon. Stone grew more talkative than he had been to date and told about the stagecoach line he'd started with his niece's husband. Mrs. Evans asked him many questions about the line and how he had gone about establishing the stations and promoting its services. Peregrin observed them with interest. He still wasn't sure exactly the nature of their relationship.

"I'm surprised you wanted to take such an active part in the business, sir," he said. "An investment, yes, but it sounds as though you did most of the buying and organizing."

"Yes, I did." Stone fixed him with a keen eye. "I've been a working man the past twenty years, Walmore. And I don't intend to stop once I reach Stoneford."

"Ah, then you have plans for the estate."

"Indeed I do. I have no idea what has happened since Richard died, but Anne has given me a fair idea of the way things were before his death. I intend to keep the farms going and perhaps add a couple of other ventures."

"What sort of ventures?"

Stone lowered his gaze and shrugged. "I'd rather not discuss it until I see how things are at Stoneford, but if things go well, I shall institute some modern methods there."

Walmore nodded, more curious than ever. "I wish you success, sir." It was too bad the man wouldn't live long enough to carry out his plans.

The train rattled on through the night, making several brief stops to take on and discharge passengers and replenish their water and coal. A gas lamp flickered low at each end of the car, and the uncurtained windows let in moonlight. When it was too dark to read, they talked as quietly as the noise of their journey would allow.

"I'm sorry that we have to sit up all night," Stone said to Mrs. Evans. "The conductor tells me that we'll change to a different train in Illinois tomorrow, and we'll be able to get berths on that one."

"Well, it is only the two nights," Mrs. Evans said. "I'm sure we'll survive it."

Peregrin couldn't help thinking what a fuss Merrileigh would make if Randolph informed her that she would have to sit up all night in a common railroad carriage.

The conductor put out all but two gas lamps, one at each end of the car. After a while, most of the passengers sank down in their seats. Peregrin drifted in and out of sleep, using his wadded jacket as a pillow.

They stopped at a small town in Illinois just after dawn.

"This is where we change trains," Stone said.

The conductor assured them that their baggage would be transferred, and they climbed down to the platform. Walmore was beginning to feel secure, but he still looked sharply about as they strolled toward the depot.

They soon learned that they must wait three hours until the Philadelphia train was ready, and the station agent suggested a boardinghouse that would serve breakfast to early travelers.

"What do you say, Mildred?" Stone asked. "Shall we sit down to a hot breakfast?"

"It sounds lovely," she replied.

"Ah, excuse me for a minute." Stone eyed a sign on the wall. "They have a telegraph office, and I believe I'll send a wire, if you don't mind."

"Of course," Mrs. Evans told him. "Mr. Walmore and I shall ramble on to the end of the platform and back." She smiled at Peregrin. "Shall we?"

"Delighted." He offered his arm as Stone strode off to the telegraph operator's window, and she placed her gloved hand inside the crook of his elbow. Was the telegram going to David's banker in New York? Or perhaps he was sending a message to be forwarded to England.

Peregrin straightened his shoulders a bit. It felt good to be perambulating with a lady on his arm. He had neglected the fair sex too long on this journey. In fact, he hadn't come into the company of any women he'd call "ladies" since a party Nigel Wallace had thrown in New York. But Mrs. Evans definitely qualified. He'd decided that much since they'd boarded the train in Independence. She lacked a certain polish that British women of the upper class possessed, but she was gracious and kind. She also had discretion, and she managed to look lovely on a sooty train journey, which was saying a lot.

Stone returned as they ambled back toward the telegraph booth. "There, that's taken care of. Oh, and I spoke for sleeping compartments for us all tonight. We shan't have to worry about a thing until tomorrow evening, when we'll approach Philadelphia."

"Excellent," Mrs. Evans said.

"That's very good of you," Peregrin added.

They took their time over breakfast, savoring fresh fruit, good coffee, and perfectly cooked eggs. Still, they returned to the depot with time to spare. At last they settled in on the new train. The seats were better padded than those on the last train, and the car looked generally cleaner and better maintained. They passed the time in pleasant conversation, and at noon picnicked out of the basket, adding hot muffins and a jug of milk that Stone purchased from a vendor at one of the stops.

The day wore on, and Peregrin grew restless. He learned from the porter that the last carriage before the baggage car was open to gentlemen who wanted to smoke. His interest piqued immediately. Surely a card game would be found there. This train was definitely a cut above the last.

Around eight o'clock in the evening, Mrs. Evans confessed she was tired and rose.

"If you gentlemen will forgive me, I'd like to retire."

"Of course," Stone said. "Let me get the porter and ask him to get your berth ready."

"Have a good night," Peregrin said. When David had gone off down the aisle with Mrs. Evans, he headed in the opposite direction, for the smoking car. He had hardly any money on him, but he'd found that Americans sometimes played for very low stakes. He hadn't so much as mentioned it earlier—one didn't discuss gambling in the presence of a lady, and he was sure Stone wouldn't like to think he would borrow from him and then risk the small amount he had left.

But Stone didn't seem to be a smoker—or a drinker either, now that Peregrin thought about it. While that was odd, the gentleman wasn't likely to make his way to the smoking car. Unless, of course, he'd been waiting for Mrs. Evans to leave them to indulge. The poor chap had been cooped up in a hotel room for weeks, after all. It was just possible he might kick up his heels now. If Peregrin got into a game, he'd have to sit where he wouldn't easily be noticed if Stone glanced in.

He had to walk through two other carriages to reach the smoking car. Porters were beginning to lower the sleeping berths that hung above the seats, and passengers were moving about, rearranging their belongings and preparing to retire.

On the open platforms between cars, the wind tore at Peregrin. The night had turned quite chilly, and he hurried to get inside again.

The atmosphere was hazy blue in the smoking car, and the occupants looked quieter than he'd imagined. Several men sat chatting amiably with glasses in their hands. Peregrin smiled. They had a small bar back here, at the far end of the car. Apparently ladies were excluded, or perhaps they weren't told about it. And there was indeed a poker game going on in a corner. Four men sat around a small table that folded down from the wall, fanning out their cards.

Peregrin was just about to step forward and ask to be dealt in when he noticed a large man getting a drink at the bar.

A very large man.

Peregrin caught his breath and glanced quickly about. Sure enough, sitting with his back to the door of the car was a smaller man whose ears and worn jacket looked suspiciously like Teddy's. Peregrin ducked back, bumping into another passenger who'd just entered.

"Oh, excuse me."

He shoved past the man, wishing he hadn't opened his mouth. His accent would draw attention. He bustled out onto the little platform between cars and stood gasping for a moment. He didn't want to go inside the next car appearing discomposed, but he couldn't stay here. If Wilkes or Teddy came out, they'd have him at their mercy in a dangerous spot. He hurried into the next carriage, not daring to look back.

How had they caught up? They would kill him; he was sure of it—unless he somehow came up with the full amount he owed them. But Peregrin hadn't the means to win it back, even if he dared waltz in there and join the poker game. No, he could never do that with Wilkes and Teddy relaxing and wetting their whistles. He'd be too nervous to concentrate on a game, assuming they let him sit down and play. With his limited funds for a stake, the best he could hope for was to come away with pocket money for the trip, and that would never make the two toughs happy.

He mustn't let them know he'd seen them. Maybe he could leave the train at the next stop and disappear into the night.

But could he survive with only a few cents in his pocket? He hadn't enough for the meanest hotel room.

The only thing he could think of that would give him a remote chance of living through this horrible journey was to do what Merrileigh had sent him to do—and to pick David's pockets before he threw him off the train. He could pay the thugs from David's plump wallet and keep whatever was left.

The thought made him feel ill, and he slumped down into the

nearest empty seat. It was the only way, he told himself. He couldn't rob David Stone and leave him alive, or he'd be arrested before he had time to count his plunder.

His short-lived notion that he could bypass his sister's plan and continue supporting himself in America had gone by the wayside. He'd failed to make good on his first attempts at bringing in more money and had in fact lost most of what he began with. When he reached New York, or whatever destination he settled on, he would need money. And if he wanted Merrileigh to help him in the future, he had to get rid of David. No other way presented itself for him to satisfy his debt to Lionel Baxter and cut loose from the savage hounds nipping at his heels.

David made his way down the aisle from the tiny washroom toward his berth. Millie had settled in for the night in hers, and he supposed he may as well get as much sleep as he could. He paused halfway down the aisle. The porters had lowered most of the berths along the length of the car, but at the one he was sure was his, a man stood with his head poked inside the curtains. A man not in uniform. David was quite certain from his clothing that it was Peregrin Walmore.

He stepped as briskly down the aisle as possible, dodging other passengers. Now the fellow had his arms inside the berth, too. David checked the numbers, just to be sure. It was his, just beyond Millie's compartment.

"May I help you?" He tapped the man on the shoulder.

Peregrin Walmore pulled his head quickly from the curtains and blinked at him, his cheeks flushing pink amid his purple and yellow bruises. "Oh, I say. Stone. Uh. . .sorry, I thought this was my berth. But I see now that it's your bag in there."

"Yes," David said coldly. "Yours is across the way."

"Pardon," Walmore said.

David didn't like it one bit. Something was fishy about this fellow's behavior and had been from the start. He glanced around. Several other passengers were within earshot, and Millie, if she wasn't sleeping already, must be able to hear them as well. He frowned at Walmore. "I'd like to speak to you privately, please."

"Well. . .uh. . ." Walmore glanced over his shoulder. "I suppose we'll have to go outside. No privacy in here."

"True enough. Shall we?"

Walmore hesitated. "If you insist."

"I do."

David followed him to the end of the car and out onto the platform. The cool night air rushed by. He paused for a moment to observe the dark countryside zooming past. They must be making thirty miles an hour. He didn't know as he'd ever gone this fast except for when he was riding a good horse at a full gallop. He thought fondly of Captain, the faithful mount he'd turned over to Anne before he left Oregon. Maybe he could build up the stable in Stoneford after he'd got his feet under him.

Hands pushed against his back—hard. David fell forward, doubling over the low iron railing. He grabbed it and held himself fast. If he'd missed his hold, he'd have tumbled right off the train.

He regained his balance and whipped around as Walmore lunged at him. David caught his wrists as the younger man dove for his throat. Squeezing with all his might, David stared into Walmore's eyes.

"What are you doing?"

Walmore grimaced. "N–nothing. I—you slipped. I was trying to help you. Gave me a fright, you did."

David shoved him, slamming him against the door of the next car. Pinning him against the door wasn't all that difficult, which surprised David, considering what little exercise he'd had lately. He was breathing a bit hard, but not nearly so desperately as Walmore, who gasped for air. The young whelp might be a gentleman of sorts, but he had no manners, and he was sadly out of shape.

"Look, we both know you attempted to kill me," David said grimly. "I think I know why."

"You do?" Walmore gulped, still staring at him, bug-eyed.

The door behind Walmore opened, and the young man almost

fell into the car. Behind him, the conductor said, "Everything all right out here?"

"Yes, thank you," David said.

The conductor shot Walmore a suspicious glance but nodded and said, "Very good, Mr. Stone. We're approaching Terre Haute." The train's doleful whistle accentuated his words. "Let me know if you need anything, sir."

"I will," David said.

The conductor closed the door, and David faced Walmore. He loosened his grip somewhat, but didn't let go altogether. "Tell me now who put you up to this. Was it Randolph?"

"N—no," Walmore said. "I wasn't—oh, please, you mustn't think me so vile."

"But I do."

"It's—it's—"

"It's what? Tell me!" David grabbed his lapels and shook him. Walmore raised a hand in supplication, and David let go of him.

"I owe some money. I know, it was stupid of me, but I thought—"

"You thought what? That I'd pay off your debt? You were disappointed, weren't you? I bought you a train ticket instead, and some meals and sundries. But you needed more. Is that what you were doing in my sleeping berth? Going through my things, looking for cash?"

The sky was quite dark, but David fancied Walmore's face went scarlet, and he didn't readily deny the accusation. The train lurched as the brake went on, and they both reached for the railing.

In the moment when they struggled to keep their balance, David considered telling the bounder to keep clear of him and Millie for the rest of the journey. But it might be wiser to keep an eye on him.

He eyed the young man sternly as they shifted their weight and the train slowed further, with the wheels squealing against the rails. "I'm warning you, Walmore. Anything short of impeccable behavior from you, and I shall have you arrested. Do you understand?"

"I—well, yes, but—"

"I mean it. If there's any more of this nonsense, I shall turn you over to the authorities."

The train had slid into the next station, where the platform was brilliantly lighted and crowded with people. David turned his back on Walmore and entered their carriage. Best to get out of the way before new passengers came on. He didn't like the idea of going to sleep with Walmore close at hand, but at least he had put the fellow on notice. Perhaps he could catch the conductor after things settled down and ask him to keep an eye on his fellow traveler.

He was about to climb into his berth when Millie poked her head out between the curtains next door.

"Is everything all right?" she asked. "I thought I heard you and Mr. Walmore having words."

David glanced about. New passengers were boarding, with porters carrying their overnight bags into the car. "Everything's fine. We'll speak in the morning."

She nodded.

"We're at Terre Haute," he added, "wherever that is."

"Indiana, I expect."

"Ah. Sleep if you can. I shall stay here now. Call out if you need anything."

She gazed at him for a moment, her green eyes full of questions. He hated to leave her wondering, but they really couldn't discuss the matter with all these people about.

"Good night then." She gave him a wan smile and withdrew her head.

David looked toward the end of the car where he'd had the altercation with Walmore, but there was no sign of the young man. He climbed onto the sleeping platform and pulled the curtains closed. One latch was unfastened on his small valise. He shoved it aside and removed his shoes.

"Now I lay me down to sleep," he muttered as his fatigue overtook him. "I pray thee, Lord. . . Up to You, really."

To Millie's surprise, David was already up when she left her sleeping compartment in the morning, and the porter was folding up his hanging berth so he could sit down. She had thought she was rising early, but there he was, looking splendid. She suspected he had given his shoes to the porter to polish last night, and perhaps had his jacket pressed as well.

David caught sight of her as she stood admiring him, and she flushed.

"Good morning, Mildred," he said with a smile. "I'm told we're nearing Cincinnati. We're stopping soon at a town on the outskirts."

"Can we get breakfast there?"

"There'll be vendors coming on with coffee and food. The train will only stop for twenty minutes, so they don't recommend that we leave it."

"That's fine," Millie said. "Did you sleep?"

"Fitfully."

She nodded. She'd slept in her brown traveling dress, and it was now rumpled and decidedly in need of a laundering, but she had managed to sleep. David had a stubble of beard shadowing his chin, and dark shadows lay beneath his eyes.

"Shall I make up your berth, ma'am?" the porter asked.

"I still have a few things in it." She turned to David. "Excuse me just a few minutes, won't you?"

"Certainly. I shall be sitting here, where we sat yesterday. Please join me at your convenience."

A short time later, when she made her way carefully back to their seats, the train had stopped. She found David perusing a newspaper. Nearly all of the sleeping compartments had been folded up out of the way.

"Where is Mr. Walmore this morning?" she asked as she seated herself. She glanced at Peregrin's sleeping berth, which was in its storage position.

"I expect he's about somewhere."

"I see his berth is made up."

"Yes. And the vendor came through a minute ago. I got us some coffee and biscuits with bacon in them, and a couple of apples."

"That sounds delightful," Millie said.

"We shall be in Philadelphia by evening." David smiled, and she wondered if he was eager to put the United States behind him and get home. He must be growing more excited as he grew nearer to his destination.

Millie, on the other hand, was headed into the unknown. She would have to try to rekindle old acquaintances and meet new people who could help her. She'd need new living quarters, a paying position, a new church. . .so much to think about. She wanted to follow David's example and anticipate these changes with optimism. But she wasn't like him—she had no estate waiting, and no counselors, and most of all, no seemingly limitless bank account.

"So soon?" She managed a smile—who couldn't smile, after all, when gazing into those stunning blue eyes?

He had set the two tin cups of coffee on the floor while he waited, and he picked one up and handed it to her.

"There you are. I'm sorry it's not tea."

"That's all right. I don't suppose I mind as much as you do. Just think—you'll soon be able to get all the tea you want."

"Yes." His eyes went sober. "It's coming right up on us, isn't it?"

She knew he meant the separation, and suddenly the morning turned gray. By evening they would part. She hated to think of a life without David. Apparently it gave him pause as well, and she took a small consolation from that.

The conductor came by. "All set, Mr. Stone? Ma'am?"

"Yes, thank you," David said.

Millie nodded, and the conductor moved on. She had noted that all the railroad employees knew David by name and showed him the utmost respect. They treated all the passengers politely but seemed to have a special preference for David and a willingness to do extra favors for him. She supposed it was because he acted like a proper gentleman and showed them respect as well.

Her thoughts turned again to her prospects in Philadelphia. She did hope she could find a paying situation quickly. She had a little money left, but not enough to keep her more than a couple of weeks at the high prices she expected in the city.

"I suppose I might find a position as a cook," she said as she took a biscuit from the packet.

"A cook." David's face fell. "Well, yes, I suppose you might."

"I was thinking at a hotel, perhaps, or a restaurant in the city. It generally pays better than housework or sewing."

"I see. But really, Mildred, do you think—"

"What?" She smiled. "You're thinking it wouldn't be proper?"

"No. Well, actually. . ." He squared his shoulders. "There's a matter I'd like to discuss with you, but this is perhaps not the place for it. Maybe when we stop again, we can take a short stroll together, if—" He looked over his shoulder.

"Yes, it is difficult to get privacy when you have a traveling companion, is it not?" she said.

"Very difficult. But—about our traveling companion." He leaned toward her and lowered his voice. "I don't trust him by half." His charming smile sent all her blue thoughts scattering, yet he seemed a bit guarded—almost worried.

"You intrigue me." Something must have happened last night, as she'd suspected. David's tone when she'd heard him speak to Walmore, close outside her sleeping berth, sounded stern—almost accusing.

He frowned for a moment, then went on in low tones, "It's distasteful for me to tell you this, but I feel I must warn you. Walmore attacked me physically last night."

"What?" She drew back to study his face. David seemed perfectly sincere, and she leaned toward him again. "Tell me more, please."

"He said afterward that he didn't mean it, but I know he did. And he was rummaging in my luggage before that—when I came back from the washroom."

"That must be when I heard you confront him."

"Yes. I didn't realize it at the time, but my cuff links are missing."

"Not the onyx ones?"

"Yes."

Neither of them mentioned Millie's own theft of the same cuff links, but it hung between them. Millie hadn't supposed they were particularly valuable. She had taken them more out of sentiment. But would Walmore take them if they were mere trinkets?

"When we went out onto the platform," David continued, "he tried to push me over the railing."

Millie tried to picture that, but Walmore seemed so unpretentious and even awkward that she found it hard to accept. "Do you really think he wanted to do that?"

"It wasn't accidental. Perhaps he wanted my wallet, but I got the impression he wanted something more. . .permanent."

Millie swallowed hard. "You think he is acting for your cousin?"

"I don't know. It's the most logical explanation."

Millie inhaled slowly. What if Walmore had succeeded last night? She wouldn't have known until now that David was missing. If the man truly wanted to kill David—or even if he merely hoped to steal his valuables, it seemed to her that they should turn him over to the police.

"Do you think he's left the train now?" she asked.

"I doubt it, since he's penniless. But maybe." David glanced back at the travelers behind them. "I say."

"Yes?"

"There's a fellow just sitting down—don't gawk, but when you think it's appropriate, take a look. I swear I saw him from my hotel window in Independence."

"Doing what?" Millie asked.

"Nothing. Just hanging about and watching the hotel."

She frowned. That didn't sound good.

"Brown jacket," David said, "in the aisle seat about four rows behind us and on the other side of the aisle. Big man—very big."

Millie eyed David for a moment. She let her gaze flicker for a moment toward the rear of the car. She saw the man he referred to and puzzled in her mind over whether she'd seen him before or not. He was too big to ignore. Her heart skipped, but she turned forward impassively.

She touched David's sleeve and, when he leaned toward her, said in his ear, "I think you are right."

"Come outside for a moment."

They rose and left the car, reaching the little platform in between cars. Millie clung to the railing with one hand and her hat with the other as she turned to face David.

"I've seen him, too," she said. "That large man was across the street from our hotel the morning we left. I saw him stand up from behind the rain barrel over there, and I wondered if he'd slept there all night. A vagrant, I supposed. He watched us as we left for the train station."

"Interesting," David said.

"But the other one, the one he's sitting with—"

"Yes?"

Millie frowned. "He looks awfully like a man who stood across the street, whittling, on more than one occasion."

David turned and peered into the carriage for a moment. "Ah, you're right. I almost overlooked him. I saw the indolent whittler myself, and I believe that is the man."

Millie grasped his sleeve. "What does it mean?"

David covered her hand with his warm one and gazed down into her eyes. "I'm not sure."

"I'm frightened." All she could think of was Scottsburg and the assassin who had stalked him. She tried to remain calm, but David looked concerned, too. She wouldn't sit by and let someone try to kill him again.

David spent the next hour deep in thought. Walmore had returned just before the train started, but he was quiet after the initial greetings and sat across from them, eating the biscuit David had saved for him.

"Sorry I didn't get you anything to drink," David said. "I couldn't handle three cups, and I wasn't sure when you wanted to eat."

Walmore waved a hand as though it was nothing, but he must wish he had something to help the biscuit go down.

David noted that while he brushed the crumbs off his clothing,

Walmore snatched repeated glances toward the suspicious men he and Millie had noted earlier.

At last a plan formed in his mind. It wasn't ideal, but David believed that the longer he stayed on the train, the more danger he was in.

"Excuse me a moment, won't you?" He got up and spoke to the porter. He wished he could discuss it with Millie first. She'd been very patient with him, considering how inconsiderately quiet he'd been. Finally, another hour into the trip, Walmore rose and excused himself, heading toward the washroom. David noted that the two suspicious men watched Walmore's every move. After he passed their seats, the larger man got up and lurched down the aisle and out the far end of the car.

"My dear," David said, leaning close to Millie's ear, "I wonder if you might be able to leave this train with me at the next stop. The conductor will see that our luggage is put off for us, and we can collect it after the train has gone on."

She arched her pretty auburn eyebrows. "Of course, if you think it is prudent. I trust your instincts."

"Well, my instincts aren't sure what to think, but they don't like this latest turn of events, if you catch my meaning. That whittler is even now sitting in the last row of this carriage, no doubt keeping an eye on us and anticipating Walmore's movements. Where his partner has got to, I have no idea."

Millie nodded gravely. "I have been wondering. . ."

"Yes?" David asked.

"Whether they are watching us or Mr. Walmore."

"A not unreasonable question. I supposed they were shadowing me, but since we took note of them this morning, I've been studying them. They may have an interest in us, but they seem to be shadowing Walmore, and I wonder if we are merely unwitting intruders in their little scheme."

"As opposed to being the objects of it?"

David nodded, though he didn't like either alternative.

"In any event," Millie said, "I am of the same mind as you, sir.

I do not like it."

"We shall get off, then? If they are following Walmore, they'll stay with him. And if they're after us, perhaps we can lose them if we move quickly. We can catch another train later in the day, I'm sure. If you don't mind a few hours' delay, that is."

"Why should I? Delay will only give me more time in your company."

Her cheeks flushed adorably, and David could not resist reaching for her hand. She had not chastised him for calling her "my dear," and now her words were tantamount to a confession that she dreaded parting from him. He dared to think her feelings mirrored his own—a pleasant thought.

They were traveling across Ohio, and after further discussion with the conductor, David chose Pittsburgh as the city in which they would disembark. He had hoped to give Millie the particulars, but when he returned to his seat beside her, he saw Walmore approaching from the opposite end of the carriage.

The erstwhile whittler had disappeared, but his companion, the big man, sat toward the rear of the car with a newspaper open before him. When Walmore walked past him, the hulk of a man watched him openly.

David considered asking Walmore if he knew the pair but decided against it. If the three were in league against him, he didn't want any of them to dream that he was about to escape their clutches.

Millie attempted a placid conversation about the lush farm country they passed through, but David's mind wandered. Was he mad to think his cousin's brother-in-law could be plotting against him? After careful consideration, he thought madness was out of the question. He might be overly suspicious, but after all, he had nearly lost his life to an assassin in Oregon. He'd thought at the time that Randolph was behind the attempt, but his solicitor sent word that his cousin swore he had nothing to do with it and was shocked and saddened at the tidings. Mr. Conrad had tried to assure David that his family had no ill will toward him and only wished to see him take his rightful place at Stoneford.

Well, David wasn't so sure. For one thing, Conrad was a doddering old man now. Anne had told him that the man was in his eighties, which confirmed David's assumption that the solicitor was well past his prime. Randolph was sly enough to put one over on the old man. And wouldn't any guilty man deny his actions when accused? Who would admit he'd hired an assassin to kill a relative for him?

They reached the outskirts of Pittsburgh late in the afternoon, and the train began to slow. "Mildred, would you like to get off here for some air?" he asked. "I understand the train is stopping for about twenty minutes."

"Let us go," she said and began to put on her gloves.

David looked at Walmore. The man eyed him uncertainly. David wanted to simply ignore him, but he could hardly do that. He'd restrained himself from confronting him about the cuff links, supposing he was more likely to get clean away if he didn't admit he knew of the theft or show his contempt toward Walmore. It would be best if he and Millie left the train casually, as though they intended to return in a few minutes.

"Let's see if we can get a cup of tea in the few minutes we have," he said aloud, and more than one passenger heard him, he was sure. "Walmore, can we bring you something?"

The young man had started to rise, and he blinked at David uncertainly. "Uh, no, that's all right. I may get a breath myself."

David had hoped he'd stay on the train, but he couldn't say so without arousing suspicion. He took Millie's arm and pulled her along quickly. Several other people soon separated them from Walmore in the aisle.

Outside the car, he turned Millie along the platform away from the windows through which Walmore and the others might watch them. Two cars down, they found the conductor helping an elderly man onto the train. David waited for him to finish and then spoke to him confidentially.

"This is the place of our departure. You will have our bags set out without any fanfare?"

"Certainly, sir," the conductor said. "And if you turn your ticket in at the window, they'll refund part of your fare."

As they turned away, David spotted Walmore leaving their car farther down the platform. He seized Millie's hand and was about to draw her away when Walmore spotted him.

"I think we need to give Walmore an errand," David said to Millie, and walked with her toward the young man.

When they drew near, Walmore eyed him with surprise. He tipped his hat to Millie.

"Mrs. Evans wants to look over the peddlers' wares yonder." David nodded toward where several vendors had set up business on the edge of the platform. He took out his wallet. "Would you mind seeing if you can change this for me at the ticket office? I might not have time, and I'd like to have a few coins later for tips and so forth."

"Of course." Walmore took the dollar bill, folded it, and tucked it in his coat pocket.

"Thank you," David said with a smile. Walmore being a gentleman would understand that his company was not welcome at present.

Walmore set off at once for the ticket window to change the bill, and David steered Millie in the opposite direction.

"What is our plan?" she murmured as they strode past the peddlers.

"We lose ourselves until the train pulls out again. With any luck, Walmore will simply think we boarded a different car. It should take him a little while to discover that we aren't on board. The conductor has been amply paid to calm him if he gets agitated, and after no less than an hour's journey, to tell Walmore they've discovered a message I left with one of the baggage handlers—that we decided on the spur of the moment to leave them."

"Do you think he'll come back and try to find us?" Millie asked.

"He'd be foolish if he did. After all, his ticket to New York is paid for. But if he tries to change it, he'll have to pay an additional fee, and I've left him with only one dollar. Unless he was lying to us since the beginning, he hasn't much more than that at his disposal."

Millie smiled. "And then what?"

"Then we go back to retrieve our luggage and take a hackney to a hotel."

"Oh." She looked a little uncertain.

"Do not worry, my dear," David said. "I intend to see that you have a fine dinner, and perhaps we can have that conversation I alluded to earlier."

"You mean. . .this isn't it?"

"No, darling, this is not it at all. In fact this is very unlike the conversation I wish to have with you."

Her cheeks flushed prettily, and David drew her hand through his arm and squeezed it. He looked back and paused, gazing over the heads of the people thronging the platform.

"What is it?" she asked.

"As I hoped—the big man has followed Walmore. I can't see whether his friend is with him or not. He could be following us."

"Do you really think so?"

"No. I think they want Walmore. But come. Let us make ourselves scarce."

Millie could hardly believe what was happening to her. The man she'd admired so long and despaired of winning was whisking her about and calling her *my dear* and *darling*. Did he mean those endearments, or did he speak without thinking, distracted by the fear that assassins were stalking him?

A bit of calm thinking did not rule out the possibility that Walmore had come to Independence to locate David for those evil men. Now that he'd insinuated his way into David's good graces and company, the murderers could choose the time and place to carry out their wicked deeds. It wasn't so far from what Peterson had tried to do in Scottsburg, using her as the go-between.

Or was David's theory that the thugs were chasing Walmore the correct one? It would explain his black eye and nervousness.

She felt a pang of compassion for Walmore. The young man

SUSAN PAGE DAVIS

didn't seem able to fend for himself in this inhospitable land. She hoped they weren't throwing him to the wolves.

Whatever their current situation, she couldn't give herself entirely over to fear. She was off on an adventure with the man she loved. Even if they were in danger, she somehow found herself enjoying every minute.

David stopped a well-dressed man on the street and asked him for the name of a nice restaurant. He then hailed a horse cab and instructed the driver to take them there.

Millie shrank back when they entered. She had never eaten in such a fine place, and she certainly wasn't dressed for it. But David drew her in, and they were soon seated at a secluded corner table. The china, the spotless linen tablecloth and napkins, the glassware—all might have been found on a rich man's table. Fresh flowers filled a ceramic vase, and the cutlery appeared to be fine silver plate. When she caught sight of the prices, she nearly swooned, but David caught her eye and smiled.

"Don't let that frighten you, Mildred. When I reach New York, I shall have an infusion of cash awaiting me."

"Oh, I—" She gulped, not knowing what to say, but she felt the heat in her cheeks. She leaned toward him. "I don't like to see you spend so much on me."

"It's my choice, dear. Enjoy it, and see if you think the chef here cooks better than you. Personally, I doubt it, but it will be a pleasant study."

Millie's heart fluttered. This was all so far from what she knew. In Oregon, she'd dreamed of living in this sort of atmosphere—or she would have, if she'd known what to dream. She couldn't have conjured up the particulars because she'd never come near to this standard of luxury.

But that was long ago when she aspired to marry her way out of poverty. Now she would gladly share a log cabin with this man and forego the social whirl she'd once craved.

She attempted to read the copious bill of fare, but she kept sneaking glances at David. He was being more than kind to her.

He was acting like a suitor. Dared she hope?

When the waiter—who was dressed finer than most preachers—reappeared, she had not come close to making a choice.

"Oh dear, there are so many dishes that sound exquisite."

"Shall I order for both of us?" David asked.

Relief settled on her, and she handed the menu to the waiter. David knew her now. He would order something she would like.

"Yes, please." She smiled at him a bit shyly, wondering how they could be so calm in the midst of life-threatening turmoil.

He ordered a chicken dish she had never heard of—the name of it sounded foreign. The waiter asked if they wanted a drink, and David asked for tea for both of them.

When the waiter had gone, David bent toward her and said quietly, "Mildred, it's time I spoke to you of what is on my heart."

"You mean. . .Walmore?"

"No, no. Forget that man—and the others as well. My dear, you must realize I've grown very fond of you." David took her hand and held it tenderly on the snowy-white tablecloth. "Might I believe that you also care for me?"

She gulped. Her face must be scarlet now, and she couldn't tear her gaze away from his earnest blue eyes if she'd wanted to, which she didn't. In fact, she thought she could stare into them for the rest of her life and never be bored.

"I. . .yes. Oh yes, David, you might. I hope you will. Because I do."

He smiled. "Ah, Mildred. You are such a delight."

"Really? Because I feel rather awkward just now."

"Please don't. It's not my intention to make you ill at ease."

Her mind whirled. Where could this lead? His words seemed directed toward a proposal of marriage, but if he was truly on his way to accept a title in the British peerage and ownership of a vast estate, how could he possibly consider her as a fitting wife? And if not marriage, then what? No, she wouldn't believe that he would suggest something more vulgar. He wasn't that type of man.

He sat back a bit but did not relinquish her hand.

"I see that you are confused. Perhaps I should have chosen a more private venue, but Mildred, I have come to admire you. In fact, I love you."

Millie's heart surged into a pounding gallop. She caught her breath but could not speak.

David smiled gently. "I am asking you to consider whether you might go to England with me, my dear—as my bride."

CHAPTER 34

The waiter returned at the most inopportune moment possible. David released Millie's hand and sat decorously silent while the food was placed before them. Millie's lovely green eyes were downcast. She seemed intent on watching how the waiter placed the dishes.

"Will that be all, sir?" the man asked.

"Yes, thank you," David said.

The man went away, and Millie raised her gaze. "I. . .I hardly know what to say, David."

"You have not said no, and I take that with optimism."

"But you. . .your position. . ."

"Ah yes. The title. I hope you won't let that put you off. But if you think you could not bear it—all that it would entail, why then I would give up the title and the estate to my cousin. I find after great deliberation that I would rather stay in America with you than return to England alone. My dear, would you accept a proposal from David Stone, commoner, who is partner in a stagecoach line?"

Millie stared at him, her cheeks going even redder. "I should be proud to if that were the case. In fact, I might say it would make me extremely happy."

"Then that is settled—you *are* willing to marry me, at least under some circumstances." He couldn't help smiling, but Millie looked astonished.

"Do you mean you would make such a sacrifice?"

He chuckled. "For me it would hardly be a sacrifice. I have done without Stoneford and all it brings for many years, and I would hardly miss it—though I do love the place, and it holds dear memories for me. But I know I could be happy with the life I established in Oregon, particularly with someone as charming and pleasant as you by my side."

Her lips twitched, and he thought perhaps he'd nearly made her smile.

"Mildred." He reached once more for her hand.

She glanced about, looking adorably timid.

"I'm sorry," he said. "I should let you eat your supper. It wasn't fair of me to raise the subject just when you're served a meal."

She did smile then. "Indeed, sir. Most inconsiderate."

He laughed aloud and picked up his fork. "Let us eat, then, but I hope you will consider my proposal while we do. We can discuss it later."

David took a bite of his salad, but he did not like to admit even to himself how nervous she had made him. He wished he'd waited until they were in a private spot—one where he could sweep her into his arms and kiss away her doubts.

Millie peered at the salad for several seconds, apparently astonished. Perhaps she had never seen fresh greens in combination with halved grapes and bits of orange and walnuts. She picked up her fork and took an experimental bite. Her expression gratified David, telling him he'd chosen well. Wait until she tried the chicken. She would probably march to the kitchen and demand a recipe or two.

However, after three bites, Millie blotted her lips with her napkin. "The food is most excellent, sir, and I thank you for it, but I must speak to your earlier point."

"Please do," David said gravely.

"I also have come to care deeply for you and to admire your character. Nothing would make me happier than to be your wife. But I know you left Oregon with a purpose in mind. I would not like to see you put aside what you felt was your duty for my sake."

Peace settled over David. He could only feel that the Lord had brought this about. "We shall speak more of this," he said, "but I assure you, I shall not shirk my duty."

She nodded. "Good. It's just that things you've said in the past have made me wonder whether you could in good conscience hand the family's heritage and responsibilities over to your cousin."

"True, my dear. For now, I will only say that you have made me the happiest man alive."

"Indeed?"

"What? Are you surprised?"

"Yes." A tiny frown wrinkled her brow. "Frankly, I am, because I had no idea I could wield such power over you."

"I hope that you shall learn in the future the strength of that power."

Millie shivered slightly, but she did not look uneasy or discontent. She fell to her dinner with enthusiasm. David relaxed and enjoyed the meal as well, and when they were nearly finished, he slipped the waiter a coin and asked him to secure a cab for them.

"Where to now?" Millie asked once they were settled in the carriage.

"Back to the depot to pick up our luggage." David took her hand and held it in both of his. At last, he had her in a place where prying eyes could not reach. "It's odd how many miles we've traveled together, but I never until these last few days wished we were the only passengers."

She laughed aloud, and he drank in the sight of her, seemingly carefree. But her face soon sobered.

"David, did you mean it?"

"What, dearest?"

"All of it. Any of it."

"Of course." He lifted his arm to encircle her shoulders and drew her near.

Millie's eyes widened then closed as he leaned in to kiss her. He was glad they hadn't trifled with romance in Scottsburg. This was as it should be—the moment when a man sealed his love for a true-hearted woman with a kiss. She brought her hand up to his collar and returned his caress with what seemed a match for his ardor, yet with enough restraint that he was encouraged. His recent assessment of the new Mildred Evans was not wrong.

"I love you," he murmured, holding her against his chest. He considered asking her to remove her hat so he could stroke her hair but decided that would come later. He may have won her love, but the time for familiarity was not yet at hand. "Let me tell you what I have in mind for us."

"I should very much like to know," she whispered.

David smiled and kissed the tip of her nose. "I know I could be happy living a simple life with you, but you're correct about my temperament. I do feel it is my duty to take on the estate at Stoneford. If there were another heir whom I thought could run it well. . . but there is not. Will you still marry me, my darling, if I go to England? Would you go with me and live as the right honorable Countess of Stoneford?"

After a moment's silence, she whispered, "If you will help me. I confess I haven't the least idea of what that means."

Peregrin returned to his seat as the train's whistle let out a blast. The places opposite his were vacant, and he looked anxiously toward the door. Instead of Stone and Mrs. Evans, the two thugs were coming toward him. Teddy plopped beside him, and Wilkes eased his big frame down onto David's seat.

Peregrin gulped. "That's Mr. Stone's seat."

"Was," Teddy said.

"What do you mean?" Panic seized Peregrin by the throat. He tried to jump up, but Wilkes grabbed his wrist and squeezed.

"Sit down, Perry. You and me's going to have a little chat."

"I told you, I'll get the money."

"Oh yes, you told us that several times," Teddy said. "Well, your so-called friend didn't give it to you. Then you said you could get it anyhow."

"You were supposed to get it last night." Wilkes leaned his massive head toward Peregrin. "So where is it?"

"He didn't have any—" Peregrin looked around and lowered his voice a notch. "He didn't have any in his suitcase. But you can have these." He fished a small wooden box out of his pocket and held it out.

Teddy snatched it and opened the lid. "What's this?"

"His cuff links. They're valuable. Close it up—he'll be back any second."

The train lurched, and Wilkes let out a guffaw. "That's what you know, genius. Your pigeon has flown."

"That he has," Teddy said.

"What do you mean?"

"Stone's cut and run. He and the lady got off and didn't get back on."

Peregrin sat very still. "You're joking."

"Not us," Teddy said cheerfully. "Guess your friend forgot to tell you."

Peregrin looked out the window. They were gathering speed, and the countryside flew past.

"We've got to go back."

Wilkes placed a weighty hand on his sleeve. "No, chum, we ain't going back. This all you got? 'Cause it don't look like much."

Peregrin swallowed with difficulty. "Those are onyx cuff links. They're family heirlooms, and they're worth a lot. You could probably sell them for a hundred pounds."

"Pounds of what?" Teddy asked.

"Sterling. Or a few hundred dollars."

"Those little things?" Wilkes made a sour face. "I doubt that."

"So do I," Teddy said, "but we'll find out when we get to New York." He pocketed the box. "You still owe us."

"Please—I'll get the money. Really. In fact, if you boys wanted to stake me, I could probably win half of it back today in the smoking car."

"I seen you play poker," Wilkes said in disgust.

"Isn't that how you got into this fix in the first place?" Teddy asked.

Peregrin had no answer. His stomach began to hurt as he contemplated his future, and the train hurtled onward.

"Have you any reason to stop in Philadelphia now, my dear?" David asked the next day, as they breakfasted in the sitting room of the suite he'd insisted on engaging for her.

"I don't think so."

"If you wish to see some of your old friends, or if you'd like to shop there for your trousseau. . ."

"My trousseau?" Millie frowned.

"Why, yes. I thought you would want some new clothes before we set sail. . ." He paused, trying to read her expression. She seemed distressed, though in his experience, most women went into raptures at the prospect of a new wardrobe.

"Oh David." Her voice faltered.

"What is it, Mildred?"

"I. . .I wouldn't know what to buy. Don't you see? I have no inkling of what a countess should wear. Have you? You must."

"Well, it's been some time since I've moved in fashionable circles." He puzzled over that for a minute, then smiled. "New York. There are always a few Londoners in New York. I'll warrant we can scare up some connections of a finer sort than Peregrin Walmore. A little hobnobbing, a few introductions, and surely within a day or two we'll unearth some lady or other who can help you choose your wardrobe for the voyage."

"It sounds so complicated. Perhaps one new dress and. . .well, some sundries." Millie wouldn't meet his gaze.

"Yes, well, I think you'll need more than that, my dear. On shipboard, people dress for dinner, you know, and there will no doubt be dancing and entertainments in the evening."

"Really?" She blinked as though the concept was quite novel.

David cleared his throat. "There are some things that will probably surprise you, dearest. I know it's all happening rather quickly, but I must return to London as soon as possible, and I'd like to make the voyage before winter sets in."

"Winter? Oh, surely. There's plenty of time, isn't there?"

"Yes. I was thinking we might stay in New York two or three weeks for our honeymoon. During that time, perhaps you can outfit yourself."

"If I have some guidance." Millie had never looked more helpless and unsure of herself.

"Yes. But the first thing, it seems to me, is the wedding. Where would you like to be married?"

She swallowed hard. "Why don't you decide?"

"All right. If there's no one you wish to include in the festivities. . ."

"I have no one now that Sam is gone."

David reached for her hand. "Mildred, I'm so sorry about your brother. He wasn't such a bad fellow."

"Yes he was, but thank you for saying that. You gave him a chance at an honest life, and he ruined it. I guess that was partly my fault. But we did get another opportunity, and I tried to steer Sam straight. He just. . .he didn't want to work hard, I think, which I don't understand. Our mother taught me to dig right in when it was needed. But Sam. . .well, it just didn't *take* with him, I guess."

"Mm, I suppose you're right." David waited a moment before easing the conversation to a happier topic. "If you wish it, we could find a minister today, in this town, and be married now, before we continue our journey."

Her eyes lit. "Really? Because it doesn't matter to me where we say our vows. I'd like to do it soon though, if we can work it out."

"I'll have to inquire. There may be regulations that require a public announcement or some such thing. If that is the case, we could go on to New York and refurbish your wardrobe while we wait."

"Oh." Millie's face fell. "David, I don't like to mention this, since I am not yet your wife, but. . .would you want to marry me in my traveling dress? I do have the calico. . . ."

"I'd be happy to buy you a new gown for the wedding," he said quickly.

She flushed. "Oh, but that wouldn't be seemly, would it?"

He gazed at her lovely face. Her green eyes remained downcast as she pondered.

"What would you like to do, Mildred?" He stroked her hand slowly.

"I am not sure. I don't think it would look well for you to buy my wedding dress."

"What of the other gown you had in your bag? The one that belonged to Anne?"

She glanced up. "Would you really wish to marry me if I were wearing that?"

"Why not? I expect that Anne will consider it a good joke when we tell her someday."

Millie caught her breath. "Do you think we shall have that opportunity?"

"I dearly hope so. One of the first things I intend to do when we get home is to write to Anne and invite her and Daniel to visit us at Stoneford, with young Richard in tow of course. I want to see my little grand-nephew."

"That would be wonderful, if she found she could forgive me."

"I'm sure she already has, my dear, and I should tell you that I've mentioned you to her in my last couple of letters. In fact, I apprised her that I'd met up with you shortly after Sam died. I shall probably find at least one letter from her waiting for me in New York."

"I. . .I don't know what to say."

David smiled gently. "Just say you will marry me today if it's possible."

She looked up at him and smiled. "All right. That doesn't seem too difficult, since you are going to make the arrangements."

"Yes. And if we find it's impossible, we'll work out when we can—the soonest opportunity." He stood and pushed in his chair. "Shall I go out now and see what I can learn?"

"I suppose so."

She rose, and David stepped closer and stooped to kiss her. "You've made me very happy, Millie."

"I hope you still feel that way a month or two from now, when all your connections, as you call them, have met me."

"They will love you as I do. But just to give you some confidence, we'll find a tutor in New York, and you shall have a couple of weeks of lessons."

"Lessons on being a countess?"

"Well, on fashion and deportment and protocol—what to call a duchess and stuff of that nature. You know—how to curtsey to the queen when you are presented."

"Oh," she said in a small voice.

David chuckled. "My dear Mildred, you look as though you're headed for the gallows. I promise you, we shall have excessive fun together. I'll buy you a horse, and when we have guests you may join our shooting parties if you like. And you will never have to wash dishes or do laundry again, or to cook unless you wish to."

"That sounds lovely."

"Good." He had no doubt she would roll up her sleeves and show the cook at Stoneford how to make American biscuits. "And I'm sure there's much more that I haven't thought to tell you. Don't be afraid to ask questions."

"I shall badger you all across the Atlantic."

"I can hardly wait." He kissed her again and reluctantly left the sitting room.

"Do you, Mildred, take this man to be your lawfully wedded husband?"

Millie sucked in a deep breath. Standing here with David, in the hotel's sitting room, wearing Anne's gown, was incredible enough, but a minister was lining out the marriage vows for her. Two simple words, and her life would never be the same.

David squeezed her hand. She glanced up into his blue eyes and knew that she wanted to make this change. Though she might find some muddy weather ahead, she would happily leave behind the Evans name and her past associations. She turned to the minister and said gravely, "I do."

Five minutes later, she was irrevocably Mrs. David Stone, and her husband was jubilantly kissing her. Nothing was said of the title, as David had felt there was no need to tell the minister about it. The preacher's wife and a bellboy had come as witnesses. David paid the minister and gave the bellboy a large tip.

"Won't you join us for a piece of cake?" Millie asked them,

blushing. David had stopped at a bakery on his way back to the hotel on a whim, and she was glad that he did. To her surprise, he'd also asked for tea to be sent up. She'd almost expected him to buy a bottle of wine, but she was relieved he hadn't. Memories of James Evans's drunken state after her first wedding had brought on some apprehension, but she ought to have known David wouldn't do such a thing.

At last the three guests left them, and David gathered her into his arms.

"Happy?" he asked.

"Yes," she whispered. "This is the happiest moment of my life."

"I believe it is for me, too. And I trust there will be many more."

CHAPTER 35

A week later, David saw Millie off for a day of shopping with Lady Ashton, the wife of a man his own age whom he'd known in his misty youth in England. They'd met in the Astor House's dining room two nights previously and again at the ballet, and Millie seemed to like Ashton's wife, so David had presumed on the marchioness's good nature and asked if she'd like to shop with his bride for suitable clothing for their upcoming voyage. Lady Ashton had jumped at the opportunity.

He'd supplied his bride of seven days with a fair amount of cash and a letter of credit from his bank. Poor Millie had looked a bit at sea, but Lady Ashton would know exactly what to do, and he wouldn't have the embarrassment of watching his blushing wife pick out undergarments and question every expenditure. He'd only succeeded in persuading her to buy one new dress so far, and she probably needed a dozen, but Millie had laughed when he said as much. He would have to do something extremely nice for Lady Ashton later, in exchange for this huge favor.

After the ladies had left the hotel, David got his hat and prepared to go out for a stroll. As he left the chamber, someone called to him, and he turned. One of the bellboys approached quickly from the stairway.

"Mr. Stone, I hoped I'd find you in. This was just delivered for you." He held out a folded sheet of paper.

"Thank you." David reached into his pocket for a coin and gave it to the young man. He took the message and opened it.

"Do you wish me to wait for a reply, sir?"

David frowned as he scanned the note. *A gentleman named Perry Walmore has been arrested for vagrancy and claims you are*

his relation and can vouch for him. Sgt. T. H. Moore, 1ˢᵗ Precinct.
"No, thank you. I shall tend to this myself."

The bellboy nodded and left. David sighed. It seemed he would have to make a stop at the police station. But it wouldn't hurt Walmore to sit there for a while. David decided to shop for some new shirts and linen first, and to order flowers for Lady Ashton while he decided how much money to withdraw from the bank. Because he had no doubt that extricating Peregrin Walmore from the police station would require cash.

Millie tried to add up the prices of all the clothes she was buying, but her head began to spin when they topped $250.

"This is too much!"

"Nonsense," said her shopping companion, Lady Sarah Ashton, known inexplicably to her intimates as Hoppy. "Your husband said the sky was the limit, and he charged me with seeing you have clothes appropriate for everything from a gallop in Hyde Park to a palace ball."

Millie gulped. "I had no idea. I mean—forty dollars for one gown? Really?"

Hoppy laughed. "Not just any gown. An elegant one worthy of the most exclusive ball. And really, my dear, that isn't so extravagant. You'll pay much more in Europe."

Millie shook her head in disbelief, but Hoppy was already fingering the skirt of another dress. "I haven't had this much fun in years! Now, if *my* husband gave me carte blanche for an entire new wardrobe, I'd buy out the stores without blinking. But Ashton is so tight-fisted, I'm lucky to get a few new gowns for the season and a promenade dress each spring. Now go try on that lavender poplin. It would be perfect for an at-home dress, though I'm not sure it's your best color." She eyed Millie critically. "Perhaps they could do it up in green."

"Oh no," Millie cried. "I can't have them doing special dress-making for me."

"Why not? Still, with a bright-colored fichu, that dress would look sweet. Perhaps the modiste can find something."

They spent another hour in the exclusive shop. The owner was only too happy to bring out garment after garment for Millie's inspection. The newlyweds had been in New York nearly a week, but Millie was still shocked at least six times a day by the sights she saw, the extravagance David surrounded her with, and the cost of it all.

She and Hoppy moved on to a millinery shop, where Millie would have swooned if she were the swooning kind of woman. Hoppy insisted she needed at least five hats for the voyage.

"Big hats are all the rage now, especially for promenades. And the sun is unrelenting on deck. Of course, you'll need a carriage bonnet and an opera bonnet—oh my dear, how thrilling to be able to buy multiple hats without guilt!"

"But I do feel guilty." Millie eyed the array of headgear in dismay. "Do you think David realizes how much hats cost?"

"I'm sure he does," Hoppy replied with a mischievous smile. "If not, we shall educate him. Oh, and it's fine to call him 'David' to me, but when you are in polite company, you must refer to him as 'Stoneford.'"

"Stoneford? But that's not his name. That's his house."

Hoppy brushed that aside with a wave of her hand, which bore a pink kid glove with a row of pearl buttons on the cuff. "It's his title, or will be within hours of your landing in England. Such a bore. Now, come, this is serious business. And we haven't been to the cobbler yet. You'll need kid boots and dancing slippers and—oh Mildred, shopping with you is *so* entertaining! But if we don't proceed with it, our dear menfolk will be wondering where we are. And you'll need at least an hour to dress for dinner this evening."

Although Millie returned to the hotel with trepidation, David seemed pleased with the plethora of parcels that had begun to arrive in midafternoon. Millie could hardly move about the bedchamber, but one of the hotel's maids assisted with unpacking everything. At the end of an hour, Millie's booty was all properly stored.

"Would you like me to draw you a bath, ma'am?" the maid asked.

"Yes, that sounds delightful, if there's time. Thank you."

Millie still wasn't accustomed to the luxury of bathing daily if she wished, or having another person dress her hair and help her put on the complicated clothing she had acquired, but she thought, with a little practice, she could get used to it. The full crinolines that were coming into fashion were a trial, but Hoppy had given her an impromptu lesson in one of the dressmakers' shops on how to manage the full skirts and petticoats.

She followed David's practice of tipping the hotel staff generously, using the ample supply of cash he'd given her for the purpose. Her own days of poverty hung close in her memory, and she didn't scruple to reward those who served her.

At last she was ready to go down to dinner, but she felt exhausted. She stepped out into the sitting room, and David leaped to his feet from the velvet-covered armchair where he'd been reading a newspaper.

"You look lovely, my darling." He walked toward her with gleaming eyes, his hands outstretched to her, and Millie was glad she'd made the effort and not suggested they take a quiet supper in their room. He was dressed in formal clothes—or at least, the most formal attire she'd ever seen him wear. How would she ever learn all the subtleties of fashion? Even David's choice of neckties seemed critical now that they were "in society." The other guests at the Astor House seemed overly preoccupied with appearance.

"Thank you." She accepted his kiss. "Hoppy was tireless, but I confess I'm a bit fatigued."

"I'm sorry."

"Well, the scented bath helped."

"We shall not make a long night of it. Ashton wanted to go to the theater, but I declined for us—I hope you don't mind."

"Not at all." Millie had enjoyed the ballet the previous evening, but in attending she had realized that David was right about her need for new clothes.

"I told Ashton perhaps we'd go with them tomorrow evening, if you felt so inclined. Apparently there is a new musical comedy program that's the talk of the town."

"It might be fun."

He stood back and looked her up and down. "That gown suits you."

"Thank you." Millie fingered the braid that trimmed her bodice. Hoppy had instructed her to wear the apple-green dress this evening, and so she felt confident it was appropriate, but what would she do when they left New York and Hoppy? David had said she would have a personal maid in England, and she supposed she needed one to help her avoid making social mistakes. That thought brought on a new anxiety. "And am I to call Ashton 'my lord'? I think that is what you said."

"Yes, darling. I'm sorry this is so nerve-racking for you."

"I don't wish to embarrass you."

David smiled. "If you make a mistake, we shall all laugh and set you straight, but it will all be good-natured. Come."

He drew her hand through his arm, and Millie raised her chin. She would study harder than she ever had in school, and somehow, by the time they reached England, she would know at least the basics of aristocratic manners. The odd thing was that, in spite of her apprehension, she was deliriously happy. One glance at David told her that he was, too. She wished Sam could see her as Lady Stoneford—but that thought flew from her head as David led her down the grand staircase.

Merrileigh greeted the caller—Mr. Iverson, from the solicitor's office—with her husband in the drawing room and took her seat on the sofa. She hoped this visit was occasioned by dire news. If Peregrin had done his job, today's tidings should be momentous, and she could begin packing up her household for the move to Stoneford.

Iverson bowed to his host and took a chair near the fireplace, while Randolph sauntered over and sat beside her.

The solicitor smiled at them. "You'll be happy to hear that we've had a new message from David Stone. He says he'll arrive in England later next month. . .with his wife."

"Wife? What—" Merrileigh stared at him.

"Well now," Randolph said, smiling, "when did this happy event take place?"

"Recently, I gather," Iverson said. "They are honeymooning in New York and plan to embark the second week of October on a steamship. We can expect them to dock by the twenty-fifth."

Merrileigh tried not to show her dismay. The last thing she'd expected—or wanted—to hear was that David was enjoying newly wedded bliss. The second-to-last was that he was alive, but she hadn't allowed herself to totally discount the possibility.

"There's time to direct congratulatory messages to the couple at the Astor House."

"I think we'll just wait until they reach England," Randolph said. "It will be interesting to meet the bride, I'm sure."

"Is she American?" Merrileigh asked.

"I assume so. He didn't give any details."

Merrileigh sniffed, thinking of Peregrin's message stating that David had a woman he'd met in the wilderness traveling with him. No doubt this was the one he had married—a person of questionable morals. The idea sickened her—that a coarse American doxy would take her rightful place as mistress of Stoneford. It was unthinkable. She would never forgive David for this, nor her brother for not preventing it.

The carriage drive at Stoneford was illuminated on Christmas Eve by two long rows of lanterns. Though the temperature outside hovered just above freezing, David had insisted that the front gardens be lit as well. All the rooms on the ground floor and second story glowed bright, and every fireplace held a coal fire that the servants replenished often.

The extravagance awed Millie. Though David was not one to waste money, he didn't stint when he had a purpose in mind. She knew that tonight his purpose was to impress the hundred guests and to prove that the Earl of Stoneford had indeed returned. She thought a small part of his show of ostentation had to do with his cousin, Randolph Stone. Randolph and his wife had accepted the invitation, and indeed were staying two nights. Most of the guests were leaving after tonight's festivities, but a select dozen would spend Christmas with Lord and Lady Stoneford. All of those staying had arrived and were settled in their rooms, preparing for the party.

Millie was terrified that she would make her husband look bad. But in the last two months, she had received a great deal of help from her staff, especially her housekeeper, Mrs. Lane, and her lady's maid, Briley. These women had been hired by the solicitor's office before the master and mistress arrived, and Mr. Iverson had assured Millie that if she was not completely satisfied with their performance, she could let them go and hire other domestics. Millie doubted she would have the heart to do so, but happily she liked both women and was thankful for their skill and their willingness to aid an inexperienced mistress.

She was confident at least in her outfit—Briley had dressed her for the evening in an elegant moiré gown of shimmering green. Though she'd purchased a full half-dozen dresses in New York, it seemed that wasn't nearly enough. This gown had been made especially for her in London. David had suggested a quick trip to the continent so that she could visit a famous dressmaker in Paris, but Millie had gently but firmly declined, reminding him of all they needed to do at home before the holidays.

She examined her gown in the long mirror in her room. She wasn't sure about the multiple flounces that graced the skirt, but the dressmaker had assured her that this style was the height of fashion.

"Our first guests are arriving, dearest. Are you ready?"

She turned toward the doorway. David stood there, resplendent in his evening clothes.

"I think so." She took a last glance at the mirror. Her hair, in a simple upsweep, looked fine to her. She lightly touched the emerald-and-gold necklace at her throat. It was finer than anything she'd ever seen, let alone owned, and she was certain David had spent a great deal of money on it, though she would never ask. He'd brought it to her their last night in New York, along with a gold ring bearing a sizable diamond. "To make up for the engagement present I should have given you," he explained, and she couldn't make him return the jewelry. He'd have been too disappointed.

She'd let him slip it onto her finger, next to her wedding ring, and she'd seen then that he drew great joy from giving her gifts. She hoped he wasn't overspending, but she could hardly deny him this pleasure. Perhaps in the future she could gently encourage him to bring her small things that would still have great meaning.

He stepped up behind her and encircled her with his arms. He bent to kiss her temple.

"You look lovely."

"Thank you," Millie murmured.

"Nervous?"

"Yes. Our first party."

"The first of many. I hope you enjoy yourself."

"I shall try. Oh—" She turned and eyed him uneasily. "What shall I say if Mrs. Stone inquires about her brother again?"

"You can refer her to me if you like. Just tell her again that you last saw him on the train, and he was fine then. I'll speak to Randolph before they go home and tell him a little more. I don't know whether they will want to do anything for Walmore or not, but I shall happily leave the matter to them now."

"Yes," Millie said. "I'm glad you got him out of custody though. I couldn't have borne it if we'd had to see his sister and know he was in jail or in mortal danger from those thugs."

David had paid a small fine for Peregrin in New York and assured the police that he was who he said he was. Then, at Millie's pleading, he had paid the young man's debt but impressed upon him that he must never ask David for help again.

"Well, we couldn't very well leave him in the situation he'd gotten into, but I shall tell Randolph I am done with it. Walmore will never receive another penny from me. What he makes of his future is up to him."

"I agree," Millie said. "And thank you."

David shrugged. "Well, I've learned more about the affair that sent him into exile, and I think it will be cleared up soon. He'll probably be back in England before another year is up. But I know you couldn't sleep if you knew he was still in danger when we sailed, and I do want you to sleep well—especially now."

She smiled and nestled into his arms for a kiss.

A few minutes later, they walked down the staircase together. She could still hardly believe her husband owned all of this—the elegant mansion and its expansive grounds, with tenant farms, a mill, and a large stable that David had already begun to stock with fine horses.

In just two months, he had put the estate to rights. The steward that had served his brother Richard had kept things going on a modest scale, but David had great plans for the spring. He was positive he could make the estate more than self-sustaining, and his employees and tenants had caught his optimism and flung themselves into the work.

Meanwhile, he told Millie, they would get used to living here and relax during the winter. Millie knew he was letting her get her feet wet slowly. The social connections she had met already had let her know that they hoped the Stones would take an active part in "the season" in London next spring. That, it seemed, involved lots of parties and entertaining, but it would not be a problem. Her husband also owned a townhouse in London's most fashionable quarter.

Among the first guests to enter the large drawing room off the front hall were Randolph and Merrileigh Stone. Millie inhaled deeply and pasted on a smile. She had met the couple once before this visit, a week after she and David had landed in England. Randolph was all right, rather bluff and hearty, and Millie suspected he wasn't overly intellectual. Merrileigh, on the other hand, seemed much more clever than her husband, but also a bit sly. She didn't quite look down her nose at the new countess, but Millie got the impression she would love to do so, if only David weren't quite so watchful.

"What a lovely gown, milady," she said as she grasped Millie's hand.

"Thank you. Yours is quite charming." Millie swept a glance over Merrileigh's gray-and-mulberry dress. She thought the colors made the wearer look older, but of course she said nothing of that. "I trust your quarters are comfortable?"

"Yes, very nice," Merrileigh said, "though I confess Randolph had hoped for the rooms overlooking the rear gardens."

David, standing beside Millie, jumped in. "I'm sorry, but I've put the Duke of Marlborough in those rooms."

Randolph, who stood before David looking very slick and over-groomed, with his hair styled a bit too foppishly and his cravat arranged in an extravagant waterfall, raised his hand in protest.

"Our rooms are fine, Cousin. Very comfortable, I assure you. I merely made a passing reference to the time we stayed in the other suite several years ago. But I'm sure every accommodation in this house is lovely. I especially like the painting over the mantel in my current chamber."

"Ah yes, the Battle of Trafalgar." David nodded. "Well, Lady Stoneford and I hope you enjoy this visit as much as you did that other, though we shall all be put in mind of Richard and Elizabeth, I'm sure, and wish they were still with us."

"Of course," Randolph murmured.

Merrileigh opened her mouth as if to speak again, but her husband steered her aside to make way for other guests. Richly dressed people were now pouring in, and the butler dutifully announced them all, but within ten minutes, Millie's head swam with names and faces. The women she tried to organize in her mind by what they wore, but soon her brain was overtaxed by the variety and sheer volume of details she'd tried to store, and she gave up.

She stuck close to David during the hour before dinner. It seemed everyone in the world—or at least in England—wanted to meet her. Most were very kind and felicitated the bride and groom with seeming sincerity. Women ogled David shamelessly, and Millie wondered how many had mourned the dashing young man when he left their circle twenty years ago.

"My dear, all the men are agog at you," he whispered in her ear midway through the hour.

"Are they?" She looked up into his eyes and smiled. "I'm afraid I've been watching the women."

"Studying their fashions? Some are rather extreme, are they not?"

"Actually, I was watching them study you."

He smiled and squeezed her gently about the waist. "I'm sure they're curious about my American bride. Let me assure you that so far you've been the perfect hostess."

She relaxed a little. It wasn't so hard when you had a score of servants keeping things flowing smoothly. At dinner, she sat between two gentlemen who seemed determined to monopolize her attention. She swiveled back and forth between them, answering their questions about life in America and how she had met David, without giving too much detail.

"We first met in the Oregon Territory," she told the duke. "But we were only in proximity for a few days then. I believe Stoneford was doing some mining business at the time. After I left the area, I didn't see him again for more than a year. We were reunited on a stagecoach journey."

That was the most she gave out about their early dealings. She and David had discussed it, and both saw the wisdom of not revealing more than the bare minimum.

Later, when the ladies had retired to what was known as the music room—which was graced by a spinet—one of them invited her to a house party in Yorkshire the last week of February.

"We'll have prodigious fun," she predicted. "And I hear you like to ride. Stoneford told my husband that he's bought you a hunter."

"Well yes," Millie said, racking her brain for the lady's name and coming up empty. "I thank you very much, but I probably shan't be doing much riding by then."

"Oh?"

Every eye turned upon her, and Millie felt her face go scarlet.

"Don't tell me you're increasing, my dear," Merrileigh said in a tone that could be construed as either horrified or merely an exaggerated surprise.

"Well..." Had she made a terrible social blunder? "I've only just seen the physician yesterday, but he thinks it likely."

The Duchess of Marlborough smiled and reached to squeeze her hand. "That's marvelous news, my dear. I wish you the best. It's high time there was a child in this house again."

After that the ice was broken. All of the women congratulated Millie and doled out advice. One assured her that motherhood was the most noble of callings, and another decreed that David would be the dotingest father ever. Merrileigh was the only one who said nothing. She sat on a brocade-covered wing chair in a corner with a dour expression on her lips—but that might be attributed to the coffee she sipped.

When at last the gentlemen joined them, all were laughing and grinning at David. Millie knew at once that he had also broken the news of the impending heir to his friends. He made his way to her side and joined her on the velvet settee.

Leaning close, she whispered, "I see the news is out."

"Yes. I hope you don't mind awfully. They're too polite to mention it now, but be sure all their wives will know before midnight."

"Oh, they know," Millie said. "I do hope I didn't cause a scandal. I didn't mean to announce it, but it just came out."

"Don't fret, my love." He raised her hand to his lips.

One of the men laughed—the Earl of something, Millie thought. Glastonbury? Hartford? How could she possibly keep all of their names and titles straight?

"Well, now, Stoneford, I'm impressed with what you've done here in such a short time," the gentleman said. "I hope you and your lady will have a long and happy life here."

"Thank you," David said. "We hope so, too." He squeezed Millie's hand, and she echoed the sentiment in her heart.

Discussion Questions

1. Millie has ambivalent feelings toward her half brother, Sam. Do you think she is wise to leave him and strike out on her own?

2. Why is it so important to Millie to explain her actions to David?

3. Why doesn't David want to talk to Millie?

4. David is considered a gentleman by nearly everyone, but Millie has to earn the right to be thought of as a lady. Why, and is this fair? Who finds it hardest to think of her as a lady?

5. If you were David, what would you have done to help Mrs. Caudle when her husband died? What would you have done to help Millie? Did David do enough? Too much? What limits do you make on charitable giving?

6. Peregrin has several weaknesses that lead him into trouble. His sister is a much stronger character—and yet her heart is no purer. Why do you think Merrileigh gets into less trouble than Peregrin?

7. After the accident, Millie concentrates her efforts on protecting David and seeing that he gets care. Do you think she acts selfishly? Should she have helped the other stagecoach passengers?

8. Halfway through the book, Mille takes care of David, but later on—once they begin their train journey—the roles are reversed, and David protects Millie. Has Millie sacrificed her independence by allowing this?

9. Given the conventions of the day and the perception of "propriety" in the 1850s, do you find Millie bold, conservative, or simply practical?

10. Describe David, Millie, Merrileigh, and Peregrin using only one definitive word for each character.

11. Millie's confidence slips near the end of the story, as she prepares to enter David's world. What things do each of them do to overcome this?

12. David slips back into the privileged class quite easily after his stint on the frontier, but Millie finds it harder to deal with menial workers and servants. Compare their relationships with porters, waiters, and maids to your own attitude toward people who serve you. Are you ever embarrassed to let a worker serve you?

13. Millie's spiritual transformation takes her on a perilous road, and her faith is tested often. One of the first rough spots she encounters is her separation from her brother. How would you handle the death of a loved one who was committing a crime?

About the Author

SUSAN PAGE DAVIS is the author of more than forty novels, in the romance, mystery, suspense, and historical romance genres. A Maine native, she now lives in western Kentucky with her husband, Jim, a retired news editor. They are the parents of six, and the grandparents of nine fantastic kids. She is a past winner of the Carol Award, the Will Rogers Medallion for Western Fiction, and the Inspirational Readers' Choice Award. Susan was named Favorite Author of the Year in the 18th Annual Heartsong Awards. Visit her website at: www.susanpagedavis.com